MONSIEUR PAMPLEMOUSSE
OMNIBUS

VOLUME 2

Monsieur Pamplemousse Omnibus

Volume 2

Michael Bond

a&b

This edition published
in Great Britain in 1999 by
Allison & Busby Limited
114 New Cavendish Street
London W1M 7FD
http://www.allisonandbusby.ltd.uk

Reprinted 1999

Monsieur Pamplemousse Takes the Cure
first published 1987 by Hodder & Stoughton Ltd

Monsieur Pamplemousse Aloft
first published 1989 by Hodder & Stoughton Ltd

Monsieur Pamplemousse Investigates
first published 1990 by Hodder & Stoughton Ltd

Monsieur Pamplemousse Rests His Case
first published 1991 by Headline Book Publishing PLC

A catalogue record for this book is available
from the British Library

ISBN 0 7490 0410 X

Design and cover illustrations by Pepe Moll

Printed and bound by Biddles Limited,
Guildford, Surrey.

Contents

Monsieur Pamplemousse Takes the Cure

Contents

1
THE IDEAL INSPECTOR

'*Entrez!*'

The director's voice sounded brisk and businesslike. It was undoubtedly the voice of someone who commanded and who also expected to be obeyed without question.

In the short space of time left at his disposal between rapping on the door and taking hold of the handle, Monsieur Pamplemousse tried to analyze it still further.

Was it, *par exemple*, the voice of a man who commanded and expected to be obeyed, and yet had also read his, Monsieur Pamplemousse's, recent article on the subject of *cassoulet* – its many forms and regional variations – which had recently appeared in *L'Escargot*, *Le Guide*'s staff magazine? And if so, was it the voice of a man who couldn't wait to hear more?

In the remaining half second or so before he turned the handle, a dry cough – an obvious clearing of the throat before getting down to business – dispelled the thought. It was scarcely the cough of a man desperately trying to conceal his excitement, but more that of someone rapidly running out of patience.

On the other hand, if the summons to the director's office wasn't to do with the article, why had he specifically mentioned the word 'Toulouse' when he rang through on the internal telephone? Toulouse, the very home of *cassoulet*. And why the note of urgency? 'Drop everything,

11

Pamplemousse,' had been the order of the day. 'Come to my office immediately.'

Perhaps the director had a cold? That was it – a cold. There were a lot around at the moment. He must have read the previous article in the December issue – the one on garlic – its use in combating man's most common ailment

The next remark, however, confirmed his worst suspicions. The director was not in a good mood. Testiness had crept in.

'Don't hover, whoever you are. Either come in or go away.'

Monsieur Pamplemousse took a deep breath, and with all the enthusiasm of an early Christian entering the lion's den, did as he was bidden.

Having entered the room, he waited for the usual nod indicating that he could sit in the chair facing the director's desk, a desk so placed that its occupant had his back to the light and his face in the shadows – just as he, Pamplemousse, had arranged his own desk in the days when, as a member of the Sûreté, he'd wished to conduct a cross-examination in his office at the *quai des Orfèvres*.

But he waited in vain. Instead, the director gave a grunt and picked up a printed form from a neat pile in front of him. Adjusting his glasses, he gazed at it distastefully for a moment or two.

'I have been studying your medical report, Pamplemousse.'

Monsieur Pamplemousse shifted uneasily. *'Oui, Monsieur le directeur?'*

'It makes unhappy reading.'

Monsieur Pamplemousse felt tempted to say, if that was the case, why bother? Why not try reading something more cheerful instead; his report concerning the continued insistence of French chefs on the use of fresh ingredients, for example. But wisely, he refrained. The director was clearly in no mood for frivolities. In any case he was speaking again, intoning from the form rather in the manner of a small-part actor who has been given the telephone directory to read while auditioning for the part of Hamlet.

'Born: nineteen twenty-eight.

'Height,' Monsieur Pamplemousse instinctively drew himself up, 'one hundred and seventy-two centimeters.'

'Weight: *ninety-eight kilograms*.'

The director made it sound like a series of misprints, each a greater travesty of the truth than the one before.

'I have large bones, *Monsieur*.'

'They have need to be, Pamplemousse,' said the director severely. 'They are bones which may well, as they grow older, have difficulty in supporting your weight. Unless … steps are taken.

'Complexion: *pique-nique*. I have never heard of that before.'

'It is a little-used medical term, *Monsieur*. It means pink, full of health. Even Doctor Labarre was impressed.'

The director barely suppressed a snort. 'Blood pressure …' he paused again and then held the piece of paper up to the light as if he could scarcely believe his eyes. 'Blood pressure … can this figure be true?'

'It was not a good day, *Monsieur*, the day of the medical examination. Madame Pamplemousse was being a little difficult, you understand, and that affected me. It had been raining and Pommes Frites had the misfortune to step in something untoward while he was out for his morning walk. We had just purchased a new carpet …'

Monsieur Pamplemousse heard his voice trail away as

13

the director reduced him to silence with a world-weary gesture of his hand.

'Facts, Pamplemousse. Facts are facts, and there is no getting away from them. It is high time we returned to first principles, principles laid down by our founder, Hippolyte Duval, without whose integrity, without whose dedication, single-mindedness, clear thinking, foresight, and devotion to duty none of us would be where we are today.'

While he was talking the director transferred his gaze to a large oil painting that occupied the centre of the wall to his right. Lit by a single spotlight, it showed an ascetic-looking man eating alone outside a hotel on the banks of the Marne. Dressed in the fashion of the day, he gazed at the artist and the world through eyes as cold and as blue as the empty mussel shells piled high on a plate beside him. With one hand he held a glass of white wine by its stem– probably a Sancerre if the artist had accurately captured the label on the bottle. With his other hand he caressed one end of a waxed moustache, the curve of which neatly echoed the handlebars of a bicycle propped against a nearby tree. It was one of many velocipedes dotted about the picture, for the motor car had yet to be invented. *Le Guide* itself was still in its infancy, confining its investigations to those restaurants in and around Paris that could be reached by Monsieur Duval on two wheels or by pony and trap.

While agreeing with the director that but for Hippolyte Duval he wouldn't be standing where he was, Monsieur Pamplemousse couldn't help but reflect that, given the present circumstances, the advantages this implied were open to debate. He'd always nursed a secret feeling that had he and the founder of *Le Guide* ever met they wouldn't necessarily have seen eye to eye. He suspected Monsieur

14

Duval lacked humor. The faint smile on his face looked out of place, rather as if it had been hired specially for the occasion. Either that, or he had just witnessed one of his fellow cyclists falling from his machine.

The director's next words confirmed this feeling. Reaching into a drawer in his desk he took out a plastic box, opened it, and withdrew a small red object, which he held up for Monsieur Pamplemousse to see.

'In his later years,' he said, 'our founder made a great study of the effect too much food can have on the body. He came to the conclusion that man can live happily on an apple a day. A dictum, Aristide, which, if I may say so, you would do well to consider.'

As the crunch that punctuated this last statement died away, Monsieur Pamplemousse gazed at the director with something approaching horror. It was a well-known fact that people often grew to look like their pets – he had himself been compared more than once to Pommes Frites, but that was different, a compliment of the highest order. It was the first time he'd encountered someone who had grown to look like another person's portrait. It hadn't occurred to him until now, but there was no denying the fact that the director bore a distinct resemblance to the erstwhile incumbent of his post, Monsieur Hippolyte Duval himself. There was the same fanatical gleam in his eyes, a gleam which brooked no interference or disagreement.

'With the greatest respect, *Monsieur*,' he said at last, 'I would not call making do with an apple a day *living* – nor would I connect it with the word *happiness*. I also feel most strongly that it is a philosophy which ill becomes a man whose whole life was dedicated to the running of a restaurant guide. Speaking personally, I would find it impossible to conduct my work for *Le Guide* were I to

15

confine myself to such a diet. An inspector has to sample to test. He has to compare and evaluate. Above all, he has to accumulate experience, experience that embraces both the good and the bad. There are times when he has to consume meals when all his natural instincts tell him to stop. People think it is easy. The few – the very few – who know how I earn my living, say to me 'Pamplemousse, how lucky you are. How wonderful to have such a job.' But if they only knew.

'Were I to confine myself to an apple a day, why ...' Monsieur Pamplemousse gazed out of the window as he sought hard to find a suitable parallel and ended up on the banks of the Seine somewhere near the *quai des Orfèvres*. 'Why, it would be like an inspector of the Sûreté patting a murderer on the head and saying, 'Go away and don't ever let me catch you doing that again.' It would make a mockery of my calling.

'Being a little overweight goes hand in hand with my work, *Monsieur*. It is an occupational hazard – a cross we inspectors have to bear, along with occasional bouts of indigestion alone in our beds at night.'

'Yes, yes, Pamplemousse.' The director interrupted in a tone of voice that all too clearly meant 'No! No!'

Rifling through some papers on his desk he extracted another sheet. Monsieur Pamplemousse's heart sank as he recognized the familiar buff colour of a form P39. It had a red star attached to it. It was the one Madame Grante in Accounts used when a decision from higher authority was needed.

'I have been going through your expenses, Pample-mousse. They, too, make unhappy reading. Unless, of course, we happened to be thinking of applying to the Gulbenkian Foundation for a grant. In those circumstances they would provide welcome evidence of the mounting cost of our operation.

'If you are so concerned about the state of your digestion, I suggest the occasional bottle of *eau minérale* instead of wine would not come amiss.

'On the tenth of January, for example, you and Pommes Frites between you consumed an entire bottle of Château Lafite with your *boeuf bourguignon*. Considering the remarks you made in your report concerning lapses in the *cuisine* – I see you compared the quality of the meat with a certain brand of shoe leather – might not a wine from a lesser *château* have sufficed? Perhaps even a *pichet* of the house red?'

'If you were to check with my P41, *Monsieur*, you would see that January the tenth was my birthday. Rennes is not the most exciting place in which to spend one's birthday – especially in mid-January. And it was raining ...'

'Be that as it may, Pamplemousse, there is no getting away from the fact that you are grossly overweight and it is high time something was done about it.' The director gestured toward the far side of the room. 'Stand over there, please, and look at yourself in the mirror.'

As Monsieur Pamplemousse turned he gave a start. In the corner behind the door stood another figure. For a brief moment he thought a third person had been a party to their conversation, and he was about to express his indignation in no uncertain terms when something about its posture made him pause. It was a dummy, an exceptionally lifelike one, complete in every detail down to the very last button on its jacket, but a dummy nevertheless.

'Allow me to introduce our latest recruit, Pamplemousse.' The director sounded pleased at the effect he had achieved. 'His name is Alphonse. No doubt you are

17

wondering why he is there?'

Glad to be able to divert the conversation away from his P39, Monsieur Pamplemousse murmured his agreement. Expenses were always a thorny subject and it was no easy matter to strike a happy balance between the need to eat at some of the most expensive restaurants in France while at the same time not to overstep the rigid boundaries laid down by an ever vigilant Madame Grante, many of whose minions were hard put to eat out at a local *bistro* more than twice a week.

The director rose to his feet. 'Alphonse, Pamplemousse, represents the *Ideal Inspector*. An ideal we must all of us strive for in the future. I have been studying the many writings of our founder and the results have been fed into a computer. From its findings I have had this model constructed.

'I think,' the director formed a steeple with his hands and tapped the end of his nose reflectively as he began to pace the room, 'I think I can say without fear of contradiction, that I know his background and his habits as well as I know my own.

'I know where he was born; where he went to school. I know where he lives. I know the number of rooms in his apartment and how they are furnished, what time he goes to bed, when he rises. I know his tastes and where he buys his clothes. I know where he goes for his holidays. In short, I know down to the very last detail what makes him tick.

'The ideal inspector working for *Le Guide*, Pamplemousse, will weigh seventy-six point eight kilos. He will lead an active life, rising at six-thirty every morning and taking a cold shower. In his leisure hours he will play tennis, perhaps a little squash from time to time enough to

18

keep his figure in trim. During his lifetime he will have no more than two point six mistresses –'

Monsieur Pamplemousse, who had been growing steadily more depressed as he listened to the growing list of what he could only interpret as his own deficiencies, could stand it no longer.

'With respect, *Monsieur*,' he exclaimed, eyeing Alphonse distastefully, 'it is hard to imagine him having point six of a mistress, let alone any more.'

'Would that we could all say that, Pamplemousse,' said the director severely. 'Two point six would be a very low estimate indeed for some of us. That unfortunate business with the girls from the Follies, the reason for your early retirement from the Sûreté – that should keep you ahead of the national average for many years to come.'

Monsieur Pamplemousse fell silent. When the director had a bee in his bonnet it was pointless to argue, and on this occasion he was clearly dealing with not one bee, but a veritable swarm. He braced himself mentally for the next blow, wondering just how and where it would land.

'I must say, Pamplemousse,' continued the director, 'that in many respects you fall sadly short of the ideal. In fairness, I have to admit you are not alone in this. Looking at the group photograph taken during the staff outing at Boulogne last year, clearly many of your colleagues would fare equally badly were they to stand alongside our friend here, but their turn will come. However, for reasons which I won't go into for the moment, it is you whom we have selected for the honor of acting as a guinea pig for what we have in mind.

'For some time now the Board of Governors has been considering various ways in which we might expand our activities – broaden our horizons, as it were. In many respects it goes against the grain, but one has to move with the times and there is no denying that some of our competitors have been forced into taking similar action. Michelin ventured into other countries many years ago. Gault-Millau currently involve themselves in areas that would make our founder turn in his grave were he to be aware of them – magazines, special offers, things I trust we shall never do.

'Nevertheless, it is our intention from time to time to test other waters, if I may coin a phrase. And first on the list is a survey of all the health farms in France.

'Pamplemousse, tomorrow we want you to dip our toes into the waters of the Pyrénées-Orientales. A room is reserved far you at an establishment north of Perpignan. I wish you luck and I look forward to welcoming the new Pamplemousse on his return in a fortnight's time.'

Having delivered himself of this salvo, a positive broadside of unexpected facts, the director came to a halt opposite Monsieur Pamplemousse, all ammunition spent, and held out his hand.

'*Bon voyage*, Aristide,' he said, eyeing the other somewhat nervously.

'A fortnight!' Monsieur Pamplemousse repeated the words with all the disbelief and bitterness he could muster. 'At a *health farm*! Has *Monsieur* ever *been* to the Pyrénées-Orientales in March? All the winter snow will be beginning to melt. It will be cascading down the mountainside in ice-cold torrents. It is not *our* toes that will suffer, *Monsieur*, it is *mine*. I hate to think what might happen to them were I to risk dipping them into such waters. At the very least they will become frostbitten. At worst, gangrene could set in and before you know where you are, *pouf*! They will fall off!'

'Come, come, Aristide, you mustn't take me too literally.'

The director stole a quick glance at his watch as he motioned Monsieur Pamplemousse toward the visitor's chair. As he feared, it was almost lunch time. It was all taking much longer than he'd planned. A good man, Pamplemousse, but not one to be hurried. Information had to be digested and slept on. A typical Capricorn, and from the Auvergne as well – a difficult combination; whereas the new model – the *Ideal* Inspector – he was definitely a Leo and from some less mountainous region.

'Dipping our toes was perhaps an unhappy turn of phrase, but don't you think, Aristide, the change will do you good?'

From the depths of the armchair Monsieur Pamplemousse listened like a man who was experiencing a bad dream. A man whose feet became more leaden the harder he tried to escape. He sat up as a thought struck him.

'I have just remembered, *Monsieur*, it will not be possible. My car is due for its two hundred thousand kilometer service. Later in the year, perhaps, when it is warmer.'

'Excellent news!' The director rubbed his hands together with a pleasure which was so obviously false that he had the grace to look embarrassed. 'It can be done while you are away,' he said hurriedly. 'I will make all the necessary arrangements. After two weeks at the Château Morgue you will be in no fit state to drive anyway. The good Herr Schmuck and his wife will see to that.'

Sensing that he had inadvertently struck a wrong note, the director hastily crossed to a filing cabinet and withdrew a green folder. Opening it up, he spread the contents across his desk. Recognizing the detachable pages contained at the back of every copy of *Le Guide*, the ones on which readers were invited to make their own comments,

Monsieur Pamplemousse wondered what was going to happen next.

'It doesn't sound so bad. Preliminary investigations have already been taking place.' The director sifted through the papers and after a moment or two found what he had been looking for. 'Look, here is one taken at random. I will read it to you: "Just like a home from home. The food was plain but wholesome, avoiding the excessive use of cream common to so many establishments. The first time we encountered genuine smiles in all our travels through France. My wife and I particularly enjoyed the early morning tramps through the snow (obligatory without a medical certificate). Our only criticism concerned the beds, which could have been softer, and the lack of pillows. It would also help if the bicycle racks were provided with locks. In many ways it reminded us both of our days in the Forces (my wife was an AT)."'

'An *at*!' repeated Monsieur Pamplemousse. 'What is an *at*?'

The director ran a hand round his collar and then glanced at the window, wondering if he should open it. The room was getting warm. 'It was some kind of paramilitary female organization operating from *Grande Bretagne* during the war.' He tried to sound as casual as possible.

'You mean the people who wrote that report were *English*?' exclaimed Monsieur Pamplemousse.

It figured. Memories of a week he'd once spent in Torquay during a particularly cold winter just after the war came flooding back to him. It had been his first visit to England and at the time he'd sworn it would be his last. An unheated bedroom. Everyone speaking in whispers at breakfast lest they incur the wrath of the landlady, a bizarre creature of uncertain temper who spoke some totally incomprehensible language and who wouldn't let anyone back inside her house until after five-thirty in the afternoon. A depressing experience. Fourteen meals of soggy fish and chips – eaten out of a newspaper! He'd spent most of his time sitting in a shelter on the sea front trying to decipher the crossword.

'It suffers a little in translation,' began the director.

'May I see the others, *Monsieur*? The *less* random ones?'

'They vary.' The director began to gather them up. 'Some, perhaps, are not quite so enthusiastic.'

'*S'il vous plaît, Monsieur.*'

The director sighed. It had been worth a try.

'Not quite so favourable!' Monsieur Pamplemousse could scarcely conceal his scorn as he glanced through the pile of reports. '*Sacrébleu*! They are like an overripe Camembert – they stink! I have never seen such reports, *never*. Not in the whole of my career. Look at them.

'"The man should be arrested ... his wife, too ... Herr Schmuck is a ... "'

There the report ended in a series of blots, rather as though the emotional strain of putting pen to paper had proved so great the author had emptied the entire contents of an ink-well over the report rather than commit blasphemy in writing.

'That settles it!' He rose to his feet. 'I am sorry, *Monsieur*.'

The director heaved another sigh, a deeper one this time. 'I am sorry too, Aristide. I had hoped that your dedication to duty, the dedication we older hands at *Le Guide* have come to admire and respect, would have been sufficient motivation. Alas ...' With an air of one whose last illusion about his fellow man has just been irretrievably shattered, he played his trump card. 'It leaves me with no alternative but to exercise the authority of my position. An authority, Pamplemousse, which I must remind you – although speaking, I hope, as a friend, it saddens me that I should have to do so – you were only too happy to accept when you first joined us. You will be leaving for Perpignan on the seven forty-one train tomorrow morning. Your tickets are with Madame Grante.'

Monsieur Pamplemousse sank back into his chair again. He knew when he was beaten. What the director had just said was true. He owed *Le Guide* a great deal. The memory of that fatal day when, out of a sense of moral duty and against the advice of many of his colleagues, he had handed in his resignation at the Sûréte, was still very clear in his mind: the sudden cold feeling of being alone in the world when he'd walked out of the *quai des Orfèvres* for the last time, not knowing which way to turn – left or right. As it turned out, the Fates had been kind. Obeying a momentary impulse, he'd turned right and headed toward the seventh *arrondissement*. And as luck would have it, his wanderings had taken him past the offices of *Le Guide*. There he had bumped into the director; a director who had cause to be grateful for the satisfactory conclusion to a case which, had it been handled differently, could have brought scandal on France's oldest and most respected gastronomic bible.

But if the director had cause to be grateful to Monsieur Pamplemousse, the reverse was certainly true. Hearing of the latter's plight, he had, without a second's hesitation, offered him a job on the spot. In the space of less than an hour, Monsieur Pamplemousse had moved from one office to another, from a job he had come to think of as his life's blood, to one which was equally rewarding.

He rose to his feet. It had been a generous act, a noble

act. A gesture of friendship he could never hope to repay. He was left with no option but to accede to the director's wishes. To argue would be both churlish and unappreciative of his good fortune.

'Come, come, Aristide,' the director allowed himself the luxury of putting an arm on Monsieur Pamplemousse's shoulder as he pointed him in the direction of the door. 'It is only for two weeks. Two weeks out of your life. It will all be over before you know where you are.'

While he was talking the director reached into an inner pocket of his jacket with his other hand and withdrew a long, white envelope. 'These are a few notes which may help you in your task. There's no need to read them now. I suggest you put them away and don't look at them until you reach your destination. What is the saying? *La corde ne peut être toujours tendue.* All work and no play makes Jacques a dull boy? Who knows, they may help you to kill two *oiseaux* with one stone.'

Monsieur Pamplemousse blinked. For a moment he was mentally knocked off balance by the director's disconcerting habit of mixing his languages as well as his metaphors when the occasion demanded. Absentmindedly he slipped the envelope inside his jacket without so much as a second glance.

'Oh, and another thing.' As they reached the door the director paused with one hand on the latch. 'I think you should take Pommes Frites with you. He, too, has been looking overweight in recent weeks. I think he is still suffering from your visit to Les Cinq Parfaits. Besides, you may find him of help in your activities.'

Monsieur Pamplemousse's spirits sank still further. It hadn't occurred to him for one moment that he might not be taking Pommes Frites. Pommes Frites always went with him. He was glad he hadn't thought of the possibility earlier, otherwise he might have said more than he had already and regretted it.

'Dogs are not normally allowed at *Établissements Thermaux*,' said the director, reading his thoughts, 'not even with the payment of a supplement. It is a question of *hygiène*. Not,' he raised his hands in mock horror at the thought, 'not that one questions Pommes Frites' personal habits for one moment. But the presence of dogs seems to be particularly frowned on at Château Morgue. *Chiens* are definitely not catered for. I had to resort to a subterfuge. I insisted on his presence on account of your unfortunate disability.'

'My disability, *Monsieur*?'

The director clucked impatiently. Pamplemousse was being unusually difficult this morning. Difficult, or deliberately unhelpful; he strongly suspected the latter.

'The trouble with your sight. I made a telephone call on your behalf late yesterday evening in order to explain the situation. I'm sure Pommes Frites will make an excellent guide dog. It's the kind of thing bloodhounds ought to be good at. You can collect his special harness along with some dark glasses and a white stick at the same time as the tickets.'

Monsieur Pamplemousse stared at the director as if he had suddenly taken leave of his senses. 'Perhaps, *Monsieur*,' he exclaimed, 'you would like me to learn Braille on the journey down?'

His sarcasm fell on deaf ears. 'Such dedication, Aristide! I knew from the outset you were the right man for the job.'

'But …' Monsieur Pamplemousse found himself clutching at straws, straws which were wrenched from his hand the moment his grip tightened. 'Would it not be easier and infinitely more satisfactory if someone else went?'

'Easier, Pamplemousse, *oui.*' The director's voice cut across his own like a pistol shot. 'More satisfactory ... *non*! We need someone with your knowledge and experience, receptive to new ideas, able to collect and collate information. Someone totally incorruptible.

'Oh, and one final thing,' the director's voice, softer now, reached Monsieur Pamplemousse as if through a haze. 'I am assuming that to all intents and purposes your *régime* has already begun. There is, I believe, a restaurant car on the *Morning Capitole*. However, I shall not expect to see any items from its menu appear on your expense sheet. It will be good practice for you and Pommes Frites, and it will put you both in the right frame of mind for all the optional extras at Château Morgue – such things as massages and needle baths. Make full use of everything. Do not stint yourselves. I will see things right with Madame Grante.

'And now,' the director held out his hand, donning his official manner at the same time, '*au revoir*, Aristide, and ... *bonne chance.*'

Although the handshake was not without warmth, the message that went with it was icily clear, delivered in the manner of one who has said all there is to say on the subject and now wishes to call the meeting closed.

The director believed in running *Le Guide* with all the efficiency of a military operation, and clearly in his mind's eye Monsieur Pamplemousse was already but a flag on the map of France that occupied one entire wall of the Operations Room in the basement; a magnetic flag which on the morrow would be moved steadily but inexorably southward as the *Morning Capitole* gathered speed and headed toward Toulouse and the Pyrénées-Orientales.

As Monsieur Pamplemousse made his way slowly back down the corridor toward the lift, he turned a corner and collided with a girl coming the other way. She was carrying a large tray on which reposed an earthenware pot, a plate, bread, cutlery, napkin, and a bottle of wine: a Pommard '72.

'*Zut!*' The girl neatly recovered her balance and then made great play of raising the tray in triumph as she recognized Monsieur Pamplemousse. '*Alors!* That was a near thing. *Monsieur le directeur* would not have been pleased if his *cassoulet* had gone all over the floor. Nor would the chef – he made it specially. *Monsieur le directeur* said to me when he phoned down a moment ago how much he was looking forward to it. I think he has had a bad morning.'

'*Cassoulet!*' Monsieur Pamplemousse repeated the word bitterly as the girl hurried on her way. '*Cassoulet!*' He had a sudden mental picture of the director clutching his apple sanctimoniously while he laid down the law. The mockery of it all! The hypocrisy!

He hesitated for a moment, wondering whether he should snatch a quick bite to eat before visiting Madame Grante, and decided against it. His digestive tracts were in a parlous enough state as it was without adding to their problems.

Besides, if he was to catch the early morning train there was work to be done. His desk would need to be cleared of outstanding papers, the contents of *Le Guide*'s issue suitcase would have to be checked. He had a feeling some of the items might come in very useful over the next two weeks – the portable cooking equipment for a start.

The thought triggered off another. He might try and persuade old Rabiller in Stores to let him borrow a remote control attachment for his Leica while he was away. He'd heard there was one in stock awaiting field trials. With time on his hands he might try his hand at some wildlife photography. An eagle's nest, perhaps? Or a mountain bear stirring after its long winter rest. He would take the precaution of stocking up on film.

Then he would need to be home early in order to break the news to Madame Pamplemousse. She would not be pleased. He had promised faithfully to decorate the kitchen before the spring. That would have to wait now, and in his weakened state after 'the cure' who knew when he might be fit enough to start work on it?

Pommes Frites, too. Pommes Frites liked his set routine. They would need to be on their way by half past six at the very latest, which would mean doing him out of his morning walk. There was also the little matter of getting him used to his new harness before they set out.

Almost imperceptibly Monsieur Pamplemousse quickened his pace. One way and another there was a lot to be done and very little time left in which to do it.

2
THE DOPPELGÄNGER

With his suitcase stowed away in the compartment at the end of the carriage, his overcoat and white stick on the luggage rack above his head, Monsieur Pamplemousse removed his dark glasses, gathered the little that was left of his breath, and gazed gloomily out of the window of the *Morning Capitole* as it slid gently out of the deserted *quais* of the Gare d'Austerlitz and then rapidly gathered speed.

The day had got off to a bad start. Trouble had set in almost as soon as they left home, a fact which Pommes Frites, already curled up on the floor as he addressed himself to the task of catching up on some lost sleep, would have been only too happy to confirm had he been asked.

Any fond hopes Monsieur Pamplemousse might have cherished about his 'condition' conferrng little extra privileges *en route* had been quickly dashed. The cup containing the milk of human kindness ran dry very early in the day on the Paris *Métro*, as he discovered when he tried to board an already crowded train at Lamarck-Caulaincourt. The *'poufs'* and snorts and cluckings which rose from all sides as he attempted to push his way through to the seats normally reserved for *les mutilés de guerre*, *les femmes enceintes* and other deserving travelers in descending order of priority, had to be heard to be believed. In no time at all he found himself back on the platform, glasses askew and suitcase threatening to burst at

30

the seams. Had he not managed to get in some quick and effective jabs with his stick, Pommes Frites might well have suffered a bruised tail, or worse – as the doors slid shut behind them and the train went on its way.

Seeing him standing there and misinterpreting the reason, a more helpful morning commuter who arrived on the platform just in time to see them alight, came to the rescue and escorted him back to the waiting lift. Monsieur Pamplemousse was too kindly a person to throw this act of friendship back into the face of his unknown benefactor, so he allowed himself to be ushered into the lift, hearing as he did so the arrival and departure of the next train.

Then, on emerging at the top, he'd collided with an ex-colleague from the Sûreté. The look on the man's face as he caught Monsieur Pamplemousse in the act of removing his dark glasses in order to get his bearings plainly mirrored his embarrassment and contempt. The news would be round all the stations by now, probably even the *quai des Orfèvres* itself. 'Old Pamplemousse has really hit rock bottom. He's trying the 'blind man on the *Métro*' routine now. Things must be bad. First the Follies and now this. No doubt about it, an *oeuf mauvais*.'

The prospect through the window as he took his seat on the *Morning Capitole* was gray. The Seine, from the few glimpses he managed to catch, looked dark and uninviting. Ahead of them lights from anonymous office blocks twinkled through the mist, beckoning to the trickle of early arrivals hurrying to beat the morning rush.

Suddenly, as the Seine joined up with the Marne and then disappeared from view, he felt glad to be heading south and away from it all. He was conscious of a warm glow that owed as much to the thought of going somewhere fresh as it did to the unaccustomed flurry of exercise. It was a feeling that was almost immediately enhanced by an announcement over the loudspeakers that breakfast was about to be served. To the devil with the director and his instructions!

Giving Pommes Frites a warning nudge, he rose to his feet. If the other passengers on the train felt as he did there would be a rush for tables.

If only Ananas had not been on the same train; worse still, he occupied the same carriage. That was the unkindest cut of all – really rubbing salt into the wound, the kind of bizarre coincidence he could well have done without. Experience in the Force had taught him that most people have a double somewhere in the world, but more often than not their paths never cross, or if they do, they pass each other by in the street without reeognizing the fact, aware only of experiencing something slightly odd – a feeling of *déjà vu*.

It was his particular misfortune to have a double whose face was constantly in the public eye, made larger than life by being plastered on billboards the length and breadth of France, and consequently in Monsieur Pamplemousse's opinion – despite the element of self-criticism it implied – made ten times less inviting.

As he led the way along the corridor toward the restaurant car, he glanced into the compartment where Ananas was holding court. Adopting a pose which ensured that his profile was clearly visible to anyone passing, he was deep in conversation with a somewhat vicious-looking individual. Monsieur Pamplemousse reflected that Ananas' companion looked as if be might have even stranger proclivities than his master, which would be saying something.

If Ananas recognized himself in Monsieur Pamplemousse he showed no sign, but then he probably didn't encounter the same problems. On occasion even the simple act of eating in a restaurant became something of a bore, with its routine of pretended mistaken identity, while other diners tried to make up their minds whether or not they were in the presence of the real thing.

Croissants, toast, *confiture*, and *café* arrived with light-ning speed, and by the time they were passing through Brétigny he was sipping a glass of *jus d'orange* and feeling better.

He wondered idly where Ananas might be going at this time of the year. Perhaps his television program was having a break. He was too sharp an operator and had too much at stake to let someone else take over while he was away. For all their present loyalty, the public were a fickle lot and he would be well aware of the double risk of having either a stand-in who was more popular than himself or someone a great deal less so. Either way he could stand to lose.

Ananas had first appeared on the scene some years before as 'Oncle Hubert' on a children's television program. 'Oncle Hubert' had a 'way' with children. Particularly, as things turned out, with little girls.

Monsieur Pamplemousse could have told his many fan clubs a thing or two. There had been a near scandal which, in the less liberal climate of the time, would have meant the end of his career had it ever come to light. As it was, strings must have been pulled by someone on high, for 'Oncle Hubert' had conveniently disappeared for a while, osten-sibly suffering from nervous exhaustion due to overwork.

When he resurfaced under his adopted name, it was as host of a particularly infantile afternoon game show, which by some quirk of fate caught the public's imagination. In a relatively short space of time the viewing figures rocketed to the top, carrying Ananas with them and the accolade of a prime spot two evenings a week. From that moment on he had never looked back. Almost overnight he became that strange product of the twentieth century – a 'television personality' – whose views on matters of moment were sought and listened to with awe. Without doubt, Ananas would be careful not to court disaster again.

At 8:25 they reached the start of the twenty kilometers or so of concrete monorail north of Orleans – test-bed for an Aerotrain that never was. By then the sun had broken through and Pamplemousse's mood was lifting. Even the sight of Ananas at a table further down the restaurant car didn't dampen his spirits. Like royalty, Ananas never soiled his hands with money, even when the need arose – which wasn't often, so the bill was being paid by his companion. A good deal of his income came from payments in kind. He was careful to endorse only those products which would enrich his own life – shoes, shirts, suits, the furnishings of his several houses; all were of the very best. Cars met him wherever he went, doors opened at his approach. The story was told that when he did pay for something by check it was seldom cashed, the recipient preferring to have it framed as a souvenir, hoping it would increase in value in the fullness of time.

Settling back preparatory to paying his own bill, Monsieur Pamplemousse reached down and fondled Pommes Frites' head. He received an immediate response in the form of a luxurious and long drawn out stretching of the legs and body. It started at the tips of the forepaws and ended up some moments later at the tail. Pommes Frites liked travelling by train; there was far more room than in his master's car, and it wasn't subject to sudden and unexpected swervings, nor bouts of thumping on the steering wheel by the driver. At least, he hadn't heard any so far. He

34

was also badly in need of reassurance, and reassurance had been very thin on the ground so far that morning.

The fact of the matter was, Pommes Frites felt in a state of utter confusion. He didn't know for sure whether he was coming or going. Or, to put it another way, he knew he was going somewhere, but he had no idea where or for what reason.

Normally it wouldn't have troubled him. Normally he looked forward to journeys with his master and he didn't really mind where they went, but the present trip seemed different. Ever since Monsieur Pamplemousse arrived home the previous afternoon he had been acting very strangely. First of all there had been the business with the glasses. No sooner had he got indoors and taken his shoes off, than he'd put on some dark glasses, darker, much darker than the ones he sometimes wore when he was driving his car, so dark you couldn't even see his eyes. Then he'd started groping his way around the apartment as if he couldn't see where he was going – which wasn't surprising in the circumstances. Madame Pamplemousse hadn't been at all pleased when he'd knocked over a vase full of flowers, particularly when they landed on the same patch of carpet he, Pommes Frites, had been in trouble over only a few days before.

But things hadn't ended there. There was also the strange contraption he'd been made to wear. At first he'd thought it was meant for carrying the shopping, something he wouldn't have minded doing at all. Pommes Frites liked shopping and he always accompanied his master on his visits to the local market. But no, it was obviously meant to serve some other purpose. What purpose he wasn't sure as yet, except that it had to do with crossing roads. Or rather, not crossing roads.

That was another thing. Normally, Monsieur Pamplemousse took charge when there was any traffic about and Pommes Frites happily followed on behind, secure in the knowledge that if he stuck close to his master's heels no harm would come to him.

Now his master had taken to hovering, holding on to the new collar and tapping the edge of the pavement with a stick – almost as though he was afraid to venture any further for fear of being knocked down. They had only been out once, but in Pommes Frites' view, once was more than enough. He'd been glad to get back home again in one piece. One way and another his confidence had been badly sapped.

Last, but by no means least, there had been the encounter with the second Monsieur Pamplemousse, the one he'd caught a brief glimpse of when they boarded the train.

True, on closer inspection the new one was quite different from the version he had known and loved for a number of years. One quick sniff had established that straight away. But outwardly the likeness had been remarkable: the same figure, the same way of walking, the same face, even down to a similar though not so dark pair of glasses.

It was all very confusing and, for the time being at least, totally beyond his comprehension. That being so, he had given up thinking about it. Pommes Frites belonged to the school of thought that believed if you waited long enough problems had a habit of solving themselves, and it was pointless losing too much sleep over them.

All the same, he was glad to feel the touch of his master's hand. It signified that at long last things were returning to normal, and he felt in a much better frame of mind as he followed Monsieur Pamplemousse out of the restaurant car, so much so he scarcely gave the ersatz edition a second glance when they passed his table.

Back in the compartment, Pommes Frites gave the scenery a cursory inspection through the window and then resumed his nap, while his master buried himself behind a *journal*.

Châteauroux and Limoges came and went unremarked, and as they drew out of Brive-la-Gaillarde, Monsieur Pamplemousse, satisfactorily up to date on current happenings in the world at large, rose and made his way toward the dining car again in order to investigate the possibility of an early *déjeuner*. He quickly shelved the idea. Ananas was already ensconced at a table, holding forth loudly on the subject of some *coquilles St. Jacques* which were apparently not to his liking. He was giving the waiter a dressing down in no uncertain terms, much to the obvious embarrassment of the other diners. Monsieur Pamplemousse reflected wryly on the aptness of the choice of dishes, for was not Saint Jacques the patron saint of money-makers? The episode left a nasty taste in his mouth and quite put him off the thought of eating. He felt relieved he hadn't woken Pommes Frites; his change of plan would have been hard to explain. It took a lot to put Pommes Frites off his food.

By Cahors hunger pangs had started to set in, and he was beginning to regret his decision. It wasn't until 13:14 precisely, as they entered the station at Toulouse, that there occurred one of those rare events which break through the thickest cloud and cause the sun to shine, restoring at one and the same time one's faith in the world.

As they drew to a halt they were assailed on all sides by the sound of cheering. Somewhere toward the front of the train a band was playing martial music, and as he went to open the door at the end of the carriage he caught sight of a group of men waving a large banner.

Toulouse, for whatever reason, seemed to be *en fête*, and the arrival of the *Morning Capitole* was obviously the high spot of the day.

Reacting rather faster than his fellow passengers, Ananas took in the situtuation at a glance and pushed his way past, waving to the crowds as he went. Donning his sunglasses in order to pay lip service to the pretence of travelling incognito, he paused momentarily to adjust his composure, and then emerged in order to greet his admirers.

The effect was magical. A great cheer went up from the waiting throng as they recognized him and word went round. A moment later he disappeared from view, swallowed up in a sea of admirers, only to reappear again seconds later as he was lifted shoulder high. It struck Monsieur Pamplemousse that his smile looked somewhat fixed as though the reception was exceeding anything even he had anticipated.

For a brief moment Monsieur Pamplemousse felt almost sorry for him. He wondered if it was like that wherever he went. In his time he'd had his own share of public attention, but it had always been a thing of the moment, a brief period of glory when he'd been responsible for solving a particularly juicy *cause célèbre*. The day after it was usually forgotten, overtaken by other events. Nowadays he was all too grateful for the strict anonymity that his work for *Le Guide* imposed. Never to be able to go anywhere without such goings-on must be dreadful.

Shortly afterward Ananas' *aide de camp* appeared, struggling beneath a large assortment of monogrammed luggage. He didn't look best pleased.

Monsieur Pamplemousse began gathering together his own belongings. At least the platform was now clear. He glanced at his watch. They had plenty of time to catch the connection to Perpignan.

Climbing down onto the platform he paused to have a brief word with the attendant.

'*Au revoir. Merci.*' He pressed a small offering into the man's hand. It disappeared with all the professional skill of one who earned a good proportion of his living by such sleight of hand. But it was worth it. Realizing that Pommes Frites was sharing the breakfast, the man had been more than generous with the portions.

'*Merci, M'sieur.*' The attendant was looking very pleased about something. After the unpleasantness with Ananas over *déjeuner*, Monsieur Pamplemousse couldn't believe he was deriving satisfaction from the latter's reception.

'Do you believe in justice, *M'sieur*?'

Monsieur Pamplemousse shrugged. 'Most of the time. Although I must admit to a certain wavering when I witness the kind of demonstration that has just taken place.'

The attendant laughed. 'That is what is known as 'rough justice,' *M'sieur*. It may get even rougher when both sides find out their mistake. It is not a demonstration of love. It is a manifestation. *Une grève sauvage*, a wildcat strike. It is over a matter of schedules. We are the last train they are allowing in today.

'I think it is one product Monsieur Ananas may regret endorsing – especially when his picture appears in the newspapers tomorrow. It could well lose him his free life pass on S.N.C.F.'

He turned and looked at Monsieur Pamplemousse with some concern. '*M'sieur* is travelling far?'

Monsieur Pamplemousse nodded. 'We hoped to reach Perpignan.'

'In that case you should hurry. The train will be coming into *quai trois*. They are allowing the connection out because the driver lives in Narbonne, but who knows? They may yet change their minds. It may not take you on to Perpignan, but it will be a start.'

Monsieur Pamplemousse thanked him and hurried down the steps and up the other side to where a train from Bordeaux had just arrived at the adjoining *quai*.

He paused as the attendant's voice called over to him. '*M'sieur*,'

'*Oui?*'

'Forgive my saying so, but has anyone ever told you ...'

'*Oui*,' said Monsieur Pamplemousse. 'Many times.'

The attendant shrugged. '*Tant pis. C'est la vie.*'

'*C'est la vie!*' The man was right – it was no use minding. He climbed into the waiting *Corail*. After the *Capitole* it felt like boarding an airplane. He almost expected to be told to fasten his seat belt.

The cheers from the other end of the platform had grown more sporadic; he could detect a note of disillusion. Perhaps Ananas was trying to pour oil on troubled waters while protecting his own position at the same time. He didn't envy him the task.

As the train moved out of the *gare* he caught a glimpse of Ananas' factotum sitting glumly on a pile of luggage. Perhaps they, too, had been hoping to make the connection. If so, they were out of luck.

He settled back to enjoy the rest of the journey, however far it took them. It had been a strange interlude, not without its compensations. Somehow it redressed the balance slightly and made up for all the little indignities he had suffered. He would enjoy relating the tale at the next year's staff outing.

He was still working it over in his mind – honing the edges as it were – when they reached Carcassonne, looking very benign as it basked in the afternoon sun, the somber history of the old town buried in shadow. The platform was deserted. In a few months' time it would be laden with produce from the surrounding countryside.

Soon they were passing through vineyards. Thirty minutes later hills ahead of them heralded Narbonne, and at Narbonne the attendant's forecast came true. There would be no more trains that day. Passengers would have to make their own arrangements.

As he joined the throng of disgruntled fellow travelers pushing their way along the subway toward the exit, Monsieur Pamplemousse decided it might be a good moment to give his accessories another airing. Perhaps the good people of Narbonne would be more sympathetic to his plight than they had been in Paris. He had happy memories of his last visit, when he'd dined at a delightful little restaurant where they played a tape of the Hallelujah Chorus to herald the arrival of the dessert 'chariot.' He glanced at his watch. The restaurant was due for another test and it might not be too late.

Leaving Pommes Frites in charge of the luggage trolley, he took hold of his white stick, had a quick look around in order to get his bearings, then donned the dark glasses.

Blackness descended, and once again he felt the awful hopelessness being struck blind must engender. Heaven alone knew where the director had found them. Perhaps Madame Grante had produced them – getting her own back for some of his expense accounts. As he groped his way along the outside of the *gare* he decided that another time – not that there would ever be another time if he had any say in the matter, but if there were – he would insist on attending some kind of training course first.

Screwing his eyes around he spied the OFFICE DE TOURISME through the side of the frames. It was closed.

On the far side of the forecourt there was a large sign marked TAXIS but the area in front of it was empty. In fact taxis were conspicuous by their absence. They must all have been taken by the fleet of foot and were probably heading for destinations many kilometers away by now.

His heart sank and he was about to give up when he heard a voice. Raising his glasses, he saw a man in a chauffeur's uniform detach himself from the bonnet of a large black Mercedes and approach him. '*Pardon, Monsieur*, you are going to the Château Morgue?'

Monsieur Pamplemousse nodded. 'That is what I had hoped to do. It is not easy.'

The man motioned him toward the car. 'I am here to take you. We had word of the *manifestation*. Herr Schmuck sends his compliments.'

Monsieur Pamplemousse rapidly revised his view of Narbonne. It was a city he remembered fondly – the birthplace of Charles Trenet, singer of love songs. The way he was feeling, the man's words could have been set to music – another contender for the hit parade. The director must have done his stuff. He pointed toward the spot where Pommes Frites was waiting patiently. 'That is very good news indeed. I have my luggage over there.'

The chauffeur followed him. 'I had not expected *Monsieur* would be accompanied,' he said, eyeing Pommes Frites unenthusiastically. 'I was not told.'

Monsieur Pamplemousse unhitched the lead. He was not disposed to enter into an argument at this stage. 'It has all been arranged,' he said firmly.

The man gave a grunt as he picked up the valise and led the way toward the car. Monsieur Pamplemousse eyed his unexpected benefactor thoughtfully as he followed on behind. His manner wasn't exactly unfriendly; unforthcoming was perhaps a more accurate description. When he spoke, it was with a touch of arrogance, rather as though in the normal course of events he was the one who was used to giving the orders.

A moment later curiosity gave way to something rather stronger. As the man bent down to open the trunk, Monsieur Pamplemousse noticed a distinct bulge high up on the left side of his jacket. It could have been a well-filled wallet. On the other hand, instinct told him it was not.

He felt for his own wallet. 'Do you happen to have change for a two hundred franc note? Two one hundreds, perhaps?'

'*Non.*' There was no question of looking. He consigned the fact to his memory for possible future use. It had been worth a try.

The Mercedes had the kind of luggage compartment, spacious and spotlessly clean, that made his valise look inadequate and shabby, rather as one felt standing in front of a tailor's mirror being measured for a new suit.

Aware of the odd look the man was giving his white stick, Monsieur Pamplemousse tightened his grip on the handle, adjusted his glasses, and slipped back into his role as he climbed unsteadily into the car. He was pleased to see there was a dividing glass between himself and the driver. With a hundred or more kilometers still to travel, conversation might have flagged a little. As he settled himself down alongside Pommes Frites he felt something hard beneath his right buttock. It was a case containing a pair of sunglasses, Bausch and Lomb, of the type with photochromic variable density lenses that change according to the light. In the circumstances they were like manna from heaven. By the time the chauffeur had climbed into his seat the change had taken place. If he noticed anything different about his passenger he wasn't letting on.

There was a faint whirr and the glass panel slid apart. 'All is for the best, *Monsieur*?'

'*Oui*,' said Monsieur Pamplemousse. '*Merci*.' He caught the man's eyes watching him in the rear-view mirror. He seemed disappointed by the reply, and faintly uneasy, rather as though he had been expecting something more than the bare acknowledgment he'd received. After an uncomfortably long pause, he pressed a button on the dashboard and the panel slid shut again.

As they moved off Monsieur Pamplemousse relaxed and turned his attention to Pommes Frites, or rather to his rear end. Like most dogs, Pommes Frites was a bit of a snob when it came to cars and he was taking full advantage of his newfound status and the fact that the rear window on his side was half open. Eyes closed in ecstasy, he presented a profile to the world in general and in particular to any local inhabitants who happened to be passing, of one to whom such luxury was an everyday event. For the second time that day Monsieur Pamplemousse felt their usual mode of transport was being held up for comparison and found to be distinctly lacking.

As they gathered speed on the highway outside Narbonne he could stand the draft no longer and, much to Pommes Frites' disgust, pressed a button on the central console which controlled the electrically operated window.

Perpignan airport flashed by at nearly two hundred k.p.h. The saying was that birds went to Perpignan to die.

Monsieur Pamplemousse couldn't help but reflect that if there was any truth in the saying and they carried on driving at their present speed, many would have their wishes granted sooner rather than later.

At Le Boulou they took the D115 and began climbing steadily. He dozed for a while. When he woke it was already growing dark and they were on a minor road. Ahead of them the Pyrénées looked gray and mysterious, outlined against the lighter sky behind, like a child's painting, simple and stark. Snow on the upper slopes shone luminously in the moonlight.

The car headlights picked out the beginnings of a small village, the houses already tightly shuttered for the night. As they shot through the square he spotted a small bar and beyond the *Mairie* some more lights. A moment later it was gone.

Almost immediately they were out of the village and he was about to close his eyes again when they rounded a sharp bend and drove past a parking area on the valley side of the road, the sole occupant of which was a long, black hearselike vehicle. The driver was standing in front of it relieving himself against a rock. Monsieur Pamplemousse had a momentary glimpse of three others dressed in black inside the car. They waved as the chauffeur gave a blast on his horn. Whether or not they had waved in recognition was hard to say, but he had an odd impression that they were waiting for something or someone. Even funeral attendants had to obey the calls of nature, but it seemed an odd time to be abroad.

Monsieur Pamplemousse turned to see if he could spot the name of the village as they passed the sign, but he missed it in the dark. The Mercedes seemed to be totally unperturbed by the steepness of the climb. His 2CV would have been in bottom gear by now and struggling.

Ten minutes later the Château Morgue came into view, its dark bulk remote and impregnable. Probably built originally to keep others out, it now served to keen people in. Not, thought Monsieur Pamplemousse as they swung in through the gates, that there appeared to be anywhere to go other than the village if any of the guests decided to play truant.

The original stone building had been hideously embellished by a monstrosity in the shape of an enormously tall, circular tower. It betrayed itself as a twentieth-century afterthought, and stood out like a sore thumb. Lights blazed from uncurtained windows at the top, but the rest of the building was in comparative darkness. The inmates of Château Morgue must retire early, probably worn out by their treatment.

Before he had a chance to take it all in and absorb the geography of the surroundings, the driver made a sharp turn and, scarcely slackening speed, they hurtled down a spiral ramp into a vast underground garage, which must have been built at the same time as the tower.

As they pulled up beside some lift doors, Monsieur Pamplemousse glanced at the other cars already parked. Wealth radiated from their bumpers. He counted five Mercedes 500 S.E.C.s, two British registered Daimlers and a Rolls-Royce, an obscenely large American car he didn't immediately recognize, a sprinkling of B.M.W. 735s – two with C.D. plates – three Ferraris with Italian number plates, and a German Porsche. Somewhat incongruously a small Renault van with the words *Château Morgue – Charcuterie* on the side was parked in a corner.

The chauffeur opened the rear door for them to alight, removed the luggage from the trunk, and then spoke rapidly into a small microphone let into the wall. It was impossible to hear what he was saying. Seconds later the lift doors slid open. Barely acknowledging Monsieur Pamplemousse's thanks, the man ushered them through the opening, then reached inside to press the button for the ground floor. He withdrew, allowing the doors to close again. For whatever reason, dislike was now clearly written across his face and he seemed glad to be rid of them.

The inside of the lift was small but luxurious, the carpet unusually thick. On the back wall, near the floor, there was a hinged panel of the kind common to lifts in large apartment blocks, easily removable for the transportation of a coffin. It reminded Monsieur Pamplemousse of their encounter on the road a few minutes earlier. Perhaps one of the patients had died. If the truth were known, death was probably never very far away at a health farm. Many of the clients only went there in the first place because they had caught their first whiff of it on the horizon. Early warning signals from on high.

They stepped out of the lift into a circular foyer which was equally luxurious, like that of a small, but exclusive, hotel: discreet and reeking of understated opulence. The flowers in the vases were out of season. A desk stood in one corner. Its only concession to being functional was a row of buttons set in a freestanding remote control panel, and a red push-button telephone alongside it. The large, leather-covered chair behind the desk was empty. The whole atmosphere was like that of certain establishments he'd come across from time to time in the sixteenth *arrondissement* of Paris. Places where anything was obtainable provided you could pay the price, and nothing was ever questioned.

As they stepped out of the lift a man in a short white coat

appeared from behind a screen and came forward to greet them.

'*Bonsoir*.' Tucking a clipboard under one arm he gave a tiny, almost imperceptible bow. 'Doctor Furze. Herr Schmuck sends his apologies. He hopes to make your acquaintance later. At present he is unavoidably detained with a patient. In the meantime, I am at your disposal.'

While he was talking Doctor Furze glanced down at Pommes Frites and, like the chauffer before him, seemed surprised by what he saw. Again, Monsieur Pamplemousse got in quickly, forestalling any possible arguments. 'This is Pommes Frites,' he said simply. 'We are never parted.'

Although Pommes Frites' inflatable kennel was packed away in the bottom of the valise in case of emergencies, he had no intention of revealing the fact for the time being. If there was any talk of his being accommodated in the stables he would resist the idea most strongly.

After a moment's hesitation, Doctor Furze turned and led the way toward the lift. Swiftly, he pressed a sequence of numbers on a panel. Old habits die hard, and Monsieur Pamplemousse found himself regretting that his dark glasses prevented him from making a mental note of them.

Inside the lift the doctor seemed even more ill at ease, rather as if he had discovered something out of place and didn't know quite what to do about it.

'You are busy?' As Monsieur Pamplemousse posed the question he realized he was lowering his guard again.

Doctor Furze seemed not to notice. He pressed a button marked four. 'We are always busy in the V.I.P. area. The regular patients are in the main building. You will not be disturbed. Special arrangements can be made if you require treatment.'

It was the kind of remark – a statement of fact – that

put a full stop to any further conversation.

The lift opened straight into another circular hallway, almost identical to the one on the ground floor, except for four doors let into the perimeter wall. It struck Monsieur Pamplemousse that, the lift doors apart, he hadn't seen any in the reception area. Perhaps there was some kind of medieval secret passage.

Doctor Furze crossed the hall and withdrew from his pocket a chain with a bunch of keys on the end. 'I trust you will find everything to your satisfaction.' He stood to one side to allow Monsieur Pamplemousse and Pommes Frites to enter.

'No doubt you will wish to unpack before you order dinner. I will arrange for your luggage to be brought up. You will find the menu and the wine list in the bureau. The control panel for the television, video equipment, and the electric shutters is beside the bed.'

Monsieur Pamplemousse gazed around. It had to be some kind of joke on the part of the director. In the course of his travels on behalf of *Le Guide* he'd been in some pretty plush places, but this one beat the band. Never before had he encountered such unadulterated luxury. The first room alone would have provided more than enough material for a feature article in one of the glossier Paris magazines: wallpaper from Canovas, crystal from Baccarat, Christofle china and silverware. On the far side of the room, through an archway, he could see a king-size four-poster bed and beyond that a bathroom. Another archway opened onto the dining-area with a table already laid, and to its right, sliding full-length windows opened onto a balcony. He crossed to look at the view, but a passing cloud temporarily obscured the moon; by daylight it must be breathtaking. He resolved to have breakfast

49

outside next morning whatever the weather.

Perhaps it was all part of a carefully hatched surprise treat on the part of the management. After his last job of work he was due for a bonus. Vague promises had been made at the time, but somehow they had never materialized. If the thickness of the carpet was reflected in the size of the bill, Madame Grante would be throwing a fit in two weeks' time.

Monsieur Pamplemousse suddenly came back down to earth with a bump as he realized Doctor Furze was talking to him.

'As I was saying, you may prefer to dine alone on your first night.' Again there was a slight hesitation. 'If not, "arrangements" can be made. If you would like company … a girl, perhaps, or two girls, you will find a list of numbers by the telephone.' He glanced toward Pommes Frites. 'It is short notice, but it may even be possible to arrange something for your dog. You must let me know his interests.'

Monsieur Pamplemousse found himself avoiding Pommes Frites' eye. Pommes Frites had an unwinking stare at times, combined with the ability to make it appear as if he were hanging onto every word, almost as though he could understand what was being said. It was nonsense, of course, but disconcerting nevertheless.

'I think we are both a little tired after our long journey.' He felt like adding that he would hardly have known what to do with one girl, let alone two, but resisted the temptation. As for Pommes Frites, heaven forbid that he speak for him or his interests, but he shuddered to think what he might make of any local *chienne*.

'As you wish. If you change your mind, you have only to ring.' The bow was accompanied by the suspicion of a heel click. 'I will leave you now. No doubt you will wish to take a bath.'

Doctor Furze opened the door, brought in the valise, which had been left standing outside, and disappeared.

As he undressed, Monsieur Pamplemousse contemplated his reflection in a mirror that occupied one entire wall of the bathroom, a reflection which was unnervingly multiplied many times by another mirror let into the ceiling. One girl? Two girls? What manner of place had he come to? It certainly bore no relation to any of the reports he'd seen lying on the director's desk. Perhaps they, too, had been a subterfuge? Perhaps even now they were laughing their heads off back at Headquarters. He had a feeling that if he'd asked for three girls it wouldn't have presented a problem.

Three girls! Luxuriating in a leisurely *bain moussant*, he devoted his thoughts to the postcards he would send back to the office; they would be a series of progress reports.

What was it the director had said? 'The change will do you good, Pamplemousse.'

Pamplemousse basked in a euphoria brought on by his surroundings, a euphoria further enhanced by the warmth of the bath and by the oils that accompanied it, by the Stanley Hall of London soap, not to mention a shave in the softest of water, followed by the refreshing sting of an after-shave lotion which bore the name of Louis Philippe of Monaco. He stretched out a toe in order to ease open the hot water tap a *soupçon*, reaching out at the same time for a Kir Royale, lovingly mixed from ingredients found in a well-stocked refrigerator by the bed. If things carried on the way they had begun, his first postcard would be to the director himself. 'Regret, problems greater than expected. May need to stay on for further week.'

No, on second thought, why stint himself? Why not play Headquarters at their own game? Why not make it two extra weeks? A month at Château Morgue would tide him over a treat until the spring.

They were sentiments which, although unspoken, clearly won the whole-hearted approval of his thoughtreading companion in the next room, revering in the luxury of his new surroundings while waiting patiently for decisions concerning the evening meal. Decisions which, knowing his master as he did, would be made quickly and expertly when the moment came, and in the fullness of time would bear fruit that would make all the waiting worthwhile.

3
READ AND DESTROY

Monsieur Pamplemousse was in his element. Gastronomically speaking, he couldn't remember having had such an enjoyable time since the occasion shortly after joining the Force when, as a young police officer, he'd been involved in his first big case outside Paris and had found himself being taken to meet Fernande Point at Vienne. Being shown around the great man's kitchen – in those days the Mecca of *Haute Cuisine* and a training ground for many of the great present-day chefs – had been akin to a small boy of the eighties being invited up to the flight-deck of a Concorde.

Since taking a bath, his pen had been fairly racing over the pages of his *aide mémoire* as he set about making preliminary notes for his report. In his mind's eye as he scanned the menu he was already hard at work planning *déjeuners* and *dîners* for the days to come, adding, subtracting, shuffling around permutations of the many delights it contained, so that he and Pommes Frites would reap full benefit in the time at their disposal, bearing in mind also that, if they were to include visits to the gymnasium during their stay, energy lost through unaccustomed exercise would need to be replaced.

The director must have been joking when he talked of *régimes*. Anything less like a *régime* would be hard to imagine. Faced with making a choice for one meal only he would have been hard put to reach a decision, but given that they were staying at Château Morgue for two weeks, hopefully more, he could afford to go wherever his fancy took him. Such an opportunity rarely came his way.

And if the menu was one of the most exciting he'd come across for a long time, the wine list, too, had been chosen by someone with an eye to the good things in life, and possessed of an unlimited budget as well. It was a positive cornucopia of riches. The Bordeaux section in particular read like the pages of that bible of the wine trade, Cocks et Féret. The Lafites, for example, contained every vintage of note stretching back to the turn of the century. There were so many good things it almost made a choice more difficult, rather like finding oneself in the position of being able to go to the theater after a long absence, and finally not going at all through sheer inability to reach a decision. In the end he opted for a bottle of '78 Château Ferrière – from the Médoc's smallest classified vineyard and a comparative rarity. He had never actually tasted it, but from all he had heard it would be a delightful accompaniment to the Roquefort, which, since they were in the area, was a must. It would also go well with the main course, earning bonus points from Madame Grante into the bargain for its very modesty.

Monsieur Pamplemousse made the appropriate note in his book and then read it back out loud for the benefit of Pommes Frites, receiving in return a reaction which could only be termed satisfactory. Pommes Frites had a sizable vocabulary of culinary terms, culled from travels with his master. There were certain key words – like *boeuf*, which invariably caused his tail to wag, and it was only necessary to add the word *bourguignon*, and he would be on his feet in a flash and ready for action. In this instance the phrase

Magret de Canard grillé au feu de bois had the desired effect, and if anticipatory dribbles weren't exactly running down his chin, it wasn't because the choice failed to receive the full support of his salivary glands, but simply the fact that his mouth was so dry from lack of sustenance they were in need of a certain amount of priming first.

In fact, he couldn't really see what his master was waiting for. If the final decision was to have duck grilled over charcoal for the main course, why not get on with it and leave the choice of the *dessert* until later. Desserts were his least favourite part of a meal anyway, and he was a firm believer in the adage that a steak on the plate was worth two meringues in the oven any day of the week.

It was a thought that gradually communicated itself to Monsieur Pamplemousse. Food took time to prepare and cook. Assuming the whole thing wasn't part of some beautiful daydream from which he would suddenly wake, a mirage that would disappear as soon as he reached out to touch it, they were losing valuable time, which would be better spent over another Kir Royale. Takng the hint from Pommes Frites' restless padding up and down the room, he looked for the appropriate button to press for service.

As he did so he caught sight of his white stick and dark glasses and was reminded once again that he had a role to play. Already he had unforgivably let it slip, first with the chauffeur, and then nearly with Doctor Furze. It wouldn't do to let it happen again.

Having pressed the button he was immediately struck by the fact that service in the Château Morgue appeared to be on a par with its other facilities. He'd barely had time to write a few brief words to Doucette on a postcard he'd found amongst some other stationery – it showed a picture of Château Morgue and he marked with a cross what he judged might be his room as he always did – when Pommes Frites paused in his perambulations and pricked up his ears, staring at the same time in the direction of the hall. A moment later he heard the soft whine of a lift coming to rest outside, then the swish of a door opening. Hastily applying the stamp, Monsieur Pamplemousse placed the card between the pages of his notebook, slipped the latter into the secret pocket of his right trouser leg, and then sat back, clasping the stick between his knees, hands on top, preparing himself for a discreet knock from without.

Prepared though he was for some kind of entrance, he hardly expected the onslaught that followed. The door burst open and a positive avalanche of people flowed into his room. First, Doctor Furze, white-faced and agitated, still clutching his clipboard, then two others, a man and a woman whom he barely had time to register before, to his even greater surprise, Ananas swam into view. But it was a very different Ananas to the one he had last seen on Toulouse station. With his jacket torn, tie missing, hair dishevelled, he was clearly in a filthy mood.

Before the others had time to speak, he pushed his way to the front and glared at Monsieur Pamplemousse. '*Enfant de garce! Imposteur! Maquereau! Opportuniste!*'

Clearly he was all set to work his way steadily through the entire dictionary of abuse, but before he could progress beyond the letter 'O', help intervened in the shape of Pommes Frites. Normally, despite his size, Pommes Frites was of a gentle disposition. He didn't often growl. Growls he kept in reserve for special occasions. But when he did give voice to them they were of a kind that in his time had caused many an adversary to stop dead in his tracks lest it be followed by even worse manifestations of his displeasure. They began somewhere deep inside his stomach and followed what must have been a tortuous path through his intestines, gathering speed as they passed through various Venturi tubes, growing in volume as they entered and left a variety of echo chambers, before finally emerging between teeth which, when bared as they were now, could well have done service as some kind of industrial shredder.

The effect was both magical and instantaneous. Ananas stopped dead in his tracks and backed away, seeking protection from the others.

Doctor Furze spoke first. 'I'm afraid there has been some confusion,' he said, consulting his clipboard. 'A case of mistaken identity.' He glanced from one to the other. 'Not unnatural in the circumstances.' A snort from the direction of Monsieur Pamplemousse's double made the point that he, for one, did not think it at all natural.

'*Pardon.*' There was a flash of gold from a Patek Philippe watch as the third man held out his hand to Ananas. 'We will rectify matters immediately. I will arrange with your manager for your luggage to be sent up while Doctor Furze escorts this – other person to his proper quarters.' He turned to Doctor Furze who was hovering nervously on the sidelines, keeping a respectable distance between himself and Pommes Frites. 'You have the details?'

For once Doctor Furze had no need to consult his board. The information was obviously indelibly etched on his memory. 'Block C, room twenty-two, Herr Schmuck.'

'Good. See that the change is carried out at once.

'Certainly, Herr Schmuck'

While the others were talking Monsieur Pamplemousse caught a brief flicker pass between the woman and Herr Schmuck; a warning, perhaps? It was hard to say. Her eyes were as black as pitch, unnervingly so.

Herr Schmuck turned and gazed intently at Monsieur

Pamplemousse, as if trying to probe behind his dark glasses. Suddenly, his arm jerked up and he clicked his fingers. Monsieur Pamplemousse, who'd been trying to rehearse focusing his gaze somewhere in the direction of infinity, reacted rather more slowly than he might normally have done. But once again he was saved by Pommes Frites, whose second warning growl came sufficiently quickly for it to divert attention away from his reflexive drawing back. To his relief Herr Schmuck seemed satisfied.

'Come, Ananas,' he said, taking the other's arm. 'You must allow us to entertain you until your suite has been made ready.'

Looking slightly mollified, Ananas gave Monsieur Pamplemousse and Pommes Frites a final glare and then allowed himself to be led away. Madame Schmuck, if it were she, followed on behind without so much as a word or a backward glance. Monsieur Pamplemousse was left with the feeling that, if it came to any kind of argument, she would have the final decision. He was also oddly aware of a faint smell of greasepaint.

'If you wish to leave your bag,' said Doctor Furze, 'I will have someone attend to it.'

'Thank you, no.' Monsieur Pamplemousse had no desire to lose sight of his valise, particularly as it contained the case belonging to *Le Guide*. Even though the latter was securely locked, he didn't want to run the risk of anyone tampering with it, and the way matters were going anything was possible.

On the way down in the lift he was tempted to inquire if the menu in C Block was the same as the one he'd just been reading, but he changed his mind. Instead, as they emerged onto another floor, he took a firm grip of Pommes Frites' harness. He needed all his faculties in order to concentrate on his role.

'You will find the accommodation a little less luxurious,' said Doctor Furze, as he led the way down a long corridor, bare and featureless, with cream-coloured walls and cord-carpeting. 'The suite you have just been in is reserved for the personal guests of Herr Schmuck himself, you understand?'

Monsieur Pamplemousse understood. Ananas was doubtless at Château Morgue under a reciprocal arrangement. A free holiday in return for a suitable endorsement.

'Your room.' Doctor Furze stopped outside a door. 'I trust you will be comfortable.'

'Comfortable!' As he entered the room, Monsieur Pamplemousse could hardly believe his eyes. 'Comfortable!' He was about to hold forth in no uncertain manner, when he realized he was in no position to. But how could the man stand there and utter such falsehoods without even so much as a change of voice? Spartan wasn't the word. Even Pommes Frites, who was rarely bothered by his surroundings, seemed taken aback. Apart from a single bed and a very small armchair, the only other furnishings were a wooden locker, a chest of drawers, a plain uncovered table, and a wooden bench. Thick pile carpet had been replaced by a piece of coconut matting. Through an open doorway in the far wall he could see a bath and a wash basin, alongside which was a set of scales.

'It feels a little – different,' he ventured, as he groped his way round the room under the pretence of getting the feel of it. His heart sank. The iron frame of the bedstead felt cold to the touch. 'Am I right in thinking the heating has been turned off?'

'*Oui.*' Doctor Furze made no attempt to enlarge on his

reply. Instead, he steered Monsieur Pamplemousse gently but firmly in the direction of the bathroom. 'While you are in here perhaps you would be good enough to remove your clothing. I will make a note of your weight. We always like to do that on the first evening, then again in the morning. Patients usually notice the difference straight away.'

Monsieur Pamplemousse brightened. Perhaps dinner wouldn't be long in coming after all. He wished now he'd ordered the *cassoulet*. It would have been interesting to see how much weight he put on. 'That reminds me,' he began, 'you might like to help me with the menu. It is a little difficult.'

'Of course,' Doctor Furze picked up Monsieur Pamplemousse's trousers and hung them on a nearby hook. 'You will find it easy enough to remember. Dinner is at six-thirty sharp each evening. I'm afraid you have missed it tonight, but in the circumstances I will see what can be arranged. Normally, for the first five days it is a glass of *eau*.'

'*Eau*?' repeated Monsieur Pamplemousse. 'Did you say *eau*?'

'*Eau*.' Doctor Furze helped him onto the scales. '*Chaude*, of course. It comes from our own special spring, which rises beneath the cellars.'

'After five days you will be allowed a little fresh lemon juice as a treat.' He took a closer look at a digital display panel on the scales and gave a grunt of disapproval. 'We are a little unhappy with our weight, *n'est-ce pas*?'

Monsieur Pamplemousse drew himself up to his full height. 'We are very happy with our weight,' he said firmly. 'It is what we are most happy with. May I have my trousers back, please?' He suddenly felt resentful at having to display his failings in a cold bathroom.

'One other thing,' Doctor Furze glanced up from his

board. 'When you wish to use the bath, please let me know and I will arrange for the issue of a plug. It is not,' he allowed himself the ghost of a smile, 'that we are short of them. It is a simple but necessary precaution. One cannot be too careful. Once the treatment begins to take effect, many of our patients find it all too easy to get into a bath, but in their weakened state they occasionally have difficulty in getting out again.

'Sign here, please.' He pushed a pen into Monsieur Pamplemousse's hand and guided it toward the clipboard. 'It is an absolution clause. It is *obligatoire!*'

While he was speaking a beeper sounded. Withdrawing a small receiver from the top pocket of his coat, he listened carefully for a moment, then spoke briefly. *'Oui.* I will come immediately.

'I am afraid I must leave you now. *Bonne nuit. Petit déjeuner* is at seven A.M. sharp.'

Monsieur Pamplemousse gazed at the door as it closed behind the doctor. On the back there was an inscription in four languages, French, German, English and Spanish: NOTHING IN THE WORLD IS FREE – LEAST OF ALL YOUR HEALTH. Underneath was a list of charges for various extra services, of which there appeared to be a great many.

'Petit déjeuner!' A glass of hot water, no doubt. Followed by another glass for *déjeuner*. He could picture it all. It wouldn't even be drinkable. It would be a dirty, filthy, foul-tasting brown liquid. Straight out of the ground and tasting like it. Its diuretic qualities would be lethal. He'd once sampled some at a spa in the Midi and had sworn there and then never to repeat the experience. Even Pommes Frites, who wasn't above stopping at the nearest puddle when he needed to slake his thirst, had turned up his nose.

Ever alive to his master's moods, Pommes Frites lifted up

his head and gave vent to a long drawn out howl. It summed up the situation admirably.

Monsieur Pamplemousse gave him an approving pat, reflecting as he did so that with all the resources of the French language at his disposal he would still have been hard pressed to find words strong enough to describe adequately his feelings; it needed a dog of Pommes Frites' sensitivity to come up with exactly the right sound.

For a moment or two he was tempted to go in search of a telephone and call the director. With luck, he might even be able to persuade Pommes Frites to put on a repeat performance down the mouthpiece.

He thought better of it. He'd had enough of groping his way around in dark glasses for one day. That apart, if he knew the director, he would be neither amused nor sympathetic, particularly if he happened to be in the middle of dinner. Dinner! He gave an involuntary groan. Pommes Frites let out another howl in sympathy. There was a protesting knock on the wall from the adjoining room.

'*Merde!*' Monsieur Pamplemousse collapsed into the armchair in a state of gloom, memories of the meal he'd so carefully planned all too clear in his mind. His gastric juices went into overtime at the thought of what might have been. His dislike of Ananas grew stronger by the minute. No doubt he was already making up for lost time.

There was a movement from somewhere nearby as Pommes Frites curled up on the floor in front of him, resting his head lovingly across his master's feet. Thank heaven for Pommes Frites. Where would he be without him? How good it was to have the company of a faithful friend in one's hour of need.

Monsieur Pamplemousse closed his eyes while he luxuriated in the warmth which was slowly enveloping his ankles.

It was really a question of who cracked first, himself or Pommes Frites. At least he had the advantage of knowing why they were there. Why and for how long they were meant to stay. Pommes Frites had no idea. He wouldn't take kindly to a glass of water for his *petit déjeuner* every morning. Had they still been at home they would be going for a stroll by now – taking the air near the vineyard by the rue Saint Vincent, walking off the after effects of one of Doucette's *ragoûts*. He could picture it all …

He sat up with a start. Thoughts of Paris reminded him that with all the things going on that day he had totally forgotten about the letter the director had given him in his office. He felt inside his jacket. It was still there.

The envelope, which bore on its flap the familiar logo of *Le Guide* – two *escargots* rampant – contained a letter and a second smaller envelope made of curiously flimsy paper. The latter was sealed with red wax, embossed with a symbol which rang a faint bell in Monsieur Pample-mousse's head. A warning bell? It was hard to say. Certainly there was something about it that left him feeling uneasy. Intrigued, he decided to put it to one side for the moment while he read the Director's covering note. It was short and to the point.

'My dear Aristide,' it began. That was a bad sign. Either the director wanted to curry favour or he had a guilty conscience.

I trust you will forgive my not being entirely frank with you in my office, but as you will see, there were very good reasons. Walls, Aristide, have ears, and the enclosed is for your eyes only. Even I, *directeur* of *Le Guide*, am not privileged to be apprised of its contents. Therefore, I can only wish you luck in what I assume is yet another of those clandestine 'missions' to which you have become so addicted, and for which you have acquired some notoriety. Take care, Aristide. Above all, take care! For once you are on your own. You can expect no help from Headquarters.

The letter, signed by the director in his usual indecipherable scrawl, ended with a postscript. 'Two other things while I write. Please assume that until such time as the order is rescinded, you have *carte blanche* with your P39s. Also, once you have read and digested the contents of the second envelope, please destroy it immediately. Both letter and envelope are made of best quality rice paper. If necessary they can be consumed with no ill effects.'

'Boiled, fried, or *nature*?' Monsieur Pamplemousse suddenly felt distinctly hard done by as he glanced at his surroundings. How dare the Director say that he had a predilection for 'missions' when as far back as he could remember he had always been a victim of outside circumstances. Not a seeker of 'missions,' but one who had missions thrust upon him whether he liked it or not. The sheer injustice of the remark rankled. As for apologizing for lack of frankness in his office, that was the understatement of the year. He picked up the second letter and held it to the light. For two pins he wouldn't even bother to read it.

As the last thought entered his mind, a slow smile gradually crept over Monsieur Pamplemousse's face. Tearing a small piece off one corner of the envelope, he applied it to his tongue and then lay back and closed his eyes again. It would have been a gross exaggeration to say that it had a pleasant taste. Comparison with Tante Marie's *gâteau de riz* would have been odious. Indeed, there was hardly any taste at all, more a sensation of blandness. All the same, it would serve them all right if hunger got the better of him and he ate the entire letter then and there, unopened and therefore, *ergo*, unread. There had been nothing in the accompanying note to say he must read it.

Dwelling again upon his meeting with the Director, other remarks and phrases came back into his mind: remarks about his weight, slurs cast on his physical features, scarcely veiled criticisms regarding his expense account. And when all those failed, appeals to his better nature and to his loyalty, neither of which had ever been held in question before.

With so much on his mind, sleep did not come easily, but gradually Monsieur Pamplemousse began to nod off, and as he did so he relaxed his grip on the letter, allowing it to flutter gently to the floor. It was an act that did not go unremarked by his companion, more especially because it landed fairly and squarely, if lightly, upon his head.

Nudged into instant wakefulness, Pommes Frites opened one eye and gazed thoughtfully at the offending object. A moment later the sound of steady chewing added itself to Monsieur Pamplemousse's heavy breathing. It was not, in Pommes Frites' humble opinion, one of the best nor the most sustaining meals he had ever eaten, but beggars can't be choosers. What was good enough for his master was good enough for him, and if it didn't exactly fill what was now a gaping void, it did at least bridge a tiny gap or two.

Hunger is not the best of bedfellows, and when Monsieur Pamplemousse woke to the sound of coughing, it was also with a sense of remorse. He realized as he sat up with a start that this sprang from a dream he'd been having – and not simply *having*, but actually *enjoying*. As he patted Pommes Frites on the back to relieve him of whatever was stuck in his throat, he could hardly look him in the eye. To have dreamed of a large suckling pig resplendent on a silver tray, an apple in its mouth, surrounded by a pile of fried potatoes, was one thing. To have transmogrified that pig into his own, dear friend was quite another matter. A shameful episode, one he would do his best to forget. Thank heavens he'd woken when he had.

He glanced at his watch and felt even more guilty. It was nearly midnight. Pommes Frites must be dying for a walk. Apart from the brief spell at Narbonne, he hadn't had an opportunity all day.

A moment later the thought was transformed into action as he led the way along a deserted corridor toward a door at the end marked SORTIE DE SECOURS. Opening it as quietly as he could, he let Pommes Frites through and then left it slightly ajar with the end of a mat so that he could come back in again when he was ready. The air outside struck cold and there was no sense in both of them suffering. He would need all his strength in the next two weeks. What a blessing he hadn't sent off a card to the director. With his present luck the request for an extra two weeks would have been granted.

Leaving Pommes Frites to his own devices he hurried back to his room. Before leaving Ananas' suite he'd had the foresight to pack a few magazines he'd seen lying about. They would help while away the time. Poor old Pommes Frites – he wondered what he was thinking about it all.

Pommes Frites, as it happened, had several very clear thoughts occupying his mind; three, to be precise, and for one not overgiven to exercising his grey matter unnecessarily, three was quite a lot.

The first thought he'd taken care of on a large bush immediately outside the door, and very rewarding it had been too. He felt much better and ready for action. He was very glad his master had made a move, otherwise he might not have been responsible for his actions, for his second thought had to do with bones. Inasmuch as Pommes Frites ever felt guilty, he was feeling it now.

He hadn't been quite so hungry for a long time, and he'd been finding it increasingly difficult to rid himself of a picture that had entered his mind while lying at his master's feet. In his mind's eye he'd suddenly seen them in quite a different light; not as objects on the end of the trouser-covered legs he had known and loved for many a year, but as bones – two lovely, juicy bones. And the longer he'd dwelt on the thought the more juicy and desirable they had become. It had been a narrow squeak. If Monsieur Pamplemousse had stayed asleep much longer he might have woken with an even greater start.

Pommes Frites' third and most constructive thought was that if his master wasn't prepared to do anything about their present situation then he, Pommes Frites, would have to take matters in hand personally. Unlike many of his human counterparts, it was not part of his philosophy to believe that the world owed him anything. The idea wouldn't have entered his head. That being so, when things weren't going right you did something about it. Which, as he set off, nose to the ground on a tour of investigation, was exactly what he intended.

It was some while later, almost an hour to be precise, that Monsieur Pamplemousse, having spent much of the intervening time searching for his letter and finding, to his growing concern, only a small piece of wet and partly chewed red sealing wax, heard a bump in the distance. A bump which was followed almost immediately by the sound of something heavy being dragged along the corridor.

Thinking it might be another patient in difficulty, an elderly lady perhaps, who was suffering from a surfeit of hot water, he put down his magazine with a sense of relief. Any diversion was better than none at all. Without exception the magazines had been porn, certainly not pure, but definitely simple in their singleminded approach to a subject that was capable of almost infinite variations. The only feeling of lust they inspired in him was the wish that some of the many *derrières* displayed could have been real. Had they been real he would have been sorely tempted to take a large bite out of them, so great was his hunger. That would have wiped the smile off some of the owners' faces as they peered around the side, or in some cases from below, tongue protruding from between moistened lips.

By the time he reached his door the thumping was almost outside. As he opened it, Pommes Frites pushed his way past, dragging a large parcel tied up with string. His face wore the kind of expression that befitted a bloodhound whose trail had led him to exactly the right spot at precisely the right time.

Having looked up and down the corridor to make sure the coast was clear, Monsieur Pamplemousse closed the door. He had no idea what the parcel contained, but at a guess, since the outside bore the name of a retailer, and below that the magic word *charcuterie*, it might with luck be a delivery of groceries. How and where Pommes Frites had managed to get hold of it was academic. The important fact was that somehow or other he had.

With trembling hands, Monsieur Pamplemousse carried the parcel over to the table and pulled the string away from the outside, up-ending the contents as he did so. To say that he was taken aback by the result was to put it mildly. Even Pommes Frites looked startled. Putting his paws up on the table he gazed down open-mouthed as a string of sausages spilled out; large ones, small ones, medium sized – as they landed so they seemed to grow in size until it was hard to believe that the parcel he had been carrying could have contained so much.

For a moment or two Monsieur Pamplemousse stood transfixed, a look of wonder on his face. He couldn't remember having seen quite so many sausages since he last attended the annual *Boudin* Festival at Mortagne-au-Perche. There were more than enough to feed a regiment. Then he sprang into action.

Undoing his valise, he removed a smaller case, the one containing the emergency kit issued to all those who worked for *Le Guide*. Designed to cover every eventuality in the minimum of space, it was a miracle of compactness; not a single cubic centimeter was wasted. Spare notebooks, maps, report forms, and writing instruments were contained in the lid. Below that was a felt-lined tray for the Leica R4, two spare lenses – wide and narrow angle – a motor winder, and various filters and other accessories. Below that again, other compartments contained a pair of Leitz Trinovid binoculars, a compass, map magnifier, water purifying tablets (Monsieur Pamplemousse slipped several into his pocket, they might come in useful later), and a book containing emergency telephone numbers. Last but not least, in the very bottom of the case there reposed a funnel, a small butane-operated folding stove, a collapsible pan, and a box of stormproof matches.

In all his years with *Le Guide* he'd never had occasion to use the last three items. Nor, for that matter, had any of his colleagues, as far as he knew, apart from Glandière, who covered the Savoie region and sometimes disappeared for weeks at a time.

Now he blessed the man who had designed it. A man of foresight, a leader among men. He turned and looked down as something long and sinewy began slapping the side of his leg.

'Pommes Frites!' he exclaimed. 'You are *très, très méchant.*' But the tone of his voice gave lie to the words, and Pommes Frites' tail began to wag even faster as he followed his master into the bathroom in search of some water.

Quite frankly, in order to save time, he would have been perfectly happy to dine on a smoked or dried sausage; a *Saucisson de Lyon*, for example, or perhaps one from *Arles*, even a raw sausage or two, but if his master intended cooking them first, then so be it.

The stove alight and the water beginning to show signs of movement, Monsieur Pamplemousse turned to the difficult task of deciding on an order of priorities. With such a wealth of sausages at his disposal, the choice would not be easy. As a member of several distinguished societies – the A.A.A.A.A., *the Association Amicale des Amateurs d'Andouille Authentique, La Confrérie des Chevaliers du Goûte-Andouille*, whose energies were directed toward the perfection of the *andouillette*, not to mention *the Confrérie des Chevaliers du Goûte-Boudin*, who were very protective about that other classic of French *cuisine*, and the *Frères du Boudin Noir et Blanc* – his loyalties were divided.

In the end, much to Pommes Frites' approval, he decided on a representative selection. One by one, *Andouillette, Saucisse de Toulouse, Saucisse d'Alsace Lorraine, Saucisse de Campagne*, and *Boudins Noirs et Blancs* disappeared into the bubbling water until the pan could hold no more.

Monsieur Pamplemousse thought the *boudins* looked particularly mouth-watering. He'd once taken part in the annual competition at Manziat to see who could eat the most – the winner had eaten over a meter at one sitting. The way he was feeling at that moment, that year's champion would have been an also-ran, a non-starter.

Reaching into the bag again, he took out a fork and plunged it into the bubbling pan. The *boudin* was beyond his wildest expectations; it would have more than upheld a reputation which stretched back into history as far as Homer. Made to the classic formula of fresh pork fat, chopped onion, salt, freshly ground pepper and spices, pig's blood, and cream, it positively melted in the mouth, like a soft ice cream on a summer's day.

Wiping the juice from his hands lest they soil the pages, he reached for his notebook. The panful in front of him had barely scratched the surface of the vast quantity still left on the table. It would be a useful exercise to start a study of the subject. Already he could see another article in the staff magazine. *Saucisses et Saucissons – A Comparative Study in Depth* by A. Pamplemousse. Perhaps, looking at the pile in front of him, with the words 'to be continued' at the end. The editor would be pleased.

At his feet, Pommes Frites gave a sigh of contentment. Oblivious to the subtle difference between an *andouillette* with its quota of chitterlings and tripe, and an *andouille* with its addition of pork meat, he'd had two of each and enjoyed them both. Now he was looking forward to rounding things off with a *boudin* or two followed by a nap. It had been a long and tiring day, a day of ups and downs, and a good nap wouldn't come at all amiss.

It was a thought that appealed to Monsieur Pamplemousse too, and shortly afterward, having taken the precaution of inflating Pommes Frites' kennel and placing it in the bathroom lest he get any ideas about sharing the bed, he started to get undressed. Soon, they were both in the land of dreams.

4
THE CAMERA NEVER LIES

Monsieur Pamplemousse slept late into the following morning. When he finally woke, it was to the sound of engines revving, the metallic slamming of car doors, dogs barking, and raised voices.

He sat up and looked at his watch. Ten o'clock! *Merde!* Such a thing hadn't happened in years. Breakfast would have been over and done with hours ago. Then he realized where he was. Breakfast was of academic importance.

Getting out of bed, he crossed to the window and drew the curtains. In the driveway near the main entrance a police van was parked alongside the car in which he had arrived. A solitary *gendarme* occupied the passenger seat, otherwise all was quiet. The view was away from the Pyrénées, southward toward the Massif du Canigou and its sacred mountain. Château Morgue was even higher than he'd expected – above the tree line. The surroundings looked as still and unspoiled as they must have been in the days when the Troubadours roamed the area crying '*oc*' instead of '*oui*.'

He opened the door to the corridor and peered out. That, too, was deserted. Outside several of the rooms reposed a tray with a solitary empty glass. The exit door at the far end was ajar, as it must have been all night. He shivered. No wonder it felt cold. Seeing it reminded him that Pommes Frites would probably be wanting to obey the call of nature.

Having seen him safely on his way, he turned his attention to the more immediate matter of running a bath. Once again he had cause to bless the man who had designed the survival kit. In a special hole let into the side of the case he found a multipurpose waste plug. Nothing had been forgotten.

As he lay back in the bath he contemplated his changed fortunes. It was certainly a case of one law for the rich and another for the less affluent. Gone were all the expensive unguents and lotions of the previous bathroom. The only aids provided for those who wished to cleanse themselves were a small bar of soap bearing the name of one of the giant combines, and a plastic shower cap. Perhaps not many inmates bothered to ask Doctor Furze for a plug. He could hardly blame them.

The disappearance of the letter was a problem and no mistake. He could hardly blame Pommes Frites, who had doubtless taken his cue from watching his master consume a corner of the envelope. All the same, it wouldn't be very easy to explain. It would be bad enough in writing, but harder still when it came to the interview which would undoubtedly follow. He could picture the looks he would get and how his simple statement – 'Pommes Frites ate it' – would be repeated in tones of utter disbelief, followed by stony silence. On the other hand, saying he'd lost it wouldn't go down too well either.

For a moment or two he toyed with the idea of phoning the director, but then he dismissed the thought. The director was obviously as much in the dark as he was. He would get no help from that quarter, and it would only bring closer the moment he was trying to put off. Far better to play things by ear for the time being. Let matters take their course.

His musings were broken into at that moment by a double click from the outside door, heralding Pommes Frites' return from his morning stroll. Pommes Frites was good at opening doors. It was a trick he'd learned on a training course when he'd first joined the Paris police. He was less good at closing them again, although in this instance politeness, or discretion, had obviously won the day.

A head appeared around the corner of the bathroom door. Its owner was wearing a distinctly thoughtful expression, but by then Monsieur Pamplemousse was much too busy drying himself to notice.

A leisurely shave and it was time for breakfast. Soon *Saucisses Viennoises*, that heavenly mixture of pork, veal, fillet steak, and coriander, were bubbling away on the stove. He leaned over as one of them rose to the surface, and pricked it with a needle to prevent it bursting.

While he was waiting for them to finish cooking he cut some slices from a *Saucisson de Bourgogne*. The slight tang of the kirsch flavouring would act as an excellent appetizer. Instinctively he made a note about the *saucisson* in his book. It was the correct length – forty-five cm – and had been well dried – in his judgment, six months at the very least. He gave it full marks, as did Pommes Frites from the speed with which it disappeared. The only unsatisfactory aspect was the lack of bread. The smell of freshly baked bread suddenly wafted into his mind. Back home the second baking at the *boulangerie* in the rue Marcadet would be just about ready. Nevertheless, given the circumstances, he couldn't grumble. It had been a more than satisfactory start to the day. Apart from orange juice and coffee, he doubted if even Ananas had fared better.

Washing-up completed, the emergency bag securely

locked and packed away, he wrapped the remaining sausages in his overcoat and stowed them away at the back of the cupboard.

Since Château Morgue obviously didn't believe in their patients enjoying the luxury of having locks on their doors – probably in case any of them shut themselves in and lacked the strength to get out again – he hung the OCCUPÉ notice on the outside handle for safety. One couldn't be too careful.

Shortly afterward, holding onto Pommes Frites' harness with his left hand and grasping the white stick with his right, he set off, tapping his way along the corridor away from the SORTIE DE SECOURS toward what an arrow on the wall referred to as THE CENTRE D'ÉTABLISSEMENT THERMAL (TOUTES DIRECTIONS). They had dillydallied long enough. It was time to take the bull by the horns and make their entry into the world of *La Cure*.

The signs on the doors of the adjoining building made gloomy reading. Everything from the coccyx to the pharynx seemed to be catered for. There was hardly a part of the body that didn't have its name written up in large capital letters. LES ECZÉMAS embraced LES ACNÉS, and the two jostled for pride of place alongside LES ULCÉRES. Parts of the body he hadn't dreamed existed were displayed in the form of illuminated x-rays, looking more like sliced portions of *andouillette* than anything remotely human. By the time he reached the end of the corridor a strange feeling of itchiness on his skin had been replaced by a dull pain in his stomach. He wasn't sure whether it was a surfeit of sausages or merely psychosomatic, but whichever it was it quickly transmitted itself to Pommes Frites who stopped scratching himself in favour of looking for a possible exit door.

Monsieur Pamplemousse decided that impurities of the skin and intestinal disorders were not high on his list of priorities that day. Far better to get adjusted to his new surroundings with the help of something less exotic.

Following a sign marked AUTRES DIRECTIONS, he turned a corner and spied a door marked OBÉSITÉ. His entry triggered off a flurry of squeals and indignant shrieks as a plethora of female bodies scattered in all directions, like over-fat mice at harvest time.

Monsieur Pamplemousse focused his attention on the nearest and undeniably most nubile of the forms. He touched his forelock with the end of his white stick.

'*Pardon, Monsieur,*' he exclaimed. '*Est-ce la bibliothèque*?'

A giggle of relief went around the room. Towels were released and fell to the ground unheeded, their owners breathing sighs of relief as they relaxed again.

It gave Monsieur Pamplemousse a chance to make a closer study of the scene. Like a small boy let loose in an ice cream parlour, he sampled a chocolate-nut sundae here, a banana split there, discarding a half-eaten Knickerbocker Glory to the right of him in favour of a pecan and hot fudge confection to his left, while yet leaving room to manoeuvre in case he had another change of mind and dipped into a tutti-frutti special. The woman he'd spoken to came toward him.

'I think you have made a mistake.'

Essaying a half-hearted attempt at sounding confused, Monsieur Pamplemousse stammered his apologies as she turned him around and gently but firmly pushed him back out through the door. He poked his head back inside for one last, lingering look. From the rear she was even more desirable. 'A thousand apologies, *Monsieur,*' he called.

Monsieur Pamplemousse went on his way with a lighter step. Life had suddenly taken on a new dimension. Quick thinking sometimes brought unexpected rewards. Saying he'd been looking for the library had been a mistake, but in the general excitement no one seemed to have noticed. There was no doubt about it, his 'affliction' had its compensations.

Farther along the corridor he came across another door marked GYMNASE. Deciding that violent exercise was not what he was most in need of at that moment, he was about to resume his perambulations when he heard a commotion coming from inside the room. It was followed almost immediately by the sound of an alarm bell ringing somewhere in the distance. Under the pretext of trying to get his bearings, he remained where he was and almost immediately his patience was rewarded. Two men in porter's uniforms came hurrying along the corridor pushing a wheeled stretcher. With scarcely a glance in his direction they opened the door to the gymnasium and disappeared inside, closing it behind them.

Intrigued, he hung around trying to decide whether or not he should follow them, when the matter was decided for him. The door opened and they emerged, moving rather more slowly than they had when they arrived, for the very simple reason that the stretcher now bore the unmistakable shape of a body covered in a white sheet.

As the men carefully manoeuvred the trolley through the doorway and into the corridor they were followed by a gaggle of white-faced women clad in leotards. Clearly all were in a state of shock as they squeezed their way past, some averting their gaze, others crossing themselves as they paid their last respects.

In the confusion, Monsieur Pamplemousse groped his

way forward and managed to make contact with the sheet to pull it a little to one side. He found himself looking down at the face of an elderly woman. She looked ominously still, her eyes dark green and lifeless against the white of her skin. There was something vaguely familiar about her. But before he had time to do anything more than record the fact, Herr Schmuck appeared in the doorway.

He seemed slightly thrown off balance by the encounter. Once again Monsieur Pamplemousse was thankful for the variable density dark glasses. The lenses had adjusted to the harsh overhead fluorescent lights of the corridor, affording him a better opportunity to study the professor than he'd had the night before. Herr Schmuck looked a good deal older than he'd thought. His skin had the kind of waxy sheen, like tightly stretched parchment, common to the very old. He was also considerably less in command of the situation than he had been on the occasion of their last meeting. Once again, there was a faint smell of greasepaint.

Taking advantage of the momentary pause, Monsieur Pamplemousse tapped the floor impatiently with his stick. 'Will someone please tell me what is going on? I do not understand. Has there been an accident?'

As he spoke he reached over toward the motionless figure on the stretcher. Almost as though he was anticipating the move, Herr Schmuck beat him to it. In a single movement he closed the woman's eyelids and pulled the sheet back over her face, but not before Pommes Frites managed to give it a quick lick. He seemed somewhat surprised by the result, rather as though it had left a nasty taste.

Herr Schmuck signaled the two men to carry on. 'My apologies for this unfortunate encounter. There is no cause for alarm. It happens from time to time. Normally we try to carry out these unpleasant tasks as discreetly as possible, but alas ...' He gave a shrug as he hurried after the others.

Monsieur Pamplemousse watched the progress of the stretcher party along the corridor, one man pushing, Herr Schmuck and the other man following on behind. Speed seemed to be the order of the day. So much so, as they went to turn a corner at the end they narrowly missed colliding with Doctor Furze who was coming the other way. His inevitable clipboard went flying and while he bent down to pick it up Herr Schmuck paused in order to exchange a few words.

Monsieur Pamplemousse was left in no doubt as to the subject of the conversation. Several times they turned and looked in his direction and at one point Herr Schmuck said something that clearly caused a certain amount of ribald amusement amongst the others.

Doctor Furze nodded, beckoned to one of the two attendants to follow him, and came hurrying down toward the gymnasium. Monsieur Pamplemousse turned to go on his way, but he had left it too late. Before he had time to take more than a few steps the other two came up on either side of him and he felt his arms being grasped gently but firmly. He tried to free himself, but the grip tightened.

'Ah, Monsieur Pamplemousse. I am pleased to see we have begun our treatment. That is good.' Doctor Furze's voice had unpleasant overtones.

'Merely a preliminary survey. A voyage of exploration. Pommes Frites and I are getting our bearings.' Monsieur Pamplemousse tried to conceal a growing uneasiness by making light of the matter. 'Or rather, Pommes Frites is getting *his* bearings. As ever, I merely follow on behind.'

'Then it is as well we came along.' Doctor Furze made a pretence of consulting his clipboard. 'You are down for a workout in the gymnasium this morning. A little toning-up of the muscles is indicated before you start your course. We have machinery for such things.' He made it sound like 'We have ways of making you talk.'

'It is, I am afraid, the moment when you and Pommes Frites will have to part company for a while. As you know, *chiens* are *interdits* at Château Morgue. An exception was made in your case, but there are certain areas where we cannot bend the rules. Others would complain.'

While he was talking Doctor Furze pushed open the door to the gymnasium and before he had time to remonstrate, Monsieur Pamplemousse found himself being propelled through the gap. There was a click as the door closed behind them, followed by a dull thud as Pommes Frites applied his full weight to the other side.

'Good. You appear to have the room to yourself.' Ignoring the interruption, Doctor Furze punctuated his remark with a metallic click as he operated a catch on the door. 'We must make sure you are not disturbed.'

Torn between wanting to protest and the need to preserve his masquerade, Monsieur Pamplemousse inwardly registered, but passed no comment on, the paraphernalia of keep-fit gadgetry surrounding him: rowing machines, stationary cycles, parallel bars, apparatus he'd only ever seen adorning the pages of glossy magazines.

Deciding that discretion was, for the time being at least, the better part of valour, he allowed himself to be helped onto a machine whose purpose he would have been hard put to define had he been asked. It looked more like the cockpit of a space module than anything remotely connected with keeping fit.

A moment later, as he lay back in a semiprone position and felt leather straps being tightened around his ankles and wrists, he wished he hadn't given in so easily. But he had left it too late. As Doctor Furze reached up and pressed a button on a panel mounted to one side of the machine, he felt his legs begin to move in a kind of pumping action, slowly at first, then gradually gathering speed. At the same time his outstretched arms were carried upward over his head, then inexorably back again. The doctor flicked another switch and there was a sudden surge of power.

Closing his eyes, Monsieur Pamplemousse was dimly aware of voices and vague movements in front of him. Then they disappeared and he heard a door close.

Fighting back the feeling of utter helplessness which came over him as he realized he was on his own, he concentrated all his efforts on trying to ride with the machine rather than resist it, knowing that if he once allowed himself to falter, panic would set in. He was determined not to give Doctor Furze the satisfaction of seeing him in a state of collapse when he returned. *If* he returned. The memory of the woman on the stretcher came flooding back and he wondered if she, too, had found herself in the 'hot seat.' It had certainly felt warm when he'd first climbed onto it.

How long his ordeal might have lasted, Monsieur Pamplemousse had no means of knowing. All he was aware of were clouds of a reddish colour filling his brain; redness, followed by purple, then total blackness enveloped him as he passed out. It was followed by a feeling of floating on air and an unaccountable warmth, a perfumed warmth which came from somewhere overhead.

He opened his eyes and saw first Pommes Frites, or rather Pommes Frites' tongue as it reached out to lick him, and beyond that an impression of peaches, a peachlike skin covered in soft down.

'Are you all right?' The peach swam into focus and formed itself into a face. 'What an awful thing to have happened. Thank goodness your dog kicked up such a fuss. I found him trying to scratch the door down. I can't think how it could have been left locked. Luckily I had my pass key with me.'

While she was talking the owner of the face set about undoing the straps and Monsieur Pamplemousse realized for the first time that the machine was no longer working.

As the last of the straps fell away he tried to dismount, then he fell back again as his legs started to buckle beneath him.

'You'd better come back to my room.' The voice took charge and a hand reached out to take hold of his. 'What I still can't credit is that anyone could be so careless. It would be bad enough at the best of times, but to let it happen to someone in your condition!'

'My condition?' Monsieur Pamplemousse suddenly remembered he had a part to play. He groped around with his free hand in search of his stick. Pommes Frites, ever alert to his master's needs, picked it up in his mouth and handed it to him.

'My room' turned out to be farther along the corridor and far enough away from the gymnasium for Monsieur Pamplemousse to breathe more freely. As far as he was concerned, the farther away the better.

He stole a quick glance at the inscription on the door as it was held open for him. It bore the name COSGROVE. MRS. ANNE COSGROVE. The label said, PÉDICURE ET MASSAGE. Below the name there was a list of appointments for the day. He considered the matter for all of a hundredth of a second. A few minutes earlier he would not have remotely considered having his toenails attended to, let alone

82

subjecting himself to a massage, and yet ... instinct told him it was an offer he shouldn't refuse.

Mrs. Cosgrove held the door open and very gently placed a hand on his left elbow. She was wearing a white suit, which must have been stock issue as he had seen other staff wearing it, but somehow she managed to make it seem as though it had been specially tailored. Perhaps it was because she had made certain modifications. The zipper, which ran the length of the jacket front, from the high-collared neck down to the bottom hem, had been replaced at some time by one in bold, black plastic, with a large ring attached to the fastener. The sleeves were short, the trousers beneath closely fitting and held firmly in place by a figure that was both full and inviting.

'I'm afraid I do not have an appointment. It is perhaps a case of – how do you English say? – pot luck.' As he allowed himself to be led into the room, Monsieur Pample-mousse drew on the small stock of phrases remembered from his stay in Torquay. In England at that time there had been a lot of pot luck.

'Oh dear.' Mrs. Cosgrove smiled ruefully. 'Is my accent *that* bad?'

'Not at all.' He was about to say he had seen her name on the door, but he stopped short in the nick of time. Instead, as she took hold of his hand to guide him into a waiting chair, he essayed a compliment. 'You have the skin of an Englishwoman – it is very smooth and flawless.'

It was true. As she leaned over and he felt the warmth of her body close to his he was reminded once again of peaches. Peaches and cream on a hot summer's day by the Marne, or perhaps even more appositely, on the banks of the river Thames, Henley, perhaps, where the English had their boat races.

83

'When you have the misfortune to inhabit the world in which I live,' he said simply, 'you acquire an extra sensitivity.' Out of the corner of his eye he caught sight of Pommes Frites watching him intently, hanging on his every word. He turned the chair slightly on its swivel. Pommes Frites could be very off-putting at times.

'Gosh, yes. I suppose so.' Mrs. Cosgrove sat down on a stool in front of him and began removing his shoes and socks. 'Is it true what they say about blind men then?'

Monsieur Pamplemousse felt himself heading toward deep water. 'People say many things about many people,' he said noncommittally. 'Some are true, some are not.'

Mrs. Cosgrove crossed one leg over the other as she reached over toward a tray of instruments. Her free leg began to swing to and fro like the pendulum of a clock. According to Didier in Planning it was a sure sign of some deep frustration, and he should know. He'd been married three times.

'I mean about their being good lovers.' Mrs. Cosgrove hastily uncrossed her legs and lifted his right foot onto her lap. 'I suppose I shouldn't really have said that.'

'It is a question you would have to ask of another woman,' said Monsieur Pamplemousse. He gritted his teeth as Mrs. Cosgrove set to work, first on the instep, then gradually moving up toward the ankle. It felt as though his foot was on fire.

'George has got very good eyesight.'

'George?'

'My husband.'

'He is here?'

Mrs. Cosgrove gave a hollow laugh. 'I should be so lucky. No, he's at home, in England. He doesn't hold with this sort of place. Too much like hard work. He's probably out

84

shooting or fishing.'

Monsieur Pamplemousse digested this latest piece of information, trying to form an equation between a man who was rich enough to spend his time out shooting and fishing on the one hand and on the other a woman massaging his ankles in a remote corner of France. Perhaps Didier was right in his theory and it accounted for the frustration.

'Life goes on.' Mrs. Cosgrove was one step ahead of him. 'They say a change is as good as a rest. I took a course years ago. Not,' she continued with feeling, 'that it's doing me much good. I seem to spend most of my time either fending off geriatric foot fetishists or digging toenails out of the curtains.'

'Every occupation has its hazards,' said Monsieur Pamplemousse. 'And few people are without their problems.'

Mrs. Cosgrove sighed. 'You can say that again. This place is full of them. It's funny really.'

'Funny?'

'Well, it's the first time I've worked anywhere like this, but it isn't at all what I expected. It's on two levels, if you know what I mean. Half the patients are barely tolerated – almost as if they are a necessary evil. They come and they go and then they are forgotten, whereas the privileged few get treated like lords. You hardly ever see them. When they arrive they have their own separate garage and they disappear into the Tower Block. But you try going up there if you haven't been invited.'

Monsieur Pamplemousse pricked up his ears. 'You have been?'

'I tried once. You'd have thought I was trying to rob Fort Knox. All hell broke loose.'

'And how about the other patients? Are there many who don't last the course?' Monsieur Pamplemousse related his experience outside the gymnasium that morning.

Mrs. Cosgrove looked as if she had heard it all before. 'That's the second this week. It's a regular occurrence. They've a set routine. The flag over the entrance gate gets lowered to half-mast. Old Schmuck puts on his black arm band. Then the hearse arrives and carts the body away and everything returns to normal as if nothing had happened.

'Mind you, they probably die happy, which is more than a lot of old dears can say. He can turn on the charm when he likes. He calls them his 'investments' and he certainly makes sure they get their dividends.'

'Is it usually women?'

Mrs. Cosgrove paused for a moment. 'You know, it's funny you should say that. I've never really thought about it before. I don't remember it being a man. Not while I've been here anyway. Mind you, it's a matter of statistics. A lot of rich old widows come here simply because they're lonely. Rich old widowers don't have the same problems.'

Monsieur Pamplemousse closed his eyes. His mind was starting to fill with facts. Facts that needed sorting and relating one to the other. Not for the first time he wished that Pommes Frites had the power of speech. There had been something odd about their encounter with the stretcher party in the corridor, something he couldn't for the moment quite put his finger on. Pommes Frites had sensed it, too, of that he was sure. It came to him suddenly. Herr Schmuck had already been wearing an arm band. He must have been very quick off the mark.

Mrs. Cosgrove glanced up at him. 'I must say your glasses are a bit disconcerting.' She reached for his other foot. 'I can't tell at all what you're thinking.'

86

'I was thinking it would be nice to see you again.' It wasn't strictly true. He was also feeling that an ally on the staff would be a great asset. 'Perhaps when you have finished for the day?'

Mrs. Cosgrove lowered her head. Her hair, he noticed, was fair down to the roots a – natural blonde. The nape of her neck looked eminently kissable.

'Staff are not encouraged to fraternize with the patients.'

'And if they receive encouragement from them?'

'Then it is expressly forbidden.'

'That is a great pity.'

'What block are you in?'

'C.'

'Mine is the adjoining block. Room thirteen. I usually have a workout around four o'clock. We could have tea together afterward.'

Monsieur Pamplemousse rose. Thirteen was his lucky number. He would leave the rest of his toes until another day. It would be good to have something in reserve. And when Mrs. Cosgrove was through with them, had he not read somewhere that the human foot contains something like twenty-six separate bones, not to mention all the attendant joints, ligaments, muscles, and supporting tissues? More than enough to cover the rest of his stay at Château Morgue.

'Shall we say four-thirty then?'

'Make it a quarter to five. I'll leave early and pop down to the village for some cakes. You must be starving.' Mrs. Cosgrove held the door open for them and once again, as she touched his elbow, he felt her warmth. '*A bientôt.*'

'*A toute à l'heure.*'

Monsieur Pamplemousse bowed and hobbled on his way, conscious of her eyes following him as he tapped his way back down the corridor. Aware, too, of a certain reserve in Pommes Frites' manner, an aloofness that hadn't been there previously, as he led the way, looking neither to the right nor to the left.

Safely around the corner, Monsieur Pamplemousse bent down and gave him a pat. The response was lukewarm to say the least. He sighed. It was to be hoped there would be no unpleasantness. If they were to share a room for the next two weeks that was the last thing he wanted. Besides, he was going to need all the help he could get.

The rest of the journey back to the room was carried out in silence. Pommes Frites clearly wanted to draw a veil over the whole proceedings, whilst Monsieur Pamplemousse, struggling to keep up with him, allowed his mind to dwell on other problems.

Apart from some minor youthful sorties in Torquay, it was his first real encounter with an Englishwoman, and he had to admit that many of his preconceptions and prejudices had received a severe dent. In no sense of the word, *par exemple*, could Mrs. Cosgrove have been called 'cold' – something he had always been brought up to believe about her compatriots. Nor was she in the slightest bit 'angular.' Again, very much the reverse. A trifle 'horsy' perhaps; she had a generous mouth and slightly protruding teeth. He could picture her on a winter's morning astride some galloping steed, clutching the reins with one hand, a whip in the other – its flanks tightly gripped between her thighs, its nostrils steaming. Perhaps hers would be too.

As they reached their room Pommes Frites brought his daydreams to a sudden halt. In an instant he froze into a position which Monsieur Pamplemousse had good cause to remember from many occasions in the past. It was as if a spring had been tightly coiled. A spring that powered twelve point five kilograms of muscle, flesh, and bone, cocked and ready to be released at the slightest signal from his master.

Someone was inside their room.

Monsieur Pamplemousse let go of the harness, carefully removed his dark glasses and placed them in his top pocket, then stood back and prepared for action. He felt a tingle of excitement as his grip tightened on the door handle. It was quite like old times. Turning the latch so slowly it was almost impossible to detect any kind of movement, he waited until it was down as far as it would go and then pushed against the door with all his might.

As it shot open and they entered the room it would have been hard to say who was the most surprised, the sole occupant or them.

'Do you always come through doors like that?' Ananas exclaimed petulantly, leaping to his feet. To say that he looked as if he'd been nearly frightened out of his wits was to put it mildly.

'Do you make a habit of entering other people's rooms without first receiving an invitation?' retorted Monsieur Pamplemousse. He took a quick glance around. Everything seemed to be in place.

'*Touché.*' Ananas pulled himself together. 'Normally, no.' He crossed and pushed the door shut. 'The fact is, I didn't want to be seen hanging around outside and I didn't know where you were. Also,' he added cryptically, 'I feel we should not be seen together.'

Without waiting for a reply he sat down and began mopping his brow with a silk handkerchief. He looked strangely ill at ease, not a bit like the blustering Ananas of the previous evening.

'To tell you the truth, I'm in a spot of bother and I wondered if you could help.'

'Me?' Not by the wildest stretch of his imagination was he able to picture how he could possibly help Ananas, a man who seemed to have everything, including friends in the highest places in the land. Nor, for that matter, did he, for the moment at least, see any good reason why he should.

'I know you, Pamplemousse. You are a man of the world. I know your *past* reputation.' The emphasis on the penultimate word did not escape Monsieur Pamplemousse. 'Why you are here, masquerading as a blind man, is not my concern. No doubt you have your reasons. And no doubt your little pretence is something you wish to keep to yourself.'

Monsieur Pamplemousse felt a growing impatience. He had not liked Ananas from the very beginning; now his dislike increased with every passing moment. 'Would you mind coming to the point?'

Ananas took the hint. He reached into an inside pocket and withdrew some photographs, which he tossed onto the table. 'The point is ... these. They were placed in my room this morning.'

Monsieur Pamplemousse picked up the top one and glanced at it. His first thought was that someone, for whatever reason, had been to a junk yard and taken a picture of a pile of old statues.

'You are holding it upside down,' said Ananas impatiently.

Monsieur Pamplemousse rotated the photograph and gradually, as he examined it more closely, a kind of pattern emerged from the montage of arms and legs and thighs and breasts It was obviously some kind of orgy, but an orgy of such enormous complexity it was hard to tell who was doing what and to whom.

'*Mon Dieu! Sapristi!*' An involuntary whistle escaped his lips. Only one part of the whole was clearly identifiable and that was the head in the middle. It was Ananas coming up for air. He looked at the other man with renewed respect. 'When was this taken?'

'Last night. I was feeling a little ... restless. Travelling always does that to me.' It was said so matter-of-factly it almost took Monsieur Pamplemousse's breath away. He thought of his own travels and they paled into insignificance.

'The trouble is,' Ananas had the grace to look slightly shifty, 'they're mostly under age.'

'Under age?' Monsieur Pamplemousse took another look at the picture. '*C'est impossible!*'

'*Si.*' Ananas peered over his shoulder. He pointed to one of the legs. 'That one is fourteen. Her sister there is only thirteen.'

Monsieur Pamplemousse gave another whistle. 'And that one? She looks thirty-five if she is a day.'

Ananas took a closer look. 'Ah, yes, that is the mother. They are all a bit, you know ... .' He tapped his head as if in doing so it absolved him of all blame. 'It comes through living in the mountains. The long winter months when they are snowed in. There is a lot of inbreeding.

'Anyway,' he dismissed the subject. 'The important thing is, someone is obviously trying to blackmail me. It is a warning. Next time there will be a note. It is not the first occasion and I cannot afford a second. It would mean the end of my career. Absolute discretion is essential – the local police must not be brought in. I have given the matter a great deal of thought and you are the ideal person for the job.'

'*Non!*' cried Monsieur Pamplemousse vehemently. '*Non!*

Non! Non!' With each exclamation he brought his fist down on the table with a thud. 'Give me one good reason why I should do such a thing.'

'Because,' Ananas took the photograph and held it up with the air of one about to play his trump card, 'people in dark glasses should not throw stones.

'It is my recollection that when you left the Sûreté it was under a cloud owing to some indiscretion at the Follies. How many girls was it? Thirty-two?'

Monsieur Pamplemousse snorted. 'A trumped-up charge. I resigned as a matter of principle.'

'Nevertheless, mud sticks. There are many who still believe what they read in the *journaux*. Those same people will be quick to recognize the face in this photograph. They will think not of Ananas, but of Pamplemousse. I must admit that the supposed likeness is something I, personally, cannot see, although it has caused me some irritation in the past. Some comparisons are more odious than others.'

Monsieur Pamplemousse gazed in disgust at Ananas as his voice droned on. He had no intention whatsoever of submitting to what was, in effect, a secondary form of blackmail, nor did he feel any great desire to render help to Ananas. On the other hand, to have his true identity revealed, not that of Pamplemousse, late of the Sûreté, but Pamplemousse, representative of *Le Guide*, would be a disaster. It would negate all his past work; it would be a betrayal of all that he now held dear. He decided to play for time.

'I will consider what steps should be taken,' he said stiffly.

'*Bon*. I knew you would understand.' Ananas reached out as if to shake him by the hand, but Monsieur Pamplemousse pretended to misunderstand. There were lengths to which he was not prepared to go. Instead, he picked up the rest of the photographs, detached one for safe keeping, and handed them over. 'No doubt you will wish to keep these as souvenirs.'

Ananas paused at the door and gave a conspiratorial wink. 'We are in this together, *n'est-ce pas*?'

Monsieur Pamplemousse barely suppressed a shudder. The thought of being in anything together with Ananas was not a pretty one.

'You will hear from me in due course,' he said gruffly.

As the door closed he sat down on his bed and considered the next move. It was two o'clock. Two and a half hours before he took tea with Mrs. Cosgrove. He studied the photograph again. How much nicer the single English peach than a whole bunch of wild Pyrenean berries.

He lay back and closed his eyes, wondering if it would be Indian tea or China. Monsieur Cosgrove was probably a retired tea planter. There were a lot of them in England. He probably had it shipped over regularly. Either that, or Earl Grey. Earl Grey from Fortnum & Mason. He'd seen it on sale in Fauchon. Yes, that would be it: Earl Grey tea, *pâtisseries*, and Madame Cosgrove. It was something to look forward to. Something to dream about in the intervening period. Ananas and his problems could wait. One thing was certain – they would not go away.

5
TEA FOR TWO

After a brief lunch of *Saucisses de Périgord*, followed by
some *Saucisson a l'Anis* – a little known variety he hadn't
come across before, and which occasioned yet another note
in his book – Monsieur Pamplemousse set off with Pommes
Frites to reconnoiter the grounds of Château Morgue.

From the outside and in daylight, it looked even more
forbidding, but as a retreat or fortress it was ideally situated.
Built on a craggy tor, with the land falling away steeply on
three of its sides, the only practicable approach was from
the south, up the narrow winding road along which they
had traveled the night before.

The Hautes Pyrénées were much nearer than he'd realized. He resolved to look at a large-scale map of the area
when they got back to the room so that he could pinpoint
their position exactly.

He glanced up at the tower, wondering at the same time
if he was being watched. There was no particular reason
why anyone should bother. There were others around,
taking the air as he was. It was simply that his white stick
and dark glasses made him feel conspicuous. He was also
aware that his coat smelled strongly of sausages. He hoped
there were no guard dogs around.

The bottom half of the tower was almost windowless.
Only the rooms on the upper floors saw the light of day,
and they must be all of sixty meters from the ground.

Anything might be going on up there. Anything – or nothing. He wished more than ever now that he'd taken note of the sequence of numbers Doctor Furze had used to operate the lift, so that he could find out at first hand.

A path ran around the outside and he was just about to set off along it when he heard the sound of an approaching car, followed a few moments later by the crunch of tires on gravel. Walking back the way they had come he was just in time to see a hearse disappearing down the ramp into the underground garage. There were four men inside it. He was too far away to be certain, but he could have sworn one of them – the driver – was the man he'd seen relieving himself against a rock the evening he arrived.

He waited and after a while his patience was rewarded. There was a whine and the hearse reappeared, the occupants sitting respectfully to attention. As it went past he instinctively reached for his hat, then stopped himself in time, but not before he'd confirmed his suspicions. It was the same men, probably in the same car, for that too had borne a Marseilles registration number.

Reflecting on how easy it was to take sight for granted, and how hard life must be for those who have lost it, having to rely on others for even the simplest scraps of information, Monsieur Pamplemousse was about to call it a day and go back inside, when he noticed that while his back was turned someone had already been at work over the entrance. The flag, which had been at half-mast when he began his walk, was now fluttering at the masthead again. The whole episode had only lasted a bare two or three minutes. Herr Schmuck wasn't joking when he said they tried to carry out such operations with discretion. Or, as Mrs. Cosgrove might have put it, they had got things down to a fine art at Château Morgue.

He felt Pommes Frites give a tug at the harness. The message was clear and to the point. He glanced at his watch. It showed 16:40. Time for tea. Tea and Mrs. Cosgrove.

Whatever else might transpire, whatever undercurrents might be read into his invitation, the thought uppermost in Monsieur Pamplemousse's mind as they made their way to the adjoining block, was that cakes of any description would make a welcome change from sausages.

He yielded to no one in his love and admiration for the sausage in all its many forms and variations, but deep down he had to admit that as a day-to-day diet, *sans* any kind of vegetable, or even a slice or two of bread, to help them on their way, they had their limitations. More than ever, he was also looking forward to some liquid refreshment.

They arrived at Mrs. Cosgrove's at almost the same moment as she did. Fresh from her workout, she was dressed in a white track suit, and if at first she seemed a trifle taken aback to see Pommes Frites, she quickly recovered.

'I suppose you have to take him with you wherever you go,' she said brightly, as she opened the door for them. 'Even indoors. I mean, I suppose he's always with you, sort of … watching over you, seeing what goes on?'

'Always,' said Monsieur Pamplemousse firmly. 'We are inseparable. Without Pommes Frites, *pouf*!'

'Yes, of course.' Mrs. Cosgrove eyed Monsieur Pamplemousse's companion somewhat nervously. He was wearing his inscrutable expression, his eyes following her unwinkingly around the room as she hurried to and fro, drawing the curtains, placing a chair ready for his master and spreading a cloth over a small table by its side.

'I'll get everything ready and then if you don't mind I'll just take a quick shower and slip into something a bit more

96

comfortable. I feel as if I've been put through a wringer.'

As she disappeared momentarily behind a cupboard door Monsieur Pamplemousse seized the opportunity to carry out a hasty inspection of his surroundings. The room was very little different in size to his own, but there the similarity ended. Apart from an air of semi-permanence, which perhaps wasn't surprising, it reflected another, more private and slightly unexpected side to Mrs. Cosgrove's character. Despite her slightly horsy, outdoor appearance, she was clearly very much into frills. Frilly doilies decorated the dressing table, matched by other frills along the edges of shelves and the bedside cupboard. The bed itself was even more extravagantly embroidered, a plumped-up *soufflé* of blue silk, edged with white lace. It looked soft and inviting, as far removed from his own orthopaedic mattress and plain thin quilt as it was possible to imagine. Altogether a very feminine room.

The dressing table was festooned with knickknacks and ornaments, from the centre of which the slightly incongruous, grayish figure of a man in a trenchcoat against a leafy background stared at him from the surround of a black picture frame. He had his coat collar turned up, rather as if it had been raining when the photograph was taken, and he was peering in through a window.

Monsieur Pamplemousse's guess as to the man's identity was confirmed a moment later when Mrs. Cosgrove removed the picture in passing and deposited it face downward in a drawer. Irrationally, he felt a sense of relief as she pushed the drawer firmly shut.

'I do hope there's enough to go around,' she said pointedly, as she placed a plate piled high with cakes on the table beside him. 'I hadn't expected three to tea and there isn't time to go down to the village again. Besides,' she lowered her voice conspiratorially, 'I'll be in for it if they find out. Patients aren't allowed in the staff quarters. They're out of bounds.' She made it sound like a schoolgirl prank.

The temptation to say that as far as he was concerned the cakes looked exactly what the doctor might have ordered was hard to resist. *Babas*, *eclairs*, almond creams lay alongside *mille-feuilles* oozing with layers of *crème chantilly*; it was a veritable symphony of the *pâtissier's* art. He could hardly wait.

Pommes Frites had no such inhibitions. He smacked his lips noisily as he peered at the table.

Once again Mrs. Cosgrove eyed him regretfully. 'Do you think he wants to go walkies?'

'Walkies? *Qu'est-ce que c'est* 'walkies'?' Monsieur Pamplemousse tried to get his tongue around the unfamiliar word.

'*Une promenade*. By himself. I could be your 'eyes' while he's gone. That is, if you'll let me.'

Monsieur Pamplemousse tried to picture persuading Pommes Frites of the need to go 'walkies' while there was a plate of cakes waiting to be eaten. He shook his head.

'It is very kind of you, but no.'

'Oh, well.' The rattle of teacups as Mrs. Cosgrove rummaged in the cupboard was tinged with disapointment; it was also mixed with the clink of bottles.

Monsieur Pamplemousse shifted slightly so that he could get a better view. As he did so he caught his breath. He could hardly believe his eyes, but there in front of him, as large as life and twice as beautiful, he could see several bottles that were unmistakably from Champagne. Behind them stood a row of high-shouldered bottles, which could only contain Bordeaux, and to one side – he shifted the other way – there was a bottle of Cognac. Not ordinary, run-of-the-mill Cognac, but a single-vineyard Marcel Ragnaud. He knew it well, although it was not often he had the pleasure of drinking it.

'Do my old ears deceive me,' he asked casually, 'or can I hear the sound of glass?'

'You can.' Mrs. Cosgrove opened the door wider still and removed one of the bottles. She placed it gently onto a shelf alongside two glasses. 'I'll put one out. Perhaps we can have it later. It's a Gruaud Larose '66 and I hate drinking alone.'

'A *Gruaud Larose soixante-six!*' Monsieur Pample-mousse repeated the words reverently, savouring each syllable – almost as if he were sipping the very wine itself. It evoked memories, one of the great wines of that year.

'George always says, if you're going to be a wino at least do it in style. He never was much of a one for plonk.'

Monsieur Pamplemousse's opinion of the British and of Monsieur Cosgrove in particular went up by leaps and bounds.

'Madame Cosgrove ...' he began.

'Do call me Anne.'

'Anne.' He felt slightly embarrassed. It was a long time since he'd asked a woman to call him by his Christian name. In the Auvergne, where he was born, there were people he'd grown up with who still called him by his surname. To such people informality came very slowly. 'You may call me Aristide.'

'Aristide!' There was a chuckle from the direction of the bathroom. 'I thought only people in school textbooks were called Aristide. There used to be one in mine – he had lots of uncles and aunts and he was always wanting the window open. I grew up thinking French people had a thing about fresh air.' Her voice became slightly muffled. There was a hiss of water from the shower.

'You were saying?' She came back into the room, lifted the frilly cover of a wickerwork basket and dropped the top half of her gym suit through the opening. There was a wriggle and the bottom half joined it. Monsieur Pamplemousse drew in his breath sharply. Mrs. Cosgrove was quite, quite naked. *En tenue d'Adam*, as the expression went.

'I was saying ...' He groped in the dark recesses of his mind for some clue as to what he might possibly have been saying and came up with nothing. *Sacré bleu!* He must take a grip of himself. 'I am sorry. It could not have been important.'

Legs wide apart, Mrs. Cosgrove stood in front of a full-length mirror for a moment or two pinning up her hair and then, catching sight of Pommes Frites watching her in the glass, she turned and hurried into the bathroom. The sound of the water changed.

'Do forgive me,' she called. 'I shan't be a moment.'

'Please, take as long as you like.' Monsieur Pamplemousse gave his glasses a quick wipe and then settled back in his chair, contemplating the stream of water as it cascaded down, over and around Mrs. Cosgrove, finding valleys here, seeking out fresh pastures there, changing course rapidly as she bent down to pick up the soap, then surging forward anew, carrying a mountain of foam before it as she lathered herself all over with a series of sensual, sucking noises.

Any pangs of conscience he might have had about his deception were quickly quashed. Without taking his eyes off the scene for a second, he reached out for a cake.

'That's good. I'm glad you've made a start.' Mrs. Cosgrove stood facing him in the doorway, rubbing her back briskly to and fro with a large towel.

'It's a bit of a bore doing gym, but George always says I must look after my best features.'

Monsieur Pamplemousse wondered which features George put top of his list. It would make interesting reading. From where he was sitting there were a number of highly desirable contenders. Did he place great store on Mrs. Cosgrove's firm but generous *balcon*, each *poitrine* topped by a nipple still erect from its final dousing in cold water? Or was he, perhaps, an *homme* addicted to the delights of the *derrière*? As Mrs. Cosgrove turned and bent down to dry her toes he had cause to find his own list of priorities wavering. It was undoubtedly a *derrière* of considerable distinction. An *arrière-train* to be reckoned with, and one, moreover, which was also extremely close. He could have reached out and touched it. By his side he sensed Pommes Frites, nose twitching, entertaining what were probably not dissimilar thoughts. Anticipating his possible intentions, he laid a restraining hand on his head.

Mon Dieu! He felt for his handkerchief. Mrs. Cosgrove would never know how close she had come to being defiled. For no particular reason he found himself wondering how Alphonse would have coped with the situation. By now he would probably have dissolved into a pool of melted wax.

'I say, are you all right?' He suddenly realized she was talking to him again. 'You've gone quite pale. And your glasses are all steamed up. Not that that matters, of course!' She covered her embarrassment with a nervous giggle as she realized what she had said. 'Forgive me. I keep forgetting.'

Monsieur Pamplemousse pulled himself together. 'It is nothing. Merely the steam from the shower.' He wiped the lenses clean and then sat back, pretending as best he could to fasten his gaze on the bathroom wall behind Mrs. Cosgrove, but somehow the tiles refused to come into focus.

'You are being very quiet.' She opened the wardrobe door and began searching inside. 'Is anything wrong?'

'The art of speech was given to us to conceal our true feelings,' said Monsieur Pamplemousse primly. It wasn't entirely apposite. In fact the more he thought about it the more he wondered why he'd said it, but it bridged a gap.

'I say, that's very clever.' Mrs. Cosgrove ran something black and lacy through her fingers, then discarded it.

Monsieur Pamplemousse wondered if he should confess that Voltaire probably thought so too when he first coined the remark, then thought better of it. He had other matters on his mind; matters not entirely unconnected with his hostess' present behavior.

Mrs. Cosgrove's liking for frills obviously extended beyond the decor of her room. One by one, undergarments made of silk, chiffon and nylon, in all possible shades of colour from lavender blue to the deepest of black, beribboned and lace-edged, came under her scrutiny and were rejected for one reason or another.

Monsieur Pamplemousse sat bemused. He wondered what the director would have thought had he been there to see him. It was the kind of fashion show one read about in glossy magazines, but never in his wildest dreams had he pictured being present in the very front row as it were at such a display; a display that said as much about the workings of Mrs. Cosgrove's mind as it did about the whims and mores of the world of fashion.

Having narrowed the choice down to two alternatives, and having weighed the relative merits of loose layered black against whiteness and tightness and decided in favour of the latter, she sat on a stool, garter-belt in place, and slowly and lingeringly drew on a pair of white stockings.

As she stepped into the briefest and flimsiest pair of matching *culottes*, Monsieur Pamplemousse reached automatically for yet another cake and found to his horror that there were only two left. He also noted a change of mind on Mrs. Cosgrove's part. The wearing of *culottes* was patently not the order of the day; an unnecessary embellishment. She had stepped out of them again.

'Poor Aristide.' Mrs. Cosgrove's voice cut across his thoughts. 'I've been neglecting you.'

The blue of her dress matched the rest of the furnishings. A transformation had taken place. She could have been dressed for afternoon tea on a lawn in England. The knowledge he possessed produced a strange feeling of intimacy. Paradoxically, to take advantage of it, even to tell someone else, would seem like an act of betrayal.

'*Ça ne fait rien.*' He brushed aside her apologies as he adjusted to the change. 'I have been very happy with my thoughts. And with your delicious *pâtisseries* too, I must confess.'

'That's good.' She reached into a handbag and took out a lipstick. 'You must have been starving. What with being on the *régime* and all that excitement this morning.'

'Excitement?' The morning seemed an age away.

'That trouble in the lecture hall. I see she's been whipped away already. You didn't happen to notice her legs, did you?'

Monsieur Pamplemousse shook his head, wondering what snippet of information he was about to receive next.

'I bet they were huge compared with the rest of her body. They've all had huge calves – like a ballet dancer's. One of the attendants told me.

'If you ask me, old Schmuck's after their money. Either that, or he's turning them into meat pies or sausages or something.'

Monsieur Pamplemousse suddenly choked on the remains of his cake. 'What makes you say that?'

'Oh, I was only joking. That would be a bit too much like Sweeney Todd. It's only that they seem to run a *charcuterie* business on the side. Funny combination really.' Satisfied with the state of her face, Mrs. Cosgrove turned away from the dressing-table mirror. 'How about a cup of tea? Or a Beaumes de Venise?'

It didn't take him long to decide. There was really no choice. Mrs. Cosgrove's revelations had triggered off an urgent need for alcohol. He was also aware of a change in the atmosphere. If he wasn't careful they would be into the area of making polite conversation.

Mrs. Cosgrove obviously felt it too as she began searching amongst a collection of cassettes in a case beside her bed. A moment later, as she went to the cupboard, the strains of 'Some Enchanted Evening' filled the room. Pommes Frites gave a deep sigh.

'I'm sorry it isn't chilled. If I'd thought, I could have stood it outside on the windowsill. The thing is, in England we drink it at the end of a meal. Whereas in France ...'

'In France it is drunk more as an *apéritif*, something to stimulate the appetite.' Monsieur Pamplemousse tried to leap the first hurdle. 'Unlike most other wines it is aged in concrete, not wood. It helps to retain the special flavour.'

The glass was large, the helping generous. He raised it to his nose; the perfume had opulence. He glanced at the label. It was a Domaine de Durban from Jacques Leydier.

As he felt the smooth lusciousness of the golden-amber

liquid at the back of his throat he began to feel better again. He drank it rather too quickly, aware that Mrs. Cosgrove was only sipping hers as she gazed at him thoughtfully over the top of her glass. He was also aware once again of the swinging leg syndrome. He wondered what she was thinking. How hard it was to read a woman's mind. Perhaps she was waiting for him to make the first move? He reached out a hand.

Mrs. Cosgrove pushed the plate of cakes toward him. 'Do finish them up.'

'*Non, merci*. It is for you.'

Pommes Frites cast a reproachful look in his direction as Mrs. Cosgrove took him at his word. Monsieur Pamplemousse pretended not to notice. In many ways he envied Pommes Frites his simple approach to life. He would have summed up the situation in a trice. Not for him the soft music, nor the Beaumes de Venise; garter belts he would have regarded as an unnecessary hazard – something he might catch his claws in. If he saw what he fancied, that was it. The worst that could happen was a bucket of cold water – like that time in the rue Ordener.

Mrs. Cosgrove ran her tongue round the edge of the last remaining *mille-feuille*. She made it look like the dress rehearsal for some more lascivious activity to come. He felt his pulse quicken as she sank her teeth slowly into the pastry.

'Scrumptious!'

Monsieur Pamplemousse waved his hand noncommittally through the air. He was not familiar with the word. 'Pastry is like mayonnaise. It is largely a matter of temperature. It needs a marble slab chilled with ice, the best butter, but most of all it is a question of *tour de main*, the "feeling in the hands." It is something you either have or you do not have. The best chefs always do it in the early morning.'

'George used to like doing it in the early morning,' said Mrs. Cosgrove sadly.

'He is a chef?' Monsieur Pamplemousse tried to picture Mrs. Cosgrove's husband in the kitchen. It wasn't easy. He seemed inseparable from his trenchcoat.

Once again, for some reason, the spell seemed to be broken. Perhaps it was his own fault this time for getting involved in culinary matters. As if to underline the fact there was a click from the direction of the bedside cabinet and the tape came to an end. It must have been set at an appropriate spot, for it had only lasted the length of the song. In the silence that followed he heard a car door banging somewhere outside. Mrs. Cosgrove crossed to the window and parted the curtains slightly.

'It's the police. They are back. Apparently there was a break-in during the night. Someone got into the kitchens and stole a lot of food. I heard on the grapevine that the police think it was an inside job and they're planning to make a room to room search.'

She let the curtain fall into place and then turned back into the room. 'I say, are you *really* all right? You're looking quite pale.'

'It is nothing.' Monsieur Pamplemousse struggled to his feet and reached for Pommes Frites' harness. 'I think perhaps I will go and lie down for a while.'

'You are welcome to stay here.' Mrs. Cosgrove tried hard to keep the disappointment from her voice.

'*Merci*.' Monsieur Pamplemousse reached out for her hand and gave it a quick squeeze. 'It is better that I return to my own room. Perhaps … perhaps you would like to visit me later when it is quiet?' He lowered his voice. 'I will let you sample my *andouillette*. *En suite*, we can drink the wine you have so kindly put out. If you open it now it will give it time to breathe.'

'Would *you* like that?' As she spoke he felt her hand tighten on his.

'It would give me very great pleasure,' he said simply.

She led him to the door and planted the lightest of kisses on his right cheek. It was like the touch of a *papillon*'s wings.

'*Au revoir*, Aristide. Until ... later.'

'*Au revoir* ... Anne.' He found it hard to make the changeover to her Christian name.

Pommes Frites gave an impatient tug and a moment later they were on their way. Once around the corner leading to the adjoining block Monsieur Pamplemousse quickened his pace. There was not a moment to be lost.

Sensing that all was not well, Pommes Frites entered into the spirit of things and by the time they reached their own corridor there was no holding him. As it was, they reached the safety of their room only just in time. As Monsieur Pamplemousse closed the door behind them he heard voices coming from the next room, voices coupled with the opening and closing of cupboard doors.

Merde! There wasn't a second to lose. By the sound of it they were making a thorough job of things.

Jamming his stick under the door handle, he rushed to his own cupboard, removed the parcel of sausages from his coat and tipped them out on to the table. As he looked around the room his heart sank. He would have done better to have made a clean breast of things with Mrs. Cosgrove and left them with her for safe keeping. It was too late now.

Grabbing a knife, he sliced a *Saucisson de Bourgogne* in half and placed the two pieces in a pair of socks. They would do service as a draught excluder along the bottom of the door. He tried slipping some *Saucisses de Bordeaux* into the hem of the curtains, but in his haste they stuck halfway. Ever anxious to help, Pommes Frites pulled them out again. Then, flushed with success, he made a dive for one of the socks.

In desperation, as he heard *au revoirs* and apologies being voiced in the corridor outside, Monsieur Pamplemousse picked up the remaining sausages and hurled them through the opening of Pommes Frites' kennel. Hardly able to believe his good fortune, Pommes Frites bounded in after them.

'*Non!*' Monsieur Pamplemousse rapped out the single word of command in a voice which left no room for argument. '*Asseyez-vous. Gardez les saucissons!*'

He was tempted to add '*Gardez les andouillettes avec un soin particulier,*' but he decided against it. At such moments beggars could hardly be choosers and Pommes Frites looked confused enough already. As his jaw dropped open with surprise at his master's sudden change of mood, a half-eaten *boudin* fell out. Honesty, precision, and simplicity of phrasing were necessary in issuing orders of the day, and Monsieur Pamplemousse knew that given those three factors his wishes would be respected without question.

Covering the front of Pommes Frites' kennel with a large towel, he closed the bathroom door, hurriedly pushed the socks back into position under the main door, then sank back into his chair. As he did so there was a peremptory knock from outside.

Adjusting his glasses, Monsieur Pamplemousse focused his gaze on a point somewhere beyond the Hautes Pyrénées and prepared himself for the worst.

'*Entrez, s'il vous plaît.*' Much to his surprise, his voice sounded almost normal.

6
THE LEADING ROLE

There was a scuffling noise outside the door, followed by a muttered imprecation from the person on the other side, then another knock, this time even louder and more peremptory than the first.

'*Ouvrez la porte, s'il vous plaît.*' It was a command rather than a request.

Monsieur Pamplemousse jumped to his feet. *Sapristi!* He had forgotten the stick. The door had been pushed with such force it had momentarily risen sufficiently to trap one of the socks containing the *Saucisson de Bourgogne* when it came down again. Already meat was showing through a weak patch in the toe, threatening to burst through the seams at any moment. He should have used a *Mortadella*, it would have been harder.

'*Un moment!*' The stick bent as he used it as a lever in order to force the door up. There was an ominous crack. A second later the socks were free. Two more and the window was open. He hurled the offending items out into the night. Almost immediately there was a loud bark followed by the sound of snarling as they landed near some unseen target. The police must have brought their dogs with them. Mercifully they had not yet penetrated the building.

Closing the window, he took advantage of the momentary lull to put his own weight against the door, removed his stick, and then stood back waiting for the storm to break.

The door opened and four people entered the room. Doctor Furze, a police inspector and two *gendarmes*. Monsieur Pamplemousse looked at them in surprise. From the rumpus outside he'd expected a whole army.

Doctor Furze eyed him suspiciously. 'Do you make a habit of barricading your door in this manner?' he demanded. 'The locking of doors is strictly forbidden at Château Morgue.'

Monsieur Pamplemousse decided that attack was the best form of defence. 'When I feel threatened, yes. I have heard there have been, shall we say, 'goings-on' during the night. I was merely taking precautions to safeguard my person. Someone in my position cannot be too careful.

'Anyway, who are you and what do you want? I recognize your voice from last night, but who are the others?'

'Furze here.' Raising his voice in the way that people sometimes do when talking to the blind, as if they must suffer from deafness as well, the doctor made it sound like a disease. 'The others are Inspector Chambard and his two assistants.'

Monsieur Pamplemousse nodded. From his looks he judged Inspector Chambard to be from the Midi or the Rhône Valley; he had a short, stocky figure and a face weatherbeaten by years of exposure to the Mistral. Not someone to fool around with – his eyes were too shrewd.

'To what do I owe the pleasure?"

Doctor Furze gripped his clipboard a trifle nervously. "As you so rightly say, there was a little unpleasantness during the night.

'An important package has been stolen,' Inspector Chambard cut in. 'It is believed that the person responsible may well be a resident of the Château. In the circumstances we feel that for the sake of peace all around there will be no objection if we make a search of the entire building.'

'Who knows where or when the thief may strike again?' agreed Doctor Furze. 'It is a necessary precaution.'

'And if I object?'

'Then we cannot, for the moment, insist.' Inspector Chambard's remark was accompanied by a shrug that said it all. Refuse and our suspicions will be aroused. And if our suspicions are aroused then we will be back with the necessary authority within the hour. Take it or leave it. There was a time when he would have reacted in exactly the same way

'Please.' His gesture embraced the whole room. Somewhere outside a dog began to choke noisily. In a flash the window was open again and Inspector Chambard disappeared through it. He returned after a moment, climbing over the sill with an agility surprising for one of his bulk. He held up the half-eaten remains of something green and woolen.

'It appears to be a sock.'

'Tccchk!' Doctor Furze looked at it impatiently

'Is that one of yours, *Monsieur*? If so, I have to tell you that the hanging of laundry outside the window is – '

'I know. It is strictly forbidden. Many things seem to be strictly forbidden at Château Morgue.'

Ignoring the interruption, Doctor Furze looked around the room. 'You have a dog.'

'Pommes Frites. He is asleep. Or rather, he is trying to sleep.' Monsieur Pamplemousse wished he'd thought to put the "Do Not Disturb" notice on the bathroom door. 'I take it that is not against the rules?'

'There is also,' continued Doctor Furze, 'a list on your door of various activities for the day. You are required to report to the doctor to whom you have been assigned for an analysis of the treatment you require. That was not done. May I ask why?'

'You may,' thundered Monsieur Pamplemousse. 'You may indeed. I did not carry out the instructions for the very simple reason that I am unable to see them; a fact which seems to have totally escaped both you and your staff. I find your attitude totally intolerable. No one, I repeat, no one has been to see me since the evening I arrived. For all you know I might have starved to death.'

He groped for the back of the chair. Already he was beginning to feel a little better, more in command of the situation.

Doctor Furze was the first to speak following his outburst.

'There is a cake crumb stuck to your moustache,' he said coldly. 'Also, there is a lump of something white adhering to your left ear. I trust it is shaving cream and not *crème pâtissière*. In which case, the patch of red on your right cheek will be blood where you cut yourself shaving rather than what it looks like – a lump of *confiture*.'

Instinctively Monsieur Pamplemousse reached up to his face, but before he had time to reply he felt himself being propelled toward the bathroom as Doctor Furze pressed home his temporary advantage.

'We do not appear to have had our daily weight check.'

'I am *not* getting undressed again,' said Monsieur Pamplemousse. 'Is there no privacy in this establishment? It is bad enough not being able to lock one's door without having to expose oneself to all and sundry.'

'There is no need. All that is necessary is to remove your shoes. I will make the appropriate allowance.' He paused and gave a sniff. 'For one who has been without food for over twenty-four hours, your breath is remarkably sweet. It is one of the first things one notices about people who are taking the *régime* – the breath.'

He helped Monsieur Pamplemousse onto the scales. 'Ah, it is as I suspected.' His voice grew even harder and colder as he glanced at the dial and then compared the figure with that on a sheet of paper attached to his clipboard. 'At the very minimum your weight has increased by over two kilos since yesterday evening.'

Leaving Monsieur Pamplemousse to his fate, he went back into the other room where Inspector Chambard and the two *gendarmes* were engaged in an inch by inch search of the furniture.

'You need look no further, Inspector. I suggest you arrest this man immediately.'

'With respect, *Monsieur, you* must allow me to be the best judge of that.' Inspector Chambard sounded piqued. 'We are not looking for someone who has overindulged in *pâtisseries*. If that were the case then in an establishment such as this we would have cause to make many arrests were it a criminal matter. Lack of food makes people desperate. I have heard tales of excursions into the village after dark. If old Pertus who runs the *boulangerie* relied on sales to the local inhabitants for his living he would not be in a position to buy himself a new Citroen every year. No, *Monsieur*, we are looking for someone who stole a large quantity of *charcuterie*, not just sufficient to put on two kilos of weight overnight, but twenty kilos. That is a lot of *charcuterie*.'

Twenty kilos! Monsieur Pamplemousse barely suppressed a whistle as he came out of the bathroom to join the others. No wonder the sausages had looked like a small mountain when he had first tipped them out.

His heart sank as there was a muffled exclamation from somewhere behind him. Pommes Frites' hideaway must have been discovered.

Pushing him to one side, the second *gendarme* went in search of his colleague. He heard their lowered voices coming from the bathroom.

'*Regardez!*'

'*Merde!*'

The appositeness of the remark triggered off a series of giggles. He could picture the nudges that went with it.

'*C'est formidable!*'

'*Oui. Tres, tres formidable!*' There was a stream of admiring whistles and "poufs."

'*Qu'est-ce que c'est?*' Unable to stand the suspense a moment longer, Inspector Chambard flung open the door of the bathroom.

'*Sacré bleu! Nom d'un nom!*' His endorsement of their findings was short, sharp, and positive. It was also accompanied by a series of warning growls. Pommes Frites enjoyed a game as much as the next dog, but he was beginning to get a bit restive with the present one.

Monsieur Pamplemousse turned. All three policemen were on their hands and knees in front of the kennel, eyeing the contents with disbelief and its occupant with a certain amount of reserve. One of the *gendarmes,* clearly under a misapprehension as to the nature of his find, held a handkerchief to his nose as he poked at a *boudin* lying on the floor near the entrance with his truncheon. He jumped back as a paw shot out. '*Merde!*'

'What did I tell you?' Doctor Furze bustled into the bathroom, anxious to declare the matter closed. For some reason best known to himself, he seemed to view the finding of the sausages as a mixed blessing, one which, while confirming his previous accusation, held other connotations of a less desirable nature.

Inspector Chambard rose from his knees and came out

of the bathroom. Ignoring the doctor, he addressed himself to Monsieur Pamplemousse.

'Will you call off your dog, *Monsieur*?'

'May I ask why? He is doing no harm; merely protecting his temporary home.'

'I wish to search it. I may need the contents as evidence. It will be sent for analysis.'

'Not without a warrant,' said Monsieur Pamplemousse finely.

Inspector Chambard gave him a long, hard stare, then shrugged. 'In that case ...' he turned back to the bathroom. 'Paradou, since you appear to be an expert on matters to do with *le petit coin*, I suggest you put that knowledge to some purpose. Get to work.'

'But, Chief ...'

'Wrap a towel around your arm. You know the drill.'

Paradou looked around for his colleague, but he had already beaten a hasty retreat and was busy looking through the pile of magazines on the table. If he was hoping for sympathy, he was disappointed.

'Chief, come and have a look at this.' As Inspector Chambard half closed the bathroom door, the other *gendarme* held up a photograph. Monsieur Pamplemousse stifled a curse. It was a diversion, but not a welcome one. He should have locked it away in his case.

'Hey, Paradou, come here.' The *gendarme* was having difficulty in hiding his excitement.

Paradou, his arm partly swathed in a towel, came out of the bathroom with alacrity. He stared at the picture. *'Tante Hyacinthe!'*

Slowly rotating the picture as he held it up to the light, he reeled off more names. 'That one is Clothilde and there is Desirée – at least, I think it is Desirée, and that must be little Josephine and …' He peered at the head in the centre, then at Monsieur Pamplemousse, comparing the two to make sure he'd seen aright.

'Don't tell me you've been with that lot?'

'Who? Where? What are we talking about?' Monsieur Pamplemousse was becoming increasingly irritated by the way things were going. The sooner his visitors left, the happier he would be.

But there was no stopping Paradou. 'When I was in the army we used to have lectures about steering clear of the local girls. Why? Because they were always poxed up to the eyebrows. Well, in the last war Tante Hyacinthe's mother was a 'local girl,' and in the war before that so was her grandmother. And if there's ever another war, that's where Tante Hyacinthe will be – up front with the troops. She, and all her family.'

Monsieur Pamplemousse began to feel profoundly relieved he hadn't taken advantage of Doctor Furze's offer the night before. He wondered if he should pass on the news to Ananas or keep it in reserve.

Doctor Furze himself had been keeping very quiet during the whole of the conversation. He was deep in thought.

'May I ask how this photograph came to be in your possession, Monsieur Pamplemousse?'

'Photograph? There is a photograph?' Aware of a sudden change in the atmosphere, Monsieur Pamplemousse played for time. At the mention of his name the two *gerndarmes* exchanged glances, then stiffened as they caught the eye of their superior. He studiously avoided looking at Paradou. 'Perhaps it was among the magazines. I heard you rustling them. Really, it is very hard to answer such questions when I cannot even see what you are discussing.'

Inspector Chambard came to his rescue. 'Paradou, you

116

get back in that bathroom.'

'Perhaps, Monsieur Pamplemousse,' he continued, 'you would like to accompany me to the *Gendarmerie*?' Both his name and the invitation were underlined by a wink. A brief, but very definite wink.

'Am I to understand that you are placing me under arrest?'

'No, but there are things you may wish to discuss.'

'In that case, the answer is no.'

Inspector Chambard looked disappointed. 'If you change your mind ... if you see the *folie* of your ways, you have only to telephone.'

It was an allusion to his past. His fame must have traveled farther than he'd ever realized. No doubt the photograph had clinched matters in Chambard's mind. It would be in character.

'*Merci.* Perhaps later.' He had no wish to get involved with the local police for the time being, but there was no sense in putting their backs up.

A thought struck him. 'In the meantime, perhaps you could do me a favour?' He felt in his pocket and took out the postcard to Doucette. 'It is to my wife. If you would be kind enough to post it for me.'

'Of course.' The wink as Chambard pocketed the card was even more meaningful. Monsieur Pamplemousse was about to reciprocate when he realized the other couldn't see it, so he removed his glasses and under the pretence of rubbing his eyes used his hand as a shield.

Doctor Furze hovered at the door. 'I find all this most unsatisfactory, Inspector. I shall report back to Herr Schmuck and no doubt you will hear further.'

Inspector Chambard looked unmoved by the implied threat. He picked up the photograph. 'If you don't mind, I will keep this for the time being.'

The bathroom door opened and Paradou emerged carrying a plastic bag. Pommes Frites must have relented. 'I'll tell you something funny, Chief – '

'Later.' Inspector Chambard waved his subordinates on their way. He suddenly seemed anxious to leave. Looking aggrieved, Paradou followed his colleague out of the room.

Chambard looked at his watch. 'Au *revoir*, Monsieur Pamplemousse.'

'*Au revoir*, Inspector.' A moment later they were gone. He heard their voices disappearing down the corridor. Doctor Furze was still holding forth. He looked at his own watch. It said 5:35. There would be time to kill before Mrs. Cosgrove put in an appearance. Time to marshal his thoughts.

Pommes Frites had clearly been trying to marshal his thoughts during the time he'd spent in his kennel. Without a great deal of success, if the furrows on his brow as he came out of the bathroom were anything to go by. The game he had played with the policeman had been enjoyable up to a point, like playing cat and mouse. Several times when he'd laid his paw gently on the man's hand it had produced a satisfactory muffled scream; but it was definitely a spectator sport. It was nothing without an audience and he was glad he'd managed to conceal the bulk of the sausages at the back of his kennel. Now he was ready for action and, patently, action was something that for the time being had a very low priority on his master's agenda. Monsieur Pamplemousse, his brow equally furrowed, was sitting at the table, a pile of forms set neatly in front of him, sucking the end of his Cross pen, torn between two items of work on his immediate agenda.

On the one hand there was his duty to *Le Guide*. So far,

apart from one or two desultory scrawlings on his pad, he hadn't made a single note. On the other hand lay the secondary, or for all he knew perhaps even the primary, reason for his being at Château Morgue. and short of paying a visit to the local vet and ordering him to carry out an immediate search for the letter, those reasons would remain entombed in Pommes Frites' stomach – if they hadn't already passed through. He was in a quandary and no mistake.

Not, he reflected, as he gazed at the pile of papers in front of him, that there was anything blank about *Le Guide*'s report forms. Quite the reverse.

They were based on the simple premise that all things are capable of being analyzed provided they are broken down into their basic component parts, like the myriad tiny dots making up the picture on the television screen, each equating its particular shade of colour with an equivalent voltage.

Although there was a large section at the end for a written report, the main bulk of the form was taken up by over five hundred basic questions to which the answer was a simple *'oui'* or *'non,'* thus ensuring that despite differences of temperament and taste, all inspectors spoke the same language. Tastes might vary, but standards never. It also provided an insurance against any kind of bribery or corruption, for in the end its findings were unassailable and unarguable, covering everything from parking facilities to the design of the cutlery; from the quality of the ingredients to the size of the portions and the way in which they were served.

Was the dish of classic origins? If so, had it been prepared in the right manner? Was the accompanying sauce too hot? Too cold? Too salty? Was it served separately? Was the waiter able to describe the dish? If not, did he find out the answer quickly and accurately?

There was an equally large section devoted to the serving of wine. Did the waiter simply sniff the cork and pour it straight away, or did he allow you to taste it first? If it was a Beaujolais was it served slightly chilled? If it was an old wine did he offer to decant it? If so, did he do it at the table? Did he use a candle? Did he take it away to do it? If so, did he bring the empty bottle back to show you? Did he bring the cork too? When he offered you some to taste was he really seeking your opinion or merely going through the motions?

The list seemed endless. In his wisdom, Monsieur Hippolyte Duval had provided for almost every eventuality. The one situation he hadn't foreseen was that of being incarcerated in an establishment where the sole form of nourishment appeared to be a glass of dirty water, and not even that much if the guest happened to arrive late.

After staring at it for something like a quarter of an hour, Monsieur Pamplemousse laid it down again. If *Le Guide* was to enter the world of *Établissements Thermaux* they would need a totally new form and a very truncated one at that.

One of his options disposed of, at least for the time being, Monsieur Pamplemousse turned his attention to the second item on the agenda. Taking a leaf out of *Le Guide*'s book, or rather, borrowing from its report forms, he began analyzing his findings to date, reducing everything to its simplest terms.

Was there something odd about Château Morgue? Most definitely *'oui.'*

Was there a Château Morgue that showed one face to the outside world and another that kept itself very much to itself? From his experience the first evening, *'oui.'*

120

Were the 'extra facilities' he'd been offered available to all and sundry? If the answer to the previous question was in the affirmative, then it had to be '*non*'.

Was the mortality rate at Château Morgue higher than at other, similar establishments? For the moment at least, he had no means of checking.

Was there any significance to be attached to the sex of those who had passed away? Instinct told him there was; logic failed to come up with an immediate reason.

Was there any significance in the size of their calves? An impossible question.

He tried another tack.

Had he been sent there for some deeper purpose than merely losing weight? Had someone heard of his impending visit and decided to take advantage of it? Without knowing the contents of the letter he couldn't be absolutely sure, but deep down he knew the answer.

Once again, he felt tempted to telephone the director and make a clean breast of things. Once again, he decided against the idea. It was a matter of pride. The director would not be sympathetic. He would assume his 'I find this difficult to grasp, Pamplemousse,' voice:

'Would you mind repeating that more slowly? You say Pommes Frites actually *ate* the letter? While you were asleep? A letter of the utmost importance! A letter from the highest authority!'

Then there would be the sarcastic tone: 'You say all those who died recently were women? And they had unusually large *mollets*? Could it be, Pamplemousse, that you are suffering aberrations brought on by lack of food? I have heard this sometimes happens.'

This would be followed by incredulity: 'What is this I

121

hear? You have *not* been on a *régime*? You have been living on *saucisses* ... and *saucissons*!' There would be silences. Silences intermingled with splutterings. Perhaps even the sound of banging on the director's long-suffering desk. He could picture it all too clearly.

He stared at his list. In all conscience, it wasn't much to go on, but at least it was a beginning.

Were the staff in general involved? He pondered the question. Starting from the top: Herr Schmuck certainly, and therefore presumably, the aloof and detached Madame Schmuck. He wondered why she had so little to say for herself. And yet she had the air of being a power behind the throne. Doctor Furze? In all probability – a tentative *'oui.'* There had been something odd about the chauffeur, but as for the rest of the staff he had met so far, *'non.'* He would have staked his reputation, for example, on Mrs. Cosgrove not being involved.

He found himself staring into space. Rubbing his chin thoughtfully and realizing he needed a shave, he looked at his watch. *Sacré bleu!* He would need to get a move on if he were to make himself look reasonably respectable in time for their *tête-à-tête*. Pommes Frites, too. If Pommes Frites was to be in a fit state to receive Mrs. Cosgrove he would need a good brush and some Vaseline rubbed on his nose; it was beginning to look dry after being cooped up indoors for so long. Mrs. Cosgrove – he still found it hard to think of her by her *prénom*.

His thoughts coincided with a knock on the door. Mrs. Cosgrove was early.

Kissing him lightly on the cheek as she brushed past, she gave a quick glance around the room; first at Pommes Frites, watching her with a red and jaundiced eye from a position he'd firmly taken up in the centre of the rug; then at the furniture, much of which was still as it had been left after the search. Finally, she looked down at Monsieur Pamplemousse's feet.

'I hope I am not too early.'

'Not at all.' Wishing he'd remembered to put his shoes back on, he went to kiss her hand, then realized she was holding something behind her back.

'I've brought the wine.' As she placed an uncorked bottle and two glasses on the table, he took the opportunity of studying her more closely, on home ground as it were. She had obviously spent the time since they'd last met in a more productive manner than either he or Pommes Frites. Her blue dress had been exchanged for a more casual one in cream. Like her uniform jacket, it had a zipper running down the front. He caught a different perfume, too. It had a discreet understatement, which left him wanting more. Her hair hung carelessly over her shoulders in a way that could only have been achieved through long and careful brushing.

Her hand trembled slightly as she began to pour the wine. He noticed, too, that she filled her own glass first and took a quick drink before attending to his. He wondered idly if she was still *sans culottes*.

'*Merci.*' He took it gratefully, conscious of a lingering touch from her fingers as they met his. Rotating the glass quickly and expertly, he swirled the liquid around until it touched the rim, then held it to his nose. The bouquet as it rose to greet him was full and fruity. He was about to hold it up to the light when he realized Mrs. Cosgrove was watching his every movement intently.

'Do you know any more party tricks?'

'Old habits die hard.' Monsieur Pamplemousse bent down and held his glass near the floor so that Pommes

123

Frites could share his pleasure. 'It is a beautiful wine. I feel highly honored. I only hope my *andouillette* stands comparison by its side. It will have a lot to live up to.'

'Aristide?' Mrs. Cosgrove sounded hesitant.

He glanced up at her. '*Oui*?'

'I don't know quite how to put this, but … it's just that in England we have a saying – 'Two's company, three's a crowd.' What I really mean is, will he be watching?'

'Pommes Frites? Watching?' Monsieur Pamplemousse considered the matter. What a strange question.

'It is possible. It depends on his mood.'

'All the time? Everything?'

'Of course. He has a very sociable nature. He likes to join in things.'

'Oh!' Mrs. Cosgrove sat down in the chair. She seemed depressed by the news. 'Oh, dear. I … I didn't think you were like that. I mean …'

'Don't worry.' Monsieur Pamplemousse tried to sound as soothing as possible. 'Despite his size he is really a very gentle dog. Normally he wouldn't hurt a fly not unless he is roused.'

'Is he very easily … roused?'

'Again, it depends. He has, how would you say? – a strong sense of what is right and what is wrong. If he feels he is being done out of what should be his, then he can get very roused. I would not like to stand in his way at such times. Then, of course, we always share things. If he feels left out then sometimes jealousy sets in.'

Mrs. Cosgrove seemed less than reassured by the reply. Having contemplated her glass for a moment or two she suddenly drained it and reached for the bottle.

'Oh, well, *c'est la vie*. In for a penny, in for a pound. When in Rome do as the Romans do.'

124

Monsieur Pamplemousse tried without success to seek the meaning behind these seemingly unconnected remarks. Taken separately they made very little sense; strung together they defied analysis. He wondered if Mrs. Cosgrove was suffering some kind of mental disturbance. She was certainly having a bad attack of the 'leg swingings' he'd noticed earlier. Perhaps it was time to get on with the matter at hand. It would be a pity to let such good wine go unaccompanied. He took a firm grip of his stick.

'*Excusez moi*. I must go to the bathroom. We are wasting precious time.'

Unaccountably, Mrs. Cosgrove blushed. 'It isn't strictly necessary you know. To take precautions, I mean.'

'Experience has taught me,' said Monsieur Pamplemousse, 'that one can never be too careful. I shall not be long.' Closing the bathroom door behind him, he bent down and peered inside Pommes Frites' kennel. It was, as always, a model of neatness. The sausages he'd cast through the opening in great haste were now lying in a neat pile at the back. There was almost a military precision about the way they had been arranged, smallest at the front, largest at the rear. *Saucisse de Toulouse* lay beside *Saucisse de Campagne, Saucisson-cervelas* snuggled up against *Saucisson de Bretagne,* but of *andouilles* and *andouillettes* there was not the slightest sign. Paradou must have decided that it was a case of *prudence est mère de sûreté,* and prudence being the better part of valour, he had gone for the nearest.

No matter. Monsieur Pamplemousse put his arm inside the kennel and groped for a likely candidate among the remaining sausages. Perhaps it wasn't meant to be. One should never judge a sausage by its skin, and *andouillettes* could be unpredictable at the best of times; some he'd come across in his travels would have tested the strongest of stomachs. Far better to choose one which would match the wine.

His hand encountered one much larger than the rest, somewhere near the back. A giant of a *saucisson*, he remembered seeing it before and at the time mentally reserving it for a special occasion.

'*Sapristi!*' He gave a gasp as he lifted it out. At a guess it must weigh all of three kilograms. Enough to keep them all happy for the rest of the evening. And afterward? Afterward, he would let matters take their course.

Clasping the *saucisson* in both hands, he rose to his feet and made for the door. Crooking the little finger of his right hand around the light cord, he gave it a tug, then manoeuvred the door handle down with his left arm and gave it a push. The door opened onto more darkness, a darkness made even more impenetrable by his glasses, stretching their photochromatic qualities far beyond anything envisaged by their designers.

'*Qu'est-ce que c'est?*'

'I hope you don't mind.' Mrs. Cosgrove's voice sounded tremulous. 'Your world is one of total nighttime, I know. So it will mean nothing to you, but to me it will mean everything. It will make us equal. I have turned out the light.'

'As you wish,' said Monsieur Pamplemousse unhappily. Life had many strange and unexpected twists – that was part of its richness – but he had to admit that a minute ago he wouldn't have remotely pictured himself groping about in his own room carrying a giant *saucisson*. It would certainly be hard to explain to others. Doucette wouldn't believe him not in a million years. That apart, he had other, more pressing problems on his mind. He wished now he'd made a more accurate mental note of the positioning of the furniture.

Steering a course as best he could to the right of centre, so as to avoid treading on Pommes Frites – assuming Pommes Frites was where he'd left him – he headed in the general direction of the table.

'*Merde! Nom d'un nom!*'

'Are you all right? Where are you? I can't see you.' Mrs. Cosgrove sounded anxious.

'I have stubbed my toe on a leg of the bed.' It was agony. It felt as though it had been broken in at least six places.

'Aaah!' Short though it was, Mrs. Cosgrove managed to imbue the word with a wealth of meaning. A moment later there was a rustle and she was by his side, breathing his name. And each time she breathed his name it was accompanied by a little sob and a wriggle. It was like standing beside a bellydancer who was having trouble with her act.

His heart missed a beat as something gossamer-light landed at his feet and he realized the truth of the matter. At least it answered an earlier question; answered it and immediately posed another.

Like most Capricorns, Monsieur Pamplemousse had a strong sense of priorities. Once a course had been set he didn't like deviating from it. Mentally he had geared himself to satisfying the desires of the inner man before anything else. The message had gone out to all departments; taste buds were throbbing in anticipation, salivary glands were at the ready, the stomach was standing by ready to receive. On the other hand ...

'Here, take this for a moment.' Holding out the *saucisson*, he started to prepare himself for a change of plan.

'Jesus!'

'*Oui, c'est ça.*' It came back to him. 'That is its name. *Jésus.*' His opinion of Mrs. Cosgrove went up several more points She obviously knew her *charcuterie* as well as she knew her *vin rouge*. She would do well on Ananas' quiz show. 'It is from the Jure. I am told it is delicious served with *pomme à l'huile.'*

Hovering on one leg as he gingerly removed the sock from his bad foot, Monsieur Pamplemousse suddenly realized he was talking to himself. Mrs. Cosgrove was no longer there. Reaching out, he made contact with her outstretched form on the bed. His reward was a long, drawn-out moan.

'Aristide!' A hand took hold of his and gently but firmly guided it toward the head of the bed. Beneath the silk of the dress her *boîte à lolo* felt warm and inviting. Warm and inviting and …

He gave a start. Someone was knocking on the door. Knocking, moreover, in a manner which suggested that whoever was responsible would not readily go away without an answer.

'Un moment.' Panic set in as he reached out and turned on the bedside light. For a split second he toyed with the idea of covering Mrs. Cosgrove with the duvet, but one look at her made him change his mind. In her present state of mind there was no knowing how she might react.

A second knock, louder this time and even more insistent, spurred him into action. Reflexes born of years in the Force took over. Putting his arms around Mrs. Cosgrove, he lifted her bodily off the bed and dragged her toward the bathroom. *En route* he essayed a kick at the *saucisson* and immediately wished he hadn't. It was his bad foot. With his other leg he hooked the *culottes* under the bed.

Pommes Frites jumped to his feet and stared at his master in astonishment. He hadn't seen such a furious burst of activity for a long time. It looked a very good game and he hurried around the room collecting all the items in

128

case they were needed for a repeat performance

'Where are you taking me? What do you want to do with me? Tell me! Tell me!' Brought to her senses at last, Mrs. Cosgrove gazed wildly around the bathroom, first at the pile of sausages on the floor, then at Pommes Frites' kennel.

'Shush!' Monsieur Pamplemousse put a finger to his lips and then planted a kiss on her forehead. 'Please. I will explain everything later.'

Closing the bathroom door before she had time to answer, he made for the other door just as it started to open. Ananas was waiting outside. He looked furtive, as if he hadn't wanted to be seen there.

'May I come in?'

'I am a little busy. Could it not wait until later?'

'I will not keep you more than a moment or two. What I have to say I would rather say in the privacy of your room.'

'As you wish.' Monsieur Pamplemousse shrugged. Clearly Ananas had no intention of leaving until he'd had his say. The sooner he got it off his chest and went away again the better.

Ananas took in the bottle and the two glasses, the state of the bed and Monsieur Pamplemousse's foot, but made no comment.

'I have come to tell you that I no longer require your services.'

Monsieur Pamplemousse raised his eyebrows. 'Really? You mean there is no one trying to blackmail you after all?'

Ananas dismissed the suggestion with a wave of his freshly manicured hand. 'Shall we say it was a little misunderstanding all around. The good Herr Schmuck was merely taking precautionary measures to ensure that I would do something I fully intended doing anyway. Château Morgue has been getting some bad press recently and he wants me to restore its respectability. You or I would have done the same thing had we been in his place.'

'You might,' said Monsieur Pamplemousse gruffly, 'I wouldn't.'

Ananas inclined his head. 'Perhaps. But in the end we all protect that which we believe to be rightfully ours. I admit I might have chosen a different means. However, we all have our methods.'

'You mean – you will give him your endorsement – after all that has happened?'

'In return for certain favours – why not? It is a business arrangement.'

'You will endorse the work of someone who is prepared to resort to blackmail when it suits him?'

'Blackmail is not a word I like. I prefer the term 'making an offer it is hard to refuse.' So much more elegant, don't you think? Believe me, if I did not wish to agree to his suggestion I would have carried on with our arrangement. As it is, I would prefer that you forget our previous conversation. We have talked too much already. However, I felt I owed you some kind of explanation and an apology for any unnecessary work you have been put to. Who knows? I may be in a position to do you a favour one day. In the meantime, perhaps you would be kind enough to let me have the photograph back and we will call it a day.'

'I'm afraid,' said Monsieur Pamplemousse, 'that will not be possible.'

'Not possible? Don't tell me that after all your moralizing, Pamplemousse, you too have thoughts of straying from the straight and narrow? Because, if so, I warn you that you will find you have picked the wrong person. You will also find that Herr Schmuck does not take kindly to being crossed either.'

Monsieur Pamplemousse took a deep breath. Really, the man was totally insufferable. 'It is not possible,' he said, drawing as much pleasure as he could from the few words, 'because the photograph is no longer in my possession. It is in the hands of the police.'

'The police!' The remark had its desired effect. Ananas went pale, his normally suave manner deserting him along with his polished accent. 'What the devil do you mean by giving it to them?'

'I didn't,' said Monsieur Pamplemousse mildly. 'They took it. There was a little confusion about the identity of the person playing what one might call the 'leading role.' It is something I still cannot entirely see myself, but ... as they probably didn't even know you were here at the time, it was understandable.'

Ananas relaxed. 'I have to admit to sharing your feelings on the subject. It is a cross we have to bear. But,' his mind raced ahead of him, 'in view of your past reputation, I agree it was an understandable error. People – even members of the police force – have a habit of putting two and two together and coming up with whatever number they choose to fit the bill.

'I would not like to be in your shoes, Pamplemousse. I shall, of course, deny all knowledge of the affair, and in the circumstances I have no doubt the others in the picture will too. They will know on which side their bread is buttered. The negative, no doubt, is still in existence, but now that is your problem.'

Ananas pressed home his advantage. 'Why are you here anyway? Herr Schmuck would not be pleased if he knew the truth – he would not be pleased at all. An ex-member of

131

the Sûreté, wandering around with a white stick and dark glasses pretending you have lost your sight, cluttering up the place with that dreadful dog.'

'Pommes Frites?' Ignoring the implied threat in the last part of the remark, Monsieur Pamplemousse took a deep breath. He was about to launch himself into the attack when there was a stirring at his feet.

Pommes Frites knew a compliment when he heard one; he was also very sensitive to the reverse side of the coin. Sensing that there was little love lost between his master and Ananas, he'd been keeping a low profile, trying to catch the drift of the conversation, but without much success. He was, despite his fearsome appearance when the occasion demanded, one of nature's mediators.

He'd been considering the matter ever since Ananas first came into the room – watching points, pricking up his ears at changes in the conversation, and he'd come to the conclusion that there was definitely a feeling of acrimony in the air.

What was needed, in his opinion, was some kind of gift. It went against the grain because on the whole he was usually fairly careful in his choice of recipient; he wasn't at all sure that he liked Ananas. In fact, sensitive to the tone of the last remark, he definitely didn't, but if it helped his master in any way, then so be it.

Pommes Frites was a great believer in gifts during moments of crisis. Slippers were his specialty. He often fetched Madame Pamplemousse's slippers if she came in with the shopping on a wet day and saw his paw marks over the floor. It almost always had a soothing effect.

Slippers were obviously out on this occasion, but his eye had caught something else that he felt sure would fill the bill. It looked like a very good present indeed. Reaching out with his paw, he drew the object toward him. Then, feeling very pleased with himself, he courteously offered it to Ananas and stood back to watch the effect. He wasn't disappointed.

A smile spread slowly across Ananas' face as he allowed Mrs. Cosgrove's *culottes* to slip through his fingers, rather like a conjuror about to turn them into a complete set of the flags of all nations.

'Good boy!' Catching them deftly in his other hand, he slipped them into his pocket, then reached down to give Pommes Frites a friendly pat.

Pommes Frites stiffened. From the look on his master's face he could see that he hadn't done the right thing.

Ananas glanced around the room again. 'My, we have been having fun, haven't we? Tit, if you will pardon the expression, for tat.' He paused with his hand on the door. 'No photograph, no present back. *A bientôt.*'

He made to close the door but Monsieur Pamplemousse swiftly intercepted him.

'I imagine you will get your photograph back when the police have finished interviewing the others involved. There is some concern about the state of their health. No doubt they will be in touch in due course.'

It was a cheap jibe, but the look on Ananas' face made him feel better.

As he went back into his room the bathroom door opened and Mrs. Cosgrove appeared. He suddenly felt guilty. In the excitement he'd totally forgotten her presence. But he needn't have worried. Her eyes were shining as she closed the door behind her and came toward him.

He held out his hands to greet her. 'I am sorry. I would have told you, sooner or later. Once you start something it is often difficult to go back on it. At least when we last met

133

I was wearing my dark glasses.'

Mrs. Cosgrove coloured as the truth of the situation came home to her. 'Oh! You mean all the time you spent in my room when I was taking a shower … Oh dear! What must you have thought?'

'I thought you were very beautiful.'

'I don't know what to say.'

'Then let us say nothing.' Monsieur Pamplemousse suddenly felt a great warmth toward her. It was as if he'd been privileged to know another human being in a way that no one, perhaps not even her husband, had ever done before. It was not to be abused. 'Misused words generate misleading thoughts.'

He reached for the wine and refilled their glasses. Sadly, it was the end of the bottle. 'Let us drink to the future – not the past.'

Tilting his glass forward he held it over the white cover of one of the books. 'Look at that colour. Think of all the love and care and attention that went into making it, and think how lucky we are to be drinking it now.'

Mrs. Cosgrove touched his glass momentarily with hers. 'I've never met a detective before. At least, not a French one. It's not a bit as I imagined it might be.'

'You're not meeting one now. Only an ex-detective.'

'I bet you were a very good detective and I don't care what you're doing here just so long as you're not on the side of that odious creature.'

'People say we are like each other.'

'You are nothing like each other. Only a fool would think that.'

He sipped the wine, tasting it properly for the first time. It was round and fruity, at its best, and yet with many years ahead of it still. Full of promise, a wine to be savoured and lingered over, not one to be hurried. The analogy between it and the person sitting opposite him was irresistible.

'You must find the negative.'

'*Pouf!* The negative! That doesn't worry me. It is all the other things things I don't understand.'

'Then we must find out about them too. I'll help.' Her eyes were sparkling with excitement again. 'We'll pool what we know. There are a lot of things I could tell you. Things I've heard. It may be gossip, but you know what they say – where there's smoke there's fire.'

Monsieur Pamplemousse hesitated. By nature and by his work with *Le Guide* he had grown unused to working too closely with others. On the other hand …

'That would be very good.' He hesitated again. 'Perhaps it is time for the *saucisson* now. If you wish I will turn off the light.' He thought he knew the answer as he posed the question and wondered what he would do if he was wrong.

Mrs. Cosgrove shook her head. 'I'm not in the right mood anymore.'

'They say that appetite comes with eating.'

'No, it wouldn't be right somehow. But thank you. Tomorrow perhaps.' She stood up. 'I know what – tomorrow evening we'll go down to the village. There's a little cafe. Strictly speaking it's out of bounds, but no one need know. We can work things out over a meal.' Pausing at the door, she turned as if she had something else to say. Monsieur Pamplemousse wondered what he would do if she asked for her *culottes* back. Should he tell her the truth, that they were in Ananas' pocket? Or should he save her embarrassment and say he wanted to keep them as a souvenir. Perhaps he could pretend Pommes Frites had hidden them.

'Do you have a car?'

'*Oui*. But not here.'

'Can you ride a bike?'

'*A bike*?' He wondered if he was hearing correctly.

'*A bicyclette*. I've got one and I know where I could borrow another for you. How about it?'

Monsieur Pamplemousse considered the matter for all of ten seconds. 'They say you never forget. There was a time – '

'Good! *Dors bien!*' Her goodnight kiss, full on the lips, took him by surprise. A moment later she was gone.

'*Dors bien!*' He wondered how much sleep he would get that night.

Pommes Frites looked at him inquiringly and then decided to try his luck again. He reached out a paw. Knowing his master's tastes and adding the fact that it was long past their dinner time, a *saucisson* – even one that was looking slightly the worse for wear through being kicked across the room – was decidedly better than nothing.

7
DINNER FOR THREE

'I'll tell you another thing,' said Mrs. Cosgrove. 'As far as I can make out, they've all been foreign. Not French, I mean. Mostly Spanish, a few Italians, a couple from South America. Come to think of it, there were no British either. They were all Latins.'

'And all with thick calves?'

'You may laugh, but it's true. I've seen enough old dears in my job. When did you last come across anyone that age with that kind of problem?'

Monsieur Pamplemousse fell silent. It was an unanswerable question. He didn't make a habit of going around looking at old ladies' legs.

Mrs. Cosgrove looked anxiously across the table. 'I say, are you all right? You haven't hurt yourself?'

'It is nothing. A little soreness. An old wound. It will soon disappear.' Slipping his pen between his left leg and the chair seat for safety, Monsieur Pamplemousse waved his other hand reassuringly through the air.

It wasn't a direct lie, merely a slight distortion of the truth. His right leg was certainly sore, but then so was the rest of him. Parts of his body he hadn't been aware of for years were aching. His back, for example. And his neck. Not to mention his *derrière*. His thighs – *mon Dieu!* His thighs felt as though they had been drawn slowly through a mangle, a mangle with rollers made of corrugated iron. As

137

for his own calves, they must be twice their normal size. If his right leg felt worse than the rest of him it was because it had never fully recovered after being peppered by shot from a gun fired at close quarters during a previous assignment.

The truth of the matter was, he'd been trying to make some surreptitious notes on his pad and it wasn't easy. During the gaps in the conversation, his pen had been fairly racing over the pages. Whether he would be able to read his writing was another matter, but the little *bistro* Mrs. Cosgrove had taken him to was a discovery indeed. To the best of his knowledge it had never received a mention in Le *Guide*, nor in any of its competitors. If the smells coming from the kitchen were anything to go by, he was hot on the trail of a very worthwhile entry, possibly Stock Pot material. It would be something of a *coup*. It might even redeem him in the director's eyes for the loss of the letter. From the occasional stirrings and lip smackings emerging from below the folds of the red-and-white checked tablecloth he sensed that Pommes Frites shared his excitement, tempering a growing impatience with anticipation of the good things to come.

'Have you had many wounds? I mean, is what you do often dangerous?'

Monsieur Pamplemousse considered the matter carefully before replying. 'The answer to the first question, *touche du bois*, is no. As to the second, it is no more dangerous than what I have just been through.'

He spoke with feeling. When Mrs. Cosgrove first suggested cycling down to the village for dinner he'd had a mental picture of setting forth on something fairly sedate; perhaps an old upright that had once belonged to the local *facteur*. In the event she had turned up with an almost brand new British Dawes, complete with a Huret fifteen-speed Dérailleur gear, Italian drop handlebars, and a Dutch all-leather racing saddle. A truly international machine, and one that could have done with a certain amount of adjustment before they set out. The lowering of the saddle, for example. He winced and shifted uneasily in his chair as he recalled the saddle. Heaven alone knew where Mrs. Cosgrove had got hold of the machine. He didn't dare ask.

The first few moments, carrying it through the under-growth leading to a back way out of the Château, had been bliss. Light as a feather, the very feel of it had brought boyhood memories flooding back. In those days he had owned an Andre Bertin, and conversation had been all about the relative merits of wooden as opposed to alloy wheel rims; of brazed versus welded frames.

Once outside Château Morgue, though, it had been a very different story. In the far off days of his youth he had barely touched sixty kilos on the scales – the optimum weight the designers of his present machine must have had in mind. The roads, too, had been much smoother, the hairpin bends more suitably cambered, of that he was sure. Seen at close quarters, the road from Château Morgue down to the village had been one *nid de poule* after another. 'Hen nests' was an understatement for such potholes. He hadn't felt quite so frightened for a long time. He now knew from personal experience how Pommes Frites must feel every time he set off head-first down a flight of stairs. Except that with stairs the end was usually in sight. The journey down to the village had seemed neverending.

Mrs. Cosgrove, on the other hand, had taken it all in her stride. Eschewing the added protection of layers of material between her *derriere* and the saddle, she'd actually lifted her skirt over the top, allowing it to drape down either side in a most provocative manner as she led the way down the hill. At any other time and under other circumstances, he would have found the sight more than a little disturbing. Instead of which he'd spent most of the time holding onto the handlebars like grim death, hardly daring to change gear lest he got into an uncontrollable wobble or, worse still, collided with Pommes Frites, who treated the whole thing as yet another new game, running on ahead and waiting in the middle of the road for his master to appear, leaving it until the last possible moment to leap to one side.

To add to his ignominious arrival in the village, Mrs. Cosgrove had greeted him rather like the last rider home in the *Tour de France,* tying onto his handlebars a large, plastic, helium-filled balloon that she'd found in a local shop, by way of consolation.

He glanced around the restaurant. There were only seven tables, two of which were already occupied by regulars. Above a pine-wood fire in a large open grate was an old-fashioned spit – a complicated arrangement of weights and pulleys – the like of which he hadn't seen for a long time. It looked as though it was still in regular use. No doubt if you ordered a steak during the summer months there would be a girl whose job it was to lay the firewood in exactly the right way, not too little, not too much, so that the meat would be cooked just as the chef thought it should be – take it or leave it.

To be true, the menu was short – again take it or leave it, but from the moment they took their seats and a plate of almond and aniseed-flavoured biscuits, fresh from the oven, was plonked on their table, automatically and without comment, he knew that he was dealing with the genuine article: a chef who definitely liked his food. More-

140

over, from the glimpses he'd caught through the serving hatch separating the kitchen from the dining room, a satisfactorily rotund chef. On the whole he tended to mistrust thin chefs, classing them alongside bald-headed barbers who tried to sell you bottles of hair restorer. Neither were any advertisement for their trade.

The *patron*'s wife, who took the orders in between sitting at her cash desk near the door, was by contrast thin-lipped and forbidding. It was a classic combination. The man happy in his kitchen. The wife out front looking after the money.

'I'm sorry. It's not very exciting.' Mrs. Cosgrove looked genuinely disappointed as she scanned the handwritten menu. 'But it makes a change.'

'Not exciting!' Monsieur Pamplemousse gazed at her. 'It is the most exciting menu I have seen for a long time. Here you will find food of a kind you will get nowhere else in France. Why? Because the chef has probably never been farther than Narbonne in his life. He knows no other *cuisine,* and even if he did he wouldn't admit to it.'

He pushed the plate of biscuits toward her, at the same time signaling to the Madame. 'Have another *resquille.* We will do them the compliment of helping them on their way with a bottle of Blanquette de Limoux – if they have one. It is a local sparkling wine. Not quite like the real thing perhaps, but I think you will like it.'

He ran a practiced eye down the menu. 'Then I suggest you try the *cargolade – escargots* grilled over vinestocks; it gives them a unique flavour. I will have mine *à la Languedocienne* – with a sauce of anchovies, ham, cognac, and walnuts. We can share with each other.'

To his pleasure the Blanquette de Limoux more than fulfilled the promise he'd made, adding to the healthy glow

141

of Mrs. Cosgrove's cheeks; a glow further enhanced by the soft light from a single candle on their table. Taking advantage of the moment he made another note on his pad. The wine had the smell of cider, characteristic of the Mauzac grape which was its main ingredient, but there was another element he couldn't quite place. Perhaps the addition of some Chardonnay. He'd read somewhere that the best *cuvées* used it to give fuller flavour.

Conscious of Mrs. Cosgrove's eyes on him, he returned to the task in hand. 'Have you ever tried *Brandade de Morue?*'

Mrs. Cosgrove shook her head. 'I've heard of it.'

'Then that is a must. Dried salt cod pounded with garlic and olive oil until it becomes a creamy paste. Then it is served on *croûtons*. Salt cod is their winter equivalent of bacon and salt pork.

'After that, since we are in Catalan country, we could try *Tranche de Mouton à la Catalane,* or *Poivrons Rouges à la Catalane* – red peppers stuffed with rice salad. Again, perhaps we can have a little of each and share. With that we can have a bottle of Côtes de Roussillon Villages – if this wine is anything to go by the *patron* will most likely know a small grower. It could be something special.'

He felt in his element. It was like composing a piece of music; a matter of rhythms, of trying to avoid striking a discordant note.

'We could finish off sharing some Roquefort over the rest of the wine.'

'We seem to be doing a lot of sharing this evening,' said Mrs. Cosgrove meaningfully. 'First the *escargots,* then the main course, now the Roquefort.'

Monsieur Pamplemousse looked up from the menu. She was back into her leg-swinging syndrome. He hoped

Pommes Frites was keeping a watchful eye on things below stairs. If she carried on at her present rate he could suffer a nasty blow to the head. He would not be best pleased.

Perhaps it was a good thing they weren't having Chambertin with the cheese. What was it Casanova had said about Roquefort and Chambertin being excellent bedfellows? 'They stimulate romance and bring budding love affairs to a quick fruition.'

He voiced his thoughts and then immediately wished he hadn't. Mrs. Cosgrove was doing well enough with the Blanquette de Limoux on its own. Pommes Frites stirred nervously at his feet.

'George swears by cinnamon. He has it a lot on toast. He always says it puts lead in his pencil.'

The mention of the word pencil reminded Monsieur Pamplemousse of his pen which was now balanced very precariously on the edge of the seat. Apart from posing an additional hazard to Pommes Frites' head, he shuddered to think what would happen to its finely engineered tip if it landed on the tiled floor. It would be like losing an extension to his right arm. No other pen would ever be quite the same.

Cautiously he reached down below the cloth and as ill luck would have it made contact with a knee which was palpably not his own.

The sigh of contentment which escaped Mrs. Cosgrove's lips coincided with the arrival of the *escargots*. Madame, her lips more tightly compressed than ever, banged the plates down in front of them, punctuating her action with a loud sniff before retiring to her cash desk.

Feeling aggrieved that his action had been misinterpreted on all fronts, Monsieur Pamplemousse seized the opportunity to withdraw his hand.

143

'Du pain, s'il vous plaît.'

There was another bang as the basket of bread landed on their table.

Mrs. Cosgrove giggled. 'You're just like George. He gets put out when things like that happen.' Her leg stopped swinging and with one swift pincer movement came together with its opposite number to embrace his own right leg in a viselike grip. Simultaneously, she reached out and clasped his left hand firmly in hers. It was like having dinner with an octopus. 'George likes his greens too!'

'Greens? *Qu'est-ce que ces* greens?'

'Oats. You know ... dipping his wick.'

Monsieur Pamplemousse didn't know, although he could guess. He wondered what Doucette would say if he arrived home one day and announced that he wanted to *plonger* his *mèche de lampe*. He withdrew the thought immediately.

His thoughts went out instead to the absent George. If Mrs. Cosgrove's present behavior was typical of their life together, his free time must be almost entirely taken up with a search for fresh stimulants. Perhaps he wasn't as old as he looked in the photograph. It really was *incroyable* the way the English gave strange names to anything that had the faintest whiff of guilt about it. They seemed to have invented an entire language to cover every eventuality. It was the same with food. They didn't eat, they 'noshed,' 'scoffed,' or had 'bites' to satisfy the 'inner man' or because they felt 'peckish,' and they followed the main course with large helpings of 'pud' which they called 'afters.'

Perhaps it had to do with being separated from their parents at an early age and the segregation of the sexes. He'd read that it still went on.

Trying to erase from his mind the vision of a dormitory

full of little Mrs. Cosgroves, all sitting on the sides of their beds swinging their legs to and fro in a demonstration of mass frustration, he wiped the earthenware dish clean with a piece of bread and passed it down to Pommes Frites.

The *escargots* had been delicious. It was no wonder they were known as 'the oysters of Burgundy.' Although these, from the vineyards of the Languedoc, were smaller, they were no less good. Catching sight of the *patron* watching him through the serving hatch, he gave the universal, rounded forefinger-to-thumb sign of approval and received a smile in return.

Over the main course he decided to bring the conversation around to more important matters. 'So what else can you tell me about Château Morgue? How about the Schmucks?'

'Herr Schmuck comes from Leipzig and is a bit of a mystery. He started out as an industrial chemist, but the middle part of his life is a bit of an enigma. According to the locals he just seemed to materialize one day. Where his wife comes from no one seems to know. She keeps herself very much to herself. I've got a theory she's escaping from something in her past. She goes on a lot of trips, but always by herself.'

Monsieur Pamplemousse looked at her curiously as he poured the wine, 'How do you know all these things?'

'People unburden themselves when they're having a manicure. You'd be surprised. They talk about the most amazing things. It's a bit like being on a psychiatrist's couch without the guilt feelings afterward.'

'And Doctor Furze?'

'He was born in Leipzig too, but he escaped from East Germany just after the war. He's no more a doctor than I am. At least, not a doctor of medicine, which is what he would like everyone to believe.'

Feeling a nudge from below, Monsieur Pamplemousse speared a generous portion of *Tranche de Mouton* and passed it down. Since they would both be smelling of garlic that night there was no point in being

parsimonious. All the same, he made a mental note to leave the bedroom window open.

The Côtes de Roussillon was young and fruity, not unlike a Châteauneuf du Pape, but softer and more rounded. Casanova might not have ascribed to it quite the same powers as a Chambertin, but it showed up well against the Roquefort. And Mrs. Cosgrove too. Her eyes seemed to have acquired an added sparkle.

His brief exchange with the *patron* brought its benefit. With *a Crème d'Homère* – the local version of *crème caramel*, but made with the addition of wine and honey – there came a glass of Muscat from Frontignan, with the compliments of the chef. Golden and honey-scented like the dessert, it made a perfect ending to the meal.

Monsieur Pamplemousse felt a great sense of well-being. A well-being threatened only by a faint but persistent unease in the middle of his chest. It had probably been brought on by overexercise; it certainly couldn't have been the food. It confirmed a theory he'd once seen propounded by an English author whose name he couldn't pronounce, that the body was filled with numerous tiny compartments full of poisonous liquids, all of which lived perfectly happily alongside each other provided they were left in peace. But if you disturbed them by running, jumping, jogging or other unnatural pursuits, then you did so at your peril. Once the fluids were mixed together the result could be fatal.

'Is anything the matter, Aristide?' Mrs. Cosgrove reached

146

for his hand again. 'Are you sure you are all right?'

He returned the squeeze while massaging his chest in a circular movement with his other hand. 'It will pass. A slight rebellion within, that is all. I should have taken some fresh carrot juice before we came out.' Carrot juice ought to have been practically on tap in an establishment like Château Morgue.

'I have a bottle of something back in my room,' said Mrs. Cosgrove. 'It is made by some monks in the Rhône Valley and it's supposed to be good for the digestion.'

Monsieur Pamplemousse declined the offer. Without wishing to appear ungrateful, he had a feeling that what was good for a monk's digestion would probably have little effect on his own after all they had eaten. In his experience monasteries were usually run on strictly business lines by Abbots with clipboards. Miracles were not on sale to the general public.

'Perhaps a little *digestif*?' he added, leaving his options open. Mrs. Cosgrove brightened.

Reminding the Madame of a doggy bag he'd ordered for Pommes Frites when they first arrived, he asked at the same time for the bill, only too well aware of the fact that food was not the only problem. It had been a mistake to order a second bottle of the Côtes de Roussillon.

The bill paid, he rose from the table, adjusted his dark glasses, took hold of Pommes Frites' plastic doggy bag in the same hand as the white stick and, after a suitable exchange of pleasantries all around, led the way by a roundabout route to the door.

'I feel very wibbley-woo,' said Mrs. Cosgrove, when they were outside.

Wibbley-woo was not the word for it. On the other hand it wasn't a bad description. Better than *joie-de-vivre*. It even lent itself to variations. Wobbley-wib ... libbley loo. He decided to make a note of it. Perhaps the English had a point after all. There was a name for everything. It was even possible to sing it. The sound of wibbley-woo echoing back from the stone buildings had a satisfying ring.

The doggy bag safely secured beneath a large clip on the carrier over the rear wheel of his bicycle, Monsieur Pample-mousse removed the balloon from the handlebars and with due solemnity attached it to Pommes Frites' collar.

Mounting the machine, even with the aid of the white stick, was something else again. As he picked himself up for the third time he felt rather than saw someone watching him, and turned to see a pair of eyes through a gap in the curtains of the bistro. They were disapproving eyes, eyes that went well with the thinly compressed mouth, as chilly and unsmiling as the night air. The owner of both was not amused.

Turning his back on the uninvited audience, he picked up the bicycle and pushed it a little way down the road before making another attempt. This time he was more successful.

'Follow me!' Mrs. Cosgrove, skirts flying, was already negotiating a corner ahead of him.

He set off in pursuit. A *pharmacie*, its windows full of large stone jars and photographic equipment, merged with a *boulangerie*, and that gave way to a *bureau de tabac*, which in turn became the souvenir shop where Mrs. Cosgrove had bought the balloon. He wondered if the owners were watching Pommes Frites from their bedroom window.

Filled with an elation brought on by a heady mixture of wine and cold air, he discovered a new courage. Suddenly, he felt confident enough to sit upright in the saddle, holding on to the handlebars, first with only one hand, then with no hands at all.

Obeying a sudden impulse, he went round the *Mairie* a second time. As he shot past the bistro he caught sight of the Madame again and waved his stick at her. His salute was not returned. She was standing beside the cash desk engaged in an earnest conversation on the telephone. He felt her eyes following him.

Soon he was out of the village and heading back toward Château Morgue. Almost immediately the road began to climb. Flushed with success, he went through all fifteen gears with an aplomb he hadn't felt in years, and then came to an abrupt halt as he tried for the sixteenth and found it wasn't there. Looking back over his shoulder he saw to his disappointment that despite everything he had barely covered a hundred meters.

Dismounting, he turned a corner and caught sight of a bicycle lying abandoned at the side of the road near the entrance to the *aire de pique-pique*. Above the wall, ghost-like and silvery in the moonlight, floated the balloon, and beyond that, stretched out on one of the tables, lay Mrs. Cosgrove. Arms locked behind her head, knees drawn up, hair streaming over the edge, she looked for all the world like a reincarnation of Aphrodite resting while gaining her second wind after her long swim in the Mediterranean.

As he laid his own bicycle gently alongside the other, Monsieur Pamplemousse felt his pulse begin to quicken and a watery sensation in the bottom of his stomach. It was a feeling which, as he bent down to remove his cycle clips, was replaced almost immediately by a sharp, stabbing pain higher up.

'*Merde!*' What a moment to get indigestion.

He was about to straighten up when he heard a long,

drawn-out animal grunt coming from somewhere close at hand. It was a complex, elemental sound, accompanied by a kind of snuffling and with overtones of such ferocity it caused him to think twice about removing his clips and to take a firm grip of his stick instead.

Pommes Frites had evidently heard it too, for the balloon was bobbing up and down as if caught in a sudden gust of wind, heading first one way and then the other. Monsieur Pamplemousse turned toward a black patch of undergrowth beneath some trees on the other side of the road, wondering if perhaps it was harbouring a wild boar. As he did so the sound came again, this time from behind. He spun around as fast as he could and immediately regretted it. Part of his head felt as if it had gone into orbit. On the other hand, he had identified the source. Unmistakably, the dying notes came from the direction of the table. Mrs. Cosgrove was enjoying a deep if not exactly soundless sleep.

From somewhere in the distance, farther down the hill, there came the roar of engines. By the sound of it two vehicles were approaching fast, their tires squealing as they took the corners at top speed. Monsieur Pamplemousse felt glad he was no longer on his bicycle. The impression that there was more than one vehicle was confirmed a few seconds later as two sets of headlights swung around a bend immediately before the village and then disappeared from view.

Instinct told him to hide. Calling for Pommes Frites to follow, he made a dive for the cover of an old workman's hut in the far corner of the picnic area. It was too late to do anything about Mrs. Cosgrove or the bicycles even if he'd wanted to. They weren't a moment too soon. He'd hardly had time to draw breath, let alone make himself comfortable, before the lights swept past, illuminating as they did so both Mrs. Cosgrove and Pommes Frites' balloon, which had broken free.

There was a screech of brakes from the leading vehicle, echoed even more urgently by the one behind, then the noise of crunching gears and engines revving as they backed down the hill a little before coming to a stop. Doors slammed as the occupants clambered out. Then came the crunch of feet on gravel, followed by the sound of familiar voices.

'It must be the woman the old girl in the cafe was talking about on the phone.' He recognized Paradou's voice, then that of his colleague as they shone a torch over the recumbent figure on the table. There were a few barely suppressed whistles, then the other *gendarme* passed a remark that provoked a coarse laugh. It was immediately stifled as another voice cut through the darkness.

Peering around the side of the hut, Monsieur Pamplemousse saw Inspector Chambard rise into view from behind the bicycles. 'Can't you wake her?'

'You try, Chief.' It was the second *gendarme*. 'She's out like a light.'

Chambard gave an impatient grunt. He crossed to the parapet and gazed up at the balloon drifting slowly across the valley. 'What the devil can have happened to Pamplemousse? It must have been him. There can't be anyone else wandering around with a white stick at this time of night.'

'I wouldn't fancy his chances if he's fallen down there.' Paradou joined the inspector and waved his torch in a desultory fashion over the side of the wall.

'*Zut alors!*' Inspector Chambard turned back to the table and gazed down at Mrs. Cosgrove. 'We can't leave her here. She'll catch her death of cold. You two had better take her back to the station. Put the bicycles in the van too. There's a bag of something on Pamplemousse's carrier – you can go through it when you get back, Paradou, and make a list of the contents.'

Paradou gave Pommes Frites' doggy bag a tentative squeeze. 'Why do I always get the dirty jobs, Chief?'

But Inspector Chambard was already in his car. The door slammed. A moment later he was on his way. Paradou waited until the car was safely around the corner before giving vent to his feelings.

'You can tell it belongs to old Pamplemousse all right. He must have some kind of kink. Feel it, go on, feel it!'

Declining the offer, his colleague picked up the other bicycle and propped it up in the back of the van. 'Did you see the analyst's report on the first lot? Sixty percent pure chicken and pork. Fifteen percent pure onion '

'Pure! That's a laugh. Wait till he gets hold of this!'

The second machine safely stowed away, they turned their attention to Mrs. Cosgrove.

From his position behind the bush, a position which was growing steadily more uncomfortable with every passing moment, it seemed to Monsieur Pamplemousse that the two *gendarmes* were making unnecessarily heavy weather of the comparatively simple task of transferring their burden from the table to the front seat of the van.

The temptation to jump out and remonstrate was almost too great to bear, but discretion won the day. He was in no mood to submit to the kind of tedious explanations that would inevitably follow such an action. Far better let things take their course.

At last they had finished. As the red tail-lights of the van receded down the hill, Monsieur Pamplemousse stood up and mopped his brow with the back of his sleeve. In spite of the cold he was sweating profusely.

He turned and gazed up the hill toward Château Morgue. The lights from the windows at the top of the tower block made it seem even more remote and impregnable than ever, and he suddenly felt very dispirited. It would need either the services of a helicopter pilot to learn what was going on inside or a bird perched on top of Pommes Frites' balloon.

Saddle sore, aching in every limb, his gastric juices in revolt, head throbbing, deprived of his sole means of wheeled transport, Monsieur Pamplemousse prepared himself for the long slog back up the hill.

Only one thing remained to render his cup of unhappiness full to overflowing. It concerned Pommes Frites and was a matter that would need to be faced up to in the not too distant future.

For the moment at least, Pommes Frites had other things on his mind. He was standing with his front paws on the parapet looking for his lost balloon, but when he mentally came back down to earth it would be with a distinct bump. He wouldn't be best pleased when it dawned on him that along with Mrs. Cosgrove and the bicycles had gone the bag containing his supper. He would feel very hard done by. Melancholy would set in. And when Pommes Frites had a touch of the melancholies, everyone else was apt to suffer. It was not a happy prospect.

'*Merde!*' Monsieur Pamplemousse picked up his stick and stabbed at a nearby bush. What a way to end an evening that had begun with such promise.

8
JOURNEY INTO SPACE

Contrary to all his expectations, Monsieur Pamplemousse went to sleep that night almost as soon as his head touched the pillow. He woke at eight o'clock the next morning feeling, if not as fresh as the proverbial daisy, at least as a daisy which required the minimum amount of attention in order to greet the new day. After a bath and a shave and a hearty breakfast of *Saucisses de Montbéliard*, he felt more than ready to start work.

To say that he spent the intervening time thinking of Mrs. Cosgrove would have been a distortion of the truth. She entered his mind more than once, but only in passing. At least he knew she was in safe hands, and doubtless she would surface again in the fullness of time.

His mind was full of little notes and observations and thoughts, all of which badly needed putting into some kind of order. In many ways it was the part he liked best, the sifting of all the available information, the analyzing, collating, and fitting together of all the various items like a jigsaw puzzle, discarding a piece here, adding a piece there, watching the overall picture gradually take shape. There was a precision about the whole activity; the knowledge that an answer must eventually be produced appealed to the mathematical side of his mind. True, in the present case there were a number of bits missing, but he had no doubt in his mind that once he'd got the edge pieces assembled, the framework and parameters within which he had to work established, the rest would follow.

With no thought of time or of Pommes Frites, he worked solidly for the best part of an hour, then he laid down his pen and sat for a while, driven to one inescapable conclusion. Whichever way he looked at it, from whatever direction he approached the problem, in order to prove his theory he needed evidence of what went on inside the Tower Block. He rose and crossed to the window, gazing out at the surrounding countryside, going over in his mind once again all that had taken place since his arrival at Château Morgue. And as had so often happened in the past when, under similar circumstances, he'd sought inspiration from the waters of the Seine via his office window in the *quai des Orfèvres,* the very act of stretching his legs and filling his mind with an entirely different view, produced almost immediate results.

By standing on tiptoe he could just see the village where he had spent the previous evening with Mrs. Cosgrove; by standing on a chair he could even see the *aire de pique-pique,* and it was while he was idly wondering what had happened to Pommes Frites' balloon, whether it was somewhere inland, or perhaps even heading toward the Mediterranean, that an idea came to him.

He stood on the chair for a moment or two, lost in thought. It would require equipment he didn't possess, equipment he probably couldn't easily get hold of at short notice. Unless ... In a flash, one idea triggered off another. He looked at his watch. Ten o'clock. Jumping down off the chair he made for the bathroom, and, watched by Pommes Frites, set to work.

At 10:13, unable to stand things a moment longer, Pommes Frites made it very clear that he wished to be elsewhere. He left the room with a worried look on his face and set off down the corridor, determined to brook no interference with his plans.

Monsieur Pamplemousse wasn't the only one to have spent his morning engaged in thought. Pommes Frites had also been exercising his gray matter, and after weighing up all the pros and cons, making all due allowances for possible errors of judgment, it was his considered opinion that his master was suffering some kind of brainstorm and that there wasn't a moment to be lost.

The signs were all there. First, there had been the business with the white stick and dark glasses; then the sudden change of eating habits – from meals of infinite variety to a diet of unrelieved sausages. The acquisition of a bicycle was yet another bad sign. Pommes Frites didn't agree with bicycles – they came at you from all angles. As for the balloon, the less said the better. The fact that his master was now playing around with his kennel was the final straw. It suggested that action of an immediate and fundamental nature was required.

No less adept, although perhaps a trifle slower than his master at sifting information, it had taken Pommes Frites some while to arrive at the truth of the matter. Now that he had, he couldn't understand why it hadn't occurred to him before. The whole thing was his fault entirely. His master was in need of care and attention and in his hour of need he, Pommes Frites, had been responsible, albeit unwittingly, for giving away something that he obviously held in great store. It was as if, and he couldn't think of a better parallel, it was as if someone had stumbled across a store of his best bones and had given them to another dog without so much as a by-your-leave.

Pommes Frites was never one for doing things by halves.

Once he had things clearly worked out in his mind, that was that – there was no stopping him. And had he been able to see his master at that moment, he would undoubtedly have quickened his pace toward his final goal, for his worst fears would have been realized.

Monsieur Pamplemousse, with the aid of a puncture repair kit normally housed in a pocket at the rear of Pommes Frites' kennel, was busily engaged in gluing down the flap over the entrance, and in so doing, effectively barring the way at one and the same time to both anyone who might seek entry and anything within hoping to escape, including, he was pleased to see as he applied his full weight to the top and bounced up and down several times, the air inside.

Pommes Frites would not have been alone in registering concern had there been others present to witness the operation, but Monsieur Pamplemousse himself seemed more than pleased as he gazed at the result of his labours; so much so it was some little while before he registered the fact that the telephone was ringing.

'Aristide.' It was Mrs. Cosgrove.

'Anne. How are you?'

'I feel awful.'

Monsieur Pamplemousse felt his forehead. 'I am not … how would you say? One hundred percent, but – '

'I don't mean that. I mean the whole thing. It's never happened to me before. I'm fine otherwise.'

Monsieur Pamplemousse decided to try again, rephrasing his original question. '*Where* are you?'

'I'm still at the police station. Some inspector or other has been questioning me. He says he knows you.'

'Chambard?'

'That's the one. He thought you were with me last night.

Apparently the woman in the restaurant gave him a description. I didn't let on. I said I was with your look-alike. The one who came to your room that night.'

'Ananas?' He felt his forehead again. The dizziness had returned. 'Ananas!'

'I don't think he quite believed me at first because of your white stick. Anyway, he does now. I didn't want to get you involved in case you wanted to keep a low profile.'

'It is very kind of you.' Monsieur Pamplemousse hesitated. For some totally illogical reason he felt slightly put out that his place had been taken, if only on paper as it were, by someone he disliked so much.

'You don't mind?' She sounded anxious.

'Of course not. I am a little jealous, that is all.'

'Oh dear. I'm sorry about that. Never mind. We'll try and make up for it later. I'll tell you something else – '

'Listen, before you do ...' Monsieur Pamplemousse cut across whatever Mrs. Cosgrove had been about to say. Her telephone call was opportune. An omen, perhaps, that what he was planning was meant. He wondered if their conversation was being overheard, and then decided to take the risk. It was too good a chance to miss. 'On your way back you can do some shopping for me. I would like you to stop off in the village and go, first of all, to the souvenir shop, the one where you bought the balloon. Then I would like you to go to the *pharmacie*. I think you will find the owner is a keen photographer. I need a number of things. I saw most of them in the window last night. You had better make a list.'

While he was talking, Monsieur Pamplemousse found himself marveling at the wonders of the human brain, able to register and retain even the most trivial details without being prompted, and all at a time when it must have been heavily engaged in supplying information to that section which was making sure he remained safely upright on his bicycle. He could still picture the window display in the *pharmacie* with the utmost clarity.

'Have you got all that?'

'I think so. Would you like me to read it back?'

'Not if you are sure.' At this stage he did not wish to arouse Chambard's interest in his activities any more than it was already. For the time being at least, he would rather work on his own. Just himself and Pommes Frites ... and Mrs. Cosgrove. Chambard was a good man, but he would be bound to ask questions. If his own theories proved correct there would soon be plenty of need for his services.

'Before you go, I must tell you. There have been some more goings-on at the Château.'

'Goings-on?,'

'Someone's been through the ladies' changing rooms like a dose of salts.' Mrs. Cosgrove's voice became muffled as she put a hand over her mouth, covering up a half-suppressed giggle. 'Apparently they all came back from their morning saunas and needle baths and found their most precious items of underwear missing. There's hell to pay. Inspector Chambard's on the phone about it right now. That's how I could ring you. He thinks it must be the same person who stole the package a couple of days ago. He says – '

Monsieur Pamplemousse looked at his watch again. Much as he liked the sound of Mrs. Cosgrove's voice, it was 10:43 and time was precious. He had a great deal to do.

'I can tell you one thing, and I will stake my reputation on it. Whoever was responsible for taking the *charcuterie* is in no way involved in the present matter.' He was about to add, 'And you can tell Inspector Chambard that from me!' but thought better of it. Conscious that he might have sounded a trifle pompous, he ended on a fonder note.

'Take care. I hope I will see you soon.'

At 10:45, just as he was in the act of laying out his camera equipment on the bed for checking, there was a loud thump on the door. He opened it and Pommes Frites staggered in. At least, he assumed it was Pommes Frites; it was hard to tell beneath the vast mound of multicoloured material he was holding in his mouth.

With all the aplomb of an elderly magician whose *pièce de résistance,* the trick he keeps for really special occasions – that of the disappearing *culottes* of all nations – has gone sadly awry, he came to a halt in the middle of the room and disgorged his load over the rug.

Suffering a feeling of *déjà vu,* Monsieur Pamplemousse shot a quick look up and down the corridor. Somewhere in the distance an alarm bell was ringing, but otherwise all was quiet. He closed the door and gazed unhappily at the pile of *lingerie.* Although black undoubtedly held pride of place, with white a close second, *culottes* of red, green, purple, and blue, all the many colours of the rainbow, manifested themselves in a variety of shapes, sizes, and degrees of laciness. At a cursory glance, if sheer weight of numbers was any criterion, Pommes Frites' latest excursion into the world of fashion had been even more successful than his earlier venture into the more mundane realms of *charcuterie.*

Well pleased with his morning's work, Pommes Frites stretched, and wagged his tail in anticipation of the words of praise to come. Although his master seemed temporarily bereft of speech, he was prepared to wait, happy in the knowledge that he had done the right thing at last. It had just been a simple case of good intentions gone wrong. Mrs.

Cosgrove had removed an article of clothing, intending it as a gift for Monsieur Pamplemousse, and he, Pommes Frites, had presented it to another. No wonder his master had been upset; small wonder, too, that he now looked so bowled over at his good fortune – it called for some more tail wagging.

Monsieur Pamplemousse stared back at Pommes Frites through eyes glazed not by tears, but with sheer incredulity. He couldn't bring himself to say *'bon garçon'*; his lips refused to form the words. On the other hand, he couldn't in fairness chastise him either. There was also the fact that he would need Pommes Frites' cooperation later that day and he couldn't afford to let any other misunderstandings come between them.

Slowly and deliberately he knelt down and began folding the garments into a neat pile. Compressing them as tightly as possible, he opened the cupboard, emptied the remains of the sausages from their wrapping paper, and used it to make a new parcel which he then pushed under the bed.

It represented yet another very good reason why he would need to work quickly. It was more than likely that Inspector Chambard would seize the opportunity to pay a return visit to Château Morgue. He was not one to be balked. No stone would be left unturned in his search for the culprit; probably no *culottes* either if Paradou had any say in the matter. The prospect of being confronted by innumerable irate ladies seeking to identify their nether garments was not a happy one. Even worse, he would be hard put to it to avoid a second request from the inspector to accompany him back to the station.

He looked out of the window to see if there was any sign of Mrs. Cosgrove returning and was just in time to see the Mercedes in which he'd arrived enter the gates. It was being towed by a breakdown lorry driven by a mechanic in blue overalls. There was no sign of the original chauffeur. The car appeared to have been in the wars since he'd last seen it. The windscreen was smashed, the front bumper twisted, and there was a sizable dent in the radiator.

The morning was clear and sunny, and he was about to open the window to let in some fresh air when his attention was caught by the pole over the main entrance. For the second time since his arrival the flag was flying at half-mast. Had his determination that it was time for action shown any signs of wavering, this was enough to give it a boost; as it was, it simply strengthened his resolve.

First there was the camera equipment to check. On his way back to the bed he closed the bathroom door. For the moment at least, he would rather Pommes Frites didn't see his kennel.

Opening up the case belonging to *Le Guide*, he lifted out the tray containing the camera equipment. Removing the Leica R4 body, the standard fifty millimeter Summicron lens and the motor winder, he began to assemble them. The motor winder responded immediately when he tested it. Loading the camera with Ilford XP1 black-and-white film, he set the program for shutter priority at a speed of one two-hundred-and-fiftieth of a second, and focused the lens at around ten yards. The combination of a lens aperture of f2 and a film speed of four hundred ASA should be auffi-cient to cover any eventuality. If not, Trigaux back at head-quarters would have means of gushing the film beyond its normal rating.

Opening up his own case, he looked for the Remote Control Unit. Once again fate seemed to have stepped in to take a hand. It was the first time he had ever had such a thing with him. Luckily he'd taken Rabillier's advice and

162

included several lengths of extension cable. It would enable him to keep hold of the unit itself and judge to a nicety when to trigger the automatic winder. With a range of anything between one frame every half second and one frame every ten seconds he ought to be able to arrive at a satisfactory optimum rate of exposure.

He would need to reconnoiter the area first and make a rough measurement of the distance along the outside wall of the Tower Block, dividing it by the total number of frames available, to gauge the exposure pattern. Even then it might result in a few blank frames – shots of the wall – but given the total window area he should be all right.

He would probably only have time for one go. There was no sense in pushing his luck, so it would have to be right first time. In the interest of safety, Pommes Frites' kennel had been made of a bright orange, light-reflecting material and would therefore be plainly visible to anyone who happened to be looking out of the windows. Unless ... He had another flash of inspiration. Unless it was covered in something that didn't reflect the light.

He felt under the bed. Covered with a suitably black, non-reflecting material, it wouldn't be any problem at all.

Pommes Frites wasn't normally given to audible expressions of pleasure He was content to leave such displays of emotion to creatures of a lower order. But anyone who didn't know him well might have been forgiven had they assumed he was undergoing some strange metamorphosis of a feline and contagious nature as he watched his master undo the parcel. Contagious, because it speedily communicated itself to Monsieur Pamplemousse. Monsieur Pamplemousse was positively purring with delight. Had he been conducting a market survey for a fashion designer who wished to prove that despite all the efforts of his rivals to dictate otherwise, black remained the most popular colour in ladies' *lingerie*, he couldn't have wished for better or more unimpeachable proof. Perhaps it had to do with the environment at Château Morgue. Perhaps many of the clients came there not so much for 'the cure' as for less laudable reasons. No matter, the plain fact was that he had more than enough material to cover a dozen kennels. Selecting several items that must have belonged to those who had benefited most from nature's generosity, and rejecting others that would have barely covered the air valve, Monsieur Pamplemousse made a fresh but smaller parcel of the ones that had failed to meet his requirements, and replaced it under the bed.

'So it *was* you after all!' At the sound of Mrs. Cosgrove's voice he jumped to his feet, colouring up like a schoolboy caught hiding something untoward beneath his desk lid. He had been concentrating so hard on the task in hand he'd totally failed to hear her enter the room. She looked deflated, like someone whose last precious illusion had just been shattered.

'It was true earlier on when I spoke to you on the phone. Now, I am afraid it is no longer so. On the other hand, *après la pluie, le beau temps.*' He picked up the nearest garment and ran it through his fingers. 'Every cloud has a silver lining. They solve a problem.' To his relief she seemed to accept this without question. It showed on her face.

'You managed to get all the things I asked for?'

Mrs. Cosgrove felt inside a carrier bag. 'I have some of them in here, the chemicals, some plaited nylon line. I got extra strong. It has a breaking point of over five kilograms. I hope I did the right thing, but not knowing what you wanted it for …'

Briefly and succinctly, Monsieur Pamplemousse ran

through his plan. At the same time he made some quick mental calculations. The camera and the lens together weighed something like nine hundred grams, the winder another four hundred. Filled with gas, the kennel should provide more than enough lift.

'The rest of the things are in my room. All except the helium cylinder. That weighs a ton and it will need the two of us. I left it in the rented car.'

'Which is where?'

'I parked it out of sight. It's well off the beaten track. I don't think anyone will find it unless they come across it by accident.'

'Excellent. I can't thank you enough.' Now that things were starting to happen he felt relaxed. His mood communicated itself to Mrs. Cosgrove.

'What are you doing for the rest of the day?'

He hesitated. 'Working.' It was an understatement. There were measurements to be taken, calculations to be made. He would need to experiment with making some kind of harness to hang beneath the kennel in order to be certain the camera remained horizontal and pointing in the right direction. If the weather stayed as it was, there shouldn't be any problem. If it changed, as it often did in the mountains, suddenly and without warning …

Mrs. Cosgrove followed him into the bathroom. She looked sceptical. 'Do you think it will ever fly?'

Monsieur Pamplemousse gave a noncommittal shrug. 'They asked the same question of the Montgolfier brothers when they set off from the Champ de Mars in 1783.' He spoke with more conviction than he actually felt. At least the Montgolfier balloon had been spherical. Aerodynamically, Pommes Frites' kennel left a lot to be desired; it was hardly in the forefront of design.

165

'And this evening?'

'This evening I shall be even busier.' He would need to make a few trial runs with Pommes Frites so that he would get used to the idea of having a miniature *dirigeable* attached to his collar. He might not take kindly to the idea. Both that and testing the helium-filled kennel would have to wait until after dark. And it would have to work first time; in all probability he wouldn't get a second chance.

Aware that Mrs. Cosgrove was looking deflated again, he turned to her. 'Perhaps,' he said gently, 'if you were to help, I might get it all done in half the time. And then ...'

'And then?' She put down her carrier bag.

'In France there is a saying: *'On s'abandonne à son imagination,'* one lets one's imagination run away with one.'

'In England,' said Mrs. Cosgrove firmly, 'we say that too. We also have one which says: 'There is no time like the present.''

As something soft and silky landed on the bathroom floor there came a sigh of contentment from the other room. Pommes Frites wasn't given to boasting or to blowing his own trumpet, but it was nice to know that his efforts at restoring his master's equilibrium hadn't been entirely wasted.

It was dark by the time Monsieur Pamplemousse followed Pommes Frites out through his bedroom window.

'Good luck!' Mrs. Cosgrove's voice came through the darkness, muffled by the bulk of the newly inflated kennel as she struggled to push it after them.

'Merci.' Privately Monsieur Pamplemousse suddenly realized he was going to need it. Or rather, Pommes Frites would need it.

A feeling of guilt came over him as he clipped the end of

the line onto the harness and the makeshift balloon rose into the air. Somewhere along the way his calculations must have gone sadly wrong. Perhaps in his ignorance he had grossly underestimated the lifting power of helium. Whatever the reason, he undoubtedly had a problem on his hands.

If only he'd given it a trial run as planned. Instead of which, his good intentions had gone for nothing, sacrificed in favour of the more immediate desires of the flesh.

Paying out the line centimeter by centimeter, he watched anxiously as the kennel buffeted to and fro against the side of the building.

Merde! If the camera broke one of the windows *en route* the game would be up and no mistake.

At his last medical Pommes Frites had weighed in at around fifty kilograms, but from the feel of things he was going to need every gram. The light breeze he'd noticed earlier in the day had freshened and was full of unpredictable upward currents. For a moment or two he toyed with the idea of adding some extra ballast, then dismissed the thought. Getting the weight exactly right would take time, and now that he'd set the wheels in motion speed was of the essence.

That Pommes Frites was beginning to share his master's anxiety was patently obvious as the end of the line was reached and he began to take the strain. There was a certain lightness to his tread as he set off along the side of the building, a lightness that caused him to gaze skyward more than once as Monsieur Pamplemousse guided him toward his starting position. Much of the time it was hard to tell what thoughts passed through Pommes Frites' mind – he could, if he chose, be very poker-faced – but for once it was patently obvious. He looked decidedly apprehensive.

'*Avancez!*' Taking advantage of a moment when the moon was temporarily obscured by a cloud, Monsieur Pamplemousse gave him an encouraging pat.

For a full two minutes their luck held. Like a jumbo jet piloted by an inexperienced captain badly in need of a refresher course and using every inch of the runway, Pommes Frites set off, following an unsteady path toward the far end of the building.

Monsieur Pamplemousse held his breath. At least one of his calculations was correct. It was hard to tell from where he was looking, but the camera appeared to be almost exactly in line with the centre of the windows. He triggered off the automatic film advance mechanism with the button on the control unit, then began counting the seconds in double rather than single figures in order to keep an accurate time check. One minute, twelve seconds later they were halfway along the side of the building. He glanced down at the control unit. The luminous display showed the figure 18. He breathed a sigh of relief. It meant his allowance of four seconds between shots had been right too.

It was as they neared the end of the building that things began to go wrong. For some reason the camera looked higher than it had at the beginning, rather too near the top of the windows for his liking. Perhaps it was that the ground sloped upward? He looked down again and saw to his horror that the worst had happened. Pommes Frites was treading air; his front paws had already left the ground and their opposite numbers at the rear were about to follow suit.

Monsieur Pamplemousse made a frantic dive forward, only to pull himself up in the nick of time as he realized he was tottering on the edge of a rocky precipice. In any case he had left it too late. Carrying the analogy with a jumbo jet to its ultimate conclusion, Pommes Frites had completed his takeoff.

Bereft of navigational lights, silhouetted in the ghostly light from the moon, now reemerged from behind the cloud, it would under other circumstances have been an awesome sight. Any local inhabitant witnessing the event while staggering home after an evening out with the boys, might well have been excused had he crossed himself and taken an immediate header off the cliffs into the valley far below. As it was, Monsieur Pamplemousse could only stand helplessly by and watch as his friend and mentor executed a steep turn to starboard and then, gaining height with every passing second, set off slowly and ponderously in the direction of the Pyrénées-Orientales.

9
A DEVELOPING SITUATION

It was well after midnight before Monsieur Pamplemousse finally got back to his room.

'Aristide!' Mrs. Cosgrove reached out to help him over the sill. 'Are you all right? You've been so long I was beginning to think the worst. How did it all go?'

She felt cold to the touch and he realized she'd probably been waiting by the open window ever since they left. He gave her a quick hug as she drew the curtains. 'I shall know for certain when we have processed the film.'

'But what happened?' They both blinked as she turned on the light. 'You look as if you've been pulled through a hedge backward.'

He glanced at his reflection in the mirror. It was an apposite description. All it needed was the word 'tree' to be substituted for 'hedge' to be true.

'Pommes Frites had an unfortunate accident. Through no fault of his own he became airborne and it was nearly the last we saw of each other. Fortunately I was still holding the control box, so I managed to pull him back safely with the cable. It was, so to speak, his umbilical cord. If that hadn't held – *alors* … !' He left the rest to her imagination. It didn't bear thinking about. Full marks to Leitz for quality workmanship. If the cable had been the product of a lesser manufacturer Heaven alone knew what might have happened.

'Poor chap.' Mrs. Cosgrove was rewarded by a grateful wagging of the tail as she bent down to give Pommes Frites a pat. 'Thank goodness you're safe.'

'I'm afraid we lost his kennel in the process. It suffered a puncture when it hit a tree.'

Monsieur Pamplemousse spoke as though the whole thing was an everyday happening, but in reality it had been a terrifying experience, seeing Pommes Frites sail off into the night. He would never have forgiven himself had the worst occurred. Climbing the tree in the dark had been nothing by comparison, although getting his precious cargo down in one piece had been another matter; the memory would probably keep him awake at night for some time to come. In the meantime there was work to be done.

'Is everything ready?'

'Just about. I've mixed the chemicals and tried to keep the solutions as near thirty-eight degrees as possible. I stood the jugs in a bowl of water and used your portable coffee heater like you said.'

'Good.' Monsieur Pamplemousse gave her another appreciative hug. 'I don't know what I would have done without you.'

As he rewound the film onto its spool he quickly checked the camera. It had survived its emergency landing with hardly a scratch. The settings were all as he had left them. The film safely back in its spool, he clicked open the back of the camera to remove it. Now for the big moment. It was a long time since he'd last done any processing. To ruin things now through some idiotic mistake would be too galling for words.

In the bathroom with the lights out, feeling his way around in the pitch dark, he was acutely aware of Mrs. Cosgrove's presence.

The film loaded into its lightproof tank, he reached for the switch. Ten minutes alone in the dark with Mrs. Cosgrove would not be conducive to good darkroom practice. He could also hear Pommes Frites sniffing along the bottom of the door.

'Do you *have* to go back to Paris tonight?'

He shrugged, trying to concentrate on what he was doing and keep an eye on the time as well. 'It depends on what's here. If my suspicions are correct then the answer has to be 'yes.' There is a train leaving Carcassonne at four thirty-three in the morning. It gets to Paris in the early afternoon.'

'I'll drive you there.'

'You don't have to. I can leave the car at the station and make arrangements to have it picked up when I get back to Paris.'

'Please. I would like to.'

'In that case I would like it too.' He couldn't deny it would be very pleasant. The thought of driving through the night in a strange car while trying to map-read at the same time over perhaps two hundred and fifty kilometers or more of mostly winding mountain roads didn't exactly fill him full of joy. Pommes Frites would be fast asleep in the back and he wasn't too sure of his own ability to stay awake.

At exactly twelve seconds before the first five minutes was up he began pouring the developer away, then quickly added the bleach-fix from another jug. Mrs. Cosgrove had done her job well.

After another five minutes he emptied out the second solution and turned on the tap over the basin. Three minutes' wash in cold water should be sufficient; four to be on the safe side.

'Will you be back?'

'It is possible.' Even as he spoke the words he knew he wouldn't be. And like the old joke, he knew that she knew that he knew he wouldn't be. To return would imply all kinds of things from which there might be no turning back.

'Who knows? It is a small world.' He turned off the tap and began unscrewing the lid of the tank. 'Did you bring the hairdryer?'

'It is in the other room.' She opened the door and went into the bedroom. Pommes Frites wagged his tail doubtfully.

Monsieur Pamplemousse held the film horizontally between his outstretched hands, keeping a watchful eye on it in case the dryer came too close. In a matter of moments all traces of wetness had disappeared.

Allowing it to spring back into a rough coil, he held the leader over a piece of white paper on the table beneath the overhead light and began pulling it through his fingers, examining it frame by frame.

The first was half wall, half window. Nothing appeared to be happening behind the latter. The second and third frames were of some kind of lounge area. There were a number of figures, mostly male, sitting or standing around in small groups, all so small as to be unrecognizable without being blown up. It looked as though there was a party in progress.

There was another shot of the tower wall. Pommes Frites must have changed his pace slightly. Momentarily diverted, perhaps, by an interesting scent *en route*, or an unexpected cross wind.

The next two or three were much more rewarding. Pin-sharp and brightly lit, they showed a gymnasium, not dissimilar to the one he'd been in on his first day, full of the

173

kind of equipment one would expect in a place where no expense was spared: parallel bars, rowing machines, weight-reducing vibratory belts, racks of dumbbells. The sole occupant was an elderly woman in a track suit who was hard at work on a cycling machine, shoulders hunched, head low down until her close-cropped hair almost touched the dial attached to the handlebars. There was something vaguely familiar about her, but without the aid of a light box or some means of reversing the image it was hard to say exactly what.

Eight and nine were again of the wall. Ten to fourteen were of individual apartments. The main lights must have been out, for they were underexposed and it was hard to tell what was going on.

Frames fifteen to twenty were again well lit. Clearly they showed a kitchen area; white cupboards lined the walls and in the background there was what appeared to be a row of stainless steel ovens. One picture showed some out-of-focus scales in close-up – they must have been standing by the window; another, a row of bowls clearly containing flour. Nearby was a pile of *saucissons*. Number nineteen showed Furze, for once minus his clipboard. He was standing in front of a second set of scales peering at a dial. From number twenty on the film was meaningless, recording for posterity Pommes Frites' journey into space. They might well yield some interesting enlargements, unique in their way, but for the moment Monsieur Pample-mousse had seen enough.

'The answer to your earlier question is 'yes.' I must catch the first train to Paris.'

'What time do you want to leave?'

'As soon as possible.' He suddenly wanted to get away from Château Morgue. Sensing her disappointment, he tried to console her. 'Look, I don't want to leave. I *have* to leave.'

It was hard to believe that his expedition with Pommes Frites had gone entirely unnoticed, and if they had been seen, word would undoubtedly filter back. There was no time to lose. 'But first there are things I must do.'

'Can I help?'

He took her arm. 'I will pack my belongings and then you can help by taking them to the car. Pommes Frites and I will join you there. When we leave we must do it quietly and quickly.'

Mrs. Cosgrove looked at him thoughtfully. Almost as if she was seeing him for the first time.

'Are you angry about something?'

'Angry?' Monsieur Pamplemousse considered the remark. Yes, he was angry. He always felt angry when he came across an injustice being done, especially when it involved the very young or those who were too old or too tired to defend themselves. In his days with the Sûréte it had been both a strength and a weakness, but he was glad his feelings had never been blunted. He attempted with difficulty to put it into words.

Mrs. Cosgrove looked relieved as she listened to him. 'I thought perhaps it was something I'd said.'

Monsieur Pamplemousse took hold of her hand. It felt instantly responsive and yet at the same time it was that of a stranger, making him aware that despite everything they hardly knew each other.

'I don't think that would be possible.' He allowed a suitable length of time to elapse before returning to business. 'There is one other thing you can do.'

'Tell me.'

'When Pommes Frites and I leave I want you to go along

175

the corridor to the right. Around the first corner you will find a fire alarm. At the exact time I give you I want you to break the glass. It will clear the building of unwanted people and it will give you an opportunity to leave with the luggage.'

'No questions?'

'No questions.' The fact of the matter was he didn't as yet have a clear picture of what he intended

to do, only the vague outline. He would play it by ear. Events would shape themselves.

Carcassonne station was unrelievedly gloomy and deserted when they arrived. A few faces stared at them uninterestedly through the windows of the waiting train.

Apart from one wrong turn crossing the Massif du Canigou, the drive had been uneventful, but the short cut through Molitg-les-Bains via the D84 had been a disaster, adding perhaps an hour to the journey. In cutting one large corner off the map they had added countless smaller ones, with the result that instead of having plenty of time to spare there was a bare ten minutes before the train was due to leave for Toulouse. Perhaps it was just as well. He didn't like prolonged goodbyes.

'You will have a long journey back.'

'That's all right. I don't mind the early mornings – once I'm up.' Mrs. Cosgrove glanced skyward. 'I shall see the sun rise. I might stop on the way and watch it.'

It was true. There wasn't a cloud in sight. It was the time of day he liked best and he almost envied her the drive across the mountains. There would be all manner of wildlife at the side of the road, looking startled as they were caught in the headlights, or shooting off in a panic. And peasants out with guns. They, too, would look affronted by the intrusion on their privacy.

He wondered what was happening back at Château Morgue. Soon after they left a fire engine passed them on its way up, followed by an ambulance and several police cars. He'd caught sight of Inspector Chambard in one of them. It looked as though they were going prepared for some kind of siege. A little later there had been another fire engine, this time with a turret ladder so large the driver was having difficulty negotiating some of the bends. They would need it if they wanted to enter the Tower Block. By the time he'd finished with the lift it would take a skilled electrician several hours to get it going again. The occupants of the Tower Block were well and truly trapped. The only other way down he'd managed to find was an emergency stair-case, which came out into the underground garage. He'd rendered that equally *hors de combat.* Sophisticated locks serve a very useful purpose if you want to keep people from making an unauthorized entry, but given a little knowledge they can be made equally effective in keeping others imprisoned.

'I expect your wife will be pleased to see you.'

He gave a start. It was the first time she had spoken of Doucette. 'How did you know?'

'You don't have to be a detective. You seem very well looked after. Sort of complete. Everything nicely ironed and no loose buttons.'

'Anyway, it won't be long before you see George again.' It was the first time he'd spoken his name out loud too. He hesitated, unsure of how to say what he wanted to say.

'I'm sorry it had to end like this. I'm sure he'll make up for it.' George would be raring to go. Deprived of his *'verts'* for so long there would be no holding him.

Mrs. Cosgrove gave a wry smile. 'I should be so lucky.

Poor old George. He isn't a bit like that really. Never has been. To tell you the truth, he likes dressing up best.' The words came out in a rush, as if she wanted to get them over and done with.

'Dressing up?'

'You know, women's clothing and all that sort of thing. He's got a better wardrobe than I have. Can't help it, poor dear – especially when there's a full moon. That's why I'm here. He had a bit of bad luck in Knightsbridge a few months ago – near the barracks. His case comes up tomorrow and he didn't want to embarrass me.'

'A few *months*. That's a long time to wait.'

'Three and a half to be exact. He elected to go for trial by jury. That delayed things a bit.'

'I trust he has a good lawyer?'

'The best. An old friend.' It was her turn to hesitate. 'I haven't … you know … for quite a few years now. Well, fifteen actually.'

'Fifteen years!'

For some reason a quotation from Tolstoy flashed through his mind. 'Man survives earthquakes, epidemics, the horrors of war, and all the agonies of the soul, but the tragedy that has always tormented him, and always will, is the tragedy of the bedroom.' He thought of all the 'Georges' he'd arrested in his time, for no better reason than that they were dressed unconventionally as members of the opposite sex. He suddenly felt very sorry for George, that gray figure in the photograph. To be married to Mrs. Cosgrove, and yet … *Mon Dieu!* Such waste! And what of her? He wondered if she had always gone in for exotic underwear just in case. Perhaps she made do with George's cast-offs.

'That is terrible.'

'I know. But there you are. They say that what you've

178

never had you don't miss. Perhaps you and I weren't meant. Still,' she lowered her eyes, 'the little we had was nice. There I go, using that dreadful word again. It wasn't just 'nice'; it was *wonderful*!' She glanced up suddenly and pressed her lips against his.

The station clock showed a minute to go. In less than a minute there would be a hiss and the doors would close automatically. Ever since train drivers had had deductions made from their statutory bonus for every minute they were late arriving they had made sure they left on time.

He hesitated. There would be other trains, other days. What was so special about catching one at 4:33 in the morning? As he took Mrs. Cosgrove in his arms and felt the warmth of her cheek against his, he caught Pommes Frites' eye. Pommes Frites didn't exactly shake his head, but his look said it all.

He was right, of course. There was no going back. Wheels had been set in motion. There would be questions to answer, forms to fill in. He would have to justify his expenses at the *pharmacie* on a P39. Despite having *carte blanche* from the director, Madame Grante would not be at all sympathetic. It would take a lot of explaining.

As the train pulled out and Mrs. Cosgrove became a lone dot on the platform he settled back in his seat and closed his eyes. He pictured her in his mind's eye stopping somewhere on the way back to Château Morgue to watch the sunrise. It was always worse for the one who was left behind. The thought of her loneliness filled him with sadness.

Perhaps he would telephone her when he got back. It would be against the rules, but at least it would let her know that he was still thinking of her; that she wasn't just a ship that had passed in the night.

He would have to think up a good reason. Something innocuous ... something ... Already a corner of his mind was thinking ahead, trying at the same time to fight off a drowsiness brought on by the motion of the train and the warmth of the carriage. The sooner he marshalled his thoughts and got down to the task of writing his report, the better. At least on the journey back he wouldn't be bothered by Ananas. Nor would he have to act out the charade of being blind. He looked down at Pommes Frites. Pommes Frites had no such problems. He was already curled up on the floor and fast asleep. It must be nice being a dog and not having to justify everything you did.

10
THE MEN FROM THE MINISTRY

'Entrez'

Monsieur Pamplemousse used the brief moment between knocking on the door of the director's office and responding to the command by taking a deep mental breath. He had totally lost track of time since his last visit. In some respects it felt like only yesterday, in other ways it could have been weeks or even months. By his side, Pommes Frites, clearly sensible to the importance of the occasion, peered at his reflection in a full-length mirror hanging in the outer office. He seemed reasonably satisfied by what he saw.

Normally, although Pommes Frites' existence was accepted (there had even been talk at one time of giving him his own P39s, but this had been quashed by Madame Grante) his visits to the office of *Le Guide* were restricted to the typing pool on the ground floor. It was a long time since he'd been invited up to the holy of holies.

'Entrez!' The voice was louder this time and slightly impatient. It coincided with his opening the door.

'Pamplemousse! Welcome back.' The director came around to the front of his desk, arms outstretched in welcome.

For one dreadful moment Monsieur Pamplemousse thought he was about to be embraced. He hoped his momentary recoil had passed unnoticed.

'And Pommes Frites.'

The director covered their mutual embarrassment by bending down to administer a pat. Pommes Frites looked even more surprised than his master. Such a thing had never happened before. He responded by jumping up and putting his paws on the director's shoulders.

'Ah, yes. *Bon chien.*' The director removed a handkerchief from his top pocket and dabbed at his face. Pommes Frites' tongue was large and rather wet.

'Gentlemen ...' He turned and Monsieur Pamplemousse suddenly realized they were not alone. Sitting beneath the portrait of Hippolyte Duval were two anonymous-looking men, immaculately clad in Identikit dark blue suits and matching ties. There was a third figure sitting to one side and slightly behind them. To his surprise he saw it was Inspector Chambard.

He wished now he had put on a suit or worn a jacket rather than a polo-necked jersey. The invitation had sounded informal, come as you are – a kind of end-of-term get-together with the headmaster. Obviously there was more to it than that.

'Gentlemen, Monsieur Pamplemousse and Pommes Frites.' The director motioned him forward. 'Inspector Chambard I think you have already met. These two gentlemen are from the *Ministère.*'

Monsieur Pamplemousse took due note of the fact that neither the Ministry nor its representatives were mentioned by name.

The taller of the two men rose to greet him. 'Monsieur Pamplemousse, we have come to offer our congratulations. We have received a copy of your report and I can only describe it as a minor masterpiece.'

Monsieur Pamplemousse tried hard to conceal his

surprise. 'It is nothing. I merely put down the facts as I saw them.'

'You are too modest.' The second of the two men joined his colleague. 'Facts, yes. It is what you did with them that matters.'

'A *tour de force.*'

'Brilliantly simple.'

'Fantastic, yet not impossible.'

The dialogue came out so smoothly Monsieur Pamplemousse found himself wondering if they had spent the morning rehearsing it. Perhaps whichever Ministry it was they worked for employed them as a roving double act.

'Tell me, Pamplemousse,' the director was not going to be outdone in his own office, 'have you ever considered taking up writing for a living? We would hate to lose you, but clearly you have a flair for plot construction. I must confess it is something that has escaped me in the past when reading your culinary reports. They are always very elegant, of course, not to say mouthwatering on occasions, but often bordering on the verbose – like some of your articles in the staff magazine. However, this ...' He sat down behind his desk and picked up what Monsieur Pamplemousse recognized as a copy of his report. Attached by means of an outsize paperclip were some blowups taken from the roll of film he'd left at the same time. 'This – '

'Could be your greatest work of fiction,' broke in the first of the two men, taking up the running again. He seemed slightly put out by the interruption. 'I shall always treasure the picture you conjure up of Château Morgue. Those little old ladies pedaling away like mad on their cycling machines.' He broke into a chuckle. 'The notion of them all developing outsize calves as a result was a master stroke.'

'And the tea parties beforehand. We mustn't forget the

tea parties.' His companion allowed himself a smile too. 'The mountains of *pâtisserie* they consumed – all fresh from the bakery in the Tower Block.'

'And for what?'

'So that their heart conditions would be exacerbated to such an extent that violent exercise immediately afterward would bring about an early death – '

'Having, of course, first rewritten their wills in favour of the Schmucks. We mustn't forget that.'

'*Ici Paris* will have a field day.'

Monsieur Pamplemousse gazed around the room. The reception being accorded to his report wasn't at all what he had expected. He listened with growing irritation to the peals of uncontrolled laughter.

'Tell me, Pamplemousse,' the director wiped his eyes in an effort to restore calm. 'What gave you the idea? You have the happy knack of making it sound as though you believe every word you have written.'

Feeling somewhat out of his depth, Monsieur Pamplemousse decided to play for time. He said nothing.

The director misinterpreted his silence. 'Gentlemen, if I may say so, that is typical of the man. Modest to a fault.'

He crossed to a cupboard and withdrew a set of keys from his hip pocket. As he unlocked and opened the door a light came on to reveal a collection of bottles. 'I think this calls for a little celebration. Aristide, you set the ball rolling. What will you have?'

Reaching inside the cupboard he opened another door at the back. A second light came on, reflected this time by a frosty interior. 'This may interest you – a Malvoisie. It comes from a small grower in the Loire. The last of a dying breed. When he goes I doubt if anyone else will make it.'

Monsieur Pamplemousse accepted with alacrity. Apart

from providing a welcome change of subject, he was looking forward to the experience. He had come across fleeting references to it in books. Made from the same grape variety as Tokay, its history dated back to the days when the trade routes of Asia Minor all passed through Malvasia. The fact that someone was still making it in the Loire was a discovery indeed.

He held his glass up to the light. The colour was pale and strawlike, the flavour on the nose sweet but not cloying, with just a hint of complexity. Altogether a delicious interlude and one which drew murmurs of appreciation all around the room. *Le Guide,* he was pleased to see, was upholding its reputation.

Tongues loosened, a common bond established, the director refilled the glasses and returned to his desk.

'You think the press will buy Pamplemousse's story?'

'If we point them in the right direction. The press will buy anything if it sells more copies. Besides, in a perverse kind of way it is too farfetched for them not to.' The leader of the two men turned to his companion for confirmation.

'I agree. And if the newspapers swallow it, then so will the public. There's nothing they like better than a good, juicy scandal.'

'The truth is somewhat more prosaic.'

'It must not go beyond these four walls.'

'Certain people are involved.'

'Members of the "International Set" ... Ministers ...'

'Governments could fall.'

'Those involved will be punished, of course, but in a roundabout way. They will quietly disappear from the public eye. There will be a number of 'early retirements' around the world. A few 'golden handshakes.' It is better that way.'

'Others will be leaned on. They will find life that much more difficult from now on. Some will disappear from the television screens for a while.' It sounded like a passing reference to Ananas. Really, the whole thing was too tantalizing for words.

Inspector Chambard reached for his wallet and took out a card. 'I must say you kept us on our toes one way and another.'

Monsieur Pamplemousse gave a start as he recognized his postcard to Doucette. No wonder she had complained about not receiving one. And to think he had blamed the office of the *Postes et Télécommunications*.

'We knew straight away that it must contain a hidden message of some kind, but you have no idea how long it took us to find it. The expression '*couscous*' had us fooled for quite a while.'

'It is what I sometimes call my wife,' said Monsieur Pamplemousse defensively. 'It is a term of endearment I use when we are apart.'

'So we discovered … in the end!' Inspector Chambard sounded reproachful.

'We had our best men working on it. They tried all the usual things. The message-under-the-stamp routine – the fact that it was on upside down bothered them. They even tried the old invisible-ink-out-of-milk ploy. And there it was – staring us in the face all the time.' He turned the card over and held it up for the others to see. 'A cross marking 'my floor' – the floor where it was all happening – and the words 'wish you were here.' It was a good thing we'd been warned, though. We had the biggest turntable ladder the Narbonne *Corps de Sapeurs-Pompiers* could provide, well able to reach up to the roof.'

'The simplest ideas are always the best in the long run, eh, Aristide?' Basking in the reflection of his subordinate's glory, the director rose and crossed to the cupboard again.

'Communication was the big problem.' Inspector Chambard turned to the other two as he held out his glass. 'We had been told to stand by but not to interfere; to await orders. We had our man in there – posing as a chauffeur. But I don't mind telling you, when we lost him I was worried.'

'The chauffeur?' Monsieur Pamplemousse found himself clutching at straws of information. 'You have lost him?'

'He was involved in an accident on the N9. The man is a fool. It seems he hit a sudden patch of sunlight, put on some dark glasses he'd found in the back of the car, and drove straight into a tree.'

'He wasn't ...'

'No. He will be out of the hospital in a couple of weeks – which is more than you can say of the car.'

'Your photographs proved most valuable.' It was back to the man from the Ministry again. 'Take this one ... *Pardon, Monsieur.*' He reached across and took one of the enlargements from the pile on the director's desk. 'What you so delightfully refer to as the kitchen is in reality Doctor Furze's laboratory. At a rough guess – and you probably know more about these things than I do – there must be over one hundred pounds of cocaine in each bowl.'

'An on-the-street value of around seventy million francs.'

'Grown in Colombia.'

'Brought in through Spain and across the Pyrénées.'

'Distributed to the larger centres in Paris and Marseilles via the coffins.'

'Delivered to the smaller markets inside hollowed-out

187

saucisses and *saucissons.'*

'Whenever the time was ripe for a major arrival or distribution there was a convenient death at Château Morgue.'

'Madame Schmuck would go into her routine. She was well equipped for it.'

'She was born of a Spanish father and an Italian mother.'

'They were both mime artists in a traveling theater in Russia; she found herself on the stage from the word go. Old ladies were her specialty – even as a teenager.'

'A change of clothes, a new set of coloured contact lenses, a different wig. It was right up her street.'

'She would arrive at the Château, expire at a convenient moment, and the wheels would begin to turn. The 'undertakers' would arrive and take her away. Then she would revert to being Madame Schmuck again.'

'No one ever stops a hearse.'

'Pouf!' Inspector Chambard gave a snort. 'To think, the number of times I have saluted that hearse! I have even held up the traffic so that it could get through.'

Monsieur Pamplemousse sank back into his chair. The picture was suddenly all too clear. The van he'd seen in the garage on his arrival: it had probably been delivering a fresh batch of *charcuterie* that very evening. No wonder its disappearance had caused such consternation. He paled at the thought of what might have happened had the *saucisses* already been filled with cocaine. Both he and Pommes Frites would have been on a high from which there would have been no return.

He glanced at the other photographs. Blown up to twenty-five by twenty, it was easy to see the likeness between Frau Schmuck and the woman he'd first met in his room, and again on the stretcher. Except that was being wise after the event. It was amazing the difference a wig and a pair of coloured contact lenses could make. No wonder they'd all had thick calves – that was one thing she couldn't change. 'The other worrying thing about it was the fact that not only had Château Morgue developed into one of the biggest drug centres we've encountered for a long time – it was rapidly becoming a major threat to Western security.'

'What started in a small way – the issuing of invitations to a few close friends – grew out of all proportion. Some very powerful people began using the Château, and not just for drugs either. Other perversions started being catered for. Herr Schmuck learned his trade after the war when Germany was in ruins and people would do anything to scratch a living.'

'His wife, Irma, was a more than willing assistant.'

'The KGB got to hear about it and began making offers to the Schmucks they couldn't refuse. There were fears of blackmail.'

The director stirred in his seat. Determined to make his presence felt, he broke into the duologue and took the photographs back. 'Two things puzzle me, Pamplemousse. The first is, how did you manage to obtain these? I gather they show rooms on the uppermost floor, and yet clearly they were taken from outside through the windows. If you had recourse to the hiring of a helicopter, I fear trouble with Madame Grante. We shall need to prepare the ground carefully before we approach her.'

'If you will forgive me, *Monsieur le directeur*,' Chambard butted in. 'There are some matters best left unexplained. I am sure you will understand me if I use the word *sécurité. Sécurité Nationale.*'

'As for the cost,' the senior of the two officials raised a beautifully manicured hand, 'rest assured it will be taken care of.'

The director looked suitably impressed. 'Of course. I understand. However, that leads me to the second matter.' As he spoke he swiveled his chair so that it faced toward the other end of the room.

Monsieur Pamplemousse followed suit and as he did so his gaze alighted first on the model of the Ideal Inspector, clean-shaven, not a hair on his head out of place, immaculately knotted tie. He gave a start as his eyes traveled downward. Sitting on a large sheet of brown paper, mud-stained and somewhat the worse for wear, rather like a captured enemy tank, stood an all too familiar object. It was held down by some large iron stage weights.

Pommes Frites saw it too. He bounded across the room, went round it several times, nearly knocking Alphonse over in the process, before finally giving vent to a loud howl as he settled down in bewilderment in order to consider the problem.

Monsieur Pamplemousse took a deep breath. 'It is a difficult matter to explain, *Monsieur*. That is, or rather was, Pommes Frites' kennel – '

'I *know* it is Pommes Frites' kennel, Pamplemousse.' The director assumed his Patience Personified voice. 'The question is, why is the entrance sealed, and why does it have a quantity of ladies' lingerie glued to the outside? *Black lingerie*. If it is like that on the outside, heaven alone knows what it is like within. The whole thing is totally beyond my comprehension.'

Monsieur Pamplemousse felt tempted to say that quite possibly the director might find the remains of some *charcuterie*, but before he had a chance to speak Inspector Chambard took over again.

'We think we know who is responsible, *Monsieur*. It is the work of a certain person in the entertainment world

190

who bears, if I may say so,' he inclined his head toward Monsieur Pamplemousse, 'a striking physical resemblance to a member of your staff. He is a person of somewhat bizarre tastes and as such he is not welcome in our part of the world. He was last seen by one of the attendants at Château Morgue carrying that object into the bushes on the night of the raid. On that evidence alone we cannot prosecute. Nevertheless, it is not something he would wish to have made public. He has been told in no uncertain terms that should he ever show his face anywhere near Narbonne again we shall *jeter le livre at* him.'

The director gazed with distaste at the object under discussion. He gave a sigh. 'We live in a sordid world. I sometimes wonder if there is any limit to man's depravity. I wouldn't have your job for all the *thé de la Chine,* Chambard. What on earth would anyone want with an inflatable dog kennel to which items of ladies' underwear have been glued? What would they do with it?'

Inspector Chambard gave a shrug which said it all. He turned to Monsieur Pamplemousse. 'With your permission, *Monsieur,* we would like to put it on permanent display in the *Musée des Collections Historiques de la Préfecture de Police* – in the *Déviations Sexuelles* division. Naturally we would pay for the cost of a replacement.'

Monsieur Pamplemousse had been about to protest, but he rapidly changed his mind. Restoring the kennel to its normally pristine condition would not be easy. He'd had to make a slit in the outer inflation tube in order to fill the inside with gas; traces of *lingerie* might be left. Besides, it would be nice to think of Pommes Frites having a place in the Hall of Fame. He might even take him to see it one day. All that apart, he'd caught Chambard's wink.

'Good. That's settled then.' The senior of the two men from the Ministry stood and drained his glass. His companion followed suit.

'You have rendered an incalculable service to your country, Monsieur Pamplemousse. Not just in the matter of drugs, which is a constant and never-ending battle – as fast as one hole is plugged another opens up – but in an area that affects us all: the security of the Western world. There will be a decoration, of course.'

'In the fullness of time. It wouldn't do to arouse too much interest for the time being.'

'Pommes Frites, too. We understand it was he who located the *charcuterie*.'

At the mention of his name, coupled with the evocative word *'charcuterie,'* Pommes Frites pricked up his ears. As far as he was concerned there had been a great deal of talk and very little action. He was also getting hungry. Perhaps things were about to take a turn for the better.

Monsieur Pamplemousse hesitated. Doucette would be pleased, but deep down he knew he couldn't possibly accept. It was easier for him; he could evaluate the risks involved. Pommes Frites, on the other hand, did things out of love and a generosity of spirit, a simple desire to please his master. He was happy to be rewarded with a kind word and a pat at the end of it all.

'What I did was nothing. At one time it would have been part of my job. However, a mention for Pommes Frites would be nice. Something small he can hang on his collar. I'm sure he would appreciate it.'

Behind his back the director raised his shoulders in a shrug which was part exasperation, part pride at Monsieur Pamplemousse's reaction.

Au revoirs said, the men from the Ministry departed; perhaps they had a matinee performance elsewhere. Inspector Chambard nodded and followed them at a discreet distance.

The director motioned Monsieur Pamplemousse and Pommes Frites to remain behind. 'There is a *soupçon* of wine left in the bottle. It would be a pity to waste it.'

'*Merci, Monsieur.*' As Monsieur Pamplemousse settled down again he glanced across at Pommes Frites' kennel and then with some distaste at Alphonse.

The director read his thoughts. 'I think Alphonse will be taking an early retirement,' he said. 'I have decided that he is, perhaps, a little too perfect for our requirements. To tell you the truth, his smile is beginning to get on my nerves. I have to cover him up from time to time.'

'Holier than thou?' ventured Monsieur Pamplemousse.

'Holier than all of us, I fear, Aristide,' replied the director. 'I think it is high time he went back to the shop window whence he came. He will be just in time for the spring sales. He has served his purpose and it seemed a good ploy at the time.

'As you will have gathered from the letter, I was under some compulsion from the powers that be to send you to Château Morgue. It came about as the result of a chance remark at an official function when I happened to talk of our plans.

'Tell me, Aristide,' the director dropped his voice. 'These things intrigue me, it is such a different world from the one I am used to. The letter ... Did you ... did you eat it?'

Monsieur Pamplemousse lowered his eyes. He couldn't bring himself to tell a direct lie.

The director followed his glance and light dawned. 'Pommes Frites again! I should have known. Some kind of emergency, no doubt. I will not embarrass you by probing too deeply.'

Draining his glass, he crossed to the cupboard and closed both doors with an air of finality. 'Ah, Pamplemousse, I do envy you at times – you people in the field. You lead exciting lives.'

Monsieur Pamplemousse took his cue. The interview was at an end.

'No doubt you will be taking Madame Pamplemousse out for a surprise *dîner* tonight. Where is it to be, Robuchon, Taillevant? Let my secretary know and I will have reservations made.'

'It is kind of you, Monsieur, but I think we shall be eating *chez nous*.' Doucette would be highly suspicious if he took her to either of the places the director had mentioned. They were reserved for very special occasions. She would think he was suffering from a guilt complex and suspect the worst.

'I understand.' As he opened the door the director assumed his man-of-the-world voice for the benefit of anyone who happened to be listening. 'We will save it for another time.'

As Monsieur Pamplemousse left the director's office and made his way down the corridor, he had an odd feeling in the back of his mind that something was missing; some piece of the jigsaw was still not yet in place. Turning a corner, he found Inspector Chambard waiting for him. They shook hands briefly and fell into step.

'*Déjeuner?*' Chambard eyed him hopefully. 'Have it on me. I am not often in Paris.'

'Why not? We can take a stroll toward the fourteenth. There is a little *bistro* I know. On Tuesdays they have *cotriade* – we can share one if you like.' The Malvoisie had sharpened his appetite for seafood. They could help it on its way with a bottle of Muscadet. Who was it who said the good Lord decreed that there should be fine wine made at the mouth of the Loire to go with the *fruits de mer*?

'The Muscadet they serve is one of the few still made *sur lie* – without racking. It is full of character.'

Pommes Frites knew the *bistro* too. He was well known there and often got invited round the back. His pace quickened as he picked up the scent. It was nice to be back in the old routine.

While they were waiting for someone to come and take their order, Inspector Chambard took out his notebook and flipped open the cover. He turned a few pages.

'I hope you will not mind my asking this. You do not have to answer, of course. It is, as it were, a matter between friends. However, I, too, have to write out a report and there are one or two loose ends. You understand?' He gave a wry smile. 'I am afraid I do not have your imagination. I have to discover the exact truth.'

Monsieur Pamplemousse nodded. He understood. Once a policeman, always a policeman. He wished Chambard would get on with it.

'Firstly, when our man met you in Narbonne you did not respond to the prearranged code message. I assume you had a good reason?'

'Ah, the prearranged code message.' Monsieur Pamplemousse found himself playing for time again.

'Our man said 'All is for the best,' and you were meant to say 'in the best of possible worlds.' It is from Voltaire.'

'One cannot be too careful,' said Monsieur Pamplemousse. 'Besides, I am used to working alone.'

Inspector Chambard looked hurt. 'Our man thought you must be Ananas after all. We'd had word that he was on the same train. I'm afraid he must have given you a rough ride. He does not consider himself one of Ananas' greatest fans.'

'He is not alone in that.'

The point was taken. 'I sympathize. But I think you will be rid of the problem for a while. If our friend knows what is good for him he will be keeping a low profile. To do him justice I don't think he realized what he was letting himself in for. A weak man himself, he was attracted by those of like mind. Such people have extrasensory perception.' There was a pause.

'One other thing. Tell me, *was* it you with the English *Madame* the other evening?'

'We had dinner in the village.' Monsieur Pamplemousse wondered what was coming now.

'And do I have your word that it was not you who was responsible for the robbery in the ladies' changing rooms?'

'You do.'

Inspector Chambard looked relieved. He methodically drew some lines across the page, then snapped the book shut, replacing a rubber band which held the covers together.

'You'd be surprised at the things that go on at a health farm. Cut people off from their food and they get desperate. I have over forty pairs of *culottes* unaccounted for. I can't tell you what a headache that is. The only ones we have retrieved so far are those on Pommes Frites' kennel. But we will find them. Never fear. We will find them.'

But Monsieur Pamplemousse was hardly listening. *'Pardon.'* He rose from the table. 'I have an urgent telephone call to make.'

How long had he been in Paris? Three days? He wondered if he had left it too late. His room might have been searched. Worse still, Mrs. Cosgrove could have already gone back to England. As the ringing tone started he found himself crossing his fingers.

'Château Morgue?' At least the switchboard was still operating. 'Madame Cosgrove, *s'il vous plaît.*'

'*Oui, Monsieur.*'

He breathed a sigh of relief. She must still be there. Conscious of a couple at a nearby table half listening to his conversation, he turned his back. In a mirror behind the bar he could see a reflection of the kitchen. Pommes Frites was busy with a bowl.

'Anne!'

'*Oui*, I am well, thank you.' He felt excited at hearing her voice again. 'I am sorry … I wanted to telephone, but … I wasn't sure if you would still be there.' It sounded a feeble excuse.

'Tomorrow? I hope you have a good journey.'

'He's got off? You must be relieved – '

'I hope so too.'

'Listen … before you go, can you do me a favour? Under my bed you will find a parcel. Could you post it for me?'

'No, not *to* me, *for* me.' That would be a disaster – if a parcel of assorted *lingerie* arrived while he was away and Doucette opened it by mistake, he would never hear the last of it.

'What address?' He thought for a moment. 'Address it to Madame Grante, care of *Le Guide.*' That would give her something to think about. He fed another coin into the slot. 'I have only a little time left.' One franc's worth to be precise and there were so many things he wanted to say.

'Who knows? One day, perhaps?'

'*Oui*, it is a small world. Listen … thank you again, *et bonne chance.* George too.'

There was a click and she was gone. The P.T.T. didn't even leave time for an *au revoir*.

He arrived back at the table at the same time as the tureen of *cotriade*. Alongside it was a bowl of the traditional heart-shaped *croûtes*. He wondered if he could distract Chambard's attention long enough to filch one. It would be a reminder of his times with Mrs. Cosgrove.

He glanced out of the window. 'It looks as if we may have snow.' It was true. There was a bitterly cold wind blowing from the north. People were hurrying by with their coat collars turned up.

He quickly transferred one of the *croûtes* onto his chair seat, holding it in place with his leg.

But his satisfaction was short-lived. As Inspector Chambard turned back he felt something push against him. Almost immediately there was a loud crunching noise from underneath the table.

Pommes Frites looked up at him gratefully. It was good to be back and to have such a thoughtful master, ever sensitive to his needs. The bowl of *navarin d'agneau* the chef had given him had been nice, but it tasted even better when it was followed by a piece of fried bread which had been well rubbed with garlic.

Life, in Pommes Frites' humble opinion, had few better things to offer. And even though he could see that for some reason best known to himself, Monsieur Pamplemousse didn't entirely share his view, instinct told him that it was only a matter of time before he would.

Monsieur Pamplemousse Aloft

Contents

1
SOMETHING IN THE AIR

Pommes Frites saw it first; a small object shaped like a sausage and about the size of a double magnum of champagne. Its silver body gleamed in the early morning sun as it emerged from the comparative gloom of the Boulevard de la Tour Maubourg in the seventh *arrondissement* of Paris and entered the Place de Santiago-du-Chili. Gliding along at roof-top level, it disappeared for a moment or two behind some trees, nosed its way slowly and silently along one side of the *Place*, eventually reappearing outside the Chilean Embassy on the corner of the Avenue de la Motte-Picquet. There it paused in its travels, gaining height momentarily, as though trying to discover what secrets lay behind the façade of the white stone building. Then, curiosity apparently satisfied, it executed a sharp 270-degree turn to port and went on its way again, following a course running parallel to the outer wall of the Hôtel des Invalides, home amongst other things, to the remains of the Emperor Napoleon.

Pommes Frites' immediate reaction on catching sight of it had been one of incredulity; incredulity which quickly gave way to apprehension. He still had vivid memories of a recent journey he had undertaken in the Pyrénées Orientales suspended beneath his inflatable kennel. It had been an unhappy experience and one he had no wish to repeat. Gathering himself together, he gave vent to a warning howl, vaguely, but in the circumstances not inaptly, reminiscent of an air-raid siren.

However, to have awarded Pommes Frites bonus points for his powers of observation would have been doing less than justice to those others who were abroad that morning. It was barely nine-thirty and most passers-by had their minds on other, more pressing matters – like getting to work on time. The overalled worker in the tiny triangular railed-in park outside the Metro station was busy watering his roses, while the taxi-drivers waiting in a line nearby had their eyes firmly fixed on lower horizons.

The truth of the matter was, Pommes Frites only happened to strike lucky because, having raced on ahead of his master, he alone in the Place de Santiago-du-Chili was gazing up at the statue of Vauban just as the object floated past. Not many, other than those with a passion for history, paused to give the statue so much as a passing glance at the best of times, and Pommes Frites was only looking at it for want of something better to do while bestowing his favours on a convenient tree. Far from centring his thoughts on the past exploits of one of France's most famous military engineers, he was wondering idly whether, if he kept very still, a pigeon perched on top of the good Marshal's hat might be lulled into a false sense of security and land on his own head by mistake. Pommes Frites didn't have a very high opinion of pigeons and although he had never actually caught one, he refused to discount the possibility.

Rotating himself as far as was practicable while standing on three legs, he watched the object pass overhead. Ignoring any possibilities the Café l'Esplanade on the corner of the *Place* might have in the way of refreshment, oblivious to the landing facilities offered up by the Esplanade des Invalides below and to its right, the object gained height again and with gathering speed disappeared over the top of some nearby buildings just as Monsieur Pamplemousse came up out of the Métro.

Much to Pommes Frites' disappointment, his master barely gave it a second glance. He, too, had other, more important things on his mind. Having registered the object, he dismissed it as a mere toy; the temporary plaything of some spoilt brat who lived in the nearby sixteenth and whose parents had more money than sense. Only the week before he'd seen a miniature tank in one of the department stores on the Boulevard Haussmann. The price had been more than the cost of his own car.

The possibility that its presence might have anything to do with his being summoned at an unusually early hour for a meeting with the Director didn't cross his mind.

Monsieur Pamplemousse mistrusted such summonses – especially when they happened to come during the middle of breakfast, and even more so when by rights he should be enjoying a well-earned week off from his travels. Doucette had not been best pleased at the news. He had promised to take her shopping that morning for some new curtain material. There had been much banging of crockery in the kitchen and he'd had to exercise care with his *croissant* lest too many crumbs found their way onto the floor. It had not been a good start to the day.

As they took advantage of a gap in the traffic and crossed the road a feeling of gloom set in. Even the all-pervading smell of fresh lime from the trees surrounding the Esplanade, normally sufficient to put him in a good humour whatever the circumstances, failed to have its usual effect. The thought he had been entertaining of telephoning Doucette when he reached the office – just to see how she was getting on – no longer seemed such a good idea. She would start asking questions about what time she could expect him back and would he want lunch and if so, what? He would become irritated because he would have no idea of the answer.

He paused at the corner of the *Place*, wondering whether he should stop by at the Café for a quick *eau-de-vie* – a little 'Dutch courage'. If he was honest he had another reason besides shopping for not wanting to go into the office that morning. Madame Grante was on the warpath, and when Madame Grante was on the warpath, 'retreat' was the only sensible course. Sniping was prevalent and mortar fire unremitting in its intensity.

The current hostilities had to do with his last assignment for *Le Guide*, an assignment which had not been of his making, and which through no fault of his own had involved him in expenditure over and above that normally agreed to in staff regulations. Expenditure of a kind which, when detailed in black and white on a P39, made Madame Grante's lips – which could never by any stretch of the imagination be described as full, let alone generous – become so compressed it was hard to tell where the bottom one finished and the top one began, except when they parted company in order to permit the escape of some freshly barbed comment. Things had reached such a pass that instead of eating in the canteen he had taken to having sandwiches sent up to his room rather than run the risk of bumping into her in a corridor, knowing full well that she was probably lying in wait for him.

He could hear her voice now as she reeled off the list from his claim sheet, savouring each and every word in tones which would not have disgraced a leading member of the *Comédie Française* reciting her favourite piece to the back row of the *fauteuils*.

'Braided nylon fishing thread, fifty metrès. One cylinder of gas, helium, large. Photographic chemicals, various. Inflatable dog kennel, one. Twenty-two pairs of ladies' *culottes*, black ... '

It was the unfairness of it all that particularly grieved Monsieur Pamplemousse. His expenses sheet should never have arrived on Madame Grante's desk in the first place, and wouldn't have done so had it not been for a clerical error somewhere along the line. It had been intended for the eyes of unnamed people in a department of the Ministry of the Interior. Promises had been made. Secrecy had been the order of the day.

In the end he had gone to the Director and asked him to put his foot down. Very reluctantly the Director had agreed.

There the matter should have ended, and in the normal course of events would have done, had it not been for the fact that it wasn't in Madame Grante's nature to let any matter rest until she was in full possession of the facts. The silence following her brief interview on the top floor didn't, in Monsieur Pamplemousse's view, mean that all was forgotten, still less forgiven.

Taking a card from an inside pocket, he paused outside an anonymous building a little way along the Rue Fabert and held it against a plate in the wall alongside a pair of wooden doors. There was an answering buzz and a smaller door set into one of the larger ones swung open. Closing it behind them he led the way across a paved courtyard and round the fountain in the centre. Noting the Director's Citroën CX25 was already in its privileged parking space he automatically glanced towards the top floor. He was just in time to see the Director himself disappearing around a corner of the balcony outside his office. He appeared to be in a hurry and he was carrying some kind of walkie-talkie, or possibly a radio-telephone. For despite *Le Guide*'s deep-rooted sense of tradition and resistance to change, he prided himself on keeping abreast of the latest developments. The operations room in the basement would not have looked out of place in the Headquarters of NATO or even a James Bond movie.

While awaiting his arrival, the Director had no doubt been enjoying the morning sunshine while indulging in his favourite pastime of counting the 'Stock Pots' of Paris. His suite of offices was a recent addition to the main offices, occupying the whole of a mansard floor which lifted it above the rooftops of the surrounding buildings. Like the bridge of a great ocean liner, it afforded an unrivalled view of everything that went on below, and from the balcony which encircled it the Director, in his role of Captain, was able to keep a weather eye on the world outside. On special occasions – such as Bastille Day – he often held parties when he treated his guests to a guided tour of those restaurants in Paris fortunate enough to be awarded a 'Stock Pot' in *Le Guide* for their culinary achievements. It was his proud boast that on a clear day it was possible with the aid of a pair of binoculars to pick out a grand total of over one hundred such establishments, no less than four of which bore the supreme accolade of three 'Stock Pots', thereby being accorded the honour of having their exact position pin-pointed by means of a brass plate engraved with an arrow let into the stone balustrade.

Monsieur Pamplemousse was about to go on his way when he stopped dead in his tracks, his eyes riveted by the spectacle above him. The object which only a few minutes before he'd seen floating above the *Place* suddenly came into view again above their heads. For a moment or two it hovered in what appeared to be an agony of indecision, and then, just as the Director came rushing back around the corner still clutching his device, it disappeared through an open door and into his office.

All in all, Monsieur Pamplemousse wasn't sorry he'd resisted the temptation to stop for a drink on the way in. At least he knew he had seen what he had seen while stone cold sober.

Pommes Frites suffered no such inhibitions. Fearing the worst as he followed his master through the revolving door of the main building, he let out another warning howl.

But Monsieur Pamplemousse's feeling of virtue was shortlived. Almost immediately he changed his mind – an *eau-de-vie* would have gone down very well indeed at that moment. Standing by the reception desk, a sheaf of papers clutched in her right hand, was Madame Grante. She was talking to the receptionist. That she had been lying in wait was patently obvious, for no sooner were they through the door than she came forward to greet them. He braced himself for the onslaught, while Pommes Frites, ever sensitive to his master's moods, almost imperceptibly but nonetheless firmly, bared his teeth.

However, both were guilty of over-reacting. For once, Madame Grante seemed all sweetness and light.

Her '*Bonjour*, Monsieur Pamplemousse!' was trilled in such spring-like tones, and the accommpanying smile was so sunny, that even Pommes Frites had the grace to look ashamed when she turned it in his direction.

'*Bonjour*, Madame Grante.' Much to Monsieur Pamplemousse's annoyance, his voice came out higher than he'd intended. He cleared his throat, wondering what to say next, but fortunately he was saved by the ping of a lift bell.

Once inside the safety of the lift he pressed the button for the top floor as quickly as possible in case she decided to follow them in.

As the doors slid shut he pondered both the Director's strange behaviour and that of Madame Grante, wondering if the two were linked in any way. Madame Grante on the warpath was one thing; at least you knew where you were. The new Madame Grante was something else again, and he wasn't quite sure how to cope with it. Had he detected another element in her welcoming smile? A gleam of triumph, perhaps? No, it had been something else. Something he couldn't quite put his finger on. Anticipation? Whatever it was he had a nasty feeling in the back of his mind that it spelt trouble. He would need to watch himself.

Exchanging greetings with the Director's secretary in the outer office he crossed the room and knocked on the inner door.

To his surprise, it was opened almost immediately.

'Aristide, *entrez*, *entrez*. And Pommes Frites. *Comment allez- vous*?'

The Director bent down to give Pommes Frites a welcoming pat and then hastily withdrew his hand as the object of his attentions bristled. It was all too apparent that flattery would be a waste of time. Pommes Frites' attentions were concentrated elsewhere.

Monsieur Pamplemousse was about to remonstrate when he, too, stiffened. There, in the centre of the Director's desk, stood a model airship. Seen at close quarters, it was not unlike the tiny replicas of aircraft one saw in the office windows of the great airlines in the Avenue des Champs Elysées, albeit, since he had seen it flying with his own eyes, much more sophisticated. Obviously the work of a master craftsman, for it was complete in every detail, even down to replicas of passengers and crew who could be seen

210

through the Perspex windows in the side, it was attached to a small mooring tower underneath which lay an open map of Europe.

The Director beamed as he followed the direction of their gaze. Crossing to his desk, he gazed reverently at the object. 'What do you think of it, Aristide?'

For a second time in as many minutes, Monsieur Pamplemousse found himself at a loss for words.

'It is a birthday present for your nephew, *Monsieur*? I'm sure he will be delighted.'

The Director made a clucking noise. 'No, Pamplemousse, it is not a birthday present for my nephew.'

Rather than risk further displeasure, Monsieur Pamplemousse decided not to essay another reply to the question, but in the event it was followed almost immediately by a second.

'Picture this dirigible inflated to several thousand times its present size,' continued the Director. 'What would you see?'

Suspecting a trick question, Monsieur Pamplemousse took his time. 'I see a lot of small pieces, *Monsieur*,' he said innocently. 'Surely it would explode?'

The Director gazed at him in silence. He had the look on his face of a man wondering whether or not he had made the right decision over some important matter. His lips moved, but nothing came out. Eventually, after what seemed like an eternity, he waved Pamplemousse towards the armchair opposite his desk and began pacing the room while gathering his thoughts.

'No doubt,' he said at last, 'you have read in the *journaux* about the inauguration of a new airship service between Brittany and *Grande-Bretagne*?'

Monsieur Pamplemousse nodded. 'I have seen pictures of

it, *Monsieur*.' The newspapers had been full of them lately.

'Good.' The Director looked better pleased. 'It is an outward manifestation of the *entente cordiale* agreement signed in 1904, the reaffirmation of which our respective governments have been working towards in recent months. It is only a small step, especially when compared with the tunnel which is at this very moment being constructed beneath *La Manche* to link our two countries by rail, but an important one nevertheless.

'The dirigible, Pamplemousse, is the transportation of the future, an elegant solution to powered flight. Word has gone out from the Elysée Palace itself that it must not fail. We are entering a new era of graciousness. It combines the best of the old with that of the new; on the one hand embracing all that we have grown up with and love and cherish, whilst at the same time reaching out towards new frontiers. Above all, it is safe. The hazardous days of the old *Graf Zeppelin* have gone forever.'

Monsieur Pamplemousse remained silent. It was hard to see where the Director's flights of rhetoric were leading him. Romantic though the possibility might be of transporting up to a dozen people in comparative luxury, it hardly compared with a direct rail link in terms of either numbers or value for money. Clearly there was more to come.

'Besides which,' continued the Director, 'it will help quieten the vociferous minority who feel Brittany is neglected and would dearly like to see it become a separate state. With an election on the horizon that is not unimportant. No doubt the scheme appeals to the British government because they will be manufacturing the dirigibles. If successful, it could well be the first of many.

'Be that as it may, both governments have their own

reasons for attaching great importance to the affair. So much so that the respective heads of state have agreed to take part in the inaugural flight four days from now.'

The Director paused by his desk and then lowered his voice. 'All I have told you so far, Pamplemousse, is common knowledge. I come now to my reason for asking you here at such short notice. We are at present in a crisis situation.'

Carefully moving the airship and its mooring tower to one side, he picked up the map. 'The inaugural flight commences at eleven hundred hours on Friday. The dirigible will take off from a small airfield north of La Baule and will touch down just over six hours later on a similar landing strip south of London – a distance of some five hundred kilometrès. What, Pamplemousse, will those aboard be most in need of during the time they are aloft? I ask, because even though I have repeated the same question to myself countless times, I still cannot believe no one thought of it.'

'You mean ... there are no facilities on board?' Monsieur Pamplemousse looked suitably staggered. 'That is indeed a grave oversight.'

'No, Pamplemousse, that is not what I mean. In the current situation "facilities" of the kind you doubtless have in mind are low on the agenda.'

'But *Monsieur*, with respect, six hours is a long time. After all that food and drink ...'

'As things stand at the moment, Pamplemousse, there will be no food and drink. There will be no food and drink for the very simple reason that no one has thought to provide any. For weeks people have been planning. Schedules have been drawn up, security arrangements tested. Everything that could possibly go wrong has been thought of. Every aspect of the programme has been covered, not once but time and time again. All except the one vital factor, sustenance.'

The Director paused to let his words sink in before resuming. 'Imagine the atmosphere aloft if thirteen hundred hours came and went and there was no sign of *déjeuner*. It would be icy in the extreme. *Entente* would be far from *cordiale*. Had the arrangements been made in *Angleterre* one might have understood. They would probably have been happy to make do with sandwiches and a thermos of hot tea – although to give them their due, even that would be better than nothing – but for *La Belle France* to make such a cardinal error – poof! It is hard to credit. We shall be the laughing-stock of Europe. Heads will roll, of course, but that doesn't solve the immediate problem. Which is where, Aristide, we come in. Or rather, *you* do.'

'I, *Monsieur*?' Monsieur Pamplemousse sat bolt upright. Had the Director suddenly let off a shotgun at close range he could hardly have been more startled.

The Director assumed his 'all has been decided, yours is not to reason why' tones. '*Le Guide* has been charged with making good the omission. We have been given *carte blanche*. Of course, Michelin will be piqued and Gault-Millau will be seething. Both will probably take umbrage, but that cannot be helped. If all goes well it will be a considerable *plume* in our *chapeau*.'

The interior of a cupboard became illuminated as he opened it to reach inside for a bottle of champagne. 'I think this calls for a celebration, although I must admit the whole thing came about by sheer chance.

'It so happened that last night I was dining with a group of friends, some of whom are highly placed, and the subject of the conversation turned to that of the dirigible.

'Purely out of professional interest I enquired as to the nature of the catering arrangements. Aristide, you could have sliced the silence which followed my remark with a *couteau à beurre*.

'I won't bore you with all that followed. Someone, whose name I cannot disclose, left the table to make a telephone call. When he returned, looking, I may say, a trifle pale, names were bandied around. One by one they were abandoned. Bocuse is in Japan on one of his tours. Vergé is in America. We went through the list, and to cut a long story short, suddenly they all turned and looked in my direction.'

The cork was removed with the discreetest of pops and the Director held up two glasses to the light to check their cleanliness before pouring. 'The honour of France is in your hands, Aristide. I need hardly say that not a word of this must be breathed to anyone. That is one of the main reasons why you have been selected. Your vast experience in matters of security coupled with your extraordinary palate and your natural sense of discretion make you an ideal choice.

'I can think of no better person for the job, Pamplemousse.' The Director raised his glass. 'Your very good health, and here's to the success of your mission. I have already drawn up some preliminary notes for a possible menu, but naturally I leave the final choice to you.'

Monsieur Pamplemousse sipped his champagne reflectively. It was his favourite – Gosset. He judged it to be a '62. There was a distinct flavour of hazelnuts. The Director must have got it in specially. All part of the softening up process, no doubt. Not that it was necessary; the whole idea sounded intriguing. He would willingly postpone his holiday. This would be a challenge.

'You say the airfield is north of La Baule, *Monsieur*?'

'It is just outside a little place called Port St. Augustin. You may know it. An ideal location for those wishing to arrive in style at what is probably the best beach in Europe.'

Port St. Augustin. Monsieur Pamplemousse remembered it well, although it was many years since he'd last been in the area.

'Madame Pamplemousse and I went there soon after we got married, *Monsieur*. We stayed at the Hôtel du Port. It is perched on the rocks overlooking the harbour ...'

'Ah, yes.' The Director looked less than enthusiastic. 'The Hôtel du Port is full, I'm afraid.'

'There was one other. The Hôtel du Centre, I believe it was called.'

'That too, is fully booked.' For some reason Monsieur Pamplemousse thought he detected a note of unease creeping into the other's voice. 'It is always the same in Brittany. The season is short and the same people go there year after year.

'However, a reservation has been made for you from tomorrow evening onwards at a small hotel just outside the village – the Ty Coz. I am told some of the rooms have a view of the sea, although the view inland is said to be equally good.

The choice is yours.'

Monsieur Pamplemousse was tempted to ask why, if everywhere else was so crowded, he could get into the Ty Coz with a choice of rooms, but the Director was in full flight.

'The Hôtel has been recommended to me in the strongest possible terms. It seems the owner has invented a whole new cuisine, *La Cuisine Régionale Naturelle*. And in southern Brittany, Aristide, we all know what that means. Luscious lobsters, fresh from their pots. Tunny fish from

216

Concarneau, sardines from La Turballe, mussels and oysters from the Morbihan ... It will be an ideal opportunity to carry out an investigation.

'Ah, Aristide,' the Director crossed to his desk and gazed lovingly at the airship. 'All that and a ride in a dirigible to boot. I wish I could come too, but alas, I am on a diet.'

He picked up the small black object which Monsieur Pamplemousse had seen him holding in his hand earlier, and which he now realised was a radio-control module. 'Would you care for a go, Aristide?'

'May I, *Monsieur*?'

The Director detached the airship carefully from its mooring and gathered it tenderly in his arms. 'If you don't mind, I will carry out the initial launch. It is the only model in existence and it wouldn't do to have an accident. Once it is airborne you will soon get the feel of the controls.'

Monsieur Pamplemousse followed him out onto the balcony and watched while adjustments were being made and the twin motors set in motion.

'It is a complete replica in every detail.' Like a small boy with a new toy, the Director could hardly keep the excitement from his voice as he licked his finger and held it up to test the wind direction. 'As I said earlier, no expense has been spared to ensure the success of the enterprise; no stone left unturned ...'

'Except one,' Monsieur Pamplemousse found the Director's enthusiasm infectious.

'Indeed, Aristide. Except one. The reason for my being given the loan of this is so that we can see for ourselves the ergonomics of the task ahead. Is there, *par exemple*, room for a dessert chariot, and if so, how large?' Shading his eyes against the sun, the Director released his hold on the craft and then watched as it set off, uncertainly at first, and then with rapidly gathering speed in the direction of the wide open space of the Esplanade des Invalides.

'You may take over now, Pamplemousse.'

Feeling slightly nervous now that the actual moment had arrived, Monsieur Pamplemousse took the control unit and began tentatively moving an array of levers.

On the square below an *autobus* was disgorging a load of Japanese tourists, all of whom were so busy rushing to and fro taking photographs of each other in groups of varying size and complexity they quite failed to see what was going on above their heads. Monsieur Pamplemousse reflected that had they but known, they were missing a golden opportunity to surprise and delight their friends back home.

He suddenly realised he'd been concentrating so hard he hadn't noticed the Director was talking again.

'I was saying, Pamplemousse, I should try and avoid flying too close to the Hôtel des Invalides. It wouldn't do to attract the attention of the guards. One of them might draw his revolver and attempt to shoot it down. I have promised to return it safely by this afternoon at the latest. The President himself has yet to see it. No doubt he will wish to have a go inside the Palace grounds.'

'*Oui, Monsieur.*' Monsieur Pamplemousse moved a lever to the left and watched as the airship began executing a turn to port. It really was most enjoyable. Perhaps when he got back from Brittany he would investigate some more modest version of the toy. A radio-controlled boat perhaps? The possibilities were endless.

As he moved another control and set the craft into a downward path which would bring it level with the top of the balcony he felt a stirring behind him. It heralded the arrival of Pommes Frites on the scene.

Pommes Frites blinked as he emerged from the Director's office onto the sunlit balcony. Having enjoyed a short nap while the others were talking, he'd woken to find he was alone and that the voices were now coming from outside. Something was going on, and feeling left out of things he decided – quite reasonably in his view – to find out what it was.

He arrived just as his master was about to carry out the delicate manoeuvre of making the final approach; a manoeuvre which would have been difficult enough at the best of times, but made more so by a sudden downward draught of cold air created by the temperature of the water issuing from the fountain in the courtyard below. It was a manoeuvre which needed the utmost concentration and which most certainly would have been brought to a more successful conclusion, had not what felt like a ton weight suddenly landed on his shoulders just at the *moment critique*.

Catching sight of Pommes Frites, and anticipating his next move, the Director issued a warning cry, but it was too late. Watched by all three, the dirigible lost height rapidly and disappeared at speed through an open window several floors below.

A feeling of gloom descended on the balcony. It was as though a large black cloud had suddenly obscured the sun.

'Let us hope,' said the Director, 'that Madame Grante manages to shut off the motors before too much damage is done. I think it was her window the dirigible entered. I trust, also, that it is not an omen.'

Without bothering to reply, Monsieur Pamplemousse bounded through the Director's office, past an astonished secretary, and out into the corridor. Eschewing the lift, and with Pommes Frites hard on his heels, he shot down three

219

floors, arriving outside Madame Grante's office without even bothering to draw breath. There was a possibility, a very faint possibility, that she would be out of her room.

But as he opened the door he came to an abrupt halt. Patently the room was far from empty. There were papers everywhere. It looked as though it had been struck by a minor hurricane.

Madame Grante was in the act of closing the door of her stationery cupboard on the far side of the room.

She turned. 'Monsieur Pamplemousse?'

'Madame Grante.' He took a deep breath and pulled himself together. 'Madame Grante, I was wondering ... that is to say ... may we have our balloon back, *s'il vous plaît*?'

With a flourish Madame Grante deposited a silver key in a place where it would have needed a braver man than Monsieur Pamplemousse to retrieve it. 'Your balloon, Monsieur Pamplemousse? I see no balloon.'

For a full thirty seconds they stood staring at each other. Once again he was conscious of a look in Madame Grante's eyes he couldn't quite make out. It was something more than mere triumph.

Wild thoughts of declaring his undying love for her crossed his mind and were instantly dismissed. Bernard always said you never could tell; still waters ran deep. But Bernard had theories about most things. The prospect of Madame Grante melting in his arms was not only remote, it didn't bear thinking about. Such a declaration might even send her into a state of shock. Not to mention the possible effect on Pommes Frites. Would it get him what he wanted? More important still, would it be worth it?

For the sake of the Director? Certainly not!

For the sake of France? No, not even for that!

Monsieur Pamplemousse knew when he was beaten. He

220

turned on his heels and left, making his way up to the top floor at a somewhat slower rate than he had come down.

The Director was waiting outside his door. His face fell as Monsieur Pamplemousse came into view. 'You are empty handed. Don't tell me ...'

Monsieur Pamplemousse nodded. 'I am afraid we are in trouble, *Monsieur*. Madame Grante has put the dirigible where she keeps her P39s.'

'And the key, Pamplemousse? Where is the key?'

'The key, *Monsieur*, is in a place which is even more impregnable than her store cupboard. It is where she keeps her *doudounes*!'

The Director clutched at the door frame for support. 'This bodes ill, Pamplemousse!' he exclaimed. 'I am not by nature a superstitious man, but I fear this bodes ill for us all.'

2
A SURFEIT OF NUNS

Monsieur Pamplemousse focused his Leica camera on the off side of his 2CV, or the little of it which could still be seen above the top of a ditch, and operated the shutter several times. As he did so he pondered, not for the first time in his life, on the immutability of the laws of fate which decreed that following a series of seemingly unconnected events one should, for better or worse, find oneself at a certain spot at a certain time, not a second before nor a split-second after that moment which had all the appearances of being pre-ordained.

His present situation definitely came under the second category. If fate had indeed had a hand in things then someone, somewhere on high, had it in for him. His star was not in the ascendant.

He shivered a little, partly from delayed shock and partly from the cool breeze which was blowing in from the sea. He licked his lips. They tasted of salt. Glancing up he registered the fact that the same breeze was bringing with it a bank of dark rain clouds and he hoped it was only a passing storm. The sky to the west still looked bright enough and the long-term forecast was good, but even a minor shower would be bad news in the circumstances. Short of getting back in the car – which wouldn't be easy – shelter was non-existent. Pommes Frites would be all right. At least he had his inflatable kennel, but there certainly wouldn't be room in it for both of them.

If only he hadn't decided on the spur of the moment to branch off the D99 at Guérande. It hadn't even been a short cut; a voyage of remembrance rather than one of discovery, an exercise in nostalgia. If he'd stuck to the main road he would have been in Port St. Augustin by now, sampling the delights of *La Cuisine Régionale Naturelle*.

Long before that there had been lunch.

Not that he regretted his meal, but it had been a far more protracted affair than he'd intended. One of his colleagues, Glandier, had left a note in his tray back at the office concerning a little restaurant he'd come across on the bank of one of the Loire's many tributaries. Any recommendation from Glandier was worth following up, and on the strength of it he'd made a detour.

In the event it had exceeded all his expectations. Over a Kir made with ice-cold *aligoté* and served at a little table under a tree by the river, he had been able to watch the work going on in the kitchen, while making the first of many notes to come during the meal.

The first course – a cucumber salad – had been exactly right. Peeled, split down the middle, its seeds removed, the cucumber had been cut paper thin and sprinkled with salt to draw out all the excess liquid, leaving it, after draining, limp, yet deliciously crunchy. The vinegar and oil in the dressing had been of good quality with just the right amount of sugar added to counteract the natural bitterness. But it was the addition of the few freshwater crayfish which had lifted the dish above the norm.

With a basketful of crisp, fresh bread and a glass or two of sparkling Vouvray to help it down, he'd been of a mind to call it a day; a refreshing break in an otherwise long and tedious journey. But then he'd caught sight of some trout being brought to the back door of the restaurant by someone he had earlier seen fishing further along the river bank and the temptation to explore the menu still further had proved too great to resist.

It had been a wise decision.

Coated in oil and rolled in flour before being seared in hot butter – quickly enough so that it didn't stick to the pan, but not so hot that the flour formed a crust – the fish had arrived at the table golden brown. A little lemon juice and some fresh blanched parsley had been added to the butter in which the trout had been cooked and made a golden foam as it was poured over the top at the last moment. The *pommes frites* were as perfect an accompaniment as one could wish for.

But it was the dessert which was undoubtedly the *pièce de resistance*. When Monsieur Pamplemousse saw a man at a nearby table – obviously a regular – tucking into a jam omelette with such gusto and dabbing of the lips with his napkin that it was like a cabaret act, he'd quickly succumbed.

As with the trout, the omelette arrived at his table at exactly the right moment. Piping hot, the icing-sugar on the top caramelised in a cries-cross pattern by the use of a red-hot metal skewer, the *confiture* inside of a quality which indicated it had never seen the inside of a shop let alone a factory. He could still taste it.

Even Pommes Frites, not normally a jam-eater, had signalled his approval, which was praise indeed. The look on his face as his master slipped him a portion said it all. Even so, with a long journey ahead of them, to have indulged in a second helping had been folly of the very worst kind. A feeling of somnolence had set in uncomfortably soon after they set off on the last part of their journey.

Snores had started to issue from the back of the *Deux Chevaux* long before they reached the N23.

Driving along, Monsieur Pamplemousse had fallen to thinking about his work, and that, too, had slowed him down. Deep inside there was the usual conflict which began when he came across somewhere new, a battle between the desire to share his pleasures and a selfish wish to keep them to himself. He had no doubt that Glandier felt the same way too. All too frequently, discovery and a mention in *Le Guide* brought success, but with success came different pressures and often changes for the worse. It would be sad to come back another year and find the tranquil field at the side of the hotel turned into a car-park smelling of petrol fumes, disturbing the peace and quiet of this lovely backwater with the sound of revving engines and slamming doors. But you couldn't have it both ways.

He gave a sigh as he regarded his 2CV. He couldn't have it both ways either. Normally he prided himself on his reactions at the wheel, but they had been dulled by over-eating; over- eating and, he had to admit, perhaps one glass of wine too many?

On the other hand, who would have expected to encounter in an area such as the Marais Salant – a vast unrelieved mosaic of grey salt pans, flat as a pancake as far as the eye could see – a car traveling on the wrong side of the road. He felt very aggrieved. It wasn't as though it had been driven by some maniac English tourist admiring the view – there would have been some excuse then; it had been full of nuns. Nuns who had so far forgotten the basic tenets of their calling that they hadn't even bothered to stop to make sure he was unharmed. For all they knew he might have needed the last rites. That they had seen him drive into the ditch he hadn't the slightest doubt; at the very last moment he'd caught a glimpse of two white faces peering out at him from the rear window of the car as it disappeared in a cloud of dust.

He wondered what the world was coming to. A few well chosen words in the ear of the Mother Superior would not come amiss, but he'd been so taken aback by the whole incident he'd failed to register the number of the car – an old Peugeot 404. Given his background and training that was unforgivable. He must be getting old.

The really galling thing about the whole affair was that he'd seen the car coming towards him long before it arrived, starting as a tiny speck on the horizon and growing in size until it had loomed inescapably large as they met on the corner, forcing him to take evasive action at the last possible moment by driving into the ditch.

Fortunately no great damage had been done, and apart from looking somewhat dazed, Pommes Frites was in one piece. The far side of the ditch was higher than the other, being part of a long platform on which salt was piled to dry off in the sun, and the grass which covered the sides had acted as a cushion. But the possibility of getting his car back onto the road again all by himself was remote. He made a few desultory attempts, but one rear wheel was lifted clear off the ground and even with Pommes Frites' weight on the back seat, that was where it stayed. He would need the help of a tractor, and looking around the area, mechanical aids of any sort seemed to have low priority in ensuring the continuing supplies of sea salt to the tables of France.

Bleak was perhaps the best way of describing the countryside; bleak, but with a strange, almost translucent light. In the distance across the empty landscape he could see the occasional figure of someone working late, but they were all too far away to notice his plight, or to do much about it if they did.

A sandpiper flew past.

Four cars came and went, but they were all going the wrong way and full of holidaymakers. He glanced at his watch. It was just after six-thirty. They were probably the last he would see for a while. Most visitors would be back in their hotels by now, getting ready for the evening meal, having left the beach early because of the approaching clouds. After a long day on the sea-front those with families were probably glad of the excuse.

Just as the first rain began to fall he saw a car coming towards him, travelling the way he wanted to go. It was being driven fast, and as it drew near he saw there was a girl at the wheel.

Signalling Pommes Frites to stay where he was, Monsieur Pamplemousse decided to abandon his own car and leapt into the road, waving his arms. Almost immediately, he jumped back again, nearly losing his balance as the black BMW shot past, swerved, then skidded to a halt a little way along the road. He might have been killed. Regardless of the rights and wrongs of stopping for strangers, there were ways of going about it. For a moment he almost regretted no longer being in the Force. In the old days he'd thrown the book at drivers for less.

There was a roar from the engine and a moment later the car reversed towards him. At least the girl wasn't leaving him to his fate like the others. It skidded to a halt and he waited impatiently for the electrically operated window to be lowered.

Sizing up the situation with a quick glance the girl reached over and released the door catch. 'You'll get soaked. You'd better get in.'

'I have a companion.' Monsieur Pamplemousse pointed to Pommes Frites. 'And some *bagages*. I'm afraid we have had an accident. Some *imbeciles* nuns driving on the wrong side of the road. If you would be so kind ...'

There was only a moment's hesitation. 'He'd better get in the back. I'll look after him. You see to the rest. The compartment is unlocked.'

Pommes Frites was in the back of the car almost before his master had time to get their luggage out, watching proceedings through the rain-spattered glass, making sure his own things were safely installed.

The boot was empty save for a small and expensive-looking valise and a roll of coarse material which he had to move before he could get his own belongings in. There was also a strong smell of pear-drops.

Monsieur Pamplemousse closed the boot and ran round the side of the car, reaching for his handkerchief as he went. He could feel the water running down his face in tiny rivulets.

'It is very kind of you.' He climbed in, mopping his brow. In the circumstances gratitude was very much in order. He could hardly complain that a moment or too earlier she had nearly run him down. 'I'm sorry if we have delayed you.'

The implication that she'd been going too fast was not lost.

'I hope I didn't frighten you too much. I was reaching for the lights as I came round the corner and your car was hidden from view. Besides, I didn't expect you to jump out from nowhere. What happened?'

'We are on our way to Port St. Augustin. We were making a detour as it happened ...'

'Port St. Augustin! But that is where I am going. I can take you all the way. Where are you staying?'

'The Ty Coz.'

'I do not know the name. I know only the Hôtel du Port, but we can look for it. The town is not large.'

As he settled back in his seat, Monsieur Pamplemousse suddenly felt warm and comfortable and at peace with the world. Out of the corner of his eye he could see that Pommes Frites felt the same way too. Dog-like, he had already assumed the proprietorial air of an owner-driver, gazing out of the window at the passing scene as if he did it every day of his life. Perhaps it was their presence in the car, not the accident leading up to it, that had been pre-ordained by the giant computer in the sky. Now there was a thought.

He stole a sideways glance at the girl. Obviously she was not a local. He doubted if she was even French. Although she spoke the language well, she sounded foreign. Italian, perhaps. Or Greek. She had a dark, olive-skinned complexion which suggested the southern Mediterranean. She was gypsy like. Her hair was long and jet-black. In a few years it would probably be too long, but time was still on her side. Her skin was smooth and unwrinkled. She drove quickly and with precision, taking advantage of every bend and camber in the road. He felt safe with her and changed his mind about the 'incident'. Perhaps, he told himself, he had been at fault for not giving her more warning.

By now they were almost out of the marshes and the giant sardine canneries of La Turballe loomed into view. They were preceded by a row of modern-looking shops and flats. He wondered about getting out there and then in the hope of finding a garage, but the first one they saw was already closed. He gave up the idea. He had no wish to be stranded with all his luggage.

Almost as quickly as it had begun, the rain stopped. Out to sea the sun was shining. Any moment now it would be shining on them too. He found himself looking for the inevitable rainbow. Keeping her eyes on the traffic ahead, which was beginning to build up, the girl switched off the wipers and leaned across to adjust the demister. Her hands looked strong, almost masculine, and yet well cared for – the nails short and business-like. If she wore any perfume it didn't register, and yet there was a curious, indefinable scent of something which stirred memories in the back of his mind. Make-up was minimal. With her looks it would have been an unnecessary embellishment.

He allowed himself a longer look while her attention was otherwise engaged.

She was wearing a loose-fitting jump suit. Dark green, the colour of her eyes. She might have been a garage mechanic for all it did for her figure, but as she leaned forward he was very conscious that what was underneath was the whole person and nothing but the person. Only someone confident enough to know the effect that would have could have got away with wearing it. Or perhaps she didn't care.

'Well, do I pass?'

He came down to earth with a jerk. 'I'm sorry. To be truthful, it is very rude of me, I know … but I was wondering what you do for a living.'

'And?'

'You don't look as though you are on holiday and you are not a housewife. At least, you do not drive like one.'

'You can tell a housewife by the way she drives?' She was mocking him, and yet it was done with good humour.

'Not exactly. But it is a process of elimination.' He felt he might be on dangerous ground. 'Housewives who own a

BMW 325i are in the minority. If it is their husband's car, then they usually drive with care – they are frightened of scratching it.'

'Being married doesn't necessarily turn you into a housewife, nor does it stop you doing something you enjoy doing well.'

Outside La Turballe they met a long line of traffic. She overtook two cars quickly and easily, then slipped into a gap behind a third.

'You are also good at making decisions.'

'Housewives do not make decisions?' Again it was said with a half smile.

'Constantly. Thousands every day. But on the whole they are minor ones. They are not usually a matter of life and death ...'

He broke off, allowing her to concentrate as she pulled out to overtake the car in front. They passed a rose-filled garden, then hedgerows with occasional patches of yellow gorse. The countryside was in full bloom. He could see giant clover and daisies everywhere. Fields of camomile bordered the road.

'That is very perspicacious of you.' She laughed. 'You will never guess.'

It was a challenge he found hard to resist. Suddenly, it was like playing a television game. It gave him the freedom to make wild statements. He almost asked to see her 'mime'.

'If I found myself in a tight corner I wouldn't mind having you beside me and I wouldn't worry about you as I might about others.'

'What a strange thing to say. Are you often in a tight corner?'

'Occasionally. I used to be at one time.'

It was her turn to look intrigued. She stole a quick sideways glance as they dropped in behind another lorry.

'Tell me more.'

He avoided the question. 'I couldn't help noticing your hands just now. They are well cared for, and yet they are also very strong. You also, if I may say so, have an extremely good figure. For what you do you must keep very fit, or vice versa.'

'That is true.'

'Fit and strong, so you must do it regularly.'

'That is also true.'

'And you are happy in your work?'

She hesitated for a fraction of a second. 'Very. It is my life. I am lucky. To be fit and well and to have work that also makes you happy is a great blessing. I couldn't wish for more.'

That, thought Monsieur Pamplemousse, is not the total and absolute truth. There are other things you wish for. He wondered what they were.

'And you? Are you happy in *your* work?'

'Very.' A quarter of an hour before he wouldn't have said that. A quarter of an hour ago, standing in the rain beside his overturned car, he had been far from happy. 'I couldn't wish for more either.'

'I think perhaps you enjoy food. There is a fresh stain on your tie, and you have – please forgive me ...' for the first time she sounded embarrassed, unsure of herself. 'You have been eating garlic recently.'

He was about to deny it. Nothing he'd eaten for *déjeuner* had contained a scrap of garlic. Then he remembered that Doucette had given him a plate of *saucisson* for breakfast on account of the journey. Between them, he and Pommes Frites had eaten the lot.

232

She was one up. 'Yes, I do like food. That is *my* life.'

'And that puts you in danger?'

Before he had time to answer, a signpost for Port St. Augustin came into view. She flicked the indicator and pulled over to the left to enter an intersection. They waited for traffic coming the other way to pass.

'Sometimes. It is a throwback from my previous work. If it is true that some people tend to attract problems, then I tend to attract "situations". Or perhaps I look for them.' He rarely brought it into conversation, preferring to remain anonymous, and he wasn't entirely sure why he was saying it now. 'For many years I was with the Paris *Sûreté*.'

She clicked her fingers. 'Of course, I knew I had seen you somewhere before. Or rather, not you, your picture. You have an unusual name.'

'Pamplemousse. I was sometimes in the *journaux*.' That was an understatement. There had been a time when, for one reason or another, it felt as though he was never out of them. Once, after being involved in a notorious case which had hit the headlines, he'd even had a feature article written about him in *Paris Match*. It had pursued him for years.

Seeing a gap in the traffic, she glanced quickly in both directions before accelerating off the main road.

He was suddenly conscious of a change in the atmosphere. It was as though a shutter had come down. She seemed nervous and kept looking in the mirror. He wondered if she had noticed something. On the pretext of seeing how Pommes Frites was getting on he turned round in his seat and took a quick look out of the back window. A dark blue van was just turning off the main road. It was too far away to identify, but the girl evidently saw it too, for he felt her accelerate and they took the next corner at a speed which startled him.

Unobtrusively, he slid his hand down and tightened his safety belt. But he needn't have worried. His companion was much too busy with her own thoughts to notice. The earthy, almost animal-like quality he had noticed earlier was now even more apparent. She was like a deer on the run. Tense, alert …

'*Alors!*' As they reached the outskirts of Port St. Augustin he glimpsed a row of posters and the penny dropped.

'You are with a circus!'

She nodded. He relaxed again. Now that he knew, it all fell into place. Her name was Yasmin. The first poster had shown her dressed in a black jacket and fishnet tights. She was holding a top hat in one hand while she kept a group of lions at bay with a whip. In the second she had been flying through the air high above the ring holding on to a trapeze by one foot. They were both artist's impressions, and no doubt he'd given full rein to his imagination, but the likeness was there.

She must be doing well to be driving a nearly new BMW. It was intriguing. He had never met a circus artist before. If the advertisements were anything to go by, no wonder she oozed confidence.

'You are a girl of many parts.'

She shrugged. 'In a small travelling circus like ours you have to be. We all do many things.' For a moment she relaxed and became animated again.

'I would like to come and see you.'

By now they were almost in the middle of the town. The harbour lay to the right and through an alleyway he caught a glimpse of the sea.

'That would be nice. Look …' She pulled up sharply. 'I

am afraid I shan't be able to take you to your hotel after all. I must drop you here.'

'*D'accord*. It was kind of you to bring us this far.' He wanted to say more, but for the first time on the journey he felt tongue-tied.

'Please hurry.' She stared back the way they had come and he saw an expression almost of fear in her eyes. She suddenly looked very small and vulnerable.

'Of course.' He was out of the car in a flash. Ever alert to his master's wishes, Pommes Frites followed suit.

Monsieur Pamplemousse paused as he shut the door. 'Thank you once again. If I can be of any help, at any time, I shall be at the Ty Coz. You know my name. You can leave a message.'

'Thank you.' She sounded genuinely grateful and he wondered if she would indeed take up the offer.

He hardly had time to shut the boot before she was on her way again. The BMW disappeared round the next corner, towards the harbour, just as the van came into view. As it slowed to negotiate the intersection he caught a glimpse of the driver. Around his neck was a gold cross on a chain. Their eyes met for a brief second and Pamplemousse knew he had seen him somewhere before. The van was on hire. It was a Renault with a local registration. Taking out his notebook he flipped through the pages and added its number to the day's notes. It might be worth a telephone call when he got to the hotel.

The garage next to the *Mairie* was closed, but if his memory served him right there used to be one near the harbour which refuelled the fishermen's boats as well. In those days he hadn't owned a car. He and Doucette had taken the train to St. Nazaire and then caught the *autobus*. It had been a big adventure. He looked at his watch again.

It was twenty to seven, but the garage might still be open. It was worth a try.

Feeling out of place in his Paris suit, Monsieur Pamplemousse gathered up the luggage and set off, his thoughts still very much on the girl. Reminders of her were pasted up everywhere, on walls and telegraph poles.

Following on behind, Pommes Frites wore his resigned expression. He knew the signs. His master was smitten.

When they reached the harbour it became clear that all the action was at the other end of the promenade. The circus was located on a patch of scrubland a little way back from the beach. The 'big top', shielded from the prevailing wind by a group of caravans and lorries, was festooned with coloured lights. A low-pitched continuous grinding sound interspersed with the spasmodic crack of rifle-fire could be heard from the fairground alongside it. He wondered how many other parts the girl played. Perhaps even now she was already drumming up custom for the hoop-la. It was a hard life.

The Quai Jules Verne was as he remembered it, except it was now called Quai Général de Gaulle. In fairness, the latter had a better claim. Jules Verne had only once in his life been to Port St. Augustin, and that only on a school outing from his home town of Nantes.

The old cobbled street leading back to the centre of town now had a 'No Entry' sign. It had been turned into a shopping precinct. The cobbles had been re-laid and everywhere there were concrete tubs filled with flowers. It was lined on either side with expensive-looking boutiques displaying the latest Paris fashions. There was even a bookshop.

Benches were dotted along the promenade, sandwiched between waste bins whose black plastic liners peeped out from beneath garish orange lids.

Three nuns came towards him. It was a good omen. To meet one or more was supposed to bring good fortune, provided you didn't see their backs. Three was especially lucky. It would make up for the earlier episode. He let them go past.

Much to his relief, the garage was still there. And it was open. Apart from a row of modern pumps it had hardly changed. In the old days they had been worked by hand.

'*Pas de problème, Monsieur*.' The owner seemed only too pleased at the prospect of an evening job outside the town. He would finish what he was doing – ten minutes at the most – then he would take *Monsieur* to his hotel, go and collect the car before it got dark and deliver it later that night. Yes, he had heard good reports of the Ty Coz, but it was not for local people. It was for the tourists.

Monsieur Pamplemousse was tempted to stroll along to the end of the promenade in order to have a quick look at the circus, but he decided instead to spend the time looking round the tiny port. Tomorrow evening would be soon enough.

A new car-park had been built and was chock-a-block. There were also many more yachts in the harbour than he remembered, the smaller ones moving gently on the swell from the incoming tide. In the old days it had been full of fishing boats. The local florist must do well. The larger the yacht, the bigger the investment in flowers. Some of them looked too immaculate and lived-in ever to put to sea.

The waitresses in the Hôtel du Port were getting ready for dinner, their starched *coiffes* bobbing up and down as they bent over the tables. There would probably be a rush of early diners wanting to go to the circus afterwards. The Hôtel now boasted an enormous electrically operated blind to protect those facing westward from the setting-sun. The bathrooms would have expensive tiles and the latest plumbing. At least the dark, solid, old-fashioned Breton furniture was still there. It was probably too heavy to move and no one else would want it anyway. It summed up modern France in a way. One foot firmly planted in the twenty-first century, the other deeply rooted in the past. In Paris uniformed men riding *Caninettes* searched the pavements for evidence of canine misdemeanours – Pommes Frites led a hunted life these days: he could hardly call his *merde* his own – while their colleagues looking after the gutters still used rolls of old carpet tied up with string to divert the water which gushed down every day from the heights of Montmartre, for the very simple reason that no one had come up with a better idea. It was the same here. The old public wash-house was still intact and looked well used, but the *pissotière* had been replaced by a concrete and steel *Sanisette*. Its predecessor had smelled to high heaven in August – worse than the fish market – but at least it had been free. Not that financial considerations seemed to make any difference these days. As he strolled past it a man carrying a small brown valise slipped a coin in the slot and stood waiting. There was a brief snatch of music as the door slid open and then closed behind him. Everything was done to music these days. Even *Le Guide* had been forced to introduce a symbol for piped music in restaurants, a loudspeaker rampant.

Monsieur Pamplemousse suddenly paused in his musings, hardly able to believe his eyes. On one of the benches further along the promenade, deeply immersed in a *journal*, sat a familiar figure. It hardly seemed possible and yet come to think of it, why not? Brittany was very much a home from home for lots of English families, some of whom took their holidays there year after year. It had

238

always been that way. He well remembered their strange habit of marking the level of wine left in the bottle before they went upstairs to bed at night. He'd always thought of it as 'the English habit', although he'd since learnt it was far from typical

A feeling of excitement came over him and he quickened his pace. Although they had spoken on the telephone several times – notably when he'd been involved in the case of the missing girls at the finishing school near Evian – it was a long time since they last met. Three years? Four?

He almost broke into a trot as he covered the last few metrès, his hand extended.

'Monsieur Pickering. How good to see you! *Comment ça va?*'

The figure on the bench glanced up from his *journal*, then looked briefly at his wrist-watch.

'*C'est dix-sept plus cinq minutes.*' It was said in a flat monotone, almost devoid of expression. Having imparted the information, the owner of the voice pointedly returned to his crossword.

'But ...' Monsieur Pamplemousse hardly knew what to say. 'It *is* Monsieur Pickering, *n'est-ce pas?* Surely you remember me?'

'Look, piss off, there's a good chap.' This time the words came through clenched teeth and were said with such feeling Monsieur Pamplemousse practically reeled back as if he had been hit.

As he made his way slowly back along the promenade he felt totally shattered; rejected on all sides. First there had been the accident with his car, then the girl. Now, Mr. Pickering – someone he had always looked on as a friend – had denied him.

So much for *entente cordiale*. Anything less *cordiale*

239

than Mr. Pickering's reception would be hard to imagine.

Feeling Pommes Frites nuzzle up against him, he reached down and patted his head. At least, come rain or shine, you knew where you stood with Pommes Frites. His was no fair weather friendship.

He directed his thoughts towards Ty Coz. When they got there they would have a good meal to make up for it. It would be a meal to end all meals; no expense spared. There would be no stinting. Madame Grante would have a fit when she saw *l'addition*. He could picture it all.

But as he crossed the road towards the garage, something else happened which gave him cause for thought. He was not unfamiliar with the workings of *Sanisettes*. Indeed, following his experience in St. Georges-sur-Lie when for a brief period he had been incarcerated in one while inspecting an hotel belonging to the Director's Aunt Louise, he'd become a walking mine of information on the technicalities of their workings.

Efficient, they might be. A minor miracle of electronics as applied to public facilities, yes. Sanitised, certainly. But fast, no. The cleaning cycle following each operation alone took exactly forty seconds, so there was no question of one out, the next one in.

And therein lay the nub of the matter. His encounter with Mr. Pickering had been brief and to the point; it had certainly taken not longer than a minute or so. And yet he'd been barely halfway across the road when the door to the *Sanisette* slid open and out came a nun. Moreover, she was carrying a small brown valise.

Clearly, the undercurrents in St. Augustin were not restricted to rocking the boats in the port. Some were hard at work on land as well.

3
TRUFFLE TROUBLE

Removing a box bearing a large red cross from the leather case provided by *Le Guide* as standard issue to all its Inspectors, Monsieur Pamplemousse opened it and began looking for a tube of antiseptic ointment and a plaster. For the latter he needed one which was both generous in its measurements and in its powers of adhesion, for Pommes Frites' nose was, to say the least, not only large but usually very wet, and he wouldn't be at all happy if the plaster fell off into his breakfast. Not that the thought of breakfast at the Ty Coz was uppermost in either of their minds at that moment. If their experience of the previous evening was anything to go by, their fast would best be broken elsewhere.

In designing the original case, which had changed very little in its basic concept over the years, the founder of *Le Guide*, Monsieur Hippolyte Duval – a perfectionist in all that he did – had sought to provide for any emergency likely to be encountered by members of his staff whilst in the field.

Monsieur Pamplemousse couldn't help but reflect as he discarded first one and then another plaster as being either too small or the wrong shape, that Monsieur Duval had probably never envisaged the need to come to the rescue of a bloodhound who had suffered injury to his proboscis from the business end of a ball-point pen, or indeed any sort of pen – given the fact that the ball-point wasn't invented until long after the Founder had passed on.

Monsieur Pamplemousse felt terrible. He would far sooner have speared his own nose than wound Pommes Frites' in the way that he had. Had he been brought up in court by an animal protection society, his excuse would have sounded very lame indeed. His head bowed in shame.

The previous evening had been an unrelieved disaster. The only good thing that had happened was the retrieval of his car, looking none the worse for its adventure. One more tribute to a design which in many respects was hard to fault.

The food in the hotel restaurant had turned out to be unbelievably bad. How the other diners could get through their meal, some with every appearance of enjoyment, was beyond him. Not even several measures of a particularly vicious Calvados had entirely taken away the salty taste. Since the bottle had been without a label he strongly suspected the chef must make it himself during the long winter evenings.

In the end he and Pommes Frites had retired to bed early armed with a large supply of Evian, the seals of the bottles unbroken to make sure the contents hadn't been tampered with. After a long drive he had hoped they might both get a good night's sleep. But hunger proved to be a poor bedfellow. Apart from which he had many things on his mind.

Mr. Pickering's strange behaviour kept him occupied for quite a while; he couldn't for the life of him think what he might have said or done to cause his old friend to act the way he had. The goings-on in the *Sanisette* were something else again. Coupled with the behaviour of the nuns in the car earlier in the day, he began to wonder whether he wasn't witnessing the total decline of the Catholic Church; the Pope must be a very worried *homme*. Thinking about the girl who had given him a lift only added to his restlessness – he couldn't get the sudden change in her behaviour out of his mind; one moment so cool and sure of herself, the next moment clearly afraid. But afraid of what? Magnified as such thoughts always are in the hours of darkness, he began to wish he'd gone to the circus after all, picturing himself in the role of rescuer from whatever it was that was troubling her.

He tried counting sheep, but that only made matters worse. They all wore frilly white collars, the kind used to decorate roast crown of lamb. He pushed the thought aside.

Last, but not least, there was the task which had brought him to Port St. Augustin in the first place: catering for the inaugural flight of the airship. Switching on the bedside light, he reached for his pen and pad. For one reason and another he hadn't even begun to think of a possible menu and time wasn't on his side. Neither as it happened, was inspiration. One thing was certain, he wouldn't find it by staying at the Ty Coz. Why on earth the Director had insisted on his going there he would never know.

In desperation he sought refuge in a game popularly known to himself and his colleagues on *Le Guide* as 'The Last Supper'. It was one they played on those occasions when they were able to meet up *en masse* as it were; the annual staff outing at the Director's weekend retreat in Normandy perhaps, or when things were comparatively slack after the March launch and they were all in the office getting ready for the next edition.

Over the years they had played it so many times the result was a foregone conclusion, but it was no less enjoyable for all that, giving rise to much smacking of lips and to

243

reminiscences which often went on far into the night.

Monsieur Pamplemousse's own choice on such occasions was clear and uncompromising. Simplicity was the keynote. Truffle soup at Bocuse's restaurant just outside Lyon. A simple grilled *filet* steak – preferably from a Charolais bull – accompanied by a green salad, at any one of a hundred restaurants he could have named without even stopping to think; followed, if heavenly dispensation made it possible to arrange, by *pommes frites* cooked by the *patron* of a little hillside café he'd once come across on the D942 west of Carpentras; light, crisp, golden, piping hot, and always served as a separate course, for they were perfection in their own right. The wine would be an Hermitage from Monsieur Chave, and after the cheese – the final choice would depend on the time of the year – a *tarte aux pommes légère*, wafer thin, and topped with equally thin slivers of almond.

His salivary glands working overtime, Monsieur Pamplemousse lay awake for a long time after that. If he were to expire during the night – and the way he felt, such an event was not entirely outside the bounds of possibility – it would not be as a happy man.

And so it came to pass that with food uppermost in his mind, he fell into a fitful sleep, dreaming, perhaps not unsurprisingly in the circumstances, of what might have been.

However, as he settled down to enjoy the meal of his dreams something very strange happened. A ton weight seemed to have settled on his stomach, pinning him to the bed. The more he struggled the harder it became to move, and panic set in.

Then, just as he was about to give up all hope of rescue, a waiter appeared bearing not the expected bowl of soup, but what could only be described as a kit of parts; a platter of pastry, a jug containing chicken stock, and a plate on which reposed a single black truffle – a magnificent specimen to be sure, the biggest he had ever seen – twice the size of a large walnut. Madame Grante would have had a fit if she'd seen it.

He reached forward to pick it up. But the surface was moist and as soon as his fingers made contact it shot out from between them and rolled across the table cloth, hovering for a moment or two before settling down again. He tried a second time, then a third, but on each occasion the result was the same. The truffle seemed to have a life of its own.

Stealth was needed. Glancing over his shoulder to make sure no one was watching, Monsieur Pamplemousse clasped his pen. Then he made a lightning stab at the object in front of him.

Alonzo T. Cross, inventor of the world's first propelling pencil – a forerunner of Monsieur Pamplemousse's present weapon – would have been well satisfied with the result, for it was a tribute to the sharpness of his products.

Not even a banshee, that spirit of Celtic superstition reputed to howl beneath the window of a house where the occupant is about to die, could have surpassed the cry which rent the air as the finely engineered point of the pen made contact with its target.

Monsieur Pamplemousse woke with a start and found himself lying half on and half off his hotel bed, with Pommes Frites eyeing him dolefully, not to say fearfully, from the other side of the room. He wore an expression, as well he might in the circumstances, of a dog who has just suffered the ultimate betrayal of a love which he had always assumed would last forever. To make matters worse it had happened at the very moment when he'd been in the middle of showing his affection for his master with a morning lick. St. Hubert – the patron saint of bloodhounds – would have been outraged had he been present at the scene.

As Monsieur Pamplemousse looked at the end of his pen and then at Pommes Frites' nose, he realised for the first time that the latter bore a distinct resemblance to the *Tuber menosporum* of his dreams and remorse immediately set in. Pommes Frites' proboscis, once the pride and joy of the Sûreté, follower to the bitter end of many a trail, sometime winner of the Pierre Armand trophy for the best sniffer dog of his year, was not something to be trifled with. Its impairment would be almost as hard to bear for those who in one way or another depended on its proper functioning as it would be for Pommes Frites himself. Reports for *Le Guide* would suffer. Tastings in restaurants across the length and breadth of France would lose their authority.

As he applied a generous helping of ointment to the end of Pommes Frites' olfactory organ and then pressed a plaster firmly into place, anger filled Monsieur Pamplemousse's soul. One look at the expression in his friend's eyes confirmed in him the need for action no matter what the consequences.

Replacing the first aid box in the case, he reached for the tray containing the camera equipment, then paused for a moment. It was tempting to take a picture of his patient for use in case there were any arguments later. But that would be unkind; it would be rubbing salt into the wound, and salt was the one culinary item any mention of which was strictly taboo for the time being.

Monsieur Pamplemousse came to a decision. Enough was enough. In this instance, more than enough. He picked up another, much larger case and placed it on the bed.

Recognising the signs, Pommes Frites wagged his tail. The possibility of spending any more time in their present surroundings was not something he could enthuse over either. Normally he had great faith in his master's ability to turn up trumps when it came to finding places to stay, but that too had undergone a severe shaking.

A few minutes later they drove out of the hotel car-park and joined the queue of traffic already heading for the beach.

As the sea came into view Pommes Frites put his head out through the open window on the passenger side and sniffed. He immediately wished he hadn't. Exhaust fumes rather than ozone filled the air; that, and a strong smell of ointment. Neither was pleasant on an empty stomach. The automatic seat belt alongside Monsieur Pamplemousse tightened as they negotiated the roundabout in the centre of the town and Pommes Frites settled back in his seat.

But if Pommes Frites was looking forward to a gambol on the sands followed by a dip in the ocean, he was disappointed. His master had other priorities. Pulling up alongside a row of telephone *cabines* at the far end of the promenade, Monsieur Pamplemousse signalled Pommes Frites to wait.

Flicking open his wallet as he entered the nearest *cabine*, he withdrew a blue plastic card from its protective covering and committed it to a slot in front of him. Sliding shut the small black door in the apparatus he pressed a series of buttons appropriate to his call; the 16-1 code for Paris, followed by a further eight digits. He noted that nineteen of the original forty units on his *Télécarte* were still available. Provided he didn't have too many interruptions they should allow him more than enough time to give vent to his feelings. During the drive from the hotel he had marshalled his thoughts into their appropriate order, rehearsing out loud his end of the conversation, honing it and polishing it until he was word perfect. Even though he hadn't understood a word, Pommes Frites had got the gist and he'd looked suitably impressed.

'*Le Guide. Puis-je vous aider*?' A familiar voice responded before the second ring was complete.

'Ah, Véronique. *Monsieur le Directeur, s'il vous plaît.*'

'Monsieur Pamplemousse! How are you? And how is the weather in Brittany?'

'The weather in Brittany,' said Monsieur Pamplemousse, 'is *très bien*. I, unfortunately, am not. I am far from *bien.*' He kept a watchful eye on the digital counter. Véronique was a nice girl, but he had little time at his disposal for pleasantries. He was short of change and he didn't want to spend time looking for somewhere to buy another *carte*.

Something in the tone of his voice must have conveyed itself via the many cables and amplifiers linking the western coast of France with the seventh *arrondissement* in Paris. Nuances of urgency had not been attenuated *en route*.

'I will put you through at once, *Monsieur.*'

Monsieur Pamplemousse murmured his thanks and waited, growing steadily more impatient with every passing second. Clearly the Director was not poised, as his secretary had been, in readiness to receive incoming calls.

He glanced across the road while he was waiting. A police car was parked outside the circus, but there was no sign of the occupants. Two men were busy setting up the *carrousel*. To the side of one of the caravans a woman was hanging out a line of washing. There was no sign of the girl, Yasmin, although he could see her car parked alongside a big generating lorry near the back. Behind the car, somewhat incongruously, there was a large menhir – one of the many 'great stones' bequeathed to that part of Brittany by a people who had inhabited the land even before the Gauls had come upon the scene.

Looking towards the port he considered the possibility that he might see Mr. Pickering, but the road was empty. Nearly everyone was down on the sand. A low stone wall separated the beach from the promenade, at the same time sheltering beds of late spring flowers from the prevailing wind. That too, was new. Beyond a beflagged sign bearing the words *Centre Sportif* children's heads rose into view, hovered momentarily, then disappeared again as their owners bounced up and down on a trampoline. Further down the beach other small figures were hard at work building sandcastles, anxious to complete them before they were enveloped by the incoming tide. He guessed they must be English. An insular race, the English, always digging themselves in. Their insularity and desire to conquer started at an early age. Even as he watched, one of them confirmed his suspicions by adding a Union Jack to one of the battlements. A provocative gesture on foreign soil – especially as he must have brought it with him with that sole purpose in mind.

A late fishing boat chugged its way towards the harbour, an escort of gulls wheeling and screeching overhead. An old biplane came into view, towing a banner. Shielding his eyes against the sun, he made out the word *cirque*.

'Aristide, how are you? And how is the weather in Brittany?' It was the Director at last, sounding slightly out of breath. Did his voice also contain a hint of anxiety? A suggestion of trepidation?

Monsieur Pamplemousse repeated the reply he had given Véronique, but with even greater emphasis.

249

'Oh, dear. I am sorry to hear that, Aristide. I was hoping the change of air would do you good. May I ask what is wrong?'

'I can give you the answer in three words, *Monsieur. Cuisine Régionale Naturelle.*'

'Don't tell me you are tired of fish already, Pamplemousse. I find that hard to believe.' The Director assumed his censorious voice. 'You have only been at Ty Coz a matter of hours. Hardly time to unpack your valise.'

'My valise, *Monsieur*, is in the back of my car, and there it will remain until Pommes Frites and I have found another hotel.'

'But, Aristide, is this not a trifle premature? It is a plum assignment. *Cuisine Régionale Naturelle* is, after all an entirely new technique. If we are to consider it for inclusion in *Le Guide*, extensive field trials will be necessary. I hesitate to say this, but it is a well known fact that our taste buds diminish in number as we grow older. One has to persevere, however ...'

'Mine will disappear altogether if I stay at Ty Coz,' said Monsieur Pamplemousse. 'They will have been pickled for posterity.'

'Come, come, Aristide. This is not like you. As with all new things, *Cuisine Régionale Naturelle is* doubtless an acquired taste.' There was a definite note of panic in the Director's voice.

'Then someone else will have to acquire it, *Monsieur*. Guilot, for example. He is always trying to lose weight. He might welcome the chance to go without food for a while.'

Over the telephone he heard the distinct sound of a cork being withdrawn from a bottle. It was followed by a 'glugging' noise. He braced himself for the attack. It was not long in coming.

'Pamplemousse. Nothing grieves me more than to have to put the matter this way, but I am afraid it is no longer a request. It is a command. Accommodation has been reserved at Ty Coz until the day after the launch. Your flag is firmly placed on the map of France in the operations room. I must warn you here and now that if you go elsewhere not only will opprobrium fall upon your head but I shall be unable to justify your P39s to Madame Grante ...'

Monsieur Pamplemousse took a deep breath as he cut across the Director's monologue, but with only five units left on his card it was essential to get his point across.

'*Monsieur*, have you tried eating *Cuisine Régionale Naturelle*?'

'I am told it is very popular in Okinawa, Aristide ...' Clearly the Director was not giving in without a fight. Monsieur Pamplemousse resisted the temptation to remark that it confirmed his worst suspicions. Whoever had recommended the hotel couldn't possibly have been a Frenchman. An oriental with a grudge perhaps?

'There are doubtless many things not to our taste which are popular in Okinawa, *Monsieur*.' In deference to Pommes Frites he turned and lowered his voice. '*Chiens en croûte* are probably considered a delicacy, whereas over here ...'

He paused.

Along the road nearer the port a man on a ladder was pasting a white paper across one of the circus posters.

'It is also possible that the waters of the Pacific are less polluted than those of the Atlantic Ocean, but even if that is true I doubt if they cook everything in sea-water. Fish is not the only speciality of the region, *Monsieur*. The Guérande peninsula is also the centre for salt production ...' Even by hanging outside the *cabine* he couldn't read the label.

'Everything? But that is not possible!'

'*Tout à fait, Monsieur*. Everything at Ty Coz is either cooked in or made with sea-water. The bread, the mayonnaise, even the coffee. Had we stayed for breakfast, I am sure even the dough for the *croissants* would have been mixed with sea-water. Pommes Frites was sick twice yesterday evening and he is not normally one to complain.

'The final straw came when I mistook the end of his nose for a truffle.'

A nun zoomed past on a *cyclomoteur*, a brace of *baguettes* clipped to the rear pannier. Monsieur Pamplemousse gave a start. He could have sworn he'd caught a glimpse of rolled-up trousers beneath her black skirt as it billowed in the slipstream. He crossed himself as he followed her progress along the promenade.

'Pamplemousse, are you there? Can you hear me? Did you say a truffle? Frankly, I am worried about you. Was the roof of your car open on the journey down yesterday? One forgets the sun can be strong at this time of the year.'

'*Pardon, Monsieur. I* was distracted momentarily. A nun went past on a motorised cycle. Her habit was caught in the slipstream and I couldn't help noticing what she was wearing underneath ...'

There was a moment's silence. 'Pamplemousse! I sometimes despair, I really do. Is there no end to your depravity? Is there nothing that can assuage your desires of the flesh? A poor girl who has forsaken all to take the vow?' Once again there was a distinct sound of something being poured from a bottle. 'Was she – was she a young novice, perhaps? I must confess, I have often wondered about these things myself.'

'*Monsieur*, whatever else she was, I suspect she was no novice, nor was she particularly young.'

'Age is immaterial, Pamplemousse. It is the principle. Or rather, the lack of principle. It is ...' There was a click and the line went dead.

Feeling that it had somehow been a less than satisfactory conversation, not quite as rehearsed, Monsieur Pample-mousse replaced the handset and left the *cabine*. Perhaps in the end if accommodation was difficult he would compromise by keeping his room at the Ty Coz and eating out. But at least he had made his point.

He hesitated for a moment. The man with the ladder was now working on another poster – slightly nearer this time. He wondered whether to take a closer look, then glanced at his watch. It showed barely a quarter to ten. His rendezvous with the airship wasn't until eleven. There would be time to take a quick look at the circus – perhaps even reserve a seat for the evening's performance – before strolling along to one of the cafés near the harbour for a leisurely breakfast. He must also remember to get a card for Doucette. That was always one of his first acts on arriving anywhere. She would start to worry if he didn't.

Pommes Frites jumped out of the car and followed his master across the road with alacrity. There was a lot to catch up on.

Monsieur Pamplemousse led the way towards the back of the waste ground. Close to, the BMW looked even more incongruous against the menhir; the blue van parked on the other side of it hardly less so. He wondered idly what the early inhabitants who had struggled to erect the stone all those thousands of years ago would think if they could see it now. No doubt they would marvel at the BMW, just as today's inhabitants marvelled at the stone. Both attracted their worshippers.

Pommes Frites had no such respect for antiquity. For

253

some reason best known to himself he appeared to have taken a violent dislike to the menhir. Having run round and round it several times growling and barking, he then bestowed his mark, not as a sign of favour, but rather the reverse, sniffing the stone at the same time, thus leaving behind a strong smell of embrocation as well. The previous evening's meal had given rise to a great thirst during the night, and Pommes Frites was clearly in no hurry.

While he was waiting, Monsieur Pamplemousse looked around. He had a strange, almost eerie sensation of being watched, but there was no one about. The whole site seemed strangely quiet. The doors to the motley collection of caravans were nearly all closed; the blinds drawn. There was no sign of the woman with the washing he'd noticed earlier. The line of sideshows still had their shutters up. No doubt when the lights were on and there were people around it was all very different, but by daylight it simply looked tatty. Tatty and rather sad. The old Gustave Bayol *carrousel* had seen better days, although nothing would ever replace the quality of the delicately carved horses with their rosettes and tassels. It must have been someone's pride and joy when it was new.

He wandered along through the fairground towards the circus tent, past the Dodgem cars and a heavily ornamented caravan belonging to a fortune-teller, its sides covered in paintings of stars and other heavenly bodies. Next to the caravan were two tents, one of which had a Jacques Cour-tois painted canvas façade advertising the only bearded lady left in Europe, the other bore a picture depicting the smallest man in the world. Both tents had their flaps tightly closed. Next came a coconut shy, and after that a helter-skelter.

He could smell the circus long before he reached it; a

mixture of sawdust and animals. It was the same smell he had noticed in the girl's car.

Some Arab ponies were tethered to a tree, and near by there was a cage containing an elderly lion. It was fast asleep, enjoying the sunshine. Clearly, it suffered from the kind of affliction even its best friend wouldn't have mentioned. But who would tell a lion? Seeing something lying on the ground, he stooped and picked it up. It was a small piece of fibreglass, newly sawn – the cut was still shiny. From force of habit he slipped it into his pocket.

To his right lay the entrance to the 'big top', fronted by a decorated pay-box. He made his way across the down-trodden grass. It was worth a try. But once again he drew a blank, and he was about to give up when he heard someone call out.

A man appeared from behind a lorry, eyeing him suspiciously. 'What do you want? We're not open yet.'

'I was wanting a ticket for the circus.'

'The *matinée* has been cancelled.'

'Tonight will be fine.'

'Tonight! *Pas de problème*! You can have as many as you like. *Vingt, cinquante, cent …*'

'I want one only.'

'Poof!' The man raised his hands. Clearly he had better things to do than open up the box office just for the sake of selling one ticket. He pointed towards the fortune-teller's caravan. 'You'd better see Madame Caoutchouc. She's the boss.'

Monsieur Pamplemousse made his way back across the fairground, threading a path through the stalls and sideshows until he reached the caravan. Signalling Pommes Frites to wait outside, he climbed the steps and knocked on the door. There was no reply. After a moment or two he turned the handle and pushed it open.

He found himself in a small area curtained off by black drapes hanging from rails fixed to the ceiling. In the middle there was a round, baize-covered table in the centre of which stood a large crystal ball. There were two chairs – one just inside the door, the other on the far side. A single shaded lamp suspended from the roof threw a pool of light onto the table.

Monsieur Pamplemousse called out, but again there was no reply. Pulling the curtain on his left to one side revealed a bedroom. A built-in bed occupied most of the space and to one side of it there was another door. It was reminiscent of a ship's cabin or the sleeping-berth on an overnight express train – all polished wood and brass. Underneath the bed he could see what looked like a long leather bag. On top of the bed there was a red cushion embroidered with a piano keyboard.

He tried parting the curtains on the other side. It was a real old-fashioned showman's caravan and no mistake. A long bow-fronted sideboard ran along one wall. The top was covered with knick-knacks collected during a lifetime of travel, old photographs in silver frames, china and brass ornaments. They must all be stowed away when the circus was on the move and brought out again at each place of call. In the centre of the sideboard, looking totally out of place, there was a Sony hi-fi – all black dials and knobs, with two miniature loudspeakers, one on either side. On the wall behind it there was a large old-fashioned mirror with a patterned border etched into the glass. On a small table in the centre of the room there was a vase full of fresh flowers, and along the remaining wall a small sink and a cooking stove let into the top of some fitted cupboards.

It was someone's whole world encapsulated in a few square metres.

It certainly wouldn't have done for Doucette, nor for him either. He found himself wondering what Madame Caoutchouc did in her spare moments – other than listen to the radio. There wasn't a single book or a magazine to be seen anywhere. His own day was rarely complete without reading something, before he went to sleep. Perhaps she didn't have any spare moments.

At that moment he heard footsteps coming up the steps. He let the curtain fall back into place and turned just as the door opened.

If Madame Caoutchouc was surprised to see such an early customer she hardly registered the fact. Instead she motioned him towards the nearest chair.

She looked worried, distracted. He could see the family likeness at once. She was an older, larger version of the girl. Yasmin in perhaps twenty years' time.

'I have told you all I know. There is nothing more to add.'

Monsieur Pamplemousse looked suitably baffled.

'I'm sorry. I do not understand …'

It was Madame Caoutchouc's turn to look confused.

'You are not from the press?'

He shook his head.

'Or the police?'

He shook his head again. 'No. I simply wanted to buy a ticket for tonight's performance.'

Madame Caoutchouc gave a short laugh. 'Tonight? Tonight, there will be no problem, *Monsieur*.' She reached for the door handle.

Monsieur Pamplemousse shrugged. For reasons best known to themselves, Le Cirque Bretagno was not in the business of selling tickets that morning. So be it. He turned and was about to leave when the memory of the man pasting over the advertising posters came back to him.

'I'm sorry. I do not understand. There *is* a show tonight?'

There was a moment's hesitation. 'You mean you haven't heard about the accident? *Morbleu!*'

Monsieur Pamplemousse felt an icy hand clutching at the pit of his stomach. He knew the answer before he even posed the question.

'It was the trapeze artiste? The girl Yasmin?'

Madame Caoutchouc nodded. 'It was terrible. I was there when it happened. I saw it all. There was nothing anyone could do. She missed the bar after a triple somersault. It was a difficult trick, but she had done it many times before. She landed in the net – that too, has happened many times – but this time ...' She suddenly had difficulty ln finding the right words.

'We did everything we could. Everything. I went with her in the ambulance ...'

Monsieur Pamplemousse asked the question uppermost in his mind.

'No, she isn't dead, but she is in a coma. If you had seen her lying there ...'

To his dismay Madame Caoutchouc suddenly burst into a flood of tears. It was as though a dam had broken. For a moment or two it was so uncontrollable he felt at a loss to know what to do or say. It was always the same when he was confronted by a woman crying; a mixture of tenderness and helplessness, which occasionally gave way to irrational anger, not with the person concerned, but with his own inability to supply the right words.

'I am sorry.' He reached out and touched her. 'If there is anything I can do.' For a moment he was tempted to tell

Madame Caoutchouc about his meeting with the girl, then he decided against it. There seemed little point.

'*Merci, Monsieur.*' With a struggle she pulled herself together. 'I'm sorry. I am a little overwrought. The police have been here asking questions. What do they know about the circus?

'There will be a show tonight – we cannot afford not to have one, but it will be without Yasmin. And without Yasmin, I think there will be no problem about tickets.'

'*Merci, Madame.*' He held her hand briefly, then turned to go. 'I am sorry to have troubled you. I did not realise what had happened.'

Madame Caoutchouc followed him to the door. Halfway down the steps Monsieur Pamplemousse paused and looked back at her.

'You say you went with your daughter to the hospital? Did she – did she say anything while you were there? Anything at all?'

'A few words in the ambulance, that is all. And they were a struggle. Nothing that made sense. I think she must have been delirious by then.'

'Do you remember what she said?'

He immediately regretted asking the question. For a moment or two it looked as though Madame Caoutchouc was about to burst into tears again, then she recovered herself.

'It was just the one word. It sounded like *pample-mousse. Pamplemousse, pamplemousse, pamplemousse*, she kept repeating it over and over again. Who knows what she was trying to say?'

'Who knows?' said Monsieur Pamplemousse. 'Who indeed knows ?'

4
THE SIX GLORIES OF FRANCE

Leaving his car parked outside the telephone *cabines*,
Monsieur Pamplemousse walked slowly back along the
beach towards the harbour. The wind had started to
freshen, but he hardly noticed it. He was sunk in gloom. He
could still hardly believe the news about the girl's accident.
There was probably nothing at all that he could have done
to help her, and yet somehow he couldn't rid himself of a
feeling of being in some way partly responsible. If only he
had gone to see her the night before, perhaps it wouldn't
have happened. Perhaps she'd had her mind on some
problem and that in turn had caused a momentary loss of
concentration. He was glad he hadn't seen her fall. That
would have been too awful in the circumstances. Sensing
his mood, Pommes Frites presented him with a stick he'd
found. It was a specially large one with some seaweed
attached.

When they reached the port Monsieur Pamplemousse
bought a postcard for Doucette in a shop which sold everything from fishing nets to wooden *sabots*, via Breton lace,
hand-painted china, and oilskins – a reminder that Brittany
had 'weather' – even in summer. The card showed a man
paddling a flat-bottomed boat through the local marshes; it
was a choice between that, views of the harbour, the salt
pans, or close-up pictures of lobsters awaiting the pot.

Coming out of the shop the first thing he saw was a

picture of the girl. Her face looked out at him from the front page of a local *journal*. They must have worked quickly. He bought a copy and led the way to a café a little way along the front.

Suddenly realising how hungry he was, he ordered a *crêpe au sucre* as well as a plate of *croissants*, a large cup of *chocolat*, and a bowl of water for Pommes Frites. Then, to the sound of halyards slapping against steel masts in the freshening wind, he settled down to read the *journal*.

In the end it didn't tell him much more than he already knew, or could have guessed. Le Cirque Bretagno was a small family-owned concern of Italian origin that had been going the rounds since before the turn of the century, handed down from father to son and currently being run by the mother. The father had died several years ago. It travelled all over Europe, seldom staying more than a night or two in any one place, and only intended being in Port St. Augustin for three nights before heading further south towards Bordeaux.

The accident had happened when Yasmin was performing a change-over on the high trapeze. It was a difficult manoeuvre – the high-spot of the act – but one which she had performed many times. No one knew quite what went wrong; a momentary loss of concentration, a split-second error of judgement; her hands had touched the other bar, but too late to tighten her grip. With such a trick there was no second chance. It underlined the ever present danger of circus life, and the fact that even with a safety net disasters could happen. Tragedy was never far away, lurking round the next corner waiting for a chance to strike. But nowadays people were so blasé; they had seen such tricks many times before on television.

Yasmin was twenty-eight. She was still in a coma, but the

local hospital hoped to issue a statement after she had undergone further examination. Her temporary loss was a great blow to the circus, but they would do their best to carry on.

Monsieur Pamplemousse folded the paper carefully, broke the remaining *croissant* in two and gave one piece to Pommes Frites, then he signalled for the bill. The clock on the church tower said ten-forty. It was time they were on their way.

Back in the car, he unlocked his issue case and removed the Leica camera and the Trinovid binoculars. The flight would give him a good opportunity to take some aerial photographs; something he had never done before. He hovered over the compartments of the felt-lined tray for a moment or two, unable to make up his mind which lenses to take, but eventually settled on the standard 50mm and the 28mm wide-angle. He had no idea how high they might be flying and he wished now he'd given the matter more thought; there might be a problem with the light. He always kept ultra-violet filters on the lenses anyway; they provided extra protection against scratches, but he slipped a couple of yellow filters into his jacket pocket to be on the safe side.

On the spur of the moment and acting on an impulse that had paid off many times in his days with the Force, he attached an auto-wind to the camera, slipped a zoom lens into place, and on the pretext of checking it, pointed the camera in the direction of the circus and shot off the rest of the reel of film. As far as he could tell, no one had seen him do it. A few moments later, the camera re-loaded, they set off.

The airship was tethered to a mooring-mast attached to the back of a large lorry. From a distance it looked like a giant wind-sock floating to and fro, the double wheels below the gondola describing a large arc as the wind blew the envelope first one way and then the other. There were more people standing around waiting for his arrival than he expected. No doubt they all had a function to perform, but it reminded him of a film set, with everyone poised for action. On the other hand, security struck him as being remarkably lax; apart from two gendarmes and a man in civilian clothes occupying a hut at the entrance to the field, no one asked to see his credentials and he was allowed to drive right up to the concrete square which served as a landing and take-off area. If the dark grey pill-boxes near the cliffs were 'anything to go by it was probably a relic of the war years. The Germans had built to last. The small office and reception room near by looked freshly painted and from two white poles alongside it the flags of France and the United Kingdom were already flying.

Monsieur Pamplemousse wasn't sure whether the airship looked bigger or smaller than he'd expected. Both in a way. Close to and seen from below, the balloon itself looked vast – vast and slightly out of control; the gondola, with its large windows and helicopter-like Perspex dome surrounding the flight deck, like a pimple which had been added as an afterthought.

Two men in dark blue uniform came out of the office to greet him.

'Monsieur Pamplemousse?' The first one, grey-haired, with a weather-beaten face and an air of quiet authority, held out his hand to introduce himself. 'Commander Winters.' He turned and nodded to the second man. 'My colleague – Capitaine Leflaix of the French navy. I'm afraid,' he looked down at Pommes Frites, 'your dog will have to stay behind.'

'Stay behind?' repeated Monsieur Pamplemousse.

'Pommes Frites? But he always comes with me. Wherever we go.'

'Company orders, I'm afraid. *Chiens* are strictly *interdits*.' Clearly there was no point in arguing.

'*Là, là*.' Monsieur Pamplemousse bent down to give his friend and confidant a consoling pat. It struck him as he did so that Pommes Frites was taking the news of his deprivation remarkably well.

Looking round, he saw why. Some dozen or so of the waiting group had detached themselves from the main body and were clutching the gondola in an attempt to keep it steady ready for boarding. They weren't achieving one-hundred-per-cent success. The remaining men were clutching two bow lines like tug-of-war teams awaiting the signal for the off.

Commander Winters looked up at the sky. 'Right!' He clapped his hands briskly. 'We'll get you weighed first and then we'd better get cracking.' He led the way into the reception room and pointed to some scales. '*Parlez-vous anglais*?'

'*Un petit peu*,' said Monsieur Pamplemousse non-committally as he watched the needle shoot round. 'A little.'

Commander Winters looked at the scales. 'Aah!' He made the word sound like a black mark. Monsieur Pamplemousse wasn't sure if it referred to his lack of English or the figure on the dial; probably both. He followed the others back outside.

'You need always to face the airship,' said Capitaine Leflaix as he helped Monsieur Pamplemousse up a small flight of steps. 'Both getting in and getting out. Otherwise, it can take you by surprise.'

As Monsieur Pamplemousse missed the first step he saw

what the other meant. Conscious of raised eyebrows and pained expressions on the faces of those trying to hold the gondola steady, he had another go, then paused momentarily in the doorway to wave *au revoir* to Pommes Frites. Pommes Frites wore his gloomy expression, as though 'goodbye – it's been nice knowing you' would have been more appropriate to the occasion. There was a clatter of feet from the other two as they followed him up the steps.

Monsieur Pamplemousse exchanged greetings with a girl in uniform as she moved forward to close the cabin door, then took stock of his surroundings. No expense had been spared for the forthcoming event. Everything smelled new. The floor was luxuriously carpeted in deep blue. There were eight spotlessly clean wine-red armchair-type seats, two at the far end of the cabin and four grouped around a small rosewood table aft of the open flight deck. Suddenly the scale of reference had changed again. Now that he could no longer see the balloon, the gondola felt unexpectedly spacious, like the sitting-room of a small flat – except, as far as he could see, there was no galley and no room to put one, only a door marked TOILETTES and what could have been a small cocktail cabinet; someone must have got their finger out already. All the same, he could see problems ahead. In the end prepared trays might be necessary – small ones at that! The Director would not be pleased.

Leflaix emerged from the flight deck carrying a small pair of portable steps. He mounted them, opened a domed porthole in the roof, and stretched up to peer through the gap.

Wondering irreverently if he was looking to see if they were still attached to the balloon or whether it had floated off without them, Monsieur Pamplemousse settled himself in one of the chairs by the table so that he would have somewhere to work and make notes.

Leflaix closed the hatch. 'I was checking the ballonet bags to make sure we are stabilised.' His expression was wry. 'You need to be a sailor as well as an airman to fly an airship.' He took his place on the flight deck.

The girl appeared and handed him a brochure. '*Monsieur* must be very important for the airship to fly on a day like today.'

Monsieur Pamplemousse gave a non-committal shrug. Nevertheless, he couldn't help feeling flattered.

He flipped through the pages. It was full of technical details: gross volume – 6,666 cubic metres, length – 59 metres, maximum speed – 60 knots, endurance – 24 hours, engines – two turbo-charged Porsche …

He had hardly finished reading the last few words when a seat belt warning light above the flight-deck bulkhead came on and there was a roar from somewhere behind him as first one and then the other of the two engines were started up. He looked through the window. The two large fans mounted towards the rear of the gondola had begun to turn.

As the crew completed their cockpit check, the men outside who had been holding the gondola steady began removing bags of ballast, while those holding the lines got ready to take the strain. He felt the pilot take control as the nose of the airship was detached from its mooring and the fans were rotated until they were at an angle of 45 degrees facing the ground.

Hand signals were exchanged and the airship began moving forward, slowly at first, then faster, until suddenly the ground started to slip away from them as the craft rose, nose down, into the air. He had a momentary feeling of guilt as he caught a glimpse of Pommes Frites. His mouth was open as though he was howling and his plaster was hanging loose. Then they turned to port and the concrete area disappeared from view.

Almost immediately they were over the cliffs, with the sea breaking angrily in clouds of white foam on the granite rocks below. It looked as though they were in for a spell of bad weather. The wind must be coming up from the Bay of Biscay.

He tried to break the ice with the stewardess. 'I think, *Mademoiselle*, we are better off up here, *n'est-ce pas?*'

She looked at him in surprise, as though the very idea was extraordinary, then disappeared behind some curtains at the rear of the compartment. Clearly she was in no mood for making polite conversation.

Monsieur Pamplemousse gave a shrug as the airship executed a wide turn to port, skirted along past St. Marc, where Monsieur Hulot spent his famous holiday, and headed for the Côte d'Amour around La Baule. He reached for his camera as he looked out of the window and saw people on the beach stand up to wave as they flew over. This was the life. There was no doubt about it – the Director was right – the dirigible was an elegant solution to the problem of manned flight. He ought to consider himself lucky to enjoy such a unique experience.

A moment later they had crossed the narrow strip of town and were over the Grande Brière, the vast area of swamp and marshland behind La Baule, home of peat-diggers and rush gatherers. Its streams were full of eels, pike, roach and wildfowl, their banks yellow with iris in spring and early summer.

Monsieur Pamplemousse began to wish he'd brought more film; his automatic winder had been working over-time. By the time they headed west towards the sea he could hardly have documented the area more fully had he been commissioned to make an aerial survey.

To his left he could see a group of islands; ahead of them was the long arm of the Quiberon peninsula. The few people out and about hardly bothered to look up as they passed over. Most of them seemed too busy packing up their belongings. A *vedette* scuttled across the bay, heading towards the harbour.

Monsieur Pamplemousse was so busy with his camera he was scarcely aware of the motion, which was not unpleasant at first – a little like drifting at sea in a small boat, rising and falling with the waves. If every so often the Captain pushed the nose down in order to pin-point a land-mark, so much the better; it gave him a better angle, as did the rolling gently first to one side and then the other. He managed to get a particularly good shot of the oyster-beds in Locmariaquer from a near vertical position. And when the nose went in the opposite direction – towards the sky – it gave him a chance to reload. He wished now he had brought his entire range of lenses and filters. Some of the cloud effects could have been quite spectacular through a dark filter; one moment black and angry-looking, the next moment like an etching as the sun broke through a gap and make a bright rim round their edge.

He could now see why so many postcards on sale in the local shops were shots taken from the air. Seen from ground level much of the countryside was flat and uninter-esting; from some three or four hundred metrès up, the Golfe du Morbihan was a wonderful series of creeks and inlets and the land behind it a maze-like pattern of fields and stone walls. With a bit of luck he would have enough pictures to warrant a whole series of articles in *L'Escargot – Le Guide*'s staff magazine.

At first Leflaix came to see him from time to time, but

gradually his visits became less frequent. He seemed more interested in the stewardess, who had joined the others on the flight-deck, peering over their shoulders at the view ahead.

Carnac appeared on the starboard side, coinciding with a break in the clouds. The sudden burst of sunshine made the rows of menhirs look like lines of Roman soldiers forming up to do battle. As they flew over, the shadow cast by the airship seemed strange, almost threatening.

Having decided to save the rest of his film for the return journey, Monsieur Pamplemousse settled down at the table. Things had gone quiet in the cabin and it was time to start work.

Feeling inside his jacket he removed a long white envelope which bore, on the back flap, an embossed reproduction of *Le Guide*'s symbol – two crossed *escargots* rampant. It contained the letter the Director had given him before he left, outlining his own plans for the inaugural flight.

Knowing how long-winded the Director could be when he got his hands on a dictating machine, Monsieur Pamplemousse had put off reading it for as long as possible. The Director was inclined to write as he spoke; brevity was not his strong point.

He skipped the first two pages, which were mostly a repeat of all that had been said in his office the day before. It read as though he had been interrupted in mid-sentence by the telephone, not once, but several times. It wasn't until the middle of page three that he got to the heart of the matter.

'... in short, Pamplemousse, my suggestion, and it *is* only a suggestion, but a good one, I think, nonetheless, is that we should confine ourselves to no more than six courses;

simple peasant dishes of the kind one might find in any little café or bistro in the area over which the dirigible will be flying. Dishes that reveal the true glory of France – its food. If there is sufficient time, we might even produce a special souvenir *carte* on the cover of which, inscribed in gold leaf, are those very words: *Les Six Gloires de la France*. Underneath one could add the symbol of *Le Guide;* two *escargots* rampant. There is no reason why we should not profit from the occasion.

'Now, to start with, one might have some of those little pastry delicacies – their correct name escapes me – but they are stuffed with *foie gras* and served alongside raw oysters. The two go particularly well together, especially when accompanied by a glass of very cold Château d'Yquem – I would suggest the '66. You may if you wish, leave that to me. I have a particularly good source.

'After that, how about some *Oeufs Pochés aux Moules*? Eggs poached in the juice in which some mussels have been cooked. I had it the other evening. The eggs and the mussels should be served with *Hollandaise* sauce. I am told that for the dish to be at its best the eggs should be as fresh as possible ...'

Suddenly aware that a gust of wind was blowing them sideways, Monsieur Pamplemousse looked out of the window. They were now flying inland. It was hard to make out where they were. He peered at the scene through his binoculars and immediately wished he hadn't. All he could see was endless fields of artichokes. They looked rather sad, as though they, too, felt they had seen the best of the day. He wondered when the Director had last eaten in a simple Breton bistro. The menu might also account for his being on a diet; a sad state of affairs for the editor of the most prestigious of France's many food guides. It sounded as though he was mentally trying to make up for lost meals.

'… lobster, of course – or a *Langouste* – perhaps *à la crème*, followed by a roast duck from Nantes. As I am sure you know, it is at its best when cooked in a sauce made from butter, cream and *eau-de-vie de Muscadet*. *I* will leave the choice of wine to you.

'By that time they should be over Normandy where cream really comes into its own. I believe *les Anglais* often prefer to have their cheese at the end of a meal a habit they most certainly didn't acquire from the Normans. However, ours is not to reason why. That being so, we could continue the theme of simplicity with some of those delicious tartlets made with eggs and almonds and cream which are a speciality of the area. I believe they are known as *Mirlitons* …'

Monsieur Pamplemousse had some difficulty focusing on the next page as the airship hit a pocket of air and fell rapidly before rising, nose-up again. Out of the corner of his eye he saw the hostess buckling herself into a seat. He thought she looked rather white.

'… then, Pamplemousse …' Monsieur Pamplemousse could almost sense from the writing – the way the letters were slanted – that the Director was about to produce one of his masterstrokes, '… then, Camembert should be served – preferably a non-pasteurised example from the Pays d'Ange. Although the season is almost over, I have a special reason for suggesting it rather than, say, a Pont-l'Evêque or a Brillat-Savarin. Legend has it that when Napoleon first tasted Camembert he kissed the waitress who had the honour of serving him. So, who knows? With the exercise of a little tact, one might arrange matters …

'Once again, Pamplemousse, I leave it to your good judgement. You have so much more experience in these affairs than I.

'To round things off, for by that time they should be on the last leg of their epic journey and nearing *Londres*, in deference to our English guests, I suggest that with the *café* we serve, instead of *petits fours*, one of their own specialities. There is one I am thinking of which they call "trifle". I have looked it up in one of their recipe books – a slim volume – it was left behind by an English girl we had staying with us a few years ago. You may remember her – a blonde girl with a predilection for a dish called "Spotted Dick". For some reason my wife took a dislike to her and she had to go, but she was something of an expert on what the English call "puddings". I believe that before she left England for France she had been a member of a well-known pudding club.'

Monsieur Pamplemousse closed his eyes. He did indeed remember the Director's *au pair*. Elsie had been her name. An unusually well-endowed girl, she had given a whole new meaning to the words '*au pair*'. He wasn't in the slightest bit surprised she had been told to leave. Puddings were probably not the only thing she was expert at.

'It seems to be a concoction which is made by emptying the contents of a can of tinned fruit over what are known as "sponge-fingers", which have themselves been previously steeped in sherry. The whole is then immersed in something they call "bird's custard". I cannot imagine what that is, nor what it tastes like – I have enquired at *Fauchon* and they have promised to telephone me back, but they have yet to do so – however, it appears to be very popular. The dish is then topped by a layer of thick cream …

'I am not sure what would go with it; the combination might prove altogether too rich, but if there is any of the Château d'Yquem left …'

272

The airship gave a lurch. Monsieur Pamplemousse suddenly felt extremely sick. Several things were abundantly clear. Not only was the Director sadly out of touch with the eating habits of both the English and the peasants of Brittany, he had never been up in a balloon either. Speaking for himself, he had never felt less like eating in his life. The *crêpe* he'd consumed at breakfast had been a ghastly mistake; the *croissants* a cardinal error; as for the *chocolat* ...

Regardless of the sign warning him to keep his seat-belt fastened, Monsieur Pamplemousse released the clip and staggered towards the rear of the airship. He beat the stewardess by a short head, but he pretended not to have seen her. Never had the word TOILETTES looked so welcoming, nor a basin coming up to greet him so inviting. Pushing the door shut behind him with his foot, he slid the catch home all in one movement. It was no time for old-fashioned gallantry, more a case of every *homme* for himself. Not the most engaging girl he had ever met. No doubt she was prone to headaches.

Like the sign on the bulkhead above the flight deck, the word OCCUPÉ above the toilet door stayed illuminated for the rest of the flight. Monsieur Pamplemousse was not in a mood to receive other callers. His head was spinning. His stomach ached – it felt as though it had been wrenched out at the roots. He was alternately bathed in sweat and shivering with cold. He hadn't felt quite so ill since the time just after the war when he'd crossed *La Manche* during midwinter on a visit to England. Death would have come as a welcome relief. He wasn't even aware they had landed until he heard a familiar scratching noise on the other side of the door and realised that the engines had been turned off.

Pommes Frites' relief at his master's safe return was

tempered with an understanding that all was not well. His welcome was suitably muted. In any case he seemed to have other things on his mind. Once he'd exchanged greetings and bestowed a welcoming lick, he disappeared outside again. There was a thoughtful expression on his face which, under normal circumstances, his master would have registered immediately and wondered at. As it was, Monsieur Pamplemousse still had problems of his own.

He began gathering up his belongings, some of which had fallen to the floor. Fortunately that didn't include the Leica, which was still on the table where he had left it. The stewardess was nowhere to be seen. She must have beaten Pommes Frites to the steps.

'Sorry about that.' Commander Winters climbed out of his seat. 'We wouldn't normally have gone up on a day like today, but your boss was most insistent when I telephoned him this morning to try and call it off. He said it was absolute top priority. Nothing must stop us. I hope you got what you wanted.'

Monsieur Pamplemousse had a mental picture of the Director sitting in his office, totally oblivious to the plight of others. He made a mental note to get his own back one day should the opportunity arise.

'Er, I wonder if you'd mind doing something about your dog? I think he is about to attack one of our chaps.'

Monsieur Pamplemousse joined Commander Winters at the cabin door and was staggered to see Pommes Frites at the foot of the steps, fangs bared, apparently engaged in a tug-of-war with one of the ground staff over a bag of ballast. The man appeared petrified, as well he might in the circumstances. When he felt like it, Pommes Frites could look extremely menacing. His plaster had disappeared and he was positively quivering with excitement as he dug his paws

274

into the ground, absolutely refusing to let go of his end. The accompanying sound effects boded ill for anyone rash enough to try and thwart him.

'*Sacrebleu!*' Monsieur Pamplemousse clambered down the steps as fast as he could go. '*Asseyez-vous!*' The command, rapped out with all the authority he could muster, had an immediate effect.

Looking suitably ashamed, Pommes Frites let go of his end and sat to attention. If a flicker of surprise entered his eyes that his master should take the other man's part, it was only momentary. He was too well trained to protest out loud.

'Never mind. I expect he's glad to see you back.' Commander Winters stifled Monsieur Pamplemousse's apologies. 'Who's a good boy, then?' He bent down to pat Pommes Frites and then thought better of it. Instead, he picked up the bag. 'Perhaps you'd like to keep this as a souvenir?'

'*Merci* – you are very kind.' Monsieur Pamplemousse would have been hard put to think of anything he wanted less as a souvenir than a ten kilogram bag of ballast. He tried to look suitably grateful as he took it, but he could see why the Commander had made the gesture. It was wet from Pommes Frites' saliva.

Leflaix clattered down the steps, his expression grieved. Perhaps he felt disappointed at having been let down by a fellow-countryman.

'You should always face the airship as you leave,' he reminded Pamplemousse stiffly. 'Otherwise it may take you by surprise.'

Monsieur Pamplemousse looked at his watch. It was midday. They had been up for less than an hour, but it could have been ten times as long. The last twenty minutes had seemed like forever. He said goodbye to the others and made his way unsteadily towards his car.

Throwing the bag in the back of the car, he started the engine and drove off.

'Don't forget to face the airship!' The words were permanently engraved on Monsieur Pamplemousse's mind as he acknowledged the salute from the man on duty at the gate and headed back towards Port St. Augustin. At that moment in time he felt as though he never wanted to look an airship in the face again. All he wanted to do was lie down somewhere and rest. But the grass at the side of the road looked damp and uninviting and the prospect of going back to the Ty Coz was not a happy one.

After a kilometre or so he opened the window to let in a welcome draught of cold air and almost at once started to feel better. He wondered if he should try his luck at the Hôtel du Port. A *digestif* of some kind might help, and if that did the trick, in the fullness of time he might even attempt an omelette; plain, of course, but with a *salade de tomates* and a slice or two of *baguette*. After that, he could explore the possibility of their having a room vacant. Whoever said 'man cannot think on an empty stomach' had a point. One way and another he had a lot to brood over.

Monsieur Pamplemousse wasn't the only one with things on his mind. Pommes Frites had remained unusually quiet during the journey, putting two and two together, first one way and then another, and each time coming up with another answer. His schooling had been based on the computer-like principle that black is black and white is white. The possibility of there being various shades of grey in between had not been introduced to his curriculum in case it led to confusion. Besides, he knew what he knew. The fact that his master didn't seem at all interested in knowing about it, he put down to a temporary lapse brought on, not unsurprisingly in his view, by the previous evening's meal followed by going up in a balloon. A lethal combination.

What, in Pommes Frites' humble opinion, his master needed most in order to restore him to good health was some grass. In fact, he fully expected him to pull in to the side of the road at any moment so that he could gather some.

Pommes Frites' training was also based on a system which recognised good work when it saw it and rewarded it accordingly – usually with a suitable tit-bit from the *boucherie. So* far that reward had not been forthcoming. Neither, for that matter, had there been much in the way of recompense for the unwarranted attack on his nose.

It was with these thoughts uppermost in his mind that he followed his master into the bar of the Hôtel du Port, and shortly afterwards outside again onto the terrace.

The bad weather had driven most of the people off the beach and into the cafés, restaurants and *crêperies* around the harbour. Monsieur Pamplemousse had to squeeze his way through a maze of beach-bags, sunshades and other impedimenta to reach the one remaining table in the corner nearest the sea. A smell of damp clothes filled the air. He felt sorry for all those who'd been looking forward to a sun-drenched holiday; even more sorry for the waitresses who were struggling to serve them.

Corks popped, plates clattered. Orders shouted over the heads of the diners were repeated by a disembodied voice from somewhere inside the hotel. Cries of '*un Muscadet*' echoed from all sides, and were repeated as bottles were plunged into buckets of ice.

He wondered if any of the old staff were still there. Most

of them had probably got married by now, or forsaken Brittany for the promise of a better life in Paris. The fourteenth *arrondissement* was full of girls who had left home in search of fame and fortune but who had got no further than the area around the Gare Montparnasse. The girl who took his order looked as though she would have happily settled for that with no questions asked. Her *coiffe* was not at its best, her matching lace apron looked decidedly ruffled.

A large and juicy steak was deposited on a nearby serving table by another waitrèss while she went off for the rest of her order. Monsieur Pamplemousse studiously averted his gaze. Steak was not what he fancied most at that moment. Despite his musings the night before, it was not high on his list of choices when he was staying in an area noted for its seafood, and in his present state of health it had very low priority indeed.

However, at that moment there occurred a strange and unexpected diversion which totally took his mind off his surroundings and made even Pommes Frites sit up and take notice.

Making her way slowly along the deserted promenade there appeared an elderly female of such bizarre appearance it almost took the breath away. The whole restaurant went quiet at the same instant. One moment it had been all noise and chatter, the next moment silence descended as everybody stopped eating and turned to watch her progress towards them.

In his time, when mingling among the down-and-outs under the bridges of the Seine had been all part of a night's work, Monsieur Pamplemousse thought he had seen everything. But even the bell which once upon a time rang at the old Les Halles vegetable market, signalling the end of trading for the day and the moment when the *clochards*

278

could take their pick of the leftovers, had never brought forth such a truly wretched specimen of humanity.

Two nuns came round a corner, crossed themselves, and then disappeared back the way they had come. A gendarme suddenly discovered he was needed urgently elsewhere and followed suit.

As she loomed nearer, the old woman looked, if possible, even more malodorous. Her putty-coloured hair hung in great knots down her back. The several layers of cardigan covering her upper half were topped by a scarf so matted it looked as though it must have been glued in place. Her feet, partially encased in a pair of ancient carpet slippers held together by string, were black with the dirt of ages. A slit up one side of a grey skirt revealed the top of an even greyer stocking held in place by yet another piece of string. String, in fact, seemed to play an important part in the old woman's attire. It looked as though anyone foolish enough – or drunk enough – to pull one of the ends would have caused the whole ensemble to collapse.

Much to Monsieur Pamplemousse's dismay she came to a halt almost directly opposite his table. Waving a battered parasol with one hand and brandishing an empty wine bottle above her head with the other, she began screaming in a shrill voice for the *patron*.

Monsieur Pamplemousse eyed her uneasily, uncomfortably aware that his was the only table on the terrace with a spare seat. The possibility of sharing a meal with such an object was not a happy one. He prayed that his omelette wouldn't arrive. It had been a mistake to ask for it *baveuse*; it could be as overdone as they liked. It could be left to cook for another ten minutes if need be.

He did his best to avoid the old crone's gaze as she swayed closer and closer, leaning back in his chair as she thrust the empty wine bottle in his face.

Fortunately, he was saved the ultimate embarrassment by the arrival of the *Madame*. She was closely followed by the chef brandishing a large kitchen knife.

His presence was unnecessary. *Madame* was quite capable of dealing with the situation; her vocabulary was more than equal to the task. No conceivable occupation, no possible country of origin was omitted from the list of permutations she flung at the unwelcome intruder. Her performance drew a round of applause.

Pursued by cries of '*vieille toupie, vieille bique, boche rastaquouère*', pausing only to indulge herself in the luxury of that classic gesture of contempt – '*le bras d'honneur*' the slapping of the right arm above the elbow by the palm of the left, causing the former to rise sharply upwards, the old woman disappeared along the promenade rather faster than she arrived.

'*Pardon, Monsieur. Poof! L'alcool!*' The *Madame* squeezed her way past.

Monsieur Pamplemousse offered his thanks, then bent down and reached under the table. In her haste to leave, the old crone had dropped her bottle. He looked at it thoughtfully, then raised it to his nose and cautiously sniffed the opening. It smelled of honeysuckle.

He wondered. The bottle was empty, but according to the label it had once contained wine from Savennières, an area just to the north of Angers; a Coulée de Serrant at that – something of a rarity. Not the usual tipple of a wino. And if the lingering bouquet was anything to go by, it had been opened quite recently.

There was something else that bothered him. The old woman had been close enough for him to have caught the full force of any bodily odours she might have had.

Expecting the worst – the nauseating, overpoweringly sweet smell which only the extremely unwashed manage to achieve – he'd instinctively drawn himself back. But it hadn't been like that at all. What little scent he'd detected had really been quite pleasant; more male oriented than female. He was no great expert, but if he'd been asked he would have said it was that of a fairly expensive after-shave.

Hearing a commotion going on behind him, Monsieur Pamplemousse turned in his seat. It didn't need any great powers of detection to see what had happened and to arrive at an immediate solution. While everyone's attention had been focused on the goings-on with the old woman, someone had helped themselves to the steak.

In looking for the culprit, the one advantage he had over the others was that he could see Pommes Frites under the table and they couldn't. Pommes Frites had his eyes closed, but his face said it all. It could have been summed up in the one word – *extase*. And if concrete rather than circumstantial evidence were called for, salivary tests would have been money down the drain. His lips were covered in meat juice. Others may have abandoned their cutlery, but it took a lot to put Pommes Frites off his food.

Monsieur Pamplemousse called for the bill. On the pretext of feeling unwell he paid it as soon as it came and left without waiting for the change. It was only a matter of time before those around him realised what had happened, and when they did, one thing was very certain, it would not be an ideal moment to broach the subject of a room for the night.

He had left the car in a space a little way along the front, and as he walked towards it felt in a quandary. He could hardly punish Pommes Frites in front of all the people in the Hôtel. It would give the game away.

On the other hand, as with a small child, punishment needed to be carried out immediately – otherwise it would be extremely unfair. Pommes Frites would think it was yet another unprovoked assault and he would be most unhappy.

That was another thing. Far from looking repentant, Pommes Frites' behaviour was entirely the opposite. Goodness as well as repleteness shone from his eyes. A halo would not have looked out of place; one of the larger sizes. He looked for all the world like a bloodhound who felt himself in line for a medal for services rendered.

Monsieur Pamplemousse was still puzzling over what to do for the best when they reached the car. He let Pommes Frites into the back and was about to climb in himself when he paused and looked across the road, hardly able to believe what he saw.

It was the old woman again. She was skulking behind the *Sanisette*. Worse still, she was clearly beckoning to him. Even as he watched she lifted up her skirt suggestively and started performing a jig. It was not a pretty sight. With the total dedication of a Cartier-Bresson and throwing caution to the winds, Monsieur Pamplemousse pointed his camera in her direction and once again used up the rest of his film. Fortunately, he had left the motor wind on his camera. At least it was all over quickly.

Slamming the 2CV into gear, Monsieur Pamplemousse manoeuvred it out of the parking space. The thought uppermost in his mind was to put as much distance between himself and Port St. Augustin as he could in the fastest possible time.

At the roundabout opposite the *Mairie* he took the road signposted to Nantes. If he did nothing else that afternoon, at least he could dispatch his films to Headquarters. If he was in time to put them on an afternoon train, Trigaux in the art department would have them first thing in the morning. With luck, they would be processed and on their way back to him by the end of the day.

After that he might call in at a local *vétérinaire*. Pommes Frites' behaviour had really been most peculiar. It was quite out of character, and totally against his past training. To behave badly once was forgivable, but twice in one morning was not. Either the wound in his nose was troubling him – it could be that there was something in the ink – or there was another, less obvious, cause. Whatever the reason, it definitely needed looking into.

And after that ... after that he would stop at a *fleuriste* and buy some flowers for the girl. He could call in with them later that afternoon.

It was early evening before Monsieur Pamplemousse finally got back to the hotel. He parked his car unobtrusively between two British cars, an elderly Rover and a Bentley, and unpacked his luggage.

The news of Yasmin was not good. She had been sent to a larger hospital in Nantes where they had more specialist treatment. He could have kicked himself for not telephoning first, for he must have passed within half a kilometre of her while he was there. At least the flowers were being sent on.

The doctor at the local hospital had been very cagey and full of questions.

'Did she drink?'

'Was she addicted to drugs?'

The answer to all of them was he didn't know. Given her occupation, it seemed unlikely.

'No, there was no point in going to see her. She wasn't

allowed visitors.' It was all very depressing.

He had hoped to creep back up to his room unnoticed, but the owner of the Ty Coz was behind the reception desk.

'*Monsieur* is back!'

'*Oui.*' He tried to make it sound as though he had never intended leaving.

The owner looked at his cases. 'We had thought ...'

'I had need of them,' said Monsieur Pamplemousse simply.

'Ah!'

'Now, if you will excuse me ...'

'*Un moment, Monsieur*. There is a letter for you. It came during *dîner* last night, but you had already retired to your room. I would have given it to you this morning with your *petit déjeuner*, but ...' Monsieur Pamplemousse was left in no doubt as to where the fault lay.

The envelope was plain. On the outside it said simply Monsieur Pamplemousse, Ty Coz. He didn't recognise the writing.

'There was no other message?' He slid his thumb under the flap and removed a single sheet of white paper.

'*Non, Monsieur*. It must have been delivered by hand while everyone was busy in the restaurant. It was found on the desk.'

He read the note several times. It was brief and to the point: the salient words were heavily underlined.

'*I must see you*. Please *do not come to me*. *I* will come to you, later tonight after the show. Take *great care!*'

It was signed Yasmin.

His mind in a whirl, Monsieur Pamplemousse slipped the note back into its envelope. If only he'd taken the bull by the horns and gone to the circus the night before ... But he hadn't, so there was no point in wishing he had. All the same, he couldn't rid his mind of Madame Caoutchouc's parting words – the one word the girl had repeated over and over again as she was taken away.

He suddenly realised the owner was talking to him.

'*Pardon.*'

'*Monsieur* will be wanting *dîner* tonight?'

'*Non.*' He folded the letter and slipped it into an inside pocket. '*Non, merci.*

'Pommes Frites and I are going to the circus. I doubt if we shall be back until late.'

5
A TOUCH OF PNEUMATICS

Madame Caoutchouc had been wrong in prophesying that no one would be going to the circus. Monsieur Pamplemousse found himself at the tail end of a long queue and spent the next fifteen minutes shuffling along at a snail's pace while he reflected on the strange make-up of human beings. Tragedy acted like a magnet. In the past he'd known people drive for miles in order to visit the scene of a particularly gruesome murder, often bringing the entire family with them so that they could make a day of it. Listening to some of the conversations going on around him it was obvious many of those present were enjoying a vicarious pleasure in discussing the gory details. Everyone had their theories. Overnight, people who had probably never done anything more adventurous than stand on the seat of a garden swing had become experts on the trapeze. He chose not to listen. Half of them wouldn't have been there normally. One couple had travelled all the way from Rennes, nearly one hundred and fifty kilometrès away. He wondered what Yasmin herself would have thought had she known.

The noise was deafening. The sideshows in the fair were doing a roaring trade. Overall there was a strange acrid-sweet smell, a mixture of candy-floss, greasy frankfurters, and smoke from a *crêperie*. He was glad they had stopped for a bite to eat in St. Nazaire on the way back, otherwise he would have felt ravenous and he might have been tempted. His liver would have suffered. As it was, once he'd got his ticket he gladly made his escape from the crowd and joined Pommes Frites in the car while he waited for nine o'clock.

A clown on stilts passed by on the other side of the road, drumming up custom; hardly necessary in the circumstances, but it was probably part of a set routine. A small group of children followed on behind, shouting words of encouragement. One, braver than the rest, tried to push him over and received a clip around the back-side from a walking-stick for his pains. A cheer went up. Loudspeakers outside the big top blared forth unintelligible announcements at intervals. He heard the sound of a lion roaring, but in the general hubbub it was hard to tell whether it was the real thing or simply a recording. If he could judge by what he had seen that morning, he strongly suspected the latter.

He glanced round. Oblivious to it all, Pommes Frites was fast asleep on the back seat next to his bag of ballast. Opening the glove compartment, Monsieur Pamplemousse took out a pocket torch and shone it on his watch. It showed five minutes to nine. There was still time enough to stroll round the outside of the circus before taking his seat. If past experience with travelling circuses was anything to go by it was unlikely to start on time. Probably most of those running the sideshows were involved in one way or another and would need to make a quick change.

He was right. By the time he reached the fair half the stalls already had their shutters up and the rest were following suit. Nearly all the crowd had disappeared. The only noise came from a giant electric generator parked near the *carrousel*. There was an air of suppressed excitement overall. Madame Caoutchouc, looking darkly voluptuous, came out of her caravan wearing a patterned dressing-gown over her costume. As she reached the tent belonging to the smallest man in the world, she paused and called out. A moment later she was joined by a midget dressed as a clown, and together they made their way towards the big top.

Monsieur Pamplemousse wondered whether to follow on behind, then he decided to explore the waste area near the back of the circus one more time. He had no idea what he was looking for, let alone where to start, but the sight of the girl's car still parked in the same place reminded him of the need to do something, however trivial-seeming.

He glanced around. There was an element missing, but he couldn't for the moment think what it could be. The BMW was in exactly the same place, alongside the generator lorry, but the blue van had been moved further away. He shone his torch on the tail-board. There were patches of mud which he hadn't registered earlier in the day. They looked fresh. The thin splashes had dried hard, but thick areas were still damp, and dark in colour. The rear wheels were covered with mud as well and there were bits of grass sticking to the walls of the tyres. He knelt down and felt the ground. There were marks which looked as though something heavy had been dragged along the surface.

Monsieur Pamplemousse was about to check the front of the van when he felt rather than saw a light go out in a nearby caravan. Switching off the torch, he backed into the shadows and waited. There was the whine of an electric motor, followed by the sound of a door being opened and shut. It was followed by the metallic click of a key being turned in a lock. The whole process was repeated. Then footsteps muffled by the grass passed him heading for the back of the tent. Whoever it was seemed to be in a hurry.

Taking a chance, Monsieur Pamplemousse peered round the side of the van and had a clear back view of a man in a dark cloak silhouetted against the light from the circus. A hood was pulled up over his head.

At that moment the muffled strains of martial music filled the air; 'The Grand March' from *Aida* played on drums and fifes, with a solitary trumpet in support by the sound of it. What it lacked in grandeur was more than made up for by sheer vigour, and any imperfections were drowned beneath the cheers from the audience.

He allowed a few seconds to pass and then made his way towards the entrance, subconsciously matching his pace to the time of the music. With luck he would catch the end of the Grand Parade and a front view of the man he'd just seen. If anyone had asked why it seemed important, he couldn't have answered.

In the event he was fortunate to get a seat. All the rows near the front were jam-packed, and he only just managed to squeeze onto the end of a bench near the back.

He recognised the man instantly even without his cloak. He had an air about him, as though he was at one and the same time both part of and yet separate from the whole. It was clear from the way he walked and the slightly arrogant look on his face as he led the parade out of the ring that he considered himself the star of the show. Perhaps he had usurped Yasmin's place. The last time Monsieur Pample-mousse had seen him he'd been behind the wheel of the van which had followed the girl into town.

Once again, Monsieur Pamplemousse had the feeling of having seen him somewhere before, some echo from the dim and distant past. Either that or a picture of him. He wasn't often wrong about such things. It was annoying because conundrums of this sort were liable to keep him awake at night, and he had lost enough sleep already.

He also recognised the man he'd spoken to outside the ticket office earlier in the day – now resplendent in the red frock-coat of a ring-master. He was introducing 'Madame Caoutchouc' in a 'death-defying act' – wrestling with a crocodile.

While the man did his build-up, Monsieur Pample-mousse took stock of his surroundings. It was a long time since he had been to a circus. Once upon a time, when he was a boy, it had been nearly all animal acts – lions, tigers, elephants, performing dogs and bears; now acrobats and jugglers were back in fashion.

Unusually for a small travelling circus, the king-poles were made of steel. Perhaps that was another sign of the changing times. It was logical. As well as being safer in a strong wind, steel poles would have allowed the height of the roof to be raised and with it the height of the trapeze. All the same the girl must have fallen many times before. Perhaps it was a case of one time too many. It happened; people injured themselves every day falling off step ladders or doing something equally mundane like tripping over a broken paving stone.

He applauded mechanically as the band reached a crescendo and the lights dimmed, only to be replaced by the flickering of a stroboscopic spot lamp as Madame Caoutchouc dashed into the ring clutching a fully-grown crocodile in her arms. She landed in the sawdust with the beast on top of her and for a moment or two it was hard to tell which way the struggle was going as they rolled around – a mass of threshing arms and legs. At first the flickering light seemed an unnecessary embellishment, but gradually it had a mesmerising effect. It was like watching a rapidly changing series of old-fashioned still pictures. First the crocodile was on top, then Madame Caoutchouc, then the crocodile again. Their positions changed almost faster than the eye or the brain could cope with. Finally, as the music reached a climax, Madame Caoutchouc managed to kneel astride the animal. Clasping it around the middle she gradually lifted it off the ground, centimetre by centimetre, until they were both upright. The tent went quiet as the crocodile thrashed to and fro, finally giving her a blow with its tail which would have floored most of those watching.

Monsieur Pamplemousse joined in the applause as Madame Caoutchouc at long last managed to extricate herself from the crocodile's grip, then forced its jaws open and placed her head inside its open mouth. Sooner her than him. The things some people did for a living; twice daily at that!

As she staggered from the ring, breathing heavily, the lights came up and the audience relaxed. A midget and another clown – an *Auguste*, the one with the red nose who always gets the custard pie – ran on and went through the age-old routine of balancing a bucket of water on the end of a pole. The shrieks as it fell off, threatening to soak those in the front row before they realised it was empty, were equalled only by the gales of laughter when a full bucket of water landed on the second clown. The rickety tiers supporting the audience swayed in sympathy. There was no gag like an old gag.

Half of him wondered if he should take the girl's note to the local police, but that would only involve a lot of tedious explanations. More than likely someone there would recognise him. They would want to know why he was in Port St. Augustin in the first place – by himself at that. It would all take up a lot more time than he could afford. The Director would not be pleased. The temptation to do a bit of ground work first was hard to resist. Afterwards he could decide on what action to take.

The clowns dashed off and were replaced by a girl doing handstands on the legs of an upturned table. The same girl repeated the trick to greater effect shortly afterwards on the back of one of the Arab ponies. Was she, he wondered, being groomed as a second Yasmin? She looked like a younger sister. Moments after her act was finished she joined the small band above the entrance to the ring, adding fife-playing to her other talents.

Madame Caoutchouc reappeared as the 'India-rubber Lady', distracting attention while a cage was erected by tying herself up in knots to the tune of 'Over the Waves', whilst at the same time making a cup of coffee.

She could have saved herself the trouble. The act which followed was something of an anti-climax. Neither the lion nor its temporary keeper made any pretence at going near each other. Perhaps they both suffered from bad breath.

Monsieur Pamplemousse found his attention wandering. Clearly it was a case of 'the show must go on', but it was a struggle. The barrel was being well and truly scraped and there was a feeling of sadness about it all.

He kept his seat during the interval, feeling that if he once got up he might not return. He wondered what on earth he was doing here anyway. Was it just the romantic notion of it all? Had he temporarily seen himself as d'Artagnan rescuing a damsel in distress? The combination of a pretty girl and the age-old lure of the circus. He corrected himself. The combination of a pretty girl, the lure of the circus and a desperate note. It was a case of locking the stable door after the horse had bolted, but he had to start somewhere.

There was something else that bothered him about the note. He took it out and read it again, even though he knew it by heart. It wasn't simply a plea for help, there was an underlying message in it for him as well. 'Take *great care.*' The last two words were even more heavily underlined than the earlier ones.

'*I must see you.* Please *do not come to me. I* will come to *you*, later tonight after the show. Take *great care!*'

It was almost as though she had wanted to tell him something, the knowledge of which would put him in some kind of danger too.

But there had been no 'after the show'. In fact, the more he thought about it the more convinced he became that Yasmin's fall had been no accident. It was too much of a coincidence. Perhaps she had been wrought up over something, perhaps it *had* been a momentary lack of concentration on her part. But even that didn't ring true. In his experience, when it came to the crunch, people working in jobs requiring total concentration were capable of switching off to everything else, including personal problems.

He wondered about the man he'd seen driving the van. He seemed to be the odd one out. 'The Great Christoph' was how he'd been billed when he'd done a brief 'strong-man' act halfway though the first half. Apart from that one appearance he'd neither played in the band nor shown his face since the opening parade.

The answer came towards the end of the second half of the programme and left him with a strange mixture of feelings. The newspaper report had made no mention of Yasmin having a partner and from the artist's impression on the poster he had assumed she was a solo act; it had really been a case of the eye reading what the brain expected it to see. It hadn't crossed his mind thee the man had also been part of her act.

A hush fell over the audience as the lights over the ring were dimmed and Christoph entered the ring and began climbing a rope hanging against one of the king-poles. It was the moment most of them had been waiting for.

No wonder the man had been keeping a low profile. It was hard to picture how he must be feeling at this moment, particularly if the accident had been the result of a row. There was no doubt in Monsieur Pamplemousse's mind that for whatever reason the girl had been avoiding her partner. Avoiding him, or ... avoiding him seeing her with anyone else.

He concentrated on the figure of Christoph as he reached a platform near the roof of the tent on the far side of the ring. Stripped to the waist, the gold cross dangling from his neck, he posed for a second or two while he regained his breath. Taking advantage of the moment, Monsieur Pamplemousse picked up his camera and zoomed in to as tight a shot as possible. The single spotlight produced a halo effect making it difficult to focus.

Perhaps it was a simple case of jealousy. Greeks were renowned for it, guarding what they considered to be their property even unto death.

He pressed the shutter six times, then Christoph made a gesture towards the ring. Another spotlight came on and a murmur went round the audience as it revealed the young girl standing at the foot of the opposite pole. It was followed almost immediately by a burst of applause as she took a quick bow and then began her climb, moving with lightness and ease, hand over hand, towards the top.

There was a low drum-roll as she unhitched a pole suspended from the roof by two ropes. It grew louder and louder as she climbed on and began to swing backwards and forwards towards her partner. There was a gasp from the audience, first of horror, then of relief as she appeared to slip and caught her heels on the pole at the very last moment, so that she was hanging upside down.

There was no doubt about it, they were both milking the situation for all it was worth. And why not? She deserved every ounce of applause for her courage. He glanced down at the ring. A group of men were standing round the safety-net. Their faces showed clearly the anxiety they felt as they followed her every movement to and fro.

Monsieur Pamplemousse slipped quietly from his seat and made his way out of the tent. It wasn't squeamishness. He simply wanted time to think, and he doubted very much if lightning would strike twice in the same place.

Outside the air was cool. There was a full moon and the sky was crowded with stars. The immediate area was totally deserted. Everyone must be inside watching the act. Another loud drum-roll sounded, followed by a burst of applause.

Almost without thinking he made his way back towards the caravan. Quite possibly, if Yasmin and the Great Christoph had formed themselves into an act, they also lived together. They might even be married. Literally putting your life in someone else's hands day in, day out, pre-supposed a closer than average relationship. But if that was the case, why had Yasmin sent the note? He still couldn't rid himself of the uneasy feeling that it had to do with something she had wished to keep from her partner.

The caravan was an American Barth. That accounted for the whine he had heard which would have come from the electrically operated steps. Even from the outside it looked as if it had everything and it probably did. A state-of-the-art multi-purpose aerial on the roof summed it all up. Again, why not? Travelling fairs and circuses were always an odd mixture of the tawdry and the up-to-date. Showmen were renowned for their caravans. It was where all the money went; an outward sign of success. The second lock on the door was a recent addition. It was French; a Vachette double cylinder multilock. Anyone breaking in would find it easier to cut a hole in the side of the caravan. There was mud on the steps, the same colour as that on the back of the blue van.

The blinds were lowered on all the side windows. Tinted glass around the driving compartment made it impossible to see inside.

Near the main door stood a portable waste-bin. It must belong to the local authorities, for it was of the same shape and dimensions as those along the promenade.

Working on the principle that it was often possible to learn more about a man in five minutes by going through his rubbish than an hour spent with him in the charge-room, he lifted the orange lid and shone his torch inside. The black polythene liner bag looked dry. Underneath a layer of old *journaux* there was an assortment of odds and ends, mostly female; old tights, make-up, several padded coat-hangers, a large bag of greyish powder – it could have been some kind of talcum. It looked as though someone had been having a good clear-out. He poked around for a moment or two longer, but it was a waste of time. There was far too much clutter.

Another, much longer burst of applause came from the direction of the circus tent. The band broke out into a loud march. It sounded as though the show was nearing its end.

Acting on the spur of the moment, he lifted the plastic bag out of the container and carried it out to the car. Accustomed though he was to his master's vagaries, Pommes Frites did not look best pleased when it landed on the seat beside him.

'*Surveille-le!*' Monsieur Pamplemousse gave him a quick pat, then hurried along the promenade in search of a suitable replacement bag.

It took him longer than he'd intended. The first two stank to high heaven, the third was nearly empty. He struck lucky at the fourth. A couple taking an evening stroll gave him an odd look when they saw what he was up to. He raised his hat and bade them a formal goodnight.

As he passed the car on his way back Monsieur Pamplemousse decided to risk Pommes Frites' displeasure once again by getting rid of the bag of ballast which was still on the back seat. Slipping the new polythene liner into the container outside the caravan, he stuffed the much-chewed bag in the bottom and covered it with some paper, plumping it up to give it more bulk. Then he closed the lid. It wasn't quite as good as he would have liked, but it was the best he could manage in the time.

By the time Monsieur Pamplemousse had finished the first of the audience were already hurrying out, anxious to reach their cars before the main rush. Lights began to come on all around him; engines roared.

He hovered for a moment or two, wondering whether to go back to his car or stay for a little while longer. He decided to stay. The fair was coming alive again. The trickle of people leaving the circus had turned into a flood, all pushing and jostling to be first. It would be some time before they dispersed.

He began to wish he'd brought Pommes Frites; at least it would have ensured a free passage through the mass of people. As it was, the very fact that he was going against the main stream was resented. Skirting round the outside of the crowd, he made his way past a row of caravans in the direction of the menhir. Almost immediately he regretted the decision. He'd been so intent on avoiding other people he failed to see a figure lurking under the trees. It was the old harridan he'd encountered earlier in the day. To his horror, as soon as she saw him coming she started to wave and began hurrying towards him.

Almost without thinking he made a dive between two of the caravans, turned sharp left at the far end and doubled back up the other side. Peering round the corner, he was just in time to see the wretched woman disappear down the route he had just taken. Clearly she wasn't giving up in a hurry. Given the incredible complications of her attire, she had a surprising turn of speed. If she kept going at her present rate, there wasn't a moment to lose.

If he took a chance and followed on behind he ran the risk of finding her lying in wait. If he tried mingling with the crowd and she caught up with him it could be even worse. He would get no sympathy; from the look of some of them they were much more likely to egg her on.

Seeing a light coming from Madame Caoutchouc's caravan he made a dive for the steps. Mounting them in one bound, he flung open the door, then closed it gently behind him. Remaining where he was for a moment or two, hardly daring to breathe, he put his ear to one of the panels. To his relief there was no pounding of feet, no sound of anyone approaching.

Relaxing a little, he let go of the door handle and took in his surroundings. The black curtains were now drawn back, turning what had in effect been a series of compartments into one large room. The little table just inside the door had gone and the crystal ball was now on top of the hi-fi. He could hear the sound of running water coming from behind the door he'd noticed that morning. Madame Caoutchouc must be having a well-earned shower. The crocheted counterpane on the bed was littered with the impedimenta of her act; unidentifiable garments covered with sequins, the cup and saucer and the coffee-maker she'd used in her act, a top hat, a white towelling dressing gown. The flowered dressing gown was lying discarded on the floor. On top of it was a whip.

To his right between the door and the sink unit was a small window. He was about to look out through a gap in the curtains when he heard the water in the shower being turned off. Abruptly the door at the far end swung open.

Madame Caoutchouc patently wasn't expecting visitors. When she caught sight of Monsieur Pamplemousse she stopped dead in her tracks and gave a gasp. Then, as she recognised him, she reached for the towelling dressing gown.

'What do you want? Didn't you see the *Fermé* notice? I am closed for the night.' She came towards him and reached for the door handle.

Monsieur Pamplemousse raised his hat. He decided to come clean. There was no great point in concocting a story.

'*Pardonnez-moi, Madame.* It is an inexcusable intrusion. The truth is, there is someone outside I would rather not see. If I may just check first ...' He motioned towards the window. 'I will not stay a moment longer than is necessary.'

'In that case I had better turn off the light, otherwise you will be seen.' Madame Caoutchouc essayed a brief and not altogether successful attempt at pulling her dressing-gown around her. Monsieur Pamplemousse averted his gaze and found himself looking at her image in the crystal ball. Her reflection as she reached for the switch near the door was distorted beyond belief.

'*Merci*. You are very kind.' He groped his way towards the window and slowly parted the curtains in the middle. The old woman was still there, skulking in the shadow of a nearby tree. From the way she was standing it looked as though she was quite prepared for a long wait.

He felt a large breast against his right shoulder. 'I can only see an old *clocharde*. Surely ...'

'That is the one.'

'*Oooh, là! là!* I understand why you would not wish to see her.' There was a slight pause for thought. 'Why did she pick on you?'

'I do not know. Perhaps it is my after-shave.' He meant it as a joke, but it immediately reminded him of the scent the old crone had left behind outside the restaurant. Until that moment it had slipped his memory.

He tried concentrating on the view outside, but it wasn't easy. For someone well into her prime, Madame Caoutchouc's breast was surprisingly, not to say disturbingly, firm. Perhaps wrestling with crocodiles was good for the mammary glands. She was also either supremely unaware of the fact – which he very much doubted – or she was being deliberately slow in removing it. It was not only surprisingly firm, it was also remarkably damp. In fact, he was conscious of creeping dampness all down his back, and he was about to let go of the curtain when he felt her stiffen. A moment later he realised why. Christoph had come into view. The old woman evidently saw him too, for she slunk back even deeper into the shadows as he went past.

Madame Caoutchouc also drew back as she followed his progress. '*Salaud!*' The word was spat out with surprising venom.

300

His interest roused, Monsieur Pamplemousse craned to see where Christoph was going. In an effort to get a better view he tried standing on a shadowy object on the floor below the window. It felt soft and yielding beneath his feet and he nearly lost his balance.

Something came up and hit the side of his leg. He tried to brush it away. It felt soft and clammy. Instinctively he drew back.

'*Merde!*'

'*Attendez!*' Madame Caoutchouc pulled him away from the window and bent down. '*Attention au crocodile!*'

'*Un crocodile!*' Monsieur Pamplemousse jumped in horror, hardly able to believe his ears.

Staggering back, he scrabbled at empty air, then toppled forward, colliding with Madame Caoutchouc as she stood up. As he clutched at her he felt himself enveloped in a damp but heady mixture compounded of flesh and fabric. It was so sudden and unexpected it was all he could do to stay upright. He was vaguely aware of making a futile grab for his hat as it slid off the back of his head – the more bizarre the situation the more man clung to the most trivial of possessions – then there was a crash of breaking glass as they collided with the table and the vase of flowers went flying. Spinning away from it, they hovered uncertainly in the middle of the caravan, then landed on the bed in a panting heap of twisted arms and legs.

He tried desperately to disentangle himself, but his body seemed to be held in place by a vice-like grip from which there was no escape. It was like a bad dream. Arms encircled him. Toes dug into his spine. Toes – or was it the coffee pot? Perhaps even – heaven forbid – perhaps even the crocodile – it was hard to tell. He had temporarily lost all feeling.

Nothing Madame Caoutchouc had done in the circus ring could possibly have prepared him for the complexity of their present arrangements. Had he been forewarned he might have been better prepared. Like a swimmer about to attempt a swallow dive from the high board, he would have filled his lungs with sufficient life-giving air to enable him to surface unharmed. As it was, all the breath had been squeezed out of him during the first few moments of their embrace and his lungs were now so tightly compressed the prospect of refilling them seemed remote in the extreme.

He called out and heard a thin voice remarkably unlike his own somewhere in the distance. There was a tramp of feet and then other voices too; voices he didn't recognise, uttering imprecations and oaths. Cries of '*Quelle horreur!*' and 'She has had an attack of her old complaint!' impinged on his brain. Hands reached out, grasping at anything within reach, in a vain attempt to pull them apart.

At the height of it all there was a loud banging sound. It seemed to be coming from outside the caravan. Irrationally it occurred to him that it might even be the old woman. The one he had been trying to escape from. It would be an ironic twist of fate if she came to his rescue, but by that time he hardly cared.

The knocking ceased and there was a blinding flash of light. It was followed by a familiar voice calling out his name. He told himself it wasn't possible. It had to be part of some dreadful nightmare from which he would wake at any moment. But as he twisted his head round to look his heart sank. Patently his senses had not entirely deserted him. His worst fears had been realised.

'*Incroyable!*' In his delivery of that one word the Director managed to convey a variety of thoughts and emotions: shock, disbelief, reprehension, condemnation – a

302

shorter word would hardly have sufficed. Pommes Frites, who was standing beside him, very wisely remained silent.

'*Monsieur le Directeur, bonsoir! Comment ça va?*' Fearful of getting a crick in his neck, Monsieur Pamplemousse lay back and having delivered himself of such pleasantries as he could manage in the circumstances, sought refuge behind the fleshy ramparts of Madame Caoutchouc.

Carefully avoiding a large breast suspended perilously close to his right eye, he took in the scene above and around him. It was one which would have caused Degas, that occasional chronicler of circus life, to reach hastily for his brush, lest he miss a golden opportunity which might never repeat itself. Although, given the confined space of the caravan, even he might have paused for a moment in order to wonder if it was too crowded a scene for his canvas.

The semi-naked figure of a woman astride a man lying on a bed; a midget dressed as a clown tugging at her left arm, a bearded lady tugging at her right; discarded sequin-covered garments strewn about the floor; and in the foreground, its mouth open wide as though it, too, could hardly believe its eyes … a rubber crocodile.

'You may well hide your face in shame, Pamplemousse,' boomed the Director. 'I knew from the tenor of our conversation on the telephone yesterday that something was amiss, but little did I dream as I was journeying down here today, nor when I came across your car parked on the esplanade, that I would find you in this … this …' For once the Director was at a loss for words.

Looking around the caravan his gaze alighted on the crystal ball. 'It does not need the services of a soothsayer, Pamplemousse, to deduce that your future looks black, very

303

black indeed. Perhaps, when you can tear yourself away, and when you have a spare moment, you would care to take a look in that ball yourself and tell me what you see. You are one of my most trusted employees, here on a mission of utmost importance, a mission, the outcome of which I need hardly say, affects us all. And what do I find? You are so engrossed in satisfying the desires of the flesh you cannot even bother to observe the basic courtesies of life by standing when I enter the room. I shall await your pleasure at the Ty Coz.'

Monsieur Pamplemousse took a deep breath and poked his head out again. 'One moment, *Monsieur. I* can explain it all ...'

But the Director had already stalked out. One by one the others crept silently after him until only Pommes Frites and Madame Caoutchouc were left; the one out of loyalty, the other for reasons best known to herself.

Pommes Frites looked somewhat aggrieved; not so much with those around him as with the injustice of the world in general. In tracking his master down, in sniffing out his trail amongst all the others and following it to the bitter end, he'd only been doing what he thought was a good deed. Praise would normally have been his due. As it was he sensed that for the second time that day he had put his foot in it, and on this occasion not just one, but all four. His master didn't look best pleased. It really wasn't fair, but as he knew all too well from past experience, the Goddess in charge of fairness did not bestow her bounties in any logical order, but scattered them far and wide in random fashion. For a brief moment he was tempted to give the piece of anatomy nearest to him a conciliatory lick, but he thought better of it. Without the benefit of a closer inspection, it was hard to tell which bits belonged to his master and which belonged to his companion of the moment.

Having decided that praise was not to be his lot, and keeping a wary eye on the crocodile, Pommes Frites settled himself down to await developments. No doubt things would sort themselves out in due course. They usually did.

'*C'est un trouduc!*'

'Now, *Madame*,' Monsieur Pamplemousse hoped the Director hadn't lingered outside. He doubted whether he would like hearing himself being called a silly old fart. He made another attempt to break free. 'Perhaps you could release me?'

'I am sorry, *Monsieur*. That is not possible.'

'Not possible! What do you mean, not possible?'

'It is as Emilio said, I have an attack of my old complaint. It happens occasionally. The last time was in Lille. It is a kind of a seizure, a form of cramp.'

'Cramp?' repeated Monsieur Pamplemousse. 'An india-rubber woman with cramp?'

'It is what the doctors call un *risque du metier*: an occupational hazard. I am not as young as I used to be. I think perhaps it is the sea air. The damp has entered my bones.'

'How long do they last, these attacks?'

'Poof!' Monsieur Pamplemousse wished he hadn't asked. Clearly, Madame Caoutchouc's thought processes involved physical as well as mental effort. He waited for the heaving to stop.

'Sometimes only a few minutes. Sometimes for several hours. In Lille it lasted all one night!'

All one night! In Lille! It was tempting to suggest that if she was so good at looking into the future the least she could do would be to sort out when he would be free, but that would have been unkind. The pain under his right shoulder was getting worse. Wriggling his left arm free he managed to twist round and feel between himself and the bedding. He withdrew a large cylindrical metal object.

'If you have a match,' said Madame Caoutchouc, 'I could make you some *café*. It would mean boiling a kettle. The *café* I make in the ring is only a trick. We could roll to the *cuisine* together.'

'I think not, *merci*.' He could envisage many more profitable ways of spending the next ten minutes than by waiting for a kettle to boil – especially with Pommes Frites looking on, watching their every move. He suddenly didn't feel thirsty any more.

'You could tell me what first gave you the idea for a crocodile made of rubber,' he suggested.

'Have you tried keeping a real crocodile, *Monsieur*?'

He shook his head.

'It is not easy in a caravan.'

As a statement of fact it was unanswerable.

'The lighting was my late husband's idea.'

'It works very well. I would never have known.'

As conversation lapsed once again, Monsieur Pamplemousse allowed his mind to drift. He wondered if he should suggest turning on the radio, but that would also involve moving. He couldn't even ask if she had read any good books lately.

'Cramp is a question of tensions.' Madame Caoutchouc was the first to speak. 'Sometimes, when things are going badly, I feel them coming on.'

'I understand.'

Monsieur Pamplemousse relaxed. Despite everything, he felt a great tenderness come over him. 'The greatest pains,' he said gently, 'are those you cannot tell others about. Perhaps what you need most of all at this moment is to relieve your tensions.'

Madame Caoutchouc looked around. 'If only I could reach my whip,' she said. 'I might be able to turn out the light.'

Monsieur Pamplemousse caught Pommes Frites' eye. He pointed towards the floor. 'I know a magic word:

'Fetch!'

Pommes Frites rose to his feet. Ever alive to the needs of others, anxious to make amends for past mistakes, he had the self-satisfied air of a dog who knew that if he waited long enough his hour would come. It was not for him to reason why his master should want to share his bed with a rubber crocodile.

Monsieur Pamplemousse heaved a deep sigh as something cold and slimy landed by his side. All the signs pointed to the fact that it was going to be a very long night.

6
THE MORNING AFTER

It was some time after dawn when Monsieur Pamplemousse finally woke. The sun was streaming in through a gap in the curtains. He looked at his watch. It showed just after seven o'clock. Moving gently so as not to disturb the figure beside him, he started to get dressed. By rights he should have felt terrible, but in fact he had slept soundly for several hours; the best sleep he'd had for a long time. Before then they had both talked far into the night. Talk had induced relaxation, and relaxation had brought with it release followed by oblivion.

Pommes Frites stirred, opened one eye to observe his master at work, then stood up and noisily shook himself. The sound woke Madame Caoutchouc.

'You are going?'

Monsieur Pamplemousse looked at her reflection in the mirror as he finished straightening his tie. 'I must.'

'You won't stay for a *café*?'

He shook his head. 'I have a lot of work to get through.' There would be a good deal of explaining to do as well and he was anxious to get back to the hotel before the Director was up and about. All that apart, without wishing to offend Madame Caoutchouc, he didn't want to be seen leaving the fairground, let alone her caravan. For no particular reason he had a sudden mental picture of Doucette waiting for him outside. It reminded him that he had not yet posted her a card.

Madame Caoutchouc reached up and took hold of his hand as he crossed to the bed. 'Then I shall not see you again?'

'Who knows? It is a small world.' He was tempted to embroider his reply with promises he knew he had no intention of keeping; to visit the circus in another town perhaps, but he thought better of it.

She pulled his hand towards her and held it for a brief moment against her breast, then lifted it higher still, looking first at his thumb, then at each of the fingers in turn.

'Your thumb shows strength and determination. It also shows you can be stubborn.'

Monsieur Pamplemousse remembered now. Like the Chinese and Indians, Gypsies placed great store on the thumb, as indeed did many Christians. To them it was a symbol of God.

'Yet the joints of your fingers are well formed, which means you are thoughtful and seek harmony. You also have a strong sense of justice. It is an interesting hand.'

She ran a finger slowly across the palm of his hand. 'You have a long life line – but take care.'

'I always take care. Life becomes more finite and therefore more precious the older one gets.'

'If you were staying longer I could tell your fortune.'

'I think I would rather not know. To be aware of one's character by the star sign is one thing. That I believe in. But to try and look into the future is something else again. It is like a mother knowing the sex of her unborn child.'

He raised her hand to his lips. Her fingers felt warm and pliant. He gave them a squeeze. '*Au revoir.*'

'*Au revoir*, and *merci*.'

Halfway across the site he turned to look back and saw her wave. The curtains were still drawn in Christoph's

309

caravan. A few workers clearing up the site gave him curious glances as he left.

The tide was out and the beach was almost deserted. Someone was exercising a dog at the far end. A small boy was out with his father trying unsuccessfully to fly a kite. Halfway along, a man was raking the sand smooth outside a beach café. A few fishermen were digging for worms. Two nuns taking an early morning stroll watched as he made his way down some steps. For some reason best known to themselves they made the sign of the cross. One of them whispered something behind her hand and the other laughed.

Pommes Frites galloped across the gleaming wet sand, sniffed the sea, then came running back, full of the joys of summer. Monsieur Pamplemousse picked up a piece of driftwood and threw it for him.

He now felt he knew all there was to know about circuses; in particular the Circus Bretagno; how it started, its family history, where they had been to, where they were going and where they had planned to go before the accident; the cost of keeping a show on the road; the dramas and scandals.

Of Christoph he knew very little more, other than that he came from one of the Greek islands and had arrived on the scene just over a year ago looking for work. They had been in Italy at the time. Madame Caoutchouc had been widowed only a few months earlier and was finding the task of running a circus by herself more than she could cope with. People needed to be paid, bookings made, advertisements placed. To be sure she had the children, Yasmin and her younger sister, but they already had more than enough on their plate. The prospect of another man to help out – an intelligent one at that – seemed heaven-sent.

At first everything in the circus had been lovely. He was tall, dark, handsome, with a mop of black, curly hair, and the inevitable happened; in a very short space of time Yasmin had fallen head over heels in love. Christoph proposed to her, and soon afterwards they were married between shows in Trieste. The BMW had been a wedding gift; the caravan arrived soon after. He'd turned up with it out of the blue shortly after the honeymoon. Any misgivings Madame Caoutchouc might have felt she kept to herself, especially when he gave her the hi-fi. It had become her pride and joy.

Pommes Frites returned with the wood. Monsieur Pamplemousse threw it for him again, further this time. It landed with a splash in a hollow left by the outgoing tide.

It wasn't until some time after the wedding that things started to go wrong. Christoph had begun to show signs of moodiness, often disappearing for days at a time. In any other job that would have been bad enough, but in the circus it was unforgivable. When he was there he threw his weight around, which gave rise to ill-feeling. He also began interfering in other ways, criticising their itinerary and going into sulks if it wasn't altered to suit him. Their present booking was typical. By rights the circus should still be in the Ardennes, not reaching Brittany until August when the holiday season would be at its peak. But once again he had got his way.

What was the phrase she had used? It was the reverse of 'you could drop him in a pig-sty and he would still come up smelling of roses'; rather, 'you could cover him with honey and he would still smell of tar'. There was obviously no love lost between them. Rightly or wrongly she was blaming him for Yasmin's accident.

Calling Pommes Frites to heel, Monsieur Pamplemousse made his way back to the car. The plastic bag was still on the back seat. It was probably too obvious what it was for anyone to bother stealing it. Thankfully, he had left the

311

camera tucked underneath it out of sight.

As they drove past the Quai Général de Gaulle he caught sight of a small group of fishermen already hard at work repairing their blue sardine nets. Others were attending to their lobster pots. They were probably all well fortified with an early-morning *marc* or two. He wouldn't have minded joining them.

At the Ty Coz he parked in the same space between the two large English cars, but once again his hopes of slipping into the hotel unobserved were doomed. The main door was still locked. The owner himself appeared in response to the bell. He eyed the plastic bag over Monsieur Pamplemousse's shoulder with some disfavour.

'*Petit déjeuner* is not until *huit heures*.'

'That,' said Monsieur Pamplemousse with some asperity, 'is why we have brought our own. We are both very hungry.' It was a cheap joke, but it made him feel better as he turned and crossed the hall. He should have asked for two plates. Half expecting to find the Director lying in wait for him, he hurried up the stairs to his room.

Bathed and shaved, he spread some paper over the bed and emptied the plastic bag over the top. Spread out, the contents looked even more of a jumble. There was something slightly depressing about handling someone else's personal belongings; it felt like an intrusion. Shoes were somehow especially evocative. One by one he put everything back into the bag until he was left with a few items of interest: several lengths of wire – multi-stranded in a variety of colours – of the kind that came in flat ribbons and was used in electronic equipment, a plain white packet containing the remains of some whitish flakes, a small plain paper bag which had once contained some white powder (he tried some between his fingers and it felt like chalk), an unused length of multi-core solder, several more pieces of sawn-off fibreglass – similar to the piece he had found on his first visit to the circus – the larger bag of greyish powder he'd come across the previous evening, two paint brushes (although the bristles had gone hard on the outside they had both been used recently and looked as though they had been bought for the job – the metal round the base of the handle was still shiny), and a small unlabelled screw-capped bottle containing traces of a colourless liquid.

Before Monsieur Pamplemousse had a chance to sniff the contents of the bottle there was a knock on the door. Hastily gathering up the remains of the things on the bed, he put them into a drawer in his beside cabinet. He was only just in time. There was an impatient rattle of the handle, then the door opened.

It was the Director. He was dressed in his yachting outfit: matching dark blue hat and blazer, the latter sporting buttons bearing the Christian Dior motif, white shirt with a knotted scarf in lighter blue, and matching two-tone blue and white rubber-soled shoes. A vision of sartorial elegance, his expression as he gazed around the room was a mixture of surprise and distaste.

'Pamplemousse, don't tell me your salary is so inadequate you have to resort to sifting through the contents of a garbage bag before you are able to face the world?'

Monsieur Pamplemousse resisted the temptation to say 'yes'. He had no wish to upset the apple-cart quite so early in the day.

'I was looking for a bone for Pommes Frites, *Monsieur,*' he said simply. 'Like me, he hasn't entirely taken to *La Cuisine Régionale Naturelle.*' *He* tried to avoid Pommes Frites' gaze as he uttered the words. It wasn't easy. Pommes Frites had an uncanny knack of knowing when he was avoiding the truth.

'Ah, yes.' The Director barely registered the reply. He seemed slightly ill at ease.

Monsieur Pampiemousse waited for the blasting which he felt could be heading his way. But either sleep had worked wonders, or second thoughts had prevailed. He strongly suspected the latter. With only a day to go before the launch the Director wouldn't want to run the risk of his walking out on the whole operation. His next remark was mild in the extreme.

'I suggest, Aristide, that if you feel up to it we drive into town and take our *petit déjeuner* at one of those little cafés near the port.'

'*Monsieur* would not prefer to stay in the hotel? I understood it was highly recommended.'

'No, Pamplemousse, I think not. It is a lovely morning and I'm sure the fresh air will do us both the world of good.'

Monsieur Pamplemousse followed the Director out of the hotel, deposited the plastic bag in the back of his 2CV, then held open the rear door of the Director's car so that Pommes Frites could climb in.

Pommes Frites gazed round approvingly while his master got into the front seat, then he settled himself down in order to make the most of things while they lasted. Soft music issued from a loudspeaker by his ear; music as soft in its way as the leather beneath him.

'*Au revoir, à bientôt.*' The Director replaced a telephone receiver and switched on the ignition. The engine purred into life. He glanced across at Monsieur Pamplemousse. 'Work, Aristide. Work must go on. I have just telephoned headquarters to tell them to stand by for further instructions. Time is disappearing rapidly. It is Thursday already.'

Monsieur Pamplemousse made a suitable noise in reply.

The picture of everyone standing by their office desks was not an easy one to focus on. Even more difficult, for experience told him where the conversation was leading, was finding a suitable answer to what he knew would be the next question. He wondered whether it would come on the journey into Port St. Augustin, or during *petit déjeuner* itself. Guessing it was likely to be the latter he closed his eyes and concentrated his mind, hoping he wouldn't be disturbed before inspiration came his way. His hopes did not go unrewarded. Hardly had they left Ty Coz than the telephone rang and the Director was once again immersed in his problems. This time it had to do with some printing technicality. It was a welcome diversion.

At a little café by the harbour they ordered *jus d'orange* and *café* for two.- After some deliberation, Monsieur Pamplemousse chose a *pain au sucre* and a *brioche* for himself and a *pain au chocolat* for Pommes Frites. The Director called for a plate of *croissants*. Then, remembering his diet, reluctantly changed the order to one.

After the rain, everything looked clean and newly washed. The cars had not yet started to arrive. The only sound came from a few seagulls wheeling and diving overhead as they greeted the arrival of a fishing boat. Further along the *quai* the men were still repairing their nets.

Blissfully unaware that his symbol in *Le Guide* was at stake – a bar stool indicating above-average food and service – the *patron* won bonus points for bringing fresh orange juice without being asked. He gained several more when he returned a moment later carrying a bowl of water for Pommes Frites. There were two ice cubes floating on the surface. It was good to have their judgement confirmed.

The Director waited until the crunching had died down, then he cleared his throat.

'Ah, Pamplemousse, this is the life.'

'*Oui, Monsieur.*' Monsieur Pamplemousse broke a *brioche* in two and automatically handed the other half down below the table top. He felt a comforting wet nose, then both disappeared.

'It is a pity, Pamplemousse, that life cannot always be *croissants* and *café.*'

'*Oui, Monsieur.*'

'And circuses.'

'*Oui, Monsieur.*'

A look of slight irritation flitted across the Director's face as he realised that he was to get no help whatsoever. Draining his cup, he dabbed at his lips with a paper serviette and embarked on a different course.

'Tell me, Aristide, in between bouts of ...' Monsieur Pamplemousse sat and listened respectfully while the Director broke into a series of whistles and grunts which were clearly meant to embrace a multitude of sins, most of which were impossible to put into words. 'Did you ... er, did you manage to give any thought to the matter in hand?'

Monsieur Pamplemousse breathed a sigh of relief. The assault he had feared was not about to materialise. 'I thought of very little else, *Monsieur.*'

The Director looked at him uneasily, clearly wondering whether or not he had been misunderstood. 'I suppose,' he continued after a suitable pause, 'that in time one gets a little blasé. What, may I ask, were your conclusions?'

Monsieur Pamplemousse placed the tips of his fingers together, forming a steeple with his hands which reflected that of the nearby parish church. He closed his eyes. The sun felt warm to his face, reminding him that he should take care. He was not by nature a sun-worshipper.

'If I may say so, *Monsieur*, your menu was a work of art.'

'You think so, Aristide?' The Director sounded better pleased.

'*Oui Monsieur*. It was like a noble wine. It had ...' Monsieur Pamplemousse paused for a moment while he sought the right words. 'It had completeness and roundness and fullness. It had flavour; rich without being cloying, it had finesse.' He wondered for a moment if he was overdoing things, but the Director's next words dispelled any such doubts.

'Then you think we should go ahead, Aristide?'

'*Non, Monsieur*.' He braced himself. It was the *moment critique*. 'With the greatest respect, I think the answer has to be *non*. It would, in its way, be too perfect.' Another way of putting it would be that with such a weight of food on board, the dirigible would never leave the ground, but he resisted the temptation. It was a moment for tact.

'Such a meal should be reserved for another, perhaps even greater, occasion: a State Banquet *par exemple*. It should not, indeed *must not*, be wasted. The great problem as I see it is that with so many other things to occupy their minds, the guests may not give it their undivided attention. They would be placed in a constant state of dilemma. It would be sacrilege to allow the *langouste* or the *canard* to grow cold, but supposing, just supposing at the very moment of their being served, the dirigible happened to be passing over somewhere like Josselin, with its magnificent castle, or crossing the Côte d'Emeraude ... It would be a tragedy if in enjoying *Les Six Gloires de la France Culinaire* they had to forgo some of the glories which lie beneath.'

He could tell by the silence that his point had gone home.

'You are quite right, Pamplemousse. I must confess that in the excitement of composition that point had escaped me.'

There was another, even longer silence.

'Do you have any suggestions, Aristide?'

'I have been giving the matter a great deal of considera-
tion, *Monsieur*.' It was true. All the way down from the hotel
he had thought of little else.

'Given all that I have just said, and bearing in mind that
space is strictly limited, I feel our keynote should be
simplicity. That simplicity, *Monsieur*, which is synonymous
with the quiet good taste and that dedication to perfection
for perfection's sake, which has always been a hallmark of *Le
Guide*.

'I suggest we start with some smoked salmon from Scot-
land.'

'*Saumon fumé?*'

'*Oui, Monsieur.*'

'From *Ecosse* rather than from France?'

'*Oui, Monsieur.*'

The Director gave a snort. 'Then one thing is certain,
Pamplemousse. The view from the dirigible will not be
wasted. I must say I am a little disappointed.'

'*Monsieur*, again with respect, the eyes of the world will
be upon us, and it will be seen as a gesture of good will, an
example of that lack of chauvinism for which we French are
renowned. That apart, in my humble opinion there is little to
equal *saumon* which has been *fumé* over a peat fire in Scot-
land. It is their one great contribution to the world of *cuisine*
and more than makes up for haggis.

'It will, of course, need to be wild *saumon*, pink from
feeding on shellfish and not from some chemical colouring
agent in their food pellets. I am told much of the *saumon* we
eat these days is farmed and that there are people who have
never actually tasted the real thing. And with it, some lemon
juice and a little fresh bread with butter from Normandy. The
whole washed down with a suitable chilled champagne,

perhaps a bottle or two of Gosset.'

'And then?'

Detecting overtones of gathering interest in the Director's voice, Monsieur Pamplemousse pressed home his advantage.

'You mentioned Fauchon at one point in your letter, *Monsieur*. It was in connection with the dessert. May I ask how many times you have tried to walk past their windows in the Place de la Madeleine and failed in the attempt, your attention caught by some exquisite arrangement of delicacies: a *tableau* of crabs and *pâtés* in one window, *terrines* and hams in another; *soufflés* juxtaposed with *fraises des bois* in a third? In short, all the ingredients for a picnic the like of which could not be assembled anywhere else in the world, and all of them but a telephone call away.'

'A picnic, Aristide?' Opening one eye, Monsieur Pamplemousse was just in time to catch the Director licking his lips. He had suspected as much. 'That is an excellent idea. Simple, and yet so right; in keeping with the spirit of the enterprise itself. And you would finish the meal how?'

'*Monsieur*, a good meal is like a well-written story. Interest has to be captured as early as possible, the main part should be satisfying, and the ending should be on a high note leaving the reader both happy and yet wishing for more. Replete, yet still hungry.'

'One moment, Aristide. Before we go any further – ' The Director clicked his fingers for the waiter. 'Another *pain au sucre*? Or a *brioche*? I think I may indulge in a further *croissant* myself. All this talk of food is making me feel hungry. No doubt Pommes Frites could toy with a second *pain au chocolat*?'

'He has never let me down yet, *Monsieur*.'

'*Encore!*' With a single grand gesture, the Director managed to embrace the whole of their erstwhile breakfast.

The fishing boat was starting to unload its catch; baskets full of sea-bass and sole landed on the *quai*, others were filled with a mixture of oddities. A few gnarled faces gathered in a small group to watch. A nun on a *Vélocette* drew up outside the P.T.T. and went inside. A car with a sailing boat in tow went past and disappeared onto the beach. Far out to sea a small flotilla of boats from the sailing school lay becalmed, waiting with resignation for the wind to freshen. Nothing in life was perfect.

'Now, Pamplemousse,' the Director could hardly conceal his impatience as the waiter disappeared again. 'Tell me about your *pièce de resistance*, your *coup de maître*.'

'It is a dish, *Monsieur*, which Madame Pamplemousse reserves for special occasions. It is called *Sabayon aux Pêches*. It is both simple and elegant and although it only requires the simplest of apparatus, there is a certain theatricality about its preparation which always heightens the effect.

'First, fresh ripe peaches are cooked in water to which sugar and the juice of half a lemon has been added. When they are tender, the skin is removed and each peach is placed in a large Cognac balloon.

'The *Sabayon is* made with a mixture of egg yolks and sugar, to which some liqueur have been added – Madame Pamplemousse always uses Marsala, but others prefer Grand Marnier or apricot brandy or even champagne. It should be whisked by hand in a *bain-marie* over a low heat until the mixture begins to ribbon, then left to simmer. At the appropriate moment it is reheated and whisked again until it fluffs up into the consistency of softly whipped cream. Then it is spooned over the peaches and served. The result, Monsieur, is pure ambrosia. It never fails to bring forth gasps of admiration, especially when accompanied by a glass of Sauternes. I would suggest a Château d'Yquem. It would, perhaps, be too much to hope for a 1904 – the year in which *entente cordiale* was born – but that was a great vintage and it would be a beautiful ending to the meal.'

'Aristide,' under the pretence of removing a speck of dust from his right eye, the Director wiped away the suspicion of a tear, 'words fail me. I have to admit that when I first arrived down here I began to entertain severe doubts concerning the wisdom of entrusting you with this mission. I had almost decided to take charge of the operation myself. But all is forgiven. It is easy enough to strike a note when asked, but to hit exactly the right one at precisely the right moment is another matter entirely. It requires that touch of God-given genius which few of us are lucky enough to possess. Leave the wine to me. In the meantime I will send for Madame Pamplemousse at once.'

Monsieur Pamplemousse gave a start. 'I hardly think that will be necessary, *Monsieur*.' The thought of Doucette arriving in Port St. Augustin filled him with alarm, especially while the circus was still in town. She might even want to be taken there. Innocent though his encounter with Madame Caoutchouc had been – a case of cause and effect – explanations would not be easy should it come to light.

'Come, come, Aristide. You said yourself that the dish is one of her specialities. Simple though you make it sound, we cannot afford to have things go wrong. Eggs can curdle; pans can catch fire. To end on a low note would be little short of disaster. We must take no risks.'

'I think, *Monsieur*, that if you send for Madame Pamplemousse you will be taking a very grave risk indeed. Curdled eggs could be the least of your problems. Madame Pamplemousse has never flown before and if she found herself in a dirigible cooking for Heads of State she might well go to pieces.'

'Then whom do we ask, Pamplemousse? As I have already told you, Bocuse is in Japan, Vergé is in America. Time is not on our side.'

For the second time that morning Monsieur Pamplemousse closed his eyes as he sought inspiration, and once again luck did not desert him.

'On my way down, *Monsieur*,' he said, after a moment's pause, 'Pommes Frites and I made a small detour ...'

The Director listened intently while Monsieur Pamplemousse described his meal, only occasionally interjecting over some technical detail or asking for elaboration of a particular dish.

'I think,' said Monsieur Pamplemousse, when he had finished describing his jam omelette for the fourth time, 'to have such a person in charge of the *cuisine* will not only be a *plume* in our *chapeau* – for he is a name as yet undiscovered by our rivals – it will also be living proof of that great strength which is France; the miracle that right across our land, in the cities and in the smallest villages, such talent exists as naturally and as unremarked as the fact that day follows night.'

'Pamplemousse, I have said it all before. To repeat it would be an embarrassment, but if you are doing nothing for *déjeuner* today we could meet and you could tell me about it all over again.

'There is also the matter of the circus. You may not wish to talk about it of course, and if so, I fully understand. I will respect your wishes to the full. But I must confess it kept me awake a good deal during the night. Images kept forming in my mind.

'I have always considered myself a man of the world. Not, of course, as experienced as your good self in the more esoteric pursuits, but we all have different tastes. It would be a very dull place if we didn't.

'Tell me, Aristide, was she ... er ... was she very ... *pneumatique*? Presumably she is not called *Madame Caoutchouc* for nothing.'

'She is a little like a child's india-rubber, *Monsieur*. She has both a hard and a soft side.'

The Director nodded. 'And the crocodile?'

'That too, was surprisingly pliable.'

'How strange. It is a variation I had not heard of before. Visits to the zoo with my young nephew will never seem quite the same again.'

'I doubt, *Monsieur*, if I shall ever look a crocodile straight in the eye again either.'

Monsieur Pamplemousse replied absentmindedly. Withdrawing the Leitz Trinovid binoculars from his jacket pocket, he trained them on a distant figure at the far end of the promenade. As the image came into sharp focus he jumped to his feet.

'*Merde!*'

'*Pardon*, Pamplemousse?' The Director looked startled.

'I am afraid, *Monsieur*, *déjeuner* will not be possible after all. There is work to be done. I must telephone Fauchon; also the chef I was telling you about. There is the printing of the menu to be arranged. Facilities for the *cuisine* must be organised.'

'The telephone in my car is at your disposal, Aristide.' The Director felt in his pocket for the keys.

'With respect, *Monsieur*,' Monsieur Pamplemousse glanced anxiously along the promenade – the old hag was getting nearer – 'they will all take time. I think it will be cheaper in the long run if I make them from a call box. I will get myself a new *carte*.'

'Ah, Aristide,' the Director tempered his obvious disappointment with a beam of approval. 'If only Madame Grante were with us now to hear you say that. I am sure she would …' He broke off and gazed in horror at the approaching figure. 'Pamplemousse, that person is waving at us! Don't tell me, I can scarcely credit it. Is there no end to your intrigues?'

'I think it must be you she is after, *Monsieur*. Perhaps she is in need of a lift.'

Oblivious to the Director's protestations Monsieur Pamplemousse signalled to Pommes Frites and together they hastened along the *quai* in the direction of the shopping precinct. It wasn't until they reached the safety of the shadows from the overhanging gables that he paused to see if they were being followed. Slipping into a shop doorway, he turned and looked back the way they had come, but the old woman was nowhere in sight. Perhaps even now she was importuning the Director.

There were occasions when retreat was definitely the better part of valour, and the present situation was one of them. Besides, the walk back to the hotel would do them both good and there was a lot to think about, not the least of which was the contents of the drawer in his room. Another trip to Nantes was indicated. After that? Who knew? It would all depend on the report of the chemist. Unless he was very much mistaken he had come across the classic recipe for manufacturing knock-out pills.

7
THE BALLOON GOES UP

The National Anthems of both countries had been played by a contingent from the French naval base at St. Nazaire, the parade had been reviewed, formal greetings had been exchanged in front of the dirigible for the benefit of the world's television cameras. A small group of children from a local school, dressed in traditional costume, performed a brief dance. Afterwards, a red, white and blue bouquet made up of poppies, cornflowers and marguerites was presented by the smallest child to the visiting Head of State. A battery of press photographers had recorded the event for posterity. Speeches of congratulation had been made, hopes for the future expressed, comparisons drawn between the present flight and that of an early pioneer, Monsieur Le Brix, an aviator from the Morbihan who in 1927, along with a Monsieur Costes, was the first to fly around the world.

Now, as lesser mortals withdrew to watch from a safe distance, the party got ready to board the airship. The ground crew, their white overalls immaculately pressed for the occasion, took the strain on the mooring ropes, although with only the lightest of breezes blowing it was scarcely necessary. The windsock hung limply from its pole, as did the flags of France and *Grande-Bretagne*.

Monsieur Pamplemousse could see Commander Winters and Capitaine Leflaix watching anxiously from their cabin window as more photographs were taken, this time of the two leaders posing in turn at the top of the aluminium steps. Capitaine Leflaix would not be pleased; they were facing outwards. No doubt both he and Commander Winters would be glad when they were airborne. At least their illustrious passengers were in for a better flight than he'd had to endure. Apart from a few wisps of strato-cumulus to the south the sky was totally blue. He almost envied them the experience.

Not for the first time that morning, Monsieur Pamplemousse found his attention wandering. He had woken with a curious feeling in the pit of his stomach that all was not well. Pommes Frites, ever sensitive to his master's moods, had obviously caught it too. From the moment they arrived at the airstrip he had been twitchy. When he caught sight of the balloon he became even more ill at ease, no doubt fearing another parting of the ways. Monsieur Pamplemousse bent down and gave him a reassuring pat.

He cast his eyes round the field as he did so. Security was as tight now as it had been lax a few days before. There were police and guards everywhere, their guns at the ready, walkie-talkies working overtime. A dozen familiar dark blue vans of the *Sûreté Nationale* were parked discreetly under the trees. As always, those behind the barred windows, having been kept in a state of enforced idleness for many hours, would be more than ready to wade in and take it out on those nearest to hand should anything untoward happen to mar the occasion.

The crowd of sightseers had been carefully selected; representatives of local government in their best clothes; heads of fish and vegetable canneries mingled with their workers. Nurses in uniform stood alongside patients in wheelchairs; boilermakers from St. Nazaire hobnobbed with building workers. A group of ubiquitous nuns kept themselves slightly apart from the rest, as was their wont.

Monsieur Pamplemousse had a lot on his mind. Like Commander Winters and his crew, he couldn't wait for the take-off so that he could get down to other matters. His suspicions about the contents of the envelope had been confirmed by a chemist in Nantes. The bottle contained the remains of some ethyl-chlorate; the white powder was calcium carbonate – common chalk; the flakes were traga-canth – commonly used as a binding agent. In short, all the necessary ingredients for manufacturing knock-out pills. The question was, had Christoph given one to Yasmin? And if he had, why ?

If she'd been given one before the performance it would almost certainly have brought on sleepiness. Had he perhaps miscalculated the dose? Perhaps he had been hoping it would take effect sooner than it did; that was the charitable explanation. But even so, the very fact of going to the trouble of making the pills in the first place suggested something more than a spur of the moment act.

There was still a query hanging over the light-grey powder in the plastic bag.

Monsieur Pamplemousse was roused from his thoughts as the airship's engines roared into life and the ground crew began removing the ballast bags. For a moment he had an uneasy feeling that Pommes Frites might take it into his head to indulge in another game of tug-of-war, but to his relief he seemed to have suddenly lost interest in the whole affair. He counted the bags; according to the handout there should be seven 10kg bags for each passenger. Fifty-six were removed. Complicated hand signals began between the cockpit and the ground-crew – they could have been selling stocks and shares in the Bourse for all the sense they made. A moment later, as the nose of the airship was released from its mooring, those manning the bow lines pulled the airship sideways towards a clear position ready for take-off.

Monsieur Pamplemousse's own camera had been working overtime. There would be no shortage of pictures to accompany his article in *Le Guide*'s staff magazine; rather the reverse. Having filled the frame with a close-up of well known faces peering out of the cabin windows, he quickly changed to a wide-angle lens.

He was just in time. As the fans were rotated groundwards and the lines released, more power was applied to the engines. The naval contingent stood to attention, the band launched into 'Anchors Away', and a cheer went up from the assembled crowd as the dirigible rose into the air, nose down at first to ensure the lower tail fin didn't make contact with the ground, then levelling out as it gained height. Slowly it executed a long and gentle turn before heading out across the sea towards the Golfe du Morbihan.

As the spectators began to disperse, drifting back to their cars and *autobuses*, Monsieur Pamplemousse saw the Director heading his way. He must have travelled with a good deal of luggage, for he was even more immaculately dressed than usual; the rosette of the *Légion d'Honneur* awarded for his services to *haute cuisine* was displayed in the lapel of his exquisitely tailored dark blue suit.

'Congratulations, Aristide,' the Director held out his hand. 'I managed to feast my eyes on your handiwork and I must say it was impossible to fault. Taste buds will undoubtedly be titillated.'

'*Merci, Monsieur. I* see you were also successful with the Château d'Yquem.'

The Director looked pleased. 'I have my sources.' Clearly

they were not about to be revealed.

'You tested the food personally, of course? It would be most unfortunate if it turned out to have been tampered with *en route.*'

'*Monsieur!*' Monsieur Pamplemousse raised his eyebrows in mute reproof. He had done no such thing, of course. The food had arrived from Paris early that morning under police escort. It would have taken a braver man than he to have got within ten metrès of it under the vigilant eyes of the men from Fauchon. *Défence de toucher* had been the by-word. Only the production of his *Guide* credentials and the fact that Trigaux had taken the opportunity of sending back his pictures in the same consignment had gained him permission to photograph it. They had been right, of course, but as the one responsible for placing the order in the first place, it had been somewhat galling.

Monsieur Pamplemousse shaded his eyes as he looked up at the sky. He reached for his binoculars. The airship seemed to have slowed down over the Baie de Quiberon, almost as though it were treading water.

The Director followed the direction of his gaze. 'No doubt they have slackened speed in order to facilitate pouring the champagne whilst overlooking the oyster-beds; a pleasing touch. We must add it to our press release. What was your final choice?'

'A Gosset '75, *Monsieur.*'

'Ah, the '75! A copybook vintage. A touch austere for some tastes, perhaps, but perfectly balanced. I wonder if they have any at the Hôtel du Port? We can have some over *déjeuner. I* have reserved a table. You look fatigued, Aristide. It will do you good.'

Although he privately doubted if the cellar at the Hôtel du Port would live up to the Director's expectations,

Monsieur Pamplemousse was more than happy to fall in with the suggestion.

Organising the meal on the airship had involved him in a non-stop round of telephone calls and other activities. It was only now, with his work virtually at an end, that he suddenly realised just how tired he felt.

'Good! In that case, I suggest we make a move.' The Director rubbed his hands together in anticipation. 'If you follow me we will meet at the Hôtel. No doubt Pommes Frites will be joining us?'

It was a redundant question. Ever alive to the nuances and undertones of conversations going on around him, Pommes Frites was already leading the way. Apart from the stop on the journey down, and the unexpected steak, the trip had not, gastronomically speaking, been a memorable one to date. There had been a lot of talk of food, but very little evidence of it. 'All words and no action' would have been his summing up had he been stopped in the street by someone conducting a public opinion poll on the state of play to date. Not normally a fish lover (fish was indelibly associated in his mind with cats and therefore hardly worth considering) he had got to the stage when he would have settled for a bowl of *moules à la marinière*, had one come his way. The sight of all the food laid out in the balloon, so near and yet so far away, had been the last straw. Putting food on display and then not eating it was beyond his powers of comprehension.

His disappointment was therefore all the more marked when, some half an hour later, having settled himself comfortably under a table, his taste buds working triple overtime as a result of listening to his master and the Director discussing at length and in savoury detail their forthcoming meal – its preparation, the sauces and other accompanying embellishments – there occurred yet another example of the strange behaviour patterns of human beings which, when they occurred, were hard to credit. The ordering of the food and then the abandonment of a meal before it even arrived was, in his opinion a prime case in point.

The first Pommes Frites knew of impending disaster was the arrival of a pair of trouser-clad legs at the side of the table and the sound of voices, but his senses told him the new arrival was the bearer of bad news. Had he looked out from under the table-cloth and seen the expression on his master's face as he jumped to his feet his worst fears would have been confirmed.

'Monsieur Pickering!'

'Aristide!'

'I have been looking for you since the day I arrived.'

'On the contrary, you have been avoiding me like the plague.' Mr. Pickering allowed himself a brief, if somewhat enigmatic smile, then immediately became serious again. 'I'm afraid I must ask you to come with me.'

'Both of us?'

There was a moment's hesitation. 'Since it involves the airship, I think, yes.'

'Forgive me.' Mr. Pickering turned to the Director. 'I know of you, of course, but I haven't had the pleasure of meeting you personally, although ...' again there was a faint smile, 'that is not entirely true. A matter of paramount importance has come up and we may well be glad of your advice.'

Flattery got him everywhere. The Director was on his feet in a flash; the bib which a moment before had been tied around his neck in readiness for a *plateau de fruits de mer* abandoned along with his napkin.

Pommes Frites heaved a deep sigh as he rose to his feet and followed the others out of the restaurant. He glanced around hopefully as they left, but history did not repeat itself. There were no unattended plates anywhere in sight.

Crossing the road, they headed towards the *Mairie*, then turned down a side street towards the *Gendarmerie.*

Mr. Pickering, having contented himself with generalities on the way, nodded to the duty officer at the desk and led them quickly up some stone stairs to a door on the first floor. Two guards standing in the corridor outside came to attention.

'Excuse me, I shan't keep you a moment.' Mr. Pickering opened the door and disappeared into the room. There was a murmur of voices which stopped abruptly, then the door closed behind him.

The Director drew Monsieur Pamplemousse to one side, out of earshot of the guards. 'Who is this man Pickering?' he hissed. 'What does he want?'

'He helped me once when I was with the *Sûreté*, *Monsieur*. It concerned a matter affecting security and I was given his name and a London telephone number. He helped me again when I was involved with that girls' finishing school near Evian. He is an expert on many things, but other than that I know little. As for what he wants ...' Monsieur Pamplemousse gave a non-committal shrug.

He could have hazarded a guess; the uneasy feeling he'd woken with that morning had returned in earnest, but he was saved the trouble. The door opened and Mr. Pickering beckoned them in.

The room was small but crowded. Heads turned as they entered, then swivelled back towards a man at the far end. He was standing in front of a blackboard to which a large-scale map of the area was pinned.

Monsieur Pamplemousse settled himself on a chair between Mr. Pickering and the Director, then concentrated his attention on what was going on. Without even seeing the faces of those already present he could have pin-pointed their rank and status. Just in front of him were two representatives of government; from the cut of their clothes he guessed they were products of one of the elite *Grandes Ecoles*, members of *les Grands Corps de l'Etat*.

In the first row he picked out the local Prefect of Police. There was an army major alongside him. Behind them came a sprinkling of British – he'd seen them grouped under the Union Jack at the launch – they were probably from the Paris Embassy. The third row were mainly military. All the occupants of the room had one thing in common; they all looked tense.

'*Messieurs*, for the benefit of those who have just joined us I will repeat what I have just told you.'

The speaker was short and stocky, but without an ounce of fat. He had to be a *Barbouze* – a member of the Special Police. His face was tanned and leathery. His hair was crewcut; his eyes light blue and totally expressionless. Not a good man to cross, or to be interrogated by, particularly in a closed room. Monsieur Pamplemousse had met his sort before. After the Algerian army revolt in November 1964 had been ruthlessly stamped on by de Gaulle, some of them had started to show their faces in Paris.

When he spoke it was with an economy of words. It was hard to tell whether he was put out at being interrupted or not.

'At 11.10 hours this morning a message was received by telephone at this station.

'I will not bother to read it to you again in full. In essence it said that a bomb is hidden on board the airship. It enumerated certain demands – the release of six Iranian terrorists at present being held in France, plus a considerable sum of money. Unless these demands are met in full by 8.30 this evening the bomb will be detonated. There is no way of communicating with the sender of the message other than by public broadcast, and there was no suggestion that he would be in touch a second time. The message was signed Andreas.'

'Could it be a hoax?' It was the Prefect of Police speaking.

'It could be, but we have reason to believe not. Until we know otherwise we have to treat it as being serious. Deadly serious.' He nodded towards a colleague in the front row. The second man rose to his feet.

'As I am sure most of you will recall, Andreas is a known terrorist who was active up until a few years ago when the pace got too hot for him and he literally vanished from the scene. We believe the message to be genuine because whoever telephoned used a code name which was established at the height of his activities so that both sides always knew whom they were talking to. He is a loner and utterly ruthless. He has never failed to carry out any threats he has ever made.' Again there was a nod and the ball was passed to a third man.

'If it is Andreas, we are not dealing with a time fuse and old-fashioned explosive situation. We are probably dealing with a sophisticated device triggered off by radio. He is a one-time associate of a Jordanian named Abu Ibrahim – a garage mechanic who turned his talents to designing high-tech detonating devices. Ibrahim has since died of cancer, but it was he who manufactured the suitcase bomb which was found on the El Al plane in 1983. That had a double

334

detonating mechanism and used a plastic explosive called Semtex H. At the time it was established that he had made five such suitcases. Only three were ever located, so somewhere in the world there are still two more.'

'The type of explosive is immaterial.' The *Barbouze* showed the first flicker of impatience. 'The important question is does it exist, and if so, what do we do about it?' The second man broke in. 'The whole airship was gone over with a fine-tooth comb this morning. Sniffer-dogs, X-ray equipment, the lot. I would stake my reputation that it was clean.'

'My point,' said his colleague, 'is that Semtex H is virtually invisible by X-ray. And if it was hidden amongst any of the mechanical parts of the wiring of the dirigible the same could be said about the detonating apparatus.'

'Then we cannot afford to take the risk. If it is Andreas he will be deadly serious. He is too old a hand to play at practical jokes. Besides, his reputation will be at stake. He is a professional and he is well paid for his work.'

'What are the possibilities of the demands being met?'

'None whatsoever. Both parties are agreed on that.'

'We are, of course, making "arrangements", but purely as a precautionary measure in case there is a last-minute change of heart.'

'Our Leaderene would never permit it.' One of the British contingent spoke for the first time. 'It would be against all her principles.'

'What are the chances of mounting a rescue attempt? A boarding party by means of a helicopter?'

'Zero.'

The questions started coming thick and fast and were answered with equal speed.

'Commander Winters and Capitaine Leflaix are carrying

out a minute search of all the possible areas inside the airship – the ones that are accessible to them that is – but the chances of their finding anything are small.'

'How long can the airship stay up?'

One of the British party rose. 'Long enough. It has loiter facilities.'

'And if the bomb goes off?'

'That depends on where it is. The differential pressure between the inside of the fabric and the outside is quite small. The fabric is laminated polyester and the airship can remain airborne for a long time with a hole in it something like the size of a saucer, but if it has a large tear, that's a different matter. If the bomb is hidden somewhere on the gondola ...'

The rest was left to the imagination.

'What if the airship returns to base?' It was the Prefect of Police again.

'The instructions are that it is to stay exactly where it is. Any movement will result in the immediate detonation of the device. So far we have managed to keep the press out of it, but it is only a matter of time before they start asking questions. The dirigible containing the Heads of State of both France and England is at present stationary over the Golfe du Morbihan. I need hardly tell you of the possible repercussions if the threat is carried out.'

He turned to the map. 'The implication of the last instruction is that Andreas is in a position where he can keep a constant eye on the airship. That would also accord with the use of a very high frequency radio device which ideally needs to be free of anything which would interfere with the path of the signal. Taking a semi-circular field radiating out from the airship, my guess is that it will be located somewhere in this area.'

He ran his finger round the lower half of the map from La Baule in the south-west to Auray in the north-east.

'But that is an impossible task. We shall never search an area that size in time.' It was someone else in the front row, who received a quick rebuff.

'*Impossible?*' Clearly it was not a word in the *Barbouze's* vocabulary. 'If we start saying things are *impossible* we might just as well all go home!

'A unit of the 11th Parachute Division based at Tarbes is being flown in. When they arrive,' he looked at his watch, 'which will be in approximately two hours from now, they will be deployed on all roads leading into and out of the area and we shall then be in a position to seal it off at a moment's notice.

'A flotilla of French navy power boats is on its way from St. Nazaire ready to carry out a search for survivors should the worst happen; a submarine will be joining them.'

Monsieur Pamplemousse was impressed. Given the short time at his disposal the *Barbouze* had worked incredibly fast. He must be in a position to exercise considerable authority.

'*Mon Dieu!*' The Director had a sudden thought. He nudged Monsieur Pamplemousse. 'If the airship is blown up,' he whispered, 'the oyster-beds of Locmariaquer will be devastated. The force of the explosion could well dislodge the baby ones from their tiles.'

'The oyster-beds of Locmariaquer will be the least of the problems, *Monsieur*,' said the man coldly. Long exposure to the North African sun had not impaired his hearing.

Conscious of a sudden chill in the atmosphere as heads turned in their direction, Monsieur Pamplemousse rose to his feet.

'May I ask a question? Why 8.30 this evening?'

'Presumably because it will be getting dark by then. Andreas will not wish to lose sight of the airship in case we try moving it under cover of darkness.'

'But the weather is good – there is a full moon. Why not nine o'clock or even midnight?'

There was a pause. '*Monsieur*, if you know of something, either you or your – *associates* ...' the stress was on the last word.

Monsieur Pamplemousse was about to reply when he felt a restraining touch on his arm and Mr. Pickering rose to his feet.

'*Monsieur, I* must congratulate you on your analysis of the situation. I need hardly add that the resources of Her Majesty's government are available should you require them.'

The pause this time was even longer. The reply when it came was directed at the other occupants of the room, but the eyes remained fixed on Mr. Pickering. 'I understand we also have at our disposal a party of "nuns" who happen to be attending a seminar in Port St. Augustin at this time. Am I correct?'

Mr. Pickering returned the other's stare with equanimity.

'That is so, *Monsieur*.' He fingered his right ear reflectively. 'I think I can safely say they belong to the only order in the world who are able to claim anti-terrorist capability. I repeat, *Monsieur*, they are at your disposal should you have need of them.'

8
DEATH BY MISADVENTURE

'In *Angleterre*,' said Mr. Pickering, 'I know a man who saws Rolls-Royce cars in half.'

'He must be one of two things,' said Monsieur Pample-mousse. 'He must either have extremely strong nerves or be unforgivably foolish.'

'He is neither,' said Mr. Pickering. 'He just happens to be very proficient with a hacksaw. He makes a good living out of welding an extra piece of bodywork in the middle and selling the "stretched" version to Arabs with large families and garages to match.'

The Director looked out of his depth. 'I fail to see what that has to do with our present problem.'

'The point I am trying to make,' said Mr. Pickering, 'is that things are not always what they seem.

'The *Barbouze* is a good man. I have a great deal of respect for him. I'm sure he is first rate at his job. But he is in command and he does not like me.'

'With respect,' said Monsieur Pamplemousse, 'I think it is not so much you he dislikes, it is the circumstances of your being here. It is a question of territories. I doubt if he likes anyone very much, particularly if he thinks they are getting in his way. He is probably a very tidy man with a mind to match.'

Mr. Pickering acknowledged the point. 'I fully understand. I would feel exactly the same way if the positions were reversed. Nevertheless, be that as it may, I – or rather *we* – are here – albeit under sufferance, and if our direct involvement is an embarrassment, then we must go it alone. I, also, have my instructions.' He turned to the Director.

'I must apologise, *Monsieur*, if I have placed you in an awkward situation because of our withdrawal from the briefing, but it seemed to me there was nothing more to be learned, and there are likely to be too many voices raised, too many egos to be satisfied, for the kind of quiet thinking which needs to be done. I will make my peace with the *Barbouze* in due course – we understand each other and we have a common objective – but for the moment at least he will have his work cut out with all the others he has to deal with.'

He turned back to Monsieur Pamplemousse. 'You asked an interesting question just before we left.'

'Why 8.30?'

'Precisely. Why not, as you say, 9 p.m. ? There is a natural tendency for people – even terrorists – to go for the round figure.'

Monsieur Pamplemousse weighed the matter carefully in his mind before replying. Other than through telephone calls and one brief meeting in Paris many years before, he scarcely knew Mr. Pickering. Yet his instinct told him he could be trusted. There was an element of mutual respect in their relationship which had been there right from the start. On the other hand, he shuddered to think what might happen if he withheld information from the proper quarters and things went wrong. At least it would earn him a place in history. Instinct won. The truth of the matter was he knew he could say things to Mr. Pickering and they would be accepted without his having to go into a lot of tedious explanations. The same certainly wouldn't be true of those in the other room.

'The circus starts at 9 p.m.,' he said simply.

'Ah!' Mr. Pickering seemed pleased with the answer. 'You think the two are connected?'

'I didn't until a few minutes ago. Now I am not so sure. There is something very wrong going on there.' Quickly and succinctly he ran through the events to date. The Director remained unusually and commendably silent throughout, only registering faint disappointment when, for the sake of brevity, Monsieur Pamplemousse sped through those areas which he judged could have no possible bearing on the matter under discussion but which, in more ways than one, simply added flesh to the bare bones of his story.

As he got to the end Mr. Pickering felt in his pocket and withdrew a small black and white enprint size photograph. He handed it over without a comment.

It was very grainy and looked like a blow-up from a small section of a larger negative. It was a head and shoulders shot of a man. He wore a black Viva Zapata-style moustache and had black, curly hair. From the angle of his head and the look on his face he appeared to be running away from something or someone. Around his neck there was a gold cross on a chain. Monsieur Pamplemousse placed his hand over the lower half of the picture. The eyes were as he remembered them.

'It is the trapeze artist, Christoph.'

'It is also the only known photograph in existence of Andreas,' said Mr. Pickering. 'It was taken during an incident in Frankfurt some years ago.'

Monsieur Pamplemousse remembered it now. It had been circulated to police forces and immigration offices all over Europe at the time.

'*Mon Dieu!*' The Director jumped to his feet. 'We must inform the authorities at once.'

'The problem with authorities,' said Mr. Pickering slowly, 'is that by definition they tend to act authoritatively, consequently their behaviour pattern tends to be ponderous and is almost always predictable.'

'But if what you say is true,' exclaimed the Director, 'if Christoph and Andreas are one and the same person can he not be arrested? Are you suggesting we should do nothing?' Clearly his involvement in matters outside his normal experience was beginning to worry him.

'No,' said Mr. Pickering, 'I am not. What I am suggesting is that although Andreas may be without mercy, he is certainly not lacking in imagination. He will have planned the whole thing meticulously down to the very last detail over a long period of time and he will have covered every foreseeable eventuality. At the first sign of anything untoward happening he will pull the plugs on the operation without a second's hesitation. If, due to a false move on our part, it is the wrong plug, that could spell disaster for everyone.

'It is abundantly clear that we must discover his whereabouts before 8.30 this evening, and having found him strike before he has a chance to act.' He glanced at his watch. 'That gives us a little over six and a half hours.'

The Director picked up the photograph. 'The man at the meeting was right. It is too big an area to cover in the time available. It will be like looking for a needle in a haystack.'

'The one clear advantage about looking for a needle in a haystack,' said Mr. Pickering, 'is that the one is very different to the other. Besides, I think we can start by eliminating a good deal of the day. If 8.30 is zero hour and the circus starts at 9 p.m., or thereabouts, he must be within half an hour's drive – probably a lot less if he has made allowances for traffic and changing into his costume for the opening parade – say, twenty minutes. That puts it within an area of not more than twelve to fifteen kilometrès away. That, in turn, would also fit in with the theory that he needs to be within sight of the airship.'

'Even so …' The Director was obviously not entirely convinced. He probably felt his *Légion d'Honneur* was at stake.

'Even so, it is a start.' Mr. Pickering took a yellow Michelin map from his pocket and opened it up. 'It eliminates the whole of the area north of the Vilaine estuary.

'What's the matter, Aristide? You look troubled.'

Monsieur Pamplemousse shrugged. There was still an element about the whole thing that troubled him. 'Is there any reason for this Andreas to go back to the circus? The girl is gone. Presumably he got rid of her because she knew too much and he felt she was about to betray him. If his plan works out and he gets what he wants, he can disappear again. There is nothing to keep him there.'

'If things don't go right,' said Mr. Pickering, 'if something goes violently wrong, his chances of getting away unchallenged will be zero – the whole area will be alive with police and troops. His best bet will be to carry on with his everyday life as though nothing had happened – at least until the first shock-waves die down. As far as he knows there is nothing to link him with the affair. The one person who could have blown his cover is gone. Once the circus moves on and is safely out of Brittany, then he can make himself scarce and we shall be back where we started.

'It has taken a long time to catch up with Mr. Andreas. The present little problem aside, it would be a great misfortune if he slipped through our hands yet again.'

Monsieur Pamplemousse looked at him curiously. Beneath the laid-back manner there was an unexpectedly steely character. In his way Mr. Pickering would be as tough a nut to crack as the *Barbouze*.

'If it is of any help,' he said, 'I may have some photos of Christoph.' Opening up his case he withdrew the large manila envelope that had arrived with the food that morning, removed a thick batch of glossy black and white enlargements, and spread them out across the table. They were even better than he'd expected. Trigaux had done his stuff as usual. The pictures taken inside the circus tent positively sparkled with life. Apart from a slight graininess, the tight shots of the figure at the top of the trapeze could almost have been taken in a studio.

'Magnificent!' Mr. Pickering's usual aplomb suffered a temporary lapse.

'I trust this is a private arrangement, Pamplemousse,' broke in the Director as he caught sight of *Le Guide*'s logo on the outside of the envelope. 'Otherwise we could have trouble with Madame Grante if she is still on the warpath.'

'I have no idea who Madame Grante might be when she's at home,' said Mr. Pickering mildly, 'but there are plenty of people who would give their eye-teeth to get their hands on these.'

'In that ease we must take them next door at once.' The Direetor tried to reassert his authority. 'After that, I suggest we wash our hands of the whole affair and leave matters to the powers that be. That is what they are there for.'

Mr. Pickering lowered the photographs and began riffling through the remainder on the table. 'I think that would be a great pity, *Monsieur le Directeur*. What do you think, Aristide?'

'Mr. Pickering is right, *Monsieur*. For what it is worth, I will see that copies of the photograph are made available. But as for the rest, I doubt if the *Barbouze* will involve us in his plans. He is interested in facts, not theories. He cannot afford to take chances and play a hunch, whereas we can. Time is not on anyone's side but at least it is worth a try. The worst that can happen is that we are proved wrong.'

'Too many cooks spoil the broth,' said Mr. Pickering, 'and the next room is full of chefs.'

'*Trop de cuisinières gâtent la sauce*.' Monsieur Pamplemousse ventured a translation in case the Director had missed the point, but he needn't have bothered. The culinary allusion had gone home; the parallel was irresistible and capitulation was at hand.

'When did you take these other photographs?' asked Mr. Pickering. He pointed to a series of shots taken from the first reel of film.

Monsieur Pamplemousse thought for a moment. So much had happened since he'd arrived in Port St. Augustin he had almost lost track of time. 'The ones of my car were taken the day I arrived. On the Tuesday.'

'Ah, yes, I heard all about that.' Mr. Pickering looked embarrassed. 'I'm afraid one of our chaps forgot to "*céder le passage*". Some of your intersections are unbelievably large and complex by our standards. He couldn't stop for fear of their breaking cover.'

Monsieur Pamplemousse wondered what story had been concocted by Mr. Pickering's 'chaps' to cover their escapade. By no stretch of the imagination could the intersection where the accident had taken place have been described as complex – but before he had a chance to enquire further he felt the Director leaning over his shoulder.

'What's this, Pamplemousse? Is that your car lying in the ditch? I trust you have filled in your P81 in triplicate and despatched it to Madame Grante. You know how she is about delay in these matters.'

'Madame Grante again. She sounds even more redoubtable than Andreas. They would make a good pair.' Mr. Pickering sounded distracted. 'It was really these ones of the outside of the circus I was interested in.'

'They were taken on the Wednesday morning. I went along to see if I could get some tickets for the evening performance. I finished off a reel of film so that I could reload before I went up in the airship. Why do you ask?'

Mr. Pickering held up one of the pictures. 'I don't remember seeing a menhir the evening I was there.'

Monsieur Pamplemousse took a closer look. There it was, just as he remembered it that first morning; a large, top-heavy, misshapen, light-grey piece of stone, standing up like a sore thumb. Yasmin's BMW was parked to the right of it, the blue hire-van further away to the left.

Mr. Pickering was right. The menhir hadn't been there that same evening. He'd sensed at the time that there had been an element missing, but it wouldn't have occurred to him in a million years that something so outwardly solid could vanish, although seeing it again made him want to kick himself.

'But it isn't possible. It must have weighed a hundred tons or more. It is as solid as a …

'*Ça y est, j'ai compris!*' The penny dropped. Suddenly everything fell into place at once; the roll of material in the boot of Yasmin's car, the smell of acetone, the bag of light-grey powder he'd found in the waste-bin – it must have been filler powder to go with the resin, the paint, the half dry brushes, the piece of sawn-off material he had come across lying on the ground, the pieces of wire and the solder.

A fibreglass menhir! It was on the face of it a preposterous idea, but the more he thought about it the more logical it seemed. As quickly and as briefly as possible he outlined his thoughts. 'It would be an ideal hiding-place. The whole area is so full of stones no one's going to notice an extra one – or if they do they're not going to report it until it is too late.'

Mr. Pickering accepted the thesis without question. 'How many menhirs do you reckon are around here?'

'How many? Probably as many as there are cafés in Paris. This part of Brittany is full of them.'

'If you wanted to erect an artificial one, where would be the best place?'

'If you went somewhere like Carnac you would have the advantage of it being one of many – it could be slipped into one of the great *alignements* – there is one which has over a thousand stones. On the other hand, Carnac is full of tourists – especially at this time of the year when the coach parties start to arrive. It would be much too public and the place is crawling with sightseers and guides and people who know the area like the back of their hand. Besides, we have already decided it has to be nearer than that.'

He paused and gazed out of the window. On the other side of the narrow street a man in shirt sleeves was working at a desk. A woman came into the room carrying a piece of paper which she gave to the man before leaving the room again. He didn't even bother looking up.

'If you simply put it in a field you would be up against the fact that anything unusual would be noticed straight away.'

'You are right.' Mr. Pickering joined him. 'It is always the same in the country. You can get away with murder in a big city, but in the country the slightest change is noticed. My guess would be in the marshes behind La Baule – the Grande Brière. It is still relatively uninhabited. An inhospitable part of the world; full of strange corners where no one goes; also the *Brièrons* are fiercely independent. They keep themselves very much apart. It might be several days before anyone bothered to report something out of the ordinary.'

The Director broke in. 'If this Andreas person is in the Grande Brière you will have your work cut out finding him, let alone his plastic menhir. It is worse than the Camargue. Over six thousand hectares of marshland and not a restaurant in sight. Most of it can only be reached by flat-bottomed boat – and then only at those times in the year when the water is high. Have you been there? Poof! You will need a guide!'

'Yes, I have been there on a number of occasions.' Mr. Pickering crossed to the table and opened up the map again. 'You are right about the restaurants, and by its very nature it is not noted for its menhirs either. There is one near Pontchâteau – at a place the English know as "Magdalen Moors", and there is a dolmen – a burial chamber – near Kerbourg. As I recall, those are the only ones Michelin marks, but doubtless there are others less worthy of note. That is what we should be looking for.

'Perhaps we shall have to deal with the *Barbouze* after all. If we get through to Washington it is possible we could get an up-to-date satellite picture of the area. The Americans are taking them all the time and they may well be monitoring this particular operation. A lot of people are interested in dirigibles these days: NASA, the US Navy, the Coastguards. Airships have a low radar profile on account of the lack of metal. We can get copies faxed over. At least we can eliminate the ones that are marked on the map and something odd may show itself.'

'That will not be necessary.' Monsieur Pamplemousse flipped through the rest of the photographs until he found the section he wanted. 'I did my own aerial survey while I was up in the balloon.'

He cleared a space on the pine-topped table and then spread the photographs out in sequence; six rows of six. In total they covered the entire Guérande Peninsula to the west, La Baule and the Côte d'Amour to the south and the Parc Régional de Brière to the north and east. Once again the combination of Leica optics and Trigaux's wizardry had not let him down. The enlargements were needle sharp. In places the pictures overlapped more than he would have liked, but it was better that way. At least there were no great gaps.

Mr. Pickering pointed to the second photograph in from the left. It included Port St. Augustin and the circus. 'The menhir has already disappeared.'

'So has the van. Andreas must have got the wind up when the police arrived and started asking questions about Yasmin. He can't have been gone more than about half an hour when I took the picture. That being so ...' Monsieur Pamplemousse ran his finger over the photographs, following the main road out of Port St. Augustin to the point where it crossed the D774 north of Guérande and then entered the Grande Brière.

They both saw it at the same time, the unmistakable shape of a van parked in a tiny lane leading towards the marshes. To one side there was a small wood and on the western side, facing towards the Baie de Quiberon, there was an area of scrubland dotted with white stones.

Mr. Pickering began counting.

'There are eight menhirs altogether. The question is, which is the odd one out?'

'It may not be any of them. It could still be in the van. There's no sign of anyone about. He may have only just arrived.'

'True. Would you recognise the one we are looking for if you saw it again?'

Monsieur Pamplemousse shook his head. 'I doubt it. There were some markings on the side, but most of them have those anyway. It depends how big the others are. It is impossible to tell from the photograph, but if they are anything like the same size – and presumably he thought of that- then the answer is no – not without getting close to it.'

'That's too risky. Andreas already knows what you look like, and if he's inside already ...'

Monsieur Pamplemousse suddenly remembered the feeling he'd had that first morning, the feeling of being watched. It was conceivable that Andreas had been inside the menhir even then. No wonder Pommes Frites had behaved the way he had.

'Presumably any kind of spy-hole he has will be facing towards the airship. We might be able to come up from behind.'

Mr. Pickering shook his head. 'It's still too risky. Unless ...' He crossed over to the window again and stood looking out. After a moment Monsieur Pamplemousse joined him. Nothing had changed. The man in the building opposite was still working away at his desk. He wondered how he would react if he knew what was happening on the other side of the street.

'What springs to mind when you think of *Bretagne*, Aristide?' said Mr. Pickering. 'Apart from menhirs and dolmens, that is.'

'Weather,' said Monsieur Pamplemousse. '*Crêperies*, cider, shellfish, rocky coasts, Muscadet, granite walls, blue roof tiles, narrow streets, fields of artichokes, thatched cottages, onion-sellers from Finistère, lace head-dresses, Tristan and Isolde, Abélard and Héloïse.' He glanced along the street. 'Churches ...'

'Carry on. You're getting warm.'

'Saints, festivals, calvaries, pardons ...'

'Exactly.' Mr. Pickering rubbed his hands with pleasure. 'Pardons. I think it is high time we held one of our own. My chaps are dying for a spot of action.'

'Now look here,' the Director, who had remained silent for longer than Monsieur Pamplemousse could remember, was unable to contain himself a moment longer. He rose to his feet. 'Enough is enough. If, as you suggest, this terrorist is concealed inside a menhir – and listening to the various arguments you have put forward, bizarre though the thought might appear to be at first sight, it does seem to be a distinct possibility – then we cannot keep the facts to ourselves. The responsibility must be shared.'

'And what decisions will those we share it with come to?' asked Mr. Pickering mildly. 'Bring in the tanks? Drop a bomb on it? Either will run the risk of triggering off a panic action which will be self-defeating. Our only hope is to use the weapon of surprise. A procession of nuns walking across a field is not an unusual sight in Brittany. There is a religious festival of one kind or another going on practically every day at this time of the year. My chaps have been in the area for a week now and no one has so much as raised an eyebrow. If Andreas does see them it will scarcely register, giving us time enough to move in on him before he has a chance to do anything.'

'And how will we know which menhir he is in?' The

Director remained unconvinced. 'Are you going to rush each and every one in turn? What happens to your weapon of surprise if he happens to be in the last one?'

'There are such things as thermal imagers,' said Mr. Pickering. 'They are used for detecting body heat. We can probably arrange to get one through the local fire-brigade.'

Monsieur Pamplemousse sighed. Thermal imagers; fax machines; satellites; dirigibles with low radar profile and hover capability; he sometimes felt as if one day the whole world would collapse under the weight of its own technology. Speaking for himself, he much preferred to entrust his fate and those of others to old-fashioned, tried and tested methods. In his experience they rarely let you down.

Opening up *Le Guide*'s case once again, Monsieur Pamplemousse removed a small tube of ointment. 'I think,' he said, 'I can suggest an even simpler solution to the problem.'

As he caught sight of the object in his master's hand, Pommes Frites rose to his feet, stretched himself, and stood waiting patiently for the next command. The smell of the ointment was one he was unlikely to forget in a hurry. An instinct, born not only out of many hours of unselfish devotion to the cause of duty, but also from encounters too numerous to mention and largely unrecorded save in the stark prose reserved for the annals of the Paris *Sûreté*, told him that his moment of glory was nigh.

Working on the principle that some achieve greatness through sheer hard work and perseverance, whilst others have it thrust upon them, he sensed that after a long period when his talents had gone unappreciated, he was now onto a winning streak. It was only a matter of time before he received his just rewards.

'Will he be all right, Aristide?' The Director peered anxiously through a gap in the trees.

'Pommes Frites?'

'It would be terrible if anything happened. Things would never be the same. His flag is always alongside yours in the operations room.'

Monsieur Pamplemousse gave a start. The operations room at *Le Guide*'s headquarters was a holy of holies. Entry without prior permission was strictly *interdite*. The position of each and every Inspector at any given moment was marked by a flag on a large map, and kept under constant review by a team of uniformed girls working in shifts. It had never occurred to him that Pommes Frites had his own flag too.

'He is well able to look after himself.'

Monsieur Pamplemousse spoke with rather more confidence than he felt. Privately, he was beginning to wish he'd let Mr. Pickering stick to his original plan of using a thermal imager. It was always the same when it came down to it. Total obedience also meant total trust. You trained an animal to obey your every command and then took advantage of it. He would sooner have gone out there himself than let anything happen to Pommes Frites. He would have loved to have told him so before they set off, but then perhaps he knew.

He watched as Pommes Frites reached the first menhir on the far side of the field, crawling on his stomach and taking advantage of every patch of heather and gorse. He sniffed it and having immediately rejected it, set off towards the next one.

It must have been the same way with Yasmin. Despite everything, when she climbed up onto the trapeze that night she must still have had total trust in her partner, otherwise she couldn't have done it. And yet, on the other side of the coin, it could be argued that she had been about to betray Andreas. Morally, she would have been right to do so, but in terms of human relationships she must have gone through agonies of doubt. The difference between her and Pommes Frites was that in no way would it have crossed his mind to betray his master. The thought didn't make Monsieur Pamplemousse feel any better.

Another menhir, nestling amongst a mass of hollyhocks, was tested and found wanting. Monsieur Pamplemousse instinctively drew back as Pommes Frites moved nearer to his hiding place in the bushes.

He looked around. If anyone had said to him a few days earlier that the following week would find both him and the Director crouched in a *Bretagne* wood dressed as nuns, he would have laughed his head off. Life had strange and unexpected twists. Doucette would be appalled if she could see him. She was probably worried enough as it was, for he still hadn't sent his postcard.

Behind him some twenty or so robed figures crouched in the undergrowth, their tense faces buried between the huge wings of their *coiffes*. He wondered what they had concealed beneath their habits – stun grenades, Browning 9mm pistols, Heckler and Koch 9mm sub-machine guns probably. They were the favourite weapons. Anyone stumbling across them unexpectedly while on a nature ramble would be in for a rude surprise.

High above on the far side of the scrubland off to his right he could see the stationary airship, a speck in the distant sky. He wondered if those aboard had enjoyed their lunch. Enjoyed wouldn't be exactly the right word in the circumstances, but it would be a pity if they had let it go to waste and it would have helped pass an hour or so. Time must be hanging very heavily by now. At least the weather was good. He didn't care to dwell on how they would have felt if it had been as bad as on the day he had gone up.

Monsieur Pamplemousse felt someone nudge him on his other side. 'Third time lucky!' Mr. Pickering pointed towards a menhir some halfway across the scrub. Pommes Frites was lying alongside it wagging his tail. He was too well trained to look their way. Instead, he slithered backwards along the ground, never for a second taking his eyes off his quarry until he reached the safety of a patch of taller shrubs.

'Here we go!' Mr. Pickering moved away and held a brief conversation with one of the nuns. In response to a hand signal the rest of them rose quietly to their feet and formed themselves into a line two abreast. A moment later, as they set off along a path through the wood which took them to a point somewhere behind the menhir, something which had been bothering Monsieur Pamplemousse ever since they had arrived on the scene crystallised in his mind. There was no sign of a vehicle parked anywhere nearby; neither the blue van nor Yasmin's car. If Andreas was planning a quick getaway it didn't make sense. He could have kicked himself for not thinking of it before, but it was too late to do anything about it. The crocodile of nuns was already emerging through a gap in the trees. Heads bowed, hands clasped in front of them, they made their way slowly but inexorably across the scrubland in a direction which would take them past the menhir. Another ten or twelve paces and the leaders would be level with it.

There was a movement in the undergrowth and Pommes Frites was back. Without taking his eyes off the scene, Monsieur Pamplemousse reached out and gave him a congratulatory pat. The hair on his neck felt stiff. He was still tense, ready to spring into action at a moment's notice.

In the event it wasn't needed. It was all over in a matter of seconds. Although seeing it all unfold before him it felt almost as though he was watching a carefully rehearsed television drama being replayed in slow motion.

Without a word being uttered, the whole column suddenly threw themselves on the ground. A moment later the menhir rocked under a hail of fire. As the echo of the shots died away two of the nuns jumped to their feet and rushed to either side of it, machine guns at the ready. A door swung open and hung drunkenly on its hinges.

For a brief moment no one moved, then there came the sound of a distant explosion. Instinctively everyone turned and looked towards the sea.

'Jesus!' Mr. Pickering crossed himself. 'I don't believe it!'

9
DINNER WITH THE DIRECTOR

Mr. Pickering removed a bottle of white wine from a large silver bucket alongside the table and poured a little of the contents into his glass. He swirled it round deftly and expertly, then held the glass to his nose. 'I think we'll dispense with the services of the waitrèss,' he said. 'I don't know about you, but I'm dying for a drink.'

After displaying the label for Monsieur Pamplemousse and the Director to inspect, he filled the rest of the glasses and replaced the bottle alongside its twin in the ice-bucket.

'A Coulée-de-Serrant. It is from the estate of a certain Madame Joly. They're not easy to find. Even in a good year only a small quantity is made and most are drunk far too young. I happened to come across three bottles in a little wine shop in Nantes soon after I arrived. I'm afraid these are the last two.'

'In that case,' said the Director, 'we are very privileged.'

Mr. Pickering looked pleased. 'It is a wine with an interesting history. The first vines in Anjou were planted by monks in the twelfth century.'

Monsieur Pamplemousse tested the bouquet. There was a familiar scent of honeysuckle. 'I remember your first bottle,' he said. 'It was discarded by an old *sorcière* outside the Hôtel du Port.'

'Ah, yes.' Mr. Pickering didn't bat an eyelid. 'The harridan. You resisted her attentions manfully. Madame

Pamplemousse would have been proud of you, I'm sure.

'I couldn't believe my eyes when I saw you coming towards me that first night. Having had reports from Interpol of Andreas being somewhere in the area, the last thing I wanted was to be seen talking to an ex-member of the *Sûreté*. He might not have known who you were, but I couldn't afford to take the risk. We didn't know at the time that he was with the circus.'

'You chose a good disguise,' said Monsieur Pamplemousse. 'I doubt if anyone would have come within a mile of you.'

'That's what I thought, but you'd be surprised,' said Mr. Pickering cryptically. He shrugged the matter off. 'I fear I am a frustrated actor at heart and like all actors I get the occasional kick out of being someone else. At school I was known for a while as "The Scarlet Pimple".

'Wine happens to be my other weakness. That's why I could never have become an Olivier. Olivier would have drunk methylated spirits if it enabled him to get inside the character of the old woman.'

Monsieur Pamplemousse was tempted to say Oliver would have chosen a cheaper after-shave as well, but that would have sounded too much like a put-down. Instead, he lifted his glass and smelt the bouquet. Then he sipped a little of the wine and let it flow over his palate. It was flinty-dry and aromatic with the taste of wild flowers. An exceptional wine by any standards. He raised his glass.

'*A votre santé*, Mr. Pickering!'

'Your very good health!'

'Congratulations to you both on a successful mission.' The Director joined them in clinking glasses.

Monsieur Pamplemousse was conscious of eyes watching them from other tables in the Ty Coz's dining-room. The sight of two nuns and a Mother Superior arriving with their own wine and imbibing it with such obvious enjoyment probably confirmed the worst suspicions of many of those present.

Mr. Pickering looked at his watch. 'The airship must have crossed the English coast by now. Their journey will be nearly at an end.'

'I still find it hard to believe,' said the Director. 'I have to confess that when I heard the explosion I thought my worst fears had been realised. I fully expected to see the dirigible coming down in flames.'

'You were not alone,' said Mr. Pickering.

Monsieur Pamplemousse inwardly voiced his agreement. It had been a nasty moment, one he wouldn't wish to repeat in a hurry. 'And the caravan?'

'Almost totally wrecked. One side has completely disappeared. Andreas ended up as a kit of parts for someone the world is well rid of.'

'There were no other casualties?'

'None, fortunately. If it had happened later in the evening when everyone was arriving for the circus it could have been a disaster area.'

'But why? I still do not understand why.' The Director pointedly made play with his empty glass. 'Did he have more explosive stored there? If so, what caused it to go off?'

Monsieur Pamplemousse exchanged a quick glance with Mr. Pickering and received the go-ahead.

'I think, *Monsieur*, it was partly to do with fate and partly to do with Pommes Frites.'

'A formidable combination.' Mr. Pickering took the hint and reached across the table in order to recharge the Director's glass. 'A case of the proverbial irresistible force teaming up with an immovable object.'

'Pommes Frites found the explosive in the first place. He picked up the scent the day I travelled on the airship. It was hidden in one of the bags of ballast.' Monsieur Pample-mousse reached down and felt under the table for the subject under discussion. He received an affectionate lick in return. 'One tends to forget that he is a dog of many talents. Long before he and I met he attended a sniffer course in Paris. I understand he was top of his class for that year. He won the Pierre Armand trophy.

'Fate then stepped in and decreed that I put the bag in the waste bin outside Andreas's caravan.'

Fate, or was it pre-ordained? If it was the latter, then it had been operating from the moment his car ended up in a ditch the day he arrived, perhaps even before that. It was an interesting point. On the same basis, the fate of two leading Heads of State in the western world had been largely determined by his spearing the end of Pommes Frites' nose with a ball-point pen. It was a sobering thought. The manu-facturers would probably love to be able to quote the fact in their literature.

He looked around the room. Strange unidentifiable agri-cultural implements adorned the walls; the whole area surrounding the huge stone fireplace was taken up with an unlikely mural of the Camargue. Wild horses were dashing towards the exit – probably trying to escape the ghastly food at the Ty Coz. He couldn't for the life of him understand why the Director had insisted on dining there in the first place.

Sitting at a nearby table was a young English family; mother, father and three children, all red from the sun and wind. The children kept looking across and giggling. A scattering of Germans and a few French families, very casually dressed, were eating noisily; the prime window seat was occupied by an elderly English couple – probably the Bentley owners. They looked as if they owned the table as well. The man was wearing a cravat, his one concession to their being on holiday. He would probably dress for dinner even if they were in the middle of the African jungle, resolutely refusing to 'go native'. A young couple, both wearing headphones, jiggled to different rhythms over a bowl of *moules*. Perhaps everyone was taking part in some pre-ordained plan. Given the abysmal food, he couldn't picture any other reason. What *had* they all done to deserve such a fate? The strangest part of all was the fact that they actually seemed to be enjoying themselves. It made a mockery of his job with *Le Guide*.

'I was explaining *to Monsieur le Directeur*,' Mr. Pickering broke into his reverie, 'the one thing we hadn't bargained for was Andreas not actually being inside the artificial menhir, but simply using it as a relay station. The main control for detonating the explosive was safely inside the caravan. Given his background and knowledge of electronics it wasn't a difficult thing to set up. It turned the whole thing into an arm's-length transaction as it were, and it also had the advantage that he could keep an eye on the airship from his window and give himself an alibi at the same time if things went wrong. No doubt when the experts search the wreckage of the caravan they will find all the evidence, but he must have had some warning device to let him know if the menhir was being tampered with. As soon as that sounded he took the decision to blow up the airship and in doing so blew himself up instead. It was, in many ways, not unjust, even an elegant solution to many people's problems.'

The Director broke in. 'But how did he manage to get the

explosive on board the airship in the first place?'

'It probably wasn't all that difficult. As Aristide will tell you, security was fairly lax in the beginning. All he would have had to do was turn up carrying a brief-case and clip-board. You can go anywhere if you carry a clip-board.'

Mr. Pickering was saved any further explanations by the arrival of his first course: *coquilles St. Jacques* – cooked the Breton way, in cider. The Director had chosen the sea-food platter which arrived on a vast oval tray placed on a stand in the centre of the table. On a bed of crushed ice lay a montage of winkles and mussels, baby shrimps, oysters, pink *langoustines*, crabs and other delicacies, nestling amongst dark green sea-weed and yellow halves of a lemon.

On the grounds that it might have been bought outside rather than made in the Ty Coz's kitchen, Monsieur Pamplemousse had ordered a portion of pork *rillettes*. It looked rather lonely on its over-large plate. Glancing at the other dishes, he almost regretted his choice, but it was a case of being better safe than sorry.

A large *faux-filet* steak, already partly cut-up. arrived in a separate dish and was placed on the floor beside his feet. Pommes Frites eyed it non-commitally from beneath the table-cloth. Like his master, he had his doubts.

As the waitress wished them '*bon appétit*' and withdrew, the Director tucked a napkin into his shirt collar and helped himself to a shrimp. 'Explosives, sabotage, hijack-ings, terrorism, fibreglass menhirs ... what is the world coming to?'

'What indeed?' said Mr. Pickering. 'Mind you, I may go into business manufacturing fibreglass menhirs myself when I retire. I'm sure there are lots of people in England who would like one at the bottom of their garden. They would make very good sheds – or homes for gnomes.'

'There must be many people in Brittany,' said Monsieur Pamplemousse, 'who wish they *hadn't* got one in their garden.'

'The grass is always greener on the other side of the fence.' Mr. Pickering reached for the second bottle of wine. Under cover of the sea-food platter the Director surreptitiously drained his glass and applied a napkin to his mouth.

'I congratulate you on your choice, Pickering. I must make a note of the vineyard. The wine has an uncommon potency.'

Mr. Pickering acknowledged the compliment. 'It is an anomaly of your otherwise excellent French wine laws. When the *appellation* was first created the vineyards mostly produced a sweet white wine so they were allowed only a very small yield per hectare and the alcoholic content had to be a minimum of 12.5 degrees. Although many of them have now turned to making a much drier wine they still have to retain the same high degree of alcohol. It is a handicap to the growers, but an enormous bonus for the rest of us ...' He broke off as a series of bleeps sounded from somewhere under his scapular. 'Please excuse me. I think I am needed. Perhaps, if you catch the eye of the waitrèss, you could ask for the condiments. That is my only complaint so far – a definite lack of salt in the cooking. It does help to bring out the flavour, you know.'

Monsieur Pamplemousse shook his head as Mr. Pickering disappeared. 'A strange race the British. Their knowledge of wine often exceeds our own, but when it comes to food ...'

'Perhaps, Aristide, your tastebuds have become jaded over the years by too much good living,' said the Director. 'You have yet to try the *rillettes*.'

Feeling rebuffed from an unexpected corner, Monsieur Pamplemousse broke off a piece of toast, reached for his knife, cut off a wedge of chunky paste, added a gherkin, set his taste buds in motion with a black olive, then sat back to contemplate the result. It was, he had to admit, better than he had expected.

The olive was jet-black and plump; the *rillettes* had clearly been made from prime meat, he could taste goose as well as pork; the gherkin had been pickled in a delicately spiced mixture of wine vinegar and dill.

Hearing a rattling noise at his feet he looked down. Pommes Frites had finished his steak and was licking his lips with relish.

'Well, Aristide?'

'I have tasted worse, *Monsieur*.' His reply was suitably guarded.

'Good. Madame Grante will be pleased.'

'Madame Grante?' Monsieur Pamplemousse paused with another portion of toast halfway to his mouth. A delicately balanced gherkin fell off and landed on the floor. Pommes Frites eyed it with interest. 'What does Madame Grante have to do with it?'

'Ah, Aristide.' The Director regarded him unhappily from behind a pair of nutcrackers which he had been about to apply to a lobster claw. 'I am very glad you asked me that. Very glad indeed.'

Monsieur Pamplemousse waited patiently while the Director busied himself with the inside of the claw. For someone who had professed himself eager to answer a question, he was being somewhat tardy.

'My reasons for suggesting you stayed here, Aristide, were several-fold.'

'*Several*-fold, *Monsieur*?' Monsieur Pamplemousse eyed

the Director suspiciously. 'Are you saying there is another fold to come?'

'That is one way of putting it.' The Director looked, if anything, even more unhappy.

'Madame Grante is a good woman, Aristide, a good woman. Much maligned by other members of staff, but a good woman for all that. However, I fear she took extreme umbrage over my intervention during the little argument you had with her recently concerning your last lot of expenses. Storm clouds were gathering over the Parc du Champ de Mars. In the end for the sake of peace I had to strike a bargain.'

'A bargain, *Monsieur*? I'm afraid I do not entirely understand what you are saying.'

'The Ty Coz, Aristide, belongs to a distant relative of Madame Grante. She approached me some while ago with a view to its being inspected for inclusion in *Le Guide*. I said to her that although she could expect no favoured treatment which, in fairness, she never sought – I would arrange for an early visit. Then, when she heard you were coming to the area she brought the matter up again, knowing she could rely on your judgement and honesty.'

'The Ty Coz, *Monsieur*? In *Le Guide*?'

The Director helped himself to an *oursin*. 'You feel it is not "Stock Pot" material, Aristide? I have to say this sea-food platter is beyond reproach.'

'Not "Stock Pot" material?' Monsieur Pamplemousse could hardly believe his ears. 'After my experience the other evening I would not recommend it for an *oeuf* saucepan – an *oeuf* saucepan riddled with holes – not even a colander! After the other evening I never want to hear the words *La Cuisine Régionale Naturelle* again.'

'Ah!' The Director visibly brightened. 'That, Aristide, is

one wish you may be sure of being granted.'

Monsieur Pamplemousse stared at the Director. 'You mentioned a bargain, *Monsieur*,' he said slowly.

The Director gave a sigh. 'The long and the short of it, Aristide, is that there is no such thing as *La Cuisine Régionale Naturelle. It* was a practical joke on the part of Madame Grante. A figment of her imagination. One which occurred to her soon after she learned you were coming here. She sent word down to her relative and clearly he was only too willing to oblige. You alone were singled out for the so-called *cuisine*.

'And you agreed to it, *Monsieur*?' Memories of the expression on Madame Grante's face the last time he saw her came flooding back; the look of triumph should have been a warning sign. The bitterest pill of all was the thought that the Director had been in on it too!

'You must understand, Aristide, that I had very little choice. You are not the only one to experience trouble with your P39s. In some ways those working out in the field are fortunate. It is hard to argue with a man who says he needed extra *essence* for his car so that he could circum-navigate a traffic jam in order to reach a restaurant on time. It is his word against Madame Grante's. I have no such advantage.

'Besides, short of committing physical assault on her person in order to retrieve the key, it was the only way I could get my balloon back. And with the Elysée Palace awaiting its return I had no alternative.

'It does show that deep down Madame Grante is not without a sense of humour. A trifle warped, perhaps. But it is there, nevertheless. All is not lost if she has it in her to concoct practical jokes.'

Warped! It was no more a practical joke than that played

by Madame Grante's mother when she gave birth to her in the first place. It was more a calculated act of revenge. Monsieur Pamplepousse was about to let forth on the subject when there was a rustle of cloth and Mr Pickering arrived back He was carrying a salt-cellar.

'Sorry I was a long time. I went into the *Hommes* by mistake and had to wait until the coast was clear before I could get out again. All very tedious.

'That was our Foreign Office on the phone. It seems the airship has now landed safely. A statement is being issued congratulating all concerned and expressing hopes for the future – the usual thing. For the time being there will be no mention of the attempt to blow it up. They will play that side of it by ear. You will be pleased to know that those in charge of catering arrangements are especially singled out for praise. Both food and wine were judged to be beyond reproach.'

The Director raised his glass. 'I would like to second that, Aristide.'

'Hear, hear.' Mr. Pickering joined in the toast. 'And my own thanks to you both once again for all your help. My men are already on their way home.'

Monsieur Pamplemousse finished off his *rillettes* and came to a decision. He signalled for the waitress.

'With your permission, *Monsieur*, I think I shall change my order.'

'Does that mean,' ventured the Director, 'that you have revised your opinion of the Ty Coz? You think it may be worthy of a mention? A recommendation? A future "Stock Pot", perhaps?'

'We shall have to see, *Monsieur*.' Monsieur Pamplemousse refused to be drawn. 'You would not expect Pommes Frites to judge a restaurant on one steak alone.'

367

He felt an approving movement at his feet.

'You are the judge, Aristide. It is your taste buds that will have to make the ultimate decision. One must not let personal matters affect the outcome.

'However, take care when ordering the dessert. I have arranged for a bottle of Château d'Yquem to be made ready the 1904. It would be a pity to waste it on something mundane.'

A 1904 Château d'Yquem! Monsieur Pamplemousse could hardly believe his ears. What riches! No wonder the Director had trouble with his P39s. It must have cost a small fortune. Suddenly all was forgiven. If it was a case of quid pro quo, then it was worth every centime. Clearly, by his expression, Mr. Pickering felt the same way.

'I ordered two bottles for the maiden voyage,' explained the Director. 'Afterwards it occurred to me that they might not even get through one and it seemed a pity to waste it. Who knows where it would have ended up?'

'Of course, *Monsieur*. I'm sure Madame Grante will understand.'

'I hope, Pamplemousse,' said the Director severely, 'that Madame Grante will never know.'

'Madame Grante again?' Mr. Pickering pricked up his ears. 'I feel I almost want to meet her.'

'It could be arranged,' said Monsieur Pamplemousse. 'You could travel back to Paris with me tomorrow.'

'Unfortunately,' said Mr. Pickering, 'I'm afraid that won't be possible. I am arranging for Mrs. Pickering to join me for a few days. The sea air will do her good. It will help blow the cobwebs away.'

He glanced around the dining room. 'We could do worse than stay here. Eunice would appreciate the décor. Perhaps you could send me some copies of those photographs you took of the old harridan outside the *Sanisette*. She would appreciate those too.'

It was hard to tell if Mr. Pickering was being serious or not. It was hard to tell a lot of things with Mr. Pickering. The English were trained from an early age not to reveal their true feelings, even when making jokes.

The restaurant was almost empty. Couples with young children had already gone up to their rooms, those without were thinking about it over a final, lingering coffee.

The d'Yquem almost defied description. Rich, fragrant, the colour of old gold, and despite its age, in perfect condition.

At the end of their meal Monsieur Pamplemousse, feeling more replete that he had for a long time, positively awash with good things and with the taste of the Director's wine still lingering in his mouth, announced his intention of taking Pommes Frites for a last stroll down to the harbour.

The Director and Mr. Pickering said their goodbyes in the foyer, then the Director went up to his room to make a telephone call, 'You go ahead, Aristide,' he called. 'I will catch up with you down at the Port.'

Mr. Pickering hesitated as they made their way out of the hotel. He obviously had something on his mind.

'I think you will find the girl from the circus much recovered, Aristide,' he said. 'I'm told you were worried about her.'

'Yasmin? You know her?'

'I know *of* her. When she came round she started calling out your name. I happened to hear about it quite by chance. Ironically, the staff at the hospital kept trying to feed her grapefruit. Having seen you the previous evening it suddenly clicked in my mind.

'When she realised the truth of what had happened she went into a state of shock. That was when she was moved. Luckily for her as it turned out; Andreas might have had another go. Now she is on the mend – it is only a matter of time.'

Monsieur Pamplemousse looked put out. 'Why wasn't I told?'

'I did my best to pass on the news,' said Mr. Pickering, sounding equally aggrieved, 'but you kept avoiding me.'

'*Touché!*' Monsieur Pamplemousse acknowledged defeat gracefully.

'One of the especially nice things about your country, Aristide,' said Mr. Pickering, as he waved goodbye, 'is that you do have exactly the right word for everything.'

It occurred to Monsieur Pamplemousse as he and Pommes Frites made their way down the road that he didn't even know where Mr. Pickering was staying. Perhaps their paths would cross again one day. It was a very small world.

The church clock was striking eleven as they reached the harbour. He led the way down to the narrow strip of beach left by a high tide which was now on the turn. Walking on the dry sand was hard work, and twice he stumbled over a discarded beer can. After a few minutes he gave up and mounted some steps leading to the promenade. The young couple from the hotel strolled past arm in arm, their Walkman sets going full blast. What it must be like on the business end of the headphones was hard to imagine. In a few years' time they would probably both be deaf; not that it would matter very much by the look of it. Strange that an invention which had its roots in communication should be death to all conversation.

The circus was in darkness. Not surprisingly, there could have been no performance that evening. Even before he got there he caught a whiff of charred wood. There was a police car parked near the wreckage. He could see the occasional glow of a cigarette from one of the occupants. For a moment or two he toyed with the idea of crossing the road and knocking on Madame Caoutchouc's door, then he thought better of it. Besides, there was nothing he could say that hadn't been said already, and he didn't want to risk a second attack of cramp. It would be another news item for the local *journal*, which must be having a field day. Perhaps it would be put down to a gas cylinder exploding.

He stood for a while thinking about Yasmin, wondering if he was pleased or sorry not to have seen her perform. Suddenly their meeting seemed an age away.

As he turned to make his way back along the promenade he caught sight of someone standing beside one of the telephone *cabines*. Pommes Frites pricked up his ears and as he ran forward a young girl wearing a thin, white cotton dress came towards them.

'Sister, please may I speak with you?'

Monsieur Pamplemousse looked round, then realised she was talking to him. She had dark, curly hair and an oval, face. Her lipstick looked brown under the artificial light.

'Of course. What is it you want?'

'*Quelle heure est-il?*'

Without thinking, he looked at his watch. 'It is fifteen minutes past eleven.' The gold Cupillard Rième gleamed momentarily in the light. Patently it was not a ladies' model.

If the girl noticed, she was unperturbed; rather the reverse it seemed, for she immediately fell into step alongside him, assuming an almost proprietorial air. It wouldn't have surprised him if she'd linked arms.

'Would you like to hear about my problems?'

'Your problems?' She looked hardly old enough to have problems, other than with her homework. The promenade was now totally deserted. Even the couple with the earphones were nowhere to be seen. He tried to keep his voice as high as possible.

'Tell me, my dear, what is troubling you?'

The girl lowered her head. 'I am afraid it is to do with men, Sister.'

'Ah, men.' Monsieur Pamplemousse managed to imbue his reply with all the sympathy at his command. His protective instincts were roused. How often had he not heard the same remark. Men! A pretty girl, young and full of innocence, still at school, and yet already at the mercy of all and sundry. Men who wanted nothing more than to use her to satisfy their selfish lusts.

'My child, you must understand that young men are not like young girls. They cannot always help themselves. It is in their nature to be the hunter. Sadly, and it is hard to understand I know, sex is often uppermost in their minds.'

'I know, Sister. It isn't always the young ones who are the worst either.' The girl ran her tongue slowly round her upper lip. Monsieur Pamplemousse did his best to pretend he hadn't noticed. His own lips suddenly felt remarkably dry.

'You must not lose faith, my child,' he began. 'Always remember, true faith needs no evidence.' He wondered where he had heard the phrase before. He was beginning to enjoy his part. Perhaps he had missed his vocation.

'But, Sister, it is not the fault of the men.' The girl stopped and stared up at him through large, round eyes. He couldn't help but notice that in the moonlight they also looked impossibly blue. 'If it was only that there would be

372

no problem. I am well able to look after myself. It is my fault. I think I must have a devil inside me. I cannot leave them alone. I think of little else. It keeps me awake at night.'

'You can't!' Monsieur Pamplemousse lowered his voice. 'I mean, it does?'

'In the long winter months when the nights seem endless and during the summer when they are hot …

'It is not just sex either, I mean, ordinary sex. It is … other things.'

'*Other* things?' Monsieur Pamplemousse looked round uneasily. Pommes Frites was pointedly relieving himself on a nearby lamp-post. He always seemed to have reserves he could draw on for such occasions. He was wearing his *déjà vu* expression. It was hard to tell whether it had to do with his task in hand or the new arrival. Strongly suspecting the latter, Monsieur Pamplemousse avoided his gaze, listening instead to the complicated tales coming from alongside him. They were growing wilder and more improbable by the minute. How much of it was true and how much a product of the girl's imagination he had no idea, but clearly she had a future in the world of letters. Had he been a literary agent he would have signed her up on the spot.

'My dear,' he exclaimed. 'This is terrible. Have you not made your confession to the good Father?'

'Many times, Sister. But sometimes it seems as though he does not really wish me to be cured. I think he looks forward to my visits. He is always asking me when I am coming next. He is excitable and lately I have become frightened of being in the same box with him. Which is why I have turned to those of your calling.'

Monsieur Pamplemousse looked round uneasily. 'That is what we are here for, my dear.'

She looked up at him again and moved a little closer. 'You nuns have been so good to me, and so generous.'

'We have?' Monsieur Pamplemousse felt his voice going again.

The girl nodded vigorously. 'Yes, all of you. Ever since you arrived. There is not one of you this past week who has not listened to me with patience and understanding, often far into the night. Some of you kept coming back for more. But now that most of you have left I don't know where to turn.'

'My child, my poor child,' Monsieur Pamplemousse looked towards the port. He reached out, intending to point her in that direction, then thought better of it. Allard was right. He always maintained there was one in every class. And he should know – he'd once been a teacher. Some of his tales about sixth-formers asking to stay on after school because they were having trouble with their biology homework were spellbinding.

'Will you listen to me, Sister? There are many more things I can tell you. Your time won't be wasted.'

Monsieur Pamplemousse took a deep breath. He sensed Pommes Frites concentrating on their every word, looking from one to the other as he waited for them to catch up.

Hearing footsteps he glanced across the road. They were heading towards the *Sanisette*. He hesitated, but only for a second. It was too good an opportunity to miss.

'I think,' he pointed towards the approaching figure. 'I think it is really a case for the Mother Superior. She is very wise in such matters. I'm sure she will listen to you.'

'Thank you, Sister. Oh, thank you.' For a moment he thought the girl was going to kiss him, then he realised she had her hand out. He reached automatically into an inside pocket and withdrew a fifty franc note.

A moment later she was gone. It was just as well. It could have been an expensive evening.

Pommes Frites registered his approval with a wag of the tail as he followed his master towards the Quai Général de Gaulle. He wasn't at all sure what had been going on, but he sensed that all was now well again. The crisis had passed.

Apart from a few lights coming from the Hôtel and from some of the yachts at their moorings, the Port was in darkness. Somewhere, far out at sea, there was a flashing beacon.

A fishing boat chugged its way out through the harbour entrance. The men on deck were busy coiling ropes, getting ready for their night's work.

Monsieur Pamplemousse stayed until the light at the masthead was a barely visible speck on the horizon, then he turned and made his way slowly back towards the town. At long last he posted Doucette's card at the P.T.T. – with luck it might even reach Paris before he did. It felt almost like an act of absolution.

He glanced along the narrow street towards the *Gendarmerie*. All the lights on the upper floors were on. The *Barbouze* must still be at it. He could picture the inquests being held. They were likely to be at it all through the night. He was glad to be out of it.

'Pamplemousse! Pamplemousse!' He heard a pounding of feet and a figure suddenly loomed out of the darkness behind them. It was the Director. He was clutching his wallet. It crossed Monsieur Pamplemousse's mind that perhaps he wanted change for a 200 franc note, then he dismissed the idea as being unworthy. The Director looked as if he was in need of help of a different kind. His habit was not at its best. At a passing-out parade in the Vatican he would not have been in line for the golden sceptre as the best turned out Mother Superior of his year. He was also patently short of breath.

'Thank goodness you're still here. You will never believe what I have to tell you.'

Monsieur Pamplemousse looked at the Director. He thought of the time that he and Pommes Frites had spent in Port St. Augustin; he thought of Mr. Pickering, the dirigible, and those who had travelled in it; he thought of the circus, of Madame Caoutchouc and of Andreas; he thought of Yasmin and the fact that tomorrow he would be able to stop off at the hospital and see her again. Then he looked up. The sky was inky-black. He could see the Milky Way and the Plough and beyond that the North Star. Glinting faintly above him were the Great Bear and a host of other heavenly bodies of greater and lesser magnitude.

'*Monsieur*,' he said innocently, 'on such a night as this anything is possible. Tell me the worst.'

Monsieur Pamplemousse Investigates

Contents

1
THE LAUNCH PARTY

It should have served as an omen. Half-way down the
Avenue Junot, while out for his early-morning walk with
Pommes Frites, Monsieur Pamplemousse encountered a
large black van parked across the pavement outside an
apartment block. As he squeezed his way through the tiny
gap left between the open rear doors and the entrance to the
building, he glanced inside and saw a series of racks running
along each wall of the interior. Five of them were filled by
leather, coffin-shaped containers. The sixth was empty,
awaiting the arrival of another customer.

It was a common enough sight at that time of the year. All
the same, it cast a temporary gloom on their outing, a gloom
which the leaden clouds almost stationary overhead did
nothing to alleviate. Even Pommes Frites hurried on his way
as though anxious to put the matter behind him as quickly
as possible.

Turning into the Rue Caulaincourt, Monsieur Pamplemousse pulled his jacket collar up to shield his neck from
the cold east wind and quickened his pace still further. He
wished now he'd worn an overcoat, but at the beginning of
the month – much against Madame Pamplemousse's advice
– he'd put it away for the year. Pride forbade that he should
take it out again, but if the bad weather continued much
longer he might have to. March, which had started warm
and springlike, was not going out without a struggle. Every

evening the news on the television had fresh tales of woe to tell.

Two sparrows having an early-morning bathe in the water swirling its way down the gutters of the Butte took off when they saw Pommes Frites approaching. A street-cleaning waggon scuttled past like a scalded cat.

Others had their problems too. Pruning had started later than usual in the little vineyard on the nearby slopes of Montmartre, and the tables and chairs which would normally have appeared by now in the Place du Tertre ready for the tourist season were still under cover. The Easter eggs in the window of the *boulangerie* looked premature.

Carrying a bag of breakfast supplies and a copy of the morning *journal,* Monsieur Pamplemousse retraced his steps back up the hill. He took a short cut this time – up the Rue Simon Dereure and through the little park opposite his apartment. It was a truncated version of what he called 'the round', but it was no morning for lingering.

Armed with a pointed stick, the park-keeper was doing his rounds, prodding at sleeping figures tucked away in odd corners, sheltering from the wind.

Out of respect for their plight, Monsieur Pamplemousse looked the other way. Windows on the upper floors of surrounding buildings were being flung open as women appeared and began draping bedclothes across their balcony railings to be aired. Some children were already hard at work on the slides in the play area, their downward progress slowed by the morning dew.

If it weren't for all the cars parked at the sides of the roads, Montmartre in the early morning wasn't so far removed from the way it must have been when Utrillo painted it.

Waiting by the Boules area for Pommes Frites he remembered the encounter with the van and wondered if perhaps there would be one player less that afternoon. One thing was certain: it wouldn't stop the game. Nothing short of an earthquake would ever do that.

Back home again, Monsieur Pamplemousse found *café* already percolating on the stove and a glass of freshly squeezed orange juice beside his plate. Pommes Frites slaked his thirst noisily from a bowl of water and then collapsed in a heap on a rug under the kitchen table while he waited for his *petit déjeuner*.

Distributing his purchases, a *croissant* on the opposite plate, and a *pain au sucre* for himself, Monsieur Pamplemousse settled down and glanced through the *journal* while he waited for Doucette to join him.

It was the usual mixture of gloom and despondency; news of the weather still predominated. He sometimes wondered why he bothered to read it, except that the day always felt incomplete without at least a cursory glance through the headlines, and he was about to discard it when his eye alighted on a brief entry amongst a list of recent bereavements. It stood out from the rest by virtue of being in bolder type. For a moment or two he could scarcely believe his eyes. Then he jumped to his feet.

'*Sacrebleu!* It is not possible!'

'What is not possible?' Madame Pamplemousse, her hair still in rollers, bustled in from the bedroom. 'You are forever telling me all things are possible.'

'The Director is *mort!*'

'What? I don't believe it!' Madame Pamplemousse automatically crossed herself.

He handed her the *journal*. 'Look for yourself.'

She scanned the entry briefly and then handed the *journal* back to him. 'Poof! It is typical. They cannot even get the date right.'

Stifling his irritation, Monsieur Pamplemousse re-read the item. It was also typical of Doucette that she should fasten on some minor detail and in so doing, lose sight of the whole. What did it matter if it was today's date, yesterday's date, or even, as in the present case, a whole week away? Which was also, by sheer coincidence, the third Tuesday in March, traditionally publication day of *Le Guide*. The fact that she was right did nothing to soften the blow. The printer's error was a trivial matter by comparison. Perhaps the compositor responsible had recognised the name and gone into a state of shock, emotion dulling his skills. There were a hundred possible explanations. The important fact was that the Director, the head of France's oldest and most respected food guide, was no longer with them. Blinds in restaurants the length and breadth of the Republic would be lowered; flags across the nation would be flown at half-mast.

He lifted the telephone receiver and dialled his office number. Not surprisingly, it was engaged. The switchboard was probably awash with incoming calls.

'It would happen today of all days.'

'If you're dead, you're dead.' Madame Pamplemousse reached for the *café*. 'It doesn't make any difference which day it is. Will you care which day it is when it happens to you? I certainly shan't.'

'Today, Couscous,' said Monsieur Pamplemousse simply, 'happens to be the very day when the text for the new edition of *Le Guide* is being sent to the printers. It is what we have all been working for over the past year. There was to have been the usual send-off party …'

'It will still go to the printers.'

'*Oui*, Couscous, it will still go. But it will not be the same.'

There wouldn't be the Director's speech for a start. Every year they all assembled in the boardroom – office staff, Inspectors, everyone connected with the production – and there was a buffet lunch. Apart from the annual staff outing in Normandy, it was the one occasion in the year when they all got together and were able to swop reminiscences and talk about the things that had happened to them over the past year. Often it went on far into the night.

'At least you'll be home early for a change, *and* you'll be spared the speech. You've always said that once the Director gets going there's no stopping him.'

Monsieur Pamplemousse finished his *pain au sucre* and rose from the table. 'I must change. I can't go looking like this.' There was no point in discussing the matter. Either you understood these things or you didn't. It was really a case of rhythms. Some things that were said half-jokingly in life did not bear repeating after death. Often the things that seemed tedious at the time were the things you missed most of all.

'You'll find your black suit in a plastic bag behind the vacuum cleaner. I had it cleaned after you went to your Tante Mathilde's funeral last May.'

He looked out of the bedroom window. Was it his imagination, or were the clouds even darker than they had been earlier? He shivered. His winter suit felt stiff after his comfortable, lived-in clothes. It also smelled of mothballs, but at least the material was warm.

He still could hardly believe the news. It was only a matter of weeks since he'd last seen the Director and he'd been looking unusually hale and hearty then. A trifle over-weight perhaps, but weren't they all? It was an occupational hazard. On an impulse he went into the bathroom and stepped on the scales, then wished he hadn't. Even allowing for the fact that his suit was made of heavy material, it was still not good news.

Pommes Frites was waiting for him when he came out of the bathroom. He had a black bow tied to his collar and his coat had been freshly brushed.

'Take care.'Doucette came to the door and kissed him goodbye. 'If you speak to *Monsieur le Directeur's* wife, do tell her how sorry I am.' Monsieur Pamplemousse gave her a squeeze. Bad news took people in different ways. He knew that deep down she was really very upset.

He gave a final wave as the lift doors started to close. '*A bientôt.*'

'I will expect you when I see you.'It was a throw-away remark, although had he but known, it would echo in his ears for days to come. In any case he had too many things running through his mind to do more than give an answering nod.

Who would take over the running of *Le Guide* for a start? It was impossible to picture anyone new. As far as he was concerned the Director had always been there. They had enjoyed a special relationship, too; a relationship which dated back to his days in the *Sûreté.* He had once done the Director a favour while working on a case, and it had later borne fruit, when he had found himself forced into early retirement and by a stroke of good fortune they had bumped into each other again. If it hadn't been for that chance meeting he wouldn't have landed a job with *Le Guide.*

He paused at the top of the steps leading down to the Lamarck-Caulaincourt Métro, then spotted a taxi waiting in the rank further down the road. It would save any possible arguments with ticket collectors over Pommes Frites' size. Like most of the other Inspectors, he had taken advantage of the lunch party to put his car in for a service. Now he was beginning to regret the decision.

It was also ironic that the Director should pass away at this particular time – just as they were about to be computerised. Under his management *Le Guide* had always been in the forefront of the latest scientific developments. It was like France itself in a way – on the one hand, firmly rooted in the best traditions of the past, on the other, paying homage at the altar of progress, and long may it remain so.

Perhaps because of the strong smell of mothballs, the driver pointedly opened his window. Once again Monsieur Pamplemousse regretted his lack of an overcoat. Pommes Frites, ever-sensitive to his master's moods, looked suitably put out as he gazed at the passing scene.

The decision to commit the entire guide to a computer had not been taken lightly. It was undoubtedly a logical step if they were to keep one step ahead of their competitors, but given the vast number of entries and the immense amount of information which flowed into *Le Guide*'s headquarters every day of the year, information which needed to be collated and analysed, weighed and debated upon before it was programmed, it was also a mind-boggling task. As he'd said to Doucette: a year's work. And there were rumours that other innovations were about to be unveiled. It was a shame the Director wouldn't be there to announce them.

As they crossed the Pont de l'Alma and swung round in a wide arc in order to circumnavigate the Place de la Résistance, Monsieur Pamplemousse asked the driver to stop when he had a suitable opportunity. It wasn't so much that he needed the walk, it was more a matter of composing himself before he reached the office. A quiet stroll along the bank of the Seine would do him good.

Half-way along the Quai d'Orsay he overtook one of his colleagues, Glandier, obviously doing the same thing.

Glandier shook hands as he came up alongside. 'A bad business.'

'Unbelievable.'

'If you ask me,'said Glandier gloomily, 'there's a jinx on the place. What with last week …'

'Last week?'

'You mean, you haven't heard?'

Monsieur Pamplemousse shook his head. 'I've been on the road for the last month.'

Glandier gave a hollow laugh. 'You missed all the fun. Someone put a piranha fish in the fountain outside the main entrance. There was hell to pay.'

Monsieur Pamplemousse whistled. 'What happened?'

'It ate all the goldfish for a start. Then it nearly did for one of the typists. Apparently she was sitting on the side having her *déjeuner*. She only put her hand in the water for a split second, and … whoosh!'

'Whoosh! Is she … ?'

Glandier raised his hand and waggled it from side to side. '*Comme ci, comme ça.* Poof! Luckily she was wearing gloves. She has regained the power of speech, but it's probably put her off sandwiches for life.'

As they turned into the Esplanade des Invalides Monsieur Pamplemousse spotted a row of large grey vans parked at the far end of the Rue Fabert. Cables were snaked across the pavement. A man wearing headphones waved a clipboard to someone inside the courtyard of *Le Guide*'s headquarters.

'They are here already!'

Both men quickened their pace until they drew level with the first of the vans, when they were suddenly stopped dead in their tracks. An open door revealed an outside-broadcast control-room, and they could just see a row of television screens showing varying shots of the same subject. Unmistakably, that subject was the Director himself.

'It must be an old film. I'm not sure I want to see it.'

Glandier was about to go on his way when Monsieur Pamplemousse stopped him.

'*Attendez!*' He pushed a path through a small knot of sightseers gathered on the pavement.

Above the hum of generators and the barking of orders from a producer seated in front of a control panel, they clearly heard snatches of a familiar voice.

'... deeply grateful for the concern everyone has shown ... a foolish prank on the part of someone as yet unidentified ... as you can see ... no, it is *not* a publicity stunt ...' The picture on the largest of the monitors – one labelled TRANSMISSION – changed to a tight close-up of the Director looking angry at the thought. '*Le Guide* has never had need for such things, nor, whilst I remain in charge, will it ever.'

The rest was drowned by a round of applause. The camera zoomed out and the picture on the monitor changed to a studio shot. The interview was over. Everyone in the van relaxed.

'*Sapristi!* What do you make of it?'Glandier hurried after Monsieur Pamplemousse as he led the way towards the entrance to *Le Guide*'s headquarters. 'I'll tell you something for nothing. There's bound to be another mishap. Things always go in threes.'

The big double gates were open and the inner courtyard was crowded with people; the television crew, already dismantling their equipment ready for the next assignment, had given way to hordes of reporters and press photographers. Standing at the top of the steps leading to the main entrance was the erect figure of the Director. He appeared to be making the most of the situation: head back, chin out, right hand thrust beneath one lapel of his jacket, he looked for all the world as though he was giving an impersonation of Napoleon addressing his troops prior to giving the off signal for their historic crossing of the Alps.

Beyond the huge plate-glass doors Monsieur Pample-mousse could see rows of familiar faces pressed against the glass. Like himself, many of those present were dressed in black. Word must have spread like wildfire.

The battery of discharging flash-guns and the accompa-nying volley of clicking shutters would have been more than enough to satisfy even the most unpopular member of government hoping to achieve re-election; no film star seeking publicity for her current extravaganza would have had any cause to complain. Certainly the Director himself looked far from displeased as he gave a final wave to the news-hungry crowd before disappearing into the building.

'So much for the anonymity of *Le Guide*,' said Glandier.

Monsieur Pamplemousse gave a grunt. 'He's probably right. Get it all over in one fell swoop. There's nothing more dangerous than an unsatisfied reporter.'

All the same, he knew what Glandier meant. Entry to the hallowed forecourt was normally only achieved by means of a magnetic card issued solely to employees of *Le Guide*. Even then, they had to pass the scrutiny of old Rambaud, the commissionaire, who had been there for longer than anyone else could remember. This furore would probably give him nightmares for weeks to come.

As they entered the building, the Director detached himself from a group congregated near the reception desk and drew Monsieur Pamplemousse to one side.

'I've been trying to get hold of you, Pamplemousse,' he complained, in the accusing tone of voice peculiar to those

whose attempts to make contact with someone by telephone have been unsuccessful.

'I called as soon as I heard the news, *Monsieur*,' said
Monsieur Pamplemousse defensively. 'All lines were
engaged.'It was not his fault if Doucette had gone out shopping.

'It is an infuriating business. I shall not rest until I get to
the bottom of it. If I discover the culprit is a member of the
staff ...' The rest was left to the imagination.

'You think it is someone within *Le Guide*, *Monsieur*?'

'I can think of no other possible explanation. Michelin
wouldn't stoop to such a thing. Besides, they have already
sent their condolences in the form of a red rocking-chair
made out of poppies. A singular honour, particularly as I am
told poppies are out of season. And Gault-Millau may have
their eccentricities, but I can't believe they would be capable
of perpetrating something so juvenile. They have denied all
knowledge.'

'Have you enquired of the *journal* concerned,
Monsieur?'

'I have indeed. I spoke with the editor at length soon after
the news broke. Apparently the entry was placed over the
telephone late yesterday evening by someone purporting to
be the proprietor. It was dealt with by a junior who has, I
gather, already departed for pastures new.

'Once today is over, Pamplemousse, I want you to take
charge of the investigation. It needs someone with a finger
on the pulse of the organisation, someone skilled in the art
of keeping a discreet ear to the ground, whilst at the same
time possessed of a nose for the scent of untoward behaviour. Your past training will be invaluable.'

Monsieur Pamplemousse absorbed this news with something less than enthusiasm. Apart from the dubious

mechanics of the Director's roll-call of his talents, which made the task ahead sound more suited to Pommes Frites, he had no wish to become embroiled in a situation which could well result in ill-feeling from the rest of the staff if they felt he was prying into their affairs.

However, any protests he might have voiced were rendered stillborn as the Director departed in order to prepare himself for his annual speech.

Monsieur Pamplemousse joined in the general throng making their way up to the boardroom on the fourth floor–some by lift, others, like himself, by the central staircase. In a matter of moments he was deep into shaking hands, greeting old friends and making new ones; Truffert asked to be reminded later to relate the story of an adventure he'd had on the Orient Express; Guilot, still persisting with his diet of fresh carrot juice before all meals, and clearly ignoring his weight problem for the day, was looking positively orange; Daladier had stumbled across a new restaurant near Strasbourg, which for the area he rated second only to that of the Haeberlin brothers; Trigaux in the art department – busily recording the event with his camera for *L'Escargot*, the staff magazine – had a new piece of photographic equipment he wanted to show Monsieur Pamplemousse when he had time.

The catering department had excelled themselves. It was their one moment of glory in the year, a chance to demonstrate that their skills extended beyond Tuesday's *cassoulet* and Friday's inevitable *ragoüt*. *Pâtés* vied with each other alongside an array of cold meats and salads; there was one table devoted entirely to fish and another to meat; tureens full of as yet undisclosed delights simmered away on a fourth. There was a display of cheese on a fifth followed by a tempting display of *desserts* for those who managed to stay the course.

Champagne greeted them as they entered the room, while on other tables at the far end were gathered an assortment of bottles to delight both the eye and the palate. Without straining too much, Monsieur Pamplemousse picked out and mentally earmarked a Bâtard-Montrachet from Remoissenet and a Charmes-Chambertin bearing the illustrious name of Dujac. On another table there was an impressive collection of old Armagnacs and Cognacs.

Given the fact that most of those present were in various degrees of mourning, ranging from a mere armband to total blackness (and those in the former category clearly regretted they hadn't taken more trouble over their dress; the Director had an eye for such things), it looked more like a convention of undertakers getting together after an unusually successful year than a gathering of hungry gourmets anxious to do justice to what lay before them.

Monsieur Pamplemousse wished now he'd been less optimistic about his chances of returning home early. He looked round, weighing up the possibility of slipping back outside in order to make a quick phone call to Doucette – he could tell her the good news about the Director at the same time – but the crush of people following on behind made it hardly worth contemplating.

Glandier clinched matters by handing him a plate.

'We shall suffer for this,' he murmured. 'But what suffering! I'm glad I've got a late pass back at the works.'

Reminded of his responsibilities by a pressure against his right leg, Monsieur Pamplemousse picked up another plate for Pommes Frites.

As he moved slowly along the succession of tables, listening to the conversation and the laughter coming from all sides, it was hard to picture there being a Judas in the camp. If such a person existed, he – or she – would be very well fed. Well fed, and ungrateful to boot. The Director might have his faults, but no one could possibly complain of being badly treated. Goodness knows what the lunch must have cost. He wouldn't like to have to foot the bill.

The thought triggered off another. So far he hadn't set eyes on Madame Grante. As Head of Accounts she was usually at the forefront of things, keeping an eagle eye on all that went on. Truffert had a theory she checked their portions and made it up afterwards when it came to going through their expense sheets. He glanced around, but she was nowhere to be seen.

Feeling suddenly in need of a little peace and quiet, Monsieur Pamplemousse made his way to the far end of the room and found himself a chair near the dais from which the Director would be making his speech later that afternoon. On the platform there was a lectern and a small table on which reposed a glass and an ominously large bottle of Badoit. To the rear there was another table bearing an object covered in a shroud from beneath which there emerged a cable connected to a wall socket.

Gradually the hubbub died down as talk gave way to the serious business of eating. Waiters in fawn-coloured uniform embroidered with replicas of *Le Guide*'s symbol – two escargots rampant – moved discreetly to and fro amongst the crowd, charging and recharging glasses.

If the Bâtard-Montrachet was grand and sumptuous, the Charmes-Chambertin was elegance personified; each was more than worthy of the occasion and both improved as the afternoon wore on. All in all, by the time the Director made his entrance, Monsieur Pamplemousse felt at peace with the world. His only regret was that he'd seated himself in a position from which there was patently no escape, right next to the dais. A quiet sleep was out of the question; a noisy one even more so. It was worse than being back at school. He wished now he'd stuck with Glandier.

'I do not propose,' began the Director, holding up one hand for silence, 'to dwell on this morning's events, nor do I intend to speculate on the possible motivation for what on the surface would seem to be an utterly senseless and irresponsible action.'

Monsieur Pamplemousse suppressed a groan. He knew the signs. When the Director said he wasn't going to dwell on something it usually meant quite the opposite. They were in for a long peroration. He hoped Pommes Frites behaved. One year, when some unidentified person had laced his water bowl with *vin rouge*, he had disgraced himself by snoring loudly during a particularly long and boring passage.

Monsieur Pamplemousse half-closed his eyes and placed one hand on his forehead in what he hoped would be interpreted as a look of deep concentration.

It was a very strange business and no mistake. If it was a practical joke, then it was in dubious taste and must have caused more heartaches than laughter. Hoaxes were all very well in their way, but there were limits.

Having relieved himself of his feelings on the subject of the morning's events, the Director devoted the first part of his speech to the usual statistics relating to the past year's activities. Out of over fifty thousand restaurants and hotels currently listed in the archives, less than ten thousand had found their way into *Le Guide*. That was not a denigration of those establishments who failed to gain entry, rather a pointer to *Le Guide*'s very high standards. Standards which, in a world where the very currency of the word was tending to become more and more debased, they must endeavour to maintain regardless of the cost. Reputations took years to build up; they could be destroyed overnight.

Out of the nine thousand eight hundred and twenty-three restaurants mentioned, eighteen had been singled out for the supreme accolade of three Stock Pots, eighty-one would receive two Stock Pots – a change in an upward direction of three over the previous year – and five hundred and nineteen teen were being awarded one Stock Pot. Congratulatory telexes were being prepared.

There were the usual moments of light relief. Reference was made to how many kilometres of *saucisses* and *saucissons* had been consumed by Inspectors in the course of duty. There were statistics relating to car mileage, the amount of wine drunk, and a pointed reference to the percentage rise in claims for expenses.

In proposing the usual vote of thanks to Madame Grante for her painstaking preparation of the figures, the Director raised a hollow laugh when he said that despite constant research a machine had yet to be perfected which would in any way replace her. Someone at the back of the room – it sounded like Truffert – triggered off a titter by shouting '*Quel dommage!*' It was instantly quelled by a strong glare from the Director.

Monsieur Pamplemousse looked round the room again, but there was still no sign of Madame Grante. Perhaps, despite the Director's words, she had taken umbrage. People were very resistant to change when their own jobs were threatened, and he'd heard rumours to the effect that all was not well in her department.

'We come now,' continued the Director, 'to the moment in the afternoon you have doubtless all been waiting for. I refer, of course, to the decision we made last year to enter the computer age.

'It was a decision, I need hardly tell you, which was not arrived at without a great deal of heart searching. *Le Guide* has always prided itself on its efficiency and in being in the forefront of all the latest scientific and managerial developments. In the past our unique filing system has been the envy of many of our rivals. However, in recent years we have been falling behind. We can no longer afford to ignore either the march of progress or the benefits which the coming of the computer has conferred on those who have acquired one. Information is our working capital, and anything which enables us to draw on that capital and make use of it quickly and efficiently can only be for the good.

'There are those who would say that we should have made the move much sooner. To them I would point out that part of our strength has always been those very same qualities which I believe make France the country it is: the will and the ability and the enthusiasm to embrace the new whilst still retaining the best of the old. We have merely taken time to make sure we are balancing the two often conflicting forces in order to achieve a harmonious whole.

'There was a time when computers were surrounded in mystery. Only highly trained operators were allowed anywhere near them, and they became the "elite" – the "high priests" as it were, acquiring power previously reserved for the higher echelons. Then, as so often happens, things turned full circle. Now, with the coming of the microcomputer, power in many companies has been transferred yet again, but this time to anyone capable of operating a keyboard. Both situations have their drawbacks and their hazards. The one is like a ship with a member of the crew who usurps the captain's position but is never seen; the other is like a ship where every member of the crew thinks he is capable of running it.

'I wish to say here and now that *Le Guide* will have but one captain. I intend to remain firmly at the helm.'

The Director took advantage of the sustained applause which greeted this last remark to help himself to a glass of Badoit.

'It is our intention to combine the best of both worlds. We have installed a central computer large enough, and powerful enough, to see us into the next century. On one level it will take care of all the information necessary to produce *Le Guide,* and this information will be accessed by only a few, thus guarding our reputation for anonymity and total secrecy. On another level it will provide us with ample facilities for the many other uses we intend putting it to. Our public information service will be enhanced. Our accounting system will be updated. Our reference library will become second to none. The list of potential benefits is almost endless.

'Concurrent with this technological leap, the first of the major changes I have to announce concerns *Le Guide*'s system of symbols; a system which, although it has amply withstood the test of time, is now in need of reassessment in order to take account of modern developments and changes in social behaviour. Over the past few years we have received many complaints, particularly from our older readers, about the problem of background music in restaurants. The most common argument advanced, and one which I have to admit strikes a chord of sympathy, is that if people feel like sharing their meal with a military band then they should take a picnic lunch in the Champs-Elysées on Bastille Day. Most people go to a restaurant in order to enjoy a meal in peace and quiet, not to have their ears assailed by discordant cacophonies from a battery of ill-concealed loudspeakers. Accordingly, we intend to institute a symbol of ear-plugs rampant for those establishments which come under the heading of "persistent offenders".

'There are to be other new symbols which you will learn about in due course – an unshaded *luminaire* for a low standard of ambience is but one example; others will be introduced in the fullness of time, but slowly, so as not to place too great a burden on you all.'

Aware that the buzz of conversation following his pronouncement had not entirely subsided and that a good part of his audience had seized on the chance to relax, the Director raised his voice.

'I come now to the major event of the afternoon. We have decided to institute a new award which I believe will be unique in the annals of catering. It will be in the form of a golden Stock Pot lid and will be presented annually to the best restaurant in France. The winner will then hold it for a year. There will, of course, be similar awards for the runners-up. A silver lid for the second and a bronze lid for the third.

'A few moments ago I made reference to our system of awarding Stock Pots to those restaurants who merit it, restaurants where the cuisine, the surroundings and the service are all exceptional and justify a special journey, much as Michelin award their stars and Gault-Millau their toques. As you all know, other guides have different systems again, none of which are entirely without merit.

'However, admirable though all these awards are, the one criticism one may level at them – our own included – is that in the final analysis they are still subjective and as such are open to human errors and human frailties; judgements can become clouded – over-indulgence by an Inspector the previous evening, indisposition of the chef on the day itself – the possibilities are endless.

'In order to arrive at a fair, indeed one might almost call it an incontrovertible decision as to which is the very best restaurant in the whole of France, and therefore, almost by definition, the whole of the world, I have decided to take full advantage of our latest acquisition. All this week staff have been busy feeding the computer with every scrap of information obtained over the past year and even while I have been talking it has been sifting this material, digesting and dissecting it, annotating the result, weighing one factor not simply against another, but against many thousand of others. It is a task which I am told would take a hundred skilled mathematicians many months to complete. And yet,'the Director turned and like a magician presenting his *pièce de résistance*, removed the shroud from the object behind him with a flourish, 'such is the miracle of modern science, the answer will be printed out the moment I issue the appropriate command on the keyboard you see in front of you; a keyboard which is connected to the mainframe in our computer room in another part of the building. I, myself, do not as yet know the result – no one does – but I can assure you that it will be as accurate and as unbiased as man could possibly devise.'

Ever one to extract the last *soupçon* of drama from a situation, the Director paused with one finger poised above the keyboard for long enough to allow a total hush to fall over the room. Then, at exactly the right moment, he struck, tapping out a series of instructions at a speed which would have earned him a place in the typing pool any day of the week and which must have taken many hours of rehearsal.

There was a moment of total silence, the barest fraction of a second, then a red lamp winked and a series of bleeps issued from the command module. The printer emitted an answering buzz and as it leapt into life a daisy-wheel rattled out its response like a machine-gun.

From his vantage point near the front, Monsieur Pample-mousse tried to calculate the possibilities, but it was a hope-less task. It was obviously too short for his own nomination Les Cinq Parfaits, near Evian. It was more than one word so it couldn't be Taillevant, or Bocuse. It was too long for Pic or Chapel. La Mère Blanc at Vézelay perhaps?

Once again the Director appeared to be milking the situ-ation for all it was worth. As a sheet of paper emerged from the machine, he tore it off and held it up to the light while his audience waited with baited breath.

They waited in vain. The Director turned white. His lips moved, but gave vent only to a strange choking noise. Clutching at the lectern for support, he slid sideways in a kind of spiralling motion, taking everything with him.

The resultant explosion of sound as both Director and microphone landed on the floor together, amplified by many decibels, produced a momentary state of shock in those nearest to the dais. A second later there was a forward rush to go to his aid. In the excitement the piece of paper he'd been clutching floated to the floor unheeded, save by Pommes Frites who, thinking it was perhaps some new kind of game, reached out his paw. Monsieur Pamplemousse retrieved the sheet before the worst happened. As he scanned the only typewritten words it bore, he too went white.

'Tell us the worst.' It was Glandier.

Monsieur Pamplemousse handed him the paper in silence, unable to bring himself to speak. He wished he'd let Pommes Frites do whatever he'd wanted to do with it.

Glandier whistled. 'No wonder the old man threw a wobbly.'

'Have you ever heard of it?'

'The Wun Pooh? I've *heard* of it. It's a Chinese take-away in Dieppe. It's supposed to be very popular with day-trippers from England. They go there on the way back from their shopping expeditions. Don't you remember? There was all that fuss last year.'

Now that Glandier reminded him, Monsieur Pample-mousse remembered it all too well. Half a ferry-boat had gone down with food poisoning.

'I told you there'd be a third thing,' said Glandier gloomily as he handed back the paper. 'But if you ask me this is the third, fourth, fifth and sixth, all rolled into one. So much for computerisation. If that's what it's come up with it means the end of civilisation as we know it. Talk about micro-chips with everything! I'm going to get myself a pick-me-up. How about you?'

Monsieur Pamplemousse shook his head. Folding the paper carefully in two, he placed it in an inside pocket. Much as he would have liked to join Glandier in a drink, or even two, it was as well to keep a clear head.

In a land where the possibilities for earning an award for culinary distinction were endless and the candidates almost without number, a Chinese take-away in Dieppe had to be fairly low on the list of hopefuls. To nominate it for what promised to be France's premier trophy had to be some kind of joke. It was black humour at its very worst.

Instinct told him that his services were likely to be called for in the not-too-distant future, and when that happened he was going to need every last gramme of stone-cold reasoning he could muster.

2
BYTES AND RAMS

'Pamplemousse, I hope I never have to live through another day like today.' The Director screwed up a sheaf of computer paper, tossed it into a nearby waste-paper bin, and then ran his hand through hair already ruffled by previous encounters.

Monsieur Pamplemousse exchanged a glance with the Staff Nurse as she clicked her case shut and made to leave. One look said it all. The Director must have been giving her a hard time. It showed too, in the state of his office. Normally it was like its incumbent, a model of all that was neat and tidy. There was rarely a paper out of place. Flowers stood to attention in their vases. Now it looked as though a hurricane had recently passed through, leaving in its wake a trail of debris picked up *en route* and then discarded. As for the Director himself, his once immaculately knotted tie hung like a hangman's noose about his neck, his jacket had fallen to the floor and his face was ashen.

'May I refill your glass, *Monsieur*?' It was a superfluous question. The Director handed it to him automatically, then leaned back in his chair.

'Help yourself while you're there. I'm sure you must be in need of one too.'

'Thank you, *Monsieur*, but no.'

'Ah, Aristide, I wish I had your strength of character.'

Monsieur Pamplemousse didn't deny himself the pleasure

of the compliment, although it was self-preservation rather than strength of character that dictated his refusal. He'd said no for the same reason that he had denied Glandier's offer. He wished to keep a clear head. The wisdom of his earlier decision had been confirmed shortly afterwards when he received an urgent but not entirely unexpected summons to the top floor.

He took the Director's glass and crossed to the drinks cupboard. The interior light was on and a half-empty bottle of Cognac stood on the shelf. Perhaps on second thoughts it was only half-full. Why did the first way of putting it always sound so much worse than the second, and why did one invariably choose the first? He picked it up and looked at the label. It was a Roullet *Très Rare Hors d'Age*. The Director didn't stint himself.

Monsieur Pamplemousse felt as if the founder of *Le Guide*, Monsieur Hippolyte Duval, was watching him as he poured a generous helping. Hanging on the wall above the cupboard, it was one of those paintings where the eyes of the subject seem to follow the viewer everywhere. Monsieur Pamplemousse couldn't but reflect that their illustrious founder would be turning in his grave if he had only half an inkling of what was going on. No doubt, were he able to see it, his disapproval would also extend to a computer terminal on its dark grey stand to one side of the drinks cabinet. Even the presence alongside the keyboard of Messieurs Cocks et Féret's tome-like but indispensable 1,800-page compendium of the wines of Bordeaux – *Bordeaux et ses Vins* – would hardly have put him in a better frame of mind. It seemed to be doing service as a paper-weight.

As Monsieur Pamplemousse glanced up at the painting, he gave a start. Monsieur Duval was now sporting a long black beard reaching almost down to his waist.

'*Qu'est-ce que c'est?*'

'You may well ask, Pamplemousse.' The Director held up a large felt-tipped pen. 'To rub salt into the wound, whoever was responsible used one of my own implements to perpetrate the deed.' He dismissed the affair with a wave of his hand. 'Graffiti can be erased – resetting *Le Guide is* another matter entirely.'

'Can the error not be put right, *Monsieur*? Surely that is the beauty of having everything on a computer ...'

The Director gave a groan. 'Would that were so, Pamplemousse. The engineers have been and gone. There is nothing they can do. It has been completely reprogrammed. They are "looking into it", and we all know what that means.'

Monsieur Pamplemousse returned to the Director's desk and handed him the glass. The Director swallowed the contents in one go. Clearly he was in a bad way. 'Pamplemousse ... ask me who won the silver award.'

'Who won the silver award, *Monsieur*?'

'The Restaurant de la Gare in Mougins!'

'The Restaurant de la Gare in Mougins? But that is crazy! For a start there is no *Gare* in Mougins. There isn't even a railway in Mougins. The nearest *Gare* is at Cannes.'

'I know, Aristide. I know. There is no need to remind me.'

'And what about the Moulin de Mougins, *Monsieur*? That is one of France's premier restaurants. It has boasted three Stock Pots for as long as I can remember. Why ...'

'According to our entry it has been relegated to a mere bar stool – the symbol we have always reserved for those wayside cafes where one is assured of a good snack. Even worse, there is an additional note saying, "They should try harder." Verge will be livid. He will undoubtedly seek legal advice.'

'And the bronze Stock Pot lid?'

'It has gone to our own canteen. Much as I like to encourage them in their endeavours, it makes a mockery of the whole thing. Apart from which it savours of nepotism.'

'And the rest of the book, *Monsieur*?'

'*Désastre!*' The Director reached down, picked up a seemingly never-ending length of computer print-out material and allowed it to slide through his fingers to the floor. '*Le Guide* is riddled from beginning to end with entries which are such a travesty of all they are meant to convey they are positively obscene; the Tour d'Argent is slated for the quality of its duck, Pic for his miserly portions, Chapel for being over-addicted to the cruet ... Need I continue?'

Monsieur Pamplemousse shook his head. He could see now why the Director was in such a state. The last time he'd had a meal at Pic he hadn't wanted to eat for days afterwards, and he'd once been present at Chapel when some other diners – a group of tourists – had asked for the salt. They had been shown the door immediately. *Le Guide* prided itself on the accuracy of its entries; the finding of a single misprint was spoken of in hushed tones for days afterwards. When it happened, which was rarely, heads were apt to roll; annual increments were set at risk. But blatant misinformation was something else again. It didn't bear thinking about. The only consolation was that the master disk hadn't gone to the printers. The thought triggered off another.

'I hesitate to mention it, *Monsieur*, but surely there must be a copy of the original somewhere – a duplicate?'

'Pamplemousse ... ?' the Director gestured towards a pile of paper on the floor, 'you are looking at the print-out from the copy. It is the same as the original. That was the first thing I thought of. As you well know, *Le Guide* has always believed in a belt and braces approach to matters of importance. Unfortunately, we failed to make a copy of the copy. Whoever perpetrated this outrage left no stone unturned.'

'And how about insurance, *Monsieur*?'

'You cannot insure against loss of confidence, Aristide. No policy in the world will cover that.'

The Director rose from his desk and crossed to the doors leading to his balcony. He opened them and went outside. For a moment or two he stood leaning over the parapet, gazing into space. Fearing the worst, Monsieur Pample-mousse hurried out to join him. Beyond the Seine, the late afternoon sun broke through a gap in the clouds and momentarily illuminated the dome of the Sacré-Coeur; to their left the Eiffel Tower cast its long shadow over the surrounding houses; to their right there were men playing Boules on the gravelled perimeter of the Parc du Champ-de-Mars. Each in its own way was a symbol of the unchanging pattern of life; both a solace and sharp reminder of their own precarious situation. The Director must have felt it too, for as he turned away he gave a little shiver.

'Never, not once in its history, Aristide, has *Le Guide* been late for publication. It must not, indeed *will* not happen now. I have been in consultation with the printers and the very latest they can hold the presses and still meet our deadline is next Friday – three days from now. It means you will need to work fast. I shall prepare a statement for the media in case the worst happens, but I trust that with your help we shall no need it.'

Monsieur Pamplemousse gave a start. It hadn't occurred to him that the Director wanted to see him for anything more than some passing advice. The name of the right person to contact in the *Sûreté*, perhaps; an expert in what was known as 'hacking', for clearly they were dealing not just with simple fault of programming, but rather an act of deliberate sabotage.

'Surely, *Monsieur,* this is a matter for the police? I know nothing about computers.'

'The police!' The Director gazed at him in horror. 'The police are the last people I wish to involve, Pamplemousse As you must know only too well, if we bring in the police word is bound to get out. With all due respect to your past profession, I doubt very much if they are equipped to deal with this kind of situation; they are bound to seek outside advice and the more people who know the harder it will be to maintain secrecy. Someone will drop a hint to the wrong person and once the story is out reporters will descend on us again like a flock of vultures. You saw what happened this morning. They will not rest until our collective bones have been picked clean. We shall be the laughing stock of the culinary world. *Le Guide*'s credibility will be destroyed forever.'

'But, *Monsieur ...*'

His protestations fell on deaf ears. The Director dismissed them with a wave of the hand. 'I do not wish to hear another word, Aristide. For whatever reason, someone has embarked on a policy clearly aimed at the destruction of *Le Guide*. The acts already carried out – the piranha fish in the fountain, that ridiculous announcement in today's *journal* about my demise, the beard now adorning the face of our founder- were but warning salvoes. Were he – or she – to be successful in their endeavours, then ruination will stare us all in the face. It is a matter for the Security Officer.'

'Ah, I had not realised we have a Security Officer.' Monsieur Pamplemousse tried to keep the note of relief from his voice. For a brief moment he had feared the worst.

'We have now, Pamplemousse.' The Director looked him

straight in the eye. 'All the resources of *Le Guide* will be at your disposal. Money will be no object. You may name your own fee.'

'It is not a question of money, *Monsieur* ...'

'Good, Aristide. Then I will not embarrass you by raising the subject ever again. I knew I could count on your loyalty. It is only a temporary appointment, of course. Once we have surmounted the present problem we shall take steps to regularise the situation, but time is not on our side.'

Monsieur Pamplemousse stared at his chief. There were times when his ability to take things for granted and ride roughshod over people's sensibilities was positively beyond belief. It would have been nice to have had the matter raised just once more; an opportunity to protest a trifle less vehemently on the subject of his remuneration would not have come amiss. But the moment was lost forever. Perhaps reading his thoughts, the Director turned on his heels and went back inside.

Almost as though it were in sympathy, the sun disappeared again. Monsieur Pamplemousse took one last look over the parapet. Paris suddenly seemed to have grown in size.

What was the population of the greater area of the city at the last count? Something over ten million people. And he would be looking for perhaps just one person in all that number – it was hard to picture a whole group waging a vendetta against *Le Guide*.

Despite his protestations, his mind was already racing with thoughts and ideas. The Director was right. Speed and secrecy were both of paramount importance. If the news did leak out they would be done for. He must get on to Glandier straight away – together with anyone else who might have seen the print-out – and impress that fact on them.

Next, he would need to know who'd had access to the computer. Was it remotely possible for it to have been an outside job? If it wasn't, then it would make his task that much easier. If it was, then he hardly knew where to start. One thing was certain: he would need to take a crash course to end all crash courses on the subject before he could even begin to ask the right questions, let alone understand the answers.

'Well, Aristide?' The Director looked up from his desk as Monsieur Pamplemousse entered the room.

'Tell me about the computer, *Monsieur*.'

'Ah, yes, the computer.' A slightly glazed expression entered the Director's eyes. 'I have to confess that once the decision was made to commit *Le Guide* to what I believe are known as "*les disques*", a term which put me in mind of a *salle de danse* when I first heard it used, and once a suitable model had been chosen – if I remember correctly, it is a Poulanc DB23, the 457 version, if that means anything to you – I left the matter very much in the hands of the experts.'

'Do you know what language it speaks, *Monsieur*?' Grabbing at straws, Monsieur Pamplemousse tried to make it sound as though he knew what he was talking about.

The Director gave a snort. 'An alien language. Pamplemousse. One which is totally beyond my comprehension. It is, I believe, largely a question of "bytes" and "rams", neither of which are terms I even remotely begin to understand, nor do I wish to. Life is complicated enough as it is without such esoteric subdivisions.'

'I was really thinking of security, *Monsieur*. How, *par exemple*, could the computer have been made to produce a print-out which is so full of inaccuracies? At this moment it isn't so much a matter of knowing who did it, but rather *how* it was done. If we know the answer to the last question it may provide us with an answer to the first.'

'Ah, there you have me, Pamplemousse. There you have me. At my insistence security is as perfect as what I believe they somewhat prosaically call "the state of the art" can make it.'

'With respect, *Monsieur,* security is usually only as good as the people who operate it.'

'True, Pamplemousse, true. However, in this case you are dealing with a situation where information relating to the new issue of *Le Guide* can only be accessed provided the correct code-word is used. A code-word which is changed on a daily basis and is known to but two people, myself included.'

'And the other person, *Monsieur*? May I know who it is?'

'It is Madame Grante. In the fullness of time we plan to extend the range of the machine to include all our accounting procedures. Naturally this will take time, but ...'

'How did she take to the thought of being computerised, *Monsieur*?'

The Director raised his hands. 'Understandably, she was not wildly enthusiastic at first. People, particularly of Madame Grante's age and disposition, are resistant to change. But gradually she came round to seeing our point of view particularly when she began to realise the very positive advantages it would have. Information which would normally take her weeks to collate will be at her fingertips by the mere pressing of a button. P39s will no longer pile up in her pending tray. It was largely because I needed her goodwill that I brought her into the project at an early stage rather than confront her with it later as a *fait accompli.* The interesting thing is that once she accepted the idea she seemed to take to it like a *canard* to water. She has been working overtime every night for the last few months, mastering the new techniques. I shudder to think what the wages bill would have been otherwise. It would not be too much to say that she has become a changed person; it has obviously been a challenge to her and she has gained a new lease of life. It was because of that I entrusted her with entering the names of all those who have qualified for Stock Pot status in this year's guide.'

'You will not object if I question her, *Monsieur*?'

The Director eyed him nervously. 'Of course not, Pample-mousse. As I said earlier, you have *carte blanche*. In fact,'he reached for a telephone, 'I will ask my secretary to have her come up straight away. It will be as well if she knows you have my full approval.'

Monsieur Pamplemousse waited patiently, listening to what appeared to be a somewhat one-sided conversation. His end of it was made up of a series of monosyllabic replies which grew steadily less assured with every passing moment. He suspected he knew the reason why. At long last the Director put the phone down. He looked worried.

'Apparently she didn't come to work today. She left early yesterday afternoon in order to visit the hairdresser and hasn't been seen or heard of since.'

'Perhaps she wanted to look her best for today's cere-mony, *Monsieur*. Something may have happened since then.'

'That is true.'The Director didn't look entirely convinced. 'However, it doesn't explain why she has not been in touch. It is most unlike her.'

They both sat in silence for a moment or two.

'What are you thinking, Pamplemousse?'

'I was thinking I would still like to see her, *Monsieur*.'

'I meant, what are you *really* thinking? You surely don't suspect anything untoward on her part. Madame Grante may have her faults, but I would stake my life on her integrity.'

Monsieur Pamplemousse spread his hands out, palms uppermost. 'At this stage, *Monsieur,* I suspect nothing and no one. I have an open mind. Nevertheless, given the circumstances, it does seem strange that she should be absent today of all days.'

If he'd given voice to his innermost thoughts it wasn't so much the possibility of Madame Grante doing anything untoward – he agreed with the Director, she was a model of rectitude – rather that something untoward might have happened to her. An accident on the way home from the office, a fall; they were just two possibilities. He didn't dare mention a third that had occurred to him. Instead, he chose another one at random.

'You say she is a changed woman, *Monsieur.* Perhaps it is not the computer at all. Perhaps she has a lover.'

The Director eyed him dubiously. 'Is that possible, Pamplemousse? A flight of fancy, surely?'

'He could be a masochist, *Monsieur.* During my time in the force I met many such men. Men who like nothing better than to be constantly punished.'

The Director fell silent for a moment, lost in thought. 'I must admit to having noticed that she has also changed her mode of dress of late. Her skirts have definitely been getting shorter and she has started wearing make-up.'

'All women are the victims of fashion, *Monsieur.* Madame Pamplemousse is always grumbling because the fashions are not what she wants.'

'My secretary also tells me Madame Grante was heard singing a selection from "Bless the Bride" recently. Appar-

413

ently it was all round the office.'

Monsieur Pamplemousse began to wish he hadn't brought up the subject. It had only been meant as a joke. A rather poor one at that.

'I think, before I do anything else, *Monsieur*, I should go and see her. If you could let me have her address.'

The Director picked up his telephone again. 'I will ask my secretary. I know it is somewhere on the right bank.' He had the grace to look slightly shame-faced. 'I should know, of course.'

It was, in fact, typical of Madame Grante that the Director didn't know. Monsieur Pamplemousse had no idea either. Occasionally on his way to the office by *autobus* he'd seen her coming along the Rue Saint-Dominique, but he'd always immediately looked the other way rather than risk having to walk to the office with her. Conversation with Madame Grante wasn't the easiest thing in the world, especially first thing in the morning. It was usually confined to mundane matters like expenses. Anything else was likely to be frowned on. Enquiries into her personal life were treated with suspicion, almost like attempted rape.

'*Merci.*' The Director reached for his pad, jotted down a number, then tore off the top sheet. He turned to Monsieur Pamplemousse. 'She has an apartment in the Rue des Renaudes in the seventeenth *arrondissement.*'

Monsieur Pamplemousse rose to his feet. 'I will go straight away, *Monsieur*.' He doubted if he would learn much more from Madame Grante than he had from the Director, but at least she would have a working knowledge of the computer. Anyway it was a case of first things first and he suddenly wanted to be on the move.

The Director looked less than enthusiastic. 'You could be wasting your time, Pamplemousse. Apparently Véronique

414

who, by the way, is the only other person who knows what has happened – has tried more than once to telephone her, but each time there has been no reply.'

'I have to begin somewhere, *Monsieur*.'

The Director gave a sigh. 'Ah, well, if you must you must. But remember, we have less than a week to go before publication. Each and every hour of the day is precious. In the meantime, while you are gone I shall put a team of girls from the typing pool to work on recompiling *Le Guide*. They will be fighting a losing battle, I fear, but it will be something to fall back on if need be. I shall also tighten security. The whole building will be put on *alerte rouge*. *As* from tomorrow no one will be allowed in or out without production of a pass and positive means of identification.'

'That sounds sensible.' Monsieur Pamplemousse couldn't but feel that it was a case of locking the stable door after the horse had bolted. He looked at the Director speculatively. Mention of there being less than a week to go before publication had reminded him of Doucette's comment during *petit déjeuner* when she had read the item in the *journal*. He wondered if the Director had noticed the misprint too. Correction: for the first time he found himself wondering if it really had been a misprint, or whether the wrong date had some deeper significance. He decided not to mention the matter, at least for the time being. The Director had enough worries on his mind.

Instead, he excused himself and was about to make his way into the outer office when the Director called him back.

'Pamplemousse, I shall be grateful if you would remove that ridiculous object from Pommes Frites' collar. I appreciate the thought, but I scarcely need a walking reminder of how black the situation is.'

'Of course, *Monsieur*.' The truth of the matter was that

what with one thing and another Monsieur Pamplemousse had totally forgotten Pommes Frites had also gone into mourning.

Anticipating his wishes, the Director's secretary had a map of Paris open on her desk. 'Madame Grante's apartment is near the Place des Ternes. Would you like me to call a taxi?'

Monsieur Pamplemousse shook his head. 'I will find my own way there.' He consulted another map in his diary. Travelling by Métro would involve changing trains twice, a tedious business in the rush hour. Madame Grante probably only did it on rainy days. More than likely she normally caught the 92 *autobus* in the Avenue Bosquet and got off in the Avenue Niel. It would be nice to do the same; a way of easing himself gradually into her way of life.

He glanced down. Taking his friend and mentor along as well would be out of the question. Rules and regulations forbade it. There was no way he could squeeze Pommes Frites into a travelling box no larger than 21cm by 10cm, still less carry it if he did. Once upon a time he could have travelled like any other normal passenger, but nowadays there was no way he would be allowed on board. Any argument and the driver would reach for the telephone beside his left ear and call headquarters. Perhaps they should take their chance on the Métro after all and hope they didn't encounter one of the roving bands of ticket Inspectors. Either that or accept the offer of a taxi, but what he wanted most at that moment was space, and time to think.

'*Permettez-moi*?' He picked up the telephone and dialled an outside number.

His call was answered almost immediately.

'Jacques, Aristide here ...'The first few questions confirmed the Director's fears. Computer crime was an area where the rapid advance in technology far outstripped the means of combating it, at least as far as the police were concerned. Help was available but it wouldn't be immediate – it was mainly left to the Fraud Squad and they were under-staffed and overworked. In any case it was a situation where the law itself was even further behind. Obtaining a conviction in a case involving computer crime was fraught with difficulties. Attempting it was often a waste of time and manpower.

Monsieur Pamplemousse listened patiently. Although it wasn't entirely unexpected, it wasn't exactly what he wanted to hear either. When he mentioned the time scale there was a hollow laugh.

'OK. Have you any other ideas then?'

'*Un moment.*' There was a pause while names were thrown around. Eventually Jacques came back to him. 'I'm told there is someone in Passy … name of Borel.'

'Could you make an appointment for me?'

'When?'

'This evening if possible.' He looked at his watch. It showed 16.30. 'Say, 18.30–19.00 hours. Before *dîner.* Tell them it is urgent.'

'*D'accord.* I'll hold on.' While he was waiting Monsieur Pamplemousse glanced at the map on the desk. The Rue des Renaudes wasn't that far. Three-quarters of an hour at the most. The walk would do them both good.

'*Merci. Vous êtes un copain.*' He put the receiver down at long last. He may have drawn a blank with help from his old department in the *Sûréte,* but at least the call had gained him an appointment with a 'consultant' who could be trusted. It was better than nothing.

He dialled his home number.

'Couscous. I fear I shall be home late.

417

'No. Something has come up. I am needed here …

'… it is not possible to say at present.

'Why don't you go and stay with Agathe?

'Good. I will see you when I see you.

'*Au revoir, chérie.* Take care.'

He replaced the receiver. Doucette had sounded resigned. How many times had they had the same conversation in his days with the *Sûreté*? He had lost count. Her sister in Melun had always been the chief beneficiary of his enforced absences.

'If you are taking Pommes Frites with you,'said Véronique, 'I should make sure he wipes his paws before he goes in. You know what Madame Grante is like.'

'*Poof!*' Monsieur Pamplemousse blew her a kiss. She caught it expertly and put it in a desk drawer for safe keeping. 'Call me if you have any news or if you need anything.'

He paused outside the door, then headed, not towards the main lift, but to a smaller one at the far end of the corridor. He had one more call to make before he left the building.

Madame Grante's secretary was new, which wasn't unduly surprising. Madame Grante got through secretaries rather quicker than most people got through writing out their expenses sheets. It would be interesting to see if the new computer stayed the course. Perhaps the current trouble was a forewarning of things to come, the electronic equivalent of a cry for help.

Madame Grante's secretary was not only new, she was less than helpful. Monsieur Pamplemousse had the feeling that the boss's absence was the best thing that had happened to the Accounts Department that week.

No, she had no idea why Madame Grante hadn't turned

up for work. Madame Grante didn't confide in her. Sniff.

No, she hadn't noticed anything different about the way Madame Grante had been behaving. She hadn't been working at *Le Guide* long enough to know. Sniff. Sniff.

She didn't actually say that she wouldn't be staying long enough to find out, but the underlying message was there, loud and clear.

Monsieur Pamplemousse took his leave. On the way down the corridor he tried the door of the new computer room. It was locked. He had been in there once – soon after it had been installed. At the time he had found it somewhat disappointing: windowless, air-conditioned and antiseptic. Even the sheer lack of size of the machine itself, standing in splendid isolation in the centre of the floor, had been a bit of a disappointment. Given the fact that one way and another it was destined to control all their working lives he would have preferred something larger, something with more wires and with glass panels he could look through in order to see what was going on inside. It was so neat and unassuming it was almost as sinister as the clicks and grunts it emitted randomly from time to time.

Apart from the computer and its associated equipment – keyboards, visual display units, and some racks containing storage disks and other items, there had, in fact, been surprisingly little to see. All the same, he would have liked to have gone inside the room again, if only to refresh his memory.

Acting on an impulse he went back to Madame Grante's department. The girl was on the telephone and she didn't look overpleased to see him.

'Do you have the key to the computer room?'

She shook her head, then put her hand over the mouthpiece. 'You could try looking in Madame Grante's desk if

419

you like.'She nodded towards an open door leading to the inner sanctum. 'She keeps a few spare keys there. If it's around at all it will be in the top drawer on the right. Otherwise they're probably all in her handbag.'

Conscious that he was being watched, Monsieur Pamplemousse tried the desk drawer. It was locked. He pulled at the others one by one, instinctively preparing himself to jump back should Madame Grante happen to appear unexpectedly. They were all locked. He was tempted to try his own keys on them, but he wasn't sure how the girl would take it.

There was a computer terminal near by. The keyboard and screen were both neatly concealed beneath grey plastic covers. He tried the one drawer below the table top. That, too, was locked.

He thanked the girl and left. As he closed the door behind him he heard her voice. 'Sorry about that. Now, about tonight ...'

Pommes Frites, glad to be out in the fresh air again, set a brisk pace and they reached the Pont de l'Alma in under ten minutes. A heavily laden barge pushing two others swept past, helped on its way by the fast-moving current. He caught a glimpse of the skipper concentrating on the view ahead before it disappeared under one of the arches. The *quais* which a few weeks before had been under water were now almost clear. Traffic was on the move again on the through-roads and the Vedettes moored further upstream were floodlit. He leaned over the parapet and looked down at the statue of the *zouave* – the French Algerian soldier who for generations had helped passing Parisians gauge the height of the Seine. His boots were now clear of the muddied waters. Bits of debris stuck to the plinth.

There was no doubt in his mind that despite all its many benefits the computer could also be a disruptive influence. For better or for worse it upset the balance of things. Get on the wrong side of one and you were in trouble. The thought of having his P39s committed to a plastic *disque,* available for instant analysis and comparison with previous entries, was hard to contemplate.

Much as one grumbled about having to indulge in arguments with Madame Grante on the subject of expenses, there was no denying the pleasure of an occasional battle won – it more than made up for all the lost ones. It wouldn't be the same thing at all with a computer.

The Inspector who used his car for a Saturday shopping trip would feel very hard done by if on Monday morning the computer deleted the mileage from his work sheet.

On the other hand, there was no good fighting it. It was here to stay. Some years before, if they had chosen to do so, he and Doucette could have had one of the Minitel terminals France Télécom distributed free on request to all their subscribers. Originally intended to replace the telephone directory, they were now used for all manner of things. Banks, the Stock Exchange, purveyors of junk mail. If you were doing a personalised mail-shot to local plumbers, it was possible to select all the men in a town of your choice whose first name was Jean. On the other side of the coin, it was said that a growing number of subscribers dialled 36 15 in order to work out their erotic fantasies via *messageries roses.* Others used the system to order their groceries. He couldn't picture Doucette doing her shopping that way. The chief beneficiaries were Télécom, who were making a fortune out of the phone calls, and the programme makers.

From the Pont de l'Alma to the Étoile took Monsieur Pamplemousse and Pommes Frites fifteen minutes. From the Étoile down the Avenue de Wagram less than another ten – he'd forgotten how much of a downhill slope there was. He hadn't been far out in his calculations. The market in the Rue Poncelet was alive and bustling. He used to shop there at one time and still occasionally bought the Christmas ham in Aux Fermes d'Auvergne. No doubt it was where Madame Grante did all her food shopping; there would be no point in going further afield.

Madame Grante's apartment was in an anonymous row of stone-clad seven-floored buildings whose uniformly vertical façades reflected the strict rules first laid down by Baron Haussmann. The architect's name was engraved in a stone high up on the wall alongside a date – 1906.

The large wooden door – normally opened by a key-operated lock – was standing ajar. On the wall just inside there was an array of entryphone buttons. He ran his finger down the list of names. Madame Grante's apartment was on the fourth floor. He pressed a button opposite her name and waited. On the other side of a glass-panelled door he could see an antiquated lift, hardly big enough for more than two people at a time.

While he was waiting, a man came in from the street, checked his mail in a row of boxes on the opposite wall, then opened the inner door. He looked at them enquiringly. The combination of Monsieur Pamplemousse's dark suit and Pommes Frites'august presence must have lent an air of respectability, for he stood to one side and held the door open for them.

'*Monsieur …*'

'*Merci, Monsieur.*' Monsieur Pamplemousse took advantage of the offer. He had a feeling he wasn't about to get anywhere with the entryphone.

On the grounds that the exercise would do him good, he

made for the stairs. It saved concocting a story. Half-way up he passed a room where someone was playing a saxophone. He was no Charlie Parker.

Madame Grante's apartment was one of two which ran the width of the building. He rang the bell and waited, but again there was no reply and he was about to leave when he heard a strange scuffling noise. Putting his ear to the door Monsieur Pamplemousse thought he detected the sound of a movement on the other side – the rustle of a gown, perhaps; it was hard to place. It was followed by what sounded like a voice in the distance, but it was impossible to make out the words. He tried pressing the bell-push a second time – the response was loud and clear – but the sound died away to nothing.

Taking out his notepad and pen, he scribbled a brief message saying he had called and asking Madame Grante to contact the office as soon as possible. Tearing the sheet of paper from its pad, he bent down and tried to slip it through the gap between the bottom of the door and the floor. It met with resistance half-way through, probably from a mat, leaving a small corner protruding into the corridor.

He crouched down on his hands and knees in an attempt to push the paper through even further, and as he did so he heard the rustling noise again, only louder this time. A moment later there was a tug and the paper was wrenched from his fingers. Pommes Frites made a dive, but he wasn't quick enough.

Monsieur Pamplemousse jumped guiltily to his feet and waited for the door to open, but he waited in vain. Once again total silence reigned. He gave a shrug. Clearly, for reasons best known to herself, Madame Grante was not at home to callers. He didn't feel inclined to press the matter, but it was hardly a good start to the evening.

On his way out of the building, he checked her mailbox. Through the clear plastic door he could see a small pile of letters – mostly circulars. Either she hadn't bothered to empty it that day, or there was some other reason for their having been left. Whatever the cause, Monsieur Pamplemousse was left with a vague sense of unease.

As they left the building he crossed over to the other side of the street and glanced up towards the fourth floor, but the windows were covered by net curtains and there was no sign of movement.

Retracing his steps in the direction of the Étoile, he called in at a little bar near the Avenue Niel and ordered a *Cardinal.* The Cassis, its freshness preserved in a refrigerator beneath the counter, was a *Double Crème* from Ropiteau Frères, rich and intensely fruity, the Beaujolais of Juliénas, purple and deliciously young; the bittersweet mixture suited his current mood. He brooded over it for a moment or two. It was good to be getting his teeth into something new, but on the other hand he wished it wasn't quite so close to home. After the first glass he began to feel better. After the second, he felt ready for the fray.

He looked at his watch. It was 17.45; time he met Monsieur Borel, the computer expert.

3
THE RIGHT CONNECTIONS

The address Monsieur Pamplemousse had been given turned out to be a smart apartment block off the Rue Raynouard in the sixteenth *arrondissement*. It was as different to Madame Grante's as it was possible to imagine. As he approached the entrance, plate-glass doors parted in the middle, opening onto an entrance hall which could have housed his own apartment several times over. He decided that if the architect – whose name was engraved on a bronze plaque let into the floor – had shares in the company who'd supplied the marble, he must have done extremely well out of the deal.

To one side of the hall there was a large desk with a bank of closed-circuit television monitors. Behind it sat a poker-faced man in uniform. It was hard to tell what he was thinking, if indeed he thought anything at all. The man gazed noncommittally at Pommes Frites while he telephoned the news of their arrival. In return Pommes Frites gave as good as he got.

There were four lifts – two either side of a rock-garden full of artificial foliage which was the centre piece of a wide passageway leading off from the rear of the hall. Monsieur Pamplemousse took the first lift to arrive and pressed a button for the tenth floor. As the doors closed he became aware of a camera lens high up in one corner. He turned his back on it. A few moments later, just as imperceptibly as it had started, the lift came to rest again. As the doors opened he found himself entering a small vestibule. The dark brown carpet was thick underfoot; pictures on the walls reflected bulk-buying rather than any artistic aspirations. They were probably the same on every floor. He wondered if the architect had shares in that company too. He pressed a bell- push on the door facing him and waited.

Even before it opened he knew exactly what Monsieur Borel would look like. He would be casually dressed, bearded – probably wearing open-toed sandals. If he wore socks they would be brightly coloured. He would have steel-rimmed spectacles and he would blink a lot as a result of having spent most of his life glued to video screens. His fore-head would be domed, his receding hair would need cutting, and he would be so intelligent he would most likely be unable to understand the few simple questions Monsieur Pamplemousse wished to ask. In his spare time he probably compiled handbooks for Eastern manufacturers of electronic equipment, translating them into a language which neither they nor their customers would understand. His large black watch would have an illuminated dial showing the time and date at any given moment in all continents of the world – even if he happened to be under water when he wanted to know. It would probably emit 'pings' at set intervals.

He was wrong on all nine counts – ten if you included the fact that it wasn't Monsieur Borel; it was Mademoiselle, and Mademoiselle Martine Borel was thirtyish, slim, well groomed, expensively dressed, cool and efficient. *Soignée* perhaps rather than chic. Her make-up was impeccably understated, and her glasses were large and round, with black frames to match her hair. Just to confuse the issue, she wore a Mickey Mouse watch on her left wrist. The flicker of surprise must have shown on his face.

'They obviously didn't tell you?'

From the way she said it and from the amused look in her eyes Monsieur Pamplemousse guessed it wasn't the first time it had happened. He covered his embarrassment by removing his hat and gesturing towards Pommes Frites.

'I hope you have no objection.'

'On the contrary. Besides, I was told you might be accompanied.'

'His name is Pommes Frites. He goes everywhere with me.'

'So I believe.'

She bent down to pat Pommes Frites, then took Monsieur Pamplemousse's hat from him and placed it on a shelf in a cupboard. She was wearing a slim gold bangle on her right wrist, but no rings. He spotted a Louis Vuitton bag on the floor and wondered if it was real or a fake. It was hard to tell these days; the *Musée de la Contrefaçon* was full of examples of the latter. If it was the former, the Director might find himself in for a sizeable bill.

As Mademoiselle Borel turned to lead the way into a large open-plan living-room he noticed she had a few grey hairs. Perhaps she was older than she looked.

From the wide picture-windows he could see across the rooftops of Paris towards the Eiffel Tower. The roads on either side of the Seine were already full of evening traffic. He glanced around the room. One wall was almost entirely covered by shelves. Most of the shelves were filled with books, interspersed with items of bric-à-brac. The remaining walls had a scattering of paintings – mostly modern. There were several pieces of modern sculpture dotted around, lit by equally modern lamps. There was also a faint, but delicious smell of something cooking. Pommes Frites licked his lips in pleasurable anticipation as he

427

settled himself down on a rug in the centre of the room, eyeing his surroundings with evident approval.

On a low glass-topped table between two black leather armchairs there was a tray on which stood two tall glasses of white wine and a bottle in an ice bucket. There was also a bowl of black olives and a plate of *amuse-gueule* in the shape of tiny tartlets. Beside the tray lay a slim black folder.

'Please help yourself.' Mademoiselle Borel crossed the room, closed a door leading to the kitchen, then returned carrying a bowl of water which she placed on the floor in front of Pommes Frites. Settling herself comfortably in one of the chairs, she draped one leg elegantly over the other, then pointed to the folder. 'My c.v.'

'*Merci.*' Monsieur Pamplemousse opened it as he took the other chair. Normally he might not have bothered, accepting the recommendation he'd been given on trust, but he was intrigued.

Born in Lyon, the only daughter of a shop-keeping family, Martine Borel had been educated first in the city itself where she had gained her *baccalauréat*, then at the *élite* Grenoble Technical University. After that had come a spell at MIT in Boston, followed by a job in California's Silicon Valley; then back to France and Honeywell-Bull before going it alone as a consultant. She had two books to her credit; one on computer security, the other with a more philosophic sounding title. She hadn't always been Mademoiselle. Somewhere along the line there had been a marriage and a divorce, so she hadn't emerged from it all entirely unscathed. Perhaps it accounted for the grey hairs.

The tartlets were warm and freshly made. They were filled with a beaten mixture of tunny fish, anchovies, chopped gherkin and mayonnaise, with a few capers to taste.

The wine was cold and unfamiliar; a total contrast to his *Cardinal.* He tried hard to place it. He could taste all kinds of fruits: peaches, plums, apples, a hint of lemon. It was a very elegant wine.

She caught him glancing at the label on the bottle as she refilled his glass.

'It is a Château Bouchamie Carneros.'

He was none the wiser.

'It is a Chardonnay from California.'

'Ah, California.'

She caught the nuance in his voice and was about to say something.

'It is very good,' he added hastily. 'In fact, it is more than very good. It is excellent.'

'One must not be chauvinistic. The Americans have a lot to learn about wine, but they are quick and dedicated. In a very short space of time they have also taught us many things – even though in the beginning we were reluctant to admit the possibility.'

He put down the file. It was time to change the subject.

'You have led a very full life.'

'Do I get the job?' Again there was a hint of amusement in the eyes. She was very sure of herself.

'If you can call it that. I am in need of advice.'

'What can I do to help? I was told only that you wish to know about computers.'

'Starting from the beginning. *Par exemple, I* know that "hardware" refers to the basic machinery you can actually touch, and that "software" refers to the programs which make it work, but beyond that ...' He spread out his hands. 'I am lost.'

She made a face. 'It is a large order.'

'It is a large problem and there is not much time.'

'I see. Well, assuming that all external connections are correct …'

Monsieur Pamplemousse's pride was stung. 'I do know a little more than that.'

'Perhaps. But is one of the most useful phrases I was ever taught. I still say it to myself whenever I have a problem. How many times have you seen people take an iron or an electric toaster to be repaired and it turns out not to have been switched on at the wall – or even plugged in? You shouldn't take it too literally. It applies to life as well as to computers.'

Monsieur Pamplemousse accepted the reproof. 'Let us assume all external connections are correct.'

'You are a brave man. Tell me, after the hall porter had announced you, what did you do?'

'I came up to your floor.'

'Exactly. And how did you reach it?'

'I pressed the button for the lift. It arrived. I got in. Then I pressed another button for the tenth floor …'

'And did you ask yourself why all these things happened?'

'No.'

'Of course not. To use a lift it is not necessary to know how it works. So why should you know how a computer works? It is usually sufficient that it does.'

'Suppose I wished to arrange matters so that when the lift reached the tenth floor it didn't stop but went on to the twelfth.'

'Ah, *then* you would need to know about lifts. You would also need to know something about aerodynamics – for the moment when it went through the roof. There are only ten floors.'

Touché! He felt himself warming towards her. 'Fortunately in my case lifts do not come into it. I only wish to know how someone might "arrange matters" with a computer. With that end in view, I feel it would be nice to know how they work.'

She nodded. 'They are like many other complicated things – taking a photograph, for example, or television – once they are broken down into their basic elements they are really very simple.

'Think of a long corridor with door after door after door. If all the doors are open you can walk straight through, but if just one of those doors is locked, then you can't. Take that a stage further. Supposing at each door there is a man who asks you a simple question to which the answer is either "TRUE" or "FALSE" . If the answer is "TRUE" you can go through. If it is "FALSE" then you are out of the game. A computer works on much the same principle. It is a series of doors.

'Think, too, of the fact that the latest IBM door can be opened and closed some thirty billion times a second.'

'Even computers occasionally come up with wrong answers. They stop people going through doors when they shouldn't, or vice versa.'

'Computers very rarely come up with the wrong answer.' For the first time there was a hint of irritation in her voice. 'If they do – if for some reason they develop a fault- then the answer is usually so wildly wrong the fact should be obvious to anyone who has half an inkling of what the right one should be. People often ask computers the wrong question, then blame it when they don't like what it tells them. It is very easy to blame something you don't understand. If computers have a fault it is that they have spawned a whole society which can't add up because it has no need to, and isn't prepared to accept responsibility for its own mistakes.'

Monsieur Pamplemousse pondered the matter for a moment or two while more wine was poured. The truth of the matter was they were playing with each other. He decided the first move was up to him. He would come clean. Instinctively he trusted her. Anyone who liked wine and had such delicious smells coming from her kitchen had to be trusted. He gave the woman a brief run-down of all that had happened to date.

'That is terrible!'

'For *Le Guide* it is worse than terrible. It could be disastrous.'

'One thing is very certain. If the entries are wrong but make sense, then it is not a mistake on the part of the computer. It has to be a deliberate act on the part of someone else.'

'Exactly.'

'For what purpose? Presumably it is not fraud. I mean, no money is involved?'

'We may not be concerned with money directly – but indirectly a great deal is involved. Over one million copies of *Le Guide* are sold each year at a published price of one hundred and fifty francs per copy. That is a lot of money.'

'And no royalties to pay!'

'No royalties to pay.'

'But that would point to a rival and from all you say that seems very unlikely.'

'I cannot picture it.'

'So if we rule that out, and if it isn't to do with the shifting of money, then how about revenge?'

'Revenge? That is a possibility, I suppose, although I can't think of a reason. Be that as it may, it is my brief to find out who is responsible, and to do that it would be helpful to find out how it could have been done.'

She thought for a moment or two. 'There are two possi-bilities. Either it was done from outside the building, or it was done by someone inside. I have to tell you here and now that the second is the more likely of the two. Most computer break-ins are made by members of staff. Do you know what kind of computer it is? What make?'

'It is – ' Monsieur Pamplemousse took out his notebook. 'It is a Poulanc DB23, 450 series. What is known as a main-frame computer I believe.'

She looked impressed. 'Nothing but the best! It has a memory of over sixty-four million bytes. They've developed a new type of laser-operated head. It gives data storage of over 500 million characters on *disque,* would you believe?'

Monsieur Pamplemousse tried his best to look fasci-nated. Words like "byte" were still as much like Greek to him as they were to the Director.

'So you probably have a number of work stations dotted about the building?' He realised she was still talking.

'There are a good many, and there are network sockets everywhere for when we need to expand.'

Mademoiselle Borel gave a shrug as if to say there is your answer. 'Are the satellites live or dumb?'

'Meaning?'

'Do they operate through the mainframe computer, or are they PCs – desk-top computers – capable of operating independently? In other words, would it be possible to feed a program into the main computer from one of them?'

Monsieur Pamplemousse had to confess he didn't know.

'There is a whole history of computers being broken into from outside, but it usually requires time, a good deal of skill and an element of luck. In 1983 a nineteen-year-old student caused consternation in high places by breaking into the Pentagon computer. Messages have been left on the NASA Space Agency computer. In England the Duke of Edinburgh's personal electronic mail was penetrated on Prestel. Mostly it is done by "hackers" for the sheer hell of it. They see it as a challenge – like climbing Mount Everest.'

'So it is possible?'

'Let us just say that nothing is impossible. Whole books have been written about computer fraud. As you saw, I have had one published myself. It has simply become more difficult, that is all. Manufacturers- try to keep one pace ahead. But it is certainly not impossible.'

'Tell me more.'

'To enter a system from the outside you need to go in through the "front door", as it were. For that, all you require is a home computer and a "modem" to connect it to the public telephone. How many people know that it exists?'

'A good many, I imagine. There is nothing secret about the installation – only the contents. It has been mentioned more than once in the trade *journaux*. You could say it is an "open secret".'

'Does *Le Guide* provide a service for outside customers?'

'An information service will be available. Two, in fact. One for members of the public via France Télécom system, and another for accredited members of various trade organ-isations. Information will be available on payment of a subscription. It will also have the capability of being accessed by members of staff feeding in information while on their travels. Ultimately all Inspectors will have their own modems.'He was beginning to pick up the jargon.

'So in one respect you have already provided a good many people with a key to the front door?'

Monsieur Pamplemousse nodded gloomily. His task

seemed to be getting more complex by the minute.

'You must also bear in mind that a newly installed computer is at its most vulnerable. A computer which has been in use for some years will have had all its bugs ironed out; a new one may have many problems. Who supplied the software the part that operates it?'

'I believe it was bought in from an outside firm and modified to our requirements.'

'There have been cases of programs being set up to go wrong on a certain date. Some software manufacturers look on it as a form of insurance against bills not being paid, or contracts not being renewed. It is not impossible for someone to have programmed the computer to sabotage *Le Guide* on a certain date right from the start.'

Once again the questions of dates seemed to have cropped up. There was an underlying feeling of everything having been pre-planned which bothered him.

'What about security?'

'*Monsieur le Directeur* has always been very security conscious,' said Monsieur Pamplemousse, glad to be on firmer ground at long last. 'As far as the physical side is concerned, no one other than staff is ever allowed inside the building without first signing the visitors'book. Members of the public are allowed entry in order to visit the shop and a reference library, but while they are there they have to wear an adhesive badge. They are then required to sign the book again on leaving.'

'How about the badge? Is it handed in?'

'Of course. Visitors aren't allowed out of the building otherwise.'

'Good. That doesn't always happen. How about the computer room itself?'

'It is kept locked.'

'Presumably cleaners go in from time to time. Some people need to have access for other reasons. Computers need servicing. So do things like air-conditioning and sprinkler systems. It is often a case of no one noticing the *facteur* when he delivers the letters. Are references always taken up when people apply for a job?'

'I imagine so.'

'Most firms don't. Will you be checking mine?'

Monsieur Pamplemousse was tempted to say 'that is different', but he knew that it wasn't. He also couldn't help reflecting on the ease with which the girl in Madame Grante's office had offered him the key to the computer room. She had been too anxious to get back to her boyfriend to worry overmuch about security. Admittedly he had drawn a blank, but he might have found it. He wondered if her credentials had been checked. Knowing Madame Grante, he was sure they would have been.

'A new computer is always a disruptive influence. People see it as a threat to old established ways of doing their job. Also, you mustn't lose sight of it having been done by someone – or a group of people – with a grudge.'

'Someone with a grudge against *Le Guide*?' It was hard to imagine.

'I agree, but it does to some extent represent the privileged. Also, such groups see any computer as a menace to society. It is their vowed intention to challenge anyone or anything connected with them. In France they go under the name of the *Comité de Libération ou de Détournement des Ordinateurs*. CLODO for short. They have been responsible for a number of attacks – mostly against big companies in the Toulouse area.'

'*Clodo* is also the slang word for a tramp.'

She shrugged. 'Granted. But even I have to admit they

have a point. For the first time it has become possible to encapsulate a man's whole life – both the good and the bad – on a tiny part of a single *disquette*. If we are not very careful, "Big Brother" could soon be watching over us, and computers are totally lacking in morals. It is not the aims of CLODO one disagrees with so much as their methods.

'Besides, they are much more likely to plant what is called a Logic Bomb – a program which is timed to go off at some predetermined date and cause irreparable damage. They are out to destroy – not to play games. Either that, or what is known as a "virus", a device which gradually eats away at the information. From all you have told me, neither seems likely.'

'But if it was an outside job?'he persisted. 'Assuming someone entered through the "front door" as you call it, how did they get any further? How did they enter the area which contains the contents of the new edition of *Le Guide*? For that it is necessary to use a password. One which is changed every day and is known to only two people.'

'What else?'

'That is not enough?'

'It is possible to place too much reliance on using a password. To use the "door" analogy once again, it is like having only one lock on the entrance but changing it every day. Sometimes it might be better to have two locks and only change them occasionally. If someone wishes to open a safe door and they don't know the combination, what do they do?'

'It depends. They can either go through all the possible combinations – which in most cases is an almost insurmountable problem because of the time factor. If they are very expert they might have listening apparatus, but that kind of thing usually only happens in films. They can blow it open – but that, too, has its problems. If it is a very small safe they might even carry it away and open it at their leisure. Or, they can try and find out the combination by other means. What is known as lateral thinking.'

'Exactly. The one advantage in looking for the "combination lock" on a computer is that provided you program another computer correctly you can use it to do all the hard work for you, particularly if the password is short – five letters or less. You say only two people know what it is?'

Monsieur Pamplemousse nodded.

'And are you one of the two?'

'No.' It hadn't occurred to him to ask the Director for it. In many ways he would rather not know.

'That is a plus.' She quickly corrected herself. 'I mean it is a plus that it wasn't given to you automatically. Now I will give you a negative. You say the password is changed every day? Presumably it is a word and not a number?'

'I was told it was a word.'

'Numbers are often safer. If you take two very large prime numbers and multiply them together it can be almost unbreakable. I will give you an example: the date of the French Revolution and the date of Hitler's rise to power 1789 – and 1933 – two prime numbers. Multiply them together and you get what is known as a "prime product" – 3,458,137 – it would take even the most powerful computer in the world years to find it.'

Monsieur Pamplemousse helped himself to another tart. 'It sounds as though I shall need a course in higher mathematics as well as electronics if I am to take part in the battle of the computer.'

Mademoiselle Borel laughed. 'I'm sorry – I wasn't trying to blind you with science. Anyway, I'm glad you said "of" not "with". The computer is entirely neutral. It is neither on your side, nor against you.'

Monsieur Pamplemousse took the point. 'I must be grateful for small mercies. So what do you suggest?'

'I think for the time being we must assume it is a word or a combination of words which is changed every day. To put it another way, there are 365 new words or combinations of words to learn in a year and as many to forget. That immediately narrows the field. Quite likely they will all be related in some way. Taken from a directory, perhaps. In the case of *Le Guide*, the chances are that it will be some word related to food or to wine. It could be the name of a cheese. Is there an official list?'

'The bible of the cheese industry is Androuet's *Guide du Fromage*.'

'So they could start at the beginning. The first one listed would be for one day, the second for day two, and so on ... Or it could be wine.'

'There is the 1855 classification for Bordeaux wines.'

'But that would only give sixty-three. Enough for two months.'

Monsieur Pamplemousse looked at her with renewed respect. He couldn't have come up with the exact number himself.

She poured the rest of the wine.

'We could always give it a try.'

'What ... now?'

'There is no time like the present. When do the staff go home?'

'Most of them leave around five thirty or six o'clock. There is a round-the-clock service operated by a skeleton staff, but as far as I know there will be no one operating the computer.'

Mademoiselle Borel looked at her watch. 'Good. It is after six. That's when most hacking is done. Weekends are usually the peak time. It's surprising how even big firms leave their systems to fend for themselves at weekends. We will carry out a little test.'

Handing him his glass she stood up and led the way towards a door on the far side of the room. He followed, and to his surprise suddenly found himself entering a room full of equipment. He could have been in a mini version of Mission Control Houston for all most of it meant to him. Mademoiselle Borel ran through a series of switches. Warning lights came on. There was a faint hum of electronic machinery. Warning bleeps issued from all sides. Screens began to glow.

On the balcony there were two small dish aerials. Beyond them he could see across the river towards his own office. If he'd had his Leitz glasses with him he would probably have been able to see the Director's office. He was glad he couldn't. He had a momentary mental vision of the Director doing exactly the same thing in reverse and their eyes meeting.

Below lay the Rue Berton, the little lane which Honoré de Balzac used when he wanted to escape from his creditors while he was living at number 47, working through the night and keeping himself awake by drinking black coffee, a combination which eventually proved lethal. A little way up the hill there was a figure in dark blue uniform clutching a machine carbine. No doubt he was guarding the Turkish Embassy.

Mademoiselle Borel glanced round as he took a closer look at the aerials. 'They are the modern equivalent of phone tapping. The air is full of information – twenty-four hours a day – flying in all directions.'

She motioned towards a second chair as she seated herself in front of a console, inserted a *disquette* and began punching in a series of commands.

Almost at once he was aware of a change in the atmosphere. Gone was the laid-back Mademoiselle Borel who had received him. In her place was a highly dedicated and knowledgeable professional.

'The first thing to do is dial up the mainframe computer. Do you have the number?'

Monsieur Pamplemousse consulted his notebook again and gave it to her.

She typed it in. There was a pause, then a welcoming BONJOUR appeared on a screen in front of them. It was followed by a request for identification.

'Any ideas?'

Monsieur Pamplemousse felt a momentary pang of guilt. It was almost as though he were breaking into his own house. Worse than that even. It felt like a betrayal of trust. 'You could try one of the other guides. Michelin, perhaps, or Gault-Millau. I'm sure they subscribe. Or any of the major *journaux*.'

'I will try *Le Monde*.'

She typed the words and they appeared on the screen.

'Which service do you require?' The reply was almost instantaneous.

She looked enquiringly at Monsieur Pamplemousse. He shrugged.

'I will ask for their HELP menu. If we are very lucky it may give the kind of vital information we need – like how to enter other areas. It has been known.'

A long list flashed on the screen. At the bottom were the words LE GUIDE.

'I don't believe it.' She selected the appropriate

command on her keyboard. 'It can't be that easy.'

MOT DE PASSE. S'IL VOUS PLAÎT appeared on the screen.

'I'll try thinking up a password at random and see what happens.'

After the third attempt the screen went blank. She made a grimace.

'It isn't as easy as it looks! The machine has been programmed to cut off the call after the third attempt. It is a common safeguard. The problem now is that it has quite probably automatically logged in the time and date. Once can be a genuine mistake, or simply someone who is interested. A whole series of repeated attempts will arouse suspicion.'

'How would you get round that?'

'If you were able to access the security section you could delete the information it has logged.'

'And if you couldn't?'

She shrugged. 'There are always other ways. Speaking for myself, I would put plan "B" into operation. I might arrange for someone to pose as a telephone engineer and insert a listening device where the lines enter the building. He could then pick up any messages via a receiver outside the building and feed it into a computer. Once you are in, there is often a device known as a "Zap Utility" which exists for all sorts of purposes – maintenance, writing of new applications. If you can enter that, the world is your oyster. You can edit away to your heart's content. Create new files ...'

Monsieur Pamplemousse sat back and closed his eyes. It was all very fascinating, but suddenly he felt himself in deep water, struggling to stay afloat. He was liable to sink at any moment under the weight of accumulated knowledge, none of which seemed to be getting him anywhere nearer his goal.

'So, to sum up, it could be a break-in from outside. That would be difficult, but not impossible. Or, it could have been from inside the building, perhaps through lack of security on our part ...'

'I'm sorry if you feel I haven't been of much help.'

'Not at all. You have been very patient. You have answered a lot of my questions. I now know a little about computers, enough to hold my own in a conversation, but ...'

He could have added that he now knew enough to realise that the problem was even greater than he had pictured. Mademoiselle Borel was right. To all intents and purposes he was no further on than he had been when he'd arrived – as he stood up he glanced at his watch – an hour ago.

'Would you care to stay and have something to eat? I can tell you a little more about computers. Or, we can talk of other things. About what it is like being an expert on food and wine for example. The grass is always greener on the other side of the fence.'

While she was talking Mademoiselle Borel led the way back into the main room and crossed to the kitchen. As she opened the door Monsieur Pamplemousse caught sight of an orange Le Creuset pot simmering on the stove. On the working top of one of the units there was a *baguette* and alongside that a plate of *saucisson*. On another working top there was a selection of cheese.

As she lifted the lid of the pot a delicious smell wafted his way; the kind of smell that could only come from long and careful preparation and even longer cooking. It was a smell he remembered well from his childhood.

'It is only a *pot-au-feu,* but there is enough to last me for several days. You are most welcome. I cook it the way my mama did when I was small – she always served the

443

bouillon on toast with the leeks.'

It had been the same in his own home. The *bouillon* from Monday's *pot-au-feu* had provided the basis for the rest of the week's meals; broth with noodles, broth with semolina and broth with rice. Then on Fridays, *potage à la fécula* – the remains of the broth thickened with cornflour. He had always hurried home from school for that.

She took a bottle of wine from a nearby rack. 'You could learn a little about Californian red at the same time. It is a Jekel Cabernet Sauvignon – Private Reserve. Or there is a Santenay if you prefer.'

Sorely tempted, Monsieur Pamplemousse hesitated. 'It is very kind of you, but I have to go. There is a great deal of work to be done. Perhaps I can take what your American friends would call a "rain check"?'

'Of course. As you see, it is a very large pot. Who knows?'As she led the way to the hall and removed his hat from the cupboard, it was her turn to hesitate. 'Would you mind if I carry on trying? Looking for a way into the computer, I mean.'

'That would be most helpful. I will keep in touch if I have any news at my end.'On an impulse he converted a hand-shake into the raising of her fingers to his lips. '*Au revoir, M'moiselle.*'

'*Au revoir.*' She waited at her door for the lift to arrive.

'Take care. I have a feeling that whoever it is you are looking for wishes to make everyone suffer for a while. If he simply wanted to hurt *Le Guide* he could have arranged for the entire program to be erased. I think he also wishes to turn the screw as well. I think it is the action of someone who is a little *en colère.*' She tapped her forehead. 'Someone with a grudge who has been brooding on it for so long it has become an obsession.'

Monsieur Pamplemousse hesitated. 'May I ask you one last question?'

'Please do.'

'The *pot-au-feu* … Do you seal the ends of the bones with potato to keep the marrow intact?'

'Of course.'

'Tied with string?'

'*Naturellement.*'

Monsieur Pamplemousse gave a sigh; a mixture of contentment and regret. It was echoed somewhat noisily and pointedly from inside the lift.

'That is how my mother used to make it too.'

On their way out Monsieur Pamplemousse acknowledged the glance from the hall porter with a nod. The man looked at his watch, then wrote something in a book.

Outside the block he stood for a moment, wondering what to do next. He almost wished now he had taken up the invitation to stay for a meal instead of opting for a rain check. He glanced up at the sky. From the look of it he might not have long to wait.

Somewhat inconsequentially, he suddenly remembered that it was in the Rue Raynouard that Benjamin Franklin had invented the lightning conductor.

What was the phrase Mademoiselle Borel had used? 'Assuming all external connections are correct.' She was right. In the end most problems turned out to have simple solutions. It was really a case of breaking them down into their essential elements – as with a computer.

The changes to *Le Guide* hadn't been made at random. They had been carefully thought out by someone with a good working knowledge of restaurants and what would cause the maximum amount of embarrassment. All of which would have taken time and thought.

Reaching a decision, Monsieur Pamplemousse set off in the direction of the Passy Metro station. It was time he returned to the office. If it was an 'inside job', then all his past experience told him to look for someone with a changed life style, and that brought him inexorably back to Madame Grante. He couldn't begin to suspect her of any kind of disloyalty. On the other hand, he couldn't get her out of his mind. For someone so very set in their ways, her 'external connections'had, by all accounts, gone very much awry.

There was a chance – a very slender chance – that if she did keep spare keys in her desk drawer he might find a duplicate set for her apartment. It was worth a try.

4
A WAITING GAME

By the time Monsieur Pamplemousse and Pommes Frites arrived at *Le Guide's* headquarters the gatekeeper had already gone off duty – he was probably holding court in the nearest bar, giving his version of the day's events. Using his entry card, Monsieur Pamplemousse let himself in and as they crossed the courtyard he glanced up towards the top floor. A light was on in the Director's office. There were lights coming from the second floor as well. It looked as though the occupants of the typing pool were working late. If the Director had his way they would probably be up all night.

A portable cabin containing a machine for taking passport-size photographs was standing near the main entrance. The issuing of special passes must have got under way soon after he'd left. It was closed for the night.

Unaware of the mental struggle his master had gone through earlier in the evening when he had turned down the offer of *pot-au-feu*, Pommes Frites was wearing his 'I am only a mere dog, mine is not to reason why – just lead the way and I'll follow on behind' look. It was a mixture of resignation – eyebrows slightly raised, mouth compressed, eyes focused on an imaginary horizon – and total lack of comprehension. As far as Pommes Frites was concerned, life was a simple matter of priorities. In an ideal world one should always know where one's priorities lay. The fact that for much of the time life was far from ideal was beside the point. The world was how you made it. Opportunities needed to be seized when they came your way, and although normally he would have stuck up for his master through thick and thin, sadly, on this occasion he was of the opinion that a golden opportunity had been passed up, perhaps never to return.

Ever hopeful, anticipating that amends were about to be made, Pommes Frites licked his lips as they entered the building. His euphoria was short-lived. Never one to be wreathed in smiles, he began to look even more woebegone as he followed Monsieur Pamplemousse along a route which took them not, as he had hoped, towards the canteen, the smell from which was already titillating his sensitive nostrils, but in the direction of the Accounts Department.

An air of Stygian gloom pervaded the corridors. The few people they encountered on the way spoke in whispers and barely acknowledged their presence.

When Monsieur Pamplemousse reached his destination, he opened the door to Madame Grante's outer office and peered inside. The lights were still on, but there was no sign of the new secretary. The coat rack was empty. No doubt she had another, more pressing engagement.

Closing the door behind them, he let himself into the inner office, mentally crossing his fingers and raising his eyes towards the ceiling as he did so.

It proved an unnecessary invocation to Saint Peter. Not only did his own key fit the one on Madame Grante's desk, which wasn't unduly surprising – they were all of a standard pattern and were meant to protect minor personal belongings for brief periods rather than to safeguard anything of great value – but when he opened the drawer he found the inside as neatly compartmented as the mind of its user.

Pens and pencils were arranged in boxes. Paper-clips, elastic bands, a ruler, an eraser, all had their allotted place; and there, in an unmarked envelope beneath a grey lift-out plastic tray, was a set of door keys, including one which was obviously meant for the outer door to an apartment block. There was no sign of any other keys.

He was about to push the drawer shut when he noticed it felt unusually weighty. Pulling it out to its fullest extent he discovered the reason. Behind more rows of plastic containers was another copy of Cocks et Féret. It was the same edition as the one he had seen in the Director's office. He flipped through it. There were enough entries to provide a lifetime of code-words.

Monsieur Pamplemousse picked up the telephone receiver, called up an outside line, and dialled Mademoiselle Borel's number. It was either engaged or it was off the hook. Perhaps she was already hard at work trying to break into *Le Guide*'s computer just along the corridor – or perhaps she was simply enjoying her *pot-au-feu* in peace and quiet.

Hearing the sound of approaching footsteps in the corridor he hastily shut the drawer, locked it, and was round the other side of the desk just as the night porter opened the outer door.

'Monsieur Pamplemousse. *Bonsoir.* Madame Grante is not working late tonight?'

'Apparently not. I can't find her anywhere.' The man looked totally unperturbed at their presence. As he turned to go, Monsieur Pamplemousse had a sudden thought. 'Were you on duty last night?'

'*Oui, Monsieur.*'

'Do you happen to know what time Madame Grante left?'

'The first or the second time, *Monsieur*?'

'You mean ... she came back?'

'*Oui*, Monsieur Pamplemousse. I was only talking about it with my colleague just now. He saw her leave early in the afternoon – about four o'clock. He remembered it because it was so unusual – especially as she has been working late for the last few weeks. But then I was assuming she must have come back, because when her brother called for her as usual ...'

'Her brother?' Monsieur Pamplemousse tried to conceal his surprise.

The porter gave a hollow laugh. 'That is what she liked to call him. If he is her brother, my uncle is a *rosbif.*' He used the slang term for an Englishman. 'Anyway, she must already have left when he came.'

'What time was that?'

'About nine thirty. It is in the book. I rang through but there was no answer. Then he went to look for her and he came back empty-handed.'

'You let him go and look for her? By himself?'

'*Oui, Monsieur.*' The man began to look worried. 'I suppose I shouldn't have, but you know what Madame Grante is like. Besides, it wasn't as if it was the first time he'd been here.'

'Can you describe him?'

'He is about the same height as Madame Grante. A little younger, perhaps. Fairly heavily built. Well dressed – he usually wears a hat and gloves. I would say he is from the Midi. Perhaps the Rhône Valley by his accent, although he could be a Corsican. He looks a little like a ...' he hesitated.

'Go on?'

The man looked embarrassed. 'I would not like Madame

450

Grante to hear me say it … but he looks like *un maquereau* … a pimp. I would not trust him with my daughter, that's for sure. Or my grandmother come to that!'

'Would you recognise him if you saw him again?'

'*Oui, Monsieur*. As I say, he has been here many times over the past few weeks. That is why I let him in.'

'And what name did he sign in the book?'

'Why, Grante of course, *Monsieur.*'

'Of course,' said Monsieur Pamplemousse drily. 'I'd forgotten. He is her brother.'

It was dark when they left the building. There was a faint drizzle in the air, so he headed up the Rue Fabert towards the taxi rank in the Place de Santiago-du-Chili.

For the first time that day he felt as though he was beginning to get somewhere. There was a glimmer of light at the end of the tunnel. It was only a very faint glimmer, and it could turn out to be an extremely long tunnel, but it was there nevertheless.

What had been said as a joke had turned out to be a distinct possibility. Perhaps Madame Grante had an '*homme*' after all. And in the circumstances, if Madame Grante had an '*homme*' then one way or another it was high time they were introduced, particularly if the porter's summing up was anything to go by.

The taxi driver took practically the same route they had walked earlier that evening, crossing the Seine by the Pont de l'Alma and then up the Avenue Marceau. Searchlights were now raking the sky above the *quai* to their right as the evening *bateaux-mouches* got ready to leave. Very soon the passengers would be dining to a running commentary on the history of Paris in four languages. The cafés in the *Place* were starting to fill.

It was strange how often life suddenly took an unex-

451

pected turn so that, within the space of a few hours, areas one hardly ever visited became a part of the daily round, rapidly becoming as familiar as the street in which one lived.

Leaving his master to his own thoughts and devices, Pommes Frites curled up beside him on the back seat and closed his eyes. He would await the call of duty, but until it came there was no sense in wasting energy needlessly.

As a precautionary measure Monsieur Pamplemousse stopped the taxi short of the Rue des Renaudes and set out to walk the rest of the way to Madame Grante's apartment. He wasn't at all sure what he expected to find when he got there, if indeed he found anything. The whole thing could turn out to be a wild-goose chase. She might well be home by now, safely ensconced in an armchair watching television. Or if she wasn't, there could be an entirely simple reason for her absence – the sudden death of a relative perhaps, an illness … And yet in his heart of hearts he knew none of those things rang true. Madame Grante was a creature of habit, meticulous in all matters to do with work – such behaviour would be totally out of character. And yet, and yet wasn't the whole business of her evening visitor out of character? During his years with the *Sûreté* he'd come across many occasions when, for one reason or another, people had done things totally out of character. The one thing he had learned from his experiences was never to take the behaviour of any human being for granted. His pace slowed as they covered the remaining hundred metres or so and he felt in his pocket for the keys.

Outside the block he looked first one way and then the other. The street was deserted.

Applying the largest of the three keys to the lock, Monsieur Pamplemousse opened the outer door. The light

452

inside the entrance hall was on. He checked the postal boxes – Madame Grante's still hadn't been emptied. There was an illuminated *minuterie* button alongside the glass-panelled inner door and as he pressed it another light came on above the lift. He tried out the Yale-type keys. The second one slid home. He held on to the first key, noting for future reference that it was the longer one of the two and by rights ought to fit the upstairs door. He took the lift this time, squeezing in alongside Pommes Frites. The only sound came from the lift motors. Even the budding saxophonist on the second floor had stopped playing.

He pressed the bell-push outside Madame Grante's apartment twice, but there was still no sound of movement. Slipping the key into the lock, he turned it gently and the door swung open to his touch, revealing a small hall. Another door on the far side stood half open and what little light there was came from a larger room beyond. He called out, but there was no response. The only sound came from the ticking of a clock somewhere nearby.

Feeling along the wall to his left, Monsieur Pamplemousse's hand made contact with a switch. As the light came on he motioned Pommes Frites to follow him in, then closed the outer door behind them and slipped the safety-catch across. He had no wish to have Madame Grante return unexpectedly and mistake him for a burglar.

The living-room was much as he would have expected it to be, although after his mistake with Mademoiselle Borel he wouldn't have stuck his neck out and laid bets on it. The furniture was large and solid, old without having acquired the status of being classed as antique, although time would rectify that. It had been made in the days when oak meant what it said, not chipboard covered with the thinnest of veneers. The atmosphere felt dry and airless as though the windows had been kept shut for a long time. He registered the fact because in the office Madame Grante had a reputation for being something of a fresh-air fiend.

A large sideboard stood against one wall. The top of it was covered with framed photographs. He scanned them briefly. They were nearly all old prints, most of them in sepia. There was certainly no one remotely like the description the porter had given of Madame Grante's 'brother'. The centre-piece, in a large silver frame, showed a man in pre-war army officer's uniform. He was posing proudly beside a section of the old Maginot Line. An inscription written across the bottom half of the photograph in small, neat handwriting said: 'To Violaine, with love. Papa.' Below the words there was a single kiss. Monsieur Pamplemousse wondered if her father had survived the war. Madame Grante never spoke of her family. Alongside it was another photograph which he assumed was of her mother. It was a strong face; not someone who would have stood any nonsense. She must also have been quite a beauty in her time.

'Violaine.' He had never heard Madame Grante called by her Christian name, and he doubted if many others had either. He certainly wouldn't have dared to ask.

On the wall there were a number of old paintings of no great interest, but doubtless each had a story to tell. Amongst them was a framed certificate of competence from a school of accountancy. There was the name again – Violaine Grante.

An inlaid sewing table occupied one corner, a small *bonheur-du-jour* bureau another. Alongside it was an old Edison cabinet gramophone with a wind-up motor. Monsieur Pamplemousse opened it and looked inside. The records were all in their original sleeves; mostly artists from the early Forties. Beside them was a small tin of steel needles.

The heavy mantelpiece supported a large clock made of gilt brass inlaid with decorated porcelain panels. Flanking it were a pair of matching side urns.

In the centre of the room there was an oblong polished mahogany table protected by a crocheted runner. On it stood a bowl of freesias which had been freshly watered. Their perfume was almost overpowering.

Some french windows leading onto a balcony were shut, as were all the other windows. He peered through the glass. The balcony ran the full width of the apartment, connecting with what must be the bedroom. At the far end on the right there was a low steel door, pock-marked with rust, which led to a fire escape. It must have been installed in the days when burglary was less of a problem, for although it was bolted on the inside, anyone with half a mind could have climbed round easily enough. Shielding his eyes from the light in the room he dimly made out the shape of a few trees in the area below; probably part of a communal garden jointly owned with those who lived in the surrounding buildings. It was starting to rain again.

In an alcove between the fireplace and the window there was a row of bookshelves. Monsieur Pamplemousse turned on a standard lamp and ran his eye along the titles. Victor Hugo, Balzac, some old school prizes, the complete works of Racine, Proust, a set of encyclopaedias; there wasn't much to choose from if you felt like a good laugh. Standing out like a sore thumb was a recent edition of a cookery book by Bocuse – put to a certain amount of use already by the look of the pages, some of which had been singled out with a strip of paper.

The top shelf was occupied by copies of *Le Guide*. The

earlier ones must be collector's items, for they dated back to when Madame Grante first joined.

Idly he reached up and removed the first one. It was for 1960. *Le Guide* had gained weight since then. Fewer restaurants had been covered in those days for a start. All the same – he skimmed through the pages; it was amazing how many entries hadn't changed, particularly outside Paris. There were fewer symbols. The reports weren't quite so long. Their founder hadn't believed in wasting words.

The Director must have been an Inspector in those days. He had been brought in by Monsieur Hippolyte Duval, by then in his nineties, unmarried and childless, to be groomed for stardom as it were. Also, according to Loudier, the doyen of the Inspectors, a certain degree of nepotism had been involved. 'Family connections', he was apt to say in his dry way. But that was probably a case of provincial jealousy.

All the same, by any standards the Director had done well. Under his leadership *Le Guide* had flourished. How terrible it would be if its downfall was at hand.

But it wasn't just the future of *Le Guide* that was at stake. It was the Director too. And why the Director? Was he simply a prime target because of his position? Or was there some other reason?

On one of the lower shelves, level with an old leather armchair, Monsieur Pamplemousse came across what he had been looking for: a copy of Cocks et Féret. He opened it up. The first few pages listing the vineyards of Bordeaux had been annotated with letters corresponding to the days of the week. That was one problem solved. Mademoiselle Borel's guess had been confirmed. He was tempted to try telephoning her again with the news.

Monsieur Pamplemousse cast his eyes round the room, half excepting to see a computer terminal tucked away somewhere, but apart from a radio the only concession to the world of electronics was an elderly television. It looked as if it might be a black and white model.

So far it had all been unremarkably neat and tidy. The bathroom was no exception. Everything was put away in cupboards. There were no errant tubes of toothpaste to spoil the effect; no signs of shared occupancy.

The kitchen, on the other hand, was more rewarding. It looked as though Madame Grante must have gone out in a hurry for some reason. A pile of unwashed crockery had been left in the sink to soak. The water was cold and greasy. It suggested something urgent must have cropped up. He couldn't picture her doing something like that without a very good reason. It wouldn't be in her nature. He poked around in the water. She hadn't been entertaining, that was for sure. There was only one of everything: one plate, one bowl, one set of cutlery. There was no wine glass.

Monsieur Pamplemousse glanced around the shelves. Most of the utensils were old and well worn, but there was a sprinkling of newer pieces of equipment: a Braun electric juicer and a Robot Coupé food processor, a new-looking set of Sabatier 'Jeune' professional knives in a wooden block, a mandoline for slicing vegetables, and rather surprisingly, a selection of much-used hand whisks – perhaps Madame Grante had hitherto unsuspected culinary talents?

The cupboards, on the other hand, were surprisingly bare. It looked as though someone had given them a good clear out.

He opened the refrigerator door. Somewhat unexpectedly, there was an unopened bottle of white Puligny-Montrachet in the door. It was from the *Domaine* of Henri Clerc; that from a woman who always said 'no' to a second glass of wine at the office Christmas party for fear of what it might do to her! Otherwise, apart from a few plastic pots containing unidentifiable left-overs, the shelves were once again almost bare.

Hanging on a hook fixed to the wall alongside the door were several carrier bags bearing the name of an *épicerie* in the Rue Cler near the office. Odd, given the fact that she had a thriving food market right on her doorstep. Why would she go to the Rue Cler? To save time? Because she was taking her purchases elsewhere? It was too early in the year for picnic lunches.

On his way out of the kitchen Monsieur Pamplemousse opened the lid of a rubbish chute and glanced inside. As was so often the case – his own was no exception – there were some odd scraps of paper trapped behind the flap. He was about to close it again when something about one of the pieces made him change his mind. It was part of a page torn from a large-scale map. There was a faintly familiar look about it which rang a bell in the back of his head. Someone – it didn't look like Madame Grante's writing – had marked one of the avenues with a cross. Nearby the word 'Beaumarchais' was printed. He folded the paper in half and put it in his jacket pocket for future reference.

Monsieur Pamplemousse left the bedroom until last. Somehow it felt almost like forbidden territory – and it certainly would have been *'interdit'* had Madame Grante been anywhere around; an unforgivable violation of her privacy.

The bed was large and old-fashioned with a crocheted cover. Again, both had probably been in the family for years. On a bedside table, between a reading lamp and the telephone, there was a small doll – it looked like an Armand Marseille – and alongside that an open box of Paul

458

Benmussa chocolates. The first layer had already gone. The sight of it made him feel hungry. He hesitated for a second or two, then resisted the temptation as he caught sight of a large thumbprint in the middle of one of the chocolates. Someone had been testing them. It looked too big to have been left by Madame Grante – and as his old mother might have said – 'you never know where it's been!'

On the dressing-table there was a bottle of Guerlain '*L'Heure Bleue*'. Again, not what Madame Grante usually wore to the office – at least, not that he had ever noticed. Once, years before, he had bought Doucette a bottle of it for Christmas. It had lasted her ages, and was only worn on special occasions.

Monsieur Pamplemousse was about to explore further when he spied something white on the carpet. Stooping down to pick it up, he reached between the legs of the dressing-table and then realised it was the note he had left on his first visit. One end was torn – torn or chewed – it was hard to say which. There was a curious series of half-round serrations – almost like tiny bites – along one edge.

He was about to hold the paper up to examine it more closely when there was a sound of flapping followed by a downward draught of air and something struck him a glancing blow on the top of the head. Almost immediately he felt a sharp needle-like pain, as if a hair had been pulled out.

Reacting in what amounted to a blind panic, Monsieur Pamplemousse automatically jumped to his feet and in so doing collided with the underneath of the dressing-table. Rolling over onto his side he clasped his head, partly in pain but also to protect it from any further blows. As he did so he made contact with something soft and wriggling. Before he had time to tighten his grasp it had gone, but not before he felt another sharp pain, this time to his index finger.

A scuffling from the direction of the doorway heralded the arrival on the scene of Pommes Frites.

'*Comment ça va? Comment ça va?*' Hearing a strange, gruff voice calling out from somewhere near at hand, Monsieur Pamplemousse tentatively opened one eye. Pommes Frites was standing in the doorway, staring in the direction of the window as though transfixed. Had he been given to dropping his jaw in moments of stress, this, clearly, would have been one of those occasions.

Following the direction of his gaze, Monsieur Pamplemousse reacted in like manner as he found himself staring at a small blue object clinging to the top of one of the curtains.

'*Nom de nom!*' He climbed to his feet and dusted himself down.

'JoJo. JoJo. *Comment ça va?*' The gruff voice repeated itself.

Without taking his eyes off his quarry and risk losing face, Pommes Frites backed away. He shared his master's dislike of birds. They were bad enough outside, where they belonged, but at least out in the open they could be chased. Indoors, they were something else again. He fully understood Monsieur Pamplemousse's panic at having one land on his head and he had no wish to take part in a repeat performance when he would be the prime target.

Taking a leaf out of Pommes Frites' book, Monsieur Pamplemousse tiptoed towards the bedroom door and closed it behind him.

A budgerigar! That was all he needed! At least it solved the problem of the snatched note. He looked round the room and saw what he should have noticed when he first came in: a birdcage on a stand. His only excuse was that it had been partially hidden from view by the door leading to the hall. Taking a closer look he saw that it had recently been cleaned out. A new sheet of sanded paper covered the floor and that in turn had been freshly sprinkled with grit. Both the seed bowl at one end and a water bowl at the other were full. The cage door was wide open, but perhaps Madame Grante usually left it that way. Along the bottom edge of the cage there was the address of a pet shop on the Quai de la Mégisserie. Thank goodness he hadn't opened any of the windows to let in some fresh air. If JoJo had escaped he would never have heard the last of it. He certainly wouldn't have fancied his chances of finding it on a dark, wet night in March.

Monsieur Pamplemousse sank down in the armchair beside the bookcase, wondering what to do next. If Madame Grante had left the bird flying loose she couldn't have intended being away all that long. In which case it might be better to carry on waiting for her. It would be silly to give up now.

To be on the safe side he unlocked the outer door in case she returned. It was a matter of balancing the weight of her wrath on finding herself locked out of her own apartment against having to explain why he was there and how he had managed to get in. Of the two alternatives, the latter was preferable. If she was locked out she might well call the police and he didn't want that to happen. The cat would really be out of the bag then.

As he reached across to replace the Cocks et Féret, he noticed something had fallen over in the space where it had been. Somewhat to his surprise, he saw it was a map of the Père-Lachaise cemetery. It had been folded inside out so that an inner section now formed the front cover. Part of it had been torn out. He felt inside his jacket pocket. The piece of paper fitted exactly into one of the corners.

Perhaps Madame Grante had a family grave there, and yet if that were so she would scarcely need a map to find the way – unless, of course, she'd wanted to direct someone else to the spot. From what he remembered of the cemetery it was so overcrowded you practically needed radar to find your way around.

Monsieur Pamplemousse slipped the piece of paper back into his pocket and closed his eyes.

He wondered whether he should telephone Doucette, but decided against it. For a start her sister, Agathe, always ate late and if Agathe answered the phone in no way would it be a short conversation. Anyway, Doucette was used to him being away for long periods without making contact – she wouldn't worry. All the same, he wished he hadn't thought of it. He was beginning to feel hungry.

The thought of food reminded him of Mademoiselle Borel. Was it his imagination or had she looked more than a little lonely standing in her doorway when she said goodbye? Lonely, and somehow, despite her chicness and poise, surprisingly vulnerable. He wondered if she often ate alone. If she did, it was a terrible waste. At least she didn't live on prepacked meals like a lot of women in her situation. Perhaps it was a case of 'once bitten – twice shy' and she found computers a safer bet than a husband – assuming all her external connections were correct. At least you could program them the way you wanted. He wondered if he would take her up on her offer when it was all over. What was it Brillat-Savarin had said? 'Tell me what you eat and I will tell you what you are.' It would be interesting to find out.

Monsieur Pamplemousse woke with a start as he realised a telephone was ringing somewhere. He reached out automatically and then remembered where he was.

Pommes Frites stirred in his sleep as his master blundered past towards the bedroom, rubbing his eyes as he went.

'*Allô!*' Monsieur Pamplemousse cursed under his breath as in his haste to grab the receiver he knocked over the box of chocolates.

In the background he could hear a police siren, but otherwise there was nothing.

'*Allô!*' He tried again. The only response was a click, then the line went dead.

He felt for a cord switch he had noticed earlier and as the light came on he looked at his watch. It was just after one thirty. He must have been asleep for several hours.

As he lay back on the bed for a moment gathering his thoughts, Monsieur Pamplemousse considered the matter. There had been something odd about the call, something he couldn't quite put his finger on. He wondered who could have been ringing Madame Grante at that time of night. Whoever it was must have been shocked to hear a man's voice at the other end. Probably too shocked to say anything. It sounded as though it had come from an outside box. The siren had been very close at one point.

'*Morbleu!*' He sat up with a start as he realised what had been bothering him. A siren had gone past the apartment at almost the same time – exactly in sync with the one on the telephone. Whoever it was must have been telephoning from very close by.

Turning out the light, he got up and crossed to the window. The rain was coming down even harder; it was no time to think of going out. He checked the locks on the french windows and then drew the curtains. As a further precaution he went back into the hall and set the safety catch on the front door.

Returning to the bedroom Monsieur Pamplemousse removed his jacket and tie, hung them over a chair, then lay down on the bed again and covered himself with the eiderdown. It was very unlikely that Madame Grante would return now, and if she did, then *tant pis* – too bad! He was not only tired, he was hungry. And if there was any truth in the old saying, *'qui dort dîne'*- 'He who sleeps forgets his hunger', that was precisely what he intended doing.

Half-way through plumping up the pillow, his fingers made contact with a piece of card. As he withdrew it and held it up to the light, his pulse quickened. It was a photograph of a man, and staring back at him from above the folds of a blue roll-neck sweater was a face which matched the description given to him by the night porter earlier that evening. He turned it over. On the back there was the name of a photographer. It wasn't much help – there was no address. He studied the face in greater detail, committing it to memory. The porter was right in his judgement. It was not the face of someone he would have trusted further than he could see. But what was of greater interest was an inscription across the bottom. POUR VIOLAINE – MON AMOUR. So, it hadn't been a joke after all. Madame Grante did have an *homme*. It must have turned her whole life upside-down, perhaps even made her a trifle unbalanced for a while.

He placed the photograph alongside the piece of map in his jacket pocket, then climbed back onto the bed and closed his eyes again. Sleep came easily.

Monsieur Pamplemousse was a great believer in committing problems to his subconscious, and as he slept he wore on his face the look of someone who felt that at long last he might be getting somewhere.

5
THE GRILLING OF JOJO

Throwing politeness to the wind, Monsieur Pamplemousse elbowed his way along the already crowded Quai de la Mégisserie, weaving in and out of the trees and shrubs, packaged rose bushes, boxes of bulbs and sundry plants, until he came across the shop he was looking for. The pavement outside was already stacked with cages of varying shapes and sizes. Pigeons vied with baby goats for attention. Cocks crowed. Other creatures, like the rabbits, gerbils and guineapigs, carried on eating regardless. If the concerted noise coming from the occupants of the cages was anything to go by, they must have been awake for ages.

Few of the *bouquinistes* who normally plied their trade on the other side of the road seemed to have followed their example. The zinc-topped wooden bookstalls were firmly padlocked and looked as if they would remain that way for some time to come. Glancing up at the sky Monsieur Pamplemousse could hardly blame them. It looked as forbidding as the Palais de Justice on the opposite bank of the Seine, and that was saying something.

Pommes Frites followed on behind at a discreet, not to say wary distance. All was not well between dog and master. Relations were, to say the least, somewhat strained.

A student of such matters, had he been making notes, would have found his pencil racing across the page. Words such as 'nadir' rather than 'apex' would have sprung to mind when trying to describe their current mood.

Had they been interviewed, Pommes Frites would have assumed his injured expression and said quite simply that in his opinion his master had got out of bed on the wrong side.

Inasmuch as he had accidentally trodden on the chocolates, Monsieur Pamplemousse would have been the first to agree that his day hadn't exactly begun on a high note. Normally he liked to sleep with a window open and today he had woken with a headache. He was also feeling both hungry and thirsty. The refrigerator had been bare of anything which looked remotely edible at that time in the morning. He'd found the end of a *baguette*, but it was rock-hard. The coffee was instant, and therefore undrinkable, and despite the presence of the juicer, fresh oranges were conspicuous by their absence.

However, all these things had paled into insignificance when he discovered that JoJo was missing. He had spent the best part of half an hour searching high and low, calling its name and uttering tweets and other endearments, but all to no avail.

In the end there was only one conclusion to be drawn. The evidence was, he had to admit, purely circumstantial; not the kind which would have stood up in a court of law. There wasn't so much as a loose feather to be seen anywhere in the apartment, let alone on Pommes Frites' person. All the same, facts were facts.

Monsieur Pamplemousse blamed himself to some extent. He should have shut the bedroom door. Pommes Frites had been deprived of his meal and so, gently and stealthily while his master was asleep, he must have let his instincts get the better of him. There was little that could be done about it. Punishment had to be meted out at the time a crime was committed. Pommes Frites would have been both hurt and confused if his master had suddenly laid into him for no apparent reason.

The only thing to do in the circumstances was buy another bird and hope that Madame Grante might not spot the difference.

'*Attendez!*' Monsieur Pamplemousse signalled Pommes Frites to wait while he entered the shop. Pommes Frites obeyed with alacrity. He was only too well aware that his star was not exactly in the ascendancy.

Inside the shop the din was even worse. It was feeding time and the noise from puppies, dogs, kittens and a multitude of birds, all shrieking their heads off, was unbelievable. Monsieur Pamplemousse glanced around and found himself opposite a glass tank containing a python. A group of white mice snuggled contentedly in its folds for warmth, blissfully unaware of their fate. He looked the other way. Even in a pet shop the rule of the jungle prevailed.

A little further along the row, beyond some tanks of tropical fish, he saw what he was searching for: a large enclosure full of blue, grey and green budgerigars. He looked for a blue one which might pass muster for the missing JoJo. To his untutored eye, apart from variations in colour, they were all remarkably alike, but he had no doubt Madame Grante would spot the slightest difference immediately. A missing heart-shaped feather on a chin would not go unremarked.

'*S'il vous plaît?*' He summoned one of the assistants and stated his requirements.

'*Monsieur* would prefer a cock or a hen?'

It was not something he had given a thought to. 'There is a difference?'

'*Monsieur,* if you are another *perruche* there is a very great difference.'

467

It was hard to tell whether the man was serious or not. No doubt he'd made the same joke many thousands of times over the years. It was probably too early in the day to accompany it with a smile.

'The cocks are the best talkers.'

Anxious to escape the din, Monsieur Pamplemousse chose one at random.

The man looked down at the floor. '*Monsieur* would like it gift-wrapped?'

Monsieur Pamplemousse's heart sank. He knew he had forgotten something. Acting on the spur of the moment he had put Madame Grante's cage out with the rubbish – there was a door at the side of the lift on the ground floor of her apartment block where large objects could be deposited ready for collection. At the time he had entertained a notion of blaming it all on a burglar, but that was before he had thought of buying another bird. It had not been one of his more fortuitous thoughts; a straw of an idea, but one worth clutching, nevertheless. Better than confessing to Madame Grante that Pommes Frites was probably responsible.

'Perhaps you have a cardboard box of some kind?'

'A cardboard box, *Monsieur*?' Clearly from his tone, the man was classifying his client as belonging to the last of the great spenders.

With a sigh Monsieur Pamplemousse reached for his wallet and pointed to a square cage hanging from the ceiling on the far side of the shop. It looked identical to the original.

'*S'il vous plaît.*'

The cage with its occupant, a small packet of seed, an iodised nibble and a millet spray came to over four hundred francs.

'I will throw in the sand, *Monsieur.*'

'*Merci.*' Monsieur Pamplemousse chose to ignore the contempt in the assistant's voice. '*Une fiche, s'il vous plaît.*'

Four hundred francs was four hundred francs; enough to keep Pommes Frites in food for a month. It was worth asking for a receipt. With luck he might be able to put it through before Madame Grante returned. Someone else must be holding the fort.

Ignoring the expression of disbelief which came over Pommes Frites' face when he saw his master coming out of the pet shop carrying his purchase, Monsieur Pamplemousse looked for a taxi. It was the wrong time of day and he was going in the wrong direction. He tried the rank by the Samaritaine store opposite the Pont Neuf and drew a blank. A small group of people were already waiting. The thought of going by Métro accompanied by Pommes Frites and a chattering budgerigar was not an appealing one. He wouldn't for the world have suggested that in the circumstances Pommes Frites was something of a liability – perish the thought! – but he was beginning to wish he hadn't taken his car in for a service. If he'd had an inkling of all that was going to happen he wouldn't have told the garage to take their time.

Hoping to avoid bumping into anyone he knew, Monsieur Pamplemousse crossed over the road and went down the first flight of steps leading to the river. The Seine was still brown and angry-looking. Branches of trees and other flotsam overtook him as he picked his way round puddles left by the retreating flood-waters. A tug pushing a quartet of heavily laden barges lashed tightly together overtook him. There was a car on its roof alongside a television aerial and he wondered if they would survive the next bridge. The *pénichier* at the wheel obviously thought they would, for he carried on at remorseless seven knots, clearing the arch by inches. A small group of early-morning tourists braving the elements waved as they went past in the opposite direction. Monsieur Pamplemousse looked the other way and caught the curious gaze of a group of *clochards* sharing a bottle of methylated spirits. If staring could wear things out he wouldn't have long to go. Pommes Frites hurried on ahead, pretending he was out for a walk on his own.

What Monsieur Pamplemousse still didn't know, of course, was where Madame Grante had gone and why. She must have intended returning home within a reasonable space of time, otherwise she would have made arrangements for her bird. He couldn't believe she was so alone in the world there was no one she could have called on. A neighbour, perhaps. Or failing that, there must be places specialising in that sort of thing. No, she had left in a hurry intending to return, and so far had not done so. It was worrying.

As they crossed the little footbridge opposite the *Musée d'Orsay* he felt the first spot of rain. There was a sudden flurry of umbrellas in the long queue outside the museum. Windscreen wipers went into action on passing cars and lorries.

Looking back on it afterwards, Monsieur Pamplemousse had to admit that stopping for breakfast at a café in the Boulevard Saint-Germain in the hope that the weather would improve was a mistake, although at the time it had seemed like a good idea; a decision that Pommes Frites had heartily endorsed. He had consumed three *croissants* in the time it took the waiter to return with his master's *chocolat*. Things, in his opinion, were looking up, and not a moment too soon.

By the time the office came into view random spots had turned into a steady drizzle. The ladies of the la Varenne School of Cookery in the Rue Saint-Dominique looked up from their stoves and watched the entourage go past. It was all too clear where their sympathies lay.

As they set out to cross the vast Esplanade des Invalides, Monsieur Pamplemousse began to curse the grandiose plans of the Emperor Napoleon. They may have looked very good on paper, but he hadn't had to go out in the pouring rain without an umbrella. Shelter was non-existent. Abandoning all attempts at keeping the cage on an even keel, he took the last fifty or so metres at a jog-trot, vying with Pommes Frites to be the first to arrive at the entrance to *Le Guide*. Pommes Frites beat him to it by a short head.

The massive double doors were shut and he was about to enter through a smaller door marked *Piétons* when he realised that someone brandishing a clip-board was hovering just inside.

'Ah, Pamplemousse!' A familiar voice boomed his name.

'Oui, Monsieur.' Monsieur Pamplemousse skidded to a halt in order to avoid crashing into the figure barring his way.

'I was wondering when you would honour us with your presence. You will be pleased to learn I have been holding a security check and things are going well. I trust they are with you. I shall look forward to receiving your first report.'

'Oui, Monsieur.' Monsieur Pamplemousse's response was terse in the extreme. It was not time for prolonging the pleasantries. He made to push his way past the Director towards the shelter of the archway only to find his way barred.

'Pardon, Monsieur. It is raining ...'

'I realise that, Pamplemousse, but have you not forgotten something?'

'*Monsieur?*'

'Your pass, Pamplemousse. May I see your pass?'

'I am sorry, *Monsieur,* I have not had time to get one as yet.'

'You have no pass, Pamplemousse?'The Director made no attempt to keep the note of incredulity from his voice. 'I can hardly believe my ears. If that is the case – and I say it with equal sorrow – you may not enter. As the person responsible for security in this establishment you must realise that no exception can be made. If one began making exceptions where would it stop?'

'But, *Monsieur …*'

'No "buts", Pamplemousse. How do I know you are who you say you are? You stand in front of me, unshaven, bedraggled, clutching a caged *oiseau …*'

'How do you know I am who I say I am?' repeated Monsieur Pamplemousse, groping for the right words. He suddenly felt as if he had entered a Kafka-like dream. 'But everyone knows me.'

He turned to the man on the gate for support. 'Tell him, Rambaud.'

Rambaud responded with an all-purpose shrug, one which allowed for whatever interpretation others might like to place on it. Monsieur Pamplemousse took it to mean. '*You* know you are right. *I* know you are right. But *Monsieur le Directeur* also knows he is right and he is the boss. I have my job to think of.'

Monsieur Pamplemousse turned back to the Director. 'I was with you in your office only yesterday afternoon, *Monsieur.*'

'That is what you say, Pamplemousse.'The Director eyed

him with a look of disfavour. 'You could be an impostor. It is not unknown.'

'How many impostors would have a dog like Pommes Frites, *Monsieur?*

'Statistically? I would need to consult the computer.'

The Director dismissed the mathematical possibilities of such an event while he took a closer look at the bird cage. A heap of wet sand had ended up in one corner of the floor, a piece of cuttlefish lay like a stranded white whale in another. The millet spray had long since disintegrated and an iodised nibble was about to do likewise. The bird clung forlornly by one leg to a central perch, its remaining leg tucked under an adjacent wing for comfort. It looked as though it wished it had never left the pet shop.

'That poor *oiseau is* soaking, Pamplemousse. It is a sorry sight.'

'*He* is soaking, *Monsieur*! *I* am soaking. Pommes Frites is soaking. That is why we wish to enter.'

'You do not have feathers, Pamplemousse.'

'Neither do I have a raincoat. I am still in mourning.'Monsieur Pamplemousse made it sound as though he wished he was mourning for the best of all reasons.

'That will do, Pamplemousse. I shall expect to see you in my office forthwith.'

'But, *Monsieur* …'

The Director raised his hand. 'No "buts", Aristide. A rule is a rule.'

'But if I am not allowed inside to get a pass and I am not allowed to enter without one, what am I to do? It is an *impasse.*'

'You should have thought of that in the first place, Pamplemousse. Having confirmed your new position as our chief security officer, I must admit to a sense of disappointment. I had hoped for better things.'

As the Director turned on his heels, Monsieur Pample-mousse played his first of two trump cards. 'Cocks et Féret,' he called.

The effect was both immediate and electrifying. Had he been playing the part of Lot's wife in a Hollywood extrava-ganza, the Director would have received rave reviews. The renewal of his contract would have been assured. He would have been typecast for ever more.

Slowly he unfroze and turned to face the gate.

'Say that again, Pamplemousse,' he exclaimed. Then he raised his hands in horror at the thought. 'No, no, please don't. Walls have ears.'

'I have not been idle, *Monsieur*. Now may I please come in.'

'Of course. Of course.' The Director dismissed the problem summarily. 'Rambaud, escort Monsieur Pample-mousse to the photographic booth and make sure the formalities are completed with all possible speed.'

He turned back to Monsieur Pamplemousse. 'I will go on up, Aristide. Follow on as soon as you can. And please get rid of that *oiseau* on the way. I find things depressing enough as they are.'

Monsieur Pamplemousse had no wish to find himself closeted for the morning with the Director. He had other more important things to do. Sensing that he was on a winning streak, he seized the opportunity to play his second card.

'Of course, *Monsieur*. I will leave the cage out here on the pavement. No doubt the garbage men will find a home for it when they do their rounds. Although what Madame Grante will say when she hears I really don't know. It is probably her pride and joy. If she loses it she will have no

474

one to talk to during the long winter evenings.

'You see, *Monsieur*, I spent last night at Madame Grante's apartment ...'

'What?'The Director gazed at him as though thunderstruck. 'You spent last night with Madame Grante. I can scarcely believe my ears. I know that over the years you have acquired a "certain" reputation, which you have always chosen to repudiate, and in the past I have always given you the benefit of the doubt. But this, Pamplemousse, this is beyond the pale. No wonder you are looking the worse for wear. Shaving must have been the very last thing on your mind. As for Madame Grante, the more I hear of her behaviour, the more worried I become. Clearly she has reached a dangerous age and something has snapped. If things carry on at the present rate none of us will be able to sleep safely in our beds.'

'*Monsieur*, with respect ...' Monsieur Pamplemousse held up his free hand to stem the flow of words. Enough was enough.

'Respect? Respect, Pamplemousse, seems to be a singularly ill-chosen word in the circumstances.' The Director was not to be silenced that easily.

'With respect, *Monsieur*, I did not say I spent the night *with* Madame Grante. I said I spent the night in her apartment. Madame Grante was not there. To be absolutely truthful I spent it with Pommes Frites. Were he endowed with the power of speech he would undoubtedly confirm the fact.'

Briefly and succinctly Monsieur Pamplemousse outlined all that had happened since he'd left *Le Guide's* headquarters the night before, omitting only that part which involved Pommes Frites' lapse from the standards normally expected of a house guest.

To his credit, the Director listened to every word. At the end of it he stared at the cage in Monsieur Pamplemousse's hand.

'Do I understand you to say that *oiseau* belongs to Madame Grante?' he exclaimed. 'And it has the power of speech? Why on earth didn't you say so in the first place. No wonder you are carrying it around with you.'

Monsieur Pamplemousse hesitated. He could hardly tell the Director that he suspected Pommes Frites of having eaten the original inhabitant of the cage.

'Strictly speaking,' he began, wondering if hairs could be sufficiently and delicately split to avoid on the one hand retracting or modifying what he had just said and on the other hand satisfying his audience. 'When I awoke this morning and discovered Madame Grante still hadn't returned ...'

But the Director wasn't listening. His mind was clearly racing on ahead, enjoying some new flight of fancy.

'It must be grilled.'

'Grilled, *Monsieur*?' Monsieur Pamplemousse looked suitably horrified at the thought. 'Surely a small towel would be sufficient.'

'No, no, no, Pamplemousse. I don't mean in order to dry it. I mean we must question it before it is too late. Judging from its present state its days may well be numbered. Pneumonia could set in before nightfall. We must send for a vet. There is not a moment to be lost. With luck it may reveal, albeit parrot-fashion and unwittingly, some vital scrap of information.'

'*Monsieur*, with the greatest respect, there are many things I have to do. You said yourself that time is of the essence.'Monsieur Pamplemousse wanted to say he had better things to do with his day than spend it grilling a budgerigar especially one which hadn't as far as he knew learnt to talk.

'Leave it with me, Pamplemousse. I will personally carry out the interrogation. It will help relieve the tedium of waiting.'

The Director reached out and poked a forefinger through the bar.

'*Qui est un gentil oiseau?*'

Somewhat unjustly in the circumstances, his kindness was not rewarded in like vein.

'*Sacrebleu!*' He jumped back as if he had been shot.

'Is anything the matter, *Monsieur*?'Monsieur Pamplemousse looked suitably solicitous as the Director nursed an injured digit. 'Would you care to borrow my handkerchief?'

The Director forbore to answer. Instead, he took the cage and headed towards the steps leading to the main entrance. Monsieur Pamplemousse resisted the temptation to call out and ask if the bird ought to have a pass. It was not the right moment.

Rambaud gave another shrug, maintaining his reputation of being a man of few words. At home he probably carried out entire conversations with Madame Rambaud that way.

His photograph duly taken, a pass issued, Monsieur Pamplemousse checked in his office tray to see if there were any messages. There was one from Doucette asking him to phone, but apart from that it was empty. He tried dialling her sister's number but it was engaged.

While he was holding on he glanced out of the window. It had stopped raining. There was even a patch of lighter sky on the horizon where the sun was trying to break through. Steam was already starting to rise from his jacket which he'd draped over a nearby radiator. He reached out and felt the shoulders. It was drying remarkably well. Picking up the contents of his pockets which were strewn over the desk, he went through them one by one. He paused at the sight of the map of Père-Lachaise. Perhaps it was time for another excursion? The thought triggered off another. Opening his wallet, he removed the photograph he had found under Madame Grante's pillow, then dialled another number.

'Administration?

'Pamplemousse here.'

'Pamplemousse. *Chef de Sécurité*. May I have the home address of the porter who was on duty yesterday evening?'

He wasn't altogether sure he liked his new title, but he might as well make use of it while he could. One thing was certain: as soon as the present fracas was over he would hand over to someone else. He couldn't wait to be out on the road again.

'*Merci*.' It was within walking distance.

Opening a desk drawer Monsieur Pamplemousse took out a pack of disposable razors. It was high time he looked respectable again. He glanced at his watch. It would help fill in time before lunch.

Washed and shaved, Monsieur Pamplemousse had one more call to make before he left the office.

The *Occupé* light was on over the darkroom door when he reached the art department, so he left the remains of Madame Grante's chocolates on the floor outside with a note outlining what he needed. Given a light dusting of powder, there were several which ought to yield quite usable thumb-prints. Blown up, they could be of value. It was a long shot, but it was worth a try, and it was the kind of job Trigaux revelled in – a welcome change from his normal routine of processing pictures of hotels and restaurants and shots of the surrounding countryside brought back by *Le Guide's* Inspectors after their travels.

No doubt the time was not far distant when they, too, would be committed to an electronic memory, available at the touch of a computer button.

A few minutes later, with Pommes Frites at his heels, he left the building.

They had gone only a little way along the Rue Fabert when he heard the sound of someone running and his name being called out. He turned and saw the Director coming towards him. It had to be something urgent for he had left his jacket behind; an unheard-of occurrence. He wondered if something was wrong with the budgerigar.

As the other drew near he saw he was clutching a piece of paper. He looked as if he had received yet another shock.

'Thank Heaven I caught you!' The Director handed him the paper. 'Read this.'

Monsieur Pamplemousse ran his eyes over the note. It was written in block capitals in a mixture of different styles and it was brief and to the point. MADAME GRANTE IS BEING HELD PRISONER. YOU WILL NOT FIND HER. DO NOT CONTACT THE POLICE. EITHER PUBLICATION OF *LE GUIDE* IS SUSPENDED OR YOU WILL RECEIVE PARTS OF HER THROUGH THE POST. THE CHOICE IS YOURS. YOU HAVE UNTIL FRIDAY. THERE WILL BE NO FURTHER COMMUNICATION.

Monsieur Pamplemousse whistled. 'When did this arrive, *Monsieur*?'

'A few minutes ago. It was pushed under Rambaud's office door while his back was turned.'

'So he didn't see who did it?'

'No. I have already delivered a severe reprimand. It won't happen again in a hurry.'

Monsieur Pamplemousse fell silent. Friday! Matters were even more serious than he'd thought. It was Wednesday already.

'What does it mean, Aristide? Parts? What parts?'

'I shudder to think, *Monsieur*. An ear, perhaps. A finger. That is where such people usually start. Something easily detachable.'

'A *finger*!' The Director clutched at a lamp-post for support. 'Would anyone dare do such a thing? If it is from her right hand, think of the problems she will have when it comes to operating the computer. Keyboards can be modified, but there are limits. The whole system will suffer.'

'I think, *Monsieur*, that Madame Grante's suffering should be our prime concern. What of her sewing and her knitting?'

The Director looked suitably shame-faced. 'You are right, Aristide. I was thinking of everyone's P39s. So much has happened over the past twenty-four hours it is hard to know where one's priorities lie. Of course Madame Grante's personal safety must come first.'

'I am also of the opinion, *Monsieur*, that when we find Madame Grante we could be well on the way to solving many of our other problems.'

'Then I must return to the *oiseau*. It may yet find itself in the witness box.'

Monsieur Pamplemousse eyed the Director dubiously. 'I doubt if a budgerigar's statement will stand up in court, *Monsieur*.'

'There is always a first time, Aristide. I have it on good authority that the testimony of a bloodhound is admissible in America. Speaking of which,' the Director glanced down. 'I take it Pommes Frites is working on the case too?'

'Of course, *Monsieur*. Rest assured we will neither of us leave a stone unturned until Madame Grante has been found.'

Monsieur Pamplemousse spoke with a confidence which

he was far from feeling. In the cold light of day the Director looked drawn and haggard.

'*Comment ça va*, Chief?' He tried not to make it sound too much like JoJo.

The Director paused. 'Between you and me, Aristide, things are not so good. The girls in the typing pool are doing their best, but they are attempting the impossible. At their present rate of progress there isn't a hope in the world of publishing on time. Even with the original material it would be pushing things, but starting from scratch ...' He gave a dispirited shrug.

As they said goodbye and went their separate ways Monsieur Pamplemousse suppressed a shiver. For some reason he was suddenly reminded of the python in the pet store. Perhaps even now Madame Grante was snuggled up to the writer of the note, blissfully unaware of the fate he had in store for her. It was a sobering thought which only served to strengthen his resolve.

As they reached the corner of the Place de Santiago-du-Chili he paused and glanced back the way they had come. The Director appeared to be engaged in an argument with someone just inside the entrance to *Le Guide*.

Could it be that Rambaud was refusing him admission? He wouldn't put it past him. An eye for an eye, a tooth for a tooth. He would enjoy getting his own back.

Life was not without its compensations. JoJo's stand-in was enjoying an unexpected reprieve. His grilling looked as though it might be delayed indefinitely.

6
THE TOMBSTONE TRAIL

Unfurling a snow-white napkin, Monsieur Pamplemousse used it to give his moustache an anticipatory dab before tucking it in behind his shirt collar. Uttering a sigh of contentment, he settled back and took in his surroundings. Although it was barely twelve thirty, the main dining area of the restaurant was already crowded and the stools lined up in front of the bar were all taken. He was lucky to have got one of the small tables situated in the window.

He ordered a *Kir Sancerre blanc* from the waiter who had shown him to his seat and it arrived a few moments later along with a small dish of biscuits and nuts.

The pace was hotting up. Somewhere in the background he could hear the familiar sound of a kitchen hand chopping *baguettes* with a guillotine. Monsieur, presiding over the bar, was busily pouring *apéritifs* in between shaking hands with old friends and filling *pichets* and *demi-pichets* with *vin rouge, vin blanc* and *vin rosé* ordered from a list, unclassified and unidentified as to year, chalked on a blackboard above the counter; wines which aspired to no greater heights than that of accompanying and washing down good, wholesome food. Than which, in Monsieur Pamplemousse's opinion, there could be few better aims in life; an outlook which was endorsed without question by Pommes Frites, noisily smacking his lips as he settled himself down at his master's feet and listened to the clink of knives and

forks hard at work on all sides. He, too, had a look of anticipation on his face.

Madame was busy writing down the lunch-time orders
on a pad, whilst at the same time keeping a weather-eye on
all that was happening around her. Other than an opening
smile of welcome and a '*Bon appétit*' when the order had
been brought, communication between the *patronne* and
her guests was minimal. Brownie points were lost if you
didn't know what you wanted by the time she arrived.
Dithering caused raised eyebrows. Last-minute changes of
mind gave rise to barely suppressed sighs of irritation. Time
was of the essence. Her wave as she caught sight of
Monsieur Pamplemousse was the equivalent of a Presiden-
tial honour.

By *Le Guide* standards there was nothing particularly
special about Les Tourelles in the Rue Bosquet. The scene
was probably being duplicated at that very moment in
similar restaurants all over France. Waiters hurrying to and
fro in their black waistcoats and white aprons, shirt sleeves
rolled up in businesslike fashion to just below the elbows.
The paper table-cloths laid over starched white linen.
Brown panelled walls with unframed copies of
turn-of-the-century posters stuck up on them. The long
banquette covered in dark red velvet against one wall; the
tables in front of it packed so close together in order to
make maximum use of the available space that there was
barely room for latecomers to squeeze between them; the
waist-high divisions which turned the centre of the room
into a group of islands surrounded by bulging coat stands.

If Monsieur Pamplemousse patronised it more than any
other establishment when he was in Paris it was as much
because it was handy for the office as for any other reason –
not so close that it was full of familiar faces, but not so far

away that walking between the two took up an inordinate amount of his lunch time; that and the sense of timeless, unchanging permanence it always gave him. He hoped it would survive the computer age and competition from *Le Fast Food*. It would certainly need a well-programmed computer to match Madame's grasp of what was going on, and the service in most of the latter was slow by comparison.

Monsieur Pamplemousse had no problems over his order. He chose, as he almost always did, from the 78F fixed-price menu, *service compris*.

Filets de Hareng Pommes a l'Huile; 1/4 Poulet Rôti pommes Frites; and a *Tarte aux Pommes* for himself, and the usual for Pommes Frites: a steak followed by a bone. Since a quarter-bottle of wine was included in the price of a meal it meant he would have a whole half-bottle to himself. He chose the red. Pommes Frites would be more than happy with a splash in his bowl of water; what was known as an *abondance*.

'*Saignant?*' Madame wrote down the second part of his order without batting an eyelid, then automatically slipped the bottom copy of the bill under an ashtray for the waiter to see when he brought the basket of bread.

'*Oui, s'il vous plaît.*' Pommes Frites wouldn't mind if his steak was underdone or not, though if pressed for a decision he would probably have opted for whichever method took the least time. Gastronomically, his master's present case had been a disaster area so far. Not at all up to par.

While waiting for his *hareng* to arrive Monsieur Pamplemousse mused on his visit to the night porter. The man's reaction to the photograph had been revealing, for he had added one useful piece of information. It was to do with the man's attire. Madame Grante's brother didn't always look quite as immaculate as he had described earlier. On the night in question he had looked much as he did in the picture. He'd been wearing a dark blue roll-neck sweater, to which could be added light blue jeans, a black leather jacket, and rope-soled shoes.

He also had a nervous tic in his right eye.

'Why didn't you tell me?'

The man had looked injured. 'You didn't ask me, *Monsieur.* You only asked me what he usually looked like.'

To which there had been no answer.

'Assuming all external connections are correct.' Martine Borel's phrase came back to Monsieur Pamplemousse as he took the photograph out of his pocket and had another look. One connection was certainly missing: where the picture had been taken; it would be nice to know. It was obviously a studio shot and the only clue was the name of the photographer on the back. It would be like looking for a needle in a haystack, unless …

In between the *hareng* and the *poulet* Monsieur Pamplemousse left his table for a moment to make a telephone call.

'Mademoiselle Borel? *Comment ça va?* I hope I am not interrupting you.

'Me? It is hard to say. I have a few leads but not much time.

'You could do something for me on your *Minitel.*

'I need to know the location of a photographer. I have the name, but no other details. Is that possible?

'No. I will give you my office Fax number. If you have any luck you can let me know there.

'*Merci.*' Once upon a time he would have used the *pneumatique* system. Using compressed air to propel messages to their destination via a network of underground pipes had seemed the ultimate in speed and efficiency. Now, he

485

didn't even know if it was still in use. Perhaps it was yet another casualty of the computer age.

The *poulet* arrived just as he got back to his table. It was large and crisp and succulent; doubtless Pommes Frites would be only too pleased to help him out if he had problems. The mound of accompanying Frites were equally crisp, verging on the golden; the bread basket had been topped up.

Between mouthfuls he gazed out of the window at the people hurrying past. Occasionally they stopped to study the menu or to peer inside before going on their way.

His thoughts turned again to Madame Grante. Since the message had been delivered by hand, the chances were that the man had done it himself – by now Monsieur Pamplemousse was convinced they were dealing with one person, although if he'd been asked to give his reasons he would have been hard put to say why; it was simply a hunch. If he was right, whoever it was would hardly have entrusted the job to anyone else – he would have wanted to make sure that it got there safely. He might even have got a kick out of doing it himself; there was a kind of sadistic element to all that had happened so far. In which case the person responsible was probably at large somewhere in Paris. But where in Paris? For all Monsieur Pamplemousse knew he could be sitting in the same restaurant at that very moment watching him from another table.

It was all very well the Director saying don't bring the police in, but there could come a point when they would have to. The whole thing had escalated beyond the mere good of *Le Guide*. Madame Grante's life was now at stake. If they left it too long they would be abused for not having done it sooner. The police were no better than anyone else at working miracles.

After the *tartes aux pommes* Monsieur Pamplemousse ordered a *café* and at the same time called for his bill. They arrived together.

Back at the office everyone else in his section was still out for lunch. He was glad in a way. He wasn't in the mood for small talk.

A large manila envelope awaited him on his desk. It was plastered with DO NOT BEND labels. Trigaux must have worked through his lunch break.

Monsieur Pamplemousse picked up the phone and called his contact at the *Sûreté*.

'Jacques? Aristide here.

'*Oui, bien, merci.*

'You might have told me it was *Mademoiselle. I* was expecting a *Monsieur* Borel.'

He got the same reply he'd been given by the night porter. 'You didn't ask me.' It was another case of 'assuming all external connections are correct.' He was stuck with the phrase now for ever more.

'*Oui*. She was very charming and helpful.' While he was talking, Monsieur Pamplemousse cupped the receiver under his chin and undid the flap of the envelope.

'Jacques, there is another small favour I would like to ask. It is a long shot, but I have some blow-ups of a thumb-print.

'Of course. When it is all over.

'At the restaurant of your choice.'

Holding the photograph between thumb and forefinger, he shook the envelope free. As he did so a piece of paper fell out and fluttered to the table. It was a note from Trigaux.

'Next time you have any chocolates you need photographed, try leaving them further away from the door.'

Monsieur Pamplemousse stared at the picture. It was in colour. Oozy, sickly, and almost uniformly chocolate brown. It was like looking at a child's idea of a moonscape. The flat area in the centre showed clearly where Trigaux had stood.

'*Qu'est-ce que c'est?*' He suddenly realised there was a disembodied voice in his right ear.

'*Non.* Forget it.'

'*Oui.* I will be in touch.'

Monsieur Pamplemousse put the receiver down and buried his head in his hands. He stayed where he was for a while, only vaguely aware of the fact that a girl had entered the room through a door at the far end and was coming towards him. She was clutching a piece of paper and she looked in a hurry.

'Monsieur Pamplemousse. I am glad I caught you. We thought you might not be coming back.'

He took the piece of paper and glanced at it mechanically. The word URGENT was stamped in red across the top.

The typed message was short and to the point. Three towns were listed: Rennes, Nice and Belfort. Each was followed by an address. '*Bonne chance* – Martine'had been added in ink.

The miracles of modern science! Where would it all end? At one time such a task would have taken many people weeks of painstaking work sifting through directories.

He glanced up and realised to his surprise that the girl was still there.

'There is no reply. Unless …' Monsieur Pamplemousse paused for a moment. 'Send a message back saying, "*Merci.*" You could add the word "Bordeaux" if you like.'

If Martine was still working on the code-word to enter

the computer, she deserved a clue. It was too late for the information to do any harm even if it got into the wrong hands. Doubtless a new code would have to be devised anyway.

'I will do that straight away, Monsieur Pamplemousse.'

The girl still showed no sign of leaving. She looked embarrassed.

'Well? What is it?'He tried not to sound too impatient.

'It is about Madame Grante, Monsieur Pamplemousse.'

'Madame Grante?'

'We were discussing your message ...'

'We? Who are "we"?'

'The other girls in the Communications Room and myself.'

'How do you know it concerns Madame Grante?'

'We put two and two together and since you are working on the case and it was marked "urgent" ...'

Monsieur Pamplemousse gave a sigh. So much for security and confidentiality. The Director would not be pleased if he knew!

'And what conclusion did you reach?'

'It isn't exactly a conclusion, Monsieur Pamplemousse. It is just that it is a funny coincidence.'

Monsieur Pamplemousse tried to conceal his growing impatience. 'A coincidence? Tell me, what coincidence?'

'Well, you see, last summer Madame Grante went on holiday to the Jura, and when she came back she was all different ...'

'Different? How do you mean – different?'

'Well, it is hard to say. She was somehow ... nicer, and she seemed more approachable. I remember she brought us back a bottle of Suze and some *tarte au fromage*. I had never tasted Suze before.'

489

Suze. He hadn't had any himself for a long time. It was an acquired taste, popular with commercial travellers and others who had to stand lots of drinks, according to George Simenon's Maigret. The *gentiane* from which it was made had medicinal qualities and it was low on alcohol.

'Anyway, we decided she must have met someone while she was there.'

Monsieur Pamplemousse sat up. He was suddenly all ears.

'And?'

'Well, it didn't last for very long. After a while she gradually dropped back into her old ways again. Worse, if anything – and we all thought that was that. Then, just recently, it happened again, only this time we really knew there was something going on. She started having flowers on her desk and once ...' The girl began to blush again.

'Go on.'

'Well, once someone saw her coming out of that shop in the Rue Cler, you know ...'

Monsieur Pamplemousse didn't know, but he didn't want to lose face either. He suspected it might be the one with the frilly-packed window. It had one of those fashionable 'In'names which could have applied to almost anything. He wondered what it was all leading up to.

'So, as I was saying, when we saw the message and the list of places we put two and two together. Belfort is in the Jura, which is where Madame Grante went to on her holiday, and well, we thought you might like to know.'

'You did well. *Merci*.'

The girl paused at the door. 'Madame Grante *is* going to be all right, Monsieur Pamplemousse? I mean, she's a funny old thing at times, but she's got a heart of gold really. Especially if anyone's in trouble. I think she's probably very lonely, so she puts up all sorts of barriers and pretends she doesn't mind.'

As the girl made her exit, Monsieur Pamplemousse gazed out of the window, lost in thought. Communication! Despite all man's endeavours, despite the invention of the computer or perhaps even because of such things, communication on its simplest level remained the great problem in the world. There he had been, living in his own little world, wrestling with his problem, and in another part of the very same building a group of young girls had been sitting around thinking about it as well, putting two and two together and coming up with one of the answers he needed. If it hadn't been for the Fax message they might never have told him.

Belfort! Opening one of the drawers he took out a copy of *Le Guide* and leafed through it. Belfort was just a name, somewhere he had yet to visit. He found it on page 221. It boasted one major hotel – the Hotel du Lion, several lesser ones with varying degrees of comfort, two restaurants with a Stock Pot, and a sprinkling of smaller ones. He wondered if Madame Grante had stayed at any of the ones listed, and if so, which. He made a note of the names on his pad, then put the book away.

'Ah, Pamplemousse.' Outside in the corridor the first person he bumped into was the Director. He had his right arm in a sling and he looked in a bad mood. There was a second finger in plaster.

'Pamplemousse, that *oiseau* is as ill-tempered as its mistress. They say pets grow to be like their owners. I fear it may never yield up its secrets. It hasn't uttered a single word since I last saw you. Its lips are sealed.'

'Its lips, *Monsieur*, but clearly not its beak.' Monsieur Pamplemousse glanced down at Pommes Frites. He must study his own face more carefully next time he was in front of a mirror to see if there were any changes. There could be worse fates.

The Director looked at him suspiciously. 'I have just been to see Sister. She has inoculated me against psitta-cosis. One never knows where its beak may have been.'

'A wise precaution, *Monsieur*. I understand the disease is highly contagious. One cannot be too careful.'

'Perhaps you would care to have a go, Aristide. You are more skilled in the art of third degree than I.'

Monsieur Pamplemousse hastily declined the offer.

'Pommes Frites and I are off to the Père-Lachaise ceme-tery, *Monsieur*.'

The Director turned momentarily pale. 'Not bad news, I trust? Nothing to do with ...'

'It is hard to say, *Monsieur*. I will let you know if anything develops.'

As they left the office Monsieur Pamplemousse decided to take a chance and catch the *autobus* to Père-Lachaise. The 69 normally had an open platform at the rear and because it started near by in the Champ-de-Mars it was rarely full.

His ploy worked. It wasn't the first time. Appreciating what his master required of him, Pommes Frites waited in a convenient doorway near a stop in the Rue Saint-Dominique until the *autobus* drew up alongside. There were no more than half a dozen passengers, all of them facing the front. As Monsieur Pamplemousse climbed aboard and flashed his pass, momentarily distracting the driver away from his rearview mirrors, Pommes Frites slipped quickly over the rail at the back and lay down out of sight. With the weather as it was, the *autobus* would need to get very crowded before anyone else was hardy enough to join him. But just in case, Monsieur Pample-mousse stationed himself on one of the rear seats with his legs stuck out across the door and his hand at the ready so that he could give the appropriate signal to abandon ship if need be.

He wanted time to think and somehow he always found the autobus more profitable in that respect than the Métro. It was somehow more soothing; there were fewer distractions. On the Métro people tended to watch you thinking for want of something better to do.

There was an element about the sabotaging of *Le Guide* which was bothering him. It had been nibbling away at the back of his mind all day.

So far he had been assuming – and he had no doubt that others, including the Director, had made the same assumption – that the version which was now committed to the computer's memory was a revised version of the forthcoming publication. He'd assumed it for the very simple reason that there had been so many other things on his mind he hadn't even bothered to sit down and think it through.

But if that wasn't the case – if it was based on last year's guide, for example – did that make any difference? It would mean it could have been prepared over a long period, rather than in the brief time between finalisation and the launch party. It would then have been a comparatively simple task either to substitute a bogus *disque* the night before – presumably only a matter of moments – or to transfer it electronically. He had no idea how long that would take.

In the Rue de la Roquette they had an encounter with a parked lorry. The road was narrow at that point and they were unable to pass. A short argument ensued which ended as it had begun with the driver of the *camion* refusing to move until he had finished unloading.

The driver of the *autobus* picked up his telephone and spoke briefly. A minute or so later there was the familiar sound of a police siren.

The lorry driver climbed into his cab and drove off. Doubtless he, too, felt himself a victim of the computer age.

They arrived at the main entrance to Père-Lachaise without further incident. Glancing up at the gathering rain-clouds, Monsieur Pamplemousse decided to remain where he was while the *autobus* skirted round the outside wall of the cemetery, climbing the steep hill towards the entrance on the far side. It would save making a similar climb on foot once he was inside the gates. Taking advantage of the general exodus towards the middle as they approached the terminus in the Place Gambetta, Pommes Frites made his own disembarkation arrangements and was already waiting on the pavement by the time the doors opened. From the way he behaved as he caught sight of his master he could have been sitting there for hours.

As they approached the entrance to the cemetery Monsieur Pamplemousse saw a woman attendant in a blue uniform peering out from her hut. She eyed Pommes Frites suspiciously as they drew near. Monsieur Pamplemousse sighed. It was yet another hazard to be overcome. For a country which allowed dogs into restaurants up and down the land and which supported a thriving industry catering to their many needs and demands, there were a remarkable number of no-go areas. He pretended not to have noticed the CHIENS INTERDITS sign.

Treading the fine line between what some might take as a compliment and others might misconstrue, Monsieur Pamplemousse raised his hat.

494

'*M'moiselle.*' He'd guessed right. The woman softened immediately.

Looking round as though to make sure no one could overhear, he leaned forward conspiratorially. As he did so he encountered a strange smell; a mixture of stale body odour and damp uniform in the ratio of two to one. It was not a pleasant experience. Reaching inside his jacket pocket with one hand, he motioned towards Pommes Frites with the other.

'*Permettez-moi, M'moiselle?* He was a great fan of the late Edith Piaf.'

'I see no *chien, Monsieur.*'

Monsieur Pamplemousse withdrew a note from his wallet. 'In that case may I invest in a map.'

The woman's hands closed around the note, held his own for rather longer than was strictly necessary – long enough for Monsieur Pamplemousse to realise that in his haste he had mistaken a hundred franc note for a twenty – then slipped it inside the top of her jacket. Without taking her eyes off him, she reached towards a shelf just behind the door of her hut. As she did so he noticed another sign: POURBOIRES INTERDIT.

Thanking her for the map, Monsieur Pamplemousse considered the situation. Patently, the transaction was considered to be at an end; negotiations as to price were not about to be entered into. For the briefest of moments he wondered whether to make up for the lack of change in some other way. He decided against it. It wouldn't do to press his luck too far. She didn't look the type of woman who gave receipts, and picture postcards were conspicuous by their absence.

'*Vous êtes très gentille, M'moiselle.*' The compliment went the way of the note.

'*Monsieur* will find the grave of Edith Piaf near the *Monuments aux Résistants et Déportés* at the far end.'

Monsieur Pamplemousse felt the woman's eyes boring into the back of his neck as he set off at right angles to the way he had intended going. Pommes Frites was already bounding along on a parallel course to his own, picking his way sure-footedly in and out of the gravestones, pausing every so often to make sure his master was still in sight, or to leave his mark.

Monsieur Pamplemousse wondered idly if his friend might encounter the giant cat said to haunt the place, albeit in search of young maidens. It was the kind of day for it: dark and gloomy. If they did meet up there would be hell to pay. Hair and fur would fly.

As soon as he could, he turned right and set off up the hill, past the memorial to Oscar Wilde, to where Pommes Frites stood waiting for him. Avoiding the vast bulk of the *Columbarium,* he took a short cut. Simone Signoret lay undisturbed but not forgotten to his right. Further still there was the usual small group gathered in silent worship around the memorial to the faith-healer Kardec. Eyes tightly closed, a middle-aged woman clung to the stone as though she was part of it. She looked as though she had been there for hours. He could have done with a bit of such blind faith himself.

Having reached the highest point, he made his way down to the little chapel and paused in the gardens for a moment in order to compare his own torn-out piece of map with the one he had just bought. As he had thought, the marked area came from the older part of the cemetery, hardly changed since the beginning of the nineteenth century, when the architect Brongniard had landscaped it, leaving the lime and chestnut trees from the original Jesuit gardens, but constructing a network of cobbled lanes and winding gravelled paths leading out from where he was standing. Abélard and Héloise were buried somewhere near the bottom of the hill, along with Chopin, Cherubini and countless others whose gravestones marked the passage of history, and where Balzac used to wander 'to cheer himself up'.

Monsieur Pamplemousse looked around as he rotated the map in order to get his bearings. Not many people were braving the weather that afternoon. The few hardy ones were mostly hidden beneath umbrellas, for it had started to rain again. He wished now he had brought one himself. If he'd thought, he could have borrowed one from the office.

There was a continuous roar from the wind in the trees and he found it hard to hold the map out straight. A sprinkling of dedicated tourists peered at their guidebooks in the dim light as they picked their way resolutely along sodden gravelled side-paths trying to reach their objectives before the gates closed. He caught an occasional glimpse of some lone person – almost always a woman – paying her respects to a loved one. You would need to miss someone very badly to be there on such a day. It wouldn't be long before the usual quota of exhibitionists, fetishists, grave-robbers, necrophiliacs, perverts, voyeurs and other bizarre inhabitants of the potter's fields put in an appearance.

He set off in a south-westerly direction along the Avenue de la Chapelle, then turned left, following a path which took him past the tombs of La Fontaine and Molière. As far as the eye could see there were thousands and thousands of tiny stone properties, many of which looked as though they had long since been abandoned, their iron gates either rusted away or hanging drunkenly by a single hinge. In parts it was more like a repository for ancient telephone kiosks and *pissoirs* rather than a cemetery. A sodden-looking black cat appeared from behind a gravestone, then beat a hasty retreat when it saw Pommes Frites.

Monsieur Pamplemousse found what he was looking for in an area occupied by some of the more illustrious Marshals of France. It somehow fitted in with the Director's preferred image. He saw the names of Ney and Masséna and Lefebvre.

The discovery wasn't a total surprise; in a way he had half expected it. All the same, it still gave him a strange feeling to see the name Leclerc engraved in the stone above the Director's family motto: *Ab ovo usque ad mala.* He supposed it meant from the egg to the apples – from beginning to end, after the Roman habit of starting a meal with eggs and ending it with apples. Given the Director's present occupation it was an apposite choice. Interestingly, the name was spelt in its simplest form, without the letter 'q'at the end. It bore out Loudier's theory that the Director himself had added it at some point in time.

The vault was better kept than most of those around it. On one side the inscription CONCESSION À PERPETUITÉ was followed by a number and a date – 1780 – but it had clearly been well maintained; the stonework was clean and the ironwork was freshly painted. Monsieur Pamplemousse climbed up a small flight of steps and peered through a glass-backed ornamental door grill. There was a vase of fresh flowers standing on a plinth at the back, and the floor looked as though it had been recently swept. Otherwise the inside was bare. Around the walls there were names engraved. The Director's grandfather had died not so long ago at the age of ninety-one – he remembered hearing about it at the time. Two uncles had died in the war. The Director's father must be still alive, the date of birth – 1892

– had been entered, but the space which had been left to record the date of his death was blank.

While his master was at the top of the steps, Pommes Frites busied himself at the bottom. There were a number of interesting, not to say unusual scents to be found on the ground around the tomb. Many of them were quite recent. Not for nothing had he won the Pierre Armand trophy as the best sniffer dog of the year during his time with the Paris *Sûreté*. Had Pommes Frites, like his human counterparts on other courses of a not dissimilar nature, kept a notebook, then he would have made entries under a variety of headings. Earth scents, which covered crushed worms and other insects, not to mention cracked and bruised vegetation. Individual scents, with subdivisions relating to Human Scent, Sex (m. or f.); and Regional Scents, covering each and every part of the body. The third category, Additional Scents, embraced types of footwear and their composition – whether they were made from leather or rubber-shoe cream, occupational scents and the kind of clothing worn.

Making full use of the long ears and hanging lips with which nature had endowed him, Pommes Frites concentrated first of all on trapping body scents, feeding them into a system which was a million times more powerful than that of any human. He registered the fact that someone whose odour he didn't immediately recognise had been very busy. Earth scents didn't yield a great deal, largely on account of the nature of the terrain. Additional scents was the most rewarding; there were several he couldn't immediately identify – but all, animal, vegetable and mineral, were duly separated and filed away in his memory for later use should the need arise.

The task completed, his mental 'in-tray' empty once

again, Pommes Frites marked the spot in time-honoured fashion and stood waiting patiently on the path, wondering what would happen next and why his master was looking so puzzled.

The simple fact was that Monsieur Pamplemousse looked puzzled because nothing he had seen so far offered up any clue as to why the piece had been torn out of the map. Perhaps it was simply, as he'd first thought, a reminder as to the exact position of the Director's family tomb. But if that was the case what was it doing in Madame Grante's apartment? It wasn't until he turned to make his way down the steps again that he saw what could be the answer: just to the right of the doorway the Director's name had been chiselled into the stone. It was followed by the beginnings of a date – the day and the month, but not the year. Perhaps whoever was responsible had been caught in the act. It was the same date as had appeared in the *journal* several days previously announcing the Director's death.

Monsieur Pamplemousse took a closer look. The work had obviously been carried out by a portable cutter of some kind; the marks were those of a saw rather than a chisel. It wasn't nearly so professional-looking as it had seemed at first sight. Nicks where the blade had overrun were crudely etched in – probably by a felt-tipped pen.

He stood up and considered the matter. If it was a joke, then it was in very poor taste. And if it wasn't a joke? In his heart of hearts he knew that whoever was responsible wasn't joking. It fitted in with all that had gone on before. The piranha fish, the announcement in the paper, the sabotaging of *Le Guide*, the kidnapping of Madame Grante; no one would go to that much trouble unless they were in deadly earnest. And if they were that serious then there was no time to be lost.

Faced with the distinct possibility that if he didn't act quickly he might have more than one corpse on his hands before the week was out, Monsieur Pamplemousse reached for his notepad and pen. It was clutching at straws, but he had to grab hold of something. Anything was better than .nothing. The chances were that anyone so totally obsessed with detail would want to come back and finish the job. It needed something to arouse his opponent's interest without giving anything away. He made two attempts, screwing both up in disgust before he finally struck the right note: MEET ME ON THE TERRACE OF AUX DEUX MAGOTS. 10.00 TOMMORROW. CARRY A COPY OF *LES GUIDE*.

If he read his adversary correctly he wasn't someone who would risk leaving such an invitation unanswered. The alternative was to hang around in the rain in the hope that someone might eventually turn up. It wasn't an attractive prospect.

The suggestion that whoever read the message should carry a copy of *Le Guide* was a master-stroke. It added a certain bizarre, yet at the same time logical note to the proceedings in keeping with the way the other's mind must be working.

Mindful of *Le Guide's* circulation figures and the possibility of confronting some innocent tourist, he added a postscript. OPEN AT PAGE 221! He plucked the figure out of the air, much as he might have picked a raffle ticket. It wasn't until some time later that he realised why he had chosen it.

Carefully making sure the first few words of his message were visible, Monsieur Pamplemousse slipped the note into the plastic cover of his season ticket in order to protect it from the rain and placed it under a stone at the bottom of the door. It would be out of sight to any casual passers-by, but clearly visible to anyone interested enough to take a closer look.

Lost in thought, Monsieur Pamplemousse set off towards the Avenue Circulaire along a route which would take them back to where they had started. Pommes Frites followed on behind wearing his enigmatic 'mine is not to reason why' look. Left to his own devices he would have gone in quite the opposite direction, but he was too well trained to protest. His moment would come. Every dog had its day. No doubt his views would be sought when the time was ripe. He only hoped it wouldn't be too late.

Anyway, there were soon other problems to contend with. As they reached the *Mur des Fédérés* in the south-east corner of the cemetery, scene of the Paris Commune's final bloody stand when the last 147 insurgents were cornered and shot, it started to rain in earnest. There weren't even any empty tombs to provide shelter; it was a part where flat grave stones predominated. He tried sheltering beneath a couple of spindly coniferous trees, but they were worse than useless. It was like standing under a colander. Any admirers of the late Edith Piaf had long since disappeared.

Making a break for it, he dashed towards the gates. The woman attendant beckoned to him invitingly from the shelter of her hut as they ran past. In her plastic bonnet she looked like an elderly pixie who had seen better days. Monsieur Pamplemousse pretended he hadn't seen her, which wasn't difficult, for by now the rain was coming down in sheets. Their departure coincided with a loud clap of thunder almost overhead.

Thinking about it afterwards, Monsieur Pamplemousse was inclined to draw a veil over the rest of the day; some things in life were best forgotten. Soaked to the skin; his already heavy suit feeling like a ton weight; failing miserably in an attempt to board an already over-crowded *autobus* whose passengers took one look at Pommes Frites and then raised their voices in a unanimous vote of protest – totally unappreciative of the fact that in similar circumstances, they too would have wished to shake themselves dry; unable to find a taxi – doubtless they had all gone home to escape the worst of the weather; their way barred on the Métro by a group of roving Inspectors anxious to justify their salaries whilst themselves sheltering from the storm; it felt like a bad dream during which one avenue after another was barred to them. He was past caring. There had come a point where nothing mattered any more.

If he had thought about it at all he would have gone back to his own apartment and got a change of clothing; but he didn't, so there was no point in wishing he had. Like a homing pigeon, he headed for Madame Grante's instead. He was far too wet to notice that in his absence someone had collected the mail from the box in the hall.

Never had anywhere looked more welcoming. As soon as they were safely inside her apartment, Monsieur Pamplemousse emptied the pockets of his suit and spread them out over the living-room table. The recent soaking had started where the first one had left off. It was doubtful if his suit would ever be the same again. He found the remains of a disintegrated mothball where his wallet had been and immediately wished he hadn't. It would probably take days for the smell to go away. Removing his jacket, shirt and trousers, he draped them over a clothes-hanger, then looked around for somewhere to hook it. The hall was out of the question. He tried hitching it over a drawer knob in the kitchen, but in no time at all there was a pool of water over the floor which grew larger with every passing moment. In the end he settled on the balcony. The wind was blowing from the west and that side of the building was sheltered from the rain.

He shivered as he went back inside, locking the door behind him and drawing the curtains. It was no night to be out half-dressed. He made his way into the living-room, switched on the electric fire, and was about to undress further when he realised Pommes Frites was behaving strangely. He was pacing up and down, sniffing here, there and everywhere, looking first in the hall, then in the bedroom and the kitchen; nothing escaped his scrutiny.

Monsieur Pamplemousse glanced around. He prided himself on having a photographic memory, and as far as he could see everything was exactly where he had left it that morning. Yet there was no denying the look of intense concentration on Pommes Frites' face. Clearly something was amiss. Equally certain was the fact that whatever or whoever was responsible was no longer in evidence.

So in the spirit of better safe than sorry, Monsieur Pamplemousse went the rounds, lowering the shutters on all the windows and putting the catch on the front door to be on the safe side. Then he carried on as before.

Removing the rest of his clothing, he filled the kitchen sink with water and left it to soak. Then he went into the bathroom and turned on the taps.

Following on behind, Pommes Frites sat watching in thoughtful mood while his master lay back, luxuriating in the warmth of the water as it crept higher and higher. He knew what he knew, and in his humble opinion having a bath was not the most important thing in the world at that moment in time, but there was no accounting for the way human beings behaved. They often did the strangest things.

It wasn't long before the inevitable happened. Monsieur Pamplemousse began to sing. It was another thing that was a constant source of amazement to Pommes Frites: the odd noises human beings made when confronted with a bath full of water.

Suddenly they both froze as a voice came from the other room. Monsieur Pamplemousse scrambled to his feet. He reached out for a towel only to discover there wasn't one. In desperation he grabbed hold of the first thing he could find. As he climbed out of the bath he caught sight of his reflection in a mirror.

There was only one consolation. Whoever the voice belonged to, it was patently not Madame Grante. She wouldn't take kindly to the sight of her best flannel being used for the purpose to which he had just put it.

7
RENDEZVOUS AT AUX DEUX MAGOTS

Signalling Pommes Frites to remain where he was, Monsieur Pamplemousse crept towards the bathroom door and peered through the crack. Hairs bristling, muscles quivering, ready to spring into action at the blink of an eyelid, Pommes Frites obeyed instructions, albeit with a certain amount of reluctance. From where he was crouching his master looked more than usually vulnerable and in need of care and protection. Bringing up his rear was not, in Pommes Frites'opinion, the best way to go about things.

'*Allô. Qui est là?*'

'*Allô. Qui est là?*' Monsieur Pamplemousse gave a start and then relaxed. The voice echoing his words from the other room had a familiar, if not particularly welcome ring to it.

He flung open the door and was greeted by a fluttering of wings as something small and blue detached itself from a nearby picture rail and took off in a wild excursion round and round the room, careering into things as it went, before finally settling on a curtain at the far end.

It was all he needed to make his cup of unhappiness complete – an *oiseau*! And not just any old *oiseau*, but clearly, from the few words it had uttered to date, the genuine article. Where JoJo had been hiding and what he had been doing during the interim period was neither here

506

nor there; a mystery which would probably never be solved. But there he was, as large as life and twice as noisy, gazing at him through beady, panic-stricken eyes. It was a problem Monsieur Pamplemousse was in no mood to deal with at that moment, even if he'd been able to. For a split second he was sorely tempted to take the easy way out and open the windows; what the eye didn't see the heart didn't grieve for, but his better nature caused him to have second thoughts. It was hard to envisage, but Madame Grante probably loved JoJo.

There was a stirring from inside the bathroom as Pommes Frites, tiring of his restricted view of the world and unable to contain his curiosity a moment longer, joined his master in the doorway. Monsieur Pamplemousse immediately felt a pang of remorse. That he could have thought the worst about his friend was unforgivable. He reached down and gave him a conciliatory pat.

Pommes Frites, for his part, looked as though he would have been only too pleased to make up for things and in so doing justify his master's earlier mistake. His better nature did not extend to love of birds, domesticated or otherwise. He licked his lips. Birds were for chasing.

Bereft of his clothes, clad only in an ill-fitting silk dressing gown belonging to Madame Grante which he had found hanging behind the bedroom door, his inner man scarcely replenished by a single slice of toasted stale *baguette* which he shared with Pommes Frites, Monsieur Pamplemousse spent an unhappy evening. The high spot came when, having washed his underclothes, he hung them out on the balcony alongside his suit. With luck they would be dry by morning. After that, time hung heavily on his hands. At around nine o'clock he had a second slice of toast. Pommes Frites devoured his half in a single crunch,

507

then sat watching through soulful unblinking eyes while Monsieur Pamplemousse eked out his portion until, unable to stand it a moment longer, he sacrificed the last corner.

He toyed with the idea of ringing Doucette to see if she could organise something, but it was late and explanations as to why he was sitting in Madame Grante's apartment *sans* his clothes would be tedious in the extreme and might not be believed.

He tried watching television for a while, but it was a panel game, *'Chiffres et Nombres',* and he wasn't in the mood. Tino Rossi singing *'Mon Pays'* began to pall after the fourth playing, and as the evening wore on he found difficulty in sharing Edith Piaf's philosophy of having no regrets.

Why on earth he hadn't gone home first he didn't know. Well, he did know, of course. Once he had his nose into a case nothing else mattered. But at least if he'd gone back to his own apartment he could have changed into some other clothes and used the time to better advantage. But doing what? He had done everything he could think of for the moment. It was now a matter of waiting. Waiting to see what his opponent's next move would be. Despite the first message saying there would be no further communication, he couldn't believe that was true. He'd already broken that vow once. He must be just as much on edge as everyone else, probably even more so. In his experience it was always the same; it was a battle of nerves – each side waiting to see if the other broke first. But would the next communication be in the form he'd threatened – a part of Madame Grante? The chances were that even if he meant what he'd said at the time, when it came to the crunch it would only be used as a last resort; certainly not until the date of *Le Guide's* publication had come and gone.

If only Trigaux hadn't stepped on the chocolates. The way he was feeling he would even have eaten the ones with the thumb-prints on.

Towards midnight he braved the lift and slipped down to the ground floor in Madame Grante's dressing-gown in order to rescue the bird cage. Luckily it was still where he had left it. After that he spent a fruitless hour trying to catch JoJo but JoJo wasn't having any. He was a past-master at the art of allowing his adversary to get within a few centimetres of touching distance, before flying off. If it happened once, it happened a hundred times. In the end, worn out by all the exertion, Monsieur Pamplemousse gave it up as a bad job, tied the cage door open with a piece of string, and lay back on Madame Grante's bed.

He stared up at the ceiling, contemplating his lot. There had to be better ways of spending an evening in Paris. Correction: there undoubtedly *were* better ways of spending an evening in Paris. Thousands of them.

He ran his eye along a row of books on a shelf in the bedside cabinet. The selection was no more exciting than it had been in the other room. He was in no mood for anything deep. Idly he removed a copy of the green Michelin *Guide de Tourisme* for the Jura. It was a recent edition. Presumably Madame Grante had acquired it when she went on her ill-fated holiday.

A folded brochure marked the town of Belfort.

Some three pages of the guide were devoted to its history and its *Curiosités,* of which there appeared to be a good many, including a statue of a giant lion eleven metres high and twenty-two metres long, carved by Bartholdi to celebrate the heroism of the town's population in defending it against the onslaught of forty thousand Germans during the siege of 1870. Situated as it was in the gap between the Vosges and the Jura Mountains it was a natural route for any invaders from the east. Its defence by Colonel Denfert-Roehereau – he who not only had an *avenue* and a *place* named after him in the capital, but also the Métro station nearest to the Catacombs – was one of the few glorious episodes of the Franco-Prussian war. Earlier still, Vauban, whose statue was not a stone's throw from *Le Guide*'s offices, had built the fortifications, from the terrace of which there was one of those *beaux panoramas so* beloved by Michelin. The Square E.-Lechten boasted a *grande variété de plantes et de fleurs*. Perhaps it was there that Madame Grante had met her *paramour*.

The river Savoureuse flowed through the town. The Canal de Montbéliard to the east joined up with the Canal du Rhône au Rhin. To the west the A36 *autoroute* provided a link between Germany and Switzerland on the one hand and Central France on the other. Perhaps not surprisingly, those factors together with its situation had been of considerable economic importance to Belfort in recent years.

He turned to the brochure. There were pictures of the lion and of the old city, with its views of the river and the surrounding mountains. Another page was devoted to the industrial area which had grown up in the eastern half of the town, burning it into a centre for many enterprises ranging from metallurgy to textiles, through plastics, to locomotives and electronic equipment. Honeywell-Bull had a factory there.

Monsieur Pamplemousse sat up in bed with a start, suddenly wide awake. Was he about to establish yet another external connection?

He picked up the telephone and dialled Mademoiselle Borel's number. It was answered almost immediately.

'Martine, forgive me, I wouldn't do this normally, but it *is* urgent.'

Despite the lateness of the hour, she didn't seem at all put out. 'I have been trying to get you. No one seemed to know where you were.'

'Tell me?'

'No, you first.'

Monsieur Pamplemousse took a deep breath. He was only too aware that the question uppermost in his mind could well have been answered by a simple call to the telephone exchange.

'I saw in your c.v. that you had a spell with Honeywell-Bull. Was it in Belfort?'

'No, it was at Angers. I was helping to develop a new mainframe computer system. But I have been to Belfort.' She pre-empted his next question. 'That is why I have been trying to get hold of you. The Poulanc factory is also there. I should have thought of it too. I was so pleased to have got the list of names I couldn't wait to get them to you.'

'There is no reason why you should have done. I only asked for the location of a photographer.'

'Even so.'

'It was of very great help. It narrowed the field. It also acted as a catalyst.' Briefly he told her of the conversation he'd had with the girl from the Communications Room.

'But you still don't have a name?'

'Not yet.'

'If you do, be sure and let me know. He may have a credit card and I could find out more about him.'

'That is possible?'

'I have a friend, back in the States. He has access to information through the International Association of

Credit Card Investigators in California. Strictly confidential, of course.'

'Of course.'

Monsieur Pamplemousse was wide awake by now. His mind was racing with questions.

'The computer uses *disques, oui*?'

'If it is the model you say it is.'

'How long would it take to change the information on one?'

'That depends. If whoever did it was able to access the mainframe and the material was pre-prepared either on *disque* or on tape, then very little time at all. An entire novel can be transferred in a matter of a few minutes.'

'And if it wasn't pre-prepared? If he was making the changes as he went along?'

'Then a very long time. Certainly no faster than a person can type. There is also the fact that he would have had to work at night when the computer wasn't being used. That would have halved the available time.'

'Whoever did it went to a lot of trouble. It wasn't simply a matter of jumbling up a few entries – he went through the entire book making outrageous alterations. Had it ever seen the light of day there would have been enough libel actions to keep the lawyers busy for years. Given the fact that *Le Guide* was still in a state of preparation and was being constantly updated, he would have had to work extremely fast.' Monsieur Pamplemousse was thinking aloud by now, acutely conscious that his questions were self-answering.

'Extremely.'

'We have been assuming all along that "all external connections were correct" and that the material on the print-out was a doctored version of the forthcoming guide, but supposing it wasn't – supposing he had simply taken the current guide and changed that?'

'Then he would have had all the time in the world. He could have done it at his leisure and then simply transferred the material at the last possible moment.'

'Like the night before the launch party?'

'Exactly.'

'And to do that quickly?'

'If it was fed in electronically it doesn't matter what the information was on. It could have been on tape – a different size of *disque* ... anything. It would simply be a matter of accessing the mainframe and feeding the signal in, erasing the original at the same time.

'If it was done manually, then provided whoever is responsible knew what they were doing and had access to the computer room it would only be a matter of seconds to make the change.

'But for the latter the *disque* would need to be physically the same as the original?'

'Clearly, yes. And since the system is peculiar to Poulanc that would imply the use of a similar machine at some stage, which makes the source of the photograph all the more interesting.'

'What would your guess be?'

There was a pause. 'If it was just an ordinary hacker, then I would say from the outside every time. A hacker would see the whole thing as a challenge. And even if they were caught he or she might get away with it. The law has yet to catch up on the complexities of electronic breaking and entering. It isn't necessarily a criminal offence. Usually they are charged with some petty offence, like stealing elec-tricity. From what you have told me so far ...'

'It has become a matter of life and death.'

'In that case my guess would be that a carefully prepared

disque was transferred physically at some point prior to the launch party. If, as you say, the copy *disque* has also been tampered with, then that could have been done at the same time, either physically or electronically. Again, my guess would be the former. It would save time.'

'So it is possible that the original and its copy are still in existence?'

'That is an area where your guess is as good as mine. He might have kept them. He might have thrown them away. It would most likely be a decision of the moment. He could have been tempted to keep them as a souvenir. Something to gloat over in his old age. Or he might simply have dropped them in a litter bin.'

'What do you really think?'

'I think you would have made a very good detective.'

'*Merci*. I am sorry to have troubled you at such an ungodly hour.'

'Do not worry. I was awake anyway. Thank you for your message. I am now deeply into the wines of Bordeaux. There are so many alternatives.'

'*A bientôt*.'

'Sleep well.'

Monsieur Pamplemousse replaced the receiver and lay back again.

Sleep well! It was easier said than done. His mind was racing with thoughts of one kind and another. He looked around for an alarm clock, but either Madame Grante relied on instinct or she had taken it with her for some reason. He toyed with the idea of telephoning Martine again and asking her to give him an early call, but for all he knew she might want to catch up on some sleep herself if she was still working. He decided against it. He might even spend the time reading.

Much as he hated wishing his life away, he couldn't wait for the morning. Either the note he'd left on the Director's tomb would produce results or it wouldn't. If it didn't? If it didn't, then perhaps he would have to go to the Director and admit defeat, hand over all he knew to the police and let them get on with it. It would go against the grain, but at least he would have done his best and it would absolve him of the responsibility if anything went wrong. Two days had gone by; two to go. The sands of time were running out.

He woke once in the night to the sound of Pommes Frites stirring. Luckily he had left JoJo shut up in the living-room, otherwise he might have suspected the worst. With that thought uppermost in his mind he went straight back to sleep again.

When Monsieur Pamplemousse woke the sun was streaming in through chinks in the shutters. The sky was as clear as though it had never rained before or ever would again. Windows were open all around him. People were emerging as though from a long sleep. He was about to fling open his own windows when he remembered JoJo.

He looked at his watch. It was just gone eight thirty. There was no need to hurry. Time enough for a leisurely bath, a shave, then breakfast with the toasted remains of the *baguette* before he got dressed.

His frugal breakfast over, he found an electric iron in one cupboard and an ironing-board in another. He looked at his watch again. It was already nine fifteen. His ablutions had been perhaps a trifle too leisurely. Time was no longer on his side.

One bright spot was that JoJo had gone back into the cage of his own accord. Monsieur Pamplemousse hastily shut the door. Perhaps it was a good omen. At least it was one problem out of the way.

Opening the doors to the balcony he went outside to get his clothes and then stopped dead in his tracks.

Ever sensitive to certain 'key' words, like *'Sacrebleu'* *'Nom de nom'* and *'Morbleu'*, to name but a brief selection of those which reached his ears from the balcony on the present occasion, Pommes Frites came rushing out to see what was happening. As he skidded to a halt alongside his master he, too, looked as though he could hardly believe his eyes. His jaw dropped and he gave vent to a loud howl. For, as with the Emperor in Hans Andersen's immortal tale, Monsieur Pamplemousse's clothes were conspicuous by their absence. All he had left in the world were the shoes he stood up in.

'Sacrebleu! Nom de nom! Morbleu!'

Monsieur Pamplemousse gave a start as he heard a small voice repeating his words somewhere inside the apartment. Trust Madame Grante to have a *oiseau* that was quick on the uptake.

'Sacrebleu! Nom de nom! Morbleu!'

It was like having a child who inevitably gravitates towards the one word you don't want it to repeat. Even Pommes Frites looked impressed.

'Sacrebleu! Nom de nom! Morbleu!'
'Sacrebleu! Nom de nom! Morbleu!'

In contemplating his lot, Monsieur Pamplemousse couldn't but feel that a profane *oiseau* – particularly one which belonged to Madame Grante – was all he needed to make his cup of unhappiness, already not far short of the brim, full to overflowing.

Given all the circumstances, for Monsieur Pamplemousse to have arrived outside Aux Deux Magots some five minutes ahead of time was little short of a miracle. The hands of the clock on the bell tower of the church of Saint-Germain-des-Prés showed 09.55 as he arrived in the *Place*. Panic had lent him speed. He had practically run the last few hundred metres from the Odéon Métro station, taking a circuitous route which kept him clear of the crowds in the Boulevard Saint-Germain itself, which was probably just as well in the circumstances. Apart from a brief, but nonetheless unpleasant encounter with a leering *clochard* at Châtelet who refused to take '*non*' for an answer, the journey had been mercifully without incident; most of those out and about had other things on their mind. All the same, he was thankful to have made it.

He was followed into the Place Saint-Germain-des-Prés at approximately 09.55 plus fifteen seconds by Pommes Frites, pointedly keeping his distance.

A dress which was patently too small by several sizes revealed parts of Monsieur Pamplemousse which, in Pommes Frites' humble opinion, would have been best kept to himself rather than shared with those passers-by who chose to take a second, and sometimes even a third, look. A student of fashion might well have had a few things to say on the subject of matching shoes, a Hermes representative would have looked askance at the way in which one of their scarves had been tightly knotted across the lower half of the face rather than draped loosely round the neck or over the head; a milliner would have thrown up his hands in disgust; Pierre Cardin, whilst applauding the choice of sun-glasses bearing his name, might have pointed out that in designing them he'd had in mind a Mediterranean beach in high summer rather than Paris in March.

Their views would have found a ready and willing listener in Monsieur Pamplemousse. Had he decided to take up a new career as a drag artist, Madame Grante's wardrobe would not have been his first choice; it wouldn't even have made the short list. But beggars could not be choosers, and he'd had no option.

Pommes Frites' reason for keeping his distance was much more basic. Although he had become accustomed over the years to his master's vagaries, he knew that others were not always quite so tolerant. He had no wish to be seen by any of his friends in the unlikely event of their straying across the river onto the Left Bank.

It was largely the presence of such thoughts that made him linger on the corner of the Place Saint-Germain-des-Prés and the Rue de l'Abbaye while he made up his mind what to do next, whether to follow his master into the cafe or wait for him outside.

As Pommes Frites stood weighing up the pros and cons of the situation he became aware of an unusual scent, one with which he had become all too familiar over the past few days. He was too well trained to react, as some dogs might have done, by seeking out the source as a matter of urgency. Instead, he remained exactly where he was. The only outward signs of anything untoward were the faintest twitching of his nostrils and a certain restlessness in the way his tail flicked to and fro, as though engaged in seeing off a swarm of unseasonable flies. After a moment or two, even those manifestations of unease died away as he mentally homed in on a nearby shop, and then more specifically on the figure of a man lurking in the doorway with his back towards the street.

Whilst gazing casually about him, Pommes Frites also noted an unusually strong police presence in and around the area. There was a blue van parked a little way along the road and two more were blocking the Rue Guillaume-Apollinaire on the far side; all were full of men in uniform.

Several police motor cycles were parked in the Boulevard Saint-Germain, their riders astride them, ready to go into action at a moment's notice. Two more policemen were directing the traffic. Another was addressing a walkie-talkie.

The information having been duly recorded, Pommes Frites decided to stay put for the time being and await further developments.

Unaware of Pommes Frites' thought processes at that precise moment, Monsieur Pamplemousse opened a current copy of *Le Guide* which he had borrowed from Madame Grante, turned to page 221, then entered Aux Deux Magots through the centre door opposite the *Place*. Pointedly flourishing the book aloft for all to see, he looked around for a vacant seat in the terrace section. His heart sank. For a start, he hadn't pictured it still being enclosed for the winter, and despite the comparatively early hour, it was already full to overflowing. Usually by that time in the year people would be sitting outside as well.

Looking very aggrieved, Monsieur Pamplemousse set off down the narrow central aisle, weaving his way in and out of the tables and wickerwork chairs in a crab-like motion. It would be a disastrous twist of fate if after all the trouble he had been to he couldn't find anywhere to sit. As he neared a table in the far corner he spotted an empty chair. It would afford him an ideal position from which he could keep an eye on things without being overlooked from behind. An elderly American couple about to start their breakfast eyed him nervously as he drew near.

Desperate situations called for desperate measures. '*S'il vous plaît*?' Before they had a chance to reply, Monsieur Pamplemousse was sitting alongside them. Pursing his heavily painted lips, he bestowed a beatific smile in their direction whilst helping himself to one of their *croissants.*

'*Merci!*'

As the couple hastily gathered up their belongings and fled the table, Monsieur Pamplemousse put his handbag firmly down on one of the vacant chairs and his guide on the other, daring anyone else to join him.

Smothering any feelings of guilt he might normally have had at inflicting such a grievous wound to Franco- American relations, he settled himself down and looked for a waiter. There wasn't one to be seen. He wondered if the *café* still came in two-cup size pots borne on a silver tray. It was a long time since he had last been there. The previous occupants of the table had been about to drink *chocolat* – the cup nearest to him was still hot. He took a quick sip. It tasted deliciously rich and warming.

Outside in the *Place* the tree buds were at bursting point. The cobbled paving was still damp from its morning wash. A 39 *autobus* went past, heading towards the Seine. For some reason best known to themselves all the passengers were looking out of the window and pointing towards the cafe.

He glanced around. In the old days the bills had been stamped *Le rendez-vous de l'élite intellectuelle.* Perhaps they still were, although nothing was for ever. Most of the present clientele could hardly be described as intellectual, let alone *élite.* If he met any of them on a dark night he would give them a wide berth. Even through his dark glasses they looked sordid enough to make the most unwashed of intellectuals appear positively angelic. Jean-Paul Sartre would turn in his grave if he saw the depths to which one of his favourite haunts had sunk; Simone de Beauvoir would have walked out, never to return. What was the world coming to? He hadn't seen such a motley collection of riff-raff since his days on the beat. The lower slopes of Montmartre at five o'clock in the morning could hardly have thrown up a more unsavoury assortment of humanity.

Monsieur Pamplemousse gave a start as he took a closer look at the occupants of the other tables. Several factors impinged on his brain at the same time. Not only was the bulk of the clientele at Aux Deux Magots that morning decidedly odd, it was also – apart from a sprinkling of unhappy looking tourists – almost completely male; if 'male'was the right word to use. Worse still, they were all clutching open copies of *Le Guide*!

'*Merde!*' There was no need for him to waste time straining his eyes to read the page number of the one nearest to him; he knew the answer without looking. The contents of his note must have circulated like wildfire to have brought such dregs of humanity crawling out of the woodwork and from under their stones. He looked at his watch. It was almost ten o'clock exactly. Even if his quarry had intended being there he must have been frightened away by now.

Monsieur Pamplemousse had barely registered the fact when his ears were assailed by the strident blast of a whistle from somewhere close at hand. Seconds later pandemonium broke out as a horde of blue-uniformed figures suddenly appeared from nowhere and began streaming in through the door. Others appeared as if by magic to bar the exit through the main cafe itself.

Monsieur Pamplemousse's first regret was that he'd chosen a table in a corner from which there was patently no chance whatsoever of escape. His second regret was that Madame Grante's handbag was full to overflowing with his own belongings. He looked in vain for somewhere to hide his copy of *Le Guide*.

'*Monsieur* ...' A stocky figure clad in a black leather jacket and riot gear appeared in front of him and held out his hand. 'May I see that?'

Monsieur Pamplemousse did a quick flick of his wrist. 'Of course, *Monsieur*. I was planning a little holiday in Brittany. You will find it somewhere near the beginning of the book.'

Looking him straight in the eye the man turned the pages back again.

'I think you have made a mistake, *Monsieur*. On page 221 you are in the Jura.'

Monsieur Pamplemousse gave up. It had been worth a try, but there was no point in arguing. It was a no-win situation. He was dealing with a member of the CRS – the *Compagnie Républicaine de Sécurité*. Purposely kept caged up behind barred windows for hours on end beforehand, like a bull getting up steam before entering the ring, the man would be spoiling for a fight. One more word and it would be a charge of resisting arrest. Two and it would be a clout around the *tête* with a baton.

As he found himself being bundled unceremoniously up the steps of a waiting van along with the other occupants of the terrace, Monsieur Pamplemousse looked around for Pommes Frites. A judiciously well-placed bite on the rear of his captor would not have come amiss, but he looked in vain. For once his friend was nowhere to be seen.

Although not visible to Monsieur Pamplemousse, Pommes Frites was, in fact, quite near at hand. He was caught on the horns of a dilemma. On the one hand loyalty to his 'master tugged him in one direction. On the other hand, all his training led him to the inescapable conclusion that he should hang on at all costs to the trail he had just picked up. He opted for the latter.

It was a difficult moment for Pommes Frites and he had the grace to avert his eyes as he saw his master being escorted from Aux Deux Magots before disappearing behind the crowd that had already collected outside, avid as ever for a free spectacle, just as they had been centuries before when on that very same spot justice had been dispensed on the gibbet and pillory by those in power.

Fortunately, looking the other way gave him a great advantage, for he was just in time to see his quarry boarding an *autobus*.

Without a moment's hesitation, he set off in pursuit. The antique shops of the Rue Bonaparte, the view from the Pont du Carrousel, the glass pyramid covering the new entrance hall of the Louvre, all passed in a flash as he strove to keep up with the *autobus* while it crossed the Rue de Rivoli and thence into the Place Palais-Royal. So intent was he on his task that when it pulled up at the first stop in the Avenue de l'Opéra he overtook it and nearly missed seeing the man get off. He was now waiting in the shelter, looking back the way he had come. Following a zig-zag course, sniffing at various objects *en route*, Pommes Frites retraced his steps and then stationed himself on the other side of the glass where he could keep a watchful eye on the man's legs.

Several more *autobus* went past before the other made a move. Then, as the fourth one arrived, he climbed on. Pommes Frites sprang into action again, following on behind as it turned right into the Rue Sainte-Anne. This time the going was much easier, for the road was narrow and progress was slow. The problem was not so much one of keeping up with the *autobus*, but occupying himself inconspicuously while it squeezed its way in between various lorries and roadworks *en route.* In the end Pommes Frites decided to keep as far behind it as possible, hoping he wouldn't be seen. He was glad that he had, for as the *autobus* made another right turn, this time into the much wider Rue du Quatre Septembre, it came to a halt again and he saw the man get off, hesitate for a moment or two, then take shelter in a nearby doorway.

As though engaged on an important errand, Pommes Frites turned left, then paused to relieve himself on the nearside wheel of a large *camion* parked at the side of the road. He positioned himself so that he would get a good look at his quarry, imprinting the image on his memory for future reference.

It was as well that he did, for he had scarcely begun to tap his ample reserves when another *autobus* drew up and he saw the man break cover and move towards it. Once again luck was with Pommes Frites: it was an *autobus* with an open rear platform. He was over the rail in a flash. The driver was too busy watching the traffic as he pulled out to notice, and if anyone else did they failed to react.

The journey this time was much longer and Pommes Frites was beginning to wonder if he'd been given the slip when, through a gap between the side and a handrail, he saw the man getting off again.

Pommes Frites waited until he was looking the other way and then, as the *autobus* stopped at some traffic lights a little further on, he seized his opportunity. He was just in time to see the man disappearing down a side-street. Hastily marking the spot in the time-honoured way that nature had intended, Pommes Frites followed on behind at a respectable distance. As he did so he sniffed the air, his brain cells beginning to work overtime as he weighed up the pros and cons of the situation.

Although relatively unversed in the thought processes which had gone into the planning of the Paris *autobus* system, he was all too conscious that if his sense of smell hadn't let him down and he was where he thought he was, then there had to be quicker ways of reaching it than the route they had taken. All of which led him to but one conclusion: the man he had been following didn't want to be followed, and if that was the case then in Pommes Frites' view, it was a very good reason for doing just that.

Having reached that decision, Pommes Frites quickened his pace, the smell of stagnant water growing stronger with every step he took.

The drive from the police station to the offices of *Le Guide* was not the happiest Monsieur Pamplemousse had ever experienced. Despite his garb, which had not improved with the passage of time, he would have preferred taking an *autobus* to riding in the Director's car. Optional extras in the way of tinted glass rendered the atmosphere even chillier than it might otherwise have been.

Monsieur Pamplemousse was the first to speak.

'It was kind of you to bail me out, *Monsieur*.'

'Frankly, Pamplemousse, kindness did not enter into the matter. The plain fact is we need you. Although, having said that, you may well be a master, or perhaps judging from your attire, *mistress* of disguise, but I fear that if nothing is forthcoming very soon, we shall have to bring in the police after all.'

Having exhausted the subject as a topic of conversation, they sat in silence for a while.

The whole episode had been a disaster. The only good

thing was the fact that Amandier had been in charge of the police operation. He was one of the 'old school'. His handshake had been acquired many moons ago from the *gendarmerie*'s standard book of etiquette, 'Advice from an Old to a Young Gendarme', and it showed. If it had been one of the younger ones who knew him only by reputation he wouldn't have fancied his chances. He would still be languishing in the cells along with the others. It was one of those occasions when the French legal system which decreed your being guilty until you managed to prove otherwise had its drawbacks. Proof of his innocence, whatever the charges, would have taken for ever. At least no one had thought of comparing his handwriting with that on the note in the Père-Lachaise. It would have been hard to talk his way out of that one.

It was the Director's turn to break the silence.

'The computer threw up an interesting fact this morning,' he began, apropos of nothing, as they turned into the Rue du Bac. 'Overnight, sales of last year's copies of *Le Guide* have risen phenomenally. Orders have been flooding in. It points to a great upsurge in our popularity.'

'Did the computer also throw up where the sales took place, *Monsieur*?'

'Strangely enough, they were all in Paris – mostly in the twentieth *arrondissement*. It seems that local bookstores there have sold out and demand has since spread to the surrounding areas. Brentano's in the Avenue de l'Opéra were in a state of siege yesterday evening and again early this morning. If the trend continues nationwide, and *if* next year's edition is ever published, we shall need to treble our print order. The projected sales graph is already off the board. I have ordered an extension.'

'I think I would hold your hand, *Monsieur*.'

The Director swerved violently and under the pretext of avoiding an oncoming *camion*, edged nearer the offside window. 'I'd rather you didn't, Pamplemousse!'he exclaimed. 'In fact, I would go so far as to suggest that after all this is over you should seek medical advice. You may be in need of a rest. A spell by the sea may not come amiss. You can have the use of my summer residence in Normandy if you wish. The cold wind blowing in from *La Manche* often works wonders.'

Monsieur Pamplemousse heaved a sigh. 'You think I should wait that long, *Monsieur*?'

His sarcasm was wasted.

'Much as it grieves me to say so, Pamplemousse, we cannot spare you at this particular time for such luxuries. It will have to wait. Every moment counts.'

'You misunderstand me, *Monsieur*.' As briefly as possible, Monsieur Pamplemousse outlined the reason for his being in Aux Deux Magots. From there it was but a short step to the possible reason behind the increase in sales. The Director listened in silence.

'I find this incredible, Pamplemousse. Did you give no thought at all to the plight of any poor innocent tourists caught up in your goings-on, had they happened to be carrying a copy of *Le Guide* as so many of them do?

'The repercussions have already begun. The American Embassy has registered a protest in the strongest possible terms. The police did not stop with those on the terrace. All the occupants of the cafe were removed for questioning; passers-by were arrested on suspicion.'

'They were quite safe, *Monsieur,* provided their copy of *Le Guide* was not open at page 221.'

'Humph.' The Director gave his passenger an odd look, then drove in silence for a while, clearly lost in thought.

'Between you, me and the *montant de barrière*, Pample-mousse,'he said at last, 'there are moments when I begin to wonder if I made the right decision in committing our entire future to an electronic chip. Management can all too easily become divorced from the assets it is supposed to be managing. The sales figures are another case in point. A snap decision based on the computer's findings would have been disastrous.'

'A computer is only as good as the information fed into it, *Monsieur*. It cannot work miracles. However, assuming all external connections are correct ...' Almost without thinking, Monsieur Pamplemousse found himself quoting Mademoiselle Borel.

The Director listened with half an-ear as he negotiated the stream of traffic converging on the Esplanade des Invalides. He stopped at the entrance to *Le Guide* in order to show his pass, watched with distaste while Monsieur Pamplemousse rummaged in Madame Grante's handbag before doing likewise, then drove round the fountain in the middle of the inner courtyard before coming to rest, not in his usual marked parking area to the right of the main entrance, but alongside a small service door some way beyond it. He withdrew a plastic entry card from his wallet and was about to hand it to Monsieur Pamplemousse when he paused. He suddenly looked tired and dispirited.

'*Comment ça va*, Aristide?'

'*Comment ça va*?' Monsieur Pamplemousse gave a shrug. What was there to say? Everything and nothing.

'You are pursuing your enquiries?'

'I have not been idle. I think I may have found out *how* it was done. I have yet to find out why, or indeed the name of the person responsible. To do that I may have to visit Belfort.'

For some reason his words had a strange effect on the Director. He went pale and for a brief moment seemed almost to shrink inside himself.

Monsieur Pamplemousse looked at him with some concern. 'Is anything the matter, *Monsieur*? Can I get you some water?'

'*Eau?*' The very thought seemed to bring about a miraculous recovery. 'If what I suspect is true, Pamplemousse, it will need something far stronger than *eau* to set matters right!

'If you will excuse me, I will just park the car. You carry on up and I will see you in my office. Before we go any further there are things I feel I should tell you.'

8
CONFESSION TIME

Monsieur Pamplemousse rose to his feet as the Director entered the office. He received a peremptory wave in return, indicating that he should return to his seat.

'Brace yourself, Pamplemousse.' The Director stationed himself behind his desk. 'I fear I have bad news.'

'*Monsieur?*'

'Pamplemousse, an attempt has been made on the life of the *oiseau!*'

'JoJo?' If the Director had announced that someone had planted a bomb under his chair, Monsieur Pamplemousse could hardly have been more surprised. It was the last thing he'd expected to hear. He glanced round automatically towards the table where he had last seen the bird cage. It was now shrouded in a dark green cloth.

'He is not … ?'

'Fortunately, no. Although he is still in a state of shock. I must confess I keep the house covered with a cloth because I cannot stand constant chirruping in the mornings.'

'*Alors?*'

'At oh, eight twenty-five this morning, Pamplemousse, shortly before I arrived at the office, a man purporting to be a veterinary surgeon called to take him away. He was allowed as far as reception and the cage was brought down. Fortunately, thanks to the vigilance of the gatekeeper, the attempt was forestalled. Rambaud came on duty just as the

530

man was about to leave. Having overheard our conversation the day before, and knowing the importance we attach to the *oiseau*'s well-being, he asked to see the man's credentials. When he couldn't produce them Rambaud refused to release the cage and threatened to call the police. After a brief tug-of-war – during which, I regret to say, the bars of the *oiseau*'s cage were nearly torn asunder, the would-be assassin made off. As he did so Rambaud heard him utter the ominous word "*Vendredi*". Today, I need hardly remind you, Pamplemousse, is Thursday. You have one day left.'

Monsieur Pamplemousse considered the matter. He couldn't help feeling that the Director's interpretation of the event verged on the over-dramatic. Trying to remove JoJo from the office hardly came under the heading of attempted murder, but doubtless his chief was beginning to feel the strain. All the same, it was certainly very strange, particularly in view of the feeling he'd had the previous evening that someone had been in Madame Grante's apartment. Perhaps whoever it was had gone there first looking for JoJo and drawn a blank. If they had then tried at the office it could mean only one thing. His own movements must have been under close scrutiny, which was disconcerting to say the least.

As Monsieur Pamplemousse sat down heavily in the visitor's chair a pained expression came over the Director's face.

'Aristide, I do wish you would either cross your legs or sit facing the other way. I find the view from my desk somewhat disconcerting.'

'*Pardon, Monsieur.*' Monsieur Pamplemousse became aware of a faint tearing sound as he struggled to reach a suitable compromise half-way between comfort and decorum. It was a simple case of trying unsuccessfully to get a generous litre into a bare demi-litre *pot*. Something went 'twang'.

'*Merde!*' It was too late, the damage had been done. He rubbed his right thigh.

'A woman's life is full of problems, *Monsieur*, not the least of which I have discovered is how to sit down gracefully without revealing that for but one glimpse of which many men would give their eye-teeth.'

'I bow to your superior knowledge, Pamplemousse,' said the Director severely. 'However, most women are more circumspect when it comes to shopping for their nether garments.'

'These came from a little *boutique* in the Rue Cler, *Monsieur* ...'

'I have no wish to know where you bought them, Pamplemousse. They make you look like an advertisement for a house of ill repute. One which has all too clearly seen better days, if I may say so.'

'I did not buy them, *Monsieur*. They belong to Madame Grante ...'

The Director gave a start. 'Madame Grante!' Sitting bolt upright, he took a closer look. 'Who would have thought it, Aristide? Women are strange creatures, they really are. A different breed. How can a mere male ever really be expected to know what goes on inside their minds? I know the shop very well. Brevity is often combined, it seems to me, with untold complexity. I invariably hurry past.'

'In the words of the song, *Monsieur*, love is a tender trap. Madame Grante must have been hit very hard.'

'Yes, yes.' A look of impatience crossed the Director's face as yet another tearing sound emerged from the depths of the chair.

'Pamplemousse, I have a spare suit in the bedroom next door. It is kept there for emergencies. Before we go any further, I suggest you make use of it. You will find it very much on the tight side, I fear, but it will be an improvement on your present mode of dress. There are also some shirts in one of the drawers.'

Monsieur Pamplemousse was only too willing to oblige. He had no wish to stay looking the way he was for a second longer than necessary. He also sensed that the Director needed a little time in which to gather his thoughts. He had mentioned having more than one matter he wished to talk about. Clearly, from the nervous way he was drumming on his desk, there was something other than the attempted abduction of JoJo on his mind.

While he was exchanging his chemise for a snow-white shirt bearing the Charvet label, Monsieur Pamplemousse's thoughts gravitated towards Pommes Frites. It was unlike him to go off on his own for so long. On the other hand, he was well able to look after himself and at least he was on home ground. Pommes Frites knew his way around Paris better than most humans – guidebooks were an unnecessary luxury. All the same, he couldn't help wondering what was keeping him.

The socks and tie were from Marcel Lassance.

The Director had been doing his wardrobe less than justice. There was not one suit hanging on a rail, but several. Monsieur Pamplemousse chose one of medium blue with a discreet pin-stripe. It fitted him like a glove. He looked at the label inside the jacket. It was by André Bardot. Considering his reflection in a full-length mirror, he found himself looking at a stranger; Doucette would hardly have recognised him. Removing a speck of invisible dust from one of the lapels, he closed the cupboard door and went back into the office.

The Director was standing at the window perusing an old copy of *Le Guide*.

He looked round anxiously as Monsieur Pamplemousse entered. 'Mind how you sit!' he exclaimed. 'I don't wish to hear any more untoward noises.'

Monsieur Pamplemousse lowered himself carefully into the chair and then draped one leg elegantly over the other. 'There is no cause for alarm, *Monsieur*. The suit is a perfect fit. It could have been made for me. I am most grateful.'

'Hmmm.' The Director looked less than pleased at the news as he turned his attention to the book he was holding aloft.

'Pamplemousse, you mentioned a certain word to me just now.'

'I am sorry, *Monsieur*. I'm afraid it slipped out.'

'No, no, Pamplemousse.'The Direetor clucked impatiently. 'I was not referring to your earlier use of an expletive, rather to something you said when we arrived. You used the word "Belfort". It confirmed my worse suspicions.'

'It did, *Monsieur*?'

'Pamplemousse, tell me what you know about *poulets de Bresse*.'

Monsieur Pamplemousse heaved an inward sigh. He had lost track of the date, but he must be coming up to his annual salary review. At such times the Director had a habit of shooting odd questions at members of staff under the guise of pretending he wanted the information for some new project. Usually it was on a subject he had only recently looked up. It was a kind of oral test paper, replacing the conventional interview.

He closed his eyes in order to concentrate his thoughts. He was getting off lightly. Everyone knew about *poulets de*

Bresse, famous for centuries as the best chicken in the world.

'They are, of course, from the plain of Bresse – Brillat-Savarin country, and birthplace of Fernand Point but more particularly from an area within the plain amounting to some 400 square kilometres – an area which was first defined as long ago as 1936. Within that area seven breeders supply day-old chicks to a thousand or so farmers, each of whom may raise a maximum of five hundred birds at a time – in other words a grand total of not more than half a million a year. The birds spend thirty-five days as chicks and then they are allowed outside to run freely on the grass, each one being allotted a minimum area of ten square metres – which is a good deal more than the average Parisian enjoys. During that time they are fed on cereals – mostly corn – and skimmed milk. At fourteen weeks they are brought inside again for fattening until at sixteen weeks they are pronounced ready for the market. The weight of each bird before and after dressing is clearly laid down. In the latter case, no bird may go to market unless it weighs at least 1.5kg and is unblemished. A true native species of Bresse chicken has white flesh and feathers, and bluish-grey legs with four toes and a red wattle and comb. In the market itself they are clearly recognisable by a lead ring around the foot attesting to the bird's origin. Strictly speaking it should be *poularde de Bresse,* for the hen is considered much tastier than the cock. They have an unmistakable delicate flavour and they are at their best when roasted simply in a very hot oven until they are golden brown and the skin is crisp. Since 1957 they have been *Appellation d'Origine Contrôlée* and any variation on the stipulations I have mentioned is strictly against the law and a punishable offence.'

'*Exactement!*' The Director sounded so much like a schoolmaster congratulating his star pupil on passing the daily test with flying colours, Monsieur Pamplemousse felt tempted to ask if he could have the rest of the day off, but clearly it was no time for levity; there was more to come. He waited patiently.

'Have you any firsthand knowledge, Aristide, of what that punishment is?'

'A heavy fine, I would imagine, *Monsieur.* Possibly, in extreme cases, a prison sentence. If the rules are administered as strictly as those which apply to wine, and doubtless they are, then there will be very little room for manoeuvre; every factor, every process, every detail from the moment of birth will be strictly enforced.'

'And what of those on the other side of the fence? What of those who sell a *poularde* which purports to be from Bresse, but is in fact an impostor?'

'Ah, that is a different matter, *Monsieur,* but they would still find themselves in trouble. That would be a matter of fraud – of "passing off". The proper authorities would deal with the problem.'

There had been a time in Monsieur Pamplemousse's own career when he had been part of the then 200-strong section of the Paris police who served as food inspectors – that had been a major reason for his becoming interested in the whole business of *cuisine* in the first place. Then it had been a matter of checking scales for accuracy, ensuring that *croissants au beurre* contained no margarine, sampling *truffled gras* to make certain it contained the real thing and not the cheaper Moroccan whites dyed black; the list of their duties had been endless and they had not been the most popular members of the force.

The Director sat down at his desk again and placed the

Guide in front of him. He gazed at it for a moment or two, then spread his hands out on the blotter, palms down.

'Some twenty-five years ago, Aristide, I was just one of the team. I had not long been with *Le Guide* and I was serving my apprenticeship as an Inspector. Our founder,' he turned and paid his respects to the freshly scrubbed portrait of Monsieur Hippolyte Duval, 'our founder believed in starting at the bottom, just as he had done himself many years before.

'One evening I found myself sitting in a restaurant about to tackle a *Poularde de Bresse en Vessie* – a dish for which I had a particular fancy at the time, and which was supposed to be one of their specialities. I had ordered it in advance an hour or two before my arrival. *Poularde de Bresse en Vessie,* as you know, consists of a Bresse chicken stuffed with its own liver and a little *foie gras* and some slices of truffle, poached very gently in a pig's bladder containing also carrots and leeks ...'

Monsieur Pamplemousse knew it only too well, for it was just such a dish that had been the cause of one of his earlier adventures.

'The owner of the establishment was a brilliant up-and-coming young chef with an assured future. He had inherited the restaurant from his father, who had died earlier that same year. At the time of his father's death it rated two Stock Pots in *Le Guide* and two rosettes in Michelin Gault-Millau didn't exist in those days – and it was heading for a third award in both. Naturally, on the death of the father, even though to all intents and purposes his son had been in charge for several years, all accolades were withdrawn. The purpose of my visit was to make a preliminary report prior to their reinstatement. At that time there was no doubt in anyone's mind that it was a mere formality, but it wasn't to work out that way.

'I knew from the moment I entered the restaurant that all was not well; there was a certain "atmosphere". The first course, *feuilleté d'asperges*, was beyond reproach, but the *maître d'hôtel* – one of the old school – was clearly ill at ease. Having presented the *poularde* to me on a silver dish, he then withdrew to a dark corner of the restaurant for it to be opened up and served, for it was still encased in its *vessie*. I can still see the pained expression on his face as he returned to my table some minutes later and placed the plate before me.

'The reason for his behaviour became all too clear the moment I took the first mouthful.

'To cut a long story short, Aristide, far from being made with a *poularde de Bresse*, the dish clearly contained a bird of the very worst kind; a cock which must have been obtained at short notice from the local *supermarché*.

'Imagine my dilemma. There I was, young and relatively inexperienced, undergoing my first real baptism of fire; not only was my own future at stake, but also the reputation of *Le Guide*. However, I had to be very sure of my facts. It is one thing making an accusation when you have proof positive – which I would have done had I seen the bird prior to its immersion in the broth. It is quite another matter when you are putting your taste-buds on the line. I took courage in a kind of sixth sense and in the end it didn't let me down.

'All the same, I have to tell you, Aristide, that when I asked to see the chef my heart was in my boots. I knew then something of what it must have been like "going over the top" in the first Great War. Heads throughout the restaurant were turned in my direction.

'It was not a pleasant experience. At first the chef tried to bluster his way out of it. He told me I didn't know what I was talking about – but his very manner betrayed his guilt. Then he offered me another dish. Finally he tore up my bill and asked me to leave the restaurant before turning on his heels and marching back to the kitchen.

'When I followed him in there and revealed the true purpose of my visit he became a changed man. First he pleaded that it had all been an unfortunate mistake – he tried to put the blame on one of the young *sous-chefs*. Then, when he saw he wasn't getting anywhere, he attempted the final insult. He took me to one side and offered a considerable sum of money if I would go away and forget the whole thing. It was at that moment that I knew I was right. I told him that my report would be submitted that very evening.

'As I uttered the words something seemed to snap. He picked up a knife – a fearsome weapon – a Sabatier *grand couteau de cuisine* with a 35cm blade – sharp as a razor – and threatened to kill me. As he advanced across the *cuisine* he removed a hair from his head and sliced it in two by way of demonstrating what he would do to parts of my anatomy before he plunged them into oil which was already boiling on the stove. He had the face of a madman, Aristide. Sweat was pouring down his face, and as he lunged at me an uncontrollable tic appeared in his right eye. For a moment or two I must confess I really did go in fear of my life. The rest of the kitchen staff had long since fled in panic, leaving me entirely on my own. Fortunately, the *maître d'hôtel* had taken it upon himself to call the police and they arrived in the nick of time.

'Two of them grabbed the man from behind, whilst a third had the presence of mind to remove the remaining tools of his trade before he was able to get his hands on them. In the ensuing struggle one of the *gendarmes* received a flesh wound. I still remember the look of naked hate on the man's face as he was led away from his restaurant, shouting and screaming and swearing revenge.

'There is no doubt in my mind that there was a screw loose somewhere, otherwise why would he have done it? There he was, a young man, just starting out in life. Granted, he had inherited the mantle of his father's success, but already he was gathering plaudits on his own account. He had no need to take short cuts or to make excuses. I can only think that false pride prevented him from saying he had run out of the real thing and, given the nature of the dish – the fact that for most of the time during its cooking the *poularde* is out of sight – he took a chance. But that doesn't excuse his action. It was an unforgivable deception.'

'What happened after that, *Monsieur*?'

'I submitted my report and in due course it was passed on to the powers that be. He suffered the usual fate. Those administering the AOC took the appropriate action. There were notices in the local *journaux*. Other notices were pasted across the window of his restaurant warning people not to patronise it. From that moment on he was ignored by his contemporaries and ostracised by the general public.

'Can you imagine what that must have meant to an up-and-coming restaurateur? No one to cook for. Above all, no one to shake hands with all day long. It would be bad enough to an ordinary Frenchman, but to the *patron* of a restaurant, it must have seemed like the end of the world.

'In due course his case came up and he was sent to prison. The restaurant struggled on for a few weeks without him, but by the time he was released it had closed down. Those in the trade made sure he was never able to work as a chef again.'

'And where was the restaurant?'Monsieur Pamplemousse knew the answer even before he posed the question.

'Need you ask, Pamplemousse? It was the very place you mentioned as we arrived. Belfort.'

'Do you remember the details, *Monsieur*?'

'They are all here, Aristide.'The Director passed the book across the table. 'The name of the restaurant and its specialities. The name of the owner. It is the edition prior to the year I made my visit. Alas, it was the last time either name appeared.'

'And there is no doubt in your mind, *Monsieur,* that the two people are one and the same?'Once again, it was a redundant question. There was no other possible explanation. The mention of the nervous tic clinched matters.

'None whatsoever. He must have been harbouring a grudge against *Le Guide* over all these years, a grudge which has been growing inside him like a cancer.'

Monsieur Pamplemousse could not but agree, with the proviso that it wasn't simply *Le Guide* against whom the man harboured a grudge, but the Director himself as the person responsible for his downfall in the first place. He glanced at the book. The entry for the restaurant had been circled in red. He copied the details into his notebook.

'It shows the kind of person we are up against, Pamplemousse.'

'*Oui, Monsieur.*'

'Clearly, he is a man who would stop at nothing. A man who would substitute a frozen bird of doubtful ancestry for a *poularde de Bresse* would be capable of anything.'

'Have you been back to Belfort since, *Monsieur*?'

'I was there several times last year in connection with the computer. On one occasion I took Madame Grante with me so that she could familiarise herself with the system.

She liked the area so much she even talked of going back there for a holiday.'

'And the restaurant?'

'It is now a coin-operated dry-cleaning establishment. A sad come-down for what could have been a temple of gastronomy.'

'And do you still not wish to call in the police, *Monsieur*, even though your own life is clearly in danger?'

'No, Aristide. Now, more than ever, the answer has to be "no" .

Monsieur Pamplemousse knew better than to argue. He was aware of the signs. Once the chief had made up his mind that was that.

'May I use your telephone, *Monsieur*?'

'Go ahead, Pamplemousse.'

He rang Martine Borel's number. She answered straight away.

'The name is Dubois. He may be using something else, but I doubt it. With a name like Dubois who needs anonymity? Why make unnecessary complications?'

'Hold on a moment while I grab a pen.'

Briefly he read out the details.

'Were you serious about finding credit information?' There was a pause during which he could hear the rattle of a keyboard. 'It is not a good time of day.' She sounded hesitant. 'The person lives in California and there is a nine-hour time difference; it may take a little while, but I will do my best.' There was another brief pause. 'I have an address for him on the Minitel.'

'Marvellous.'The wonders of science! He listened as she reeled it off. 'If I am not in the office try me on …' He flipped back through his notebook and gave her Madame Grante's number.

He tried dialling a second number.

Jacques was out on a case; there was no knowing when he would be back. He left the details with an underling. The man seemed less than enthusiastic.

'That is a long time ago ...'

'Anything would be helpful. He has a record, back in ...' he looked at the date on the outside of *Le Guide*, '1963'.

'It might be worth trying the hotels. He must have been staying somewhere.

'I'll get a photo over to you as quickly as possible.

'No, I don't know if he is still using the same name ...'

'*Oui*, I know you will have to check with Jacques ...'

One thing was for sure, he wasn't going to end up with dinner at Les Tourelles. The way things were going it would be Taillevant or nothing.

'*Oui*, it is urgent.'

It was worth a try. At least it meant he had more than one iron in the fire.

'What do you think we should do about the *oiseau*?' asked the Director as Monsieur Pamplemousse replaced the receiver. 'It seems to have assumed some importance in the eyes of our adversary. He may well try again.'

Monsieur Pamplemousse raised his eyes heavenwards. He'd forgotten about JoJo's stand-in. 'You are right, *Monsieur*. The *oiseau* must be put in a place of safety.' It was better to go along with the idea than try to explain.

'A matter for security, would you not agree?'

'*Oui, Monsieur.*'

'*Bon.*' The Director rose to his feet and crossed to the cage. 'In that case, Pamplemousse, I suggest you take him with you. I have had the bars straightened, and clearly the *oiseau* knows something, otherwise why would the man wish to remove it? I have tried to break down the barriers of communication and failed. It is your turn now.'

'But, *Monsieur* – '

'No "buts", Pamplemousse. That is an order.'

'In which case, *Monsieur*, speaking as Head of Security I suggest that you remain in this building until such time as it is safe to leave.'

'Aristide, is that strictly necessary?'

'That, too, is an order, *Monsieur*. Unless, of course, you would prefer me to resign?'

The Director gave a sigh as Monsieur Pamplemousse stood up to leave. '*Touché*, Pamplemousse. But I hope it will not be for too long.'

'I hope so too, *Monsieur*.' Monsieur Pamplemousse spoke with rather more confidence than he felt.

'One last thing, Aristide ...'

Monsieur Pamplemousse paused at the door. '*Monsieur*?'

'Don't forget the *oiseau*!'

9
POMMES FRITES TAKES THE PLUNGE

On his way back to Madame Grante's apartment Monsieur Pamplemousse called in at the Rue Poncelet and did some shopping. He bought a *baguette*, still slightly warm to the touch from the second baking of the day, and a *tarte aux fraises*. Further along the street he called in at a *charcuterie* and purchased a thick slice of *jambon,* smoked in oak from the forests of the Ardennes, and some slices of underdone Charolais beef. To this he added a generous helping of black olives and another of gherkins, ten quail's eggs, a selection of salads, a portion of Camembert Fermier- true, it was a little early in the year, the milk would not yet have reached its best quality, but unpasteurised cheese was becoming more and more difficult to find and it was hard to resist – and a portion of smooth, buttery-looking Roquefort. Laid out on the counter in front of him it added up to a simple enough repast, but it would help tide him over until he was able to order a proper meal. As an afterthought he asked for a slice of *pâté forestière* – it would go well with the gherkins. Better safe than sorry: he might have a long wait.

In truth, although he had talked to the chief about going to Belfort, there really didn't seem much point – even if he'd had the time. He now knew all he really needed to know. Paris was where the action was. If necessary he would carry on playing cat and mouse until something concrete turned up.

At an *épicerie fine*, he treated himself to a bottle of Volnay; an '80 Clos des Chênes from Michel Lafarge.

He half hoped to see Pommes Frites waiting for him outside Madame Grante's block, but the street was deserted.

As he took the lift up to her apartment for the third evening running, Monsieur Pamplemousse found himself looking out for signs of life on the other landings. Already he had established a nodding acquaintance with several of the tenants. It was amazing how quickly one was accepted with no questions asked. The saxophone player was at it again.

Once inside the apartment he set to work laying the table, but gradually his pace began to slacken, until by the time he finally drew up a chair and sat down he found he had lost his appetite. It was the kind of meal which needed company.

He poured himself a glass of Volnay instead. It was an impeccable balance of fruit and perfume, an elegant wine, but again, a wine to be shared.

And that was the truth of the matter. He suddenly felt very lonely without Pommes Frites. They would have enjoyed the evening together.

After toying in a desultory fashion with the *pâté* he tried telephoning the caretaker back at his own apartment. It was just possible that Pommes Frites might have gone home – but he drew a blank. There was no report of his having been seen for several days.

Monsieur Pamplemousse looked out of the window. The gardens at the back of the block were deserted. Lights were beginning to come on in the surrounding buildings. He drew the curtains and then turned on the television. It was '*Chiffres et Nombres*' again. It was always '*Chiffres et Nombres*'.

At least, judging from the din they were making, JoJo and his companion were enjoying it. In desperation he switched the set off.

Going through the pile of records he found an old Yves Montand selection. Half-way through '*C'est si bon*' the needle stuck. He tried the Tino Rossi again. It reminded him of his early cinema-going days when he had been courting Doucette. Tino Rossi was forever playing double roles – twin brothers – the good guy and the bad guy. He'd always worn a pencil moustache and had his hair slicked down for the latter part. They were about the only changes he'd made, but for purposes of plot it had always fooled the rest of the cast, especially the girls, so that one had longed to cry out a warning.

Over the cold meats and salads he took the photograph of Madame Grante's lover from his wallet and propped it up against the bottle of wine.

Dubois. Being able to put a name to the face somehow helped bring it to life. In a way, the man wasn't unlike the characters in the Tino Rossi films. He wondered which one Madame Grante had met first of all. The good guy or the bad guy? Either way, there had been no one to shout out a warning, if indeed she would have heeded it. People in love rarely did.

Dressed one way, he could imagine that all the porter had said about Dubois was probably true; he knew the type. On the other hand, wearing his casual clothes there was nothing about the man that would have caused him to stand out in a crowd. Monsieur Pamplemousse certainly didn't hold out much hope of his being picked up simply on the off-chance of someone recognising him from the picture. In a small town, possibly. People had to go out if only to do the shopping or to eat. But in a city of over ten

547

thousand restaurants, it was too much to ask, and Paris had more than its fair share of sleazy hotels where no questions were asked provided the bill was paid.

What he needed was a break.

It came a few minutes after ten o'clock in the form of a telephone call from Martine.

Monsieur Pamplemousse listened in silence as she reeled off a list of details. There had been no credit problems. Bills had always been paid promptly. Apart from the usual selection of odds and ends most of them were to do with eating out and paying domestic accounts: gas and electricity, local taxes. All related to the Belfort area, and all very innocuous, but he could tell from the tone of her voice that there was more to come.

In early February the pattern had changed. Bills started coming in from farther afield: Montbéliard, Clerval, Laisey, then several from Besançon, two from Dole. They were over a period of several days. Some were from restaurants, but mostly they were for fuel. Whatever the reason for his journey he didn't seem to be in any particular hurry.

'Hold on a moment. I will see if I can find a map.' He remembered seeing a gazetteer in the other room.

'If it's of any help I have done that already. Montbéliard is the nearest big town south of Belfort. It is on the Canal du Rhône au Rhin. Besançon is another eighty-four kilometres or so to the south-west. Dole follows on from that. They are all on the same canal. Soon after Dole it heads north and joins the river Saône at Saint-Symphorien. North of that again it meets up with the Canal de la Marne à la Saône.'

'And on to Paris.'

'Exactly. I have checked with a friend of mine who knows about these things and he says Dubois could have

548

taken another route via the Canal de Bourgogne. That's shorter and reckoned to be the more beautiful of the two but the first is more modern and there are far fewer locks. One hundred and fourteen as against one hundred and eighty-nine.'

Monsieur Pamplemousse was listening with only half an ear. He could have kicked himself for not having thought of it before. All along he had been picturing his quarry holed up in some small hotel. Either that or in a rented apartment. A boat was the obvious answer. The picture of him dressed in sailing gear should have provided the clue; the porter's mention of rope-soled shoes another.

'I'm sorry I can't be of any more help.'

'You have done more than enough.'

'*Bonne chance.*'

'*Merci.*'

After he had replaced the receiver Monsieur Pamplemousse lay back and thought for a while. If Dubois had set out to travel from Belfort via the Marne, then he would have arrived in Paris to the east of the city. The chances were that he would either have tied up in some backwater outside the limits – in which case the boat could be anywhere – or he might have taken it as far into Paris as it was allowed. Of the two alternatives, that seemed far more likely. In which case, entering from the east, the logical place to aim for would be the Paris-Arsenal Marina where the Canal Saint-Martin joined the Seine. That would offer a choice of escape routes if things went wrong: either back the way he had come, or on down the Seine towards Rouen and Le Havre. Failing that, he could always head northwards up the Canal Saint-Martin *en route* to Belgium and beyond.

On the other hand, if that were the case – if he had ended up in the Arsenal basin – he wouldn't be able to go anywhere without passing through a lock. There was one between the Marina and the Seine and a whole series in the Canal Saint Martin itself. All of them were electrically powered and needed an attendant to operate them.

Monsieur Pamplemousse's knowledge of the inland waterways of France was fairly hazy, but as far as he knew none of the locks were manned during the hours of darkness. He looked at his watch, then fumbled for his shoes. There was only one way to find out for certain. Go there and look for himself.

The main gates to the Marina were still open and as Monsieur Pamplemousse made his way down the cobbled slip road leading to the water his heart sank. There were boats as far as the eye could see. At a rough guess, there must be well over two hundred of all shapes and sizes tied up on either side of the basin.

A line of yellow lamps along the deserted *quai* was still switched on, contrasting with the brighter lights from the streets high up on either side. A few of the boats were showing lights, and from one or two he could hear the sound of a party in full swing, but the majority were in darkness.

A restaurant at the top of a flight of steps to his left was just closing for the night. During the winter months most of its trade probably came from the few resident boat-owners who were tired of cooking in cramped galleys, and they probably ate early. In the summer things would be different. Then it would attract the tourist trade as well.

To his right lay the entrance to the long tunnel which ran beneath the Place de la Bastille and then followed the line of the Boulevard Richard-Lenoir before finally emerging some two kilometres away near the Place de la République.

From there it continued via a series of old-fashioned locks and swing bridges until it reached the basin at La Villette. It was Simenon country, an area of artisans, and popular with film-makers who went there in search of 'atmosphere'.

A red traffic light to the left of the tunnel entrance forbade entry.

The area in front of him was laid out as formal gardens with rose-covered archways, paths and symmetrical rows of low-cut hedges. He could see the mast of a giant model schooner rising up out of what must be a children's play area.

On the cobbled quayside, a sign pointed the way to the Harbour Master's office at the far end, near the entrance to the Seine. The building was in darkness. He would get no help there.

Beyond it, a Métro train rattled across a bridge, its wheels shrieking in protest at the sharp curve which took it into the Quai de la Rapée station.

As he reached the water's edge Monsieur Pamplemousse stood for a moment or two considering what he was looking for. By process of elimination, it was unlikely to be one of the sailing boats moored on his side. Most of them were so large they had been tied up lengthways on to avoid causing an obstruction. They would have far too big a draught for a journey across France by canal. Most likely they had been brought up river from Le Havre to spend the winter inland.

The bulk of the smaller boats were moored on the far side of the Marina. He ran his eye along them. Given the time of the year, it was unlikely that Dubois would be in an open boat, and in view of the weather and some of the currents he must have encountered between canals *en route*, he would have needed something with a fairly powerful motor.

A medium-size cabin cruiser perhaps, one with an inboard engine. Even so, that still left a wide choice. In their various ways, practically ninety per cent of the craft came into that category. Each had its own mooring position with a selection of utility services it could plug in to.

Suddenly, he felt rather than saw a movement at his side, and his spirits rose. It was Pommes Frites; large as life and in the circumstances, twice as beautiful. If Pommes Frites didn't actually say 'Sssh', he made his meaning very clear as he stretched out on the ground beside his master. Only the faintest movement of his tail betrayed his pleasure.

Monsieur Pamplemousse bent down and gave his friend a pat. Pommes Frites' neck felt cold and damp and he was trembling all over, but whether it was a simple case of cause and effect or sheer excitement it was hard to tell. From the alert expression on his face and from the way he was lying, ears pricked up, nose twitching, legs ready to spring into action at a moment's notice, Monsieur Pamplemousse strongly suspected the latter. He turned to look back at the Marina.

Pommes Frites' gaze was firmly fastened on a boat moored, stern on, almost opposite them on the far side of the basin. It was a motor cruiser some ten metres in length, with a closed-in wheelhouse aft of the forward cabin. Even to Monsieur Pamplemousse's inexpert eyes it looked solid and workmanlike compared with those tied up on either side of it. The decks were of varnished teak and there was a businesslike array of radio aerials attached to a stubby mast. From where he was standing it was impossible to see the stern.

Straining his eyes, Monsieur Pamplemousse thought he detected a momentary glimmer of light from inside the wheelhouse, but a second later it disappeared.

He looked to his right and then to his left, trying to decide the best way of getting across to the far side. It was a case of swings and roundabouts. The boat was moored rather nearer the Place de la Bastille than the Seine, but there was another Métro station between the *Place* and the Marina and if they went that way it would mean losing sight of it for a while, then taking a chance that the entrance near the tunnel on the far side was open.

If they went to the left and crossed over via the lock they would be able to keep the boat in view the whole time, but against that they would have to travel much further and then run the risk of being seen as they made their way along the opposite *quai* which looked totally empty and bereft of any kind of shelter.

He tossed a mental coin and chose the first way.

The pavement area above the tunnel was packed with parked cars and they had to squeeze a tortuous path in and out of them. It took rather longer than Monsieur Pample-mousse had bargained for. Worse still, when they finally reached the other side, although the gate at the top of the steps was open, a second one half-way down was securely padlocked. He glanced through the bars at the Marina.

'*Merde!*' Slowly, almost imperceptibly, the boat was edging away from the *quai*. Already there was a good metre between the prow and the mooring post.

Somehow or other they must have been spotted. He could see someone lying prone on the foredeck, inching the boat along by pushing against the one in the next berth. Even from a distance he was clearly recognisable as the man in the photograph.

Signalling Pommes Frites to follow on behind, Monsieur Pamplemousse slowly backed up the steps, keeping as close to the shadow of the wall as possible.

Having reached the top, he set off across the Place de la Bastille as fast as he could go. Although he was acting out of pure instinct, Monsieur Pamplemousse was also aware that Dubois had very little choice in the matter. He was hardly likely to make for the Seine. His exit would be blocked by the lock. If he went through the tunnel he could either hide in there until morning – in which case there would be ample time to bring in reinforcements – or tie up just beyond the far exit near the Place de la République, some two kilometres away.

Given the fact that Dubois would most likely want to put as much distance as he could between himself and his pursuer, the latter course seemed the more likely of the two. If the worse came to the worst, once Dubois reached the far end he could always abandon Madame Grante and make good his escape. The prime object uppermost in Monsieur Pamplemousse's mind as he tried to ignore the agony in his calves was to get there ahead of him.

In the beginning luck was with him. He'd picked a moment when the main stream of traffic was flowing off to his left towards the river and he reached the island in the centre of the *Place* in double quick time. But as he set out to cross to the far side, he encountered a mass of cars and buses sweeping round from the new Opera House. Dodging in and out of it, he left in his wake a cacophony of screaming tyres, horns, shouts, and an ominous dull crunch of metal hitting metal. The insurance companies would be busy in the morning.

As he reached the safety of the wide central reservation which divided the Boulevard Richard-Lenoir in two, Monsieur Pamplemousse's pace began to slow. It dawned on him that in no way was he going to make the other end of the tunnel before the boat, if indeed he got there at all.

Already his feet felt as though they were made of lead. His heart was pounding, and his temples were beginning to throb.

Pommes Frites had no such worries. He was just getting into his stride. Galloping on ahead, he looked good for another thirty kilometres at least. Clearly, as he stood waiting for his master to catch up, he was anticipating further instructions. Equally clearly, he was going to have to wait awhile.

Monsieur Pamplemousse bent down in a vain effort to touch his toes. Almost immediately he felt a sharp pain in his side. It was nature's warning; the beginnings of a stitch.

He looked around for a taxi, but as always at such moments, there wasn't one in sight, and he certainly didn't intend braving the wrath of those in the *Place* by going back in search of a rank.

After a moment or two, having got his second wind, Monsieur Pamplemousse moved off at a slower pace, trying to keep up a steady, if less ambitious jog trot. At least he had a head start, although it was a moot point as to how long that would last once Dubois started the engine and got up speed.

Once upon a time, the central reservation had been open to the sky, the canal itself separating the fourth from the eleventh *arrondissements*. As he skirted round some railings he was reminded of a boat trip he had once taken on the canal with Doucette.

Dotted along the length of the tunnel there were a number of round openings, each about two metres across. Basically intended to provide ventilation, during the daytime they also gave those below the benefit of a series of strange, almost translucent shafts of light. It stuck in his mind because at the time he had tried to capture the effect on film and had wildly misjudged the exposure.

The top of each opening was protected by a domed steel frame covered in thick wire mesh, and these were further screened off from the public by railed-off areas planted with shrubs and roses. During the summer months the holes themselves were scarcely visible.

Monsieur Pamplemousse vaulted over the first set of railings. Ignoring the thorns tearing at his trouser legs, he reached down and tugged at one of the covers. It remained firmly in place. He tried a second one. That showed no sign of movement either. Feeling along the inside of the rim he came across some stout metal cleats let into the concrete.

He ran on to the next enclosure, but once again luck was against him.

The fifth cover shifted slightly when he pulled at it, but it was beyond his strength to lift the frame clear of the stonework. In desperation he looked around for something he could use as a lever, but there was nothing.

Lying prone on the ground, Monsieur Pamplemousse put an ear to the opening and heard the faint chug-chug of an approaching engine. Pommes Frites heard it too and began pawing the ground impatiently.

About half-way along the first leg of the Boulevard, just before the Richard-Lenoir Métro station, Monsieur Pamplemousse found what he was looking for. As he pulled at one of the frames it gave slightly and he heard a splash of falling masonry in the water below.

Gathering all his strength, he made another attempt to shift it and this time managed to lift the metalwork clear of its concrete surround. Bracing himself, he pushed upwards and outwards on the frame as hard as he could and as it rolled over he flung it clear into the nearby shrubs.

Bending down, Monsieur Pamplemousse peered into the

darkness below, but it was impossible to make out anything. He took hold of a loose piece of masonry and dropped it through the opening. From the time it took to hit the water he judged the distance to be about five metres at the most. Given the height of the boat, that would make the deck a little over three metres away – always assuming Dubois was steering a course down the middle of the canal, which would be the natural thing to do.

Above the sound of traffic flowing past on either side of the island, he could hear the engine again – much closer this time, and faster.

Monsieur Pamplemousse lowered himself over the edge of the shaft and, as ill luck would have it, caught his jacket on some kind of projection. He felt himself dangling in space, his feet clear of the bottom of the opening. He held his breath as he caught sight of an approaching spotlight. Luckily it was pointing in a downward direction. The water below showed up inky black in its rays. Even if he'd had the strength to lift himself up again, there wasn't time – the boat was almost on him.

In retrospect, although he wouldn't have been prepared to swear on oath that Pommes Frites actually pushed him with intent – giving him the benefit of the doubt, it was probably more a case of the excitement of the chase getting the better of him – the effect was much the same, as some fifty kilograms of bone, muscle and flesh landed on Monsieur Pamplemousse's shoulders.

Even above the roar of the engine echoing around the walls of the cavern-like tunnel, Monsieur Pamplemousse was aware of a rending sound as he parted company with whatever it was that had been holding him back and he felt himself falling.

The next few seconds felt like a clip from some modern

'pop video', the kind where no single image lasted long enough to leave more than a fleeting impression.

As he landed awkwardly on the foredeck he sprawled over on all fours, carried forward by the speed of the boat. He clutched at the mast to stop himself falling over the side, acutely conscious that if his fall had been delayed by even a fraction of a second he might well have been impaled on the end of it.

While he was struggling to regain his balance, he heard a second crash just behind him, followed immediately by the sound of splintering wood.

Once again, viewed in retrospect, it would have been hard to say whether Pommes Frites was in total control of the situation. Inasmuch as he landed fairly and squarely on the middle of the wheelhouse, which was considerably higher than the foredeck, he was luckier than his master, for he had less far to travel. On the other hand, honours were rendered more or less equal when he went straight through the roof.

As his rear end disappeared from view the boat rocked violently and went out of control, heading at speed towards the starboard side of the canal. There was a brief exchange of growls and oaths, followed by a cry of pain, then two splashes in quick succession.

As Monsieur Pamplemousse crawled across the roof of the wheelhouse and lowered himself down through the hole he caught a brief glimpse of two dark shapes in the water. It looked as though the second was gaining rapidly on the first.

There was a crash and the boat rocked even more violently as they struck the granite edge of the towpath a glancing blow. Monsieur Pamplemousse made a grab for the wheel. He had no idea how deep the canal was at that point, and there were better ways of finding out than by sinking.

With his other hand he reached for the throttle control and slowly eased it back, but not before they hit the towpath on the opposite side.

From somewhere astern of the boat he heard a cry of pain. Pommes Frites must have caught up with his quarry. One thing was certain. If he had got his teeth into Dubois there would be no letting go. He would hang on until the bitter end.

Monsieur Pamplemousse eased the throttle lever back still further until they were barely moving, then he tried the door leading to the forward cabin. It was locked. He called out but there was no reply.

For the second time in as many moments the sound of splintering wood echoed round the walls of the chamber.

Monsieur Pamplemousse felt round the edge of the door frame until he found a switch. He clicked it on.

Bathed in the light from a single overhead bulb he saw a figure stretched out on a bunk at the far end. From the way it was lying it was patently obvious why there had been no reply.

10
THE FINAL PRINT-OUT

Monsieur Pamplemousse studied a long, hand-written list of 'things to do' as he paused for a moment outside the Director's office, mentally ticking off the items as he went.

JoJo was in his rightful place in Madame Grante's apartment; the stand-by *oiseau* from the pet shop was back with the Director. That in itself hadn't been as easy as it sounded. The first mistake – and one he wouldn't make again in a hurry – had been to let both birds out for their morning fly at the same time. Catching one had been bad enough; catching two was more than one too many. With the early-morning traffic building up behind him in the Rue des Renaudes, the taxi driver had not been pleased at being kept waiting.

On the way back to Madame Grante's apartment he had visited her in hospital. Outwardly at least, she was very little the worse for her experience and, subject to a favourable report from the doctor, she would be going home later that same day.

Before leaving the Rue des Renaudes for good, he had been through the apartment with a fine-tooth comb. Sheets and pillow cases had been taken to the launderette and were freshly ironed, and every last trace of Pommes Frites'hairs had been removed from the carpet and rugs with a vacuum cleaner. JoJo's supplies had been 'doctored' to make it look as though they had never been replenished. Monsieur Pamplemousse was particularly pleased with the last touch.

It was what separated the professional from the amateur. He'd very nearly slipped up and filled both water and seed bowl to the brim. The sand on the floor of the cage looked as though it hadn't been touched for days. With luck Madame Grante would have so many other things on her mind she would never know he had been there. Any missing items of food she would put down to her erstwhile lover.

He'd ordered some flowers and a large box of chocolates for the girls in Communications. They should arrive at any moment.

A message of thanks had gone out to Jacques asking when and where he would like to be taken out to dinner. The fact that in the end he'd been able to do without his help was beside the point, there were still things to be done.

Only one vital piece of the jigsaw was missing – the fate of the missing *disques*, and that he could do nothing about.

Suddenly conscious from the odd glances Pommes Frites kept giving him, that he wasn't exactly looking his best, Monsieur Pamplemousse made a half-hearted attempt at straightening his tie, before knocking on the door.

'Aristide!' The Director jumped to his feet and came bounding round his desk as they entered. 'Congratulations!'

Monsieur Pamplemousse gave a shrug. 'It is not quite as satisfactory as I would have wished, *Monsieur.*' Personally he would have awarded himself eight out of ten at the most. Without the vital *disques*, publication of *Le Guide* would have to be delayed indefinitely.

'At least we can sleep safely in our beds from now on. What do you think will happen to him?'

Monsieur Pamplemousse gave another shrug, even more non-committal than the first. How long was a piece of string? It was out of his hands now.

'Time alone will tell, *Monsieur.*'

Like a visiting dignitary inspecting his guard of honour, the Director stood back in order to get a better view of his guests.

'I trust Pommes Frites' head will soon be better.'

'The *vétérinaire* has said the bandages can be removed in a few days.'

'Good. Good. As soon as they are we must make sure he is suitably rewarded.' The Director fastened his gaze on Monsieur Pamplemousse.

'I must say you have surpassed yourself this time, Aristide. Before we go any further I must let you divest yourself of your disguise, although if I may venture one criticism, I doubt if even the most hard done-by of the working classes – an artisan who has seen his livelihood submerged beneath a tidal wave of cheap imported Japanese goods, or someone practising what has become a dying trade, a wheelwright, perhaps, or soothsayer – would hardly venture forth knowing there was a large tear in his trouser leg. As for the jacket lapels hanging by a thread, do you not think that is a trifle over the top?'

'I am afraid, *Monsieur*, I had a little accident. I was climbing through a ventilation shaft and it got caught in a projection of some kind. As for the trousers, I had an encounter with some rose bushes. I will ask Madame Pamplemousse to see what she can do before I return them.'

The Director stared at him, glassy-eyed. 'You mean that is my suit you are wearing?'

'*Oui, Monsieur,* it is the one you were kind enough to lend me.'

'But that was one of my best suits, Pamplemousse. It came with a ten-year guarantee!'

'In that case, *Monsieur*, there is no problem. You have good cause to complain.'

'They are not designed for use below ground, Pample-mousse,' said the Director severely, 'least of all in *les égouts*!'

Monsieur Pamplemousse took a deep breath. He could see he was in for a difficult time. 'It was not in the sewers, *Monsieur*,' he began. 'It was in the Canal Saint-Martin ...'

'Canals, sewers, they are all one and the same, Pample-mousse.' The Director sounded less than mollified.

'Perhaps, *Monsieur*, you could catch Madame Grante while she is in a good mood. In the circumstances she can hardly turn down a claim for expenses.'

'Hmmph. You don't know how much it cost. She will need to be in a very good mood indeed. I suggest you choose something a little less costly for the time being – you will find a sports jacket somewhere in the wardrobe.'

'You are very kind, *Monsieur*.' Before the Director had time to comment further, Monsieur Pamplemousse disap-peared into the other room. Ever sensitive to the atmosphere, Pommes Frites followed on behind.

When they returned, the Director was busying himself in front of his drinks cupboard, opening some wine. He looked in a better mood. Monsieur Pamplemousse caught a glimpse of the label on the bottle. It was a Bâtard-Montrachet from Remoissenet, an '83. It must have been left over from the launch party. Perks were not confined to the office staff making free telephone calls.

'I have put another bottle on one side for you, Aristide. I think you deserve it.' The Director must have read his thoughts.

Monsieur Pamplemousse murmured his appreciation as he took a large Burgundy glass and held it to his nose. So much had happened it hardly seemed possible that only a few days had passed since he had last tasted it. 'Twice in one week is a very great privilege, *Monsieur*. It is not often I am able to afford such nectar.'

The Director brushed aside the compliment. 'Good wine is never expensive, Aristide. Only bad wine is expensive.' He crossed the room and opened one of the french windows leading to his balcony.

'I do believe we are in for a change in the weather. Look, the sun is shining.' He stepped outside and took in a deep draught of fresh air. 'A perfect spring day at last!'

Monsieur Pamplemousse joined his chief on the balcony. All around there was the hum of traffic. The Boules players were still at it.

'I am dying to hear everything. Tell me about Madame Grante, how is she? What did she have to say when you found her?'

Monsieur Pamplemousse hesitated. The truth was that in the event it had all been strangely formal. When he removed her gag she had said 'Monsieur Pamplemousse' and he had said 'Madame Grante'. They might have just bumped into each other in the street. Afterwards, on the way to the hospital, he had held her hand and she had said his name again.

'She is little the worse for her adventure, *Monsieur*. It is largely a matter of getting her circulation back. When I went to see her she was already asking about the P39s, wondering if they were beginning to pile up. I did my best to reassure her.'

'Ah, with some people, Pamplemousse, recovery is a mixed blessing. Tell me, was she … was she complete? Did she have her full complement of digits? There was nothing missing, I trust?'

'As far as I could tell, *Monsieur*, Madame Grante was complete in every detail. Those that were visible. I cannot, of course, vouch for what lay or did not lie beneath the sheets.'

The Director had the grace to blush. 'You know what the mail is like these days, Aristide. There might have been something still in the post. I wouldn't have forgiven myself if anything had happened.

'Has she … has she recovered in other ways?'

'It is hard to say, *Monsieur*. Time alone will tell.'

'I wonder what made her do it?'

'Love clouds judgement, *Monsieur*.'

'Do you think there was any love on his part, or was it totally a matter of expediency?'

'Perhaps a little of each.' Secretly, Monsieur Pamplemousse found himself hoping there was a lot of the first. It would be unbearably sad if there wasn't.

'It is certainly hard to picture.'

'*La nuit, toutes les chattes sont grises, Monsieur*. They say that all cats are grey in the dark.'

'Do you really believe that, Pamplemousse?'

'*Non, Monsieur.*' Monsieur Pamplemousse shook his head. 'No, I have never believed that.'

'I am pleased to hear it. Were that true there would be little hope for mankind.'

Monsieur Pamplemousse couldn't help thinking it would also mean an end to romance. He took in the scene before them. The Eiffel Tower to their left, in front of them the Seine, and beyond that the Grand Palais and the Tuileries. On the horizon there was the Sacré-Coeur to remind him that he would soon be home again. The whole added up to a feeling of permanence.

The Director read his thoughts.

'France may be a country divided into fifty-five million inhabitants, Aristide, but with all our faults, God loves the French best. We don't have a future, we have a destiny, a destiny rich in memories of the past, We are indeed a favoured nation. That is my belief.'

Monsieur Pamplemousse resisted the temptation to remark that the poet Péguy had thought of it first. The Director was definitely feeling better. He was about to enter one of his Napoleonic moods. It was one of the great disadvantages of being situated within sight of the Emperor's tomb. He chose the line of least resistance.

'It is a very reassuring view, *Monsieur*. It makes it even harder to believe that such a small mistake made by one person so many years ago could have caused so much disruption.'

'No, Aristide, there I beg to differ. It was not a small mistake, it was a blatant and unforgivable act of deception, one which brought dishonour not only to his calling, but to his father's memory as well. It had to be stamped on.

'Curnonsky, the Prince of gastronomes, once said: "Never eat the left leg of a partridge, for that is the leg it sits on." A counsel of perfection perhaps, but one must have standards. Gastronomy is not just a matter of pots and pans, it is also a mental attitude.

'We must maintain our standards. I have read that there are more nutrients in a cornflake packet than there are in the actual cornflakes themselves. There are undoubtedly people out there who are only too willing to take advantage of that fact. We must guard against the erosion of our taste-buds in the name of convenience. The world is full of people who care so little about standards they would be only too willing to meet the demands of those who eat to live rather than live to eat in order to make a profit.

'Do you wish to eat neurotic tasteless birds, brought up on antibiotics, killed before they have acquired any taste, frozen solid until they are like rocks before being dumped into a freezer cabinet, with nothing left to thaw out except water?

Or do you want to eat birds which have been brought up on a proper diet of maize and dairy products; chicken which taste as though they have led a happy life?

'It may sound a small matter, Pamplemousse, but it is the tip of the iceberg. In the end it is a matter of how you want things to be. What kind of world you wish to inhabit. That was the question uppermost in my mind that evening many years ago, and once I had posed the question, I had no doubt in my mind as to the answer.'

The Director was right, of course. Monsieur Pamplemousse would have done exactly the same thing in his place, otherwise what was he doing in his present job?

'And now, Aristide, for my little morsel of news.' The Director turned and led the way back into his room. 'I think I may say with all due modesty that I have achieved something of a breakthrough myself. When I woke this morning and found you had returned the *oiseau* to my office, I must say I felt somewhat piqued, but at long last patience has reaped its due reward. Somewhat late in the day the *oiseau* and I have established a rapport. Conversation is limited at present to a few basic pleasantries, and the language is, I fear, not all that one might expect from a creature who has spent most of its life either in the nest or in the company of a maiden lady, but who knows where it may lead, perhaps even to the recovery of the missing *disques*?'

Crossing to where the bird cage was standing, the Director removed the cloth with a flourish.

'*Comment ça va,* JoJo?'

The effect, as far as at least one member of his audience of two was concerned, was no less magical than it would have been had they been watching the great Robert-Houdin performing at the peak of his career.

'*Comment ça va,* JoJo?' The Director's words were

echoed by a smaller, though in its way, and size for size, hardly less powerful voice. There then followed a stream of expletives which would not have disgraced a stevedore who had suffered the misfortune of having a bulk container break loose from a dockside crane and land on his foot.

'*Merde!*' Monsieur Pamplemousse involuntarily added his quota to JoJo's list of adjectives as the truth of the matter sank in. Somehow or other he must have got the two birds mixed up. His heart sank as he looked at his watch. In all probability Madame Grante would be getting ready to go home by now if she wasn't already on her way. There wasn't a moment to be lost.

'I am sorry, *Monsieur*. I shouldn't have inflicted JoJo on you. I will remove the cage at once. In any case I must return him to Madame Grante.'

'I shall miss it, Aristide.' The Director looked genuinely sorry. 'Birds are strange creatures. They are like women. Who knows what goes on in their minds?'

Monsieur Pamplemousse decided to strike while the iron was hot.

'*Monsieur*, I know someone whose *oiseau* has recently received a great shock. In all probability it has temporarily lost the power of speech. Given your success with JoJo ...'

'You're a good fellow, Aristide. I don't know what I would have done without you these last few days.' The Director crossed to his drinks cupboard. 'You must have two bottles of wine. I insist.'

If Monsieur Pamplemousse had a twinge of conscience, it was only momentary. After all he had been through, he felt as though a whole vintage would not have come amiss. He paused at the door.

'I shall be back very soon, *Monsieur*.'

It was with a feeling of *déjà vu* that Monsieur Pamplemousse climbed out of a taxi in the Rue des Renaudes for what he fervently hoped was the very last time plus one. He was beginning to get the feeling that he was somehow caught up in an avant-garde play, doomed to trudge the streets of Paris for ever carrying a bird cage as a penance for past misde-meanours. His mood transmitted itself to his companions. Pommes Frites clearly felt much the same way about things as he gazed gloomily up and down the street, and the object of the exercise, JoJo himself, had remained mute for the whole of the journey.

As they paused outside the entrance to Madame Grante's apartment, Monsieur Pamplemousse felt in his pocket for the keys, then stifled an oath. In his anxiety to restore the status quo and return things to normal he'd put them back in Madame Grante's drawer at the office. He turned and waved, but the taxi had already disappeared round the nearest corner.

It was then that he made his second mistake. Truly, misfor-tunes never came singly. Glancing towards the upper floors of the block he caught sight of Madame Grante looking out of her window. She must have beaten him to it. It was also abundantly clear from the look on her face that she had seen everything, including the cage.

He made his way into the entrance hall and pressed the button for her apartment. He would have to put a brave face on things. In response to a buzz, he pushed open the inner door, signalling at the same time for Pommes Frites to remain where he was. Pommes Frites was only too pleased to obey.

The lift was waiting. On the way up it struck Monsieur Pamplemousse that it seemed to be going faster than usual. The door to the apartment opened before he had a chance to touch the bell-push.

'Madame Grante … I know you are not going to believe this …'

'In that case, Monsieur Pamplemousse, why bother to tell me.'It was a statement rather than a question.

'As you may have gathered, when we became alarmed for your safety I visited your apartment.'

'I trust Pommes Frites did not come too. JoJo is terrified of dogs. He either goes berserk or else he goes into hiding. Once, when I had a friend for *déjeuner,* he hid in a fold of the curtains. It took me until the evening to find him.'

Monsieur Pamplemousse held up the cage. 'I realised that, Madame Grante. Which is why I thought it best to remove him to a place of safety. JoJo has been in good hands. He has been staying with the Director. The one in your cage is merely a stand-in.'

As JoJo jumped from his perch and clung to the bars of the cage nearest Madame Grante, Monsieur Pamplemousse had a sudden thought. 'I believe *Monsieur le Directeur* has been trying to teach him a few new words. He seemed very pleased with the result.'

It was an insurance policy. There was no knowing what the real JoJo might say once he found himself back in familiar surroundings.

'Perhaps you would like to change the *oiseaux* over. I'm sure you are much better at it than I am.'

He wondered if Madame Grante would invite him in, but she made no attempt. Instead, she disappeared for a moment or two before returning with the cage containing its rightful occupant. In her other hand she held a large manila envelope.

'This is for you. I suggest you open it when you get back to the office.'

Monsieur Pamplemousse obediently relieved her of both.

He held his breath. Already he could hear JoJo holding forth.

'I believe you have something of mine?' said Madame Grante.

'I do?'

'I left it under my pillow.'

It definitely wasn't his day. Putting the cage down for a moment, he felt for his wallet, then handed Madame Grante the photograph. She took it without a word.

'I am very sorry.' Monsieur Pamplemousse found himself at a loss for words. 'It must have been a very distressing experience for you. Did you and he … ?' The words slipped out before he could stop them.

'Did we what, Monsieur Pamplemousse?'

'*Pardon, Madame.*' It was unforgivable. Not at all what he had meant to say.

'We had a wonderful time together, while it lasted.'

As she closed the door he saw there were tears in her eyes.

On the way down the lift seemed to have reverted to its normal slow pace again. What was it Proust had said? The true paradises are paradises we have lost.

The Director removed two film-wrapped *disques* from the envelope and gazed at them. 'Do you mean to say, Pamplemousse, these were hidden in the *oiseau's* cage all the time? I can hardly believe it.'

'I could hardly believe it myself, *Monsieur.* It is the old story of the man on the building site who every day was seen removing a brick in a wheelbarrow. No one bothered to challenge him for taking just one brick. It wasn't until it was too late that they discovered he was really stealing wheelbarrows.'

The Director frowned. 'I'm not sure that I follow you.'

'We thought our man was after the bird, whereas in fact what he wanted to get hold of was the right cage.'

'The right cage, Pamplemousse? I still don't understand what you are getting at.'

Realising that he was about to get himself into deep water, Monsieur Pamplemousse hastily changed tack. 'What I am saying, *Monsieur*, is that he must have hidden the *disques* in JoJo's cage at some point. According to her note, it wasn't until Madame Grante returned home and removed the sheet of sanded paper in order to clean it out properly that she discovered them. They fitted almost exactly into the bottom of the tray.'

Fortunately the Director had other things to think about. 'It is a great weight off my mind, Aristide.' He picked up the telephone. 'I must warn the printers to stand by. With luck, the first copies of *Le Guide* should start rolling off the presses tonight. Review copies will be despatched immediately they become available.'

It seemed a good moment to leave, but as Monsieur Pamplemousse turned to go the Director waved him to remain.

'I have something addressed to you, Aristide. It came through on the computer just before you arrived back. It appears to be in some kind of code.'

Monsieur Pamplemousse reached across and took a sheet of computer print-out from the Director. As always, the length of the message bore no relation to the amount of paper. It was short and to the point: MORE RAIN IS FORECAST. AMPLE FUNDS ARE AVAILABLE IF YOU WISH TO CASH YOUR CHEQUE, BANK OF PASSY. Ten out of ten to Martine for persistence.

The Director put a hand over the mouthpiece of the receiver. 'What do you think it means, Aristide? Can it be that someone else has already entered the system?'

'Perhaps the engineers are conducting some kind of tests,

Monsieur. I will investigate the matter straight away.'

'Please do, Aristide, there's a good fellow. And don't forget your bottles of wine. They are with Véronique.'

Monsieur Pamplemousse hesitated at the door. 'I have a little something for you, *Monsieur*. It is also with Véronique.'

It wasn't a bad swop – two bottles of Bâtard-Montrachet for one *perruche*. At least it solved the problem of what to do with JoJo's stand-in.

Back at his desk, Monsieur Pamplemousse found another note awaiting him. This time it was from Jacques. He ran his eyes down it.

'… A few years later he tried again with a restaurant boat on the river but someone shopped him. After that he drifted for a while, worked as a radio operator on board ship; he even tried his luck working the canals in the Paris area, but eventually he gave that up and returned to Belfort. Computers were coming into their own, and because of his experience as a radio operator, he landed a job with Poulanc …' Congratulations followed, then: 'Next time, be a good fellow and bring us in earlier. It'll save an awful lot of tedious explanations.'

Next time! Monsieur Pamplemousse gazed out of the window for a moment or two. He hoped there would never be a 'next time'. With luck, Dubois should be out of the way for some while to come and would have learned his lesson. He wondered if, during his time in Paris, he had ever come near *Le Guide*'s offices. If he'd seen the Director driving out through the gates in his usual splendour, the grievance he had been nursing over the years would have come flooding back, enlarged out of all proportion. Probably when his journeyings on the Seine took him past the Esplanade des Invalides he'd taken to thinking out ways of getting his revenge. It was hard to imagine the surprise he must have felt when suddenly, years later, the Director turned up out of the blue at the Poulanc factory.

Monsieur Pamplemousse gave a sigh. It all seemed academic now. Around him the rest of the staff were rushing about their work as news filtered through that all was well again.

Monsieur Pamplemousse picked up the telephone. He suddenly felt very flat.

Pile ou face? Heads or tails?

He took out a coin and tossed it. Tails. He dialled a number.

'Couscous. I have finished what I was doing. I shall be home this evening.'

'*Oh, la! la!*' Doucette sounded flustered. If only he had phoned earlier. Her sister was already hard at work preparing the evening meal. *Tripe à la mode de Caen.* They were having it for the simple reason that Agathe knew he didn't like it.

Monsieur Pamplemousse felt tempted to say that an even simpler reason why he didn't like the dish was because of the way Agathe made it. Tripe needed to be cooked for a long time, preferably in a casserole which had been hermetically sealed with flour and water paste. If you didn't, it was a sure recipe for indigestion. Agathe couldn't be bothered with such niceties, and he almost always suffered accordingly.

'We have plenty. It can be divided. You will be more than welcome.'

'No, no, Couscous, I shall be all right, really I shall. Tomorrow night we can go out and make up for it.

'You, too, *ma chérie.*'

Clearing the call, he allowed all of two seconds to elapse, then he dialled Martine's number.

'Bank of Passy? I have a cheque I wish to cash. What time do you close?'

'We are open until late this evening.'

'In that case I will be with you as soon as possible.'

'Would you like to know what I have planned?'

'Tell me.'

'*Moules aux amandes.*'

Mussels with almonds. That was more like it. He felt his mouth watering at the thought. It was a Basque speciality. The last time he'd tasted it had been in a little restaurant in Saint-Jean-de-Luz. It had been helped on its way with a *pousse-rapière* beforehand – Armagnac, sparkling white wine and a slice of orange. The memory lingered.

'And after that?'

'*Poularde en demi-deuil.*'

'Aaaah!' Monsieur Pamplemousse felt his salivary glands begin to work overtime at the mere mention of the name. It was a dish made famous by one of the *Mères Lyonnaises*. Chicken with slices of truffle placed in splits between the skin and the breast. It was an apt name – chicken in partial mourning.

'And the *poularde* is from where?'

'Bresse, of course.'

'Of course! Where else?' In the circumstances it couldn't possibly be otherwise.

The bird would be stuffed with sausage meat mixed with white of egg, cream and breadcrumbs, then it would be poached in a *court-bouillon* containing leeks, carrots, turnips and celery. It was *not* something his mother had ever cooked. Even on fête days, truffles had been way beyond their reach.

'Then some cheese. I have managed to get something special from near home which you may like to try.

'And to finish, there are orange sorbets ...'

'Served inside the orange with meringue on top?'

She laughed. 'There are other ways?'

'I will see you soon. May I bring the wine? I have something I think you will appreciate.'

Monsieur Pamplemousse suddenly realised how hungry he felt. Even so, he knew someone who must be feeling even hungrier.

'May I also bring Pommes Frites?'

'Of course. I will lay another place.'

Pommes Frites pricked up his ears at the sound of his name. Given the various other evocative words he had overheard during the course of the conversation, words like *poularde* and *Bresse,* add to them the look of anticipation on his master's face – a look he knew only too well – and it all sounded distinctly promising.

He stood up as his master replaced the receiver. It was time to reorganise his filing system. Certain smells could now be relegated to the archives; new ones would soon be taking their place.

And the very nice thing about that, he decided as he followed Monsieur Pamplemousse down the corridor and into a room at the far end, was that he would be sharing them with the person who meant most to him in the world.

Only one thing puzzled Pommes Frites. Why on earth at such a moment waste valuable time bothering to shave? There were some things about his master he would never understand.

Monsieur
Pamplemousse
Rests His Case

Contents

1
HANDS ACROSS THE OCEAN

The Director settled himself comfortably in the leather armchair behind his desk, shuffled a few papers nervously to and fro across the top, carefully covering as he did so a large map of the United States of America, then cleared his throat as he brought both hands together to form a miniature steeple with his fingertips.

Recognising the signs, Monsieur Pamplemousse sought reassurance by giving the top of Pommes Frites' head a passing pat, then sat back waiting for the worst. He wondered idly if it would be a case of being addressed by his surname or by his Christian name. From the shape of the steeple – high and severely orthodox – he guessed at the former. The Director was wearing his official look: a mixture of barely concealed disapproval and distaste of what he was about to say. He cleared his throat a second time.

'Pamplemousse, I have no doubt that in your previous occupation – I refer, of course, to your years with the Sûreté – you had need from time to time to consult the *Code Napoléon*?'

Monsieur Pamplemousse made a non-committal grunt. There had been more than one occasion when he would gladly have seized hold of a copy, preferably a leatherbound edition, and used it in order to batter a particularly belligerent or uncooperative offender into telling the truth, but he sensed it was neither the time nor the place to say so.

'Good.' The Director picked up a sheet of paper. 'That makes my task easier. I would like, if I may, to draw your attention to Article 1101: the definition of a contract.

'It states, and I quote: "A contract is a convention by which one or several persons commit themselves towards one or several other persons to give, to do, or not to do something."

'I'm sure you will agree that the extract I have just read is a masterpiece of construction. The wording is concise – a mere twenty-eight words; the meaning crystal clear and unassailable.'

Seeing that something more than a mere grunt was expected of him, Monsieur Pamplemousse nodded his agreement. There was no point in doing otherwise.

'I am pleased you agree, Pamplemousse. To carry matters a stage further, in accepting your present post as an Inspector with *Le Guide*, you committed yourself to a contract. Why, then, when I arrived at my office this morning, did I find a letter of resignation on my desk? I have, of course, torn it up, but I think I deserve an explanation.'

'The answer is perfectly simple, *Monsieur*. It was in response to your memo of yesterday's date asking me to stand by for further instructions. By the merest chance I happened to be passing the Operations Room and when I went inside I saw where they had put my flag. Not, as I had every good reason to expect, in the *Section Vacances*, but lying on its side in the pending tray. The staff were unusually evasive and I began putting two and two together. It did not take me long to come up with an answer. One which, if I may say so, is certainly not covered by the *Code Napoléon*.'

The Director made a clucking noise. 'My dear Pample-mousse, everything is covered by the *Code Napoléon*. If it is not in the *Code Napoléon*, then it does not exist. In their wisdom, its authors made sure the document covered every conceivable eventuality; from the laws which govern our country, to the way one should behave when visiting a public garden; from the manner in which letters should be written – the various forms of address and the correct phrasing of salutations – down to the time it should take a *concierge* to clean her front door-step.'

He rose to his feet, went to the window, and gazed out across the esplanade towards the Hôtel des Invalides and the vast golden dome which protected its illustrious occu-pant from the elements.

'Were he alive today, Pamplemousse, the Emperor would not be best pleased. If one believed in such things, one might hazard a guess that he is at this very moment turning in his tomb, thus causing consternation among those tourists from all over the world who have tendered good money in order to pay their respects.'

'With equal respect, *Monsieur*, were he alive today and in my shoes I think he would have good reason to be restive. The Emperor Napoléon may have covered every eventuality which he could possibly have foreseen at that period in history, but times change. Had he been born a century and a half later, and had he found himself working for *Le Guide*, he could well have had second thoughts on the subject; he might even have toyed with the idea of introducing a possible escape clause to Article 1101; an "in so far as" perhaps, or even a simple phrase like *sauf exceptions* – "with certain exceptions"; *par exemple*, requests beyond the call of duty, particularly if it had been his understanding that he was about to enjoy a well-deserved holiday with the Empress Joséphine.'

The Director heaved a sigh and turned away from the window. Clearly, as he crossed to his drinks cupboard and removed a bottle from the ice-bucket he was preparing himself for another form of attack; a diversionary move of some kind aimed at lulling his adversary into a false sense of security prior to a sudden flanking movement.

A brief glimpse of the label confirmed Monsieur Pample-mousse's suspicions. The Chief must have been expecting trouble, otherwise why would he have had a bottle of Gosset champagne chilled and at the ready when his normal preference was for Louis Roederer? The answer was simple. He knew the tastes of his staff.

'Come, come, Aristide ... you must not take too narrow a view of life. There are wider horizons than the one which can be seen from this window, or even from wherever it was you and Madame Pamplemousse intended spending your holiday together. Horizons which have much to offer. It is my belief that if *Le Guide* is to flourish and prepare itself for entering the twenty-first century we cannot afford to stand still. We must lay the foundation stones for the future, and we must lay them now. The recent computerisation was but a first step. Now that that particular mountain has been successfully conquered, we must put our facilities and our expertise to good use. We must expand into other areas. In particular we must look towards the New World. I am sure it is what our founder, Monsieur Hippolyte Duval, would have wished.'

The Director diverted his attention momentarily towards a painting which occupied a goodly portion of the wall above his head. Following the direction of the other's gaze, Monsieur Pamplemousse couldn't help but reflect that its principal subject, depicted by the artist toying with a bowl of *moules marinières* outside a country inn, might not have looked quite so relaxed had the river which formed the background to the picture been the Hudson rather than the Marne. By all accounts he might have felt the need to keep a more watchful eye on his bicycle, chaining it to a convenient fire hydrant for a start, instead of leaving it unattended against a nearby tree.

'Others have made a stab at it. For several years now Gault-Millau have published a guide to New York – and a very good little book it is too, even though it suffers from their usual inability to avoid the *bon mot* at other people's expense. But no one on this side of the *Atlantique*, not even Michelin, has attempted a gastronomic guide to the whole country. It is an enormous, a mind-boggling task ...'

Monsieur Pamplemousse half rose from his seat. He didn't like the turn the conversation was taking. 'You are surely not suggesting, *Monsieur*, that I should move to America? Madame Pamplemousse would never agree to it. As for Pommes Frites ...'

Hearing his name mentioned, Pommes Frites opened one bloodshot eye and fastened it unblinkingly on the figure hovering by the drinks cabinet. It signalled his agreement in no uncertain manner to whatever point his master might be making.

'No, no, Aristide, of course not.' The Director made haste to relieve his audience of any possible misunderstanding. 'I am merely looking into the future – the very distant future. For the moment we must content ourselves with exploring the possibilities. To that end, while I was in New York recently I made contact with the publisher of an up and coming gourmet magazine – a Mrs Van Dorman. She is a charming lady, but I suspect life in the Big Apple has passed her by to some extent. She has already carved out one successful career in the perfume business. Now she finds herself heading a publishing conglomerate which has set its sights on Europe.

'We established a certain *rapport*, the upshot of which is that she has given me a long list of establishments in the USA which could well form the basis of a guide, and in return I promised her that if she was ever in this country and in need of help I would be happy to reciprocate to the best of my ability. That moment has arrived, Pamplemousse; rather sooner than expected I have to admit – it is only a matter of weeks since we first discussed the matter – but a promise is a promise and I must do my best to slot her in.'

Monsieur Pamplemousse winced. Ever since he had arrived back from America, the Director – normally a staunch upholder of all that was sacred in the French language – had taken to peppering his speech with words and phrases which would have caused even the most catholic member of the Académie Française to reel back in horror had they been present. 'Slotting things in' was the least of his transgressions. Ideas had become 'creative concepts', and 'potentials' were constantly being 'maximised'.

'It is her first visit to Europe and I can think of no one better qualified to act as her guide and mentor while she is in La Belle France than your good self. I would take on the task myself, but alas ...' The Director raised his hands in despair. 'It is one of the problems of going away, Aristide. There are a thousand things to catch up on ... planning next year's edition of *Le Guide* ... making sure those who qualify receive their annual increments.' He paused for a moment. 'I believe your own salary comes up for review quite soon ...'

Monsieur Pamplemousse stared at the Director's reflection in the mirrored interior of the cupboard. At least he had the grace to concentrate on the task in hand – the removal of the cork, silently and expertly, and the pouring of the champagne, tasks which kept his head bowed, thus enabling him to avoid a direct meeting of the eyes.

'What I am suggesting is surely not so outrageous? It could be a pleasant break from routine.'

'Madame Pamplemousse will certainly consider it outrageous, Monsieur. She will say I am an Inspector, not a tour guide.

'And what of the language problem?'

'Mrs Van Dorman has a little French, I believe. Enough. Besides, it does not seem to have hampered you in the past. What you cannot put into words you manage to convey all too successfully by whatever other means are at your disposal. What was the name of that English woman in the Hautes Pyrénées? Madame Cosgrove? As I recall, inhibitions were somewhat thrown to the wind on that occasion; lack of a common language did not prove to be an insurmountable barrier.'

Monsieur Pamplemousse chose to ignore the remark. Instead he tried another tack.

'I have to take my car into a blacksmith for a major repair, *Monsieur*.'

'A blacksmith, Pamplemousse?'

'I am having trouble with one of the doors. It has to do with the hinges. As you know, it is an early *deux chevaux* and the particular part is in short supply. I have been teaching Madame Pamplemousse to drive and it is not easy. We had an encounter with a *camion* in the rue Marcadet. As you may know, it is a one-way street. Unfortunately we were travelling in the wrong direction ...'

'Why is it, Pamplemousse, that whenever you don't wish to go somewhere there is always trouble with your car? I sometimes suspect you use it as an excuse. It's high time you either bought a new one or made use of a company car like everyone else. Anyway, it will have to wait.'

'I did promise Doucette I would try and slot her in for another lesson this week in preparation for our holiday, *Monsieur*.'

The Director eyed him suspiciously as he returned to his chair. He placed two long-stemmed glasses on the desk, motioning Monsieur Pamplemousse to help himself.

'Many people would consider my proposal a signal honour, Aristide. But perhaps I haven't explained myself sufficiently well.'

Drinking deeply from his glass, he uncovered the map and set about the task of unfolding it. 'America is a large country; a land of boundless opportunity.

'So far I have only tasted the delights of *La Grande Pomme*, but I cannot wait to savour other areas. New York is an exciting city, of course: a mixture of extremes. There are undercurrents which are hard to put a finger on, let alone explain. But in the same way that Paris cannot be called France, neither is New York the be all and end all of the New World. *Amérique du Nord* isn't all hamburgers with French fries on the side ...'

'I understand they also have frankfurters, *Monsieur* ... and doughnuts.'

'Don't be so chauvinistic, Pamplemousse. It is unworthy of you. It ignores the fact that they also have *homards* from Maine, red snappers from the Gulf of Mexico, crayfish from Louisiana, salmon from Oregon, prawns from Monterey, suckling pigs from Amador County, beef from Texas, and wines from the Napa Valley ... the list is endless.

'They also, I may say, possess boundless enthusiasm for whatever project they happen to be involved in; a quality many of us would do well to emulate.' The Director paused in order to allow the implied criticism time to reach its target and sink in.

'Currently, Pamplemousse, as I am sure you know, there is a fashion in certain gastronomic circles for recreating some of the great meals of the past – both in fact and fiction. The worst excesses of *nouvelle cuisine* are now behind us and people are turning to their history books.'

'I understand there is a restaurant in London which has recreated on more than one occasion the meal on which the film *Babette's Feast* was based. I, myself, was lucky enough to be present only recently at a very grand occasion in the Bois de Boulogne when a whole bevy of chefs, Robuchon, Lenôtre, Dutournier, and others, prepared a Pre-Revolutionary Banquet at the behest of one of the great Champagne houses.'

'But when it comes to the grand gesture, the kind of function where money is no object, then one has to hand it to our friends on the other side of the Atlantic. In order to achieve their objective the question of money doesn't arise. In 1973 the Culinary Institute of America held a feast commemorating Sherlock Holmes at which a hundred guests sat down to a feast of some thirteen courses culled from the works of Conan Doyle.

'It is a quest of this nature which brings Mrs Van Dorman to our shores and she has sought my advice. She is acting as escort to a group of American crime writers who have a particular interest in culinary matters. They are members of a very elite society – *Le Cercle de Six*. They meet only once a year and on each occasion they choose a different venue.

'Last year it was Death Row in Alcatraz. The year before

589

that they diced with the possibility of their own demise by eating fugu fish in Tokyo. This time it is the turn of Vichy.'

'Vichy?' Monsieur Pamplemousse looked at his chief in surprise.

'That seems a very odd choice, *Monsieur*. With all due respect to the chefs of that estimable city, some of whom have a place in *Le Guide*, I do not recall Stock Pots lying thick on the ground. People usually go there for the waters. They are more concerned with not eating rather than the reverse.'

'The good chefs of Vichy may well surprise us, Aristide. It could be that they will seize the opportunity with both hands. Think what it must be like to spend one's life cooking for people whose main preoccupation lies in the contemplation of their liver. How they must long to be able to tear up their calorie charts, throw caution to the wind, add a little extra cream here, another slab of *beurre* there, and indulge themselves just for once ...'

'Nevertheless, *Monsieur*, it is not a place one would normally choose for a gastronomic extravaganza.'

The Director made a clucking noise. 'Not all the establishments in Vichy are like the Merveilleux, Aristide.'

Monsieur Pamplemousse gave a start. In all the time he had been working for *Le Guide* it was the first occasion on which the Director had dropped so much as a hint that he might have been involved in something that had happened soon after he'd joined: a kind of initiation ceremony.

The Merveilleux had been one of his first ports of call. He'd been sent there in order to determine whether or not the Hôtel restaurant was suitable Stock Pot material – the award given by *Le Guide* when the cuisine was above average and worthy of a special visit; on a par with Michelin's *rosettes* and Gault-Millau's *toques*.

The memory of that evening had remained with him for a long time; the hush which had fallen over the other diners when he'd asked for the *à la carte menu*, only to be told there was no choice. The meal that followed was indelibly etched on his mind – *velouté de tapioca* followed by *carrottes Vichy* followed by *fruits de saison*. Clearly, from the meagre offering of the last course, it had been a bad season for fruit farmers.

Never had he eaten so many grapes at one sitting. In the end the waitress had taken the bowl away from him. And never had he felt so lonely.

Sleep had eluded him that night, as it had Pommes Frites, who was convinced he had done something wrong and was being punished; a conviction which wasn't helped through his having drunk too deeply of the local water, losing his voice as a result.

Monsieur Pamplemousse had got his own back by writing a report eulogising in great depth on his meal, fabricating a story which involved a change of ownership and a young chef destined for stardom. Another Inspector had been dispatched post haste, and from that moment on, although the Director had never referred to the matter, he had been accepted as part of the team.

'Anyway, Pamplemousse,' the Director broke into his thoughts, 'ours is not to reason why. I have to admit I asked myself the same question when I first heard of the venue. But it appears it is one of those occasions when outsiders know more about the history of a country than do its inhabitants.

'In order to find the answer one has to turn to the life and works of Alexandre Dumas. You know, of course, that he compiled one of the great culinary works of all time: *Le Grand Dictionnaire de Cuisine*.'

Monsieur Pamplemousse had to confess it was a gap in his education. 'I am aware of it, Monsieur, but I have never read it.'

'Ah, then you must, Aristide, you really must. It is more than a mere cookery book – it is a distillation of things learned during a whole lifetime of good eating and entertaining. It deserves to stand alongside the works of Brillat Savarin. Sadly, it was his last work. He delivered the manuscript to his publisher, Alphonse Lemerre, in March 1870. Shortly afterwards the Franco-Prussian War broke out and publication was delayed. He died at his house just outside Dieppe while it was still at the printers.' Reaching down, the Director opened a desk drawer and removed a large, leather-bound volume. 'I will lend you my copy. I'm sure it will appeal to you.'

'*Merci, Monsieur.*' Feeling that in accepting the offer he was somehow entering into a commitment, but unable to see a way out of his predicament, Monsieur Pamplemousse reached across and took the book.

'As is so often the case,' continued the Director, 'love of food and cooking went hand in hand with the appreciation and love of other good things in life; art – he was a great friend of Monet – conversation, and, naturally, of women. One summer he took a house called the Villa André on the outskirts of Vichy in order to begin work on yet another sequel to *The Three Musketeers*. Before he started work he decided to put himself in the right frame of mind by preparing a banquet for a few close friends who were staying with him at the time. His collaborator, Auguste Maquet, was there … the painter Courbet … and Courbet's mistress, Madame de Sauvignon.

'And what a meal, Aristide. Let me read you a little of the menu.

They began with a recipe of Dumas' own invention –
Potage à la crevette, and for an *hors d'oeuvres* they had
lampreys – cooked as they should be – in their own blood;
a rare delicacy these days. *Asperge* came hard on the heels
of the lampreys, followed by *ortolans* roasted on the spit.

'But the main course, the *pièce de résistance*, served
after palates had been cleansed by water ices, was *Rôtie à
l'Impératrice*.

'You start with an olive, remove the stone and replace it
with some anchovy. Then you put the olive into a lark, the
lark into a quail, the quail into a partridge, the partridge
into a pheasant, the pheasant into a turkey, and then the
turkey into a suckling pig. The rest is up to the chef.

'They ended the meal with peaches in red wine, pears
with bacon, and *fromage*.

'Think of the ergonomics of preparing such a feast, Aristide. Imagine going into a *boucherie* or a *poissonnerie*
today with such an order and asking them to ensure that
every ingredient is in exactly the right state of readiness.
And remember, this was long before the days of electric
refrigeration.

'No doubt after such a feast the rest of the company
departed to take the cure in nearby Vichy and left him in
peace to write.'

'And it is that feast *Le Cercle de Six* are hoping to
recreate, *Monsieur*?'

'Down to the very last detail.'

In spite of all he had said, Monsieur Pamplemousse felt
himself wavering. It was an opportunity that might never
occur again. Already he could see an article for *L'Escargot*
– the staff magazine. Feeling a movement at his feet he
glanced down and then wished he hadn't. The Director
would not be pleased when he saw the state of his carpet.

Pommes Frites, who had been hanging on his every word, was positively trembling with excitement. Drool issued unregarded from his mouth.

'I will see what Madame Pamplemousse has to say.' He knew exactly what Doucette would have to say when he arrived home and broke the news to her that their holiday would have to be put back. He was in for a bad evening. Lips would be pursed; sighs interspersed with recriminations. It wouldn't be the first occasion. His time in the *Sûreté* had been one long series of cancelled holidays.

'I will do my best, *Monsieur*. I cannot say more.'

'Good. I knew you wouldn't let me down.' The Director rose from his chair. 'Let us shake hands on it, then I will recharge our glasses so that we may drink to the venture.' For some reason he appeared to be growing agitated again; his hand, usually firm and dry, felt moist.

'You must have your photograph taken on the night, Aristide,' he called. 'Madame Pamplemousse may like one for the mantelpiece.'

Monsieur Pamplemousse contemplated the back of the Director's head. He seemed to be taking an inordinately long time over the simple task of pouring a second glass of champagne.

'May I ask, *Monsieur*, what is so special about the occasion that Madame Pamplemousse would like a photograph of me for the mantelpiece? She is well used to seeing me eat.'

Privately he felt it would be the last thing he would want to give Doucette. It would act as a constant reminder of things that might have been. It would always be 'the picture taken of Aristide enjoying himself the year we had to postpone our holiday'.

He realised the Director was speaking again.

'I was saying, Aristide, it isn't often we see you, how shall I put it? – *à travesti.*'

'*Comment, Monsieur?*' Monsieur Pamplemousse came down to earth with a bump, wondering if he had heard aright. 'Did I hear the words "fancy dress"?'

'You did, Aristide. I have given the matter a lot of thought and I think it will be singularly apposite if you go to the banquet dressed as d'Artagnan. It is not, I will freely admit, what is known in the world of the cinema as "type casting" – I would hardly describe you as the athletic sort. "Dashing" is not a word which springs immediately to mind, neither is "swashbuckling". However, beggars can't be choosers.'

Monsieur Pamplemousse rose to his feet. It was the final straw. 'In that case, *Monsieur,*' he said coldly. 'I suggest you send someone else.'

'Sit down, Pamplemousse. Sit down. You make me nervous when you jump up and down like that. Mrs Van Dorman is entering into the spirit of things. She is going in costume of the period. You can hardly let France down by appearing in a lounge suit.

'Anyway, it isn't possible to send anyone else.' The Director strove hard to keep a note of irritation from his voice. 'As you are well aware, June is a busy time of the year. We drew lots yesterday morning and you eame up with the short straw. Or rather, in your absence Glandier drew it for you.'

'Glandier!' Monsieur Pamplemousse stared at the Director. Things were starting to fall into place. He knew at the time it had been a mistake to take time off in order to go shopping with his wife. Shopping with Doucette was never a happy experience at the best of times; tempers were liable to become frayed. When she couldn't find the dress she wanted she had a habit of staring at the empty rack as though hoping something would materialise. That it never did and never would made no difference. All the same, it hadn't occurred to him that while he was drumming in Galeries LaFayette dark deeds were afoot.

'Have you not seen Glandier at the staff annual outing, *Monsieur*? He is the one who always brings along his conjuring outfit. He does the three-card trick better than anyone I know. He can make a *lapin* appear out of his hat as soon as look at it. They say he even has a black cloth on the table when he dines at home so that he can practise in front of his wife!'

'Pamplemousse!' The Director looked mortally offended. 'You are surely not suggesting …'

'*Oui, Monsieur*. That is exactly what I am suggesting. I demand another draw.'

'I am sorry, Pamplemousse. That is quite out of the question. The straws have been returned to the canteen. Besides, you are the only one left. The rest of the staff have gone their separate ways.'

'As quickly as possible I would imagine,' said Monsieur Pamplemousse drily. 'You probably couldn't see them for dust.'

He ought to have known something was afoot from the smug way Glandier had said '*Bonne chance*' when they met on the stairs that morning. He'd been carrying his going-away valise as well.

Other encounters came to mind; or rather, non-encounters. Looking back on it everyone had seemed only too anxious to hurry about their business, which was unusual to say the least. Most of them were away from base so much during the year they were normally only too pleased to seize on any chance of catching up on the latest gossip.

'As part of our contribution to the event I have engaged a group of local thespians to play the part of Dumas and his guests – it will add a touch of colour. Mrs Van Dorman has expressed a wish to go as d'Artagnan's projected mistress in the new work, a certain Madame Joyeux. All in all, it promises to be an exciting evening.'

'I do not think that is a very good idea, *Monsieur*. It may be apposite if I go as d'Artagnan, but being accompanied by my mistress is fraught with danger.'

The Director clucked impatiently. 'Must you take everything so literally, Pamplemousse? It will be in name only.'

'It is precisely the name, *Monsieur*, which will bother Madame Pamplemousse most. She is even more likely to take it literally than I do when I tell her.'

The Director looked startled. 'Tell her, Pamplemousse? Is that wise? Is it strictly *nécessaire*?'

'*Oui, Monsieur.*'

'But this is most unlike you. Need she ever know?'

Monsieur Pamplemousse raised his eyebrows. 'You have met Doucette, *Monsieur*. She will know. Over the years she has developed a sixth sense in such matters.'

'Mmm. Yes, I see what you mean.'

'Besides,' said Monsieur Pamplemousse virtuously. 'I have decided to turn over a new leaf. Life is too short to spend it arguing. Ever since La Rochelle ...'

'La Rochelle?' The Director sat bolt upright and gazed at Monsieur Pamplemousse with interest. 'What happened in La Rochelle, Aristide? You did not tell me about it.'

'Nothing happened, *Monsieur*.'

'Then what are you talking about?'

'There was an unfortunate misunderstanding. Madame Pamplemousse telephoned me about something and the call was put through to my room.'

'And?'

'The chambermaid happened to pick up the receiver. She was turning the mattress at the time, and naturally she was breathing somewhat heavily.'

'I must say, Pamplemousse,' said the Director severely, 'that in view of your past reputation I would be somewhat suspicious were I your wife – which, thank *Le Bon Dieu*, I am not – and I heard a young girl breathing heavily on the other end of the line.'

'She was not young, *Monsieur*. That is why she was breathing heavily. I took a photograph of her to prove my point. Unfortunately, she happened to bend over just as I pressed the shutter release and Madame Pamplemousse came across the enlargement before I had a chance to explain. The matter has come up on a number of occasions since.'

'All women nag, Aristide. They deny it, of course, but it is in their nature. Why only this morning my own dear wife informed me for the fourth or fifth time over breakfast that she never nags, and when I pointed out that repetition of certain remarks was in itself a form of nagging, all logic deserted her.'

'I am simply saying, *Monsieur*, that in view of the present atmosphere I am – how shall I say? – on trial as it were. I wouldn't wish Doucette to think I was deceiving her. Life would not be worth living. In the circumstances I shall have to tell her that I am being "accompanied" and I am not sure how she will take it.'

'So be it, Pamplemousse.' Clearly, now that he had got over the shock, the Director had filed it away in his mind as a domestic problem, and therefore no concern of his. 'If it is of any consolation, I think you will find Mrs Van Dorman is hardly one of the *grandes horizontales*. As a captain of her profession she has too many other things on her mind. Success can be very time- and energy-consuming as I know to my own cost.'

The Director managed to combine his dismissal of the problem with an airy wave of the hand which suggested he, too, had other more important matters awaiting his attention and that it was high time Monsieur Pamplemousse went on his way. For his part, Monsieur Pamplemousse was more than willing to oblige before anything else happened to disturb his peace of mind.

'Your costume will be ready on the night. Fortunately there is an opera house in Vichy, much given I am told to revivals of works of the period. Everything has been arranged. It will be delivered to your Hôtel two days from now. Your *cheval* will be waiting at the gates to the Villa André so that you can make your entrance.'

Monsieur Pamplemousse was in the outer office before he absorbed the full import of the Director's last words. He hesitated, wondering if he had heard aright, then knocked on the door again.

'*Entrez.*'

The Director's face fell as he caught sight of Monsieur Pamplemousse hovering in the doorway.

'You used the word *cheval*, Monsieur? Do you mean … my *deux chevaux*?'

Once again the Director had difficulty in stifling his impatience.

'No, Pamplemousse, I do *not* mean your *deux chevaux*, I mean *un cheval*. Had I meant *deux* I would have used the plural. If you are to play the part of a musketeer you must do things properly. You can hardly arrive for a nineteenth-century banquet at the wheel of a Citroën 2CV. It would be an anti-climax to say the least; somewhat akin to Cleopatra journeying down the Nile on a pedalo.'

'But, *Monsieur* ...'

'Pamplemousse! I must say you are in a singularly difficult mood today. It is surely not asking too much of you to
relinquish your car for one evening in the year. In short, to
exchange your *deux chevaux* for the real thing. Besides,
you said yourself you are having trouble with the door. It
will be a good opportunity to have it mended. Vichy is
known for equestrian pursuits. It must be full of black-
smiths.'

'I shall need riding lessons, *Monsieur*.'

'There is no time for such luxuries, Pamplemousse!'
barked the Director. 'You will hardly need lessons in order
to travel the hundred metres or so up the driveway to the
Villa ... A child of five could do it blindfold.

'In any case, I am not asking you to spring from the
saddle as if you were representing France in the Olympics.
Help will be near at hand.'

'But I am not insured,' protested Monsieur Pamplemousse.

The Director picked up his telephone receiver. 'I will get
Madame Grante to deal with the matter immediately. She
can arrange for a cover note to be issued. All it needs is a
simple document. Fire and theft are hardly necessary. Third
party possibly ...'

'It is not the third party I am worried about, *Monsieur*.'

'Pamplemousse! I do not wish to hear another word.

'I have arranged for you to meet Mrs Van Dorman
tomorrow morning at the Hôtel de Crillon where she is
staying. I will accompany you to effect an introduction,
then I must leave you. It so happens I have an appointment
there for *déjeuner*.'

Monsieur Pamplemousse listened to the Director with a

growing sense of doom, wondering if there was more to come. He hadn't long to wait for an answer.

'One last thing before you go …' The Director opened his desk drawer again and took out a small wicker-work container. Undoing the lid, he withdrew a graduated tumbler. 'You may as well take this. It will save buying a new one. I used it once a long time ago when I was taking the cure at Vichy. I have washed it out, but if I were you I would give it another rinse before using it. My wife finds it useful when she is spraying the roses for greenfly.'

He slid the drawer shut. 'You are fortunate to be going now. The season proper begins on 15th June, so you will miss the worst of the rush. After the 15th you can hardly get into the 'Palais des Sources' for fear of being crushed by what our American friends call *les Wrinklies*.

'*A votre santé*, Aristide. We will touch base at the Hôtel de Crillon tomorrow.'

2
FAMOUS LAST WORDS

Fresh from a last-minute briefing at *Le Guide*'s headquarters off the esplanade des Invalides, Monsieur Pamplemousse crossed the Seine by the pont de l'Alma, turned right along the cours Albert l, negotiated the stream of traffic thundering round the place de la Concorde, and drew up outside the Hôtel de Crillon at precisely twelve noon.

As a commissionaire came forward to greet them, the Director consulted his watch. 'Good work, Pamplemousse,' he exclaimed. 'I must say ...'

Monsieur Pamplemousse never did discover what further accolade his chief was about to bestow on him, for the sentence remained unfinished, cut off in mid-flight as it were, as its begetter suddenly vanished out of the side of the car.

The look of disbelief on the Director's face as he disappeared from view was equalled only by that of the commissionaire as he stood clutching the door of Monsieur Pamplemousse's car, unsure whether to give priority to restoring it to its rightful place or rendering assistance to the figure sprawled on the pavement at his feet.

'*Pardon, Monsieur.*' The man's normal air of aplomb deserted him as he made a fumbling attempt to hook the door back on. 'Such a thing has never happened to me before.'

'You will be hearing from my *avocat* in the morning,' said Monsieur Pamplemousse coldly. 'It may teach you to take more care in future.' He leaned across and peered out at the Director.

'I am sorry, *Monsieur*, but I did warn you. As I said in your office only yesterday, since Madame Pamplemousse had her accident, opening the door is not always easy. It is an acquired knack.'

The Director stared up at him. 'It might have become detached while we were going along!' he exclaimed. 'What then?'

'Oh, no, *Monsieur*. Once it is shut it is shut. It is when anyone tries to open it that trouble begins.'

The Director rose to his feet and dusted himself down. 'I trust it doesn't happen *en route* to Vichy. I shall never forgive myself if Mrs Van Dorman is deposited on the *autoroute*. The repercussions if she happened to be struck by a passing *camion* do not bear thinking about.'

He turned abruptly on his heels and waited by the entrance long enough for Monsieur Pamplemousse to carry out the necessary repairs, then led the way into the hotel.

'Henri!' As they entered the foyer a tall, elegant woman in her late thirties rose to greet them. Monsieur Pamplemousse caught a whiff of perfume, strong and assertive. It was not one he recognised; probably one of her own manufacture. He was aware, too, of an unexpectedly healthy tan enhancing a smile which revealed whiter than white, slightly protruding teeth. Dark sunglasses rested on a pile of blonde hair, cut to within an inch of the collar of an immaculate two-piece suit. It was not what he would have chosen for a long journey in a 2CV.

The Director was already into his 'Welcome to France' routine; an essay in Gallic gallantry. The meeting of the eyes, the slight bow, the delicate clasping of the fingertips as he raised them to his lips; the uttering of the single word '*Enchanté*' in a tone half an octave lower than normal. Mrs Van Dorman looked as though she had encountered it on previous occasions, but wasn't averse to a repeat performance.

As he was carrying out the latter part of his routine the Director gave a slight start.

'You are prepared for the journey I see.'

Monsieur Pamplemousse glanced down. In striking contrast to the rest of her outfit, Mrs Van Dorman was sporting a pair of brightly coloured designer sneakers.

'I use them when I travel. I went for an early morning jog round the Tuileries. It makes a change from Central Park. It's like I always say, a healthy body is a healthy mind.'

'I hope you are listening, Pamplemousse,' said the Director pointedly.

'*Comment?*' Monsieur Pamplemousse did his best to suppress a shudder as the Director introduced him to their guest. 'I am afraid my Eenglish is, 'ow do you say? a little covered in rust.'

Conscious that the Director was glaring at him across Mrs Van Dorman's shoulder, he was about to emulate the other's welcome when he thought better of it. Instead he contented himself with a brief handshake. It was reciprocated coolly but firmly. As he let go, he gave a quick glance round the foyer, half expecting to see Doucette lurking behind a potted palm. He wouldn't have put it past her. His edited version of all that had passed between himself and the Director had not gone down as well as he had hoped; the seeds of suspicion had been sown. Given the fact that Mrs Van Dorman didn't match up in any way whatsoever with his description, the quicker they made their getaway the happier he would be. Better safe than sorry.

'I am sure you will have things to talk about with *Monsieur Le Directeur,*' he said. 'If you will allow me I will supervise the loading of the luggage.'

The Director eyed him approvingly. 'A good idea, Pamplemousse. And ... *bonne chance.* I shall await your report with interest.'

Not quite certain how to take the last remark, Monsieur Pamplemousse made his way out of the Hôtel to the side door in the rue Boissy d'Anglas, where the baggage of the rich and famous normally came and went.

His heart sank as he took in a pile of monogrammed valises waiting on a trolley just outside the entrance. They looked like an advertisement for a complete set of round-the-world baggage. He knew even before he saw the initials on the side whom they belonged to. Already he could see problems with Pommes Frites.

The porter's eyes said it all as Monsieur Pamplemousse led the way back into the *place* and stopped by his car. The commissionaire, his white gloves streaked with black oil, studiously turned his back on them. Monsieur Pamplemousse reached for his wallet. In a world where most things had a price he felt he could be in for an expensive time.

He became aware of the perfume again and turned to find Mrs Van Dorman standing just behind him.

'Do we have to go to all this trouble?' she asked. 'There must be an easier way. Can't we get the Car Jockey to bring the motor here, or else ask the Bell Captain to organise the porters to take the baggage straight to the car? It can't be that far away.'

'This *is* the car,' said Monsieur Pamplemousse.

Mrs Van Dorman gazed at him thoughtfully. 'You know what I thought you said?'

'*Comment?*' Monsieur Pamplemousse sought refuge in the language barrier again. 'I am afraid you will have to talk slowly. *Lentement s'il vous plaît.*'

'Oh, God!' It was hard to tell what Mrs Van Dorman might be thinking behind her dark glasses, now firmly in place over her eyes.

'As you see,' said Monsieur Pamplemousse, rolling back the canvas roof, 'the top comes away.'

'Along with the door?' The Director had obviously been recounting his experience.

'It is what we call a *deux chevaux.*'

'It looks more like a *faux pas* to me. In America we call it a roll-top desk.'

Even with the roof open, Mrs Van Dorman's luggage took up almost the whole of the back seat, rising up through the opening like a miniature Eiffel Tower. Squeezed into what little space there was left behind the passenger seat, Pommes Frites assumed one of his mournful expressions. He kept a stock of them especially for such occasions. Clearly the seating arrangements did not meet with his approval. In Pommes Frites' opinion anyone who travelled with that amount of luggage should personally suffer the consequences and not visit them on others.

They took the Porte d'Orléans exit out of Paris and then drove via the *Périphérique* on to the A6 autoroute. Even simple pleasantries like 'the Director is a nice man' (a statement which elicited a slightly less than enthusiastic '*oui*' from Monsieur Pamplemousse) and 'I should make sure your seat belt is tight in case the door falls off again' (greeted with even less enthusiasm by Mrs Van Dorman), which had served to break the ice while driving the length of the boulevard Raspail, dwindled away to nothing as heavy lorries roared past on either side of them. For the time being the noise of their engines drowned any further attempt at conversation.

Mrs Van Dorman, who had been growing steadily more restless as time went by, began shifting about in her seat as though she was trying to escape something unpleasant. As they stopped at the toll barrier just before entering the Forest of Fontainebleau she reached down and felt inside a black leather case at her feet.

Monsieur Pamplemousse glanced across with interest as she produced a Filofax built like a miniature desk which she spread out on her lap.

'I have a secret compartment in my right trouser leg,' he said as they moved off. 'It was made for me by Madame Pamplemousse. You will never guess what I keep in there.'

'I think I'd rather not know.'

Glancing nervously at the woods on either side, Mrs Van Dorman buried herself in an instruction booklet for a moment or two, then pressed a series of keys. A loud bleep emerged, followed by an electronic voice with Japanese overtones. Monsieur Pamplemousse made out the words 'Spume, foam, spindrift, meringue and nimbostratus'. It seemed an unlikely combination.

'Shit!' Mrs Van Dorman seemed to be expressing disappointment rather than searching for a further synonym.

'You have a problem?'

'Why is it you can look up every kind of goddamn eventuality except the one you want. If I go to the dentist and he takes out the wrong tooth I can tell him to put it back in six different languages, but ask it something simple ...'

'What is the word you are looking for?'

'Dribble.'

'*Comment?*'

'Dribble. Your dog happens to be dribbling down the back of my neck.'

Monsieur Pamplemousse narrowly avoided careering out of his lane and into the barrier as he stole a quick glance over his shoulder. Pommes Frites, the lower part of his jaw joined to the nape of Mrs Van Dorman's neck by a rivulet of viscous liquid, returned his gaze unblinkingly.

'*Mon Dieu!*' Monsieur Pamplemousse regained control of the car. 'It is probably the heat. In French we use the word *dégouter.*' There were others he could think of. The phrase 'Every dog has his day' sprang to mind.

Mrs Van Dorman snapped her case shut. 'You want to know something? I'm past caring. Right? It feels the same in any language. Right?'

'*D'accord!*' Monsieur Pamplemousse felt inside his pocket.

'Would you care for a *mouchoir* – a handkerchief?' As he removed a freshly ironed square of white linen from an inside pocket and unfolded it, something round and black fell out on to Mrs Van Dorman's lap. It looked like a badly squashed beetle.

'Jesus! What's that?' Only the seat belt prevented her disappearing through the open roof.

'It is a raisin – an aid to digestion. I have been reading Monsieur Dumas' *Grand Dictionnaire de Cuisine*. In it he recommends eating several large raisins after a meal. They need to be seeded, of course.'

Mrs Van Dorman greeted the news in silence.

Monsieur Pamplemousse made a mental note to stick to the main roads. He had entertained thoughts of showing his guest something of France on the way to Vichy, perhaps taking in the cathedral of Notre-Dame at Chartres, or making a detour via the hardwood forest of Troncais which had been laid down by Louis XIV's farsighted minister, Colbert. But it was no time for history lessons. He decided to stick to the shortest route possible. Pommes Frites had a tendency to feel indisposed if he sat in the back for too long and the signs were not good.

'The book is full of interesting facts,' he continued, a note of desperation in his voice. 'Did you know, *par exemple*, that when the storks fly south for the winter and they rest for the night, the ones who are on guard duty stand on one leg in order to conceal a pebble in their other claw. Thus, if they fall asleep they will relax their grip on the pebble and the sound of it hitting the ground will cause them to wake.'

'I have to say I didn't know that.' Mrs Van Dorman gave him a strange look.

'Another interesting fact,' said Monsieur Pamplemousse, 'is that one ostrich egg is equal to ten hens' eggs.'

'I can't wait to tell my cook next time I ask her to make me an omelette.'

'There is also an interesting section on bakers and baking,' said Monsieur Pamplemousse defensively. Mentally, he was beginning to agree with Pommes Frites' summing up of the situation. Since Mrs Van Dorman was helping to organise the banquet, the least she could do was show a little interest in the subject.

His thought waves evidently struck home. 'Your English is better than you let on,' said Mrs Van Dorman. 'Tell me about where we are going.'

'Vichy?' Glad to be on firmer ground at last, Monsieur Pamplemousse considered the question for a moment or two. 'Vichy is ... Vichy. It is like nowhere else. You will see when you get there. To me, its one great asset is that it happens to be on the edge of the Auvergne, and the Auvergne is on the edge of another world; part of the Massif Central. Six hundred million years ago there was a cataclysmic upheaval of the ground. In consequence it is a landscape full of strange nooks and crannies. Everywhere you go you will see patches of black lava, and dotted about the countryside there are *puys* – unlikely peaks formed by the molten lava.

'People from the Auvergne are renowned for keeping their wealth under the mattress. They also bottle it. All over the area there are spas where the water gushes up out of the ground – sometimes hot, sometimes cold. Ever since Roman times people have gone there for their health; to St Nectaire for the kidneys, Royat for the heart, Le Mont Dore for asthma and to Vichy for the digestion. There are many more besides. Each town has its speciality.

'In the spring the countryside is alive with wild flowers; cowslips, celandines, snowdrops and daffodils. You open the car window as you drive along and you can smell their perfume. There are trout and salmon and crayfish in the streams and the hills are covered with yellow gorse. In summer it can be very hot. In the autumn there are crocus and spiraea.

'But I am prejudiced. It is where I was born.'

'If it's so perfect, why did you leave?'

'For the same reason as everyone else. What I have been describing is only true for part of the year. There is a price to pay for everything – especially perfection.

'The winters are cold and hard. If you live in a remote village you can be snowed up for weeks on end. There is little work. When the railways came it was hoped they would bring prosperity to the region; instead the men took advantage of it to leave home for the capital. Even the success of the spas turned against them. People began to feel that if they could buy the water at home, why bother to make the journey. Traditionally those who left became restaurateurs; they set up the first *bals musettes*; Paris became known as the biggest city in the Auvergne.'

'Have you ever thought of becoming a *restaurateur*?'

'Often. Then I go behind the scenes and I change my mind. It is also a hard life. Working for *Le Guide* I have the best of both worlds.'

They drove in silence for a while, but it was a different silence this time.

'If there is time,' said Monsieur Pamplemousse, 'I would like to take you into the mountains.'

'It makes a change from being asked to look at etchings!'

'*Comment?*'

'I'm sorry. I'm being crabby. The truth is I have bad vibes about this trip.'

'Vibes? I am sorry. I do not understand.'

'Vibrations. Feelings. Have you ever tried acting as nursemaid to six authors? Individually they're fine. But together … yuch!'

'Is that why you are not travelling with them? As tour leader should you not be with your troops?'

'Are you kidding? I don't mind laying on the feast; it's good publicity and we can go to town on it in the next issue. But before and after it they can look after themselves. On the surface everything is sweetness and light, but underneath it all they're as jealous as hell of each other. Do you know something? Before I left New York we had a meeting in my office. I happened to have a book written by one of them on my desk. One of the others threw it in the trash can. He made it seem like a joke, but I caught the look on his face.'

'Why do they go then?'

'Search me. I guess it's one of those things – they've been doing it for years and once you start a thing it's hard to stop. Anyway, they've all been in Annecy on some kind of mystery writers' festival. They're coming on to Vichy under their own steam.'

'Tell me about them.'

'What do you know?'

'I know only their names.' Monsieur Pamplemousse felt in a folder below his seat. The Director had given him a list that morning during the briefing.

Without taking his eyes off the road he handed a sheet of paper to Mrs Van Dorman. She scanned it briefly.

'Harvey Wentworth specialises in culinary mysteries.'

'Don't they all?'

'To a greater or lesser extent. But Harvey's hero is the only one who is actually a chef. He solves all his mysteries over a hot stove. *The Case of the Sagging Soufflé, Stoolpigeon Pie, Dinner for Two and a Half, Mayhem with Mustard*. His restaurant has such a high casualty rate you wonder why anyone ever goes there. He's a reviewer's delight; they can let loose with all the puns in the book. On the other hand, he knows his onions, if you'll pardon an unintentional one. He often writes for our magazine under the pseudonym of Harvey Cook.

'Then there's Harman Lock. His hero is a classical conductor who happens to be a mixture of gourmet cum detective on the side. *Schubert's Third* was all about a little old violinist called Arnold Schubert who had just one incurable weakness: little old ladies. He used to invite them up to his room to hear him play "Air on a G String", wait until they had their eyes closed, then garotte them.'

The last service area before the D7 spur beyond Nemours came and went. Monsieur Pamplemousse sensed Pommes Frites' disappointment. Pommes Frites was good on autoroute signs – especially those that had to do with food. He could recognise a set of crossed knives and forks a kilometre away. The car swayed slightly as he shifted his weight to look back the way they had come.

'Ed Morgan, on the other hand, writes tough gangster novels full of one-liners, with as many dead bodies to match. They have to run a shuttle service to the morgue at the end of every book while the hero goes off to a lay his current girl-friend after a good homespun all-American cook-out of clam chowder followed by planked charcoal-grilled porterhouse steak, washed down by ice-cold Budweiser. His speciality is the dressing that goes with the salad. The girls can't refuse it. He has the knack of making the simple act of opening a tin of sweetcorn and stir-frying it in a saucepan sound like heaven.'

'That takes more than a knack. That takes genius. I wish I could do that.'

Mrs Van Dorman looked at him suspiciously. 'Are you taking the mickey?'

'I am being totally serious. I never knock other people's success. If I had that kind of talent it might help to sell more copies of *Le Guide*. Except the Director would never allow it.'

'When Ed Morgan writes about food, I get hungry.'

'You are hungry now?'

'I thought you'd never ask. Maybe we could pull in off the *autoroute* somewhere and grab a snack. Or get something for a picnic?'

'I'm afraid I don't have my table and chairs with me. I

613

had to leave them out otherwise we wouldn't have got all the luggage in.'

'Do we need a table and chairs? Can't we just find a patch of grass somewhere. I could do with a good stretch.'

Monsieur Pamplemousse took the spur road. 'Only corrupt people – like the Romans and the Ancient Greeks – or those who don't care about their food lie down to eat. I know of a restaurant not far from here. It is nothing special, but for many years it has earned itself a bar stool in *Le Guide.*'

The girl at the *péage* gave Mrs Van Dorman a look of commiseration as she relieved them of 12 francs. She probably thought they were moving house on the cheap. If he'd been on his own she might well have charged commercial rates.

'Tell me about the others.' Monsieur Pamplemousse slowed down to join the N7. 'How about … what is the name? Monsieur Robard. I have seen his name in bookshops.'

'Paul K. Robard? Paul K. Robard has struck a rich seam in soft porn. He writes for American housewives who work out their fantasies in the long, lonely afternoons. I'm told he's good on research too! His particular forte is recipes with sexual overtones. Five hundred unputdownable pages full of people sinking their teeth into warm, juicy peaches covered in sugar and cream, washed down with a bottle of Château d'Yquem or whatever Californian equivalent is currently available in the local supermarkets – he always makes sure he has a tie-in of some kind. The fact that the peaches may have been steeped in arsenic is beside the point. He has more fan mail than Michael Jackson. On a hot summer afternoon the bedrooms of America must be awash with scantily clad housewives drooling over their pillows.'

614

As they passed through Montargis Monsieur Pamplemousse found himself wondering if Mr Van Dorman had
ever come home early and found his wife covered in peach
juice, drooling over her pillow. It sounded unlikely – she
probably worked late at the office too. Perhaps the Van
Dormans were too busy ever to meet up.

Sensing from her silence he was on delicate ground,
Monsieur Pamplemousse glanced across at the list. 'And
Elliott Garner?'

'Elliott? He's the odd one out. He keeps himself to
himself. I guess his books are more intellectual than the
others; more wide ranging. He travels a lot. His hero is apt
to sit on his hacienda nibbling dry biscuits over an even
drier sherry. Do you know about sherry?'

Monsieur Pamplemousse shook his head.

'Then you should try reading *Bad Deeds at the Bodega*.
By the time you've finished it you'll know everything there
is to know, including the ins and outs of cask making …
where the wood comes from … what particular part of the
forest. How they bend it the way they do. He's meticulous
on detail. If Elliott says something happened a certain way,
you can bet your bottom dollar that's the way it was.

'This whole trip was Elliott's idea. It's his turn this year,
and I'll tell you something – if nothing else it'll be well
documented. Elliott's a keen photographer. And it'll go like
clockwork. Not like last year when they let Spencer Troon
loose and he organised a get-together in an old Death Row
cell at Alcatraz.'

Monsieur Pamplemousse pondered for a moment on
what a condemned man might choose to eat. 'I know what
my last meal would be.'

'I wonder? I'm not sure I'd want anything – I'd be too
sick with fear. The whole thing was a disaster anyway. They

picked on a multiple murderer who happened to be vegetarian. Vegan at that! They had water to drink. Can you imagine?

'Spencer's high on ideas but low on research. His middle name is "Wallow". He revels in the macabre. You only have to read the list of his book titles to see the type of mind he's got: *Clinging Slime*, *Pus … Pus …* , *Death by Ordure*, *Worms in the Caviar …*' Mrs Van Dorman broke off and peered out of the window as Monsieur Pamplemousse turned off the road and parked in the last available space between a giant DAF lorry and trailer with a Dutch number plate and an even larger Mercedes from Germany.

'Is this it? The place is full of freight trucks.'

'That is because it is a *Relais Routier*. I am not sure, but they may even have awarded it a casserole at one point.'

'You French! Stock Pots … stars … toques … casseroles. You have it all tied up.'

'Life is for living,' said Monsieur Pamplemousse simply. 'Besides, to have so many *camions* outside a restaurant is a recommendation in itself.'

Mrs Van Dorman took a quick check of her appearance in the driving mirror. 'Go ahead. I'm in your hands.'

As they entered the packed restaurant there was a noticeable drop in noise level for a moment or two. Then it resumed as everyone went on with their eating.

Monsieur Pamplemousse spotted an empty table for two halfway down one wall and, after exchanging formal greetings with three men at the next table, pulled a chair out for Mrs Van Dorman.

Mrs Van Dorman looked round curiously as she sat down. 'You know something, this wouldn't happen in America.'

'You mean … rubbing shoulders with lorry drivers? Why

not? I have always thought of America as a democratic society.'

'It is, but it is also a matriarchal society and a moneyed one too. Most women who could afford it wouldn't be seen dead in a place like this.'

'Do you mind?'

'I don't mind, but if I'd known I would have dressed differently.' She gave a sniff. 'Can you smell something funny?'

Monsieur Pamplemousse glanced around him. 'It is probably a compilation; an amalgam of many smells which have permeated the woodwork over the years. *Pot au feu*, *navarin*, *café*, *Gauloise* ...'

'I majored in chemistry when I was at college,' said Mrs Van Dorman. 'And it isn't any of those. There's something else.'

Monsieur Pamplemousse wondered if he should point out that it might have something to do with the fact that the door leading to the toilet was just behind Mrs Van Dorman's left ear, but he forbore.

'It is perhaps nothing more than honest sweat. When you have been cooped up in a hot cab all morning ...' He took refuge in the *carte*.

The solitary waitress slapped a basket of freshly sliced baguette on the table, glanced across at another table, shouted '*Commencez la tarte*' in the direction of an open hatch at the far end of the room, then stood by with a pencil poised over her pad. It boded well.

'*Vous avez choisi?*'

At a nod from Mrs Van Dorman, Monsieur Pample-mousse took charge.

He gave a quick look round the other tables and ordered the soup of the day followed by *cassoulet*.

'You know it?'

Mrs Van Dorman shook her head. 'I know of it, but I've never eaten it.'

'Ah, then you are in for a treat. From the menu I suspect the owners are from that area. We will also have a Côtes de Rhône.'

Monsieur Pamplemousse slapped the *carte* shut and handed it to the waitress. He would reserve judgement on the sweet until he'd seen what the others were eating. If the *tarte* were freshly made it could be good.

'They don't waste much time.'

'With only one waitress and forty *couverts* they can't afford to. It is a study in time and motion, perfected over the years.'

The wine arrived in a cream and brown *pichet*, along with a *carafe* of water and a plate and bowl of water for Pommes Frites.

While they were waiting for the first course Mrs Van Dorman removed a photograph from her bag and laid it on the table.

'Take a look at what you're letting yourself in for.'

It was like all group photographs. It could have been a party of chartered accountants getting ready for their annual conference, or *Le Guide*'s staff outing in Normandy.

'They don't look as I imagined they would from the things you have already told me.'

'Who does in this world?'

That was true. Mrs Van Dorman didn't for a start. He caught a glimpse of something crisply white and taut as she leaned forward and pointed to a slight, bespectacled figure in the centre of the group.

'That's Jed Powers. And in case you're wondering why that makes seven when there are only six in the picture, it's also Ed Morgan, and if you think Ed Morgan writes toughies you should read Jed Powers. Jed Powers makes Ed Morgan read like Snow White and the Seven Dwarfs.'

'Now that does surprise me.'

'It surprises everyone who meets him. His real name's Norm Ellis and Norm Ellis is not only a hypochondriac with a capital H, he's frightened of his own shadow. The story goes that he passed out on the way over because he found a spider in the aircraft toilet and was in such a hurry to escape its clutches he couldn't unlock the door. It took two stewardesses and half a bottle of Scotch to bring him round. Everybody who reads his books thinks they're auto-biographical, but the truth of the matter is he's so unlike his heroes his publishers daren't let him go on a promotion tour for fear of what it might do to the sales figures. He's their biggest money-spinner. He has two desks in his study and a chair on a set of rails so that he can work on the film script at the same time as he writes a book.

'Have you read *Lay Me Down to Die*?'

Monsieur Pamplemousse was forced to admit he hadn't.

'Maybe it isn't over here yet, but it will be. He's in over thirty languages. It's been on the *New York Times* Best Seller list for over six months. For a crime novel that has to be something of a record, much to the disgust of all who know him. I'm afraid our Norm is very adept at stealing other people's ideas, putting them all into the mixing-bowl he calls his head and coming out with something which he likes to think is all his own. Funnily enough, the really tough bits are. They crackle like an electric pylon in a thunderstorm.'

The soup of the day was leek and potato. Sprigs of chervil had been added and it came with croutons and a bowl of grated *Gruyère*. It was more than adequate: a meal in itself.

The *cassoulet* arrived in the pot in which it had been cooked. It was the Castelnaudary version – made without mutton or lamb, but with haricot beans, *saucisses* of the area, pork and ham. The pot was left on the table.

Monsieur Pamplemousse served two generous portions, then put some on Pommes Frites plate; a little sausage and a portion of ham. He went easy on the beans. There was no point in asking for trouble and they still had some 250 kilometres to go.

'There is much rivalry as to which is the true version. In Carcassonne they use mutton. In Toulouse they add tomato. To be truly authentic the one we are eating should have been cooked in an oven fired with gorse from the Montagne Noire. It imparts a special flavour.'

'Tell me something. How can a nation with such abysmal taste in décor serve such wonderful food?'

Monsieur Pamplemousse looked around the room. Walls panelled with plywood in imitation matchboard; radiators with inset doors for tiny heating stoves in winter supported shelves laden with china flower-filled ducks; light fittings made of wrought iron; the patterned stone-tiled floor worn almost bare in places; pink table-cloths sporting plastic imitation straw mats; a board covered with wine labels advertising Ed. Kressman et Cie., alongside pictures of humanised dogs doing unseemly things to each other with evident enjoyment; wooden, hardbacked chairs. It was par for the course. There were thousands of places like it all over France. It wasn't the best he had ever seen, but he felt compelled to rise to its defence.

'It is a question of priorities. The food is good – that is the main thing. You might just as well ask how a nation who are able to put men on the moon and take photographs of Mars can commit so many atrocities when it comes to cooking? I have read that you cook steak in Coca-Cola.'

'You're just prejudiced. I could take you places ... Le Cirque and Lafayette in New York. Chez Panisse in Berkeley ...'

'So could I. You mustn't judge France by what you see here. I could take you to places where the décor and the plumbing would put anything in America to shame.'

'I bet you never put maple syrup on top of your pancakes or cinnamon on top of the coffee foam, or eat blueberry corn muffins, or put balsamic vinegar on your raspberries.' It was Mrs Van Dorman's turn to be on the defensive. 'You should try that some time. Sprinkle sugar on top and leave them to soak for two or three hours.'

'That happens to be an Italian way of doing it.'

'You French are so chauvinist. If it wasn't invented by a Frenchman it might just as well not exist.'

'We did invent the word restaurant,' said Monsieur Pamplemousse mildly. 'They came about when a certain Monsieur Boulanger began selling soups which he called "restoratives".'

While the waitress's back was turned Mrs Van Dorman surreptitiously scraped what was left on her plate into Pommes Frites' dish. 'I'm not going to make it.'

'For what it is worth, you have made a friend for life.'

'If he helps me out he'll have one too!'

Monsieur Pamplemousse wiped the inside of the tureen with the remains of his bread, toyed with the idea of ordering *tarte aux pommes*, then called for *café* and the bill instead.

'This one is on me.' Mrs Van Dorman touched the back of his hand lightly for a moment as she reached for her bag. 'I'm sorry if I'm being crabby. It's like I said earlier – I shan't rest until all this is over.'

Getting back into the car was less easily accomplished than it had been on the first occasion. Once settled, Pommes Frites closed his eyes and was soon fast asleep. It wasn't long before Mrs Van Dorman did likewise.

Feeling inside the secret pocket of his right trouser leg, Monsieur Pamplemousse helped himself from a store of raisins. He chewed on it reflectively as he drove, wondering what he had let himself in for.

Halfway between Nevers and Moulins, feeling in need of some company, he turned on the radio and was just in time to catch the tail end of an item about Vichy. A man – as yet unidentified – had died while taking the waters. It must have only just happened for the details were very sketchy. No more than the bare facts. In all probability the authorities would try and play it down anyway. It wouldn't be very good publicity.

He was glad Mrs Van Dorman wasn't awake to hear it. She might have had her worst fears confirmed.

It was the middle of the evening by the time they arrived. As he tried to move his stiff and aching limbs into action, Monsieur Pamplemousse reflected they must look as though they were in Vichy for the cure, and none too soon either. Like two superannuated jockeys, they mounted the well-worn steps of the Hôtel Thermale Splendide, negotiated as best they could the vast revolving door, and checked in at the desk. Pommes Frites chose to wait outside. He mistrusted revolving doors.

Complaining that she might never walk again, let alone eat, Mrs Van Dorman said goodnight and disappeared into the lift along with her luggage and an elderly night porter with a long-suffering look on his face. Having committed his own bag to temporary safe-keeping at the desk, Monsieur Pamplemousse took Pommes Frites for a walk in the Parc des Sources by the river.

The sky was blue and cloudless; the water sparkling in the evening light. He'd forgotten how wide the Allier was at that point. Taking off from a strip of sandy beach, Pommes Frites essayed a quick dip in the river. Monsieur Pamplemousse could hardly blame him – he wouldn't have minded one himself, but given the fact that they would be sharing a room that night it wasn't the best news he'd had that day.

While he was waiting he stopped by a small riverside café and ordered a sandwich and a bottle of beer.

'Bad news about the death today.'

The man behind the counter gave a shrug. 'It's a wonder it doesn't happen more often when you look at some of the people who go there. Not that this one was old. Only in his forties, so they say.' He poured half the beer into a glass. 'Bet you can't guess what his last words were.'

It was the kind of question Monsieur Pamplemousse could have done without at the end of a long and tiring drive, but fortunately it was rhetorical.

'Bring me a bottle of Bâtard Montrachet and some fish.'

Monsieur Pamplemousse expressed suitable surprise.

'Now, I bet you're going to ask me "what year?" and "what sort of fish?".'

As it happened it was the last thing on Monsieur Pamplemousse's mind, but clearly he was stuck with the subject until he'd finished his snack. The man seemed glad of a new audience for a story he'd obviously repeated many times.

'He didn't specify!'

'I think,' said Monsieur Pamplemousse, 'in similar circumstances I would have tempered desire with availability. I would have settled for a bottle of Muscadet and some lobster – a cold lobster, with mayonnaise and a little green salad.'

623

'Me, I'd have chosen a good *vin rouge* and *steak frites*.'

Several others round the bar nodded their agreement. They were about to join in when Pommes Frites, having heard his name mentioned, arrived on the scene and set about shaking himself dry.

Monsieur Pamplemousse gave him the remains of his sandwich, then beat a hasty retreat. On the way back through the old part of the town he looked for a *tabac-journaux* in the hope of buying a newspaper, but they were all closed. He toyed with the idea of searching out the house where the banquet was to take place – it was somewhere near the Pavillon Sévigné, one-time home of France's most famous letter writer, the Marquise de Sevigne – but he thought better of it. His mind was on other things. Something of Mrs Van Dorman's sense of unease had entered into him and all he really wanted to do was go to bed and get some sleep.

To his relief when he arrived back at the Hôtel his room was already prepared for the night; the shutters were wound down over the balcony window and the bed sheets had been turned back.

Too tired to have more than a token wash, Monsieur Pamplemousse reserved the luxury of a bath until morning and climbed straight into bed. He had hardly settled down and made himself comfortable when the telephone rang. He groped for the receiver.

'Aristide?'

It was Mrs Van Dorman. She was one up on him. He had no idea what her Christian name might be.

'*Oui.*'

'It's DiAnn … Can I ask you something?'

'Of course.' He wondered what was coming.

'Do you think it's safe to drink the water?'

It wasn't until he had put the phone down and turned out the light once again that the irony of the question struck him. It was a good job Mrs Van Dorman had asked him and not the night porter. The latter might well have taken umbrage.

On the other hand ... he closed his eyes, allowing himself the luxury of drifting to sleep on thoughts which floated in and out of his mind like the waves of an incoming tide ... on the other hand, there was one person in Vichy who might well have had a different answer had he still been alive to voice it.

3
TROUBLED WATERS

Monsieur Pamplemousse woke to the sound of a road cleaning machine making its early morning rounds outside the Hôtel. If the noise was anything to go by, the driver was a strong union man. One up the lot up.

Pommes Frites opened one jaundiced eye and, when he saw the room was still in semi-darkness, closed it again. Monsieur Pamplemousse tried following suit for a while, but he had too much on his mind to go back to sleep and in the end he got out of bed and wound open the shutter covering the balcony window. Then he opened the door and went outside.

The road below was still gleaming where it had been freshly sprayed with water; the locals must be expecting the early summer they had been enjoying to stay for a while. The temperature in Paris had been in the upper seventies; today looked as though it might be even hotter. Looking eastwards over the rooftops he could barely make out the foothills of the Monts de la Madeleine, some twenty kilometres away, for the intervening countryside was shrouded in a heat haze.

Monsieur Pamplemousse looked at his watch. It was already nine o'clock. He hadn't slept so late in years.

While he was shaving he ran the bath. It was a giant of a thing, with taps and pipework to match; the product of a bygone age. Undoubtedly it would confirm Mrs Van

Dorman's worst suspicions about French plumbing. On the other hand, she couldn't have grumbled about the water. It was what his old mother would have called 'piping hot'. In its heyday the Hôtel must have needed a boiler the size of an ocean liner's. At least it still worked, which was more than could be said for the row of bell-pushes alongside the bed; one marked *Femme de Chambre*, another *Valet de Chambre* and a third *Sommelier*. At some point in time the wires had been severed at the skirting board, the paint-covered ends still protruded from beneath the well-worn patterned carpet. As he lay back in the bath, Monsieur Pamplemousse reflected on how nice it must have been to stay in bed of a morning and summon help from all directions when you felt like it, instead of having to hang a breakfast order on a door knob outside the room the night before.

One came across such places from time to time, mostly in old spa towns or once fashionable seaside resorts. Dinosaurs of the Hôtel trade, they were mostly staffed by old retainers who had nowhere else to go, and when they died the Hôtel would die too.

Hearing the sound of splashing, Pommes Frites came into the room and rested his chin on the side of the bath. Even he looked a little taken aback by its size. Monsieur Pamplemousse hoped it wouldn't occur to him that there was room for them both, or even that he should essay an attempt to rescue his master.

He was saved by a knock on the outer door, reminding him that he'd ordered his breakfast for nine-fifteen.

'*Entrez!*' Reaching for the flannel, he sank down into the water.

The chambermaid was unperturbed. '*Sur le balcon, Monsieur?*' She didn't give him time to reply as she bustled past the open bathroom door carrying a tray. There was a rattle of crockery from somewhere outside and the sound of chairs being moved, then a '*Bon appétit, Monsieur,*' and she was gone again.

She was right, of course. It was no morning for sitting in one's room eating *croissants* by electric light.

Swathed in a voluminous towelling dressing-gown, courtesy of the Hôtel, Monsieur Pamplemousse found the town plan the Director had provided him with, then went out on to the balcony and poured himself a cup of *café*.

He gazed across the town. Apart from a few desultory figures taking the air, the Parc des Sources was deserted. Dozens of white, wrought-iron chairs were scattered in small groups along the crisscrossing paths as though waiting for something to happen, their filigree backs casting photogenic shadows from the morning sun. Two workmen in blue overalls were busy attending to the steps in front of the Opera House, their besoms making long arcing motions as they swept all before them with the practised ease of those who performed the same task day in day out all through the year. A large billboard advertised a programme of opera music, but it was at too much of an angle for him to read the small print. A miniature white train appeared out of a side turning, crossed the street into the park and drew up on a path near the bandstand to await the first load of tourists for the day.

Monsieur Pamplemousse decided that if he had any time to spare he might load up his camera and set out on a voyage of exploration later in the day.

Vichy looked as though it had changed very little since his last visit; or even since he had been there as a small child. In those days it had been an annual treat, but that was before its name had gone down in history as the seat of wartime capitulation. He doubted if his parents had ever gone there again, such was their shame. The centre of the town was uniquely pre-war. Seedy in places, but still with a certain dignity.

True, it now had its modern side – the area by the river – the *Bassin International D'Aviron-Voile-Motonautisme - Ski* as it was grandly marked on the map; but the old part, the arcaded walks around the park, the antique shops, the kiosks selling 'Vichy Pastilles' and the facilities for 'taking the cure' were still there. Before the war visits to the spa had been the prerogative of the rich and well to do. Now it was mostly on the National Health.

He sat up and concentrated his attention on the far side of the park as a familiar figure came into view. It was Mrs Van Dorman, weaving her way in and out of the chairs as she returned from a jog.

She was wearing a dark blue towelling track suit, with a matching blue sweat-band round her forehead. She looked undeniably healthy. Healthy and chic. Central Park's loss was undoubtedly Vichy's gain. She was keeping up a fast pace – running rather than jogging. He wondered idly how she would look without her suit. In shorts perhaps? Would bare muscles ripple in the morning sun? It was one of life's little mysteries which would probably never be revealed.

Fancy asking if it was safe to drink the water! He couldn't wait to tell his colleagues back in the office. If it had been anyone else he might have suspected an ulterior motive behind the call, but as it was he felt on safe ground.

As Mrs Van Dorman drew near, Monsieur Pample-mousse saw she was carrying a tiny plaited straw case by its handle. It was similar in size to the one the Director had given him – *de rigueur* for anyone 'taking the cure'. Six times a day the Parc des Sources would be full of people carrying identical cases as they made their way to and fro between their Hôtel and the Hall at the far end. In between times the park would be almost empty again. Perhaps Mrs Van Dorman had bought a drinking glass as a souvenir for her husband, or she might even have decided to take the waters herself.

As she crossed the road and disappeared from view somewhere below him, Monsieur Pamplemousse turned back into his room. Seeing him go, a waiting sparrow fluttered down on to the table. Keeping one beady eye on Pommes Frites, it lost no time in pecking up the crumbs. Pommes Frites, for his part, eyed the bird with the air of one who couldn't be bothered with such trifles.

The maid had left a copy of *La Montagne* on a table in the room. Monsieur Pamplemousse picked it up and glanced at the headlines. Sport and agriculture seemed to be the dominant topics. It wasn't until he reached the back page that he came across the item he was looking for. It was under the headline VICHY TRADÉDIE – LE MYSTÉRE. There followed a non-committal statement from the local police to the effect that they were pursuing their inquiries, but it told him nothing new; rather less in fact, for there was no mention of the man's last request. Perhaps that bit of it was a joke on someone's part. It did sound highly unlikely. The whole thing was a journalistic exercise in filling up the maximum amount of space with the minimum number of facts. By tomorrow it probably wouldn't even get a mention.

Remembering that in his haste to have breakfast he hadn't emptied the bath Monsieur Pamplemousse went into the other room and turned a large wheel between the two taps. The water made an interesting noise as it ran away; a series of rhythmic bangs and thumps reminiscent of a blacksmith hard at work.

It was only after the last of the water had disappeared with an extra loud 'glug' that he realised the knocking was being augmented by someone outside. Cursing the maid under his breath for not leaving him in peace – she probably wanted the tray back so that she could get away early – he went into the bedroom and opened the door.

To his surprise it was Mrs Van Dorman. Her face was devoid of make-up and he realised for the first time how blue her eyes were; they matched her track suit. Holding the door open he was also very aware of the warmth from her body as she squeezed past him.

'Have you heard the news?'

'Tell me.'

'That man who died yesterday. The one in the spa. It was Norm Ellis.'

'Norm Ellis? *Morbleu*!' No wonder Mrs Van Dorman had been in a hurry. 'Is he not the short one with glasses who writes under several different names?'

'Right ... Ed Morgan ... Jed Powers and others he was trying hard to forget. Apparently he was tasting the waters in the Parc des Sources yesterday afternoon when he collapsed in a heap. It was all over before anyone could do anything. They called for an ambulance, but by the time it arrived he was dead.' Mrs Van Dorman swallowed hard. 'You're not going to believe the next bit.'

Monsieur Pamplemousse couldn't resist it. 'Before he died he asked for a bottle of Bâtard Montrachet and some fish.'

Mrs Van Dorman stared at him. 'How did you know that?'

'No matter. What I didn't know was that it was Monsieur Ellis. There was no mention of it in the *journal*.'

'But do you know something even stranger? According to the others Norm Ellis not only doesn't know one wine from another, but if you gave him a bottle and a corkscrew he wouldn't know which end to open without looking up the instructions. Budweiser is more his line.'

'*Extraordinaire!*'

'Is that all you can say? We're talking about Norm Ellis. The same Norm Ellis who's been on the best-seller lists for over six months. Someone's going to have to break the news to his publishers, and you know who that's going to be.'

'How about his wife?'

'He doesn't have a wife. He lives with his mother.'

'His mother, then.'

'I guess you're right. I'd better phone his agent.' Mrs Van Dorman looked at her watch. 'Anyway, I can leave it for a while. It'll be three o'clock in the morning there. I'm sorry ...' she perched herself on the edge of the bed, 'but I still can't believe it. I feel responsible in a way. If only I'd been here earlier.'

'Death comes to us all in the end,' said Monsieur Pamplemousse. 'Even to those who spend their life writing about it.' It sounded too sanctimonious for words, but it was all he could think of on the spur of the moment.

'But Norm of all people. He never goes outside the door without a medical. What a way to go – in a French spa!'

'Are you certain it was him?'

'It's Norm all right. It has to be. He checked in at his Hôtel yesterday lunchtime along with the others. Then he said he was off to take the waters and explore the town, so he might not be back until late. They all agreed to meet up for an early breakfast. It was only when he didn't put in an appearance that they started to get worried. When they checked his room they found the bed hadn't been slept in. All the others are convinced it's him. Spencer Troon is off to identify the body. Trust him. Offer Spencer a trip to the morgue and he's there like a shot.'

'You have seen the others already?' Monsieur Pamplemousse began to wish he'd asked for an early morning call. Everyone else seemed to have been up for hours.

'They're staying just down the road from here. I called in to see how they were doing. That's how I found out about Norm. They'd been trying to phone me.'

'How are they taking it?'

Mrs Van Dorman shrugged. 'OK, I guess. It's hard to say. It doesn't seem to have hit them yet. Harvey had gone back to his room by the time I got there, and Elliott was already round at the Villa Andre. It hasn't put the rest of them off their breakfast, that's for sure. They were tucking in like there was no tomorrow when I saw them. You know what Harman Lock said?'

Monsieur Pamplemousse shook his head. It was too early for guessing games.

'"Trust Norm to pull a fast one!" Anyone would think he'd done it on purpose.'

She held up the case she'd been carrying. 'Do you realise that's all we have left of him – apart from his luggage! Jesus – that's another thing. I guess I'll have to do something about that.'

Monsieur Pamplemousse stared at the case. 'You mean that was his? Where did you get it?'

'One of the attendants at the spa gave it to me. As soon as I said I was a personal friend she went to a cupboard and fished it out. They came across it yesterday after he had been taken away. Apparently some little old lady went off with it to see if she could get some wine for him and by the time she got back Norm had been taken away, so she handed it in.'

'May I see it?'

She hesitated for a moment before passing him the case. 'I guess maybe I ought to hand it over to the police, although it's hardly "exhibit A".'

Monsieur Pamplemousse turned it over in his hand. The initials N. E. were stamped on the leather fastener. Further proof of the identity of the corpse, if proof were needed.

'Would you like me to see them? I may be able to find out more.'

'Would you? That'd be great. If I go there could be a communication problem. There's just so far you can get with sign language. Besides, I've got so much to do today what with the banquet and now this.'

'You are still going ahead with it?'

'I guess so. It would be crazy not to after all the work that's gone into it. I tell myself Norm would have wanted it that way. Maybe he had it on his mind when he collapsed – that's why he said what he did.'

'Where will I see you?'

'I shall be at the Villa André most of the time. I have to make sure they have all the food and that the chefs are happy ... then I have to go for a costume fitting.' She paused at the door. 'Is what the Director told me true – you're going as d'Artagnan?'

Monsieur Pamplemousse nodded dolefully. He had almost forgotten about that side of the affair.

'And I am your mistress?'

'That also is true.'

Mrs Van Dorman gave a giggle. 'I was reading up about Alexandre Dumas last night. His last affair was with a stage horseback rider called Adah Menkin. He was sixty-five at the time would you believe?'

'It is no age,' said Monsieur Pamplemousse firmly.

'Dumas had a reputation for being very active in all his pursuits. They say in many respects he had the strength of ten men.'

'I can't wait.'

While he finished dressing, Monsieur Pamplemousse began exploring the room, pondering over Mrs Van Dorman's last remark as he did so. There was a row of books on a shelf let into one of the alcoves: *Memoires de Guerre* by someone called Lloyd George; Simenon's *Le Testament Donadieu*, and a set of encyclopaedias.

A picture of a sailing ship caught in a storm at sea adorned the wall above the huge brass bedstead.

The built-in wardrobe was vast – like another small room. On the inside of the door there was a yellowing inventory of fixtures and fittings. It read like a wedding list and was comprehensive enough to have furnished many a small household.

The only concessions to modernity were a remotely controlled television standing in a corner near the balcony and a large refrigerator which he came across in yet another cupboard. It accounted for the faint hum he'd heard during the night. Hoping it might be stocked with goodies, he opened the door. It was completely bare.

He tried out the television. It was a children's panel game. He was about to switch channels when the phone rang. It was the Director. With the briefest of *bonjours* he waded straight in.

'This is bad news, Pamplemousse.'

Unsure as to exactly how much the Director knew, Monsieur Pamplemousse essayed a non-committal '*Oui, Monsieur*' in reply.

'I heard about the death on television yesterday evening, but I had no idea it was one of Madame Van Dorman's party.' Already the Director was distancing himself from the affair.

'It is very sad, *Monsieur*. I gather he was only in his early forties. It is no age.'

'Yes, of course. *Trés triste. Trés triste.*' There followed a short, but nicely judged pause of respect for the departed during which Monsieur Pamplemousse could almost feel the appropriate number of seconds being counted off. 'However, I was really thinking of how it might affect *Le Guide*. I have already taken the precaution of speaking to an old friend of mine – a Deputy. We were at school together. He has promised to do his best to hush matters up. You know what the *journaux* are like when they get a sniff of something.'

'You have been told what his last words were, Monsieur?'

'*Extraordinaire*, Pamplemousse, do you not think? And why a Bâtard Montrachet? Why not a Montrachet itself? That would have had the twin merits of being less of a mouthful to say and being a marginally better wine.'

'May I ask how you got to know, Monsieur?'

'You may well indeed. I was woken in the early hours of this morning by a telephone call from the police. It seems that for some strange reason the man's pockets were devoid of anything which might provide a clue as to his identity. The only thing the police could find was the address of *Le Guide* written on a scrap of paper. The night staff at the office put them through to me. I managed to stall on the true reason for his being in Vichy, and in particular our own association with the event ...'

'But surely, *Monsieur*, it is not the end of the world. By the law of averages such things must happen in a spa from time to time. It is unfortunate he was one of our party, but

I fail to see how it could reflect badly on us. There is nothing sinister about it. People die every day.'

'Be that as it may, Pamplemousse, it is the kind of thing a reporter might make capital of, particularly if jogged into action by one of our rivals. That is why I am saying we must exercise extreme caution. I am relying on you to keep a watchful eye on things at your end to make sure they don't get out of hand.

'The fact of the matter is we have an ongoing situation with Mrs Van Dorman. It is a meaningful relationship, and one which I hope will enable us to maximise our potential in the years to come ...'

Monsieur Pamplemousse listened to his chief with only half an ear. The Director was wearing his new hat again – the one he had brought back from Bloomingdales on Lexington Avenue. Cupping the receiver between his head and his shoulder, Monsieur Pamplemousse idly opened the case Mrs Van Dorman had given him and removed the drinking glass. His first reaction was that it was almost identical to his own. They probably all came like it. He had used the one the Director had given him for a glass of water when he went to bed. Picking it up he compared the two. They both had the same gradations on the side – from 0 to 150. He raised the second glass up to the light. It was clean apart from some kind of clear deposit round the inside near the bottom. He held it to his nose. He could still detect the characteristic volcanic sulphury smell of the waters; that, and potassium nitrate, but underlying it there was some-thing else again which he couldn't quite place.

Seeing Pommes Frites watching his every movement he held it out for him to examine. Using his large ears as a shield, Pommes Frites applied the smell receptors at the tip of his nose to the opening, sniffed deeply, then committed the result to that section of his olfactory system which contained his comparison charts. After a moment's hesitation while wheels turned and mental card indexes were consulted in order to form an evaluation, his face took on a thoughtful expression.

'Are you there?' A petulant voice in Monsieur Pamplemousse's left ear brought him back to earth.

'*Oui, Monsieur.*'

'I was saying, it is too late now to go back on our undertaking to Mrs Van Dorman – the die is cast – but it is not a good start. I suggest you play down our involvement. Above all, Pamplemousse, keep a low profile; merge into the background as much as you can.'

Monsieur Pamplemousse contemplated the end of the telephone receiver for a moment or two while he counted up to *dix*. It was sometimes hard to come to terms with the Director's conflicting demands. On the one hand the constant desire for publicity, on the other a fear of it back-firing.

'With respect, *Monsieur*, it will be a little difficult to merge into the background if I am to attend tonight's banquet dressed as a character from *Les Trois Mousquetaires*.'

'Pamplemousse, whenever you begin a sentence using the phrase "with respect", I know full well you are about to be difficult. All I ask is that you behave as d'Artagnan would have done. No more, no less. If I remember correctly, he was constantly merging. What was the phrase? "They seek him here, they seek him there" ...'

'I think *Monsieur* is mixing him up with the Scarlet Pimpernel. In any case he had the advantage of being dressed as others were at that period in time. I shall not be. Also, he did not have to drive through Vichy in a *deux chevaux*.'

'Then don't do it, Pamplemousse. Go by some other means.'

'Very good, *Monsieur*. I will hire a taxi. I am sure that in the circumstances Madame Grante will agree to the added expense. Or perhaps if it is a fine evening I might even arrange to have the horse delivered to my hotel instead of having it wait for me at the Villa André. No doubt the town will be full of others doing the same thing.'

There was a pause and when the Director spoke again it was in tones of resignation.

'Aristide, I am not a superstitious person, but I have to tell you the air in Paris is rife with ill omens. Last night I was kept awake for several hours by the sound of a screeching barn owl outside my window. As if that wasn't bad enough, this morning as I was about to enter the office building I walked under a ladder. Naturally I immediately retraced my steps in order to spit through its rungs three times, and in so doing I inadvertently stepped in a large pot of paint.'

The Director paused. 'I will leave you to guess what happened next.'

Monsieur Pamplemousse hesitated. It was hardly possible there could be more, but luckily the Director didn't expect an answer.

'When I carried out my intention of spitting through the rungs in order to counteract the ill luck brought on by walking under the ladder in the first place, my *salive* landed on a black cat which happened to be passing behind it at the time. Furthermore, Aristide, the animal was crossing my path in the worst possible direction – from left to right. It was not amused.

'One might argue that if a *chat*, whatever its colour, chooses to walk under a ladder, then it, too, is tempting fate and must expect to suffer the consequences. However, I cannot help thinking that someone, somewhere is trying to tell me something. That is all.' There was a click and the line went dead.

Monsieur Pamplemousse replaced his own receiver. He could see now why the Director wasn't bubbling over with happiness. Crossing to the balcony, he looked out across the red-tiled rooftops of the town while he adjusted his tie. The background mist had lifted and he could now see the countryside clearly. Below him the park was suddenly full of people; blue and white parasols adorned the tables. The sweepers had finished their work and were in consultation with each other over what to do next.

It would be very easy to laugh off the Director's fears, but on the other hand he had to admit the whole thing was really rather odd.

For a start it was strange that Norm Ellis should have nothing on him in the way of identification. In his own experience almost everyone – unless they happened to be completely down and out – carried something about their person; a diary, a wallet containing odd items, credit cards. He could hardly have been robbed. By the sound of it there had been too many people around. Perhaps, for some reason best known to himself, Norm hadn't wanted to be identified. But if not, why not? He wished now he'd thought to ask Mrs Van Dorman if any of those things had been found in his Hôtel.

Monsieur Pamplemousse went back into his room and picked up the tumblers again, holding them up to the light and comparing the two. Apart from the slight roughness which he'd noticed earlier in the bottom of the one used by Norm Ellis, they both looked identical. Someone, somewhere, must turn them out in their thousands. Wetting his index finger, he reached down inside the second glass and just managed to press it against the deposit. It felt slightly sticky to the touch.

Resisting the temptation to taste it, Monsieur Pamplemousse hesitated for a moment, then picked up the phone and dialled the code for an outside line, followed by his office number.

'Operations?

'Pamplemousse here.

'Oh, *ça va, ça va*. Tell me, do you have Glandier's number?

'*Merci. Au revoir.*'

Glandier was roughing it in Reims. No doubt preparing himself for a visit to Boyer to check on its three Stock Pots.

Dialling the number he had been given, Monsieur Pamplemousse struck lucky. Glandier was about to set off on his travels.

'How are things in Vichy?'

'Oh, *ça va, ça va*. Tell me about trick glasses; the sort magicians use.'

'What do you want to know?'

'Can anyone buy them?'

'It depends how sophisticated you want them to be. If you mean the drinking beer out of a tankard type – the sort where a small amount of liquid is contained inside a double skin between the inner and the outer glass – you can buy those in any good magic shop, or even in one of those joke shops. You know – the kind of place that sells "whoopee cushions" or plastic dog's *merde*, blood capsules – that kind of thing.'

'How about a tasting glass? The sort they would have at a spa?'

'A tasting glass?' Glandier pondered the question for a

moment. 'I haven't ever come across one. You can get wine glasses. You've probably seen them. They look as though they're full of wine, but when you hold them upside down nothing comes out. You would need to go to someone who specialises ... I could give you the name of a firm in Paris. In New York there's a shop on West 34th Street called "The Magic Center". I've sent away there for things myself from time to time. That sort of place is usually run by an ex-pro., so if you want something really special they always know people who will make it for you – at a price.'

'How about other kinds of tricks?' He tried a long shot. 'Water into wine for example.'

'That's usually a case of the quickness of the hand deceiving the eye. Plus a few chemicals. Take a jug of water mixed with ten per cent sulphuric acid, pour it into a glass containing a pinch of potassium permanganate and hey presto! you have a glass of red wine. Only get rid of it quickly before anyone has a chance to sample the result.

'Hey! Don't tell me you're taking up conjuring too?'

Avoiding the question, Monsieur Pamplemousse thanked Glandier and hung up. He sensed the other's interest being roused. Another moment and he would be offering advice on how to saw Mrs Van Dorman in two.

As he replaced the receiver Pommes Frites stood up, wagging his tail. Monsieur Pamplemousse took the hint. Clearly, fifty per cent of the room's occupants thought it was high time they went for a walk.

He wondered whether he ought to contact the police as he'd promised. But that was before he'd spoken to the Director. No doubt if he rang an ex-colleague in Paris he would be given a name, but that would mean explaining why he was there and even if they were being 'leant on' from on high by a Deputy, the chances were that someone might pass on the news if only out of pique.

The phone rang. It was Mrs Van Dorman.

'I've been thinking. There's no reason on earth why you should be saddled with my problems. If you like to drop Norm's glass back I'll take it into the police on my way to the Villa André.'

'It is no trouble …'

'No, really. It'll be a good test of my French. Besides, they're bound to ask questions you may not be able to answer. I'm about to have a bath but the maid is doing the room so you can leave it with her.'

Feeling somewhat deflated, Monsieur Pamplemousse sat on the edge of his bed for a moment or two lost in thought. Then, acting on an impulse he would have been hard put to explain, let alone justify, he swopped the two glasses over. If anyone queried it he could always plead a mistake on his part. Whether or not he would be believed was immaterial.

The room maid was busy with a feather duster. He watched while she put the case on Mrs Van Dorman's dressing table. The sound of running water came from the bathroom.

'My room is free if you wish to clean it.' He pre-empted the question he knew she was about to ask.

Strolling through the old town, Monsieur Pamplemousse tried to get himself in the mood for the evening's event, picturing what it must have been like in Dumas' time. The whole history of the writing of *Les Trois Mousquetaires*: the fact that the characters of Athos, Porthos and Aramis – even that of d'Artagnan – were based on real people, made fascinating reading. Dumas had certainly done well out of it, as he had from *The Count of Monte Cristo*. Long queues had formed in Paris whenever a new episode was due, and outside the capital crowds gathered to greet the arrival of the stage coach carrying copies of those *journaux* serialising the story.

By the time Dumas arrived in Vichy to begin work on yet another sequel his fame as a gourmand and *bon viveur*, as well as a womaniser, must have gone before him. At the height of his success, with over 400 literary works to his credit, he had built a mansion outside Paris – the Château Monte Cristo – to accommodate his many guests, and then he'd had to build another small house alongside – the Château d'If – as a retreat where he could escape from it all in order to work! The penalties of fame!

Having explored the town to his satisfaction, Monsieur Pamplemousse took a short cut down the rue du Docteur Fouet – *Superintendent des Eaux Minérales de Vichy 1646–1715* – an achievement commemorated some three centuries later by Pommes Frites who paused at the corner to leave his mark, and together they made their way towards the Villa André.

Nothing in Monsieur Pamplemousse's musings had prepared him for what he found. After the sunshine the house felt darker than it probably was, but clearly, he was witnessing a no-expense-spared operation. The Villa André, which by all accounts had remained empty for some years, had undergone a transformation. It was hard to tell whether the heavy oak furniture had been brought in specially for the occasion or if it had been there all the time, but as he picked his way in and out of the rooms it felt like the opening night of some theatrical extravaganza. Girls were busy dusting and polishing chairs and tables which looked as though they could well have been there when Dumas was staying; others were cleaning silver.

In the kitchen someone – from the Nikon slung round

his neck at the ready he guessed it must be Elliott Garner – was engaged in a technical argument with the *chef-de-cuisine* over the method of serving. According to Elliott the dinner had taken place on Friday 23rd June 1862, eight years before Dumas died.

The problem centred over whether the serving should be *à la Française*, as it would have been up until about 1860, when all the dishes were brought in and presented at table before being taken away to be carved, or *à la Russe* introduced soon after that date – in which the carving was done in advance and brought in to be eaten straight away.

It was hard to tell who was winning, but Elliott Garner was obviously taking it to heart and looked as though he was ahead on points. It struck Monsieur Pamplemousse as being a little late in the day.

The *Rôtisseur* was keeping his thoughts to himself as he tackled the daunting task of preparing the *pièce de résistance* – the *Rôtie à l'Impératrice*. If it was only half as complex as the Director had described it, he would be occupied for the whole of the morning.

Monsieur Pamplemousse drifted away to explore the rest of the house. No stone seemed to have been left unturned, no expense spared to ensure the evening's success. In the dining-room silver candelabra graced a huge table laid for twelve. He arrived just as a waiter was about to remove one of the place settings.

One thing was for sure, if the number of glasses was anything to go by Norm Ellis would have made up for lost time in his consumption of wine. He might even have got to taste the Bâtard Montrachet he'd hankered after.

He bumped into Mrs Van Dorman in the corridor outside. She was dressed in white overalls.

'Am I glad to see you!'

Monsieur Pamplemousse looked suitably gratified.

'Do you feel like an *apéritif*?'

'If an *apéritif* means what I think it means – an appetiser before lunch – then the answer is "no". I'm saving myself for tonight. But I could use a drink.' Mrs Van Dorman looked at her watch. 'Anyway, it's time I went back to the Hôtel. I have a fitting for my dress at twelve-thirty. Maybe we could have a quick one there.'

'Since we are about to enter into the mood of d'Artagnan, why not a *Pousse Rapière* – a "rapier thrust", or even a *Badinquet*?'

'Tell me?'

'The first is made from Armagnac and sparkling white wine – ideally a *vin sauvage* from the region of Gers, garnished with orange peel. For the second a teaspoon of *Crème de Cassis* is mixed in with the Armagnac and a still white champagne is used.'

The barman at the Hôtel professed never to have heard of either. It was said in the tone of voice implying that if he didn't know about it then it didn't exist. Monsieur Pamplemousse settled for two Kirs. It wasn't worth an argument. Once again he found himself apologising.

'I know the type. He is like the people from Bordeaux who pretend they have never heard of Burgundy, and vice versa. The drinks I mentioned come from the Pyrénées and to him they don't exist.'

He looked at Mrs Van Dorman as she sipped her Kir reflectively.

'Is anything the matter? You look worried.' It was a stupid question. She must have a lot on her mind.

'You know it definitely is – or was – Norm. Spencer confirmed it when he got back from the morgue. He looked like he'd seen a ghost.'

'Was there any doubt?'

'I didn't think so, but the others did apparently. Either that or it's only just hit them. I was there when Spencer broke the news. You could have knocked any of them down with a feather. All except Elliott, and he was too busy arguing with the chef. Harman Lock was all for calling the whole thing off. *And* there's going to be an autopsy.'

'That is normal when someone dies away from home.'

'All the same, I shall feel happier when tonight's over.' Mrs Van Dorman finished off her drink. 'Talking of which, it's time I got ready for my fitting.'

'I, too, have a fitting,' said Monsieur Pamplemousse gloomily. 'I am not looking forward to it.'

He paid the bill and having collected the keys at the desk they went up in the lift together, each lost in their own thoughts.

'See you!' Mrs Van Dorman paused at her door. 'Good luck.'

'*A bientôt.*'

Further along the corridor, Monsieur Pamplemousse turned a corner, unlocked his own door, and was in the act of removing his jacket when the telephone rang.

'Aristide – can you come quickly.' It was Mrs Van Dorman. She sounded distraught.

'Of course. I will be right with you.'

With Pommes Frites hard on his heels Monsieur Pamplemousse retraced his steps as fast as he could go. He found Mrs Van Dorman waiting for him just inside her room. She looked flushed, as well she might.

'*Merde!*' Monsieur Pamplemousse took in the scene. It was familiar to anyone who had spent time in the police; drawers half open, clothes scattered, suitcases upended. Whoever had done it had been in a hurry.

'Did you leave anything of value?'

Mrs Van Dorman shook her head. 'I had all my money and travellers' cheques with me. My jewellery is in the Hôtel safe.'

'Passport?'

'That's OK too. It was in my handbag.'

Monsieur Pamplemousse crossed to the balcony and tried the French windows. They were locked from the inside.

'And the main door was locked?'

Mrs Van Dorman nodded. 'I remember trying it when I left this morning. And it was certainly still locked when I came back in just now.'

'Then whoever did it must have had a key.'

'It certainly wasn't mine. You saw me pick it up from the desk.'

Monsieur Pamplemousse shrugged. 'Someone may have "borrowed" it on a pretext. In a Hôtel this size they would stand a good chance of getting away with it. It might even have been someone who's stayed here before and "lost" the key. It wouldn't be the first time that's happened. There are a dozen ways.'

'You don't think it could be one of the staff?'

'I doubt it. They wouldn't have made such a mess. Have you reported it yet?'

'No, I rang you first.' While they were talking Mrs Van Dorman went through her belongings. 'Anyway, nothing seems to be missing. Unless …' she paused by the dressing table. 'That's strange. I can't see Norm's glass anywhere.'

'You mean you hadn't taken it to the police.'

'No. In the end I was running late, so I thought I'd do it this afternoon. What do you think it means?'

Monsieur Pamplemousse gave a non-committal grunt,

but behind it his mind was racing.

Mrs Van Dorman reached for the phone. 'I guess I'd better call the desk.'

While she was talking, Monsieur Pamplemousse took a last look round the room – under the bed, in the bathroom, and finally in the wardrobe.

'If you like I will leave Pommes Frites with you.'

'I'll be all right once the mess is cleared up. Besides, the costumier should be here any moment.'

'Well, you know where I am. You only have to call.'

'Thanks.' Mrs Van Dorman reached out and gave his hand a squeeze. 'I'm beginning to wonder what I'd do without you.'

Back in his own room, Monsieur Pamplemousse prowled around for a while lost in thought. He wasn't normally superstitious, but he was beginning to think that perhaps the Director was right in his fears. Come to think of it, on the journey down even Mrs Van Dorman had admitted to having "bad vibes".

For want of something better to do he picked up the case containing Ellis's glass and opened it. Removing the glass, he tried sniffing it again, this time warming the outside with his hands first to release the vapour, then emulating Pommes Frites by forming them into a screen so that the smell would be trapped. Ignoring the prickle in his nose and at the back of his throat from the sulphur and the very definite odour of potassium nitrate, he concentrated on the third smell. As with a wine, it needed only a moment – anything longer was a waste of time. First impressions were the most reliable. He tried again and this time it came to him – a very faint trace of almonds; the kind of smell which in its bitter form indicated a badly fined wine. The Germans had a good word for it – *mandelbitter*.

Mandelbitter, or ... Monsieur Pamplemousse put the glass down and gazed at it thoughtfully. Perhaps he was wrong to think in terms of wine; perhaps it wasn't so much a matter of *vin rouge*, but rather *hareng rouge*. What the English would call a 'red herring'.

It was largely a matter of what one was conditioned to, of reading what one expected to read. Working as he did for *Le Guide*, his immediate reactions were inclined to be gastronomic. Had he still been with the *Sûreté* they would have taken him in quite another direction.

Cyanide, *par exemple*?

4
DINNER WITH DUMAS

Monsieur Pamplemousse gazed up at his mount, silhouetted in the cold light from what, given the circumstances,
seemed an unnecessarily, not to say an embarrassingly
overbright moon. The horse was not only a good deal
bigger than he had expected, it also lacked certain fundamental items of equipment which made his own *deux
chevaux* seem, by comparison, positively over-endowed
with optional extras; little things like a wheel at all four
corners or, more particularly, a handbrake to ensure that it
remained stationary when parked. The latter was conspicuous by its absence.

To carry the motoring analogy a stage further, the horse's
progenitors had obviously been of like mind to the late
Henry Ford, who had offered would-be purchasers of his
Model T the choice of any colour under the sun provided
they asked for black, for black it certainly was. Black as the
ace of spades.

Nor did Monsieur Pamplemousse entirely trust the look
in its eyes. Rapport between man and beast seemed fairly
low on its agenda for the evening.

'Why is there steam issuing from its nostrils?' he
demanded.

'It is mostly the effect of the night air, *Monsieur*. After
the heat of the Opera House ...' The groom wiped some
foam from the horse's lower lip with the back of his sleeve.

'The Opera House?'

'He is appearing all this week in *The Best of Wagner*. Unfortunately, rehearsals this afternoon did not go well. Madame Trenchante, the soprano, is not the lightest of singers, you understand? ... and the members of the orchestra behaved badly. He is not used to being applauded when he obeys the call of nature. We are hoping for better things at tonight's performance.'

The man suddenly bent down, grasped the offside front leg of the horse with both hands, and gave it a twist. Taken by surprise, the animal promptly lay down on the gravelled driveway.

'See, he is feeling better already!'

Monsieur Pamplemousse had no wish to argue with such an obvious expert in equestrian behaviour, but it struck him as being a very moot point. He was uncomfortably aware of an eye gazing up at him, watching his every move. It was a large eye, unblinking and heavily veined. Set against a colour chart it would have registered yellow rather than white. It struck him as the kind of eye which belonged to an animal merely biding its time until the moment arrived when it could get its own back on those around it.

'That is most kind of you.' Taking a deep breath, he made to clamber on.

'*Monsieur!*' The man grabbed at his arm. 'I would not advise it. Not unless you wish to end up in the river. I was merely demonstrating one of his many tricks, but he is not called *Le Diable Noir* for nothing.'

Monsieur Pamplemousse jumped back. The latest snippet of information did little to assuage his feeling of gloom; a gloom which had set in soon after he left the Hôtel. The news about the opera explained why there had been so much traffic. In the end he had abandoned all thoughts of using his own car for fear of losing his parking space, choosing instead to walk the half kilometre or so to the Villa André. It also explained why he had been stopped several times on the way for his autograph. He wished now he had taken advantage of the situation. Placido Domingo might have looked even more impressive than Charles de Batz Castelmore – the name of Dumas' human model for the character of d'Artagnan – and P. Domingo would certainly have been much quicker to write.

The groom relaxed his grip on the horse, withdrew a silver hunting-cased watch from one of has waistcoat pockets, and flicked open the cover with his thumbnail.

'If *Monsieur* will forgive me. It is almost time for the evening performance and we have to be in our places five minutes before the curtain goes up.'

As the horse rose to its feet, Monsieur Pamplemousse looked around for something to stand on – a pair of steps, perhaps? A car roof? – but there was nothing in sight. He glanced towards the house at the end of the short drive. The lights were on and through the open door he could see waiters flitting to and fro. To his relief there was no sign of the photographer the Director had threatened him with. Posterity and Mrs Van Dorman's magazine would have to do without. Taking a deep breath, he braced himself. It was now or never.

'*Monsieur* has ridden before?'

'*Oui.*' Monsieur Pamplemousse dismissed such a foolish question with a wave of his hand. 'Many years ago.' He forbore to mention that the last time – the one and only time – had been on a camel in the Bois de Boulogne. It would have been a sad confession for one born and brought up in the Auvergne.

'Aah!' The tone of voice suggested that his reply was not

entirely unexpected. 'Then I would suggest that if *Monsieur* wishes to mount he faces the way he is going so that he can place his other foot in the *trier*.'

Grasping Monsieur Pamplemousse's left foot in much the same manner as he had used earlier in demonstrating his command over the horse, the groom guided it into a stirrup. Then he cupped his hands together to form a step, placed it under the other foot, and gave a quick heave.

It was hard to say which of those present was most surprised by the events which followed, or who reacted the fastest.

Had the promised cameraman been present, and had his finger been on the button, he might have resolved matters by capturing a photo finish with his lens, but he would have needed to be quick for it was all over in a matter of seconds.

Monsieur Pamplemousse, expecting to find himself flying straight over the top of the horse and therefore bracing himself accordingly, met instead with unexpected resistance, spun round, and collapsed in a heap on the driveway.

Pommes Frites, having until that moment remained coldly aloof from the proceedings, sprang into action. Anticipating the outcome by virtue of his vantage point near the ground, he was already at his master's side by the time he landed, his tongue at the ready in case first aid was required.

The horse, taken completely unawares by Monsieur Pamplemousse's sword as it swung round and up, stood for a brief second registering a mixture of shock and disbelief, then gave vent to a cry, more shriek than whinny, before leaping several feet into the air.

Last, but by no means least, although compared to the other three, undoubtedly an also-ran, the groom added his shouts to the *mêlée* as he struggled to regain control of his charge.

'Aristide! Are you all right?'

Groping under a nearby bush for his hat, Monsieur Pamplemousse looked up and found himself gazing into the eyes of Mrs Van Dorman.

'*Oui et non*. I fear I have lost part of my hat.'

'By the sound of it you're lucky if that's all you've lost. I tell you something else. How about we take your entrance as read? The photographer's still tied up inside the house. Besides, we can leave all that until after we've eaten.'

Monsieur Pamplemousse considered the matter for all of a second or two. Mrs Van Dorman wouldn't have to fill in a P.39 at the end of her trip justifying to Madame Grante in Accounts the reasons for claiming a new set of plumes. He doubted very much whether, as an item, they would have been programmed on to *Le Guide*'s computer. There would be innumerable complications. He could picture it all. The section on the form for explanations wouldn't be large enough for a start. Once again he would have to resort to writing 'please see attached sheet'.

He was also distracted from his task by the nearness of Mrs Van Dorman's bosom. She was wearing a high-waisted dark blue dress with a lace-edged off-the-shoulder *décolletage*, the squareness of which emphasised and even enhanced the roundness and fullness of her snowy white *balcons*. *Balcons* which, unlike *Le Diable Noir*, benefitted from being bathed in moonlight. The effect was unexpectedly ravishing, not to say disturbing.

Climbing to his feet with as much grace as possible, Monsieur Pamplemousse adjusted his sword and turned to the groom.

'*Madame* is right. I will see you after the performance. I hope it goes well.'

'*Oui, Monsieur.*' The man sounded as relieved as he did.

Monsieur Pamplemousse glanced at Mrs Van Dorman as they made their way towards the house. 'You are looking very beautiful.'

'Thank you, Aristide. And you are looking very dashing. Doublet and hose suit you. You should always wear them. As for the black beard ...'

'I think not. It would make life much too complicated in the mornings.'

Monsieur Pamplemousse spoke with feeling. Even with the help of two men from the theatrical costumiers it had taken him most of the afternoon to get ready. As for undressing again, he wouldn't know where to begin. All the same, as he took Mrs Van Dorman's arm he couldn't help feeling a little *je ne sais quoi* – 'a certain something'; his step was undoubtedly lighter. His spirits had been raised and he felt on top of the world; it was a night when anything was possible.

Pausing by the steps leading up to the door he became aware, too, of an unseasonable smell of jasmine – jasmine and honeysuckle: strong and heady. It wasn't difficult to locate the source. Mrs Van Dorman read his thoughts.

'I hope you don't find my perfume too overpowering. I picked it up from Jean Laporte when I was in Paris. It belongs to the period – along with the beauty spots.' She pointed to a black patch adorning her right cheek. 'They both served their purpose in covering up bodily imperfections – B. O. and pock-marks. They didn't call Louis XIV a "sweet-smelling monarch" for nothing. He had them build a blue and white pavilion at Versailles and filled it with flowers. They say he used to spend most of his time there –

in between bouts of making love.'

'Do you have a perfume for every occasion?'

'I try to. I'm always experimenting. It has to do with the chemistry of the skin. I'll tell you about it some day.

'Anyway, here goes …' She led the way into the house and on into the dining-room where two distinct groups were clustered at the far end.

Monsieur Pamplemousse's spirits took a sudden nose-dive again. He'd completely forgotten the thespians the Director had engaged for the occasion. He hoped their expectations of his own acting abilities weren't running too high. If so, they were in for a shock.

Not that it looked as though the expectations of anyone in the room were exactly at fever pitch. As he followed Mrs Van Dorman round the long candle-lit table in the centre of the room, awash with gleaming silver cutlery and sparkling glassware, it struck Monsieur Pamplemousse that the atmosphere was decidedly low key. Apart from their dress, it wasn't hard to distinguish which group was which. The theatricals appeared to be in a state of suspended anima-tion, as though awaiting a cue from some unseen Director before taking the stage. Either that, or they had been given orders not to mingle. The rest of the occupants, perhaps not surprisingly, looked as though they were trying to strike a balance between anticipation of things to come and remembrance of things past.

Someone he recognised as Elliott Garner detached himself from the group of writers and came forward to greet them.

'DiAnn! Or should I say Madame Joyeux? Congratula-tions. You are looking wonderful.'

'Thank you, Elliott. You haven't met Monsieur Pample-mousse … Aristide. And Pommes Frites …'

Elliott nodded briefly. 'We saw each other across a crowded kitchen this morning. Although I must admit, I would hardly have recognised you.' His hand felt cold to the touch.

'I am sorry if I have held you up,' said Monsieur Pamplemousse. 'I had a little disagreement with my *cheval*. I feel we may neither of us ever be quite the same again.'

'What is the saying? "Beware of all enterprises that require new clothes."' Elliott glanced down at Pommes Frites. 'Now I know we are in France.'

Monsieur Pamplemousse looked at him enquiringly.

'In New York dogs are not allowed in restaurants.'

'Now, now, Elliott,' said Mrs Van Dorman. 'Pommes Frites is an honoured guest. Besides, this isn't a restaurant, it's a private gathering.'

'I didn't say he shouldn't be allowed in.' There was a hint of petulance. 'I was only pointing out one of the differences between our two countries.'

'I think perhaps dogs come under the heading of popular misconceptions,' said Monsieur Pamplemousse. 'Perhaps because of our eating habits, we are not usually thought of as a nation of animal lovers – but *chiens* are almost always welcome. If they weren't people would soon take their custom elsewhere.'

Conscious that Pommes Frites, aware that his name was being taken in vain, had his eye on Elliott Garner as though making notes for future reference, Monsieur Pamplemousse tried to make it crystal clear that if the need arose, he, too, would happily take his custom elsewhere. It was hard to tell if Pommes Frites was grateful or not.

Mrs Van Dorman touched his arm. 'Come and meet the rest of the party, Aristide.'

'Paul Robard ... Spencer Troon ... Harman Lock ... Harvey Wentworth ...'

Monsieur Pamplemousse took his time. In their formal attire they were hardly recognisable from the pictures he'd seen in the group photograph and he wanted to get them fixed in his mind.

Mrs Van Dorman turned to the second group. 'Alexandre Dumas, I'm sure you know. Madame de Sauvignon, Monsieur Courbet and Monsieur Auguste Maquet.'

Monsieur Pamplemousse eyed them curiously as they bowed and curtsied. It was type-casting with a vengeance. Alexandre Dumas, in his sixties, portly, wearing a waistcoat several sizes too small, beneath which was one of the soft, pleated and embroidered shirts he had made famous; Madame de Sauvignon, slim, poised, undeniably attractive in a long black dress done up at the collar, but with a revealing area of black net across her front; Courbet every inch the 'artist', Maquet, thin-lipped, jealous of Dumas' success, on which he was later to lay claim.

Monsieur Pamplemousse was so taken up with his own responses, making sure he didn't have a second, perhaps even more embarrassing accident with his sword, it was a moment or two before he realised that not one of the second group had spoken a word, and another few seconds before the truth dawned on him. They were all having to mime. For no obvious reason he found the thought immensely cheering. It was probably one of the Director's little economies – or what was perhaps even more likely, having made the Grand gesture, he had encountered opposition from Madame Grante. He could see it all. The endless hairsplitting arguments. The triumphant expression on Madame Grante's face as she had delivered her *coup de grâce*; the fact that actors came a lot cheaper if they didn't have speaking parts.

'You know something,' Harvey Wentworth joined them. 'The last time I was in Paris doing an article for *Gourmet* magazine I took the boat across to that island in the Bois de Boulogne – the one with the restaurant. There's a notice by the ferry saying dogs are forbidden unless they are going there to eat! Can you imagine that happening back in the States?'

'A few years ago,' said Monsieur Pamplemousse. 'Someone opened a restaurant in Nice for dogs only.'

'No kidding? What happened if one of them brought an owner in?'

'He got chained to the table like the rest of them,' said Spencer Troon.

Everyone laughed.

'Let's drink to that.' Harvey took a ladle from a silver bowl on the sideboard and filled a glass with a sepia coloured liquid. 'Punch *à l'Alexandre Dumas*. One of his own inventions. Perfected over years of party giving.'

Monsieur Pamplemousse took the glass and held it to his nose. He hazarded a quick guess. 'Lemon tea? Lemon tea with something much more potent added.'

'Right in one. If you want a repeat order when you get back home – put some sugar into a large bowl and mix in some rum. Light the blue touch paper and stir until it reduces to a third. Add hot Souchong tea and some lemon juice, then top up with mystery ingredient "X" – white Batavian arrack.'

'I wouldn't bother writing it down,' said Paul Robard, 'the recipe'll be in Harvey's next book.'

'So?' Harvey looked unabashed. 'Something new comes your way – you use it. That's what it's all about, right? Old "motormouth" Norm himself would have been on to it like a shot. He's probably making notes even now.'

'In all that heat?' Paul Robard gave a snort.

Harman Lock drained his glass. 'Let us not speak ill of the dear departed.'

The ice broken, everyone suddenly began talking at once, and finding some of the accents difficult to follow Monsieur Pamplemousse took the opportunity to cast his eye over the wine on a sideboard to his right. With the exception of some white Burgundy and a bottle or two of Loire poking out from a pair of large ice-buckets, it was all from Bordeaux. He caught sight of a Mouton-Rothschild and a Château Léoville. In the centre of the sideboard, in a position of honour, stood a decanting machine with a bottle already in place. The original label had long since disappeared, but he couldn't resist looking at a hand-written tag dangling from the neck.

Elliott came up behind him. 'You approve?'

'Lafite 1884? How could I not?'

'I acquired it for the occasion at a wine auction in California. It is our one big extravagance for the evening. I tell myself Dumas would have approved. He was an extremely generous host.'

He was also, thought Monsieur Pamplemousse, a teetotaller. Clearly, Elliott wasn't living up to his reputation of being meticulous on research. He let it pass, deciding instead to watch out for other mistakes. Elliott invited a challenge.

'Where did you learn about this particular event?'

Elliott shrugged. 'I don't even remember. Someone must have told me. As I'm sure you know only too well, research often throws up all kinds of strange facts.'

'I congratulate you on the Lafite. It is a great coup.'

'I read somewhere that it was the favourite drink of Queen Victoria. The cellar book at Windsor Castle lists the 1862 vintage as being the house wine.'

'She has gone up in my estimation,' said Monsieur Pamplemousse. 'I had always pictured her as being a little *formidable*.'

'It only goes to show. Things are seldom what they seem.' Elliott ran his eyes over the other bottles, making a last-minute check that all was well.

'Ideally, it would have been nice if all the wines could have been of the period, but there is a limit. However, I suspect namewise they would have been much as you see here. It was the beginning of a golden age for Bordeaux. The 1855 classification had just taken place and the vines had yet to be stricken by phyloxera. Mouton-Rothschild had begun its long fight to be recognised as a first growth – it was fetching the same prices, and Léoville already belonged to an Irish family named Barton.'

'You must have done a lot of research.'

'It's fun. And you learn a lot on the way.'

'It has been said that *Les Trois Mousquetaires* could not have been written without all the research carried out by Auguste Maquet.'

Elliott Garner looked at him with interest. 'You're a scholar of Dumas?'

Monsieur Pamplemousse shook his head. 'Only from around forty-eight hours ago. As as child I was brought up on *The Count of Monte Cristo*, but I have a lot of catching up to do.'

The reply was casual enough, but somehow he sensed a momentary feeling of relief in the other. It would have been hard to put into words, and in any case further conversation was cut short by the sound of a dinner gong from the other end of the room.

He looked at his watch. It was exactly eight o'clock.

As they made their way towards the table Elliott motioned the actor playing Dumas to sit at the head. 'I feel that is where you should be. I have put your mistress, Madame de Sauvignon, on your right. Paul, you are next to her, then Harman and Auguste Maquet.'

'I guess we're going to have to talk to each other, Paul,' said Harman.

'You win some, you lose some.' Paul Robard looked as though he would be perfectly happy if he spent the evening miming to Madame de Sauvignon. Harman was in for a thin time.

'I shall be at the other end of the table,' continued Elliott. 'On my right, Monsieur Courbet. Then Harvey, Madame Joyeux, Monsieur d'Artagnan, and Spencer.'

Almost imperceptibly a bevy of waiters moved into position. Chairs were pulled back, then rearranged as the guests seated themselves.

As the waiters disappeared to begin preparations for serving the first course, the *sommelier* and his assistant began pouring the wine. Monsieur Pamplemousse had to admire Elliott's attention to detail. All the same, he couldn't resist a dig as the waiters reappeared.

'I see the service is *à la Russe*. Does that mean you won your battle this morning?'

Elliott looked at him in surprise. 'Of course.'

'Beware of Elliott,' said Harman. 'Elliott treats any form of disagreement as a confrontation and he has to come out top. Right, Elliott?'

Elliott didn't even bother to reply.

'*Potage à la Crevette, Monsieur.*' One of the waiters moved in alongside Monsieur Pamplemousse and served him from a tureen.

'Another of Dumas' own inventions,' said Elliott, for the

benefit of the assembly. 'He adored shellfish – shrimps especially.

'He made it with tomatoes, onions, white wine and the *bouillon* from a *pot au feu*. The tomatoes and onions are cooked in one pan, the shrimps with white wine in another. He always added a pinch of sugar to bring out the flavour of the tomato. I'm sure when you taste it you will agree the amalgamation is superb.'

While Elliott was talking, Monsieur Pamplemousse sipped the wine. It was a Pouilly Fumé: deliciously flinty. Its bouquet mingled perfectly with that of the soup.

He settled back and tried to make himself comfortable. Dressed in all his finery, it wasn't easy. Already there was a large smear of butter on his right sleeve. He looked around for some bread. D'Artagnan would probably have speared some from across the table with his sword. Monsieur Pamplemousse resisted the temptation.

The soup brought back memories of his childhood: the *bouillon* from Sunday's *pot au feu* which appeared as a base for other dishes all through the week. If the rest of the meal lived up to its early promise, then as a *restaurateur* Elliott would undoubtedly have been in line for a Stock Pot or two in *Le Guide*.

'Boy, this is something,' Harvey Wentworth smacked his lips.

'Dumas was lucky to have lived by the sea during an age of abundance,' said Monsieur Pamplemousse. 'Food was there for the taking and it was going to last for ever.'

'The field which ploughs itself,' said Elliott. 'And it's cheap. Compare an acre of the Atlantic with an acre anywhere in the States. But for years people ignored the fact that it still has to be sown.'

'It's the same all over the world,' agreed Harman. 'When

I was a kid in California you couldn't walk on the beach without treading on clams. Now they fine you if you're caught picking them up under a certain size.'

'You know something?' said Harvey. 'Take crabs, right? You get on an airline and what do they serve you? Crab meat, right? Or lobster. You know where most of it comes from? The Orient. They call it "blended sea-food product" which is supposed to make it OK, right? But what you're really eating is cod, plus starch, chemical seasoning and boiled down crab shells to give it the flavour. It's got to be big business, but the sad thing is people will grow up thinking it's the real thing.'

The *Lamproie à la Bordelaise* came and went while everyone started talking at once about the difficulties of living in such a profligate, uncaring world. Monsieur Pamplemousse decided it was probably a good thing. Prepared in the traditional way, the story of the lamprey's journey from the Gironde to the plate was not for the gastronomically fainthearted, even if in many people's eyes the end justified the means.

He concentrated instead on the second wine; a Grand Cru Chablis from the Domaine de la Maladière. Palish yellow in colour, with just a hint of green, it was steely dry, and richly perfumed without being cloying. From choice, he would have preferred a red; it would have gone better with the dark sauce made from the lamprey's own blood, but he wasn't grumbling.

The asparagus tips which followed were served with scrambled eggs to which a chicken *bouillon* had been added. It was a very smooth combination. Monsieur Pamplemousse reached instinctively for the notepad he normally kept concealed in his right trouser leg. As he did so he encountered a wet nose.

The sigh of contentment which emerged from beneath the table as he took the hint and delivered a sizable portion on a piece of bread didn't pass unnoticed. It was rewarded with a second helping.

Elliott called across. 'Don't tell me Monsieur d'Artagnan is flagging already. You disappoint me.'

'On the contrary. Pommes Frites is very fond of *asperge*. I was interested in his views.'

'You want my views?' Harman Lock broke off from a conversation he'd been having with Paul Robard. 'I reckon it's a good thing Norm wasn't here tonight. If drinking spa water did for him he would have died of a heart attack twice over by now.'

Monsieur Pamplemousse shrugged. 'Perhaps. They thought the Emperor Claudius died of indigestion through eating too many mushrooms until they found that whoever tickled his throat to make him vomit had used a poisoned feather.'

Harvey Wentworth leaned forward and looked along the table. 'What are you trying to say?' he demanded. 'That Norm didn't have heart failure?'

'No. Only that until the result of the post mortem no one knows why it stopped beating. It could have been for a variety of reasons.'

'It's the one certain thing that happens when we die,' agreed Paul.

'He didn't need the insurance money, that's for sure,' broke in Spencer Troon. 'I heard he got an advance of over a quarter of a million bucks for his next three books. A quarter of a million bucks without a word being written, would you believe?'

'I know one person who'll be in deep mourning at the funeral,' said Harman. 'His agent. I doubt if he's gotten a single word on paper.'

'He was probably waiting to see what we did next before he got started,' said Paul.

'I don't know so much,' said Harvey. 'At least he came up with something original before he died. Can you imagine having "Bring me a bottle of Bâtard Montrachet and some fish" written on your tombstone?'

Monsieur Pamplemousse caught Mrs Van Dorman's eye. She gave a slight shrug as much as to say 'What did I tell you?'

'Hey, fellers ...' It was Harman Lock. 'Can't we talk about something else tonight?'

Elliott rapped his knife against a glass, calling the table to order.

'Harman's right. It's time for the *ortolans*. In a moment I will ask you to cover your heads in the traditional manner. Special napkins will be provided. But before that ...' he glanced along the table towards Monsieur Pamplemousse, 'perhaps our honoured guest would like to tell you something about them. In his role of d'Artagnan they can be said to inhabit his part of the country, and I understand that in real life he is something of an expert.'

Monsieur Pamplemousse wasn't sure whether it was an attempt to put him down, or whether he was being paid a compliment. He decided to give Elliott the benefit of the doubt.

'I have to admit I have never eaten them – the nearest I have experienced is larks, but they are really at their best in winter. In the Auvergne, when I was a boy, I used to see *ortolans* fly over twice a year – in May and October. Once *en route* to Burgundy where they built their nests in the vineyards, and again on their way back south after the breeding season.'

He glanced towards Elliott. 'I must congratulate you on your detective work. In Alexandre Dumas' time they were a symbol of richness. Nowadays, like the fish we were talking about earlier, they have become something of a rarity. Tracking them down cannot have been easy.'

In view of the conversation round the table he was sorely tempted to point to a moral about shared guilt, but he decided that would be out of place.

As his dish was placed before him he was pleased to see that the birds had been cooked in the simplest way possible; wrapped in vine leaves and roasted in a pan rather than on a spit. There were three to a plate, resting on slices of toast. Each bird had a quarter of lemon beside it.

The *sommelier* offered up two bottles of wine. Monsieur Pamplemousse chose the Mouton in preference to the Léoville, then leaned back while a waiter tied a fresh napkin over his head. It was like the preparation for a sacred rite, which indeed it was in some people's eyes.

He felt a pressure against his left leg. Patently it didn't emanate from Pommes Frites. Pommes Frites wasn't given to sending messages in that way; the placing of a paw on the foot or knee perhaps, but not lingeringly on the calf. He glanced along at Mrs Van Dorman, but she had already disappeared beneath her napkin. It was hard to say whether she had been trying to attract his attention about something or was looking for support. Perhaps she didn't like the sight of small birds peering up at her. A sudden movement by Madame de Sauvignon on the other side of the table suggested that others were taking advantage of the situation.

The toast had been prepared by first cooking it in goose fat and afterwards spreading it with Roquefort cheese. It would test Alexandre Dumas' theory about raisins to the limit.

As he placed both hands beneath the canopy his napkin had formed over the *ortolans* and began dissecting the birds, Monsieur Pamplemousse found himself wondering about the evening. Mrs Van Dorman was wrong about one thing. It wasn't so much that her party bickered amongst themselves, rather that they all shared a common dislike of the late, but obviously not greatly lamented, Norm Ellis.

His first reaction on hearing of Ellis's death had been that he must have committed suicide. But if that were the case, it was a slightly bizarre way of going about it. On the surface he had everything to live for, but success didn't necessarily bring happiness, and as Elliott had so rightly said, things weren't always what they seemed. All the same, in his experience potential suicides very rarely used cyanide; in fact in all his time in the force, he couldn't remember having come across such a case.

Peeling off a piece of meat, he reached under the table, but Pommes Frites was no longer there.

Pommes Frites, in fact, had gone on a voyage of exploration. There were certain matters to attend to; things he wanted to get straight in his mind before he was very much older. Pommes Frites had an orderly, almost computer-like mind. It relied on the breaking down of problems into a series of short questions to which the answer was either yes or no. 'Perhaps' and 'maybe' were not words which formed part of his vocabulary, and there were currently too many of both for his liking.

Unaware of the reason for Pommes Frites' absence, Monsieur Pamplemousse consumed the offering himself, then took the opportunity to feel for his glass. Anyway, why choose Vichy of all places? Unless, of course, Ellis was going to extreme lengths to make it appear as though he had died from natural causes. Insurance perhaps? It hardly seemed likely. People committing suicide were seldom that thoughtful of the effect it would have on others, and he hardly seemed in great need.

The wine was rich and opulent, with an aroma of ripe plums and spicy oak. It was Mouton at its best.

And if Ellis hadn't committed suicide, what then? That thought and the ones which followed on took on a slightly eerie aspect in the circumstances. Sitting with his head in a shroud made him feel vulnerable, as he always did in a shower during the moment when his eyes were closed to protect them from the soap. Perhaps Mrs Van Dorman had been feeling it too and that was why she had reached out. He decided a call to the Poison Control Centre in Paris in the morning would not come amiss; although quite what he would ask them was another matter.

Quickly polishing off the remains of the dish, Monsieur Pamplemousse uncovered his face and reached for a finger bowl. He was the first to finish. The neat pile of tiny bones on his plate looked as though they had been picked clean by a hungry buzzard and then left to whiten in the desert sun.

Out of the corner of his eye he caught an approving look from the waiter as he removed the napkin from around his neck.

One by one the others emerged from beneath their hoods. Mrs Van Dorman was next. The heat had brought a flush to her cheeks. The beauty patch on her cheek seemed to have slipped slightly. It was probably one of the hazards of the period. He reached up and felt his beard to make sure it was still in place.

Feeling that some kind of comment was due, he called across to Elliott. 'My compliments to the chef. Brillat Savarin was right: "One becomes a cook, but one is born a roasting cook."'

670

Mrs Van Dorman looked at her own plate. 'I have a feeling I'm not going to make the finishing line,' she whispered.

Monsieur Pamplemousse glanced round the table. 'I think you are not the only one.'

'You do this kind of thing every day? For a living? How do you manage it?'

Monsieur Pamplemousse shrugged. 'All occupations have their hazards. I rarely accept second helpings. Sometimes I follow the example set by one of our rivals – Monsieur Christian Millau. He insists on being given half portions wherever he goes. When it is possible, I drink a glass of fresh carrot juice half an hour before a meal. It is very effective provided it is fresh – not bottled. And since I started reading Alexandre Dumas I have taken to carrying raisins for afterwards.'

'And they work?'

'I will tell you tomorrow. In between I rely on Pommes Frites. He never lets me down.' He was about to amend that to 'rarely', then thought better of it.

Mrs Van Dorman looked past him. 'I know one person who's enjoying himself. He hasn't been so quiet all evening.'

Monsieur Pamplemousse glanced to his right where a waiter was hovering behind the one remaining guest still wearing a shroud. Catching the man's eye, he gave a brief nod. Others bearing trays laden with sorbets were already waiting outside the door, and he could sense Elliott's impatience at the hold-up. No doubt he was anxious to reach the high spot of the evening – the *Rôtie à l'Impératrice*.

Neatly and deftly the waiter undid the knot holding the napkin in place and with a barberlike flourish shook it free. As he did so, almost as though he had withdrawn a cork from a bottle, there came an unearthly groan which sent a shiver round the room. For a moment there was total silence as the rest of those around the table stared aghast, then someone – it must have been Madame de Sauvignon – let out a scream.

Jumping to his feet, Monsieur Pamplemousse reached out, but he was a fraction of a second too late. With a crash which sent china and glass flying, Spencer Troon hit the table and lay motionless where he had landed. The dribble of blood which oozed from his lips mingled with the half-eaten remains of the *Ortolans à la Landaise*, giving the effect not so much of a classic dish of days gone by, but nouvelle cuisine at its most macabre.

With a sense of timing perfected over the years, Pommes Frites chose that particular moment to return from his wanderings. Taking in the situation at a glance he lifted his head and added his mite to Madame de Sauvignon's scream of horror. As a howl, it was not so much one of alarm or grief, but rather of indignation. The indignation of one who felt that if only he had been consulted earlier all this might not have happened.

5

THE LONE STRANGER

'Of all the Goddamn crazy things!' Elliott looked as though he was about to burst a blood vessel. Monsieur Pample-mousse had seldom seen anyone so furious. He was posi-tively white with rage.

'And what's with all the tomato ketchup?'

Spencer Troon, dabbing at his mouth with a napkin, looked bloody but unbowed.

'How the hell should I know? I haven't worked that bit out yet. Anyway, if you want to know, it isn't tomato ketchup. I got it from a joke shop in town.'

'I haven't worked that bit out yet,' mimicked Elliott. 'Typical! It's like everything else you do.'

'These things take time,' said Spencer. 'You should know that. Maybe I had a poisoned bone. Like that story Aristide here told about the feather.' He turned to Monsieur Pamplemousse for help. 'What was the guy's name? That Emperor ... the one who ate too many mushrooms?'

'Claudius?' Monsieur Pamplemousse was still recovering from his surprise – he wouldn't have admitted to the word shock – at finding Spencer return from the dead as it were. The whole episode had a strange surrealistic feel to it. One moment he'd been lying sprawled across the table looking as though he had breathed his last, the next moment he'd jumped to his feet uttering a triumphant cry as though nothing had happened. The others seemed to share Elliott's irritation, and he had to agree with them. In the circumstances it seemed a particularly tasteless joke to play.

'That's the one,' said Spencer. 'Claudius. He had a poisoned feather with his number on, right? So – in my case it was a bone. Like with Norm. Norm's number was called. That's why he's up there working away at the Great Word-Processor in the sky, right?'

'Jesus!' said Harman. 'Why can't you just say he's dead? How many different ways are there of not saying it?'

'You name it,' broke in Paul Robard, 'they come up with it. "Non-viable condition"; "negative patient care outcome"; "paying a call on the perpetual rest consultant"; "patient failed to fulfil his wellness potential". They've got a million.'

'You're right there,' conceded Harman. 'Anything to pass the buck. You know, I even read the other day of a guy who took an overdose and put himself into a "non-decision-making mode". Can you beat that? The poor sap tries to end it all and what do they call it? A "non-decision-making mode". Decisions don't come any bigger than wanting to do away with yourself.'

'What happened to him?' asked Harvey Wentworth.

'They botched the treatment. Some intern took a decision for him and it just so happened it was the wrong one. He suffered a "negative mortality experience". In other words, same as Norm. He died.'

'What the hell?' said Spencer. 'I had you all fooled there for a moment and somebody had to be runner-up. I know one thing, though. If Norm *is* working away at his word-processor, the rest of us are going to suffer "inventory shrinkage" when it comes to stock-appraisal time.'

Elliott gave a deep, deep sigh as he rose to his feet. 'I suggest we change the subject. I refuse to allow the evening to be spoilt because of a petty, childish prank.'

He crossed to the sideboard where the *sommelier* had placed a lighted candle behind the neck of the bottle held in the decanting machine. The cork had been drawn some time previously. A row of seven glasses arranged alongside the machine provided an answer to another of Monsieur Pamplemousse's earlier unspoken questions. The thespians were having to do without. He could hardly blame Elliott. Considering what the wine must have cost it would be carrying generosity a bit far to share it amongst the whole table, although from the look on one or two of the actors' faces it was not a view shared by all. Alexandre Dumas in particular had so far forgotten his role that he was looking most aggrieved. Method acting was obviously not his particular forte.

'Anyway,' Elliott bent down and cranked the handle very gently until almost imperceptibly the bottle, already some ten degrees or so off the vertical, began to tilt still further, 'we're all wasting our breath. The contest is null and void.'

'What do you mean – null and void?' exclaimed Spencer. 'I chipped in the same as everyone else.'

'Ssh!' Aware that the *sommelier* was casting a critical eye over his right shoulder, watching his every move, Elliott was not disposed to argue.

'Do what the man says,' broke in Harman. 'Can't you see he's busy?'

While all eyes turned to watch Elliott at work, the sorbet arrived, replacing the absinthe of Dumas' day.

'It is a lemon *granité*, Monsieur,' whispered the waiter with evident approval. 'It is made with the addition of a little *anisette*.'

'Jesus!' exclaimed Paul Robard as he took a mouthful. 'What are they trying to do – poison us?'

Monsieur Pamplemousse tasted a little. Judged simply as a palate cleanser it was undervaluing itself. A confirmed alcoholic would have been kept happy for days; a furniture restorer would have looked no further for some polish remover. No wonder the waiter's hand had been a little shaky.

He pondered over the conversation that had just taken place, wishing once again that his command of the language was better. It was hard to tell what the others were thinking; the dialogue might well have been lifted out of any of their books – delivered in a brittle, poker-faced fashion. But beneath it all he sensed undeniable nuances and undercurrents, the true meaning of which escaped him for the moment. He resolved to question Mrs Van Dorman later. In the meantime he broke off a piece of bread and chewed it for a moment or two in order to take away the taste of the *granité*.

'I suggest we all do the same,' said Elliott approvingly, as he returned to the table and stood hovering like a mother hen over her chicks while the waiter distributed the glasses.

Monsieur Pamplemousse studied his own offering for a moment or two, almost afraid to touch it in case the contents of the glass disappeared or he shook up some vital element which would cause the wine to break up. Elliott had done a good job. Not only had he managed to extract seven moderate servings from the bottle, but the liquid was crystal clear with no tell-tale traces of murkiness which would have occurred had any of the sediment been disturbed during the pouring.

He picked up his glass and held it at arm's length. The wine was a deep amber colour. It showed well against the soft candle-light. The glass was a Riedel Bordeaux – shaped so as to enhance the wine rather than show up its defects, throwing the contents towards the back of the mouth and away from the tip of the tongue and the 'sweet' taste buds.

The Director would have envied him, in fact most of those who had wangled their way out of the assignment would have envied him at that moment. It served them right.

He was soon so lost in thought he was hardly aware of the *Rôtie à l'Impératrice* arriving.

It must have tested the chef to the full; not only in the preparation and the cooking, but in the serving of it as well. It must have been no easy matter to ensure that everyone received their fair share of all the component parts; the pork, the turkey, the pheasant, the partridge, the quail and the lark. The juice came separately in silver serving bowls, along with a simple salad of fresh dandelion leaves; it was exactly right; anything more would have been unnecessary – a case of over-gilding the lily – and the slightly bitter taste would counterbalance the richness of the dish.

'The next-question', said Elliott, 'is whether we drink the wine by itself or savour it along with what is, after all, the main event of the evening. Aristide, what do you think?'

Once again Monsieur Pamplemousse had the feeling he was being tested. 'In my view,' he said, 'a wine such as this deserves our full attention. Look at that colour.' He held the glass to his nose. It was rich and fragrant; spicy. 'And smell the bouquet.'

He paused for a moment. 'It is *formidable* ... *merveilleux*. I think we should, perhaps, do both. Drink a little of the wine by itself first, then test it against the *rôtie*. In that way we can have the best of both worlds and there will be no argument afterwards.'

The truth of the matter was he would have been more than happy just to savour the wine. It would be a memorable way of rounding off the evening. He had a feeling the *Rôtie à l'Impératrice* might come under the heading of 'experiences I have known' or possibly even 'experiences I wish I hadn't known'. It represented the worst excesses of the period. Contemplating his plate, he was reminded of the time when he had taken Doucette to see a film called *La Grande Bouffe*. They hadn't wanted to eat for days afterwards. Now the thought had entered his mind he couldn't rid himself of it, and he was relieved when he felt a stirring at his feet. Even if he had been an avid cinema goer, Pommes Frites would have suffered no such inhibitions.

'Spoken like a true diplomat,' said Elliott. 'D'Artagnan himself couldn't have put it better. How about the bouquet? Has anyone got any ideas?'

'I guess I can pick up some kind of spices,' said Harman. 'Don't ask me what.'

'I get a bit of Eucalyptus.' said Harvey.

'A touch of resin, maybe?' Paul Robard hazarded a guess.

'I'd go for raspberries,' said Spencer. 'Raspberries and currants – fruit anyway.'

'DiAnn?'

'I think I would agree about the fruit,' said Mrs Van Dorman. 'But there are so many things. Does anyone else get almond? It comes over quite strongly in my glass.'

There was a murmur of dissent from around the table. Suddenly alert, Monsieur Pamplemousse leaned forward.

Mrs Van Dorman raised the glass to her lips. 'Well someone has to start, I guess.'

'*Attention!*' Leaping to his feet, Monsieur Pamplemousse made a grab for Mrs Van Dorman's hand. Somehow or other, as she jerked back her head the glass eluded him and flew out of her hand. As it landed with a crash on Elliott's plate, a rivulet of dark red liquid slowly spread out across the table.

For a second or two everyone sat in stunned silence. Pommes Frites was the first to move. He put his front paws on the table, gave the remains of the wine a desultory sniff, then settled himself down alongside his master to await further developments. They weren't long in coming.

Elliott rose to his feet. 'I don't know what occasioned that behaviour, nor do I wish to ruin what until now has been a thoroughly delightful evening by enquiring into the matter further. I assume you had good reasons for behaving as you did …'

Monsieur Pamplemousse also rose. 'I can assure you, Monsieur Garner, I had very good reasons, although I would rather not elaborate on them at this moment in time. Please accept my sincere apologies.'

Elliott gave a brief nod. 'I think we are all a little on edge this evening.'

'I hope …' Monsieur Pamplemousse picked up his own glass and handed it to Mrs Van Dorman, 'I hope Madame Joyeux will accept this in recompense.' It was the least he could do.

'I won't say no to sharing.'

Elliott left the table. 'If you will excuse me … I must go and wipe myself down. Please carry on.'

Suddenly you could feel the relief in the air as Elliott left the room.

'If that was me,' said Harman Lock, 'I'd be wanting to squeegee my pants into the nearest glass.'

'There'll be a third thing,' said Paul darkly, as he speared a mouthful of meat with his fork. 'Any guesses as to what it'll be?'

There were no takers.

It was, to all intents and purposes, the end of the evening. For all its uniqueness, the *Rôtie à l'Impératrice* came as something of an anti-climax. There were no takers for a second helping.

By the time Elliott returned, most of the guests were either ready for the next course, or only too willing to do without it. The peaches in wine had few takers. Sadly, Monsieur Pamplemousse watched his pears with bacon begin its journey back to the kitchen, untouched even by Pommes Frites. The cheese board followed swiftly in its wake. Coffee was a muted affair. The farewell speech by Elliott and the vote of thanks by Mrs Van Dorman were both mercifully brief.

'What did you make of all that?' asked Monsieur Pamplemousse as they took their leave of the others and headed towards the door.

'I thought Elliott took it remarkably well. I felt so sorry for him. Do you know how much that bottle cost? They say he nursed it all across the Atlantic. Sat with it between his knees and wouldn't let it out of his sight. It's almost as bad as that time at the Four Seasons in New York when a waiter hit a bottle of 1787 Château Margaux with his tray. Remember? Over four hundred thousand dollars of wine disappeared into the carpet.'

'Indeed I do.' It wasn't what he'd meant, but clearly Mrs Van Dorman was blissfully unaware of the fact that for a moment he had feared for her life.

'What came over you? I couldn't believe my eyes.'

Monsieur Pamplemousse wondered if he should tell the truth – it was hard to know how she would take it – but as they were about to leave the house she abruptly changed the subject.

'Oh, God! I'd completely forgotten. We have a reception committee.'

'I have been wondering,' said the photographer, 'if perhaps we should try something in *contre-jour*. *Madame* could stand exactly where she is ... perhaps a little further out ... so that she is framed in the doorway with the light behind ... a handkerchief in her hand to stem the tears as she waves goodbye. *Monsieur* can be in the foreground, mounting his charger.'

Monsieur Pamplemousse considered the idea for a moment. He could think of no very good reason why d'Artagnan would have wished to leave his mistress at that moment – unless, of course, another adventure called. On the other hand, flushed with good food, awash with even better wine – the memory of his share of the Lafite '84 still lingering in his mouth – he felt in an obliging mood.

'Whatever you suggest. *Pas de problème!*'

Mrs Van Dorman opened a small purse she had been carrying all the evening and searched for something suitable to wave. 'Do be careful, Aristide. Remember what happened last time.'

'This time,' said the groom, 'I have brought a *montoir* – a mounting block.'

'You see,' said Monsieur Pamplemousse, as he accepted the other's outstretched hand. 'It is as I said ... *pas de problème*.'

'I have also taken the precaution of fitting *Le Diable Noir* with blinkers so that he cannot see you,' said the man. He sounded anxious to get to bed.

Pommes Frites did a double-take as he joined Mrs Van Dorman in the doorway and contemplated the scene before him.

'*Excellent!*' exclaimed the photographer. 'The finishing touch! *Ne quittez pas, s'il vous plaît!*'

In assuming that Pommes Frites had taken up the pose of a hunter ready to spring into action at a moment's notice simply because he wished to be in the picture, the photographer was doing him a grave injustice. Pommes Frites was not so much riveted to the spot for artistic reasons as glued to it because he could hardly believe what was going on. Although in the normal course of events Monsieur Pamplemousse could do no wrong in Pommes Frites' eyes, if questioned on the subject he would have been forced to admit that there were moments when in his humble opinion his master came very close to pushing his luck a bit too far. Patently this was one of those occasions.

But even Pommes Frites was hardly prepared for the events of the next few seconds.

Emboldened on the one hand by the wine, and if he'd been totally honest, a sudden desire to impress Mrs Van Dorman, Monsieur Pamplemousse flung caution to the wind. As a schoolboy he had learned the lesson that bravery is often a mixture of foolhardiness coupled with the fear of being laughed at. Given something nobody really wants to do, there are positive advantages in being first to have a go; at least you get it over with. In that way he had gained something of a reputation for bravery; leading the rest of the class into the water when it was time for a swimming lesson on a cold winter's day, or being first up a tree when a kite became entangled in its uppermost branches.

It was in much the same spirit that he snatched the purse from Mrs Van Dorman and in one swift movement leapt into the air, landing more by luck than judgement fairly and squarely in the middle of the saddle.

For the second time that evening the photographer

missed his big moment. There was no possibility of another chance. As Monsieur Pamplemousse landed on its back, *Le Diable Noir* gave a loud whinny and reared into the air like a bucking bronco determined to free itself of its rider. The fact that horse and rider remained as one was simply because Monsieur Pamplemousse had got his own impedimenta entangled with that of his steed. Clutching Mrs Van Dorman's purse in one hand, holding on like grim death to the *pommeau* with his other, stirrups flying in the wind, he disappeared down the drive and out through the open gate as though shot from a canon.

A moment later Pommes Frites woke from his trance and set off in hot pursuit.

Whichever of Monsieur Pamplemousse's guardian angels was unlucky enough to be taking the late shift that night must have been torn between watching over his charge and keeping an up-to-the-minute record of the events which followed. Doubtless in the circumstances he was forgiven for lapsing into some kind of heavenly shorthand.

X'd boulevard Pres. Kennedy. Entered Parc du Soleil by r. On to D426 then N. on to D270 and D175.

Had he dared, Monsieur Pamplemousse would gladly have swopped Mrs Van Dorman's purse for *Le Diable Noir's* blinkers.

As they headed towards open country the telephone in the local gendarmerie began to ring. It was the first of many calls from late-night motorists and startled householders wakened by the clatter of hooves. But by the time it was answered Monsieur Pamplemousse was already lying in a ditch. The Monts de la Madeleine, which only that morning had seemed so far away, now loomed uncomfortably close.

Thankful to be alive and in one piece, he lay for some while where he had landed. Mercifully the ditch was devoid of water. It was even, by comparison with the saddle, remarkably soft and comfortable and he had no great desire to move.

Gradually growing accustomed to his surroundings and having assured himself that there were no broken bones, Monsieur Pamplemousse relaxed. As he did so he became aware of the sound of an approaching car. Struggling into a sitting position, he gave a desultory wave. Almost immediately he wished he hadn't.

Temporarily blinded by the headlights, which remained pointing straight at him as the car skidded to a halt, Monsieur Pamplemousse raised an arm to shield his eyes from the glare.

It was too late to hide. Hands reached out and helped him clamber to his feet. There was a pause while he recovered his balance and then the first of the two *gendarmes* spoke.

'*Monsieur*, may I see your papers?'

'I have no papers,' said Monsieur Pamplemousse. 'At least, not on me. They are in my Hôtel room.'

The men exchanged glances. 'Your name, *Monsieur*?' enquired the second *gendarme*.

Monsieur Pamplemousse essayed an attempt at the jocular. 'I am Charles de Batz-Castelmore, but you may call me d'Artagnan.'

'*Oui, Monsieur*,' said the first, 'and I am Robespierre.'

Monsieur Pamplemousse recognised the type. Sound in many ways. Painstaking. Given the right instructions, he would be indefatigable in following up an inquiry. But no sense of humour whatsoever.

'All right,' he said wearily. 'My name is Pamplemousse. Late of the *Sûreté*.'

The two men looked at each other again. '*Oui,*

Monsieur,' said the second one. 'Now, will you please turn around.'

Monsieur Pamplemousse knew better than to argue. He would have done the same thing in their place; a quick frisk to check for concealed weapons; no guns concealed in the ruff, no hidden knives. Better safe than sorry. There was room for a whole armoury inside his sleeves. He waited patiently while the officer subjected him to a brief body search. First the top half, then the lower. Suddenly he felt his arms being grasped from behind. There was a tightening round his wrists followed by a series of rapid clicks.

'*Sacrébleu!*' He struggled to free himself, but it was too late.

'What is the meaning of this?'

'The meaning, *Monsieur*,' said the first *gendarme*, 'is quite simple. You are under arrest.'

'Arrest? On what charge?'

'You really wish to know?' The man's voice sounded pained. He turned to his colleague for support. 'First of all he terrorises half the neighbourhood by rampaging through the streets at one o'clock in the morning on a horse. Then he is found lying in a ditch wearing fancy dress and smelling of drink. Next he gives a series of false names ... And he wants to know why we are arresting him!'

The second *gendarme* gave a hollow laugh.

'All right,' said Monsieur Pamplemousse. He could see there was little point in arguing. 'I can explain it all when we get to the station. But in the meantime – what about my horse?'

'Your horse, *Monsieur*? What horse?'

Monsieur Pamplemousse nodded towards a small clump of trees on the far side of the road. 'He is somewhere over there. You can hardly leave him to roam around loose all

685

night. Who knows what damage he may cause?

'*Ici! Ici!*' Warming to his theme, he emitted a series of whistles which, if they did nothing else, produced a satisfactory and clearly recognisable response from further down the road. A single bark indicated that Pommes Frites wasn't far away.

'*Attendez un moment, Monsieur.*'

The possibility that he might do anything other than wait clearly didn't enter the mind of the *gendarmes* as they crossed the road. One of them produced a torch and began waving it around in a desultory fashion.

Monsieur Pamplemousse held back until they reached the trees, then he turned and took a flying leap across the ditch. As he landed on the far side he slipped on the turf. For a brief moment he thought he was going to fall. Then, regaining his balance with an almost superhuman effort, he was away. Oblivious to the shouts calling him to stop or else, he set off across the open country as fast as he could.

From somewhere behind him he heard the sound of barking; barking followed by snarls. There were several shrill blasts on a whistle, then silence. By the sound of things Pommes Frites was doing his bit.

Monsieur Pamplemousse wasn't sure how long he carried on running; it was probably only a matter of minutes, but it seemed like hours. Heart pounding, his breath becoming shorter with every passing moment, he kept going; across fields, in and out of ditches, over rocks, until gradually the running dwindled into a jog, and the jog into a walk. Finally, stumbling over a boulder, he sat down in order to regain his breath.

He still wasn't sure quite why he had done it. Instinct; a spur of the moment decision. But he'd burned his boats and no mistake.

The irony of the situation suddenly struck home. He, Aristide Pamplemousse, late of the *Sûreté*, on the run like a common criminal. It was too late to do anything about it now. It had been too late after the first few metres. There was no going back and saying he was sorry. That would go down like a lead balloon. Overcome by a sudden burst of self-pity at the idiocy of the whole thing, he banged his handcuffs against the rock in the hope of dislodging the ratchet – but it only made them tighter still.

Running away when he'd first seen the car headlights was one thing – a not unnatural reaction – he could have pleaded he didn't realise he was dealing with the police. Escaping from custody was something else again. They would throw the book at him. It sounded bad enough sitting in the middle of a field in the early hours of the morning, but read out in court in the cold light of day, or plastered over the front page of a *journal*, it could mean the end of everything.

He tried to remember what the *gendarmes* had said. It was unlikely that they would have linked him with the banquet, if they even knew of its existence. They probably thought he'd been to a fancy dress party, or perhaps they'd assumed he was one of the singers from the Opera House suffering from over-indulgence following an after-the-show party. It wouldn't take them long to discover the truth. Or would it? It depended how seriously they took the matter, or what else came up. He had a feeling the senior of the two *gendarmes* wouldn't rest until he'd got to the bottom of the matter.

One thing was certain. Sitting on his backside would get him nowhere. At all costs he must return to the hotel as quickly as possible. Onee daylight came, discovery would be only a matter of time. He made one last effort to free himself, but it was hopeless. The handcuffs were on the last possible notch – they were biting into the flesh. In doing them up behind his back the *gendarmes* had known a thing or two. At least they hadn't bothered to double-lock them. In any other circumstances he could have freed himself in a matter of seconds with the aid of a piece of bent wire. It was a simple matter of lifting the ratchet wheel away from the bar. If he had a piece of bent wire!

What he needed most of all was a telephone. Making use of it with his hands behind his back would be something else again, but he would cross that bridge when he came to it. He felt tempted to give a shout – just one – in the hope that Pommes Frites might hear. But that would be tempting providence.

Everything seemed to have gone remarkably quiet. At least it wasn't raining. The sky was inky black and full of stars. He heard a twig snap somewhere close by. It was followed by a grunting noise, then silence as whatever was responsible stopped in its tracks. Conscious that something unseen was probably watching him, Monsieur Pamplemousse gave a shiver. The cold air was beginning to penetrate his costume.

He wondered what the real d'Artagnan would have done. For a start he would more than likely have been wearing the then equivalent of thermal underwear. He certainly wouldn't have been without his horse. Ever resourceful, had he lived in the present age he would doubtless have had a portable telephone tucked away somewhere as well.

Clambering to his feet, Monsieur Pamplemousse went on his way. After about a quarter of an hour he saw what he was looking for. Showing up against the skyline were two sets of cables. The first looked like a power line. The second had to be a telephone. Tossing a mental coin as to which way to go, he followed the line of posts up the side of a hill towards a small patch of woodland. Sure enough, when he came out on the other side of the trees he stumbled across a narrow track. The surface looked well worn from frequent use, and at the end of it there was a cluster of farm buildings.

Hopes raised, he made his way towards an iron gate. As he drew near a dog barked a warning. It was quickly taken up by a second animal. He waited for a moment or two, expecting to hear the sound of pounding feet, but they must have been tied up somewhere, for it didn't materialise. He heard an upper window being flung open and a shout. At least whoever lived there was already awake.

As Monsieur Pamplemousse reached the main building he backed up to the front door and thumped on it with his fists, then turned and stepped back a pace to see if it had any effect. Out of the corner of his eye he sensed a movement from one of the attic windows. Some curtains parted and he had a brief glimpse of three faces peering out at him. He assumed they must be the daughters of the house, for they were all young and patently female. Essaying a wave, he nearly fell over in the attempt, but before any of them had a chance to respond they were pushed to one side and another figure appeared. A double-barrelled shot-gun gleamed momentarily in the moonlight, then the curtains fell back into place.

He had almost given up waiting when he heard the sound of a bolt being withdrawn on the other side of the door, then another. It was followed by the metallic click of a gun being cocked.

As the door slowly opened he braced himself. '*Monsieur* … please forgive me for waking you at such an hour. I fear

I have had an accident with my horse. I wonder if I might use your telephone?'

'You leave my daughters alone. I saw you waving at them.' The speaker had an accent you could have cut with a knife. Only a very dim light came from inside the house, but from the colour of the man's skin he guessed he was dealing with a North African, although what an Arab was doing ensconced on a hillside in the Auvergne goodness only knew. It was no moment to enquire.

'I assure you, *Monsieur*. I only wish to use your telephone.'

'That's what they all say.'

'*S'il vous plaît, Monsieur*? I will not be ungenerous.'

The man peered out at him as though making a swift evaluation of his worth. 'How much?'

Monsieur Pamplemousse hesitated, thinking once again of his P.39s. Unexpected expenses were starting to mount. It was hard to say how much Madame Grante might consider reasonable in the circumstances.

Inspiration struck as he remembered he was still clutching Mrs Van Dorman's purse. Struggling as best he could to avoid letting the man see the handcuffs, he made a half turn and waved it to and fro. 'Let us just say "whatever you think is right and proper".'

The man thought it over for a moment or two. 'Where are you from?'

'Gascony.' It was as good a place as any and it seemed to satisfy the other, for he stood back and motioned with the shot-gun for Monsieur Pamplemousse to enter.

'All right, then. Just one call. But no wanting funny business afterwards.'

'*Vous êtes très gentil, Monsieur.*'

As he entered the house Monsieur Pamplemousse was

greeted by a smell of stale air. It was so overpowering he wanted to reach for his handkerchief. Stale food, unwashed bodies, cheap perfume, cats; a public health inspector would have had a field day. Halfway across the room he tripped over something. It felt like a ball and chain.

There was no sign of the other occupants of the house. Everything had gone deathly quiet again. If he hadn't seen them with his own eyes they might not have existed.

'Any funny business and I'll have your *couilles* off and fry them in batter for *déjeuner.*' There was a cackle from halfway up the stairs. He groped his way towards it.

'It wouldn't be the first time,' said the voice.

'Nor the last.'

Monsieur Pamplemousse was glad when they reached the landing. The conversation was getting both one-sided and tedious. Nor did he much care for the gratuitous sound effects which accompanied the remarks.

He stood waiting while the man unlocked a door and then motioned him to enter. There was no doubt about it; he was *un bicot*; *un bicot* of the very worst kind. He should have stayed in North Africa where he belonged.

'In here. And don't take too long about it.'

Anxious to get the matter over with, Monsieur Pamplemousse did as he was told. The room was in darkness and as he stood waiting for his eyes to get accustomed to the gloom the door slammed shut behind him.

'*Merde!*' It was the second time that evening he'd been caught unawares. He made a dive for the door, but before he was halfway there he heard the sound of a key being turned.

'*Bougnoule! Melon!* Come back! Let me out!'

The only response was another cackle.

In desperation Monsieur Pamplemousse delivered a kick

in the direction of the sound, then immediately regretted it as he made contact with the door.

Having felt in vain for a light switch and drawn a blank, he hobbled across to the window and looked out. Any hope of making a jump for it faded fast. Immediately below him there was a pile of old farm implements. Monsieur Pamplemousse didn't fancy his chances if he landed on them. The old man's wishes might be granted sooner than he expected. Even in the moonlight their barbs and prongs looked lethal.

Seeing everything from a different angle showed that he was in some kind of scrap-yard. Pieces of rusty farm machinery lay everywhere. Most of it looked as though it had been there for years. An old open-topped bus stood in one corner, its chassis broken. Weeds sprouted from unlikely places. Somewhat surprisingly there was a tarmac area which seemed to have been set aside for a makeshift car park. There were lines painted on it to mark the spaces, but there was no sign of a car.

Somewhere amongst it all there had to be a ladder, or at least something that would serve as one. If only he could get at it. He turned away from the window hoping there might at least be a bed with some sheets, but the room seemed totally devoid of furniture. He couldn't even find anywhere to sit.

Monsieur Pamplemousse spent the next ten minutes or so pacing up and down in a state of growing frustration. After a while he thought he detected a noise coming from the corridor. He crept towards the door and put his ear to it. He could hear someone whispering. It was followed by a giggle.

'*Qui est là?*' At the sound of his voice the noise stopped abruptly.

He tried again. 'Who is there? Can you open the door?'

'No. It is not possible. He has the key.' The voice was female; the accent a softer version of the man's.

'In that case, we have an *impasse*.' Nice though it was to hear another voice, there seemed little point in pursuing the conversation.

A piece of paper appeared under the door. It was followed by more giggles. Crouching down, Monsieur Pamplemousse managed to pick it up. He took it across to the window, placed it on the sill, then turned and peered at it. He could hardly believe his eyes. Expecting a message of some kind, he was confronted instead with a coloured drawing.

'*Sacrébleu!*' He couldn't help himself. Even without the aid of a torch it was clear that anatomically correct though the result might be, its influences owed more to readings of the Kama Sutra than from any medical publication. Explicit was hardly the word. *Extraordinaire* was more like it.

In a fit of desperation Monsieur Pamplemousse opened Mrs Van Dorman's purse and felt inside it. There was a small comb, a handkerchief, several articles he couldn't immediately identify, and then ... he found what he was looking for. Undoing the top of a lipstick he put the holder in his mouth, turned the paper over, and began laboriously writing out a message.

MY HANDS ARE TIED. PLEASE FREE ME.
I WILL PAY YOU WELL. NAME YOUR PRICE.

His task completed, he passed it under the door and waited for some kind of reaction. His only reward was another burst of giggling.

He was about to remonstrate when a dog barked. The

others must have heard it too, for without another word they disappeared down the corridor. Once again there was a shout followed by silence.

Peering through the open window he made out the familiar shape of Pommes Frites crouched in a patch of weeds on the far side. Pommes Frites was much too well trained to give any sign that he had seen his master, but he gradually eased his way across the yard on his stomach until he reached the pile of machinery below the window where he waited, his tail moving gently to and fro.

Monsieur Pamplemousse allowed himself to be seen for a brief moment, then threw Mrs Van Dorman's purse down to him. Pommes Frites sniffed it once. The message was clear without his master having to utter so much as a word.

Once again, as had so often happened in the past, it was a case of *cherchez la femme*.

Following a trail carefully laid at strategic points on the outward journey, Pommes Frites set off into the darkness, glad that at long last there was something concrete to do.

Monsieur Pamplemousse watched until he had disappeared from view. It would be some while before he would see Pommes Frites again, but that he would see him before the night was over he had little doubt.

He wondered if the recipients of his note were making equal efforts on his behalf. Somehow, he doubted it. Perhaps all three were tucked up in bed hard at work on more drawings.

Unable to check the hour by virtue of a handicap which Messrs Cupillard Rième could scarcely have been expected to foresee when they designed the dial of his wrist watch, Monsieur Pamplemousse sat down to wait, counting off in his mind first the seconds, then the minutes.

As an exercise in passing the time it soon began to pall,

and he had long since given up making the effort when he heard the sound of an engine. And not just any old engine; it was the unmistakable noise made by the 602cc flat-twin, air-cooled engine of a Citroën *deux chevaux*.

It stopped some distance away and then there was silence again. Mrs Van Dorman was learning fast. Straining his eyes for any sign of movement, Monsieur Pample-mousse stationed himself by the open window. Doubtless Pommes Frites would lead the way; and what was perhaps even more important, it would be done quietly and stealthily so as to avoid waking any of the others. He would be in his element. With luck, there wouldn't be much longer to wait.

6
COMINGS AND GOINGS

Monsieur Pamplemousse lay back on the bed, too tired even to remove the sword dangling from his belt. Closing his eyes for a moment, he concentrated all his energies on fighting off a growing feeling of claustrophobia at still having his hands securely fastened behind his back. Never before had he felt quite so powerless, or so frustrated.

'Are you sure you have nothing?' he called. 'No safety-pins? Not even a paper-clip?'

'I have pins galore.' Mrs Van Dorman searched through a tray on her dressing table. 'Long ones, short ones, fat ones, thin ones ... you name it. I just don't have anything I can use to make a right angle bend in one.'

'*Merde!*' If only he'd been in his own room. If he'd been in his own room he would have had his emergency case – the one issued by *Le Guide*; designed to cater for all eventualities. The possibility of having to bend the end of a safety-pin or a piece of stiff wire in order to break open a set of hand-cuffs, although not specifically envisaged in the list of basic requirements, would have been *pas de problème*. One twist with the small pair of pliers included in his wisdom by the founder, and he would have been home and dry.

'Poor Aristide. Are you feeling very frustrated?'

Monsieur Pamplemousse opened his eyes and raised them ceiling-wards as he felt a tug, first on his right leg, then on his left. It was a self-answering question.

Mrs Van Dorman slid his boots under the bed. 'What are you thinking?'

'I was thinking that you are very kind. I don't know what I would have done tonight without you. If it wasn't for you I would still be incarcerated in that dreadful farmhouse.' In truth he was thinking many other things as well. His mind was awash with thoughts.

'What else? You are very quiet.'

'I was wondering about Pommes Frites' sense of smell. I am a little worried that he may be losing it.'

'How can you say that after all he's been through? He followed you to the farmhouse, then back here. Then he led me all the way back to the farmhouse again while I drove the car. Listen to him ... poor thing ... he's quite worn out.'

Almost as though he was aware in his sleep that he was being talked about, Pommes Frites gave a loud snore. It was the first of many to come.

Monsieur Pamplemousse was less than sympathetic. 'Following me there the first time was second nature; that is what he is trained to do. Going back to it again was simply a matter of covering old ground. As for finding his way to the hotel between whiles – he has his methods. After all the *asperge* he ate earlier in the evening he could hardly have gone wrong. No, it was something else which makes me wonder. As you say, his nose cannot be entirely redundant, but I wonder if it is only firing on three cylinders.'

'I think we probably all are at the moment.' Mrs Van Dorman plumped up his pillow. 'And what else do we have on our mind?'

'I was thinking I must send a fax message.'

'Now? Right this minute? Can't it wait until morning?'

'The sooner the better. In Paris I have a set of skeleton keys.'

'How do you know one of them will fit?'

'It will. All I have to do is match a key to the make. The mechanism is really very basic. In most cases one key will fit all locks from the same manufacturer.' Given time he was sure he could instruct Mrs Van Dorman in the ancient art of lock-picking, but to have a set of keys would be an insurance policy in the event that he failed. For all he knew she might be totally impractical; unable to open a can of soup, let alone a pair of *menottes*.

It would have sounded ungracious to add that for the moment at least he wanted nothing more than to be left alone with his thoughts. He was at a stage when normally he would have made a list of questions that needed answering. If he'd had his notebook ... and if he'd been in a position to hold a pen. He let out a sigh. There were so many 'ifs'.

'OK.' Mrs Van Dorman took the hint. 'Tell me what you want to say. I'll see if I can wake the night clerk. If he's not around I'll send it myself. Where do you want it to go?'

'It is to my office.' Monsieur Pamplemousse gave her the number, then dictated as succinct a message as possible. 'Mark it for the attention of the Director's secretary – Véronique. She will know what to do.'

As the door closed behind Mrs Van Dorman, he tried to get out of bed, but after a moment or two gave up the struggle. His whole body was aching. It felt as though no part of it had gone unscathed from the ride on the horse. Bits that he didn't know existed were making their presence felt. He glanced at a clock on the bedside table. It was after three o'clock. Alongside the clock was an open box of fudge. It was nice to think of Mrs Van Dorman having a guilty secret.

Monsieur Pamplemousse lay back and closed his eyes

again. Beginning at the beginning, he started running through the various questions uppermost in his mind.

That Norm's demise had cast little more than a passing shadow on the previous night's proceedings was patently obvious, but he couldn't help feeling there was some other element involved.

There was the question of Spencer Troon's performance over dinner for a start; pretending he'd been poisoned. That it hadn't exactly endeared him to Elliott was hardly surprising in the circumstances. But what had been behind Spencer's remark that at least it made him 'runner-up'? Runner-up to what? Or to whom?

And then there was Pommes Frites' strange behaviour, which had occasioned his remark to Mrs Van Dorman. Why had he ignored her glass of wine when it was knocked over? He hadn't given it so much as a passing sniff, treating it almost with contempt. And yet there definitely had been a scent of bitter almonds, reminiscent of the smell they had both received from Ellis's tasting glass. If he, Pample-mousse, had noticed it, why hadn't Pommes Frites? Normally he would have been in there like a shot.

His thoughts were broken into at that point by the return of Mrs Van Dorman. She looked flushed as she let herself into the room, opening and closing the door as quietly as possible.

She put a finger to her lips. 'The *gendarme* is still outside your room. I think you'd better stay here for the time being.'

Monsieur Pamplemousse didn't feel disposed to argue.

'Let me cover you up – you'll get cold.' Mrs Van Dorman pulled the eiderdown up over him. 'There's nothing else we can do until morning. The fax has gone off. And I had a word with the night clerk. I've asked him to arrange with the telephonist tomorrow morning to have any calls for you transferred to this room.'

'You think he will oblige?'

'I'm sure he will if he wants to earn the rest of his bonus. Besides, the whole place reeks of nepotism. The bell captain is his uncle, and the switchboard operator just happens to be the granddaughter of a friend. He's promised to pass the word around to the rest of the staff. I get the feeling he doesn't like the police.'

Monsieur Pamplemousse nodded. It was probably an echo of some unmentionable wrong dating back to the war years. The police must have gained a lot of enemies in Vichy during the time the pro-Hitler puppet government was in residence.

'How about the man outside my door? Do you think he heard you coming up in the lift?'

'No way. I used the back stairs.'

The thought of Mrs Van Dorman bothering to come up the back stairs on his behalf made Monsieur Pamplemousse feel strangely excited. What was the old saying? The most beautiful moment of a love affair is the one when you are climbing the stairs. Even if the sentiment were true, it didn't seem like a moment they were destined to share.

Mrs Van Dorman hovered for a moment. 'Do you mind if I have a quick shower? I'm dying to get out of these clothes. I've been corseted long enough.'

'Of course not.'

Monsieur Pamplemousse wondered if he should take her into his confidence. Obviously the whole thing was giving her a kind of vicarious pleasure, but he was reluctant to give voice to thoughts that were still only half formed in his own mind, and the sound of running water put paid for the time being to any hope of conversation.

He had to hand it to her. Not once during the drive back had she questioned his behaviour. Not once had she asked him about his encounter with the police. Nor had she hesitated for a moment, as some women might have done, when she learned they were awaiting his arrival back at the hotel. Rather the reverse; clearly it had set the adrenalin flowing.

Grudgingly, Monsieur Pamplemousse took his hat off to the locals. They had got on to him far quicker than he'd expected them to.

Wriggling his hands behind his belt, he managed to turn it until the buckle was at the rear and he was able to grapple with the fastening. There was a clunk as belt, scabbard and sword landed on the floor. The relief was indescribable.

'Are you OK? It sounded as though you'd fallen out of bed.' Mrs Van Dorman arrived back in the bedroom. She was wearing a pair of pink silk pyjamas with bell-bottom trousers. The jacket had her initials embroidered on the pocket. The wig had gone, but the beauty spot was still in place. Perhaps she had forgotten it was there, or perhaps she felt it lent an air of abandon to the situation.

'Mind if I join you?' Without waiting for an answer she turned out the bedside light.

Monsieur Pamplemousse felt a draught of cool air overlaid with a waft of the perfume she had been using earlier in the evening. A moment later the bedclothes were in place again.

He lay silent for a while drinking in the smell of honeysuckle and jasmine. It was like a breath of blossom- time encapsulated between the sheets, refreshing and at the same time curiously disturbing.

'Now what are you thinking?'

'I was wondering, statistically, how many men there are in France at this moment dressed as d'Artagnan, in bed with a beautiful lady, their hands powerless behind their

701

back.' Perhaps in some establishments on the foothills of Montmartre, or in rooms off the rue St Denis where they catered for bizarre tastes.

'I guess the answer would have to be pretty minimal. And not just in France.'

He sensed a hesitation in her voice. 'Anyway, you shouldn't pay compliments you don't mean.'

'But I do mean it.'

'You know something? No one has said that to me for a very long time.'

Monsieur Pamplemousse rolled over on his left side and immediately wished he hadn't.

'What are you thinking?' he asked, masking his discomfort.

'I was thinking, Aristide, you really should remove your sword when you are in bed with a lady.'

'And I feel it is only fair to warn you,' said Monsieur Pamplemousse, ' that is not cold steel you feel.'

'Oh?'

There was a slight movement beside him as she moved closer, then a moment's silence.

'Nor is it!'

'Tell me,' it was his turn to ask the questions. 'How do you think Monsieur d'Artagnan would have behaved in similar circumstances?'

'From all I have heard he wouldn't have been above asking a lady for her assistance. It is a question of where your priorities lie.'

The response came in the form of a deep sigh. 'I doubt,' said Monsieur Pamplemousse, 'if he had my problem.'

Unable to contain himself a moment longer, he sat up in bed. Ever since they had set off on the journey back to the Hôtel, there had been one thought above all others uppermost in his mind. He had tried his best to ignore it, but it was no longer possible. The ride down from the hills had been bad enough. The sound of the shower had been the last straw.

'*Excusez moi* … I, too, have a priority … it is one which is of the utmost urgency.'

Easing himself down beneath the eiderdown, Monsieur Pamplemousse encountered a hand. He kissed it briefly, then rolled off the end of the bed.

As he groped his way round the foot and headed towards the bathroom his feet encountered something solid. Giving voice to a yelp of pain, Pommes Frites leapt to his feet and sent his master spinning in the direction of the dressing table.

As the sound of the crash echoed round the room, Mrs Van Dorman switched on the bedside light. 'Boy!' she exclaimed, taking in the scene. 'Do you ever need help!'

Monsieur Pamplemousse stirred in his sleep, gradually becoming aware that horizontal shafts of sunlight were filtering through the shutter. He opened one eye. Mrs Van Dorman's head was on the adjoining pillow, barely inches away from his own. In the half-light she looked different; almost as though there was something missing. He noticed, not for the first time, how blue her eyes were.

'*Bonjour*, Aristide.'

'*Bonjour* …' He wanted desperately to rub his own eyes as he tried to force himself awake.

'You went out like the proverbial light last night. It was all I could do to get you back to bed.'

It was true. He hardly remembered a thing. The combination of the food and the wine and all that followed, had acted like a 'knock-out' drop. For the second night running he had slept like a log.

'What is the time now?'

'Almost twelve o'clock.'

'*Morbleu!*'

'I don't plan on going anywhere, Aristide,' said Mrs Van Dorman. 'Do you?'

Monsieur Pamplemousse felt the handcuffs biting into his wrists. His arms were like lead weights. 'I couldn't go anywhere,' he said ruefully, 'even if I wanted to.'

There was a stirring from somewhere nearby as Pommes Frites stood up and shook himself awake at the sound of voices. A face appeared over the end of the bed. Monsieur Pamplemousse recognised the signs; the doleful look, the chin resting on the cover, the soulful eyes gazing up at the ceiling. An artist searching for models to illustrate a series of paintings based on well-known phrases would have needed to look no further when he came to 'hang-dog expression'. No doubt Pommes Frites would be making his way towards the door at any moment, pointedly asking for his morning stroll; he was no respecter of moments.

'DiAnn ...'

'You can call me Dee if you like. Most of my friends do.'

'Dee ...' It felt strange enough using her Christian name, let alone in a truncated form. 'May I ask you something?'

'Go ahead ...'

Monsieur Pamplemousse hesitated as he heard settling down noises. Perhaps Pommes Frites' instincts were telling him to build up his reserves again. After all his activity during the night they could probably do with replenishment.

A moment later the subject was driven from his mind as the telephone rang. The sound was so loud and unexpected he nearly fell out of bed.

'I guess that's another problem d'Artagnan wouldn't

have had to face.' Mrs Van Dorman sounded resigned.

'If we ignore it, perhaps it will go away.'

Monsieur Pamplemousse reckoned without Pommes Frites. Ever alive to his master's needs, he rose to his feet again and padded round the side of the bed. As far as he was concerned there was too much talk and too little action. The sooner the talking was over and done with and he could go out for a walk the better.

Something hard and wet landed on the pillow beside Monsieur Pamplemousse's head. As it did so a familiar voice issued from one end.

'Pamplemousse! What *is* going on? Are you there?' The Director's voice came through loud and clear.

'*Oui, Monsieur*. I am here.'

He exchanged a glance with Mrs Van Dorman. It mirrored that worn by Pommes Frites a moment earlier.

'Pamplemousse, you must remain exactly where you are. Do not move.'

'*Oui, Monsieur*. I shall be most happy to oblige.'

Mrs Van Dorman tried, not entirely successfully, to smother a giggle.

'Pamplemousse ... did I hear another voice just then? Do I take it you are not on your own?'

Monsieur Pamplemousse parried the question. 'Possibly it was a crossed line, *Monsieur*.'

'Hmm.' The Director didn't sound entirely convinced. Fortunately, he clearly had other things on his mind.

'Pamplemousse, how long have you been in Vichy?'

'Two days, *Monsieur*.'

'Two days, Pamplemousse, and two nights! I put you in charge, and what happens?

'One of America's foremost gastronomic magazine publishers goes missing, two *gendarmes* have been

705

attacked, three maidens ravished, the police forces of four continents are on the look-out for you, and *Le Cercle de Six* has become *Le Cercle de Cinq*. It is no wonder you are on the run from the authorities.'

Monsieur Pamplemousse stirred uneasily. The Director made it sound like a new arrangement with variations for words and music of 'The Twelve Days of Christmas'.

'What is wrong, Pamplemousse? Are you listening?'

'*Oui, Monsieur*. It is simply that I am lying with my left ear on the telephone receiver and it is very painful.'

In the few moments it took the Director to absorb the information, Monsieur Pamplemousse managed to adjust to a more comfortable position.

'May I ask, Pamplemousse, what is wrong with your right ear? Do you have to use your left?'

'It is difficult to explain, *Monsieur*, but the simple answer is "*Oui, c'est tres necessaire*". I am sore from all that has happened. Turning is difficult.'

'In view of the reports I have received concerning your activities over the past twenty-four hours I am not surprised.'

'It is not what you think, *Monsieur*. It is mostly from the horse.'

'When I arranged for you to have a *cheval*, Pamplemousse, I did not expect you to use it in order to live the part of d'Artagnan to the full – roaming the countryside, terrorising the local populace, pillaging and raping, *gauche, droit et centre*.

'It would have been better if I had sent you to the banquet dressed as Henri V – a prince known to all and sundry as *Le Vert galant*. If my memory serves me correctly, he was awarded the title on account of his excessive sexual activities; activities which remained undiminished until he met his death at the hands of an assassin. Had he been alive today he would have had to look to his laurels, lest he forfeit the title.

'A warrant has been issued for your arrest. Interpol has been alerted. All manner of crimes have been laid at your doorstep; crimes culled from files which have been gathering dust over the past decade. Years of unsolved cases are beginning to surface. Everything from attempted rape in Yugoslavia to fire-raising in Provence. Fortunately, the description they have of you is somewhat hazy. I suggest you either remove your beard at the earliest opportunity or have it dyed another colour.'

Monsieur Pamplemousse settled back. The Director had the bit well and truly between his teeth. He could be in for a long session.

'There is absolutely nothing they can charge me with, *Monsieur*. I may have run away from the police, but who wouldn't at that hour in the morning on a lonely country road? How was I to know they were who they said they were. They produced no form of identity.'

'*Ortolans*, Pamplemousse. *Ortolans*. Aiding and abetting in the cooking and eating of *Ortolans* – a serious offence.'

'*Ortolans*, Monsieur? But I did not know ...'

'I'm sure you don't need to be reminded, Pamplemousse, that ignorance of the law is no excuse in the eyes of the authorities. I must admit I was unaware of a change in the regulations myself, but due to over-indulgence – mostly in the area of the Landes – the EEC in their wisdom have deemed *ortolans* to be a protected species, along with fig-pickers and the Pyrenean brown bear.'

Monsieur Pamplemousse hardly listened. It was true. If they wanted to they could get you on anything. If it hadn't been *ortolans* it would have been something else – like stealing the handcuffs. It was one of the first things he had learned in the force. If all else failed, accidentally push them over and charge them with resisting arrest.

'I wish to goodness I had never got involved in this whole thing,' continued the Director. 'We shall be the laughing stock of France if it ever emerges that one of our staff has indulged in nefarious culinary practices.'

'It was hardly my fault, *Monsieur*.' Monsieur Pamplemousse felt obliged to protest. 'I did not devise the menu.'

He felt Mrs Van Dorman nodding her head vigorously in agreement. 'Besides, for all anyone knows I might not even have touched the *ortolans*. My conscience could well have forbidden it. The evidence is all circumstantial.'

'That is as may be, Aristide, but it was Thoreau, was it not, who said "Some circumstantial evidence is very strong – as when you find a trout in the milk"?'

'With all due respect to Thoreau, *Monsieur*, he did not have to stand up in court and explain to the good burghers of Vichy how he happened to be knocking on the door of a lonely farmhouse in the early hours of the morning dressed as d'Artagnan.'

'Ah,' broke in the Director. 'I am glad you mention that, Pamplemousse. It brings me to the matter of the three maidens. How you came to be there in the first place is beyond me, but the fact remains that notes were sent. Money was proffered. An obscene drawing is to be exhibit "A". An obscene drawing passed during the hours of darkness to three innocent creatures.'

'One note, *Monsieur*, and no money exchanged hands. The "obscene drawing" as you put it, happened to be on the back of the note. As for their innocence, that is something I am unable to comment on since I only caught a brief glimpse of their faces at an upper window.'

'I hardly think that is a good defence, Pamplemousse. You were the one who pushed the note under the door in the first place. There are three witnesses who are willing to swear to it.'

'Not in the first place, *Monsieur*. In the second. They pushed it under the door to me first.'

'It is your word against theirs, Pamplemousse. One against three.'

'Are you saying you do not believe me, *Monsieur*?'

'No, Pamplemousse, I am not saying that. What I choose to believe or disbelieve is really immaterial. What matters is what those in court believe. I do not fancy your chances. The evidence against you is overwhelming. The wording of the note, MY HANDS ARE TIED. PLEASE FREE ME. I WILL PAY YOU WELL. NAME YOUR PRICE," speaks volumes. They are words which will be hard to explain if you are confronted by a skilled interlocutor.'

Monsieur Pamplemousse drew a deep breath and prepared to play his trump card. 'It will need a very skilled interlocutor indeed, Monsieur, to demonstrate in court precisely how I was able to execute a drawing in such great and explicit detail while my hands were tightly secured *behind* my back.'

The silence gave him much-needed breathing space. Arguments with the Director always left him feeling drained. He stole a glance at Mrs Van Dorman. It struck him that she was looking unusually thoughtful.

'You say your hands were secured behind your back?'

'*Oui, Monsieur*. With a pair of *menottes*.'

'Ah, I see your dilemma. So you did not climb into bed with intent to ravish these girls as their father maintains.'

'No, *Monsieur*. I did not. I did not even see their bed, for the very simple reason that I was locked inside another room. A room from which I have since escaped. Furthermore, *Monsieur*, my hands are still cuffed together. Short of cutting the jacket free, I cannot even undress …'

'Cut your jacket free!' The Director reacted in horror at the thought. 'I trust you will do no such thing, Aristide. It was hired at great expense. I cannot begin to tell you the trouble I experienced clearing the bill with Madame Grante in the first place. If it is damaged in any way I shall never hear the last of it. Nor, I fear, will you.'

'In that case, *Monsieur*, perhaps you would be kind enough to suggest an alternative.'

'Can you not telephone Glandier? If he is as good a magician as you say he is, I am sure he will know of a method of removing a jacket without undoing the *menottes*. It is the kind of thing one has seen done many times on the stage.'

Monsieur Pamplemousse relaxed. Having let off steam, the Director was obviously going off the boil. Now it was his turn. 'I'm sure you are right in what you say, *Monsieur*. It would not do to appear in court alongside you wearing a jacket which has been ripped apart from top to bottom, the lining protruding …'

'Alongside me, Pamplemousse?'

'I assume you will be speaking on my behalf, *Monsieur*. After all, the whole enterprise was your idea. I am only here as your representative.'

The Director sounded dubious. 'I will, of course, engage a good lawyer to act on your behalf. That is the least I can do. But as for appearing myself, I am not sure that would be wise. The adverse publicity …' He paused for thought. 'I shall have to await progress reports before I make a decision.'

'You shall have one, *Monsieur*, just as soon as my hands are free. I am working on the case. But if you would rather I didn't, I can always make a clean breast of things. Before going to the police I could telephone the local *journal* and try to enlist their sympathy. No doubt they would welcome an article on the banquet ...'

It had the desired effect.

'Don't misunderstand me, Aristide. Of course I don't want you to stop what you are doing. I value your judgement in these matters. And if anyone is to receive the benefit of an article I trust it will be the Staff magazine. I shall look forward to seeing the photographs as well in due course, but in the meantime ...'

'In the meantime, *Monsieur*, in certain areas I have made a good deal of progress. *Par exemple*, I know the exact whereabouts of Mrs Van Dorman ...'

'You do? Good work, Aristide! This is incroyable. When news started filtering through during the early hours of this morning I tried to telephone her. I was told she was not in her room. Naturally I assumed the worst ...'

'She is safe and well, *Monsieur*.'

'But where is she? Tell me. You must bring her back to Paris at once.'

'I am afraid that is not possible, *Monsieur*.'

'Not possible?'

'There are things I must do before I leave Vichy. I need to satisfy my curiosity over certain matters.'

Out of the corner of his eye he saw Mrs Van Dorman nodding vigorously.

'Besides, I have to wait until the postman arrives.'

'Ah!' The Director sounded more cheerful. 'Now there I have good news for you, Pamplemousse. If you are referring to your fax message about the keys, the night staff alerted

Véronique and she came into the office early this morning. She has already taken the necessary action and she assures me they will be with you shortly.

'As for my being with you, I will do my best to slot you in. However, as you know, the new edition of *Le Guide* has not long been out and it is always a busy period. In the meantime I will get on to my good friend the Deputy again. I'm sure he will do his best, but in order to pull strings one first has to find the right ends and it is not his region ...'

'*Oui, Monsieur.*' Monsieur Pamplemousse allowed the Director sufficient time to justify to his own satisfaction the many reasons why he might not be able to make the journey to Vichy, then uttered his '*aux revoirs*' and signalled Mrs Van Dorman to cut the call. There was a click as the line went dead.

As she stretched across him to replace the receiver in its cradle, he lay back exhausted.

It was a moment or two before either of them spoke.

'You know, Aristide,' said Mrs Van Dorman. 'You are the only man I've ever kissed whose beard tasted of glue.'

'You have kissed many men with beards?' asked Monsieur Pamplemousse.

'Come to think of it, no. Come to think of it, you're the very first.'

'Perhaps it is a fact of life that all men's beards taste of glue.'

'I'll let you know. You've given me a taste for it. I'll tell you something else. When you kissed me back I heard the proverbial bell ringing.'

'I heard it too,' said Monsieur Pamplemousse. 'I am afraid I can still hear it. It is very persistent.'

'Maybe you'd better take the call,' said Mrs Van Dorman. 'I don't think it's going away.'

Reaching across for the receiver again, she held it against his ear, brushing her lips across his forehead as she did so. Pommes Frites, who had been on his way to render service, assumed his resigned 'here we go again' expression and went back to bed.

The voice, when it emerged was even more familiar than the first. Monsieur Pamplemousse's heart sank.

'*Couscous*! How wonderful.' He made faces at Mrs Van Dorman 'And how clear your voice is. You could be right here in Vichy.'

'I *am* in Vichy, Aristide. I am waiting for someone to show me up to your room. For some reason the staff seem very reluctant to do so.'

In a sudden panic, Monsieur Pamplemousse pressed his head against the mouthpiece. '*Merde!*' he hissed. 'It is my wife – Madame Pamplemousse. She is here. In Vichy!'

'Jesus!' Mrs Van Dorman was out of bed like a shot.

'I am sorry, *chérie*. What was that you said?'

'I said why are you covering the mouthpiece, Aristide? Is there someone else with you? If it is another chambermaid ...'

'*Couscous*. I promise you ... on my honour. Have you *seen*' the chambermaid. She is old enough to be my mother ...'

'That did not seem to bother you in La Rochelle.'

'Once and for all, Doucette ...' Playing for time, Monsieur Pamplemousse watched helplessly while Mrs Van Dorman swept as many of her belongings as she could into a case and bundled it into the wardrobe. 'La Rochelle is not what you think it was. If only you wouldn't jump to conclusions. I can explain everything ...' He suddenly realised the receiver had gone dead and he was talking to himself.

713

'Quick, she must be on her way.' Even as he spoke he heard the faint sound of lift doors opening and closing.

Mrs Van Dorman dived into the cupboard. She wasn't a moment too soon. As the door swung shut behind her, the one leading to the corridor opened and the porter peered nervously round the corner.

'*Monsieur …*'

'*Entrez. Entrez.*' Monsieur Pamplemousse did his best to keep the note of impending doom from his voice. '*Couscous,* what a wonderful surprise!'

Doucette looked round suspiciously as she followed the porter into the room. 'Why are the shutters still drawn, Aristide? Do you know what time it is? I have been up since dawn. The train left Paris at eight forty-three.'

'And I', said Monsieur Pamplemousse virtuously, 'have hardly *fermé les yeux* all night.'

'*Monsieur?*' Hovering nervously on the sidelines, the porter gestured towards the window.

'Please do. It is time I was up.'

As the man slowly and laboriously wound up the shutter and the room was flooded with light, Monsieur Pamplemousse took a quick glance at his surroundings. He breathed an inward sigh of relief. Mrs Van Dorman had done a good job. As far as he could tell there was nothing untoward in view. Nothing that he couldn't talk his way out of.

The porter looked equally relieved as he made good his escape. He was probably worried about his bonus.

As soon as they were on their own Doucette flung open the balcony doors. 'This room smells like a brothel.'

Monsieur Pamplemousse resisted the temptation to ask how she knew. It was no time for scoring cheap points.

'Do you have the keys?'

Rummaging in her capacious handbag, Doucette found what she was looking for. 'Are these the ones? They were in the bureau drawer.'

Spreading them out on the bedcover, she waited while Monsieur Pamplemousse glanced through them.

'How on earth did this happen – to you of all people?'

'It is a long story ...'

'An Inspector in the Paris *Sûreté.*'

'Ex,' said Monsieur Pamplemousse.

'I'm not surprised.'

Monsieur Pamplemousse chose to ignore the last remark. 'Try the small one next to the Yale. That should do it.'

Rolling over on to his side he waited patiently for Doucette to undo the first lock. As she bent over him she paused and gave a sniff. 'What is that scent?'

'Scent?' repeated Monsieur Pamplemousse.

'Ah, *oui*, the scent. It is of the period. I wore it at the banquet last night. I resisted the idea at first, but the costumiers insisted. In those days many men of a certain class wore perfume. It was said to be a particular favourite of Louis XIV. That is why they called him the "Sweet-smelling Monarch". It is made from the petals of jasmine and honeysuckle. If you like it, *chérie, I* will buy you some when I get back to Paris. It is from Jean Laporte.'

'You have become very expert at perfume all of a sudden,' said Doucette suspiciously.

Monsieur Pamplemousse broke off in mid-flight. She was right, of course. He mustn't overdo it. There was nothing more incriminating than being over-enthusiastic. How often had he not witnessed the same thing in the old days when he was questioning a suspect; a sudden burst of eloquence over some trivial matter in the hope of diverting attention. Apart from which, now that the moment was so near, he could hardly wait to be released.

'Hurry, *Couscous.*'

He waited impatiently while his wife fiddled with the keys.

'It is difficult with so many. The others get in the way.'

A moment later his hands were free. The relief was indescribable. For a second or two his shoulders felt so stiff he could hardly move, let alone bring his arms round in front of him, but at last he managed it. Taking the bunch of keys from Doucette, he undid the second lock.

'Your poor wrists. They are almost raw.' She leant forward to embrace him. 'I shall stay and look after you until they are better.'

Monsieur Pamplemousse stopped rubbing himself immediately. 'That is not necessary, *chérie.* In a matter of a few hours they will be as right as rain again. It is only a little redness ...' He broke off as he realised Doucette was hardly listening. Instead, she was staring in horror at something behind his left shoulder.

'What is wrong, *Couscous*?' he asked nervously.

'Aristide! There is something on the other pillow. Something round and black.'

Turning his head, Monsieur Pamplemousse followed the direction of his wife's gaze. His heart nearly missed a beat. There, on the pillow, was Mrs Van Dorman's beauty spot. It must have fallen off during the night. No wonder she had looked different in the morning.

'*Voilà!*'

Regardless of the pain in his wrists, he made as though to swat the object. As he did so he managed to scoop it up in his fingers. In desperation he handed it to Pommes Frites, who was also giving the matter his undivided attention. Pommes Frites' gratitude at receiving his master's benefaction was short lived. Pleasurable chomping noises gave way almost at once to violent choking. It sounded as though he might be having trouble with a tooth. Either that or the object had stuck to the back of his throat.

'Poor thing,' said Doucette. What do you think it could have been?'

'A bed bug of some kind.' Monsieur Pamplemousse dismissed the matter as hardly worthy of discussion.

'But it looked enormous. I have never seen such a big one.'

'Doubtless it became bloated through feeding on me all through the night,' said Monsieur Pamplemousse. He wriggled inside his costume. 'This hotel is full of such creatures. It is disgraceful. I feel itchy all over.'

Taking his cue, Pommes Frites, who had been listening to the conversation with growing concern, put two and two together on his master's behalf. Pausing in his retching, he began scratching himself vigorously. He looked a sorry sight.

Doucette reached for her handbag. 'If that is the case, I am certainly *not* staying here a moment longer.'

'Are you sure, *Couscous*? Is there nothing I can say to make you change your mind?'

Madame Pamplemousse wriggled. 'Indeed not.' She cast a disapproving eye around the room. 'I am surprised you even suggest it. *And* I shall tell them at the desk exactly why I am not staying.'

'I would rather you didn't, *Couscous*. Not before I make out a report to Headquarters.'

'I think the sooner you get back to Paris and submit it the better.'

Monsieur Pamplemousse gave a sigh. 'I know you sometimes think life is all champagne and roses when I am away, Doucette, but as you see ...' He gave the pillow a thump and immediately wished he hadn't. Apart from a searing pain which shot up his right arm, the blow released a fresh cloud of invisible esters, filling the room with perfume as they rose into the air.

'As for the smell ...' Madame Pamplemousse's sniff said it all. 'It's no wonder France had to suffer a revolution if that's what men went about wearing.'

'I think you will find there is a fast train at thirteen-thirty-eight.' Monsieur Pamplemousse glanced up from a plasticised information sheet on the bedside table. 'It will get you to Paris just before five o'clock. There is a restaurant car, so you will be able to have lunch. I don't wish to hurry you, but if you go now you should just catch it.'

'Are you sure?' Doucette hesitated. 'I feel as though I am deserting you.'

'Don't worry about me,' said Monsieur Pamplemousse. 'I shall be all right. Besides, I have work to do.' He raised his hands as far as the pain from the slowly returning circulation would allow, then let them fall again. There was no point in overdoing the protestations.

'Your beard', said Doucette, as she kissed him goodbye, 'tastes of glue!'

Monsieur Pamplemousse listened at the door for the lift gates to close and as soon as he heard a satisfactory clang he slid a security bolt into place and turned towards the cupboard.

Opening the door, he put his head inside. The blue track suit was hanging in one corner. He recognised the outfit worn on the journey down. The dress for the banquet hung in an opposite corner. In between the two there were summer frocks and evening gowns galore.

718

'DiAnn! It is safe. You can come out now.'

Parting the hangers in the middle, he slid them to one side and began groping in the area behind, half expecting Mrs Van Dorman to jump out at him.

Gradually faint irritation at playing games gave way to surprise, then a sense of shock. It was hard to take in for a moment, but a second and then a third search confirmed the simple truth. To all intents and purposes both Mrs Van Dorman and her suitcase had vanished into thin air.

7
PUTTING OUT THE CREAM

Glandier would have been pleased; it would have appealed to his sense of humour.

As a stage act, it might not have lived up to the high standards set by the great magicians of the past; illusionists of the calibre of Maskelyne and Devante, who were able to make elephants disappear before your very eyes. For a start they would have insisted on the inside of the cupboard being painted matt black, thus ensuring there would be no tell-tale reflections of light from an unpainted knob or hinge; gleams which would have revealed the existence of an old door built into the wall at the back.

'I guess I must have noticed it when I got unpacked,' said Mrs Van Dorman, 'but it didn't register. It wasn't until I hid behind the things hanging up and felt something digging into me that I thought of trying the handle. Who'd have guessed it would open into the next room?'

Who indeed? It was yet another echo from the past, a throwback to the days when whole families stayed in Vichy to take the cure. However, the simple question gave rise to a number of others. Why, for instance, had the door been unlocked in the first place? Had it always been left that way, or had someone unlocked it recently, perhaps when they entered Mrs Van Dorman's looking for Ellis's glass.

'Your wife has gone back to Paris?'

Mrs Van Dorman broke into his thoughts.

'Positive.' Doucette had a horror of unclean sheets. She wouldn't be happy until she was back home again.

'I couldn't help overhearing most of what was going on. I was petrified she might look inside the cupboard. All my clothes are still there. And what was all that about a bed bug?'

'I'm afraid you will have to ask Pommes Frites. He has swallowed it.'

Mrs Van Dorman took the hint.

'So what happens now – aside from wanting me to keep quiet?'

'First I shall get out of these clothes. Then I intend taking a long, leisurely bath. I need time to think. After that I shall get dressed again.'

'The first two shouldn't be a problem, but I can't help much with the third. Unless you fancy using one of my track suits. You're welcome. But without wishing to be rude, it could be a tight fit.'

'There is another way round the problem,' said Monsieur Pamplemousse. 'You could go to my room and get a change of clothing for me.'

Mrs Van Dorman looked dubious. 'I don't see how. If the guard is still in the corridor outside …'

Monsieur Pamplemousse picked up his keys. 'There are precedents. What has been done once can be done a second time. Especially if I show you how.'

'If anyone had told me two days ago,' said Mrs Van Dorman, 'that I'd be taking a crash course in lock-picking, I'd have told them where to go.'

'And now?'

'Go ahead. I'm all yours. This whole thing is like a bad dream anyway.'

'*La première leçon*,' said Monsieur Pamplemousse. 'Do

not be put off by something which looks more complicated than it actually is. The point about locks is that although very often the key may look elaborate, the basic mechanism of the lock itself is really very simple. Much of the design centres on preventing any key other than the correct one from operating it. This is done by building in pieces of protruding metal called "wards" which will stop it turning unless there is a slot cut into the blank in exactly the right place.'

'I think I understand.'

'Here, I will show you.' Taking a sheet of paper and a Biro from the Hôtel folder on the bedside table he drew out the rough shape of a key. 'The long tubular section fits over the "post" of the lock, that is to say the projection inside the round part of the opening on which the key turns. The flat piece is called the "blank" – until the required cuts are made in it – at which point it is known as the "bit". In essence a skeleton key is an ordinary key with as much cut away from the blank as possible, leaving just enough "bit" to turn the mechanism.'

'Can anybody buy one?'

'If you know where to look. There are books and magazines on the subject. Any crime writer used to doing research would have no problem at all. Failing that, once you know what to do it is easy enough to make up a set yourself. All you need is some blanks, a vice, a hacksaw, some files and a little practice.

'Now, I will show you how to use it.'

Going into the cupboard, Monsieur Pamplemousse slid the dresses to one side and selected a key. He was right first time. A moment later there was a metallic rattle and the lock on the communicating door clicked shut.

'*Voilà!*'

'You've done it before.'

'Now you have a go.' Monsieur Pamplemousse stood back and let Mrs Van Dorman take his place, watching over her as she struggled with the key.

'Take it gently. Not too much force. Try moving it in and out a little and from side to side until you feel something begin to move. Remember … I have just locked it. You are trying to unlock it again.'

'Eureka! It works!' Mrs Van Dorman looked as pleased as Punch as the mechanism slid open again. 'How soon before we start lesson two? I see a whole new career ahead of me.'

'Have another go while I run my bath. When you are sure you know how to do it without making too much noise, go downstairs and tell your friend the porter that you want to change rooms. Say you do not like the view from this one.'

Monsieur Pamplemousse crossed to the window and looked out. On the other side of the street immediately opposite him an elderly couple were sitting on a balcony playing cards. They were probably relaxing between treatments.

'It would be a reasonable request. From here you look out on to another Hôtel. From my side of the Hôtel there is a view across the whole of Vichy. Ask if room 607 is free. I'm sure they will be understanding. There is almost certain to be a connecting door. It was common practice in the days when this Hôtel would have been built. There is an identical cupboard in my room.'

'What are you doing?' said Mrs Van Dorman. 'Trying to ruin my reputation? Anyway, supposing 607 isn't free?'

'I didn't hear anyone in there the first night. It is worth a try. The season proper hasn't started, so most of the customers will be passing trade and won't have arrived yet. If it is already occupied we will have to think again. If it is not, see if you can borrow the key to the outside door.'

'If it's that easy, why did someone go to the trouble of breaking into my room through the cupboard?'

'It could simply have been fortuitous. A room-maid may have left the door of the room next to yours open.'

Monsieur Pamplemousse didn't mention the other possibility – that whoever it was hadn't entered via the room next door, but had gone straight to Mrs Van Dorman's. Having discovered the connecting door, he would have opened it to provide an escape route. She could well have disturbed him while he was going through her things. That would explain why the door between the two rooms had been left unlocked. Whoever it was would have wanted to make as quick a getaway as possible. Or even come back in again when the coast was clear.

'Assuming I do manage to get the key to 607, what do you want me to do?'

'Open the connecting door and go into my room. Only make sure whoever is on duty outside doesn't hear anything.

'Apart from a change of clothing, there are things I need. There is a small case belonging to *Le Guide* which may be useful. And on the shelves you will see a set of encyclopaedias. If you can't manage them all, then I would like the one which includes the letter "D".

'If there is a new guard on duty in the corridor – which is almost certain to be the case – then I suggest that when you leave the room you bring my bags with you. He will assume you are checking out of the Hôtel.'

Mrs Van Dorman tried the key in the communicating door several times before finally locking it.

She stepped out of the cupboard. 'Here goes. If I'm not back inside half an hour, send out a search party.'

'If you are not back in half an hour,' said Monsieur Pamplemousse. 'I shall come myself.'

Unable to wait for the bath to fill, he added a generous helping of oil, then climbed in and lay wallowing in the running water, adjusting the taps from time to time with his big toe as the bubbles rose higher and higher until they were level with his chin. He hoped the perfume wouldn't linger for days and days. Doucette would have something to say if he arrived back smelling of sandalwood. It must be Mrs Van Dorman's flavour of the day.

As he luxuriated in the water he allowed his mind to wander over the events of the past two days. But for once the warmth, which he had hoped would be conducive to thought, failed to work. He realised all too clearly that apart from Mrs Van Dorman's briefing on the way down and the encounter over dinner, he hardly knew anything about the people involved. Elliott Garner he had spoken to most. Spencer Troon he'd listened to. Harvey Wentworth had struck him as being the most interesting of the five, but that was probably because his leading character was a chef. Sandwiched between two non-speaking actors, Harman Lock and Paul Robard had spent most of the dinner talking to each other.

He tried to remember what Mrs Van Dorman had said about them all on the way down, but he'd been kept so busy the first day – getting dressed for the part of d'Artagnan, trying to picture life in Dumas' time, and if the truth be known suffering 'first night' nerves – and so much had happened since, it was almost impossible.

There was something else hovering tantalisingly in the back of his mind, something he couldn't quite put his finger on. Each time he tried to concentrate his thoughts it disappeared again.

He focused on his watch which he had left lying on its side by the wash-basin. It showed nearly one-thirty. Mrs Van Dorman had been gone nearly twenty minutes. He hoped she was all right. At least he had Pommes Frites to keep guard over him.

Putting thoughts of a leisurely bath to one side, he climbed out, half dried himself, and took one of the Hôtel dressing-gowns from a rack near the door.

Partly as a means of passing the time, he put through a call to Paris and got the number for the Poison Control Centre. In turn they gave him a contact at the Information Centre in Lyons; a specialist in cyanide.

'You have a pen?'

'*Oui*. Go ahead.'

Once he had established his credentials the information flowed thick and fast.

Most of it only really confirmed what he already knew in a hazy kind of way, and he began to wish he'd waited for Mrs Van Dorman to get back. His Cross pen would have coped better than the hotel Biro, which had seen better days.

Lucrezia Borgia responsible for popular belief that poisoning largely prerogative of women murderers. Medical profession thrown up quite a few in its time ... on account of easy access, specialised knowledge, etc.

In response to his specific question: cyanide exceptionally quick acting; one of the fastest known poisons. For that reason had been favourite with Nazi criminals and undercover agents ... cyanide gas used in American gas chambers ... fatal dose can be as little as 50 milligrams ... about the same weight as postage stamp ... that amount gave it ten times more molecules than the total number in human body – whatever that might mean.

He was out of his depth trying to picture it and his wrist was starting to ache. Already he could feel the pain beginning to creep up his right arm.

Paralysis of respiratory centre of the brain causing loss of oxygen. Pulse weakens ... rapid loss of consciousness. Signs: convulsions ... coldness of extremities ... pupils dilated and don't react to light ... sometimes traces of froth at mouth. Death usually within a few minutes – five at most. When crystals combined with water to produce prussic acid fumes can cause death in as little as ten seconds. Few visible signs ... skin and body may show irregular pink patches ... characteristic odour of bitter almonds at mouth. Cyanides quickly altered by metabolic activity once in body, and converted into sulphocyanides which are normally present. Presents problem if no reason to suspect foul play and post mortem not quickly carried out.

Spelling sulphocyanides gave Monsieur Pamplemousse problems of his own and he missed a large chunk to do with ancient Egyptians having distilled cyanide from peach stones, and the fact that Leonardo da Vinci experimented with it until he became an expert poisoner. In his time Leonardo da Vinci had experimented with most things. There were even those who maintained he'd perfected a method of introducing it beneath the bark of trees and then used the fruit to poison one Giangaleazzo Sforza at a banquet in the house of Lodovico il Moro.

Monsieur Pamplemousse gave up writing at that point. He'd had more than enough.

Repeating Ellis's last words produced a loud guffaw at the other end of the line; the first in what had otherwise been a one-sided, not to say sombre conversation. It was quite a plus. The person at the other end didn't sound as though he was normally a bundle of laughs.

Ellis would have done better to have called out for some dicobalt edetate instead of Bâtard Montrachet and fish.

Monsieur Pamplemousse thanked the man for his trouble, then replaced the receiver and sat for a while lost in thought.

At long last he picked up the phone again and made a telephone call to England. He was in the middle of a long conversation when he heard a knock.

'Can you call me back?'

'*Oui*. As soon as possible …'

'Yesterday would be even better!'

'Au revoir.'

Opening the door, he found Mrs Van Dorman standing outside. She was doing a balancing act with his working case and the encyclopaedias. Perched precariously on top of it all, looking as though it was about to slide off at any moment, was Norm Ellis's tasting glass. He grabbed it in the nick of time.

'Sorry if I've been a long time.' She sounded out of breath.

'You had a problem?'

'You can say that again. I managed to get the key to the room next to yours, and I didn't have too much trouble with the lock on the connecting door. It was the door itself. It must have been a tight fit to start with, and sometime or other it had gotten itself painted over while it was still shut. It took for ever to get it open.

'Then, when I came out the policeman on duty insisted on carrying everything to the elevator for me. To make matters worse, when it arrived there was someone in there already. I had to go all the way down to the ground floor and bring as much as I could carry in one go up the back stairs. If the desk clerk saw the encyclopaedias he must wonder what's going on. I thought I'd bring the lot just in case.'

While Mrs Van Dorman was talking Monsieur Pamplemousse opened his case and spread the books out across the table.

'Can you manage the rest of the things?'

'I've packed everything in the one bag. One bag! Some people believe in travelling light! How do you manage it?'

'When you spend much of your life on the road,' said Monsieur Pamplemousse, 'you learn not to waste energy carrying around things you don't need.'

'*Touché!*'

By the time Mrs Van Dorman returned with his valise Monsieur Pamplemousse was deep into the encyclopaedias. He could have done with Alexandre Dumas' assistant. According to one entry Auguste Macquet had been 'a tireless searcher out of historical documents' on behalf of his master. On the other hand, Auguste Macquet could doubtless have answered the question that was at the back of his mind without resorting to an encyclopaedia.

'I told them I'd decided not to take the other room after all. Who needs a view?'

Mrs Van Dorman laid his clothes out on the bed and then began hanging them up for him alongside her own as though it was the most natural thing in the world.

'Do you really think someone poisoned Norm?' she asked as she draped his jacket over the back of the chair.

'I think there is nothing more certain.'

'Why?'

'If you mean "why do I think it?" – let us just say it is the ex-policeman in me. Instinct tells me I am right. If you mean "why did they do it?" that is something only the person concerned can answer.

'Either way, something must be done. There is always the possibility that a person who kills once will kill again given sufficient reason. I think it nearly happened again last night.'

'You mean the wine?' Mrs Van Dorman gave a shiver. 'If you're right, then it must have been the same person who broke into my room. In which case, he could try again.'

'I think there is nothing more certain.'

'That gives me goose bumps.'

Monsieur Pamplemousse looked up from a list he'd been compiling. 'I don't think you should spend another night on your own anyway.'

If Mrs Van Dorman read anything into the remark she showed no sign.

'But how did he get at Norm?'

Monsieur Pamplemousse handed her his list. 'If you manage to find all these things for me, perhaps I can answer that question too.'

Mrs Van Dorman read the list carefully.

'Are you OK? Do you need a doctor?'

'I am A1, thank you.'

'Then why do you need a thermometer?'

'I have it in mind to test the temperature of the water in the Parc des Sources.'

'If you want a walk – fine. But if you really want to know how warm it is I can save you the trouble.'

Monsieur Pamplemousse looked at her enquiringly.

'It's all in the hand-out.' Mrs Van Dorman crossed to the dressing table and opened a large plastic pack in the shape of a briefcase.

She took out a folder and flipped through the pages.

'Here we are. Célestin comes out at 21 degrees centigrade. In the Source du Parc you have a choice … anything from 27 degrees centigrade to 42.5 degrees.' Unfolding the centre pages she spread it out across the table. 'There's a map showing exactly where they are. The Parc de Célestin is down near where we were the other evening …'

'May I see that?' Monsieur Pamplemousse took the map from her and studied it intently for a moment or two. The notion that had been nagging at him in the bath had surfaced again.

'Is there something wrong?' Mrs Van Dorman broke into his thoughts.

'You must have a good travel agent,' said Monsieur Pamplemousse vaguely. 'They seem to have thought of everything.'

'Call it American efficiency. It came along with the tickets, an itinerary, and a spare roll of film – compliments of the management.'

'It must have been an expensive operation.'

'More so than average, I guess, but not as bad as it sounds. I gather they've accumulated a lot in the kitty over the past few years. They all chip in with a fixed amount each spring. Besides, they've managed to save quite a lot on the last few trips. When they went to Japan they were guests of some writers' society or other and in return for a mention or two all their expenses were paid for by one of the big electronic companies. Spencer's ill-fated "last breakfast" saved them a bundle; that was eating out on the cheap with a vengeance. This year they were going to the conference at Annecy anyway and I daresay a lot of it goes down on expenses.'

Monsieur Pamplemousse had a sudden thought. 'How about the tasting glasses? Did they come with the other things?'

Mrs Van Dorman hesitated. 'I guess they must have done. They're the kind of firm that thinks of everything.'

She looked at the list again. 'You're sure there's nothing else? I mean, while I'm out you wouldn't like me to get you a kitchen sink? What's a *quincaillerie* when it's at home?'

'A *quincaillerie*,' said Monsieur Pamplemousse, 'is like your travel agent – it is the kind of shop where they have everything. They will help cut the glass for you, and if they can't do it themselves they will know where you should go.'

'I've just learnt something fundamental,' said Mrs Van Dorman. 'Sarcasm doesn't cross language barriers.'

'*Comment?*'

'Forget it. Seriously – is there anything else you need?'

Monsieur Pamplemousse considered the matter for a moment or two.

'If you come across a good bookshop you might see if you can find any books by our friends down the road.' It was a long shot, but it might tell him something. 'Get as many as possible. And don't forget to ask for *une fiche*.'

Madame Grante probably wouldn't wear it, but there was no harm in getting a receipt – just in case.

'You can take Pommes Frites with you, if you like. He could do with the walk. Only make sure you go down the back stairs in case the guard sees you both and puts two and two together.'

'Thanks a heap!' Mrs Van Dorman paused at the door and looked at Pommes Frites. '*Pardonnez-moi*. I didn't mean it. It'll be nice to have someone to talk to. One last question. Why do you need sugar?'

'Let's just say I have a sweet sooth.' Taking the Cross pen from his jacket pocket, Monsieur Pamplemousse twisted the barrel. It was a good 'thinking' pen. He always felt lost without it. 'Talking of which, on the way out could you order me a sandwich and a bottle of wine? I will leave the choice to you.'

'You know something, Aristide,' said Mrs Van Dorman thoughtfully. 'Given time, you could be really infuriating.'

As the door closed behind her, Monsieur Pamplemousse picked up the map again and studied it carefully, a slight frown on his face. Turning the pages of the guide until he came to what he wanted, he took a clean sheet of paper from his case and started to write.

The telephone rang once. It was his call from England.

A room-maid arrived with a bottle of Côtes du Rhone and a ham sandwich. While he was eating the sandwich Monsieur Pamplemousse telephoned the Bibliothèque Municipale and had a brief but satisfactory conversation with the head librarian.

He had barely replaced the receiver when Mrs Van Dorman and Pommes Frites arrived back. Pommes Frites looked suitably refreshed and Mrs Van Dorman was obviously feeling very pleased with herself.

'You look as though you have just discovered the wheel.'

She put her shopping down on the bed. 'I feel like I have. Do you want to know something crazy?'

Listening with only half an ear, Monsieur Pamplemousse went through the contents of the bags. He toyed with the idea of telling her his own news, then thought better of it. 'You have done well.'

'Aren't you going to ask me what's happened?'

'*Pardon*.' He gave her his undivided attention. 'Tell me, what has happened?'

'I've solved a mystery. You're not going to believe this.'

'Try me and see.'

'Well, I bumped into Paul Robard while I was out and we got talking. You remember all the hoo-ha over dinner when

Spencer Troon pretended he'd been poisoned. The cracks he made about having everyone fooled and how it made him runner-up ...'

Monsieur Pamplemousse nodded.

'Apparently it all had to do with a wager they'd made with each other while they were in Annecy. The first one to come up with a plot for the perfect murder got the jackpot. The catch was that whoever won it had to convince the rest that his idea would work. When Norm died everyone assumed at first it was as a result of a heart attack. Then, as time went on, they began to wonder if maybe he was trying out an idea and it had gone horribly wrong. Either way, no one felt like going into deep mourning and it was tacitly assumed by all but Spencer that the bet was off.'

'Do you know whose idea it was in the first place?'

'I asked that, but Paul's not sure – he says he thinks it just kind of happened. Harvey swears it was Norm himself, which would be rough justice. Harman reckoned he was bugged because they were all getting at him for pinching their material over the years. Apparently he'd actually had the gall to get up at the conference and deliver a speech on how he thought up his plots. He even gave a for instance of one he'd worked out which involved suspending a block of dry ice above someone while they were asleep. The idea being that the vapour would flow down and displace the surrounding air so that the victim would be deprived of oxygen and suffocate in his sleep.'

'I'm sure it happens all the time,' said Monsieur Pample- mousse drily. It sounded like the plot for a book.'

'You can't prove it doesn't,' said Mrs Van Dorman.

He didn't feel inclined to argue. What was the figure for undetected murders? Years ago he'd read a quote from an American survey. It had been something like ten to one –

and that didn't include deaths classed as accidents or suicides. If you pushed someone off the edge of a cliff when no one was watching who was to say it was murder?

'Anyway,' continued Mrs Van Dorman, 'it was the start of an argument afterwards because Harvey swore he'd read the same idea in a book and accused Norm of plagiarism. That was more or less how it all began.'

Monsieur Pamplemousse turned the information over in his mind for a moment or two.

'What time are the others leaving?'

'They're booked for New York on the last flight out of Paris. The Air-Inter connecting flight leaves Clerment-Ferrand for Orly at 17.55. I'm catching the same one tomorrow.'

'So they leave here at what time?'

'The car picks them up at a quarter past four.'

Monsieur Pamplemousse looked at his watch again. Fourteen-fifteen. Two hours to go.

'Will you do one more thing for me? I'm afraid it will mean going out again.'

'It beats jogging,' said Mrs Van Dorman. 'I haven't had so much exercise in years.'

'I think the time has come when we should put out some bait,' said Monsieur Pamplemousse. 'I think before the others leave you should go to their Hôtel and wish them *bon voyage*.'

'I planned to do that anyway. Apart from Paul, I haven't seen them since the dinner.'

'Good. In that case, while you are there perhaps you would be kind enough to give them my felicitations and apologise for the fact that I cannot be with them in person. Tell them I am busy; that something has come up over the death of Ellis. Say I have made an important discovery and

I am writing out a report in my capacity as an ex-member of the Paris *Sûreté*. At the same time you can let slip the fact that I am working alone here in your room and do not wish to be disturbed.'

'Putting it out for the cat and seeing who comes to lick it up?'

'Something like that.' He must try and remember the phrase to add to the Director's collection. 'I suggest you take Pommes Frites with you again. He will make sure no harm comes to you.'

'How about you?'

'I shall be all right. It is better that I am seen to be entirely on my own.' It also occurred to him that it was probably better if Mrs Van Dorman wasn't.

As they left the room Monsieur Pamplemousse caught Pommes Frites' eye. Pommes Frites was endowed with extra-sensory perception when it came to summing up situations, and he was wearing his enigmatic expression. It would have been nice at that moment to know what he was really thinking.

The knock on the door came even sooner than he had expected. It was followed by the sound of someone trying the handle. Purposely leaving his papers spread out across the table, Monsieur Pamplemousse crossed to the door and opened it.

'*Entrez.*' He stood to one side, allowing room for his visitor to squeeze past. '*Comment ça va?*'

'I'm OK. I hope I'm not disturbing you. DiAnn said I might find you here.'

'Please take a seat.' Monsieur Pamplemousse motioned towards a chair.

'I won't stop, thank you. I have a plane to catch. I really

only dropped by to say *au revoir* and to ask if you enjoyed the other evening.'

'I could hardly fail to have done. As a meal it was an exercise in sheer gluttony, but there ...'

'I've heard tell the Romans had a similar dish – the Trojan roast pig. They stuffed it with fig-pickers, thrushes and oysters. In the end their Senate banned it on the grounds that it was too extravagant.'

'In that case, I am even more privileged than I thought.'

'You've read Alexandre Dumas' original recipe for *Rôtie á l'Imperatrice*?'

'I am working my way through *Le Grand Dictionnaire de Cuisine*. I dip into it when I go to bed at night, but in a very random fashion.'

'Well, I guess it's a bit like the house that Jack built. The chef starts off with an olive from which he first removes the stone, replacing it with an anchovy. The olive is then placed inside a lark, the lark inside a quail, the quail goes into a partridge and the partridge into a pheasant. The pheasant then goes inside a turkey, which is finally placed inside a suckling pig.'

Monsieur Pamplemousse listened patiently. He could hardly do otherwise. But he was beginning to wonder where the conversation was leading. 'It was a triumph for the *Rôtisseur*. To have cooked such a combination to perfection cannot have been easy.'

'You know what Dumas said about the dish?'

'Tell me.'

'The true gourmet discards the meat. He eats only the olive and the anchovy.'

'It sounds remarkably like yet another of Monsieur Dumas' extravagant statements,' said Monsieur Pample-mousse. 'Sadly, like many of his pronouncements we shall never know the truth.'

'On the contrary. After you and DiAnn left the other night the rest of us paid a visit to the kitchen and managed to rescue the olive from under the very noses of the staff before it disappeared along with the rest of the remains.

'And now, at DiAnn's request, and out of respect for a true gourmet, that is what I have brought you ...' Monsieur Pamplemousse found himself being handed a small jar ... a present from us all before we return home.' Unscrewing the cap, he put his nose to the opening. Shrivelled though the olive was from the cooking, the smell was redolent with all that had gone into the *Rôtie à l'Imperatrice*; the rich juices from the pork combined with the ripeness of a pheasant which must have been hung until the feathers practically fell from its breast – it was a wonder the bird had held together when they stuffed it inside the turkey – and that in turn mingled with the smell of partridge, quail and lark. Above it all there was the unmistakable pungent odour of anchovy.

'It is most kind of you. A very great honour. But I cannot be the only one to benefit. I insist that you share it with me.'

'In no way. It's for you. Besides, there's hardly enough to share.'

'In that case, perhaps you will join me in a toast?' Monsieur Pamplemousse went into the bathroom and returned a moment later with a second glass into which he poured the remains of his wine. It was young and crystal clear and he allowed the bottle to drain.

'You know what they call that final drip? The *larme* – the teardrop.'

'You French always have a word for it, right?'

'*Oui, c'est ça.*' He handed over the glass.

'Your good health, Aristide.'

'*A votre santé.*'

Monsieur Pamplemousse sipped a little of the wine, then picked up the jar again. He gazed reflectively at the contents for a moment or two. Then, placing it to his lips, he threw his head back, uttering a sigh of contentment at the thought of the unique pleasure to come.

Conscious that his every movement was being watched, he closed his eyes and allowed the contents of the jar to rest in his mouth for a while, prolonging the experience before slowly beginning to chew, savouring each and every morsel until the very last had disappeared.

'I guess that was something else again, right?'

Monsieur Pamplemousse opened his eyes and was about to reply when a sudden change came over him. The ecstatic expression on his face changed into a look of agony. His breathing became short gasps. The jar slipped unheeded from his hand as he clutched at his throat. Choking, he turned and clutched desperately at the bedclothes, pulling them with him as he fell to the floor. The convulsions lasted at the most a matter of five or six seconds before he gave one final shudder and then lay still, tongue protruding, eyes wide-open and staring.

The long silence which followed was eventually broken by the faint click of the door being closed.

The sound of footsteps disappearing down the corridor had hardly died away when he heard the rattle of a key in the lock and a moment later felt a faint draught of cool air on his face as the door was opened.

Monsieur Pamplemousse waited a moment or two, then opened one eye tentatively, but he was too late – his second visitor had vanished without uttering a word.

It was several minutes later that the phone rang. He recognised the desk clerk's voice.

'*Monsieur* ...'

'*Oui?*'

The man sounded taken aback. '*Monsieur* is all right?'

'*Oui.*'

'We received a telephone call a moment ago saying that you had been taken ill.'

'As you can hear I am perfectly well.'

'*Monsieur* has no need of an ambulance?'

'No need whatsoever,' said Monsieur Pamplemousse. 'It must have been a hoax. But thank you for calling.'

He replaced the receiver. A hoax? Or someone with a guilty conscience at having left him to his fate. Harvey, or his second visitor?

Mathematically, the permutations were limited, but emotionally ... emotionally, he needed time to think.

8
THE BALLOON GOES UP

There was bright yellow gorse everywhere and fields carpeted with buttercups, exactly as he had promised there would be when they were driving down from Paris. It was another cloudless day and the sun sparkled from a myriad tiny mountain streams. Every so often they rounded a corner and a totally new landscape came into view. Here and there he spotted the remains of a broken-down shepherd's hut on a distant hillside, but the higher they went the fewer were the signs of civilisation.

After being cooped up in the hotel room for hours on end, the freedom of driving along deserted country roads exceeded all Monsieur Pamplemousse's expectations. He found himself changing gear just for the fun of it.

Slowing down as they reached a piece of straight road, he opened the car window and took a deep breath.

'You promised to tell me all about perfume one day. Speaking as an expert on the subject, don't you think that is the most satisfactory, the most rewarding scent of all?'

'I wouldn't argue. It's also the most difficult to capture and the most expensive, believe you me. You know what they say – you pay through the nose for perfume. Do you realise it takes a ton of rosebuds to make one kilo of essence? That's a lot of rosebuds.'

'For us at this moment,' said Monsieur Pamplemousse, 'the smell is as free as the air. With all due respect to your last profession, one of the best laws ever passed in France was that which forbade the picking of wild flowers. Left to humanity the countryside would be stripped bare and turned into one enormous car park.'

'I wouldn't argue with that either.'

Anxious not to be left out of things, Pommes Frites stood up on the back seat of the *deux chevaux* and stuck his head out through the opening in the roof, surveying the countryside with a proprietorial air. He, too, gave an appreciative sniff.

'I still can't believe we're here,' said Mrs Van Dorman. 'When I saw you stretched out on my bedroom floor yesterday I'm afraid I panicked. I just ran.'

'You weren't the only one,' said Monsieur Pamplemousse. 'Harvey Wentworth was convinced he'd poisoned me.'

'You're sure you're all right to drive?' Mrs Van Dorman seemed nervous and ill at ease. She glanced down at Monsieur Pamplemousse's wrists. They still showed red marks from the handcuffs.

'The exercise will do them good.'

All the same, a few minutes later he stopped the car and they got out for a moment to stretch their legs. The only sound came from a stream bubbling its way over some nearby rocks. He wished he'd thought to bring a bottle of champagne. They could have sat and talked while it chilled. Even in early June there was still unmelted snow to be seen on the distant peaks. The water flowing down the mountainside would be ice-cold.

'I shall miss all this,' said Mrs Van Dorman. 'Life will seem very quiet on Fifth Avenue.'

'Paris will seem quiet too,' said Monsieur Pamplemousse. 'It always does. Life in the country is really much busier.'

'What things do you miss most?'

'Partly the wildness and the neglect, the crumbling buildings; many of the things which, when I was young, were my reasons for leaving. But France is a big country and each part of it has its own special character and influences. To the south, there is the Italian influence. To the west, that of Spain. To the east, Germany. If I had been brought up in the south I would miss the colour of the roof tiles, or turning a corner and seeing a sun-bleached advertisement for Dubonnet painted on a wall.'

He was glad she had said 'things'. If the question had been more specific, he might have been tempted to give a more direct answer.

'I shall miss the Hôtel Thermale Splendide with its bath-tubs,' said Mrs Van Dorman. 'Tomorrow it's back to central heating, air-conditioned apartments, and hotels with sanitised toilet seats.'

'… and Monsieur Van Dorman.'

She shook her head, then hesitated for a moment as though weighing up the pros and cons of what to say next. 'There is no Monsieur Van Dorman. There never has been.'

'No Monsieur Van Dorman? Never? How can that be?'

'I guess in the beginning he was a kind of insurance policy; a protection in what was a man's world. I still bring him out from time to time and dust him down. In a funny kind of way he's become part of my life. He's been around so long now I take him for granted. We even have rows sometimes when I want to let off steam. It's like the real thing, but without the hassles.'

And also, thought Monsieur Pamplemousse, without the feeling of having someone else to snuggle up to on a cold winter's night. Perhaps it was part of the price you paid for the benefits of central heating.

'Why did you not tell me before?'

'Would it have made any difference?'

Monsieur Pamplemousse considered the matter for a moment, then side-stepped the question. 'It seems a terrible waste.'

She shrugged. 'It's like we said last night – the night before last – whenever – I've lost track of time; it's a matter of priorities. You can't have everything you want in life. In the beginning my priority had to do with making a career, not finding a husband. First it was perfume, now it's the magazine business. It seemed a good idea to acquire a mythical husband and shelve the problem for the time being. The trouble is, it's the kind of situation that can back-fire. After a certain point if you're not married men wonder what's wrong, and if they think you're married but available, it attracts the wrong sort of person. Anyway, men get frightened by successful women. You can't win.'

'I was a little nervous of you at first,' said Monsieur Pamplemousse, 'but for other reasons. At first I thought you were a little *formidable*.'

'More than a little by the look on your face driving down. And now?'

'Now?' Monsieur Pamplemousse went to the car and fetched his camera. 'Now I see you in a different light.'

Crouching down in order to use a low-hanging branch from a tree as foreground interest and to give the picture depth, he framed Mrs Van Dorman sitting on a rock against a background of snow-capped mountains. Hoping she wouldn't notice, he zoomed in for a closer shot and checked the focus. The sun acted as a key-light, picking out the highlights in her eyes. Looking away for a moment under the guise of checking the background, he pressed the shutter release.

'Will you promise to send me a copy?'

'Of course. Although, you may be disappointed. A photograph is the sum of many parts. A split second in time. Often it is the things which are not shown that matter most. The person you are with, where you have just been or where you are about to go.'

'And where are we going?'

'Now? Now I shall take you to a place called Thiers and there, over *déjeuner*, I will tell you everything you want to know. I refuse to talk on an empty stomach. Besides, it is an interesting little town – another side to the Auvergne, and another reason why I left. The people who hanker after the Midi forget the Mistral, just as I often forget that not so long ago, when Thiers supplied France with seventy per cent of its cutlery, the town was full of men who spent their working lives lying flat on their stomachs over the raging streams, their noses literally to the grindstone. They all had a dog lying on top of them. Why? To protect their kidneys from the intense cold. It could have been me; it could have been Pommes Frites.'

'If I say I can't wait,' said Mrs Van Dorman, 'it's only because I know I'm going to have to.'

But in Thiers they struck lucky. Feeling saturated from a surfeit of cutlery following a tour of the town, they turned a corner into an alleyway and came across a tiny restaurant. Tucked away behind it they discovered an even smaller courtyard with just three tables set for lunch.

The sun was high overhead and they felt its warmth rising from the paving stones as they took their seats beneath a tree grown tall to escape the surrounding buildings.

Monsieur Pamplemousse ordered a *pichet* of *vin rose* and while they scanned the brief menu the *patron* brought them a plate of home-cured ham cut into thick slices. He returned a moment later with a basket of freshly baked bread, a bowl of butter and a stone jar filled with gherkins.

Monsieur Pamplemousse chose an *omelette au fromage* and Mrs Van Dorman a *quiche*. While they were waiting they shared a *salade de tomates*.

The omelette, when it came, was exactly as it should have been – *baveuse* in the middle. The *quiche* was filled with egg and ham. There was a plate of *pommes frites*, which they also shared.

For a while they ate in silence. Then Monsieur Pamplemousse, having wiped his plate clean with the remains of the bread, felt inside the secret compartment of his right trouser leg and removed a raisin.

'You're still a believer?'

'Now more than ever, but for a very different reason. Yesterday, when I went to your bathroom to fetch another glass, I managed to substitute one for the olive. It got me out of a sticky situation.'

He leaned back in his chair to escape the sun, which had moved round while they had been eating. Recalling the moment, he couldn't help thinking that Glandier would have been proud of him.

'As for their efficacy as a cure for indigestion, I am not sure. Who ever knows if a headache might not have gone away of its own accord without the help of an aspirin? Dumas had a penchant for making statements that were as hard to disprove as they were to prove.'

'Like the storks?'

'Like the storks. He also stated categorically that coffee, far from being the drug we now know it to be, actually served as an antidote to many poisons. I doubt if Monsieur

Ellis would have benefited very greatly from the theory – even if he'd had time to test it out.'

'He certainly wasn't calling for coffee when he died,' said Mrs Van Dorman. 'What do you think he did want?'

'I asked myself the same question many times over,' said Monsieur Pamplemousse, 'and on each occasion I gave up because I came to a *route barrée*. In the end I telephoned an old friend of mine, a Monsieur Pickering. He is an Englishman who specialises in crossword puzzles. He has helped me several times in the past. They have very devious minds, the English; they adore riddles. He is also a Francophile and he came up with the answer almost straight away.

'Everyone assumed Ellis had been talking French, whereas Monsieur Pickering's theory is that it was probably a mixture of the two. What those who were present at the time thought he said was "Bâtard Montrachet" followed by "*poisson*".

'Pickering suggested that Ellis was already fighting for breath through the effect of the poison and that what he might actually have said was: "Bastard!" in English. Then, lapsing into French, he called out "*mon trachée*" – meaning "my windpipe".

'As Pickering rightly pointed out, Ellis unfortunately got his genders wrong. Had he said "*ma trachée*" it wouldn't have mattered. As it was he said "*mon*", and to any French people around "*mon traché*", coupled with the previous word "bastard" sounded like Bâtard Montrachet which, as I'm sure you know, is a white wine from Burgundy.

'Then, when he started calling out "poison", they naturally assumed he was saying "*poisson*" because he wanted some fish to accompany the wine.'

'I don't see what's so natural about it,' said Mrs Van Dorman.

'You are in France,' said Monsieur Pamplemousse mildly. 'Whatever the situation, the thoughts of a Frenchman naturally turn to food. *Par exemple*, do you know the French term for grilling a suspect?'

Mrs Van Dorman shook her head.

'It is called to *cuisinade*. Likewise, the slang for a police van is *panier à salade*. I could give you many more examples. I think Pickering is right. To a Frenchman, Ellis's last words probably seemed a sensible request. One might quibble over his choice – that is a matter of personal taste – but one wouldn't question the sentiment behind it. Besides, until someone has actually died, how is anyone to know they are uttering their last words? To judge from some lines you see quoted, those who speak them must have been polishing and honing them for a long time, and once they have given voice they feel they cannot say another word for fear of spoiling the effect. It is better to be remembered for a stirring phrase like "Not tonight, Josephine" than for something mundane, like "I think I am going to be sick".'

Monsieur Pamplemousse closed his eyes. 'You want to know what I think. The truth is, I don't know, and perhaps no one ever will know the exact truth. Why did someone want to murder Ellis? Who knows? Lots of people probably felt like it. But feeling like it and actually doing it are two very different things.

'My guess, for what it is worth, is that he was the victim of a trick; an elaborate charade which had been carefully planned in advance and which, once the wheels were set in motion, was hard to stop. Perhaps in planning it, the murderer became so involved in the sheer mechanics of the whole thing he lost sight of the moral aspects. One could argue, and if it comes to court, no doubt a good lawyer *will* argue, that in the circumstances "death by misadventure" is the only possible verdict, but my belief is that someone virtually handed Ellis a kit of parts to do the job himself.

'For a while I puzzled over how it could have been done. I pictured a trick glass having being made, one which would have enabled the murderer to conceal cyanide in the bottom, but other than traces of some hard deposit on the inside I could see nothing different about the one you gave me. Besides, having one specially made would have had its dangers, for if whoever did the job got to hear of Ellis's death, as he quite likely would have done, the chances are he would call in the police.

'Thinking about it, I decided it needn't have been as complicated as I first imagined. All the tasting glasses come in the same shape, that is to say they taper towards the bottom. All it needed was a circle of plain glass cut slightly larger than the narrowest point. The poison could be placed in the bottom of the glass – it would require only a minute amount – according to my source less than that needed to cover a postage stamp. The bottom of the tasting glasses is like thick bottle glass, so once the circle was in place any crystals would be scarcely visible to the naked eye. The circular glass could be held in place with something like a sugar solution which, when it set, would be reasonably transparent and yet would dissolve as soon as warm water came into contact with it, thus releasing the glass and the poison.'

'Ingenious.' Mrs Van Dorman looked thoughtful. 'So that's why you wanted to know the temperature in the Parc des Sources?'

'*Exactement*. It also answered another question which had been bothering me. Why a spa? It was the one place where one could guarantee the drinking water would be warm. The deeper the source the warmer it is. I tested my

749

theory while you were out yesterday and it worked.

'As I see it, the argument which took place in Annecy – the wager as to who would be first to plan a perfect murder – were all part of an elaborate and carefully worked out set-up. Once the bait was laid the murderer would have taken Ellis on one side and casually fed him with the bones of the plot, perhaps asking him to treat it as a matter of confidence – which would have been about as much good as asking him to fly. He probably showed him the glass he had already prepared, and then left it lying around anticipating that Ellis wouldn't be able to resist the temptation of swapping it for his own when he thought no one was watching. He judged well. Once they all arrived in Vichy Ellis couldn't wait to unpack before he rushed round to the Parc des Sources in order to try it out.'

'Not dreaming that the crystals in the bottom of the glass were the real thing?' Mrs Van Dorman reached for her sunglasses. 'And you figured that out all by yourself?'

'Not all by myself,' said Monsieur Pamplemousse modestly. 'I could hardly have done it without your help, DiAnn. Besides, for many years I was with the *Sûreté*. Figuring things out was part of my job.

'As I said earlier, a good lawyer would argue that in stealing the glass Ellis sealed his own fate. In a sense he took his own life. The murderer would plead that he was working on a plot for a book and that in order to make sure it was feasible he had to get all the details exactly right. How was he to know someone would steal the glass? It would also have salved his own conscience to a certain extent. The question then was which of the other five was the culprit?'

'Which is why you got me to put the cream out for the cat so that you could see who came to lick it up.'

'That is so. For a while, given his penchant for writing gastronomic mysteries, I was convinced it would turn out to be Harvey Wentworth. As it happened, one of the books you brought me was by him and it had to do with a man poisoning his wife with cyanide. She took sugar in her coffee and he didn't. He doctored one of the lumps in the sugar bowl with cyanide, so it was only a matter of time before she used it.

'Ellis must have stolen the idea because two years later it surfaced again in a book he'd written under the name of Jed Powers – *Vomit in the Vestry* – a cosy little tale about a homicidal priest who dealt out punishment to his flock by tampering with the communion wafers.

'When Harvey Wentworth appeared clutching the olive and went into his long explanation about why he was giving it to me I was sure I had it right. My guess was that he'd taken fright after hearing that I was actively working on the case and wanted to get rid of me. Then I saw the look on his face as I keeled over and I knew I was wrong.

'What I hadn't bargained for was the cat sending someone else to lick up the cream for him. It was most unfeline behaviour. Perhaps the murderer felt that Wentworth was the only one who might put two and two together and he had in mind killing two birds with one stone. If Harvey Wentworth got himself arrested for my death there's no way he would have got out of it.'

'To think I bumped into Harvey in the corridor as he was leaving,' said Mrs Dorman. 'He must have gone straight back to whoever gave him the olive.'

Monsieur Pamplemousse nodded. '*D'accord.*'

'And Pommes Frites followed him.'

Monsieur Pamplemousse nodded again. 'Other than Harvey Wentworth, Pommes Frites is probably the only one in the world who knows for certain who the murderer is, and there is no way he can tell us.'

He glanced down at Pommes Frites, but Pommes Frites clearly had his mind on other things. He was gazing up at Mrs Van Dorman with a faraway look in his eyes. Perhaps he, too, had fallen under her spell.

'So what's your guess?'

'It isn't so much a guess,' said Monsieur Pamplemousse, 'as an accumulation of arrows, each one pointing in the same direction.

'As I lay on the floor of your room my mind went back to something which had been bothering me ever since I arrived in Vichy. It wasn't until I looked at your map that it began to come clear, and even then it took me a while to grasp the full significance.

'In France, we have a predilection for naming our streets after famous people. In Vichy, for example, your town map lists no less than three hundred and sixty different names. There are four streets called after American Presidents. There is a square Georges Pompidou, a place General de Gaulle, and a rue Napoléon III. There are some streets named after saints, and others after generals, doctors and scientists, from Saint-Barbe to Foch; from Colas to Pasteur. There is even a street named after a seventeenth-century Superintendent of Waters, a certain Docteur Fouet; a worthy man I am sure, and fully deserving of having his name recorded for posterity, but there is no mention what-soever of a *rue* Alexandre Dumas. I asked myself why? If you have achieved fame as a writer in France and have a connection with a place, however tenuous – you need only have stayed there for a night *en route* to somewhere else – you are assured of a *place* at the very least. Over the years Voltaire has been honoured by the authorities in Vichy, as have Romains and Victor Hugo, but there is no mention whatsoever of Dumas. I cannot think that if he had stayed at the Villa André in order to begin work on a new novel the occasion would have passed unremarked.

'The truth is that the whole episode was a fabrication from start to finish. According to the encyclopaedias Dumas certainly wrote two sequels to *The Three Musketeers* – *Vingt ans après* and *Le Vicomte de Bragelonne* – but I can find no mention of him embarking on a fourth book. I telephoned the library and they had no knowledge of it either, and they should know if anyone does.

'The question I then asked myself was did Elliott dream up the story or was he himself the victim of a hoax? If he concocted the whole thing, then given his pedantic approach and ingrained perfectionism, he must have glossed over the truth for a very good reason.

'Should the matter come to court, and were I appearing for the prosecution, that is an area I would concentrate on. I would put it to him that someone wanted Ellis in Vichy for a very good reason.'

'He certainly did a very good job,' said Mrs Van Dorman. 'He had me fooled.'

'He had everybody fooled. On the other hand, there was no reason why anyone should check up his story. It sounded perfectly authentic, and it would have required a more than averagely erudite Dumas scholar to say otherwise.'

'Where would he have got the cyanide?'

'It is not that difficult. Cyanide turns up in all sorts of different guises. Anyone involved in chemicals can probably get hold of it. As someone once involved in the perfume industry, you should know that. Besides, cyanogenic glucosides are found in lots of natural products – kernels of bitter almonds, apricots, peaches, plums … apple seeds. A cupful of apple seeds is known to have been fatal. The leaves from the wild black cherry tree contain amygalin which the stomach converts into hydrogen cyanide. It is used in the manufacture of plastics and as an intensifier in photographic processing. Elliott is a keen photographer.

'If you simply swallow the crystals there is time for treatment. But given the right combination and mixed with water to form prussic acid, a gas is given off and death can take place in a matter of seconds. The one thing which is always present is a smell of almonds, although interestingly a good twenty per cent of people can't detect it.

'By the time we had our dinner Elliott must have had an inkling that I was more than a little interested in Ellis's death. I can only think he must have been trying to throw me off the scent by doctoring the wine with something like almond, suggesting that someone else was trying to poison him. Somehow or other his glass got mixed up with yours.

'So Pommes Frites' sense of smell wasn't at fault after all?'

'I ought never to have doubted it. As you may remember, he treated the episode of the spilt wine with the contempt it deserved.'

As though to prove his point, Monsieur Pamplemousse picked up the remains of the ham in his fingers and held it under the table. He felt Pommes Frites sniffing it carefully. Then, a moment later, the inspection complete, it disappeared.

'So … what are you going to do about it?'

Monsieur Pamplemousse gave a shrug. 'I am a food inspector, not a judge. I comment on the world as I find it – not as I would wish it to be. I shall make out a report and pass it on to the proper authorities – in my position it would be hard to do otherwise, my conscience wouldn't allow it and I have my sleep to think of. After that it will be up to others.'

'What do you think will happen?' persisted Mrs Van Dorman.

Monsieur Pamplemousse repeated his previous 'who knows?' gesture. From the ease with which they had left the Hôtel that morning he suspected that wheels were already beginning to turn.

'I see endless complications ... or none at all. The party has already left for America. The authorities will have a field day making up their minds. It will be a matter of looking up the rules ...'

'Rules?' repeated Mrs Van Dorman. 'Here we are in a country where people happily park on pedestrian crossings or come at you with murder in their eyes if you dare to use one in order to cross the road, and you talk about "rules".'

'That is not the point,' said Monsieur Pamplemousse. 'In truth, France is a country which is steeped in rules. There are rules laid down for everything. Some rules are meant to be obeyed, others are not. The important thing is that when it comes to a disagreement they are there to be referred to. If there is an argument in a taxi about whether or not the window should be open, the passenger has the final say. That is the rule. By the same token, if there is an argument between two passengers on an *autobus* over the same matter, the final arbiter is the driver. That, also, is a rule.

'There is only one area I can think of at this moment which is not governed by rules.'

'And that is?'

Monsieur Pamplemousse picked up the menu. 'Whether to have the *tarte aux fraises* or the *tarte au fromage blanc*. I noticed them both as we came in. The strawberries looked mouth-wateringly fresh – they must be the first of the season. The *tarte au fromage* is a speciality of the region. The Auvergne is known as "the cheese table" of France.'

'Perhaps,' said Mrs Van Dorman, 'we could have one of each and make our own rules as we go along.'

They drank their coffee slowly, savouring each remaining moment.

'All good things come to an end sooner or later,' said Mrs Van Dorman. 'I feel as though I could stay here for ever.'

'I doubt it,' said Monsieur Pamplemousse. 'You would miss New York with its skyscrapers and its way of life, just as I would now miss Paris. Even though there are times when I want to escape, I am always happy to be back there.'

He called for the bill. 'It is my turn this time.'

'If you ever come to New York,' said Mrs Van Dorman, 'I'll take you to the Deli on West 57th. That's something else again. I'll buy you a bagel with cream cheese and lox, or maybe Lukshen Kugel with apple sauce and a potato pancake on the side. Apple strudel and coffee to follow.'

'And when you are next in Paris,' said Monsieur Pamplemousse, 'I will take you to La Coupole for oysters followed by *choucroute*. That, too, is something else again.' He could have listed a hundred other places he would have liked to take her to.

They drove back to Vichy in silence. It was hard to tell what Mrs Van Dorman was thinking behind her sunglasses. Even Pommes Frites was looking unusually thoughtful.

When they reached the hotel a car was waiting to take Mrs Van Dorman on to the airport. Her baggage was already loaded.

She put her hand on his shoulder as they said goodbye. 'I wish you could come as far as Paris – you could wave me goodbye at the airport.'

'I wish I could. But, it is not possible. I have my car.'

'You could leave it. It'll still be here tomorrow.'

'There is also Pommes Frites. He will be lonely without me.'

Mrs Van Dorman gave a mock sigh. 'Excuses.'

'*Raisons*,' said Monsieur Pamplemousse.

'Aristide! *Entrez! Entrez!*' The Director looked to be in an expansive mood as he rose from behind his desk. 'And Pommes Frites. It is good to see you both.

'You have arrived at an opportune moment. The photographs have just come in. A successful operation, by all accounts. It is unfortunate that the pictures taken of you on the *cheval* haven't come out.' He held a strip of negative up to the light. 'It is hard to tell what went wrong. Everything seems blurred. I suspect you must have moved at the crucial moment.'

'I will have a word with Trigaux in the art department, *Monsieur*. He may be able to do something.' Monsieur Pamplemousse didn't add that there was a little private matter he wanted to see Trigaux about too; a matter of some prints of his photographs of Mrs Van Dorman. They should be nearly ready.

The Director crossed to his drinks cabinet. 'I have been going through your report, Aristide. It came through on the fax early this morning. You have done well. A victory over the forces of adversity. It deserves another bottle of Gosset I think.

'I particularly liked the way you ran the-flag up the pole, so to speak, and then waited to see who saluted it.'

In acknowledging the compliment Monsieur Pamplemousse also privately had to admit defeat over another matter. When it came to American phraseology, the

Director was a clear winner. He also wondered if in watering down his report he'd omitted some essential detail, so that it no longer made sense. In the end he had left out more than he had put in. But the Director was much more interested in peripherals.

'Tell me again about Ellis's last words,' he said. 'I don't want to get the story wrong when I repeat it, and it is too good not to repeat.'

Monsieur Pamplemousse obliged. Doubtless his chief would be dining out on it many times in the months to come.

'I am reminded,' said the Director when Monsieur Pamplemousse had finished, 'of a story my father used to tell me. It is an English joke from the First World War and therefore somewhat convoluted as English jokes often are. It also requires a knowledge of the language and of the somewhat bizarre currency system in use at the time, for it took place long before they had the good sense to become decimalised.

'The message started off as "Send reinforcements, we are going to advance." It was passed down the line by word of mouth and eventually, by the time it reached headquarters, it had become "Send three and fourpence, we are going to a dance."'

Monsieur Pamplemousse laughed dutifully. His old father had told him a similar story, not once but many times.

'Another piece of good news', continued the Director, as he poured the champagne, 'is that you are no longer on the "wanted" list. My very good friend, the Deputy, has stepped in. Strings have been pulled.'

'I am delighted to hear it,' said Monsieur Pamplemousse. All the way up the *autoroute*, in between listening to a tape of Ben Webster and thinking of Mrs Van Dorman, he'd kept a wary eye on the driving mirror in case he was being followed.

'That is what Deputies are for,' said the Director. 'Without Deputies to oil the machinery from time to time, life would be intolerable. France would grind to a halt.

'Anyway, it wasn't difficult. It seems the man at the farmhouse where you spent the night was running a brothel, catering in the main for the somewhat exotic tastes which are often prevalent in those parts of the world where the winters are long and hard and time hangs heavy. When you arrived dressed as d'Artagnan, brandishing a lady's purse, and wearing *menottes* into the bargain, they not unnaturally assumed you were a new customer anxious to be chastised. It is an establishment popular with the local farming community, some of whom are sufficiently elevated they would rather their proclivities were kept under the bed as it were, instead of on top for all to see. When you failed to give the correct response to a simple code message – something to do with "wanting funny business afterwards"— panic set in. The police were contacted and their first reaction was to throw the book at you. Early reports were somewhat exaggerated. They simply wanted to frighten you enough to make quite sure you never set foot in the area again.'

'I think it will be some while before I do, *Monsieur*.'

'Good, Pamplemousse. I am glad to hear it.' The Director raised his glass. 'I never cease to marvel at the way nature manages to produce a constant stream of bubbles from a point source of such minuscule dimensions.

'Tell me, Aristide, the man's daughters, were they ... how shall I put it? ... were they very ... ?'

Monsieur Pamplemousse sighed inwardly as the Director

lapsed into the series of short whistles and other sound effects which he invariably brought into play when he was discussing 'delicate matters'. Clearly, he was not going to accept the plain, unvarnished truth. Embroidery was the order of the day.

'They were not without talent, *Monsieur*. The eldest one sang the Marseillaise while she performed with contraro-tating tassels attached to her *doudons*.'

'*Mon Dieu!*' The Director gave another whistle and then reached for his handkerchief. 'And the others?' he asked, dabbing at his forehead.

'The second one specialised in tricks she had obviously learned in the Casbah.

'The third did amazing things whilst suspended by one leg from a chandelier. They catered for all tastes.'

The Director looked at him suspiciously for a moment, then he rose to his feet and began shuffling the papers around on his desk.

'You look tired, Pamplemousse. I suggest you take the rest of the day off. Put work on the back burner for a while.'

'I was awake for a long time last night, *Monsieur*. I found it hard to sleep after all the excitement.'

'I trust you have no regrets. If you do, I would strongly advise you to go and see Matron.'

'Regrets, *Monsieur*?' Monsieur Pamplemousse raised his eyebrows. 'I think one of my few regrets is that there will be no more Jed Powers books. Or Ed Morgan. I acquired several while I was in Vichy. They are, as they say in the blurbs, quite "unputdownable".'

The Director accompanied him towards the door. 'You will be pleased to know, Aristide, that I, too, have won a minor victory.

'I had an encounter with Madame Grante earlier today.

It seems the thespians are causing trouble. Some of them are claiming extra payment for their performance at the banquet. They claim that when Monsieur Troon pretended he had been poisoned, they were unable to prevent themselves uttering cries of *"Ooooh, la! la!"* and *"Mon Dieu! Mon Dieu!"* Their union says it puts them in another category.

'Madame Grante was in her element. I saw the light of battle in her eyes. All the same, I fear I had to intervene and persuade her to let it go through in return for the exercise of a certain amount of discretion on the other side.'

Monsieur Pamplemousse wondered what life would be like if there were a union of food inspectors. Madame Grante wouldn't know what had hit her if he submitted a claim asking to be recompensed for half the things that happened to him over and above the normal call of duty.

'She is a good sort,' said the Director. 'However, there is one item on your P.39 she is querying. It seems that before you left for Vichy you purchased a large quantity of ... raisins.'

Monsieur Pamplemousse heaved a sigh. Now he knew he was back in earnest.

'If it is of any consolation,' said the Director, 'I have received a very complimentary note from Mrs Van Dorman. I have a feeling she thinks well of you.'

'That is nice to know, *Monsieur.*'

'An attractive lady. I have to admit I fell for her when I was in New York. It is a good thing she is married, otherwise who knows? One evening over a drink she bared her soul to me. Apparently her husband, whom I never met, is of an extremely jealous disposition. He is also an expert in Karate. A Black Belt, I believe.'

Monsieur Pamplemousse had difficulty in keeping a

straight face. He was beginning to see the advantages of Mrs Van Dorman's invention.

'Mind you, I would not like to upset her either. She is not a woman to be crossed. There is another side to her character – a hard streak. Not altogether surprising – even in this day and age a woman does not reach the top of her profession without it. I had evidence of it both in New York and again the other evening in Annecy.'

Monsieur Pamplemousse paused for a moment with his hand on the door knob. 'Did you say Annecy, *Monsieur*?'

'I did.'

'You mean Mrs Van Dorman didn't arrive straight from New York?'

The Director looked at him in some surprise. 'Of course not,' he said a trifle impatiently. 'These matters don't just happen, Pamplemousse, as you should know only too well. They require weeks of careful planning. Naturally, as it was her idea rather than Elliott's to hold the event in Vichy, she wished to make absolutely certain everything was going according to plan. She flew into Annecy a couple of days early before coming on to Paris. I joined her there for the first evening to ensure she had all she needed.'

'And did she, *Monsieur*? Have all she needed?' Even as he posed the question, Monsieur Pamplemousse felt his mind racing over the events of the past few days. It felt as though his whole world had suddenly been turned upside down. And yet ... and yet all kinds of little things began to make sense. It was no wonder Pommes Frites had been giving Mrs Van Dorman some funny looks.

'There was nothing she had not thought of. Everything had been meticulously planned down to the very last detail – I couldn't have done a better job myself. Brochures, itineraries; she even presented each member of the party with his own tasting cup in an initialled carrying case. I need hardly have bothered. The idea for initiating a competition involving the plot for a perfect murder was merely icing on top of the cake ...'

The Director broke off and looked at Monsieur Pample-mousse with some concern. 'Is anything the matter, Aristide? You have gone quite pale.'

'It is nothing, *Monsieur*. A momentary dizziness, that is all.' Monsieur Pamplemousse pulled himself together. 'You mentioned another side to Mrs Van Dorman's character ... something which happened in New York.'

The Director glanced uneasily at the door in order to make sure it was properly shut, then lowered his voice.

'We were dining *tête-à-tête* at one of those restaurants one normally sees only in Hollywood films. The sort where they bring a telephone to your table.

'Halfway through the meal Mrs Van Dorman received a call. It gave rise to the most extraordinary outburst. Not once did she raise her voice, but I tell you, Pample-mousse, my vocabulary that evening was considerable enhanced; my grasp of the American vernacular improved by leaps and bounds. Hell hath no fury like a woman scorned.

'After she put the receiver down she behaved as though nothing had happened, but it left me considerably shaken. I honestly believe that for the first time in my life I was in the presence of a genuine schizophrenic.

'It was only later I discovered the caller was none other than our friend, the late Monsieur Ellis. He was waiting for her outside the restaurant. She passed it off by saying he had been seeking her advice as an expert on perfume for one of his books – *Charnel No. 5* I think she said it was called. But I was left with the uneasy feeling that there was considerably more involved than that. I beat a hasty retreat.'

'And in Annecy, *Monsieur*? What happened in Annecy?'

'Ah. it was there, Pamplemousse, that I had my original suspicions confirmed in no uncertain manner. Feeling my presence was redundant, I went for a post-prandial stroll round the town. Imagine my surprise, when on the way back to my apartment I saw Mrs Van Dorman entering Ellis's room. I think they planned a "night-cap" together. She was carrying a tasting glass.

'An odd combination, don't you think? One wonders what brought them together in the first place.'

'Perhaps it was loneliness, *Monsieur*.'

'Perhaps.' The Director gave a shrug. 'Now, of course, the question is academic.'

'*Oui, Monsieur*. It is, as you say, *académique*.'

As he let himself in through the entrance door to his apartment block Monsieur Pamplemousse encountered yet another reminder that he was home.

He was about to enter the lift when the *gardien* came out of his office clutching an enormous white cardboard box. He glanced at Monsieur Pamplemousse's luggage.

'It is addressed to you, *Monsieur*, but if you like I will give it to Madame Pamplemousse. She will be back at any moment. She is only out shopping.'

Instinct told Monsieur Pamplemousse to decline the offer. Instinct proved right, as he discovered when he arrived upstairs and opened the box. Anxious to lend a paw, Pommes Frites jumped back in alarm as his master lifted the lid. A large, gas-filled balloon in the shape of a heart floated out and attached itself to the ceiling.

There was card tied to the ribbon. It read 'To my very

own Musketeer' and it was signed 'Madame Joyeux'.

Monsieur Pamplemousse read the card a second time, then he detached it and slipped it into his wallet alongside the photograph of Mrs Van Dorman he'd collected from Trigaux. Taking hold of the ribbon, he crossed to the French windows and went out on to the balcony.

He stood for a while lost in thought as the balloon floated across the rue Girardon towards the little park opposite. As it passed over the *boules* area one of the players made a grab for it and missed. He heard the sound of laughter from the man's companions. Further up the hill some children stopped playing for a moment and watched as it drifted higher and higher, gradually losing its heart shape until it was only a speck in the sky.

As it finally disappeared from view Pommes Frites gave vent to a brief but poignant howl and then followed his master back into the room.

With a heavy heart Monsieur Pamplemousse picked up the telephone and dialled a number. He shivered. After the warmth of the balcony the room felt cold and he had little taste for what was to come.

While he waited to be connected he took out his wallet and removed the photograph, laying it out on the table in front of him. It hardly seemed possible that only a few days before he had never set eyes on the face staring back at him. So much had happened since.

'Aristide! You are back!'

Monsieur Pamplemousse jumped. He had been so intent on looking at the photograph he hadn't heard the door open.

'*Couscous*! You startled me.' Rising to his feet he replaced the receiver and held out his arms.

"Who is that?' Doucette glanced at the photograph as

she bustled in and set down her shopping.

'She is a colleague of *Monsieur Le Directeur*. I had dealings with her concerning the banquet.' It was no good fabricating a yarn.

'What a strange expression she has.'

'Do you think so?' He took another look. His judgement was clouded by a host of events, but now that Doucette mentioned it there was something odd about the way Mrs Van Dorman was looking. In snatching an unguarded moment he had managed to capture a slightly haunted look; a mixture of triumph and apprehension. And yet, underneath it all there were traces of the warmth he'd grown to know. As a picture it defied analysis.

'If it wasn't for the fact that she isn't your type I would say she is a little in love.'

'Really?' Monsieur Pamplemousse held it up to the light.

'I pity the man whoever he is. She would probably twist him around her little finger, then throw him on the rubbish dump when she'd finished with him.'

Monsieur Pamplemousse eyed his wife curiously. It was the second time in less than an hour that he'd heard the same reservation voiced.

'That is very perspicacious of you.'

As Madame Pamplemousse turned and picked up her shopping bag she spied the box. 'What on earth do you want that for, We have enough cardboard boxes to last us a life-time.'

Monsieur Pamplemousse slipped the photograph into his pocket. 'One can never have too many, *Couscous*,' he said. 'But if it pleases you I will throw it out when I take Pommes Frites for a walk. He has been cooped up in the car all day and he is a little restive.'

'Don't be too long,' said Doucette. 'I have prepared your

favourite stew. It has been simmering all day.'

Monsieur Pamplemousse gave her a quick embrace. It was good to be back.

'You look sad, Aristide. Is anything the matter?'

'Sad?' Monsieur Pamplemousse considered the matter for a moment or two. 'No, just a little disappointed, that is all. Also, I have a report to rewrite.'

'Life is full of disappointments – you are always telling me that.' Madame Pamplemousse pushed him away as she bustled about her work. 'Aren't you going to finish making your telephone call?'

'It can wait,' said Monsieur Pamplemousse. 'I am not sure what I was going to say anyway.' He signalled to Pommes Frites and Pommes Frites, ever alive to moments when his master was in urgent need of a diversion, obliged with alacrity, making his way towards the outer door.

'And Aristide ...'

'*Oui?*' He turned in the doorway clutching the box in both

'While you are about it don't you think you should get rid of the rest of your rubbish?'

Outside the apartment block, Monsieur Pamplemousse opened the box under the watchful eye of Pommes Frites and put the label inside. After a moment's hesitation, he added the photograph, stirring the plastic packing with his fingers until both were lost from view. Then he closed the lid, pressing the ends of the sticky tape back into place so that it was safely sealed.

'Allow me, *Monsieur*.' The *gardien* came out of his room and took the carton from him. '*Monsieur* is having *un grand nettoyage*? A spring clean?'

'*Non,*' said Monsieur Pamplemousse firmly. 'It is Madame Pamplemousse who is having *un grand nettoyage*.

Pommes Frites and I are going on a balloon hunt. 'He gazed up at the sky. '*Entre nous*, *Monsieur*, sometimes when you throw one up in the air you never know quite where it is going to land.'